*"The Orc King* finds Drizzt's whirling scimitar blades tackling both familiar foes and refreshingly ambiguous moral challenges . . . The story line marks the continuation of Salvatore's maturation as a writer, introducing more complex themes into a frequently black-and-white fantasy landscape."

—*Kirkus*

"(R.A. Salvatore) is not only skilled enough to create fantastic worlds littered with dozens upon dozens of magnificent characters, creatures, landscapes, and wonders, but he has been born with the additional talent of being able to take what appears within the fabric of his mind's eye, and bring it to life with descriptive, colorful, rich, and meaningful verbiage."

—Todd McFarlane

"There's good reason this saga is one of the most popular—and beloved—fantasy series of all time: breakneck pacing, deeply complex characters and nonstop action. If you read just one adventure fantasy saga in your lifetime, let it be this one."

—Paul Goat Allen, *B&N Explorations* on *Streams of Silver*

"When reading . . . the Legend of Drizzt, I believe you will wonder whether (R.A. Salvatore) is writing fiction, or whether he is describing a secret place he's been to, a secret history he's really experienced and is kind enough to reveal to us."

—James Merendino, Director of *SLC Punk*

"Salvatore's fight scenes are probably the best I've ever read. His description, though detailed, is very fast paced. Every time I read one, my heart races and my hands shake. It is pure brilliance . . ."

—SFFWorld on *The Legacy*

"The action sequences are parallel to none and I have discovered what an extraordinary writer R.A. Salvatore is. *Sojourn* is the perfect fantasy novel and Drizzt Do'Urden is the most exceptional fantasy character ever created. Any way you look at it, this book is stupendous, a masterpiece of fantasy that any reader will love."

—*Conan Tigard* for *Reading Review* on *Sojourn*

## The Legend of Drizzt®

*Homeland*
*Exile*
*Sojourn*
*The Crystal Shard*
*Streams of Silver*
*The Halfling's Gem*
*The Legacy*
*Starless Night*
*Siege of Darkness*
*Passage to Dawn*
*The Silent Blade*
*The Spine of the World*
*Sea of Swords*

## The Hunter's Blades

*The Thousand Orcs*
*The Lone Drow*
*The Two Swords*

## Transitions

*The Orc King*
*The Pirate King*
*The Ghost King*

## The Sellswords

*Servant of the Shard*
*Promise of the Witch-King*
*Road of the Patriarch*

FORGOTTEN REALMS

# R.A. SALVATORE

## The Legend of Drizzt® Collector's Edition • Book I

HOMELAND

EXILE

SOJOURN

# THE LEGEND OF DRIZZT
Collector's Edition, Book I



Published by Wizards of the Coast LLC



Printed in the U.S.A.

Cover art by Todd Lockwood

Collector's Edition First Hardcover Printing: February 2008
This Edition First Printing: January 2010

This book collects the complete text from the December 2005 edition of Homeland, the March 2006 edition of Exile, and the June 2006 edition of Sojourn.

9 8 7 6 5 4 3 2

ISBN: 978-0-7869-5370-7
620-25143000-001-EN

U.S., CANADA,
ASIA, PACIFIC, & LATIN AMERICA
Wizards of the Coast LLC
P.O. Box 707
Renton, WA 98057-0707
+1-800-324-6496

EUROPEAN HEADQUARTERS
Hasbro UK Ltd
Caswell Way
Newport, Gwent NP9 0YH
GREAT BRITAIN
Save this address for your records.

Visit our web site at www.wizards.com

# Dedications

## Homeland

To my best friend,
my brother,
Gary

## Exile

To Diane,
with all my love

## Sojourn

It is time for me to acknowledge the two people whose belief in me and whose creative influence helped to make Drizzt's tales possible.
I dedicate Sojourn to
Mary Kirchoff and J. Eric Severson,
editors and friends, with all my thanks

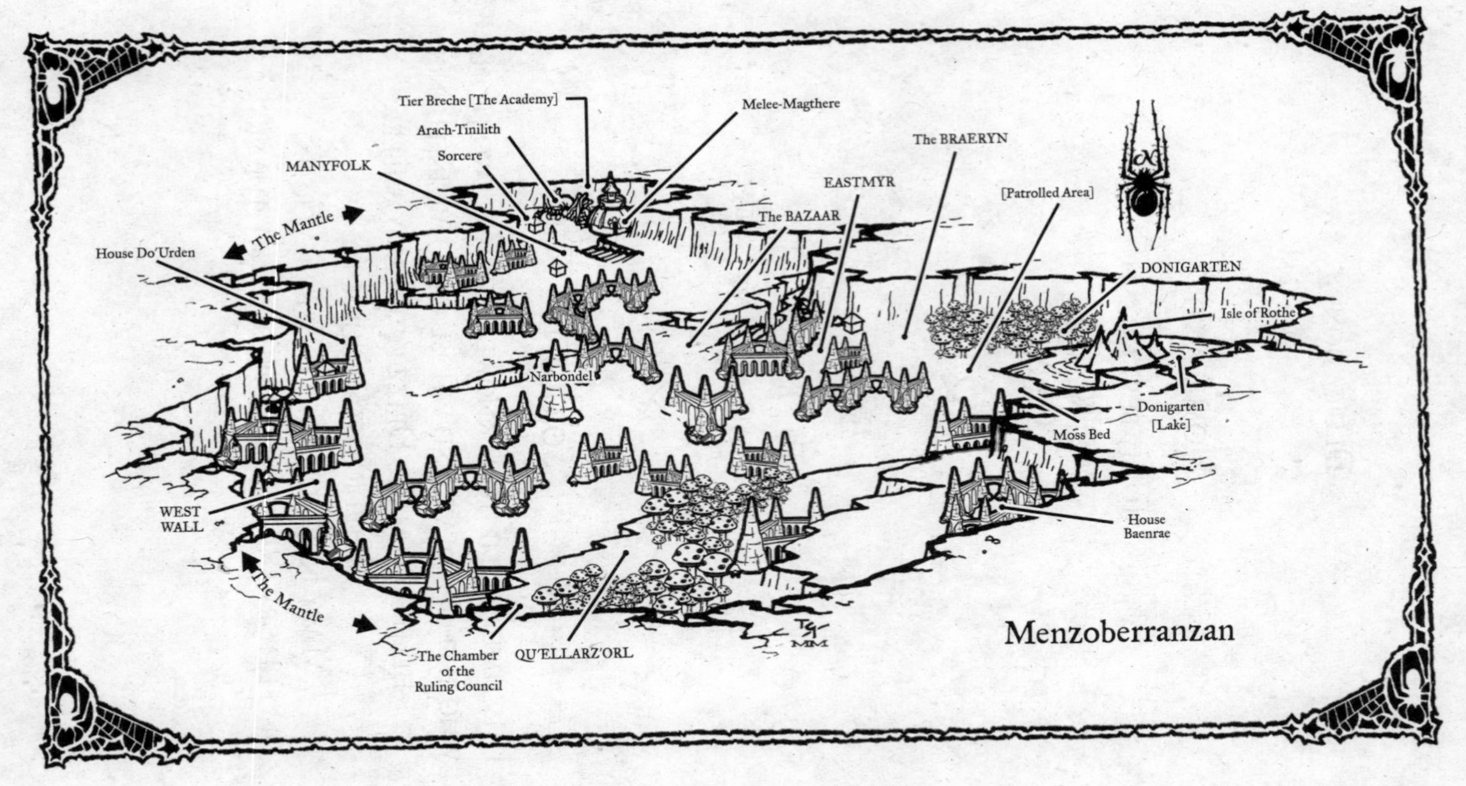
Menzoberranzan
Tier Breche [The Academy]
Arach-Tinilith
Sorcere
Melee-Magthere
MANYFOLK
The Mantle
House Do'Urden
The BAZAAR
EASTMYR
The BRAERYN
[Patrolled Area]
DONIGARTEN
Isle of Rothe
Donigarten [Lake]
Moss Bed
Narbondel
WEST WALL
The Mantle
The Chamber of the Ruling Council
QU'ELLARZ'ORL
House Baenrae

HOMELAND
THE LEGEND OF DRIZZT
BOOK I

# Prelude

Never does a star grace this land with a poet's light of twinkling mysteries, nor does the sun send to here its rays of warmth and life. This is the Underdark, the secret world beneath the bustling surface of the Forgotten Realms, whose sky is a ceiling of heartless stone and whose walls show the gray blandness of death in the torchlight of the foolish surface-dwellers that stumble here. This is not their world, not the world of light. Most who come here uninvited do not return.

Those who do escape to the safety of their surface homes return changed. Their eyes have seen the shadows and the gloom, the inevitable doom of the Underdark.

Dark corridors meander throughout the dark realm in winding courses, connecting caverns great and small, with ceilings high and low. Mounds of stone as pointed as the teeth of a sleeping dragon leer down in silent threat or rise up to block the way of intruders.

There is a silence here, profound and foreboding, the crouched hush of a predator at work. Too often the only sound, the only reminder to travelers in the Underdark that they have not lost their sense of hearing altogether, is a distant and echoing drip of water, beating like the heart of a beast, slipping through the silent stones to the deep Underdark pools of chilled water. What lies beneath the still onyx surface of these pools one can only guess. What secrets await the brave, what horrors await the foolish, only the imagination can reveal—until the stillness is disturbed.

This is the Underdark.

⚔ ⚔ ⚔ ⚔ ⚔

There are pockets of life here, cities as great as many of those on the surface. Around any of the countless bends and turns in the gray stone a traveler might stumble suddenly into the perimeter of such a city, a stark contrast to the emptiness of the corridors. These places are not havens, though; only the foolish traveler would assume so. They are the homes of the most evil races in all the Realms, most notably the duergar, the kuo-toa, and the drow.

In one such cavern, two miles wide and a thousand feet high, looms Menzoberranzan, a monument to the other worldly and—ultimately—deadly grace that marks the race of drow elves. Menzoberranzan is not a large city by drow standards; only twenty thousand dark elves reside there. Where, in ages past, there had been an empty cavern of roughly shaped stalactites and stalagmites now stands artistry, row after row of carved castles thrumming in a quiet glow of magic. The city is perfection of form, where not a stone has been left to its natural shape. This sense of order and control, however, is but a cruel facade, a deception hiding the chaos and vileness that rule the dark elves' hearts. Like their cities, they are a beautiful, slender, and delicate people, with features sharp and haunting.

Yet the drow are the rulers of this unruled world, the deadliest of the deadly, and all other races take cautious note of their passing. Beauty itself pales at the end of a dark elf's sword. The drow are the survivors, and this is the Underdark, the valley of death—the land of nameless nightmares.

# PART ONE

## STATION

Station: In all the world of the drow, there is no more important word. It is the calling of their—of our—religion, the incessant pulling of hungering heartstrings. Ambition overrides good sense and compassion is thrown away in its face, all in the name of Lolth, the Spider Queen.

Ascension to power in drow society is a simple process of assassination. The Spider Queen is a deity of chaos, and she and her high priestesses, the true rulers of the drow world, do not look with ill favor upon ambitious individuals wielding poisoned daggers.

Of course, there are rules of behavior; every society must boast of these. To openly commit murder or wage war invites the pretense of justice, and penalties exacted in the name of drow justice are merciless. To stick a dagger in the back of a rival during the chaos of a larger battle or in the quiet shadows of an alley, however, is quite acceptable—even applauded. Investigation is not the forte of drow justice. No one cares enough to bother.

Station is the way of Lolth, the ambition she bestows to further the chaos, to keep her drow "children" along their appointed course of self-imprisonment. Children? Pawns, more likely, dancing dolls for the Spider Queen, puppets on the imperceptible but impervious strands of her web. All climb the Spider Queen's ladders; all hunt for her pleasure; and all fall to the hunters of her pleasure.

Station is the paradox of the world of my people, the limitation of our power within the hunger for power. It is gained through treachery and invites treachery against those who gain it. Those most powerful in Menzoberranzan spend their days watching over their shoulders, defending against the daggers that would find their backs. Their deaths usually come from the front.

—Drizzt Do'Urden

# I
# Menzoberranzan

To a surface dweller, he might have passed undetected only a foot away. The padded footfalls of his lizard mount were too light to be heard, and the pliable and perfectly crafted mesh armor that both rider and mount wore bent and creased with their movements as well as if the suits had grown over their skin.

Dinin's lizard trotted along in an easy but swift gait, floating over the broken floor, up the walls, and even across the long tunnel's ceiling. Subterranean lizards, with their sticky and soft three-toed feet, were preferred mounts for just this ability to scale stone as easily as a spider. Crossing hard ground left no damning tracks in the lighted surface world, but nearly all of the creatures of the Underdark possessed infravision, the ability to see in the infrared spectrum. Footfalls left heat residue that could easily be tracked if they followed a predictable course along a corridor's floor.

Dinin clamped tight to his saddle as the lizard plodded along a stretch of the ceiling, then sprang out in a twisting descent to a point farther along the wall. Dinin did not want to be tracked.

He had no light to guide him, but he needed none. He was a dark elf, a drow, an ebon-skinned cousin of those sylvan folk who danced under the stars on the world's surface. To Dinin's superior eyes, which translated subtle variations of heat into vivid and colorful images, the Underdark was far from a lightless place. Colors all across the spectrum swirled before him in the stone of the walls and the floor, heated by some distant fissure or hot stream. The heat of living things was the most distinctive, letting the dark elf view his enemies in details as intricate as any surface-dweller would find in brilliant daylight.

Normally Dinin would not have left the city alone; the world of the Underdark was too dangerous for solo treks, even for a drow elf. This day was different, though. Dinin had to be certain that no unfriendly drow eyes marked his passage.

A soft blue magical glow beyond a sculpted archway told the drow that he neared the city's entrance, and he slowed the lizard's pace accordingly. Few used this narrow tunnel, which opened into Tier Breche, the northern section of Menzoberranzan devoted to the Academy, and none but the mistresses and masters, the instructors of the Academy, could pass through here without attracting suspicion.

Dinin was always nervous when he came to this point. Of the hundred tunnels that opened off the main cavern of Menzoberranzan, this one was the best guarded. Beyond the archway, twin statues of gigantic spiders sat in quiet defense. If an enemy crossed through, the spiders would animate and attack, and alarms would be sounded throughout the Academy.

Dinin dismounted, leaving his lizard clinging comfortably to a wall at his chest level. He reached under the collar of his *piwafwi*, his magical, shielding cloak, and took out his neck-purse. From this Dinin produced the insignia of House Do'Urden, a spider wielding various weapons in each of its eight legs and emblazoned with the letters "DN," for Daermon N'a'shezbaernon, the ancient and formal name of House Do'Urden.

"You will await my return," Dinin whispered to the lizard as he waved the insignia before it. As with all the drow houses, the insignia of House Do'Urden held several magical dweomers, one of which gave family members absolute control over the house pets. The lizard would obey unfailingly, holding its position as though it were rooted to the stone, even if a scurry rat, its favorite morsel, napped a few feet from its maw.

Dinin took a deep breath and gingerly stepped to the archway. He could see the spiders leering down at him from their fifteen-foot height. He was a drow of the city, not an enemy, and could pass through any other tunnel unconcerned, but the Academy was an unpredictable place; Dinin had heard that the spiders often refused entry—viciously—even to uninvited drow.

He could not be delayed by fears and possibilities, Dinin reminded himself. His business was of the utmost importance to his family's battle plans. Looking straight ahead, away from the towering spiders, he strode between them and onto the floor of Tier Breche.

He moved to the side and paused, first to be certain that no one lurked nearby, and to admire the sweeping view of Menzoberranzan. No one, drow or otherwise, had ever looked out from this spot without a sense of wonder at the drow city. Tier Breche was the highest point on the floor of the two-mile cavern, affording a panoramic view to the rest of Menzoberranzan. The cubby of the Academy was narrow, holding only the three structures that comprised the drow school: Arach-Tinilith, the spider-shaped school of Lolth; Sorcere, the gracefully curving, many-spired tower of wizardry; and Melee-Magthere, the somewhat plain pyramidal structure where male fighters learned their trade.

Beyond Tier Breche, through the ornate stalagmite columns that marked the entrance to the Academy, the cavern dropped away quickly and spread wide, going far beyond Dinin's line of vision to either side and farther back than his keen eyes could possibly see. The colors of Menzoberranzan were threefold to the sensitive eyes of the drow. Heat patterns from various fissures and hot springs swirled about the entire cavern. Purple and red, bright yellow and subtle blue, crossed and merged, climbed the walls and stalagmite mounds, or ran off singularly in cutting lines against the backdrop of dim gray stone. More confined than these generalized and natural gradations of color in the infrared spectrum were the regions of intense magic, like the spiders Dinin had walked between, virtually glowing with energy. Finally there were the actual lights of the city, faerie fire and highlighted sculptures on the houses. The drow were proud of the beauty of their designs, and especially ornate columns or perfectly crafted gargoyles were almost always limned in permanent magical lights.

Even from this distance Dinin could make out House Baenre, First House of Menzoberranzan. It encompassed twenty stalagmite pillars and half again that number of gigantic stalactites. House Baenre had existed for five thousand years, since the founding of Menzoberranzan, and in that time the work to perfect the house's art had never ceased. Practically every inch of the immense structure glowed in faerie fire, blue at the outlying towers and brilliant purple at the huge central dome.

The sharp light of candles, foreign to the Underdark, glared through some of the windows of the distant houses. Only clerics or wizards would light the fires, Dinin knew, as necessary pains in their world of scrolls and parchments.

This was Menzoberranzan, the city of drow. Twenty thousand dark elves lived there, twenty thousand soldiers in the army of evil.

A wicked smile spread across Dinin's thin lips when he thought of some of those soldiers who would fall this night.

Dinin studied Narbondel, the huge central pillar that served as the timeclock of Menzoberranzan. Narbondel was the only way the drow had to mark the passage of time in a world that otherwise knew no days and no seasons. At the end of each day, the city's appointed Archmage cast his magical fires into the base of the stone pillar. There the spell lingered throughout the cycle—a full day on the surface—and gradually spread its warmth up the structure of Narbondel until the whole of it glowed red in the infrared spectrum. The pillar was fully dark now, cooled since the dweomer's fires had expired. The wizard was even now at the base, Dinin reasoned, ready to begin the cycle anew.

It was midnight, the appointed hour.

Dinin moved away from the spiders and the tunnel exit and crept along the side of Tier Breche, seeking the "shadows" of heat patterns in the wall, which would effectively hide the distinct outline of his own body temperature. He came at last to Sorcere, the school of wizardry, and slipped into the narrow alley between the tower's curving base and Tier Breche's outer wall.

"Student or master?" came the expected whisper.

"Only a master may walk out-of-house in Tier Breche in the black death of Narbondel," Dinin responded.

A heavily robed figure moved around the arc of the structure to stand before Dinin. The stranger remained in the customary posture of a master of the drow Academy, his arms out before him and bent at the elbows, his hands tight together, one on top of the other in front of his chest.

That pose was the only thing about this one that seemed normal to Dinin. "Greetings, Faceless One," he signaled in the silent hand code of the drow, a language as detailed as the spoken word. The quiver of Dinin's hands belied his calm face, though, for the sight of this wizard put him as far on the edge of his nerves as he had ever been.

"Secondboy Do'Urden," the wizard replied in the gestured code. "Have you my payment?"

"You will be compensated," Dinin signaled pointedly, regaining his composure in the first swelling bubbles of his temper. "Do you dare to doubt the promise of Malice Do'Urden, Matron Mother of Daermon N'a'shezbaernon, Tenth House of Menzoberranzan?"

The Faceless One slumped back, knowing he had erred. "My apologies, Secondboy of House Do'Urden," he answered, dropping to one knee in a gesture of surrender. Since he had entered this conspiracy, the wizard had feared that his impatience might cost him his life. He had been caught in the violent throes of one of his own magical experiments, the tragedy melting away all of his facial features and leaving behind a blank hot spot of white and green goo. Matron Malice Do'Urden, reputedly as skilled as anyone in all the vast city in mixing potions and salves, had offered him a sliver of hope that he could not pass by.

No pity found its way into Dinin's callous heart, but House Do'Urden needed the wizard. "You will get your salve," Dinin promised calmly, "when Alton DeVir is dead."

"Of course," the wizard agreed. "This night?"

Dinin crossed his arms and considered the question. Matron Malice had instructed him that Alton DeVir should die even as their families' battle commenced. That scenario now seemed too clean, too easy, to Dinin. The Faceless One did not miss the sparkle that suddenly brightened the scarlet glow in the young Do'Urden's heat-sensing eyes.

"Wait for Narbondel's light to approach its zenith," Dinin replied, his hands working through the signals excitedly and his grimace seeming more of a twisted grin.

"Should the doomed boy know of his house's fate before he dies?" the wizard asked, guessing the wicked intentions behind Dinin's instructions.

"As the killing blow falls," answered Dinin. "Let Alton DeVir die without hope."

⚔ ⚔ ⚔ ⚔ ⚔

Dinin retrieved his mount and sped off down the empty corridors, finding an intersecting route that would take him in through a different entrance to the city proper. He came in along the eastern end of the great cavern, Menzoberranzan's produce section, where no drow families would see that he had been outside the city limits and where only a few unremarkable stalagmite pillars rose up from the flat stone. Dinin spurred his mount along the banks of Donigarten, the city's small pond with its moss-covered island that housed a fair-sized herd of cattle-like creatures called rothe. A hundred goblins and orcs looked up from their herding and fishing duties to mark the drow soldier's swift passage. Knowing their restrictions as slaves, they took care not to look Dinin in the eye.

Dinin would have paid them no heed anyway. He was too consumed by the urgency of the moment. He kicked his lizard to even greater speeds when he again was on the flat and curving avenues between the glowing drow castles. He moved toward the south-central region of the city, toward the grove of giant mushrooms that marked the section of the finest houses in Menzoberranzan.

As he came around one blind turn, he nearly ran over a group of four wandering bugbears. The giant hairy goblin things paused a moment to consider the drow, then moved slowly but purposefully out of his way.

The bugbears recognized him as a member of House Do'Urden, Dinin knew. He was a noble, a son of a high priestess, and his surname, Do'Urden, was the name of his house. Of the twenty thousand dark elves in Menzoberranzan, only a thousand or so were nobles, actually the children of the sixty-seven recognized families of the city. The rest were common soldiers.

Bugbears were not stupid creatures. They knew a noble from a commoner, and though drow elves did not carry their family insignia in plain view, the pointed and tailed cut of Dinin's stark white hair and the distinctive pattern of purple and red lines in his black *piwafwi* told them well enough who he was.

The mission's urgency pressed upon Dinin, but he could not ignore the bugbears' slight. How fast would they have scampered away if he had been a member of House Baenre or one of the other seven ruling houses? he wondered.

"You will learn respect of House Do'Urden soon enough!" the dark elf whispered under his breath, as he turned and charged his lizard at the group. The bugbears broke into a run, turning down an alley strewn with stones and debris.

Dinin found his satisfaction by calling on the innate powers of his race. He summoned a globe of darkness—impervious to both infravision and normal sight—in the fleeing creatures' path. He supposed that it was unwise to call such attention to himself, but a moment later, when he heard crashing and sputtered curses as the bugbears stumbled blindly over the stones, he felt it was worth the risk.

His anger sated, he moved off again, picking a more careful route through the heat shadows. As a member of the tenth house of the city, Dinin could go as he pleased within the giant cavern without question, but Matron Malice had made it clear that no one connected to House Do'Urden was to be caught anywhere near the mushroom grove.

Matron Malice, Dinin's mother, was not to be crossed, but it was only a rule, after all. In Menzoberranzan, one rule took precedence over all of the petty others: Don't get caught.

At the mushroom grove's southern end, the impetuous drow found what he was looking for: a cluster of five huge floor-to-ceiling pillars that were hollowed into a network of chambers and connected with metal and stone parapets and bridges. Red-glowing gargoyles, the standard of the house, glared down from a hundred perches like silent sentries. This was House DeVir, Fourth House of Menzoberranzan.

A stockade of tall mushrooms ringed the place, every fifth one a shrieker, a sentient fungus named (and favored as guardians) for the shrill cries of alarm it emitted whenever a living being passed it by. Dinin kept a cautious distance, not wanting to set off one of the shriekers and knowing also that other, more deadly wards protected the fortress. Matron Malice would see to those.

An expectant hush permeated the air of this city section. It was general knowledge throughout Menzoberranzan that Matron Ginafae of House DeVir had fallen out of favor with Lolth, the Spider Queen deity to all drow and the true source of every house's strength. Such circumstances were never openly discussed among the drow, but everyone who knew fully expected that some family lower in the city hierarchy soon would strike out against the crippled House DeVir.

Matron Ginafae and her family had been the last to learn of the Spider Queen's displeasure—ever was that Lolth's devious way—and Dinin could tell just by scanning the outside of House DeVir that the doomed family had not found sufficient time to erect proper defenses. DeVir sported nearly four hundred soldiers, many female, but those that Dinin could now see at their posts along the parapets seemed nervous and unsure.

Dinin's smile spread even wider when he thought of his own house, which grew in power daily under the cunning guidance of Matron Malice. With all three of his sisters rapidly approaching the status of high priestess, his brother an accomplished wizard, and his uncle Zaknafein, the finest weapons master in all of Menzoberranzan, busily training the three hundred soldiers, House Do'Urden was a complete force. And, Matron Malice, unlike Ginafae, was in the Spider Queen's full favor.

"Daermon N'a'shezbaernon," Dinin muttered under his breath, using the formal and ancestral reference to House Do'Urden. "Ninth House of Menzoberranzan!" He liked the sound of it.

⚔ ⚔ ⚔ ⚔ ⚔

Halfway across the city, beyond the silver-glowing balcony and the arched doorway twenty feet up the cavern's west wall, sat the principals of House

Do'Urden, gathered to outline the final plans of the night's work. On the raised dais at the back of the small audience chamber sat venerable Matron Malice, her belly swollen in the final hours of pregnancy. Flanking her in their places of honor were her three daughters, Maya, Vierna, and the eldest, Briza, a newly ordained high priestess of Lolth. Maya and Vierna appeared as younger versions of their mother, slender and deceptively small, though possessing great strength. Briza, though, hardly carried the family resemblance. She was big—huge by drow standards—and rounded in the shoulders and hips. Those who knew Briza well figured that her size was merely a circumstance of her temperament; a smaller body could not have contained the anger and brutal streak of House Do'Urden's newest high priestess.

"Dinin should return soon," remarked Rizzen, the present patron of the family, "to let us know if the time is right for the assault."

"We go before Narbondel finds its morning glow!" Briza snapped at him in her thick but razor-sharp voice. She turned a crooked smile to her mother, seeking approval for putting the male in his place.

"The child comes this night," Matron Malice explained to her anxious husband. "We go no matter what news Dinin bears."

"It will be a boy child," groaned Briza, making no effort to hide her disappointment, "third living son of House Do'Urden."

"To be sacrificed to Lolth," put in Zaknafein, a former patron of the house who now held the important position of weapons master. The skilled drow fighter seemed quite pleased at the thought of sacrifice, as did Nalfein, the family's eldest son, who stood at Zak's side. Nalfein was the elderboy, and he needed no more competition beyond Dinin within the ranks of House Do'Urden.

"In accord with custom," Briza glowered and the red of her eyes brightened. "To aid in our victory!"

Rizzen shifted uncomfortably. "Matron Malice," he dared to speak, "you know well the difficulties of birthing. Might the pain distract you—"

"You dare to question the matron mother?" Briza started sharply, reaching for the snake-headed whip so comfortably strapped—and writhing—on her belt. Matron Malice stopped her with an outstretched hand.

"Attend to the fighting," the matron said to Rizzen. "Let the females of the house see to the important matters of this battle."

Rizzen shifted again and dropped his gaze.

⚔ ⚔ ⚔ ⚔ ⚔

Dinin came to the magically wrought fence that connected the keep within the city's west wall with the two small stalagmite towers of House Do'Urden, and which formed the courtyard to the compound. The fence was adamantine, the hardest metal in all the world, and adorning it were a hundred weapon-wielding spider carvings, each ensorcelled with deadly glyphs and wards. The mighty gate of House Do'Urden was the envy of many a drow house, but so soon after viewing the spectacular houses in the mushroom grove, Dinin could only find disappointment when looking upon his own abode. The compound was plain and somewhat bare, as was the section of wall, with the notable exception of the mithral-and-adamantine balcony running along the second level, by the arched doorway reserved for the nobility of the family. Each baluster of that balcony sported a thousand carvings, all of which blended into a single piece of art.

House Do'Urden, unlike the great majority of the houses in Menzoberranzan, did not stand free within groves of stalactites and stalagmites. The bulk of the structure was within a cave, and while this setup was indisputably defensible, Dinin found himself wishing that his family could show a bit more grandeur.

An excited soldier rushed to open the gate for the returning secondboy. Dinin swept past him without so much as a word of greeting and moved across the courtyard, conscious of the hundred and more curious glances that fell upon him. The soldiers and slaves knew that Dinin's mission this night had something to do with the anticipated battle.

No stairway led to the silvery balcony of House Do'Urden's second level. This, too, was a precautionary measure designed to segregate the leaders of the house from the rabble and the slaves. Drow nobles needed no stairs; another manifestation of their innate magical abilities allowed them the power of levitation. With hardly a conscious thought to the act, Dinin drifted easily through the air and dropped onto the balcony.

He rushed through the archway and down the house's main central corridor, which was dimly lit in the soft hues of faerie fire, allowing for sight in the normal light spectrum but not bright enough to defeat the use of infravision. The ornate brass door at the corridor's end marked the secondboy's destination, and he paused before it to allow his eyes to shift back to the infrared spectrum. Unlike the corridor, the room beyond the door had no light source. It was the audience hall of the high priestesses, the anteroom to House Do'Urden's grand chapel. The drow clerical rooms, in accord with the dark rites of the Spider Queen, were not places of light.

When he felt he was prepared, Dinin pushed straight through the door, shoving past the two shocked female guards without hesitation and moving boldly to stand before his mother. All three of the family daughters narrowed their eyes at their brash and pretentious brother. To enter without permission! he knew they were thinking. Would that it was he who was to be sacrificed this night!

As much as he enjoyed testing the limitations of his inferior station as a male, Dinin could not ignore the threatening dances of Vierna, Maya, and Briza. Being female, they were bigger and stronger than Dinin and had trained all their lives in the use of wicked drow clerical powers and weapons. Dinin watched as enchanted extensions of the clerics, the dreaded snake-headed whips on his sisters' belts, began writhing in anticipation of the punishment they would exact. The handles were adamantine and ordinary enough, but the whips' lengths and multiple heads were living serpents. Briza's whip, in particular, a wicked six-headed device, danced and squirmed, tying itself into knots around the belt that held it. Briza was always the quickest to punish.

Matron Malice, however, seemed pleased by Dinin's swagger. The secondboy knew his place well enough by her measure and he followed her commands fearlessly and without question.

Dinin took comfort in the calmness of his mother's face, quite the opposite of the shining white-hot faces of his three sisters. "All is ready," he said to her. "House DeVir huddles within its fence—except for Alton, of course, foolishly attending his studies in Sorcere."

"You have met with the Faceless One?" Matron Malice asked.

"The Academy was quiet this night," Dinin replied. "Our meeting went off perfectly."

"He has agreed to our contract?"

"Alton DeVir will be dealt with accordingly," Dinin chuckled. He then remembered the slight alteration he had made in Matron Malice's plans, delaying Alton's execution for the sake of his own lust for added cruelty. Dinin's thought evoked another recollection as well: high priestesses of Lolth had an unnerving talent for reading thoughts.

"Alton will die this night," Dinin quickly completed the answer, assuring the others before they could probe him for more definite details.

"Excellent," Briza growled. Dinin breathed a little easier.

"To the meld," Matron Malice ordered.

The four drow males moved to kneel before the matron and her daughters: Rizzen to Malice, Zaknafein to Briza, Nalfein to Maya, and Dinin to Vierna. The clerics chanted in unison, placing one hand delicately upon the forehead of their respective soldier, tuning in to his passions.

"You know your places," Matron Malice said when the ceremony was completed. She grimaced through the pain of another contraction. "Let our work begin."

⚔ ⚔ ⚔ ⚔ ⚔

Less than an hour later, Zaknafein and Briza stood together on the balcony outside the upper entrance to House Do'Urden. Below them, on the cavern floor, the second and third brigades of the family army, Rizzen's and Nalfein's, bustled about, fitting on heated leather straps and metal patches—camouflage against a distinctive elven form to heat-seeing drow eyes. Dinin's group, the initial strike force that included a hundred goblin slaves, had long since departed.

"We will be known after this night," Briza said. "None would have suspected that a tenth house would dare to move against one as powerful as DeVir. When the whispers ripple out after this night's bloody work, even Baenre will take note of Daermon N'a'shezbaernon!" She leaned out over the balcony to watch as the two brigades formed into lines and started out, silently, along separate paths that would bring them through the winding city to the mushroom grove and the five-pillared structure of House DeVir.

Zaknafein eyed the back of Matron Malice's eldest daughter, wanting nothing more than to put a dagger into her spine. As always, though, good judgment kept Zak's practiced hand in its place.

"Have you the articles?" Briza inquired, showing Zak considerably more respect than she had when Matron Malice sat protectively at her side. Zak was only a male, a commoner allowed to don the family name as his own because he sometimes served Matron Malice in a husbandly manner and had once been the patron of the house. Still, Briza feared to anger him. Zak was the weapons master of House Do'Urden, a tall and muscular male, stronger than most females, and those who had witnessed his fighting wrath considered him among the finest warriors of either sex in all of Menzoberranzan. Besides Briza and her mother, both high priestesses of the Spider Queen, Zaknafein, with his unrivaled swordsmanship, was House Do'Urden's trump.

Zak held up the black hood and opened the small pouch on his belt, revealing several tiny ceramic spheres.

Briza smiled evilly and rubbed her slender hands together. "Matron Ginafae will not be pleased," she whispered.

Zak returned the smile and turned to view the departing soldiers. Nothing gave the weapons master more pleasure than killing drow elves, particularly clerics of Lolth.

"Prepare yourself," Briza said after a few minutes.

Zak shook his thick hair back from his face and stood rigid, eyes tightly closed. Briza drew her wand slowly, beginning the chant that would activate the device. She tapped Zak on one shoulder, then the other, then held the wand motionless over his head.

Zak felt the frosty sprinkles falling down on him, permeating his clothes and armor, even his flesh, until he and all of his possessions had cooled to a uniform temperature and hue. Zak hated the magical chill—it felt as he imagined death would feel—but he knew that under the influence of the wand's sprinkles he was, to the heat-sensing eyes of the creatures of the Underdark, as gray as common stone, unremarkable and undetectable.

Zak opened his eyes and shuddered, flexing his fingers to be sure they could still perform the fine edge of his craft. He looked back to Briza, already in the midst of the second spell, the summoning. This one would take a while, so Zak leaned back against the wall and considered again the pleasant, though dangerous, task before him. How thoughtful of Matron Malice to leave all of House DeVir's clerics to him!

"It is done," Briza announced after a few minutes. She led Zak's gaze upward, to the darkness beneath the unseen ceiling of the immense cavern.

Zak spotted Briza's handiwork first, an approaching current of air, yellow-tinted and warmer than the normal air of the cavern. A living current of air.

The creature, a conjuration from an elemental plane, swirled to hover just beyond the lip of the balcony, obediently awaiting its summoner's commands.

Zak didn't hesitate. He leaped out into the thing's midst, letting it hold him suspended above the floor.

Briza offered him a final salute and motioned her servant away. "Good fighting," she called to Zak, though he was already invisible in the air above her.

Zak chuckled at the irony of her words as the twisting city of Menzoberranzan rolled out below him. She wanted the clerics of House DeVir dead as surely as Zak did, but for very different reasons. All complications aside, Zak would have been just as happy killing clerics of House Do'Urden.

The weapons master took up one of his adamantine swords, a drow weapon magically crafted and unbelievably sharp with the edge of killing dweomers. "Good fighting indeed," he whispered. If only Briza knew how good.

# 2

# The Fall of House DeVir

Dinin noted with satisfaction that any of the meandering bugbears, or any other of the multitude of races that composed Menzoberranzan, drow included, now made great haste to scurry out of his way. This time the secondboy of House Do'Urden was not alone. Nearly sixty soldiers of the house walked in tight lines behind him. Behind these, in similar order though with far less enthusiasm for the adventure, came a hundred armed slaves of lesser races—goblins, orcs, and bugbears.

There could be no doubt for onlookers—a drow house was on a march to war. This was not an everyday event in Menzoberranzan but neither was it unexpected. At least once every decade a house decided that its position within the city hierarchy could be improved by another house's elimination. It was a risky proposition, for all of the nobles of the "victim" house had to be disposed of quickly and quietly. If even one survived to lay an accusation upon the perpetrator, the attacking house would be eradicated by Menzoberranzan's merciless system of "justice."

If the raid was executed to devious perfection, though, no recourse would be forthcoming. All of the city, even the ruling council of the top eight matron mothers, would secretly applaud the attackers for their courage and intelligence and no more would ever be said of the incident.

Dinin took a roundabout route, not wanting to lay a direct trail between

House Do'Urden and House DeVir. A half-hour later, for the second time that night, he crept to the mushroom grove's southern end, to the cluster of stalagmites that held House DeVir. His soldiers streamed out behind him eagerly, readying weapons and taking full measure of the structure before them.

The slaves were slower in their movements. Many of them looked about for some escape, for they knew in their hearts that they were doomed in this battle. They feared the wrath of the dark elves more than death itself, though, and would not attempt to flee. With every exit out of Menzoberranzan protected by devious drow magic, where could they possibly go? Every one of them had witnessed the brutal punishments the drow elves exacted on recaptured slaves. At Dinin's command, they jumped into their positions around the mushroom fence.

Dinin reached into his large pouch and pulled out a heated sheet of metal. He flashed the object, brightened in the infrared spectrum, three times behind him to signal the approaching brigades of Nalfein and Rizzen. Then, with his usual cockiness, Dinin spun it quickly into the air, caught it, and replaced it in the secrecy of his heat-shielding pouch. On cue with the twirling signal, Dinin's drow brigade fitted enchanted darts to their tiny hand-held crossbows and took aim on the appointed targets.

Every fifth mushroom was a shrieker, and every dart held a magical dweomer that could silence the roar of a dragon.

". . . two . . . three," Dinin counted, his hand signaling the tempo since no words could be heard within the sphere of magical silence cast about his troops. He imagined the "click" as the drawn string on his little weapon released, loosing the dart into the nearest shrieker. So it went all around the cluster of House DeVir, the first line of alarm systematically silenced by three-dozen enchanted darts.

⚔ ⚔ ⚔ ⚔ ⚔

Halfway across Menzoberranzan, Matron Malice, her daughters, and four of the house's common clerics were gathered in Lolth's unholy circle of eight. They ringed an idol of their wicked deity, a gemstone carving of a drow-faced spider, and called to Lolth for aid in their struggles.

Malice sat at the head, propped in a chair angled for birthing. Briza and Vierna flanked her, Briza clutching her hand.

The select group chanted in unison, combining their energies into a single offensive spell. A moment later, when Vierna, mentally linked to Dinin, understood that the first attack group was in position, the Do'Urden circle of eight sent the first insinuating waves of mental energy into the rival house.

Matron Ginafae, her two daughters, and the five principal clerics of the common troops of House DeVir huddled together in the darkened anteroom of the five-stalagmite house's main chapel. They had gathered there in solemn prayer every night since Matron Ginafae had learned that she had fallen into Lolth's disfavor. Ginafae understood how vulnerable her house remained until she could find a way to appease the Spider Queen. There were sixty-six other houses in Menzoberranzan, fully twenty of which might dare to attack House DeVir at such an obvious disadvantage. The eight clerics were anxious now, somehow suspecting that this night would be eventful.

Ginafae felt it first, a chilling blast of confusing perceptions that caused her to stutter over her prayer of forgiveness. The other clerics of House DeVir glanced nervously at the matron's uncharacteristic slip of words, looking for confirmation.

"We are under attack," Ginafae breathed to them, her head already pounding with a dull ache under the growing assault of the formidable clerics of House Do'Urden.

A second signal from Dinin put the slave troops into motion. Still using stealth as their ally, they quietly rushed to the mushroom fence and cut through with wide-bladed swords. The secondboy of House

Do'Urden watched and enjoyed as the courtyard of House DeVir was easily penetrated. "Not such a prepared guard," he whispered in silent sarcasm to the red-glowing gargoyles on the high walls. The statues had seemed such an ominous guard earlier that night. Now they just watched helplessly.

Dinin recognized the measured but growing anticipation in the soldiers around him; their drow battle-lust was barely contained. Every now and came a killing flash as one of the slaves stumbled over a warding glyph, but the secondboy and the other drow only laughed at the spectacle. The lesser races were the expendable "fodder" of House Do'Urden's army. The only purpose in bringing the goblinoids to House DeVir was to trigger the deadly traps and defenses along the perimeter, to lead the way for the drow elves, the true soldiers.

The fence was now opened and secrecy was thrown away. House DeVir's soldiers met the invading slaves head-on within the compound. Dinin barely had his hand up to begin the attack command when his sixty anxious drow warriors jumped up and charged, their faces twisted in wicked glee and their weapons waving menacingly.

They halted their approach on cue, though, remembering one final task set out to them. Every drow, noble or commoner, possessed certain magical abilities. Bringing forth a globe of darkness, as Dinin had done to the bugbears in the street earlier that night, came easily to even the lowliest of the dark elves. So it went now, with sixty Do'Urden soldiers blotting out the perimeter of House DeVir above the mushroom fence in ball after ball of blackness.

For all of their stealth and precautions, House Do'Urden knew that many eyes were watching the raid. Witnesses were not too much of a problem; they could not, or would not, care enough to identify the attacking house. But custom and rules demanded that certain attempts at secrecy be enacted, the etiquette of drow warfare. In the blink of a red-glowing drow eye, House DeVir became, to the rest of the city, a dark blot on Menzoberranzan's landscape.

Rizzen came up behind his youngest son. "Well done," he signaled in the intricate finger language of the drow. "Nalfein is in through the back."

"An easy victory," the cocky Dinin signaled back, "if Matron Ginafae and her clerics are held at bay."

"Trust in Matron Malice," was Rizzen's response. He clapped his son's shoulder and followed his troops in through the breached mushroom fence.

⚔ ⚔ ⚔ ⚔ ⚔

High above the cluster of House DeVir, Zaknafein rested comfortably in the current-arms of Briza's aerial servant, watching the drama unfold. From this vantage, Zak could see within the ring of darkness and could hear within the ring of magical silence. Dinin's troops, the first drow soldiers in, had met resistance at every door and were being beaten badly.

Nalfein and his brigade, the troops of House Do'Urden most practiced in the ways of wizardry, came through the fence at the rear of the complex. Lightning strikes and magical balls of acid thundered into the courtyard at the base of the DeVir structures, cutting down Do'Urden fodder and DeVir defenses alike.

In the front courtyard, Rizzen and Dinin commanded the finest fighters of House Do'Urden. The blessings of Lolth were with his house, Zak could see when the battle was fully joined, for the strikes of the soldiers of House Do'Urden came faster than those of their enemies, and their aim proved more deadly. In minutes, the battle had been taken fully inside the five pillars.

Zak stretched the incessant chill out of his arms and willed the aerial servant to action. Down he plummeted on his windy bed, and he fell free the last few feet to the terrace along the top chambers of the central pillar. At once, two guards, one a female, rushed out to greet him.

They hesitated in confusion, though, trying to sort out the true form of this unremarkable gray blur—too long.

They had never heard of Zaknafein Do'Urden. They didn't know that death was upon them.

Zak's whip flashed out, catching and gashing the female's throat, while his other hand walked his sword through a series of masterful thrusts and parries that put the male off balance. Zak finished both in a single, blurring movement, snapping the whip-entwined female from the terrace with a twist of his wrist and spinning a kick into the male's face that likewise dropped him to the cavern floor.

Zak was then inside, where another guard rose up to meet him . . . but fell at his feet.

Zak slipped along the curving wall of the stalactite tower, his cooled body blending perfectly with the stone. Soldiers of House DeVir rushed all about him, trying to formulate some defense against the host of intruders who had already won out the lowest level of every structure and had taken two of the pillars completely.

Zak was not concerned with them. He blocked out the clanging ring of adamantine weapons, the cries of command, and the screams of death, concentrating instead on a singular sound that would lead him to his destination: a unified, frantic chant.

He found an empty corridor covered with spider carvings and running into the center of the pillar. As in House Do'Urden, this corridor ended in a large set of ornate double doors, their decorations dominated by arachnid forms. "This must be the place." Zak muttered under his breath, fitting his hood to the top of his head.

A giant spider rushed out of its concealment to his side.

Zak dived to his belly and kicked out under the thing, spinning into a roll that plunged his sword deep into the monster's bulbous body. Sticky fluids gushed out over the weapons master, and the spider shuddered to a quick death.

"Yes," Zak whispered, wiping the spider juices from his face, "this must be the place." He pulled the dead monster back into its hidden cubby and slipped in beside the thing, hoping that no one had noticed the brief struggle.

By the sounds of ringing weapons, Zak could tell that the fighting had almost reached this floor. House DeVir now seemed to have its defenses in place, though, and was finally holding its ground.

"Now, Malice," Zak whispered, hoping that Briza, attuned to him in the meld, would sense his anxiety. "Let us not be late!"

⚔ ⚔ ⚔ ⚔ ⚔

Back in the clerical anteroom of House Do'Urden, Malice and her subordinates continued their brutal mental assault on the clerics of House DeVir. Lolth heard their prayers louder than those of their counterparts, giving the clerics of House Do'Urden the stronger spells in their mental combat. Already they had easily put their enemies into a defensive posture. One of the lesser priestesses in DeVir's circle of eight had been crushed by Briza's mental insinuations and now lay dead on the floor barely inches from Matron Ginafae's feet.

But the momentum had slowed suddenly and the battle seemed to be swinging back to an even level. Matron Malice, struggling with the impending birth, could not hold her concentration, and without her voice, the spells of her unholy circle weakened.

At her mother's side, powerful Briza clutched her mother's hand so tightly that all the blood was squeezed from it, leaving it cool—the only cool spot on the laboring female—to the eyes of the others. Briza studied the contractions and the crowning cap of the coming child's white hair, and calculated the time to the moment of birth. This technique of translating the pain of birth into an offensive spell attack had never been tried before, except in legend, and Briza knew that timing would be the critical factor.

She whispered into her mother's ear, coaxing out the words of a deadly incantation.

Matron Malice echoed back the beginnings of the spell, sublimating her gasps, and transforming her rage of agony into offensive power.

"*Dinnen douward ma brechen tol,"* Briza implored.

"*Dinnen douward. . . maaa . . . brechen tol!*" Malice growled, so determined to focus through the pain that she bit through one of her thin lips.

The baby's head appeared, more fully this time, and this time to stay.

Briza trembled and could barely remember the incantation herself. She whispered the final rune into the matron's ear, almost fearing the consequences.

Malice gathered her breath and her courage. She could feel the tingling of the spell as clearly as the pain of the birth. To her daughters standing around the idol, staring at her in disbelief, she appeared as a red blur of heated fury, streaking sweat lines that shone as brightly as the heat of boiling water.

"*Abec*," the matron began, feeling the pressure building to a crescendo. "*Abec*." She felt the hot tear of her skin, the sudden slippery release as the baby's head pushed through, the sudden ecstacy of birthing. "*Abec di'n'a'BREG DOUWARD!*" Malice screamed, pushing away all of the agony in a final explosion of magical power that knocked even the clerics of her own house from their feet.

⚔ ⚔ ⚔ ⚔ ⚔

Carried on the thrust of Matron Malice's exultation, the dweomer thundered into the chapel of House DeVir, shattered the gemstone idol of Lolth, sundered the double doors into heaps of twisted metal, and threw Matron Ginafae and her overmatched subordinates to the floor.

Zak shook his head in disbelief as the chapel doors flew past him. "Quite a kick, Malice." He chuckled and spun around the entryway, into the chapel. Using his infravision, he took a quick survey and head count of the lightless room's seven living occupants, all struggling back to their feet, their robes tattered. Again shaking his head at the bared power of Matron Malice, Zak pulled his hood down over his face.

A snap of his whip was the only explanation he offered as he smashed a tiny ceramic globe at his feet. The sphere shattered, dropping out a pellet that Briza had enchanted for just such occasions, a pellet glowing with the brightness of daylight.

For eyes accustomed to blackness, tuned in to heat emanations, the intrusion of such radiance came in a blinding flash of agony. The clerics' cries of pain only aided Zak in his systematic trek around the room, and he smiled widely under his hood every time he felt his sword bite into drow flesh.

He heard the beginnings of a spell across the way and knew that one of the DeVirs had recovered enough from the assault to be dangerous. The weapons master did not need his eyes to aim, however, and the crack of his whip took Matron Ginafae's tongue right out of her mouth.

⚔ ⚔ ⚔ ⚔ ⚔

Briza placed the newborn on the back of the spider idol and lifted the ceremonial dagger, pausing to admire its cruel workmanship. Its hilt was a spider's body sporting eight legs, barbed so as to appear furred, but angled down to serve as blades. Briza lifted the instrument above the baby's chest. "Name the child," she implored her mother. "The Spider Queen will not accept the sacrifice until the child is named!"

Matron Malice lolled her head, trying to fathom her daughter's meaning. The matron mother had thrown everything into the moment of the spell and the birth, and she was now barely coherent.

"Name the child!" Briza commanded, anxious to feed her hungry goddess.

⚔ ⚔ ⚔ ⚔ ⚔

"It nears its end," Dinin said to his brother when they met in a lower hall of one of the lesser pillars of House DeVir. "Rizzen is winning through to the top, and it is believed that Zaknafein's dark work has been completed."

"Two score of House DeVir's soldiers have already turned allegiance to us," Nalfein replied.

"They see the end," laughed Dinin. "One house serves them as well as another, and in the eyes of commoners no house is worth dying for. Our task will be finished soon."

"Too quickly for anyone to take note," Nalfein said. "Now Do'Urden, Daermon N'a'shezbaernon, is the Ninth House of Menzoberranzan and DeVir be damned!"

"Alert!" Dinin cried suddenly, eyes widening in feigned horror as he looked over his brother's shoulder.

Nalfein reacted immediately, spinning to face the danger at his back, only to put the true danger at his back. For even as Nalfein realized the deception, Dinin's sword slipped into his spine. Dinin put his head to his brother's shoulder and pressed his cheek to Nalfein's, watching the red sparkle of heat leave his brother's eyes.

"Too quickly for anyone to take note," Dinin teased, echoing his brother's earlier words.

He dropped the lifeless form to his feet. "Now Dinin is elderboy of House Do'Urden, and Nalfein be damned."

⚔ ⚔ ⚔ ⚔ ⚔

"Drizzt," breathed Matron Malice. "The child's name is Drizzt!"

Briza tightened her grip on the knife and began the ritual. "Queen of Spiders, take this babe," she began. She raised the dagger to strike. "Drizzt Do'Urden we give to you in payment for our glorious vic—"

"Wait!" called Maya from the side of the room. Her melding with her brother Nalfein had abruptly ceased. It could only mean one thing. "Nalfein is dead," she announced. "The baby is no longer the third living son."

Vierna glanced curiously at her sister. At the same instant that Maya had sensed Nalfein's death, Vierna, melded with Dinin, had felt a strong emotive surge. Elation? Vierna brought a slender finger up to her pursed lips, wondering if Dinin had successfully pulled off the assassination.

Briza still held the spider-shaped knife over the babe's chest, wanting to give this one to Lolth.

"We promised the Spider Queen the third living son," Maya warned. "And that has been given."

"But not in sacrifice," argued Briza.

Vierna shrugged, at a loss. "If Lolth accepted Nalfein, then he has been given. To give another might evoke the Spider Queen's anger."

"But to not give what we have promised would be worse still!" Briza insisted.

"Then finish the deed," said Maya.

Briza clenched down tight on the dagger and began the ritual again.

"Stay your hand," Matron Malice commanded, propping herself up in the chair. "Lolth is content; our victory is won. Welcome, then, your brother, the newest member of House Do'Urden."

"Just a male," Briza commented in obvious disgust, walking away from the idol and the child.

"Next time we shall do better," Matron Malice chuckled, though she wondered if there would be a next time. She approached the end of her fifth century of life, and drow elves, even young ones, were not a particularly fruitful lot. Briza had been born to Malice at the youthful age of one hundred, but in the almost four centuries since, Malice had produced only five other children. Even this baby, Drizzt, had come as a surprise, and Malice hardly expected that she would ever conceive again.

"Enough of such contemplations," Malice whispered to herself, exhausted. "There will be ample time . . ." She sank back into her chair and fell into fitful, though wickedly pleasant, dreams of heightening power.

⚔ ⚔ ⚔ ⚔ ⚔

Zaknafein walked through the central pillar of the DeVir complex, his hood in his hand and his whip and sword comfortably replaced on his belt. Every now and a ring of battle sounded, only to be quickly ended. House Do'Urden had rolled through to victory, the tenth house had taken the fourth, and now all that remained was to remove evidence and witnesses. One group of lesser female clerics marched through, tending to the wounded Do'Urdens and animating the corpses of those beyond their ability, so that the bodies could walk away from the crime scene. Back at the Do'Urden compound, those corpses not beyond repair would be resurrected and put back to work.

Zak turned away with a visible shudder as the clerics moved from room to room, the marching line of Do'Urden zombies growing ever longer at their backs.

As distasteful as Zaknafein found this troupe, the one that followed was even worse. Two Do'Urden clerics led a contingent of soldiers through the structure, using detection spells to determine hiding places of surviving DeVirs. One stopped in the hallway just a few steps from Zak, her eyes turned inward as she felt the emanations of her spell. She held her fingers out in front of her, tracing a slow line, like some macabre divining rod, toward drow flesh.

"In there!" she declared, pointing to a panel at the base of the wall. The soldiers jumped to it like a pack of ravenous wolves and tore through the secret door. Inside a hidden cubby huddled the children of House DeVir. These were nobles, not commoners, and could not be taken alive.

Zak quickened his pace to get beyond the scene, but he heard vividly the children's helpless screams as the hungry Do'Urden soldiers finished their job. Zak found himself in a run now. He rushed around a bend in the hallway, nearly bowling over Dinin and Rizzen.

"Nalfein is dead," Rizzen declared impassively.

Zak immediately turned a suspicious eye on the younger Do'Urden son.

"I killed the DeVir soldier who committed the deed," Dinin assured him, not even hiding his cocky smile.

Zak had been around for nearly four centuries, and he was certainly not ignorant of the ways of his ambitious race. The brother princes had come in defensively at the back of the lines, with a host of Do'Urden soldiers between them and the enemy. By the time they even encountered a drow that was not of their own house, the majority of the DeVirs' surviving soldiers had already switched allegiance to House Do'Urden. Zak doubted that either of the Do'Urden brothers had even seen action against a DeVir.

"The description of the carnage in the prayer room has been spread throughout the ranks," Rizzen said to the weapons master. "You performed with your usual excellence—as we have come to expect."

Zak shot the patron a glare of contempt and kept on his way, down though the structure's main doors and out beyond the magical darkness and silence into Menzoberranzan's dark dawn. Rizzen was Matron Malice's present partner in a long line of partners, and no more. When Malice was finished with him, she would either relegate him back to the ranks of the common soldiery, stripping him of the name Do'Urden and all the rights that accompanied it, or she would dispose of him. Zak owed him no respect.

Zak moved out beyond the mushroom fence to the highest vantage point he could find, then fell to the ground. He watched, amazed, a few moments later, when the procession of the Do'Urden army, patron and son, soldiers and clerics, and the slow-moving line of two dozen drow zombies, made its way back home. They had lost, and left behind, nearly all of their slave fodder in the attack, but the line leaving the wreckage of House DeVir was longer than the line that had come in earlier that night. The slaves had been replaced twofold by captured DeVir slaves, and fifty or more of the DeVir common troops, showing typical drow loyalty, had willingly joined the attackers. These traitorous drow would be interrogated—magically interrogated—by the Do'Urden clerics to ensure their sincerity.

They would pass the test to a one, Zak knew. Drow elves were creatures of survival, not of principle. The soldiers would be given new identities and would be kept within the privacy of the Do'Urden compound for a few months, until the fall of House DeVir became an old and forgotten tale.

Zak did not follow immediately. Rather, he cut through the rows of mushroom trees and found a secluded dell, where he plopped down on a patch of mossy carpet and raised his gaze to the eternal darkness of the cavern's ceiling—and the eternal darkness of his existence.

It would have been prudent for him to remain silent at that time; he was an invader to the most powerful section of the vast city. He thought of the possible witnesses to his words, the same dark elves who had watched the fall of House DeVir, who had wholeheartedly enjoyed the spectacle. In the face of such behavior and such carnage as this night had seen, Zak could not contain his emotions. His lament came out as a plea to some god beyond his experience.

"What place is this that is my world; what dark coil has my spirit embodied?" he whispered the angry disclaimer that had always been a part of him. "In light, I see my skin as black; in darkness, it glows white in the heat of this rage I cannot dismiss.

"Would that I had the courage to depart, this place or this life, or to stand openly against the wrongness that is the world of these, my kin. To seek an existence that does not run afoul to that which I believe, and to that which I hold dear faith is truth.

"Zaknafein Do'Urden, I am called, yet a drow I am not, by choice or by deed. Let them discover this being that I am, then. Let them rain their wrath on these old shoulders already burdened by the hopelessness of Menzoberranzan."

Ignoring the consequences, the weapons master rose to his feet and yelled, "Menzoberranzan, what hell are you?"

A moment later, when no answer echoed back out of the quiet city, Zak flexed the remaining chill of Briza's wand from his weary muscles. He found some comfort as he patted the whip on his belt—the instrument that had taken the tongue from the mouth of a matron mother.

# 3
# The Eyes of a Child

Masoj, the young apprentice—which at this point in his magic-using career meant that he was no more than a cleaning attendant—leaned on his broom and watched as Alton DeVir moved through the door into the highest chamber of the spire. Masoj almost felt sympathy for the student, who had to go in and face the Faceless One.

Masoj felt excitement as well, though, knowing that the ensuing fireworks between Alton and the faceless master would be well worth the watching. He went back to his sweeping, using the broom as an excuse to get farther around the curve of the room's floor, closer to the door.

⚔ ⚔ ⚔ ⚔ ⚔

"You requested my presence, Master Faceless One," Alton DeVir said again, keeping one hand in front of his face and squinting to fight the brilliant glare of the room's three lighted candles. Alton shifted uncomfortably from one foot to the other just inside the shadowy room's door.

Hunched across the way, the Faceless One kept his back to the young DeVir. Better to be done with this cleanly, the master reminded himself. He knew, though, that the spell he was now preparing would kill Alton before the student could learn his family's fate, before the Faceless One could fully complete Dinin Do'Urden's final instructions. Too much was at stake. Better to be done with this cleanly.

"You . . ." Alton began again, but he prudently held his words and tried to sort out the situation before him. How unusual to be summoned to the private chambers of a master of the Academy before the day's lessons had even begun.

When he had first received the summons, Alton feared that he had somehow failed one of his lessons. That could be a fatal mistake in Sorcere. Alton was close to graduation, but the disdain of a single master could put an end to that.

He had done quite well in his lessons with the Faceless One, had even believed that this mysterious master favored him. Could this call be simply a courtesy of congratulations on his impending graduation? Unlikely, Alton realized against his hopes. Masters of the drow Academy did not often congratulate students.

Alton then heard quiet chanting and noticed that the master was in the midst of spellcasting. Something cried out as very wrong to him now; something about this whole situation did not fit the strict ways of the Academy. Alton set his feet firmly and tensed his muscles, following the advice of the motto that had been drilled into the thoughts of every student at the Academy, the precept that kept drow elves alive in a society so devoted to chaos: Be prepared.

⚔ ⚔ ⚔ ⚔ ⚔

The doors exploded before him, showering the room with stone splinters and throwing Masoj back against the wall. He felt the show well worth both the inconvenience and the new bruise on his shoulder when Alton DeVir scrambled out of the room. The student's back and left arm trailed wisps of smoke, and the most exquisite expression of terror and pain that Masoj had ever seen was etched on the DeVir noble's face.

Alton stumbled to the floor and kicked into a roll, desperate to put some ground between himself and the murderous master. He made it down and around the descending arc of the room's floor and through the door that led into the next lower chamber just as the Faceless One made his appearance at the sundered door.

The master stopped to spit a curse at his misfire, and to consider the best way to replace his door. "Clean it up!" he snapped at Masoj, who was again leaning casually with his hands atop his broomstick and his chin atop his hands.

Masoj obediently dropped his head and started sweeping the stone splinters. He looked up as the Faceless One stalked past, however, and cautiously started after the master.

Alton couldn't possibly escape, and this show would be too good to miss.

⚔ ⚔ ⚔ ⚔ ⚔

The third room, the Faceless One's private library, was the brightest of the four in the spire, with dozens of candles burning on each wall.

"Damn this light!" Alton spat, stumbling his way down through the dizzying blur to the door that led to the Faceless One's entry hall, the lowest room of the master's quarters. If he could get down from this spire and outside of the tower to the courtyard of the Academy, he might be able to turn the momentum against the master.

Alton's world remained the darkness of Menzoberranzan, but the Faceless One, who had spent so many decades in the candlelight of Sorcere, had grown accustomed to using his eyes to see shades of light, not heat.

The entry hall was cluttered with chairs and chests, but only one candle burned there, and Alton could see clearly enough to dodge or leap any obstacles. He rushed to the door and grabbed the heavy latch. It turned easily enough, but when Alton tried to shoulder through, the door did not budge and a burst of sparkling blue energy threw him back to the floor.

"Curse this place," Alton spat. The portal was magically held. He knew a spell to open such enchanted doors but doubted whether his magic would be strong enough to dispel the castings of a master. In his haste and fear, the words of the dweomer floated through Alton's thoughts in an indecipherable jumble.

"Do not run, DeVir," came the Faceless One's call from the previous chamber. "You only lengthen your torment!"

"A curse upon you, too," Alton replied under his breath. Alton forgot about the stupid spell; it would never come to him in time. He glanced around the room for an option.

His eyes found something unusual halfway up the side wall, in an opening between two large cabinets. Alton scrambled back a few steps to get a better angle but found himself caught within the range of the candlelight, within the deceptive field where his eyes registered both heat and light.

He could only discern that this section of the wall showed a uniform glow in the heat spectrum and that its hue was subtly different from the stone of the walls. Another doorway? Alton could only hope his guess to be right. He rushed back to the center of the room, stood directly across from the object, and forced his eyes away from the infrared spectrum, fully back into the world of light.

As his eyes adjusted, what came into view both startled and confused the young DeVir. He saw no doorway, nor any opening with another chamber behind it. What he looked upon was a reflection of himself, and a portion of the room he now stood in. Alton had never, in his fifty-five years of life, witnessed such a spectacle, but he had heard the masters of Sorcere speak of these devices. It was a mirror.

A movement in the upper doorway of the chamber reminded Alton that the Faceless One was almost upon him. He couldn't hesitate to ponder his options. He put his head down and charged the mirror.

Perhaps it was a teleportation door to another section of the city, perhaps a simple door to a room beyond. Or perhaps, Alton dared to imagine in those few desperate seconds, this was some interplanar gate that would bring him into a strange and unknown plane of existence!

He felt the tingling excitement of adventure pulling him on as he neared the wondrous thing—then he felt only the impact, the shattering glass, and the unyielding stone wall behind it.

Perhaps it was just a mirror.

⚔ ⚔ ⚔ ⚔ ⚔

"Look at his eyes," Vierna whispered to Maya as they examined the newest member of House Do'Urden.

Truly the babe's eyes were remarkable. Though the child had been out of the womb for less than an hour, the pupils of his orbs darted back and forth inquisitively. While they showed the expected radiating glow of eyes seeing into the infrared spectrum, the familiar redness was tinted by a shade of blue, giving them a violet hue.

"Blind?" wondered Maya. "Perhaps this one will be given to the Spider Queen still."

Briza looked back to them anxiously. Dark elves did not allow children showing any physical deficiency to live.

"Not blind," replied Vierna, passing her hand over the child and casting an angry glare at both of her eager sisters. "He follows my fingers."

Maya saw that Vierna spoke the truth. She leaned closer to the babe, studying his face and strange eyes. "What do you see, Drizzt Do'Urden?" she asked softly, not in an act of gentleness toward the babe, but so that she would not disturb her mother, resting in the chair at the head of the spider idol. "What do you see that the rest of us cannot?"

⚔ ⚔ ⚔ ⚔ ⚔

Glass crunched under Alton, digging deeper wounds as he shifted his weight in an effort to rise to his feet. What would it matter? he thought. "My mirror!" he heard the Faceless One groan, and he looked up to see the outraged master towering over him.

How huge he seemed to Alton! How great and powerful, fully blocking the candlelight from this little alcove between the cabinets, his form enhanced tenfold to the eyes of the helpless victim by the mere implications of his presence.

Alton then felt a gooey substance floating down around him, detached webbing finding a sticky hold on the cabinets, on the wall, and on Alton. The young DeVir tried to leap up and roll away, but the Faceless One's spell already held him fast, trapped him as a dirgit fly would be trapped in the strands of a spider's home.

"First my door," the Faceless One growled at him, "and now this, my mirror! Do you know the pains I suffered to acquire such a rare device?"

Alton turned his head from side to side, not in answer, but to free at least his face from the binding substance.

"Why did you not just stand still and let the deed be finished cleanly?" the Faceless One roared, thoroughly disgusted.

"Why?" Alton lisped, spitting some of the webbing from his thin lips. "Why would you want to kill me?"

"Because you broke my mirror!" the Faceless One shot back.

It didn't make any sense, of course—the mirror had only been shattered after the initial attack—but to the master, Alton supposed, it didn't have to make sense. Alton knew his cause to be hopeless, but he continued on in his efforts to dissuade his opponent.

"You know of my house, of House DeVir," he said, indignant, "fourth in the city. Matron Ginafae will not be pleased. A high priestess has ways to learn the truth of such situations!"

"House DeVir?" The Faceless One laughed. Perhaps the torments that Dinin Do'Urden had requested would be in line after all. Alton had broken his mirror!

"Fourth house!" Alton spat.

"Foolish youth," the Faceless One cackled. "House DeVir is no more—not fourth, not fifty-fourth, nothing."

Alton slumped, though the webbing did its best to hold his body erect. What could the master be babbling about?

"They all are dead," the Faceless One taunted. "Matron Ginafae sees Lolth more clearly this day." Alton's expression of horror pleased the disfigured master. "All dead," he snarled one more time. "Except for poor Alton, who lives on to hear of his family's misfortune. That oversight shall be remedied now!" The Faceless One raised his hands to cast a spell.

"Who?" Alton cried.

The Faceless One paused and seemed not to understand.

"What house did this?" the doomed student clarified. "Or what conspiracy of houses brought down DeVir?"

"Ah; you should be told," replied the Faceless One, obviously enjoying the situation. "I suppose it is your right to know before you join your kin in the realm of death." A smile widened across the opening where his lips once had been.

"But you broke my mirror!" the master growled. "Die stupid, stupid boy! Find your own answers!"

The Faceless One's chest jerked out suddenly, and he shuddered in convulsions, babbling curses in a tongue far beyond the terrified student's comprehension. What vile spell did this disfigured master have prepared for him, so wretched that its chant sounded in an arcane language foreign to learned Alton's ears, so unspeakably evil that its semantics jerked on the very edge of its caster's control? The Faceless One then fell forward to the floor and expired.

Stunned, Alton followed the line of the master's hood down to his back—to the tail of a protruding dart. Alton watched the poisoned thing as it continued to shudder from the body's impact, then he turned his scan upward to the center of the room, where the young cleaning attendant stood calmly.

"Nice weapon, Faceless One!" Masoj beamed, rolling a two-handed, crafted crossbow over in his hands. He threw a wicked smile at Alton and fitted another dart.

⚔ ⚔ ⚔ ⚔ ⚔

Matron Malice hoisted herself out of her chair and willed herself to her feet. "Out of the way!" she snapped at her daughters.

Maya and Vierna scooted away from the spider idol and the baby. "See his eyes, Matron Mother," Vierna dared to remark. "They are so unusual."

Matron Malice studied the child. Everything seemed in place, and a good thing, too, for Nalfein, elderboy of House Do'Urden, was dead, and this boy, Drizzt, would have a difficult job replacing the valuable son.

"His eyes," Vierna said again.

The matron shot her a venomous look but bent low to see what the fuss was about.

"Purple?" Malice said, startled. Never had she heard of such a thing.

"He is not blind," Maya was quick to put in, seeing the disdain spreading across her mother's face.

"Fetch the candle," Matron Malice ordered. "Let us see how these eyes appear in the world of light."

Maya and Vierna reflexively headed for the sacred cabinet, but Briza cut them off. "Only a high priestess may touch the holy items," she reminded them in a tone that carried the weight of a threat. She spun around haughtily, reached into the cabinet, and produced a single half-used red candle. The clerics hid their eyes and Matron Malice put a prudent hand over the baby's face as Briza lit the sacred candle. It produced only a tiny flame, but to drow eyes it came as a brilliant intrusion.

"Bring it," said Matron Malice after several moments of adjusting. Briza moved the candle near Drizzt, and Malice gradually slid her hand away.

"He does not cry," Briza remarked, amazed that the babe could quietly accept such a stinging light.

"Purple again," whispered the matron, paying no heed to her daughter's rambling. "In both worlds, the child's eyes show as purple."

Vierna gasped audibly when she looked again upon her tiny brother and his striking lavender orbs.

"He is your brother," Matron Malice reminded her, viewing Vierna's gasp as a hint of what might come. "When he grows older and those eyes pierce you so, remember, on your life, that he is your brother."

Vierna turned away, almost blurting a reply she would have regretted making. Matron Malice's exploits with nearly every male soldier of the Do'Urden house—and many others that the seductive matron managed to sneak away from other houses—were almost legendary in Menzoberranzan. Who was she to be spouting reminders of prudent and proper behavior? Vierna bit her lip and hoped that neither Briza nor Malice had been reading her thoughts at that moment.

In Menzoberranzan, thinking such gossip about a high priestess, whether or not it was true, got you painfully executed.

Her mother's eyes narrowed, and Vierna thought she had been discovered. "He is yours to prepare," Matron Malice said to her.

"Maya is younger," Vierna dared to protest. "I could attain the level of high priestess in but a few years if I may keep to my studies."

"Or never," the matron sternly reminded her. "Take the child to the chapel proper. Wean him to words and teach him all that he will need to know to properly serve as a page prince of House Do'Urden."

"I will see to him," Briza offered, one hand subconsciously slipping to her snake-headed whip. "I do so enjoy teaching males their place in our world."

Malice glared at her. "You are a high priestess. You have other duties more important than word-weaning a male child." Then to Vierna, she said, "The babe is yours; do not disappoint me in this! The lessons you teach Drizzt will reinforce your own understanding of our ways. This exercise at 'mothering' will aid you in your quest to become a high priestess." She let Vierna take a moment to view the task in a more positive light, then her tone became unmistakably threatening once again. "It may aid you, but it surely can destroy you!"

Vierna sighed but kept her thoughts silent. The chore that Matron Malice had dropped on her shoulders would consume the bulk of her time for at least ten years. Vierna didn't like the prospects, she and this purple-eyed child together for ten long years. The alternative, however, the wrath of Matron Malice Do'Urden, seemed a worse thing by far.

* * * * *

Alton blew another web from his mouth. "You are just a boy, an apprentice," he stammered. "Why would you—?"

"Kill him?" Masoj finished the thought. "Not to save you, if that is your hope." He spat down at the Faceless One's body. "Look at me, a prince of the sixth house, a cleaning steward for that wretched—"

"Hun'ett," Alton cut in. "House Hun'ett is the sixth house."

The younger drow put a finger to pursed lips. "Wait," he remarked with a widening smile, an evil smile of sarcasm. "We are the fifth house now, I suppose, with DeVir wiped out."

"Not yet!" Alton growled.

"Momentarily," Masoj assured him, fingering the crossbow quarrel.

Alton slumped even farther back in the web. To be killed by a master was bad enough, but the indignity of being shot down by a boy. . . .

"I suppose I should thank you," Masoj said. "I had planned to kill that one for many tendays."

"Why?" Alton pressed his new assailant. "You would dare to kill a master of Sorcere simply because your family put you in servitude to him?"

"Because he would snub me!" Masoj yelled. "Four years I have slaved for him, that back end of a carrion crawler. Cleaned his boots. Prepared salve for his disgusting face! Was it ever enough? Not for that one." He spat at the corpse again and continued, talking more to himself than to the trapped student. "Nobles aspiring to wizardry have the advantage of being trained as apprentices before they reach the proper age for entry into Sorcere."

"Of course," Alton said. "I myself trained under—"

"He meant to keep me out of Sorcere!" Masoj rambled, ignoring Alton altogether. "He would have forced me into Melee-Magthere, the fighters' school, instead. The fighters' school! My twenty-fifth birthday is only two tendays away." Masoj looked up, as though he suddenly remembered that he was not alone in the room.

"I knew I must kill him," he continued, now speaking directly to Alton. "Then you come along and make it all so convenient. A student and master killing each other in a fight? It has happened before. Who would question it? I suppose, then, that I should thank you, Alton DeVir of No House Worth Mentioning," Masoj chided with a low, sweeping bow. "Before I kill you, I mean."

"Wait!" cried Alton. "Kill me to what gain?"

"Alibi."

"But you have your alibi, and we can make it better!"

"Explain," said Masoj, who, admittedly, was in no particular hurry. The Faceless One was a high-level wizard; the webs weren't going anywhere anytime soon.

"Free me," Alton said earnestly.

"Can you be as stupid as the Faceless One proclaimed you?"

Alton took the insult stoically—the kid had the crossbow. "Free me so that I may assume the Faceless One's identity," he explained. "The death of a master arouses suspicion, but if no master is believed dead . . ."

"And what of this?" Masoj asked, kicking the corpse.

"Burn it," said Alton, his desperate plan coming fully into focus. "Let it be Alton DeVir. House DeVir is no more, so there will be no retaliation, no questions."

Masoj seemed skeptical.

"The Faceless One was practically a hermit," Alton reasoned. "And I am near to graduation; certainly I can handle the simple chores of basic teaching after thirty years of study."

"And what is my gain?"

Alton gawked, nearly burying himself in webbing, as if the answer were obvious. "A master in Sorcere to call mentor. One who can ease your way through your years of study."

"And one who can dispose of a witness at his earliest convenience," Masoj added slyly.

"And what then would be my gain?" Alton shot back. "To anger House Hun'ett, fifth in all the city, and I with no family at my back? No, young Masoj, I am not as stupid as the Faceless One named me."

Masoj ticked a long and pointed fingernail against his teeth and considered the possibilities. An ally among the masters of Sorcere? This held possibilities.

Another thought popped into Masoj's mind, and he pulled open the cabinet to Alton's side and began rummaging through the contents. Alton flinched when he heard some ceramic and glass containers crashing together, thinking of the components, possibly even completed potions, that might be lost by the apprentice's carelessness. Perhaps Melee-Magthere would be a better choice for this one, he thought.

A moment later, though, the younger drow reappeared, and Alton remembered that he was in no position to make such judgments.

"This is mine," Masoj demanded, showing Alton a small black object: a remarkably detailed onyx figurine of a hunting panther. "A gift from a denizen of the lower planes for some help I gave to him."

"You aided such a creature?" Alton had to ask, finding it difficult to believe that a mere apprentice had the resources necessary to even survive an encounter with such an unpredictable and mighty foe.

"The Faceless One—" Masoj kicked the corpse again—"took the credit and the statue, but they are mine! Everything else in here will go to you, of course. I know the magical dweomers of most and will show you what is what."

Brightening at the hope that he would indeed survive this dreadful day, Alton cared little about the figurine at that moment. All he wanted was to be freed of the webs so that he could find out the truth of his house's fate. Then Masoj, ever a confusing young drow, turned suddenly and started away.

"Where are you going?" Alton asked.

"To get the acid."

"Acid?" Alton hid his panic well, though he had a terrible feeling that he understood what Masoj meant to do.

"You want the disguise to appear authentic," Masoj explained matter-of-factly. "Otherwise, it would not be much of a disguise. We should take advantage of the web while it lasts. It will hold you still."

"No," Alton started to protest, but Masoj wheeled on him, the evil grin wide on his face.

"It does seem a bit of pain, and a lot of trouble to go through," Masoj admitted. "You have no family and will find no allies in Sorcere, since the Faceless One was so despised by the other masters." He brought the crossbow up level with Alton's eyes and fitted another poisoned dart. "Perhaps you would prefer death."

"Get the acid!" Alton cried.

"To what end?" Masoj teased, waving the crossbow. "What have you to live for, Alton DeVir of No House Worth Mentioning?"

"Revenge," Alton sneered, the sheer wrath of his tone setting the confident Masoj on his heels. "You have not learned this yet—though you will, my young student—but nothing in life gives more purpose than the hunger for revenge!"

Masoj lowered the bow and eyed the trapped drow with respect, almost fear. Still, the apprentice Hun'ett could not appreciate the gravity of Alton's proclamation until Alton reiterated, this time with an eager smile on his face, "Get the acid."

# 4 The First House

Four cycles of Narbondel—four days—later, a glowing blue disk floated up the mushroom-lined stone path to the spider-covered gate of House Do'Urden. The sentries watched it from the windows of the two outer towers and from the compound as it hovered patiently three feet off the ground. Word came to the ruling family only seconds later.

"What can it be?" Briza asked Zaknafein when she, the weapons master, Dinin, and Maya assembled on the balcony of the upper level.

"A summons?" Zak asked as much as answered. "We will not know until we investigate." He stepped up on the railing and out into the empty air, then levitated down to the compound floor. Briza motioned to Maya, and the youngest Do'Urden daughter followed Zak.

"It bears the standard of House Baenre," Zak called up after he had moved closer. He and Maya opened the large gates, and the disk slipped in, showing no hostile movements.

"Baenre," Briza repeated over her shoulder, down the house's corridor to where Matron Malice and Rizzen waited.

"It seems that you are requested in audience, Matron Mother," Dinin put in nervously.

Malice moved out to the balcony, and her husband obediently followed.

"Do they know of our attack?" Briza asked in the silent code, and every member of House Do'Urden, noble and commoner alike, shared that unpleasant thought. House DeVir had been eliminated only a few days before, and a calling card from the First Matron Mother of Menzoberranzan could hardly be viewed as a coincidence.

"Every house knows," Malice replied aloud, not believing the silence to be a necessary precaution within the boundaries of her own complex. "Is the evidence against us so overwhelming that the ruling council will be forced to action?" She stared hard at Briza, her dark eyes alternating between the red glow of infravision and the deep green they showed in the aura of normal light. "That is the question we must ask." Malice stepped up onto the balcony, but Briza grabbed the back of her heavy black robe to stay her.

"You do not mean to go with the thing?" Briza asked.

Malice's answering look showed even more startlement. "Of course," she replied. "Matron Baenre would not openly call upon me if she meant me harm. Even her power is not so great that she can ignore the tenets of the city."

"You are certain that you will be safe?" Rizzen asked, truly concerned. If Malice was killed, Briza would take over the house, and Rizzen doubted that the eldest daughter would want any male by her side. Even if the vicious female did desire a patron, Rizzen would not want to be the one in that position. He was not Briza's father, was not even as old as Briza. Clearly, the present patron of the house had a lot at stake in Matron Malice's continued good health.

"Your concern touches me," Malice replied, knowing her husband's true fears. She pulled out of Briza's grasp and stepped off the railing, straightening her robes as she slowly descended. Briza shook her head disdainfully and motioned Rizzen to follow her back inside the house, not thinking it wise that the bulk of the family be so exposed to unfriendly eyes.

"Do you want an escort?" Zak asked as Malice sat on the disk.

"I am certain that I will find one as soon as I am beyond the perimeter of our compound," Malice replied. "Matron Baenre would not risk exposing me to any danger while I am in the care of her house."

"Agreed," said Zak, "but do you want an escort from House Do'Urden?"

"If one was wanted, two disks would have floated in," Malice said in a tone of finality. The matron was beginning to find the concerns of those around her stifling. She was the matron mother, after all, the strongest, the oldest, and the wisest, and did not appreciate others second-guessing her. To the disk, Malice said, "Execute your appointed task, and let us be done with it!"

Zak nearly snickered at Malice's choice of words.

"Matron Malice Do'Urden," came a magical voice from the disk, "Matron Baenre offers her greetings. Too long has it been since last you two have sat in audience."

"Never," Malice signaled to Zak. "Then take me to House Baenre!" Malice demanded. "I do not wish to waste my time conversing with a magical mouth!"

Apparently, Matron Baenre had anticipated Malice's impatience, for without another word, the disk floated back out of the Do'Urden compound.

Zak shut the gate as it left, then quickly signaled his soldiers into motion. Malice did not want any open company, but the Do'Urden spy network would covertly track every movement of the Baenre sled, to the very gates of the ruling house's grand compound.

⚔ ⚔ ⚔ ⚔ ⚔

Malice's guess about an escort was correct. As soon as the disk swept down from the pathway to the Do'Urden compound, twenty soldiers of House Baenre, all female, moved out from concealment along the sides of the boulevard. They formed a defensive diamond around the guest matron mother. The guard at each point of the formation wore black robes emblazoned on the back with a large purple-and-red spider design—the robes of a high priestess.

"Baenre's own daughters," Malice mused, for only the daughters of a noble could attain such a rank. How careful the First Matron Mother had been to ensure Malice's safety on the trip!

Slaves and drow commoners tripped over themselves in a frantic effort to get far out of the way of the approaching entourage as the group made its way through the curving streets toward the mushroom grove. The soldiers of House Baenre alone wore their house insignia in open view, and no one wanted to invoke the anger of Matron Baenre in any way.

Malice just rolled her eyes in disbelief and hoped that she might know such power before she died.

She rolled her eyes again a few minutes later, when the group approached the ruling house. House Baenre encompassed twenty tall and majestic stalagmites, all interconnected with gracefully sweeping and arching bridges and parapets. Magic and faerie fire glowed from a thousand separate sculptures and a hundred regally adorned guardsmen paced about in perfect formations.

Even more striking were the inverse structures, the thirty smaller stalactites of House Baenre. They hung down from the ceiling of the cavern, their roots lost in the high darkness. Some of them connected tip-to-tip with the stalagmite mounds, while others hung freely like poised spears. Ringing balconies, curving up like the edging of a screw, had been built along the length of all of these, glowing with an overabundance of magic and highlighted design.

Magic, too, was the fence that connected the bases of the outer stalagmites, encircling the whole of the compound. It was a giant web, silver against the general blue of the rest of the outer compound. Some said it had been a gift from Lolth herself, with iron-strong strands as thick as a drow elf's arm. Anything touching Baenre's fence, even the sharpest of drow weapons, would simply stick fast until the matron mother willed the fence to let it free.

Malice and her escorts moved straight toward a symmetrical and circular section of this fence, between the tallest of the outer towers. As they neared, the gate spiraled and wound out, leaving a gap large enough for the caravan to step through.

Malice sat through it all, trying to appear unimpressed.

Hundreds of curious soldiers watched the procession as it made its way to the central structure of House Baenre, the great purple-glowing chapel dome. The common soldiers left the entourage, leaving only the four high priestesses to escort Matron Malice inside.

The sights beyond the great doors to the chapel did not disappoint her. A central altar dominated the place with a row of benches spiraling out in several dozen circuits to the perimeter of the great hall. Two thousand drow could sit there with room to stretch. Statues and idols too numerous to count stood all about the place, glowing in a quiet black light. In the air high above the altar loomed a gigantic glowing image, a red-and-black illusion that slowly and continually shifted between the forms of a spider and a beautiful drow female.

"A work of Gromph, my principal wizard," Matron Baenre explained from her perch on the altar, guessing that Malice, like everyone else who ever came to Chapel Baenre, was awestruck by the sight. "Even wizards have their place."

"As long as they remember their place," Malice replied, slipping down from the now stationary disk.

"Agreed," said Matron Baenre. "Males can get so presumptuous at times, especially wizards! Still, I wish that I had Gromph at my side more often these days. He has been appointed Archmage of Menzoberranzan, you know, and seems always at work on Narbondel or some other such tasks."

Malice just nodded and held her tongue. Of course, she knew that Baenre's son was the city's chief wizard. Everybody knew. Everybody knew, too, that Baenre's daughter Triel was the Matron Mistress of the Academy, a position of honor in Menzoberranzan second only to the title of matron mother of an individual family. Malice had little doubt that Matron Baenre would somehow work that fact into the conversation before too long.

Before Malice took a step toward the stairs to the altar, her newest escort stepped out from the shadows. Malice scowled openly when she saw the thing, a creature known as an illithid, a mind flayer. It stood about six feet tall, fully a foot taller than Malice, most of the difference being the result of the creature's enormous head. Glistening with slime, the head resembled an octopus with pupil-less, milky white eyes.

Malice composed herself quickly. Mind flayers were not unknown in Menzoberranzan, and rumors said that one had befriended Matron Baenre.

These creatures, though, more intelligent and more evil than even the drow, almost always inspired shudders of revulsion.

"You may call him Methil," Matron Baenre explained. "His true name is beyond my pronunciation. He is a friend."

Before Malice could reply, Baenre added, "Of course, Methil gives me the advantage in our discussion, and you are not accustomed to illithids." Then, as Malice's mouth drooped open in disbelief, Matron Baenre dismissed the illithid.

"You read my thought," Malice protested. Few could insinuate themselves through the mental barriers of a high priestess well enough to read her thoughts, and the practice was a crime of the highest order in drow society.

"No!" Matron Baenre explained, immediately on the defensive. "Your pardon, Matron Malice. Methil reads thoughts, even the thoughts of a high priestess, as easily as you or I hear words. He communicates telepathically. On my word, I did not even realize that you had not yet spoken your thoughts."

Malice waited to watch the creature depart the great hall, then walked up the steps to the altar. In spite of her efforts against the action, she could not help peeking up at the transforming spider-and-drow image every now and.

"How fares House Do'Urden?" Matron Baenre asked, feigning politeness.

"Well enough," replied Malice, more interested at that moment in studying her counterpart than in conversing. They were alone atop the altar, though no doubt a dozen or so clerics wandered through the shadows of the great hall, keeping a watchful eye on the situation.

Malice had all that she could handle in hiding her contempt for Matron Baenre. Malice was old, nearly five hundred, but Matron Baenre was ancient. Her eyes had seen the rise and fall of a millennium, by some accounts, though drow rarely lived past their seventh—and certainly not their eighth—century. While drow normally did not show their age—Malice was as beautiful and vibrant now as she had been on her one-hundredth birthday—Matron Baenre was withered and worn. The wrinkles surrounding her mouth resembled a spider's web, and she could hardly keep the heavy lids of her eyes from dropping altogether. Matron Baenre should be dead, Malice noted, but still she lives.

Matron Baenre, seeming so beyond her time of life, was pregnant, and due in only a few tendays.

In this aspect, too, Matron Baenre defied the norm of the dark elves. She had given birth twenty times, twice as often as any others in Menzoberranzan, and fifteen of those she bore were female, every one a high priestess! Ten of Baenre's children were older than Malice!

"How many soldiers do you now command?" Matron Baenre asked, leaning closer to show her interest.

"Three hundred," Malice replied.

"Oh," mused the withered old drow, pursing a finger to her lips. "I had heard the count at three-hundred fifty."

Malice grimaced in spite of herself. Baenre was teasing her, referring to the soldiers House Do'Urden had added in its raid on House DeVir.

"Three hundred," Malice said again.

"Of course," replied Baenre, resting back.

"And House Baenre holds a thousand?" Malice asked for no better reason than to keep herself on even terms in the discussion.

"That has been our number for many years."

Malice wondered again why this old decrepit thing was still alive. Surely more than one of Baenre's daughters aspired to the position of matron mother. Why hadn't they conspired and finished Matron Baenre off? Or why hadn't any of them, some in the later stages of life, struck out on their own to form separate houses, as was the norm for noble daughters when they passed their fifth century? While they lived under Matron Baenre's rule, their children would not even be considered nobles but would be relegated to the ranks of the commoners.

"You have heard of the fate of House DeVir?" Matron Baenre asked directly, growing as tired of the hesitant small talk as her counterpart.

"Of what house?" Malice asked pointedly. At this time, there was no such thing as House DeVir in Menzoberranzan. To drow reckoning, the house no longer existed; the house never existed.

Matron Baenre cackled. "Of course," she replied. "You are matron mother of the ninth house now. That is quite an honor."

Malice nodded. "But not as great an honor as matron mother of the eighth house."

"Yes," agreed Baenre, "but ninth is only one position away from a seat on the ruling council."

"That would be an honor indeed," Malice replied. She was beginning to understand that Baenre was not simply teasing her, but was congratulating her as well, and prodding her on to greater glories. Malice brightened at the thought. Baenre was in the highest favor of the Spider Queen. If she was pleased with House Do'Urden's ascension, then so was Lolth.

"Not as much of an honor as you would believe," said Baenre. "We are a group of meddling old females, gathering every so often to find new ways to put our hands into places they do not belong."

"The city recognizes your rule."

"Does it have a choice?" Baenre laughed. "Still, drow business is better left to the matron mothers of the individual houses. Lolth would not stand for a presiding council exacting anything that even remotely resembled total rule. Do you not believe that House Baenre would have conquered all of Menzoberranzan long ago if that was the Spider Queen's will?"

Malice shifted proudly in her chair, appalled by such arrogant words.

"Not now, of course," Matron Baenre explained. "The city is too large for such an action in this age. But long ago, before you were even born, House Baenre would not have found such a conquest difficult. But that is not our way. Lolth encourages diversity. She is pleased that houses stand to balance each other, ready to fight beside each other in times of common need." She paused a moment and let a smile appear on her wrinkled lips. "And ready to pounce upon any that fall out of her favor."

Another direct reference to House DeVir, Malice noted, this time directly connected to the Spider Queen's pleasure. Malice eased out of her angry posture and found the rest of her discussion—fully two hours long—with Matron Baenre quite enjoyable.

Still, when she was back on the disk and floating out through the compound, past the grandest and strongest house in all of Menzoberranzan,

Malice was not smiling. In the face of such an open display of power, she could not forget that Matron Baenre's purpose in summoning her had been twofold: to privately and cryptically congratulate her on her perfect coup, and to vividly remind her not to get too ambitious.

# 5 Weaning

For five long years Vierna devoted almost every waking moment to the care of baby Drizzt. In drow society, this was not so much a nurturing time as an indoctrinating time. The child had to learn basic motor and language skills, as did children of all the intelligent races, but a drow elf also had to be grilled on the precepts that bound the chaotic society together.

In the case of a male child such as Drizzt, Vierna spent hour after endless hour reminding him that he was inferior to the drow females. Since almost all of this portion of Drizzt's life was spent in the family chapel, he encountered no males except during times of communal worship. Even when all in the house gathered for the unholy ceremonies, Drizzt remained silent at Vierna's side, with his gaze obediently on the floor.

When Drizzt was old enough to follow commands, Vierna's workload lessened. Still, she spent many hours teaching her younger brother—presently they were working on the intricate facial, hand, and body movements of the silent code. Often, though, she just set Drizzt about the endless task of cleaning the domed chapel. The room was barely a fifth the size of the great hall in House Baenre, but it could hold all the dark elves of House Do'Urden with a hundred seats to spare.

Being a weanmother was not so bad now, Vierna thought, but still she wished that she could devote more of her time to her studies. If Matron Malice had appointed Maya to the task of rearing the child, Vierna might already have been ordained as a high priestess. Vierna still had another five years in her duties with Drizzt; Maya might attain high priestesshood before her!

Vierna dismissed that possibility. She could not afford to worry about such problems. She would finish her tenure as weanmother in just a few short years. On or around his tenth birthday, Drizzt would be appointed page prince of the family and would serve all the household equally. If her work with Drizzt did not disappoint Matron Malice, Vierna knew that she would get her due.

"Go up the wall," Vierna instructed. "Tend to that statue." She pointed to a sculpture of a naked drow female about twenty feet from the floor. Young Drizzt looked up at it, confused. He couldn't possibly climb up to the sculpture and wipe it clean while holding any secure perch. Drizzt knew the high price of disobedience, though—even of hesitation—and he reached up, searching for his first handhold.

"Not like that!" Vierna scolded.

"How?" Drizzt dared to ask, for he had no idea of what his sister was hinting at.

"Will yourself up to the gargoyle," Vierna explained.

Drizzt's small face crinkled in confusion.

"You are a noble of House Do'Urden!" Vierna shouted at him. "Or at least you will one day earn that distinction. In your neck-purse you possess the emblem of the house, an item of considerable magic." Vierna still wasn't certain if Drizzt was ready for such a task; levitation was a high manifestation of innate drow magic, certainly more difficult that limning objects in faerie fire or summoning globes of darkness. The Do'Urden emblem heightened these innate powers of drow elves, magic that usually emerged as a drow matured. Whereas most drow nobles could summon the magical energy to levitate once every day or so, the nobles of House Do'Urden, with their insignia tool, could do so repeatedly.

Normally, Vierna would never have tried this on a male child younger than ten, but Drizzt had shown her so much potential in the last couple of years that she saw no harm in the attempt. "Just put yourself in line with the statue," she explained, "and will yourself to rise."

Drizzt looked up at the female carving, then lined his feet just out in front of the thing's angled and delicate face. He put a hand to his collar, trying to attune himself to the emblem. He had sensed before that the magic coin possessed some type of power, but it was only a raw sensation, a child's intuition. Now that Drizzt had some focus and confirmation to his suspicions, he clearly felt the vibrations of magical energy.

A series of deep breaths cleared distracting thoughts from the young drow's mind. He blocked out the other sights of the room; all he saw was the statue, the destination. He felt himself grow lighter, his heels went up, and he was on one toe, though he felt no weight upon it. Drizzt looked over at Vierna, his smile wide in amazement . . . then he tumbled to a heap.

"Foolish male!" Vierna scolded. "Try again! Try a thousand times if you must!" She reached for the snake-headed whip on her belt. "If you fail . . ."

Drizzt looked away from her, cursing himself. His own elation had caused the spell to falter. He knew that he could do it now, though, and he was not afraid of being beaten. He concentrated again on the sculpture and let the magical energy gather within his body.

Vierna, too, knew that Drizzt would eventually succeed. His mind was keen, as sharp as any Vierna had ever known, including those of the other females of House Do'Urden. The child was stubborn, too; Drizzt would not let the magic defeat him. She knew he would stand under the sculpture until he fainted from hunger if need be.

Vierna watched him go through a series of small successes and failures, the last one dropping Drizzt from a height of nearly ten feet. Vierna flinched, wondering if he was seriously hurt. Drizzt, whatever his wounds, did not even cry out but moved back into position and started concentrating all over again.

"He is young for that," came a comment from behind Vierna. She turned in her seat to see Briza standing over her, a customary scowl on the older sister's face.

"Perhaps," Vierna replied, "but I'll not know until I let him try."

"Whip him when he fails," Briza suggested, pulling her cruel six-headed instrument from her belt. She gave the whip a loving look—as if it were some sort of pet—and let a snake's head writhe about her neck and face. "Inspiration."

"Put it away," Vierna retorted. "Drizzt is mine to rear, and I need no help from you!"

"You should watch how you speak to a high priestess," Briza warned, and all of the snake heads, extensions of her thoughts, turned menacingly toward Vierna.

"As Matron Malice will watch how you interfere with my tasks," Vierna was quick to reply.

Briza put her whip away at the mention of Matron Malice. "Your tasks," she echoed scornfully. "You are too yielding for such a chore. Male children must be disciplined; they must be taught their place." Realizing that Vierna's threat held dire consequences, the older sister turned and left.

Vierna let Briza have the last word. The weanmother looked back to Drizzt, still trying to get up to the statue. "Enough!" she ordered, recognizing that the child was tiring; he could barely get his feet off the ground.

"I will do it!" Drizzt snapped back at her.

Vierna liked his determination, but not the tone of his reply. Perhaps there was some truth to Briza's words. Vierna snapped the snake-headed whip from her belt. A little inspiration might go a long way.

⚔ ⚔ ⚔ ⚔ ⚔

Vierna sat in the chapel the next day, watching Drizzt hard at work polishing the statue of the naked female. He had levitated the full twenty feet in his first attempt this day.

Vierna could not help but be disappointed when Drizzt did not look back to her and smile at the success. She saw him now, hovering up in the air, his hands a blur as they worked the brushes. Most vividly of all, though, Vierna saw the scars on her brother's naked back, the legacy of their "inspirational" discussion. In the infrared spectrum, the whip lines showed clearly, trails of warmth where the insulating layers of skin had been stripped away.

Vierna understood the gain in beating a child, particularly a male child.

Few drow males ever raised a weapon against a female, unless under the order of some other female. "How much do we lose?" Vierna wondered aloud. "What more could one such as Drizzt become?"

When she heard the words spoken aloud, Vierna quickly brushed the blasphemous thoughts from her mind. She aspired to become a high priestess of the Spider Queen, Lolth the Merciless. Such thoughts were not in accord with the rules of her station. She cast an angry glare on her little brother, transferring her guilt, and again took out her instrument of punishment.

She would have to whip Drizzt again this day, for the sacrilegious thoughts he had inspired within her.

⚔ ⚔ ⚔ ⚔ ⚔

So the relationship continued for another five years, with Drizzt learning the basic lessons of life in drow society while endlessly cleaning the chapel of House Do'Urden. Beyond the supremacy of female drow (a lesson always accentuated by the wicked snake-headed whip), the most compelling lessons were those concerning the surface elves, the faeries. Evil empires often bound themselves in webs of hate toward fabricated enemies, and none in the history of the world were better at it than the drow. From the first day they were able to understand the spoken word, drow children were taught that whatever was wrong in their lives could be blamed on the surface elves.

Whenever the fangs of Vierna's whip sliced into Drizzt's back, he cried out for the death of a faerie. Conditioned hatred was rarely a rational emotion.

# Part Two

# The Weapons Master

Empty hours, empty days.

I find that I have few memories of that first period of my life, those first sixteen years when I labored as a servant. Minutes blended into hours, hours into days, and so on, until the whole of it seemed one long and barren moment. Several times I managed to sneak out onto the balcony of House Do'Urden and look out over the magical lights of Menzoberranzan. On all of those secret journeys, I found myself entranced by the growing, and dissipating, heat-light of Narbondel, the timeclock pillar. Looking back on that now, on those long hours watching the glow of the wizard's fire slowly walk its way up and down the pillar I am amazed at the emptiness of my early days.

I clearly remember my excitement, tingling excitement, each time I got out of the house and set myself into position to observe the pillar. Such a simple thing it was, yet so fulfilling compared to the rest of my existence.

Whenever I hear the crack of a whip, another memory—more a sensation than a memory actually—sends a shiver through my spine. The shocking jolt and the ensuing numbness from those snake-headed weapons is not something that any person would soon forget. They bite under your skin, sending waves of magical energy through your body, waves that make your muscles snap and pull beyond their limits.

Yet I was luckier than most. My sister Vierna was near to becoming a high priestess when she was assigned the task of rearing me and was at a period of her life where she possessed far more energy than such a job required. Perhaps, then, there was more to those first ten years under her care than I now recall. Vierna never showed the intense wickedness of our mother—or, more particularly, of our oldest sister, Briza. Perhaps there were good times in the solitude of the house chapel; it is possible that Vierna allowed a more gentle side of herself to show through to her baby brother.

Maybe not. Even though I count Vierna as the kindest of my sisters, her words drip in the venom of Lolth as surely as those of any cleric in Menzoberranzan. It seems unlikely that she would risk her aspirations toward high priesthood for the sake of a mere child, a mere male child.

Whether there were indeed joys in those years, obscured in the unrelenting assault of Menzoberranzan's wickedness, or whether that earliest period of my life was even more painful than the years that followed—so painful that my mind hides the memories—I cannot be certain. For all my efforts, I cannot remember them.

I have more insight into the next six years, but the most prominent recollection of the days I spent serving the court of Matron Malice—aside from the secret trips outside the house—is the image of my own feet.

A page prince is never allowed to raise his gaze.

—Drizzt Do'Urden

# 6
# "Two-Hands"

Drizzt promptly answered the call to his matron mother's side, not needing the whip Briza used to hurry him along. How often he had felt the sting of that dreaded weapon! Drizzt held no thoughts of revenge against his vicious oldest sister. With all of the conditioning he had received, he feared the consequences of striking her—or any female—far too much to entertain such notions.

"Do you know what this day marks?" Malice asked him as he arrived at the side of her great throne in the chapel's darkened anteroom.

"No, Matron Mother," Drizzt answered, unconsciously keeping his gaze on his toes. A resigned sigh rose in his throat as he noticed the unending view of his own feet. There had to be more to life than blank stone and ten wiggling toes, he thought.

He slipped one foot out of his low boot and began doodling on the stone floor. Body heat left discernible tracings in the infrared spectrum, and Drizzt was quick and agile enough to complete simple drawings before the initial lines had cooled.

"Sixteen years," Matron Malice said to him. "You have breathed the air of Menzoberranzan for sixteen years. An important period of your life has passed."

Drizzt did not react, did not see any importance or significance to the declaration. His life was an unending and unchanging routine. One day, sixteen years, what difference did it make? If his mother considered important the things he had been put through since his earliest recollections, Drizzt shuddered to think of what the next decades might hold.

He had nearly completed his picture of a round-shouldered drow—Briza—being bitten on the behind by an enormous viper.

"Look at me," Matron Malice commanded.

Drizzt felt at a loss. His natural tendency once had been to look upon a person with whom he was talking, but Briza had wasted no time in beating that instinct out of him. The place of a page prince was servitude, and the only eyes a page prince's were worthy of meeting were those of the creatures that scurried across the stone floor—except the eyes of a spider, of course; Drizzt had to avert his gaze whenever one of the eight-legged things crawled into his vision. Spiders were too good for the likes of a page prince.

"Look at me," Malice said again, her tone hinting at volatile impatience. Drizzt had witnessed the explosions before, a wrath so incredibly vile that it swept aside anything and everything in its path. Even Briza, so pompous and cruel, ran for hiding when the matron mother grew angry.

Drizzt forced his gaze up tentatively, scanning his mother's black robes, using the familiar spider pattern along the garment's back and sides to judge the angle of his gaze. He fully expected, as every inch passed, a smack on his head, or a lashing on his back—Briza was behind him, always with her snake-headed whip near her anxious hand.

Then he saw her, the mighty Matron Malice Do'Urden, her heat-sensing eyes flashing red and her face cool, not flushed with angry heat. Drizzt kept tense, still expecting a punishing blow.

"Your tenure as page prince is ended," Malice explained. "You are secondboy of House Do'Urden now and are accorded all the . . ."

Drizzt's gaze unconsciously slipped back to the floor.

"Look at me!" his mother screamed in sudden rage.

Terrified, Drizzt snapped his gaze back to her face, which now was glowing a hot red. On the edge of his vision he saw the wavering heat of Malice's swinging hand, though he was not foolish enough to try to dodge the blow. He was on the floor then, the side of his face bruised.

Even in the fall, though, Drizzt was alert and wise enough to keep his gaze locked on to that of Matron Malice.

"No more a servant!" the matron mother roared. "To continue acting like one would bring disgrace to our family." She grabbed Drizzt by the throat and dragged him roughly to his feet.

"If you dishonor House Do'Urden," she promised, her face an inch from his, "I will put needles into your purple eyes."

Drizzt didn't blink. In the six years since Vierna had relinquished care of him, putting him into general servitude to all the family, he had come to know Matron Malice well enough to understand all of the subtle connotations of her threats. She was his mother—for whatever that was worth—but Drizzt did not doubt that she would enjoy sticking needles in his eyes.

⚔ ⚔ ⚔ ⚔ ⚔

"This one is different," Vierna said, "in more than the shade of his eyes."

"In what way, then?" Zaknafein asked, trying to keep his curiosity at a professional level. Zak had always liked Vierna better than the others, but she recently had been ordained a high priestess, and had since become too eager for her own good.

Vierna slowed the pace of her gait—the door to the chapel's antechamber was in sight now. "It is hard to say," she admitted. "Drizzt is as intelligent as any male child I have ever known; he could levitate by the age of five. Yet, after he became the page prince, it took tendays of punishment to teach him the duty of keeping his gaze to the floor, as if such a simple act ran unnaturally counter to his constitution."

Zaknafein paused and let Vierna move ahead of him. "Unnatural?" he whispered under his breath, considering the implications of Vierna's observations. Unusual, perhaps, for a drow, but exactly what Zaknafein would expect—and hope for—from a child of his loins.

He moved behind Vierna into the lightless anteroom. Malice, as always, sat in her throne at the head of the spider idol, but all the other chairs in the room had been moved to the walls, even though the entire family was present. This was to be a formal meeting, Zak realized, for only the matron mother was accorded the comfort of a seat.

"Matron Malice," Vierna began in her most reverent voice, "I present to you Zaknafein, as you requested."

Zak moved up beside Vierna and exchanged nods with Malice, but he was more intent on the youngest Do'Urden, standing naked to the waist at the matron mother's side.

Malice held up one hand to silence the others, then motioned for Briza, holding a house *piwafwi*, to continue.

An expression of elation brightened Drizzt's childish face as Briza, chanting through the appropriate incantations, placed the magical cloak, black and shot with streaks of purple and red, over his shoulders.

"Greetings, Zaknafein Do'Urden," Drizzt said heartily, drawing stunned looks from all in the room. Matron Malice had not granted him privilege to speak; he hadn't even asked her permission!

"I am Drizzt, secondboy of House Do'Urden, no more the page prince. I can look at you now—I mean at your eyes and not your boots. Mother told me so." Drizzt's smile disappeared when he looked up at the burning scowl of Matron Malice.

Vierna stood as if turned to stone, her jaw hanging open and her eyes wide in disbelief.

Zak, too, was amazed, but in a different manner. He brought a hand up to pinch his lips together, to prevent them from spreading into a smile that would have inevitably erupted into belly-shaking laughter. Zak couldn't remember the last time he had seen the matron mother's face so very bright!

Briza, in her customary position behind Malice, fumbled with her whip, too confounded by her young brother's actions to even know what in the Nine Hells she should do.

That was a first, Zak knew, for Malice's eldest daughter rarely hesitated when punishment was in order.

At the matron's side, but now prudently a step farther away, Drizzt quieted and stood perfectly still, biting down on his bottom lip. Zak could see, though, that the smile remained in the young drow's eyes. Drizzt's informality and disrespect of station had been more than an unconscious slip of the tongue and more than the innocence of inexperience.

The weapons master took a long step forward to deflect the matron mother's attention from Drizzt. "Secondboy?" he asked, sounding impressed, both for the sake of Drizzt's swelling pride and to placate and distract Malice. "Then it is time for you to train."

Malice let her anger slip away, a rare event. "Only the basics at your hand, Zaknafein. If Drizzt is to replace Nalfein, his place at the Academy will be in Sorcere. Thus the bulk of his preparation will fall upon Rizzen and his knowledge, limited though it may be, of the magical arts."

"Are you so certain that wizardry is his lot, Matron?" Zak was quick to ask.

"He appears intelligent," Malice replied. She shot an angry glare at Drizzt. "At least, some of the time. Vierna reported great progress with his command of the innate powers. Our house needs a new wizard." Malice snarled reflexively, reminded of Matron Baenre's pride in her wizard son, the Archmage of the city. It had been sixteen years since Malice's meeting with the First Matron Mother of Menzoberranzan, but she had never forgotten even the tiniest detail of that encounter. "Sorcere seems the natural course."

Zak took a flat coin from his neck-purse, flipped it into a spin, and snatched it out of the air. "Might we see?" he asked.

"As you will," Malice agreed, not surprised at Zak's desire to prove her wrong. Zak placed little value in wizardry, preferring the hilt of a blade to the crystal rod component of a lightning bolt.

Zak moved to stand before Drizzt and handed him the coin. "Flip it."

Drizzt shrugged, wondering what this vague conversation between his mother and the weapons master was all about. Until now, he had heard nothing of any future profession being planned for him, or of this place called Sorcere. With a consenting shrug of his shoulders, he slid the coin onto his curled index finger and snapped it into the air with his thumb, easily catching it. He then held it back out to Zak and gave the weapons master a confused look, as if to ask what was so important about such an easy task.

Instead of taking the coin, the weapons master pulled another from his neck-purse. "Try both hands," he said to Drizzt, handing it to him.

Drizzt shrugged again, and in one easy motion, put the coins up and caught them.

Zak turned an eye on Matron Malice. Any drow could have performed that feat, but the ease with which this one executed the catch was a pleasure to observe. Keeping a sly eye on the matron, Zak produced two more coins. "Stack two on each hand and send all four up together," he instructed Drizzt.

Four coins went up. Four coins were caught. The only parts of Drizzt's body that had even flinched were his arms.

"Two-hands," Zak said to Malice. "This one is a fighter. He belongs in Melee-Magthere."

"I have seen wizards perform such feats," Malice retorted, not pleased by the look of satisfaction on the troublesome weapons master's face. Zak once had been Malice's proclaimed husband, and quite often since that distant time she took him as her lover. His skills and agility were not confined to the use of weapons. But along with the pleasures that Zaknafein gave to Malice, sensual skills that had prompted Malice to spare Zak's life on more than a dozen occasions, came a multitude of headaches. He was the finest weapons master in Menzoberranzan, another fact that Malice could not ignore, but his disdain, even contempt, for the Spider Queen had often landed House Do'Urden into trouble.

Zak handed two more coins to Drizzt. Now enjoying the game, Drizzt put them into motion. Six went up. Six came down, the correct three landing in each hand.

"Two-hands," Zak said more emphatically. Matron Malice motioned for him to continue, unable to deny the grace of her youngest son's display.

"Could you do it again?" Zak asked Drizzt.

With each hand working independently, Drizzt soon had the coins stacked atop his index fingers, ready to flip. Zak stopped him there and pulled out four more coins, building each of the piles five high. Zak paused a moment to study the concentration of the young drow (and also to keep his hands over the coins and ensure that they were brightened enough by the warmth of his body heat for Drizzt to properly see them in their flight).

"Catch them all, Secondboy," he said in all seriousness. "Catch them all, or you will land in Sorcere, the school of magic. That is not where you belong!"

Drizzt still had only a vague idea of what Zak was talking about, but he could tell from the weapons master's intensity that it must be important. He took a deep breath to steady himself, then snapped the coins up. He sorted their glow quickly, discerning each individual item. The first two fell easily into his hands, but Drizzt saw that the scattering pattern of the rest would not drop them so readily in line.

Drizzt exploded into action, spinning a complete circle, his hands an indecipherable blur of motion. Then he straightened suddenly and stood before Zak. His hands were in fists at his sides and a grim look lay on his face.

Zak and Matron Malice exchanged glances, neither quite sure of what had happened.

Drizzt held his fists out to Zak and slowly opened them, a confident smile widening across his childish face.

Five coins in each hand.

Zak blew a silent whistle. It had taken him, the weapons master of the house, a dozen tries to complete that maneuver with ten coins. He walked over to Matron Malice.

"Two-hands," he said a third time. "He is a fighter, and I am out of coins."

"How many could he do?" Malice breathed, obviously impressed in spite of herself.

"How many could we stack?" Zaknafein shot back with a triumphant smile.

Matron Malice chuckled out loud and shook her head. She had wanted Drizzt to replace Nalfein as the house wizard, but her stubborn weapons master had, as always, deflected her course. "Very well, Zaknafein," she said, admitting her defeat. "The secondboy is a fighter."

Zak nodded and started back to Drizzt.

"Perhaps one day soon to be the weapons master of House Do'Urden," Matron Malice added to Zak's back. Her sarcasm stopped Zak short, and he eyed her over his shoulder.

"With this one," Matron Malice continued wryly, wrenching back the upper hand with her usual lack of shame, "could we expect anything less?"

Rizzen, the present patron of the family shifted uncomfortably. He knew, and so did everyone—even the slaves of House Do'Urden—that Drizzt was not his child.

⚔ ⚔ ⚔ ⚔ ⚔

"Three rooms?" Drizzt asked when he and Zak entered the large training hall at the southernmost end of the Do'Urden complex. Balls of multicolored magical light had been spaced along the length of the high-ceilinged stone room, basking the entirety in a comfortably dim glow. The hall had only three doors: one to the east, which led to an outer chamber that opened onto the balcony of the house; one directly across from Drizzt, on the south wall, leading into the last room in the house; and the one from the main hallway that they had just passed through. Drizzt knew from the many locks Zak was now fastening behind them that he wouldn't often be going back that way.

"One room," Zak corrected.

"But two more doors," Drizzt reasoned, looking out across the room. "With no locks."

"Ah," Zak corrected, "their locks are made of common sense." Drizzt was beginning to get the picture. "That door," Zak continued, pointing to the south, "opens into my private chambers. You do not ever want me to find you in there. The other one leads to the tactics room, reserved for times of war. When—if—you ever prove yourself to my satisfaction, I might invite you to join me there. That day is years away, so consider this single magnificent hall—" he swept his arm out in a wide arc—"your home."

Drizzt looked around, not overly thrilled. He had dared to hope that he had left this kind of treatment behind him with his page prince days. This setup, though, brought him back even to before his six years of servitude in the house, back to that decade when he had been locked away in the family chapel with Vierna. This room wasn't even as large as the chapel, and was too tight for the likings of the spirited young drow. His next question came out as a growl.

"Where do I sleep?"

"Your home," Zak answered matter-of-factly.

"Where do I take meals?"

"Your home."

Drizzt's eyes narrowed to slits and his face flushed in glowing heat. "Where do I . . ." he began stubbornly, determined to foil the weapons master's logic.

"Your home," Zak replied in the same measured and weighted timbre before Drizzt could finish the thought.

Drizzt planted his feet firmly and crossed his arms over his chest. "It sounds messy," he growled.

"It had better not be," Zak growled back.

"Then what is the purpose?" Drizzt began. "You pull me away from my mother—"

"You will address her as Matron Malice," Zak warned. "You will always address her as Matron Malice."

"From my mother—"

Zak's next interruption came not with words but with the swing of a curled fist.

Drizzt awoke about twenty minutes later.

"First lesson," Zak explained, casually leaning against the wall a few feet away. "For your own good. You will always address her as Matron Malice."

Drizzt rolled to his side and tried to prop himself up on his elbow but found his head reeling as soon as it left the black-rugged floor. Zak grabbed him and hoisted him up.

"Not as easy as catching coins," the weapons master remarked.

"What?"

"Parrying a blow."

"What blow?"

"Just agree, you stubborn child."

"Secondboy!" Drizzt corrected, his voice again a growl, and his arms defiantly back over his chest.

Zak's fist curled at his side, a not-too-subtle point that Drizzt did not miss. "Do you need another nap?" the weapons master asked calmly.

"Secondboys can be children," Drizzt wisely conceded.

Zak shook his head in disbelief. This was going to be interesting. "You may find your time here enjoyable," he said, leading Drizzt over to a long, thick, and colorfully (though most of the colors were somber) decorated curtain. "But only if you can learn some control over that wagging tongue of yours." A sharp tug sent the curtain floating down, revealing the most magnificent weapons rack the young drow (and many older drow as well) had ever seen. Polearms of many sorts, swords, axes, hammers, and every other kind of weapon Drizzt could imagine—and a whole bunch he'd never imagine—sat in an elaborate array.

"Examine them," Zak told him. "Take your time and your pleasure. Learn which ones sit best in your hands, follow most obediently the commands of your will. By the time we have finished, you will know every one of them as a trusted companion."

Wide-eyed, Drizzt wandered along the rack, viewing the whole place and the potential of the whole experience in a completely different light. For his entire young life, sixteen years, his greatest enemy had been boredom. Now, it appeared, Drizzt had found weapons to fight that enemy.

Zak headed for the door to his private chamber, thinking it better that Drizzt be alone in those first awkward moments of handling new weapons.

The weapons master stopped, though, when he reached his door and looked back to the young Do'Urden. Drizzt swung a long and heavy halberd, a polearm more than twice his height, in a slow arc. For all of Drizzt's attempts to keep the weapon under control, its momentum spun his tiny frame right to the ground.

Zak heard himself chuckle, but his laughter only reminded him of the grim reality of his duty. He would train Drizzt, as he had trained a thousand young dark elves before him, to be a warrior, preparing him for the trials of the Academy and life in dangerous Menzoberranzan. He would train Drizzt to be a killer.

How against this one's nature that mantle seemed! thought Zak. Smiles came too easily to Drizzt; the thought of him running a sword through the heart of another living being revolted Zaknafein. That was the way of the drow, though, a way that Zak had been unable to resist for all of his four centuries of life. Pulling his stare from the spectacle of Drizzt at play, Zak moved into his chamber and shut the door.

"Are they all like that?" he asked into his nearly empty room. "Do all drow children possess such innocence, such simple, untainted smiles that cannot survive the ugliness of our world?" Zak started for the small desk to the side of the room, meaning to lift the darkening shade off the continually glowing ceramic globe that served as the chamber's light source. He changed his mind as that image of Drizzt's delight with the weapons refused to diminish, and he headed instead for the large bed across from the door.

"Or are you unique, Drizzt Do'Urden?" he continued as he fell onto the cushioned bed. "And if you are so different, what, then, is the cause? The blood, my blood, that courses through your veins? Or the years you spent with your weanmother?"

Zak threw an arm across his eyes and considered the many questions. Drizzt was different from the norm, he decided at length, but he didn't know whether he should thank Vierna—or himself.

After a while, sleep took him. But it brought the weapons master little comfort. A familiar dream visited him, a vivid memory that would never fade.

Zaknafein heard again the screams of the children of House DeVir as the Do'Urden soldiers—soldiers he himself had trained—slashed at them.

"This one is different!" Zak cried, leaping up from his bed. He wiped the cold sweat from his face.

"This one is different." He had to believe that.

# 7
# Dark Secrets

"Do you truly mean to try?" Masoj asked, his voice condescending and filled with disbelief.

Alton turned his hideous glare on the student.

"Direct your anger elsewhere, Faceless One," Masoj said, averting his gaze from his mentor's scarred visage. "I am not the cause of your frustration. The question was valid."

"For more than a decade, you have been a student of the magical arts," Alton replied. "Still you fear to explore the nether world at the side of a master of Sorcere."

"I would have no fear beside a true master," Masoj dared to whisper.

Alton ignored the comment, as he had with so many others he had accepted from the apprenticing Hun'ett over the last sixteen years. Masoj was Alton's only tie to the outside world, and while Masoj had a powerful family, Alton had only Masoj.

They moved through the door into the uppermost chamber of Alton's four-room complex. A single candle burned there, its light diminished by an abundance of dark-colored tapestries and the black hue of the room's stone and rugs. Alton slid onto his stool at the back of the small, circular table, and placed a heavy book down before him.

"It is a spell better left for clerics," Masoj protested, sitting down across from the faceless master. "Wizards command the lower planes; the dead are for the clerics alone."

Alton looked around curiously, then turned a frown up at Masoj, the master's grotesque features enhanced by the dancing candlelight. "It seems that I have no cleric at my call," the Faceless One explained sarcastically. "Would you rather I try for another denizen of the Nine Hells?"

Masoj rocked back in his chair and shook his head helplessly and emphatically. Alton had a point. A year before, the Faceless One had sought answers to his questions by enlisting the aid of an ice devil. The volatile thing froze the room until it shone black in the infrared spectrum and smashed a matron mother's treasure horde worth of alchemical equipment. If Masoj hadn't summoned his magical cat to distract the ice devil, neither he nor Alton would have gotten out of the room alive.

"Very well, then," Masoj said unconvincingly, crossing his arms in front of him on the table. "Conjure your spirit and find your answers."

Alton did not miss the involuntary shudder belied by the ripple in Masoj's robes. He glared at the student for a moment, then went back to his preparations.

As Alton neared the time of casting, Masoj's hand instinctively went into his pocket, to the onyx figurine of the hunting cat he had acquired on the day Alton had assumed the Faceless One's identity. The little statue was enchanted with a powerful dweomer that enabled its possessor to summon a mighty panther to his side. Masoj had used the cat sparingly, not yet fully understanding the dweomer's limitations and potential dangers. "Only in times of need," Masoj reminded himself quietly when he felt the item in his hand. Why was it that those times kept occurring when he was with Alton? the apprentice wondered.

Despite his bravado, this time Alton privately shared Masoj's trepidation. Spirits of the dead were not as destructive as denizens of the lower planes, but they could be equally cruel and subtler in their torments.

Alton needed his answer, though. For more than a decade and a half he had sought his information through conventional channels, enquiring of masters and students—in a roundabout manner, of course—of the details concerning the fall of House DeVir. Many knew the rumors of that eventful night; some even detailed the battle methods used by the victorious house.

None, though, would name that perpetrating house. In Menzoberranzan, one did not utter anything resembling an accusation, even if the belief was commonly shared, without enough undeniable proof to spur the ruling council into a unified action against the accused. If a house botched a raid and was discovered, the wrath of all Menzoberranzan would descend upon it until the family name had been extinguished. But in the case of a successfully executed attack, such as the one that felled House DeVir, an accuser was the one most likely to wind up at the wrong end of a snake-headed whip.

Public embarrassment, perhaps more than any guidelines of honor, turned the wheels of justice in the city of drow.

Alton now sought other means for the solution to his quest. First he had tried the lower planes, the ice devil, to disastrous effect. Now Alton had in his possession an item that could end his frustrations: a tome penned by a wizard of the surface world. In the drow hierarchy, only the clerics of Lolth dealt with the realm of the dead, but in other societies, wizards also dabbled into the spirit world. Alton had found the book in the library of Sorcere and had managed to translate enough of it, he believed, to make a spiritual contact.

He wrung his hands together, gingerly opened the book to the marked page, and scanned the incantation one final time. "Are you ready?" he asked Masoj.

"No."

Alton ignored the student's unending sarcasm and placed his hands flat on the table. He slowly sunk into his deepest meditative trance.

"*Fey innad . . .*" He paused and cleared his throat at the slip. Masoj, though he hadn't closely examined the spell, recognized the mistake.

"*Fey innunad de-min . . .*" Another pause.

"Lolth be with us," Masoj groaned under his breath.

Alton's eyes popped wide, and he glared at the student. "A translation," he growled. "From the strange language of a human wizard!"

"Gibberish," Masoj retorted.

"I have in front of me the private spellbook of a wizard from the surface world," Alton said evenly. "An archmage, according to the scribbling of the orcan thief who stole it and sold it to our agents." He composed himself again and shook his hairless head, trying to return to the depths of his trance.

"A simple, stupid orc managed to steal a spellbook from an archmage," Masoj whispered rhetorically, letting the absurdity of the statement speak for itself.

"The wizard was dead!" Alton roared. "The book is authentic!"

"Who translated it?" Masoj replied calmly.

Alton refused to listen to any more arguments. Ignoring the smug look on Masoj's face, he began again.

"*Fey innunad de-min de-sul de-ket.*"

Masoj faded out and tried to rehearse a lesson from one of his classes, hoping that his sobs of laughter wouldn't disturb Alton. He didn't believe for a moment that Alton's attempt would prove successful, but he didn't want to screw up the fool's line of babbling again and have to suffer through the ridiculous incantation all the way from the beginning still another time.

A short time later, when Masoj heard Alton's excited whisper, "Matron Ginafae?" he quickly focused his attention back on the events at hand.

Sure enough, an unusual ball of green-hued smoke appeared over the candle's flame and gradually took a more definite shape.

"Matron Ginafae!" Alton gasped again when the summons was complete. Hovering before him was the unmistakable image of his dead mother's face.

The spirit scanned the room, confused. "Who are you?" it asked at length.

"I am Alton. Alton DeVir, your son."

"Son?" the spirit asked.

"Your child."

"I remember no child so very ugly."

"A disguise," Alton replied quickly, looking back at Masoj and expecting a snicker. If Masoj had chided and doubted Alton before, he now showed only sincere respect.

Smiling, Alton continued, "Just a disguise, that I might move about in the city and exact revenge upon our enemies!"

"What city?"

"Menzoberranzan, of course."

Still the spirit seemed not to understand.

"You are Ginafae?" Alton pressed. "Matron Ginafae DeVir?"

The spirit's features contorted into a twisted scowl as it considered the question. "I was . . . I think."

"Matron Mother of House DeVir, Fourth House of Menzoberranzan," Alton prompted, growing more excited. "High priestess of Lolth."

The mention of the Spider Queen sent a spark through the spirit. "Oh, no!" it balked. Ginafae remembered now. "You should not have done this, my ugly son!"

"It is just a disguise," Alton interrupted.

"I must leave you," Ginafae's spirit continued, glancing around nervously. "You must release me!"

"But I need some information from you, Matron Ginafae."

"Do not call me that!" the spirit shrieked. "You do not understand! I am not in Lolth's favor . . ."

"Trouble," whispered Masoj offhandedly, hardly surprised.

"Just one answer!" Alton demanded, refusing to let another opportunity to learn his enemies' identities slip past him.

"Quickly!" the spirit shrieked.

"Name the house that destroyed DeVir."

"The house?" Ginafae pondered. "Yes, I remember that evil night. It was House—"

The ball of smoke puffed and bent out of shape, twisting Ginafae's image and sending her next words out as an indecipherable blurb.

Alton leaped to his feet. "No!" he screamed. "You must tell me! Who are my enemies?"

"Would you count me as one?" the spirit image said in a voice very different from the one it had used earlier, a tone of sheer power that stole the blood from Alton's face. The image twisted and transformed, became something ugly, uglier than Alton. Hideous beyond all experience on the Material Plane.

Alton was not a cleric, of course, and he had never studied the drow religion beyond the basic tenets taught to males of the race. He knew the creature now hovering in the air before him, though, for it appeared as an oozing, slimy stick of melted wax: a yochlol, a handmaiden of Lolth.

"You dare to disturb the torment of Ginafae?" the yochlol snarled.

"Damn!" whispered Masoj, sliding slowly down under the black tablecloth. Even he, with all of his doubts of Alton, had not expected his disfigured mentor to land them in trouble this serious.

"But . . ." Alton stuttered.

"Never again disturb this plane, feeble wizard!" the yochlol roared.

"I did not try for the Abyss," Alton protested meekly. "I only meant to speak with—"

"With Ginafae!" the yochlol snarled. "Fallen priestess of Lolth. Where would you expect to find her spirit, foolish male? Frolicking in Olympus, with the false gods of the surface elves?"

"I did not think . . ."

"Do you ever?" the yochlol growled.

"Nope," Masoj answered silently, careful to keep himself as far out of the way as possible.

"Never again disturb this plane," the yochlol warned a final time. "The Spider Queen is not merciful and has no tolerance for meddling males!" The creature's oozing face puffed and swelled, expanding beyond the limits of the smoky ball. Alton heard gurgling, gagging noises, and he stumbled back over his stool, putting his back flat against the wall and bringing his arms up defensively in front of his face.

The yochlol's mouth opened impossibly wide and spewed forth a hail of small objects. They ricocheted off Alton and tapped against the wall all around him. Stones? the faceless wizard wondered in confusion. One of the objects then answered his unspoken question. It caught hold of Alton's layered black robes and began crawling up toward his exposed neck. Spiders.

A wave of the eight-legged beasts rushed under the little table, sending Masoj tumbling out the other side in a desperate roll. He scrambled to his feet and turned back, to see Alton slapping and stomping wildly, trying to get out of the main host of the crawling things.

"Do not kill them!" Masoj screamed. "To kill spiders is forbidden by the—"

"To the Nine Hells with the clerics and their laws!" Alton shrieked back.

Masoj shrugged in helpless agreement, reached around under the folds of his own robes, and produced the same two-handed crossbow he had used to kill the Faceless One those years ago. He considered the powerful weapon and the tiny spiders scrambling around the room.

"Overkill?" he asked aloud. Hearing no answer, he shrugged again and fired.

The heavy bolt knifed across Alton's shoulder, cutting a deep line. The wizard stared in disbelief, then turned an ugly grimace on Masoj.

"You had one on your shoulder," the student explained.

Alton's scowl did not relent.

"Ungrateful?" Masoj snarled. "Foolish Alton, all of the spiders are on your side of the room. Remember?" Masoj turned to leave and called, "Good hunting," over his shoulder. He reached for the handle to the door, but as his long fingers closed around it, the portal's surface transformed into the image of Matron Ginafae. She smiled widely, too widely, and an impossibly long and wet tongue reached out and licked Masoj across the face.

"Alton!" he cried, spinning back against the wall out of the slimy member's reach. He noticed the wizard in the midst of spellcasting, Alton fighting to hold his concentration as a host of spiders continued their hungry ascent up his flowing robes.

"You are a dead one," Masoj commented matter-of-factly, shaking his head.

Alton fought through the exacting ritual of the spell, ignored his own revulsion of the crawling things, and forced the evocation to completion. In all of his years of study, Alton never would have believed he could do such a thing; he would have laughed at the mere mention of it. Now, however, it seemed a far preferable fate to the yochlol's creeping doom.

He dropped a fireball at his own feet.

⚔ ⚔ ⚔ ⚔ ⚔

Naked and hairless, Masoj stumbled through the door and out of the inferno. The flaming faceless master came next, diving into a roll and stripping his tattered and burning robe from his back as he went.

As he watched Alton patting out the last of the flames, a pleasant memory flashed in Masoj's mind, and he uttered the single lament that dominated his every thought at this disastrous moment.

"I should have killed him when I had him in the web."

⚔ ⚔ ⚔ ⚔ ⚔

A short time later, after Masoj had gone back to his room and his studies, Alton slipped on the ornamental metallic bracers that identified him as a master of the Academy and slipped outside the structure of Sorcere. He moved to the wide and sweeping stairway leading down from Tier Breche and sat down to take in the sights of Menzoberranzan.

Even with this view, though, the city did little to distract Alton from thoughts of his latest failure. For sixteen years he had forsaken all other dreams and ambitions in his desperate search to find the guilty house. For sixteen years he had failed.

He wondered how long he could keep up the charade, and his spirits. Masoj, his only friend—if Masoj could be called a friend—was more than halfway through his studies at Sorcere. What would Alton do when Masoj graduated and returned to House Hun'ett?

"Perhaps I shall carry on my toils for centuries to come," he said aloud, "only to be murdered by a desperate student, as I—as Masoj—murdered the Faceless One. Might that student disfigure himself and take my place?" Alton couldn't stop the ironic chuckle that passed his lipless mouth at the notion of a perpetual "faceless master" of Sorcere. At what point would the Matron

Mistress of the Academy get suspicious? A thousand years? Ten thousand? Or might the Faceless One outlive Menzoberranzan itself? Life as a master was not such a bad lot, Alton supposed. Many drow would sacrifice much to be given such an honor.

Alton dropped his face into the crook of his elbow and forced away such ridiculous thoughts. He was not a real master, nor did the stolen position bring him any measure of satisfaction. Perhaps Masoj should have shot him that day, sixteen years ago, when Alton was trapped in the Faceless One's web.

Alton's despair only deepened when he considered the actual time frame involved. He had just passed his seventieth birthday and was still young by drow standards. The notion that only a tenth of his life was behind him was not a comforting one to Alton DeVir this night.

"How long will I survive?" he asked himself. "How long until this madness that is my existence consumes me?" Alton looked back out over the city. "Better that the Faceless One had killed me," he whispered. "For now I am Alton of No House Worth Mentioning."

Masoj had dubbed him that on the first morning after House DeVir's fall, but way back then, with his life teetering on the edge of a crossbow, Alton had not understood the title's implications. Menzoberranzan was nothing more than a collection of individual houses. A rogue commoner might latch on to one of them to call his own, but a rogue noble wouldn't likely be accepted by any house in the city. He was left with Sorcere and nothing more . . . until his true identity was discovered at last. What punishments would he then face for the crime of killing a master? Masoj may have committed the crime, but Masoj had a house to defend him. Alton was only a rogue noble.

He sat back on his elbows and watched the rising heat-light of Narbondel. As the minutes became hours, Alton's despair and self-pity went through inevitable change. He turned his attention to the individual drow houses now, not to the conglomeration that bound them as a city, and he wondered what dark secrets each harbored. One of them, Alton reminded himself, held the secret he most dearly wanted to know. One of them had wiped out House DeVir.

Forgotten was the night's failure with Matron Ginafae and the yochlol, forgotten was the lament for an early death. Sixteen years was not so long a time, Alton decided. He had perhaps seven centuries of life left within his slender frame. If he had to, Alton was prepared to spend every minute of those long years searching for the perpetrating house.

"Vengeance," he growled aloud, needing, feeding off, that audible reminder of his only reason for continuing to draw breath.

# 8
# Kindred

Zak pressed in with a series of low thrusts. Drizzt tried to back away quickly and return to even footing, but the relentless assault followed his every step, and he was forced to keep his movements solely on the defensive. More often than not, Drizzt found the hilts of his weapons closer to Zak than the blades.

Zak then dropped into a low crouch and came up under Drizzt's defense.

Drizzt twirled his scimitars in a masterful cross, but he had to straighten stiffly to dodge the weapons master's equally deft assault. Drizzt knew that he had been set up, and he fully expected the next attack as Zak shifted his weight to his back leg and dived in, both sword tips aimed for Drizzt's loins.

Drizzt spat a silent curse and spun his scimitars into a downward cross, meaning to use the "V" of his blades to catch his teacher's swords. On a sudden impulse, Drizzt hesitated as he intercepted Zak's weapons, and he jumped away instead, taking a painful slap on the inside of one thigh. Disgusted, he threw both of his scimitars to the floor.

Zak, too, leaped back. He held his swords out to his sides, a look of sincere confusion on his face. "You should not have missed that move," he said bluntly.

"The parry is wrong," Drizzt replied.

Awaiting further explanation, Zak lowered one sword tip to the floor and leaned on the weapon. In past years, Zak had wounded, even killed, students for such blatant defiance.

"The cross-down defeats the attack, but to what gain?" Drizzt continued. "When the move is completed, my sword tips remain down too low for any effective attack routine, and you are able to slip back and free."

"But you have defeated my attack."

"Only to face another," Drizzt argued. "The best position I can hope to obtain from the cross-down is an even stance."

"Yes . . . " Zak prompted, not understanding his student's problem with that scenario.

"Remember your own lesson!" Drizzt shouted. "'Every move should bring an advantage you preach to me, but I see no advantage in using the cross-down."

"You recite only one part of that lesson for your own purpose," Zak scolded, now growing equally angry. "Complete the phrase, or use it not at all! 'Every move should bring an advantage or take away a disadvantage.' The cross-down defeats the double thrust low, and your opponent obviously has gained the advantage if he even attempts such a daring offensive maneuver! Returning to an even stance is far preferable at that moment."

"The parry is wrong." Drizzt said stubbornly.

"Pick up your blades," Zak growled at him, taking a threatening step forward. Drizzt hesitated and Zak charged, his swords leading.

Drizzt dropped to a crouch, snatched up the scimitars, and rose to meet the assault while wondering if it was another lesson or a true attack.

The weapons master pressed furiously, snapping off cut after cut and backing Drizzt around in circles. Drizzt defended well enough and began to notice an all-too-familiar pattern as Zak's attacks came consistently lower, again forcing the hilts of Drizzt's weapons up and out over the scimitars' blades.

Drizzt understood that Zak meant to prove his point with actions, not words. Seeing the fury on Zak's face, though, Drizzt wasn't certain how far the weapons master would carry his point. If Zak proved correct in his observations, would he strike again to Drizzt's thigh? Or to his heart? Zak came up and under and Drizzt stiffened and straightened. "Double thrust low!" the weapons master growled, and his swords dived in.

Drizzt was ready for him. He executed the cross-down, smiling smugly at the ring of metal as his scimitars crossed over the thrusting swords. Drizzt then followed through with only one of his blades, thinking he could deflect both of Zak's swords well enough in that manner. Now with one blade free of the parry, Drizzt spun it over in a devious counter.

As soon as Drizzt reversed the one hand, Zak saw the ploy—a ruse he had suspected Drizzt would try. Zak dropped one of his own sword tips—the one nearest to the hilt of Drizzt's single parrying blade—to the ground, and Drizzt, trying to maintain an even resistance and balance along the length of the blocking scimitar, lost his balance. Drizzt was quick enough to catch himself before he had stumbled too far, though his knuckles pinched into the stone of the floor. He still believed that he had Zak caught in his trap, and that he could finish his brilliant counter. He took a short step forward to regain his full balance.

The weapons master dropped straight down to the floor, under the arc of Drizzt's swinging scimitar, and spun a single circuit, driving his booted heel into the back of Drizzt's exposed knee. Before Drizzt had even realized the attack, he found himself lying flat on his back.

Zak abruptly broke his own momentum and threw his feet back under him. Before Drizzt could begin to understand the dizzying counter-counter, he found the weapons master standing over him with the tip of Zak's sword painfully and pointedly drawing a tiny drop of blood from his throat.

"Have you anything more to say?" Zak growled.

"The parry is wrong," Drizzt answered.

Zak's laughter erupted from his belly. He threw his sword to the ground, reached down, and pulled the stubborn young student to his feet. He calmed quickly, his gaze finding that of Drizzt's lavender orbs as he pushed the student out to arm's length. Zak marveled at the ease of Drizzt's stance, the way he held the twin scimitars almost as if they were a natural extension of his arms. Drizzt had been in training only a few months, but already he had mastered the use of nearly every weapon in the vast armory of House Do'Urden.

Those scimitars! Drizzt's chosen weapons, with curving blades that enhanced the dizzying flow of the young fighter's sweeping battle style. With those scimitars in hand, this young drow, barely more than a child, could outfight half the members of the Academy, and a shiver tingled through Zak's spine when he pondered just how magnificent Drizzt would become after years of training.

It was not just the physical abilities and potential of Drizzt Do'Urden that made Zaknafein pause and take note, however. Zak had come to realize that Drizzt's temperament was indeed different from that of the average drow; Drizzt possessed a spirit of innocence and lacked any maliciousness. Zak couldn't help but feel proud when he looked upon Drizzt. In all manners, the young drow held to the same principles—morals so unusual in Menzoberranzan—as Zak.

Drizzt had recognized the connection as well, though he had no idea of how unique his and Zak's shared perceptions were in the evil drow world. He realized that "Uncle Zak" was different from any of the other dark elves he had come to know, though that included only his own family and a few dozen of the house soldiers. Certainly Zak was much different from Briza, Drizzt's oldest sister, with her zealous, almost blind, ambitions in the mysterious religion of Lolth. Certainly Zak was different from Matron Malice, Drizzt's mother, who seemed never to say anything at all to Drizzt unless it was a command for service.

Zak was able to smile at situations that didn't necessarily bring pain to anyone. He was the first drow Drizzt had met who was apparently content with his station in life. Zak was the first drow Drizzt had ever heard laugh.

"A good try," the weapons master conceded of Drizzt's failed counter.

"In a real battle, I would have been dead," Drizzt replied.

"Surely," said Zak, "but that is why we train. Your plan was masterful, your timing perfect. Only the situation was wrong. Still, I will say it was a good try."

"You expected it," said the student.

Zak smiled and nodded. "That is, perhaps, because I had seen the maneuver attempted by another student."

"Against you?" Drizzt asked, feeling a little less special now that he knew his battle insights were not so unique.

"Hardly," Zak replied with a wink. "I watched the counter fail from the same angle as you, to the same result."

Drizzt's face brightened again. "We think alike," he commented.

"We do," said Zak, "but my knowledge has been increased by four centuries of experience, while you have not even lived through a score of years. Trust me, my eager student. The cross-down is the correct parry."

"Perhaps," Drizzt replied.

Zak hid a smile. "When you find a better counter, we shall try it. But until then, trust my word. I have trained more soldiers than I can count, all the army of House Do'Urden and ten times that number when I served as a master in Melee-Magthere. I taught Rizzen, all of your sisters, and both of your brothers."

"Both?"

"I . . ." Zak paused and shot a curious glance at Drizzt. "I see," he said after a moment. "They never bothered to tell you." Zak wondered if it was his place to tell Drizzt the truth. He doubted that Matron Malice would care either way; she probably hadn't told Drizzt simply because she hadn't considered the story of Nalfein's death worth telling.

"Yes, both." Zak decided to explain. "You had two brothers when you were born: Dinin, whom you know, and an older one, Nalfein, a wizard of considerable power. Nalfein was killed in battle on the very night you drew your first breath."

"Against dwarves or vicious gnomes?" Drizzt squeaked, as wide-eyed as a child begging for a frightening bedtime story. "Was he defending the city from evil conquerors or rogue monsters?"

Zak had a hard time reconciling the warped perceptions of Drizzt's innocent beliefs. "Bury the young in lies," he lamented under his breath, but to Drizzt he answered, "No."

"Then against some opponent more foul?" Drizzt pressed. "Wicked elves from the surface?"

"He died at the hands of a drow!" Zak snapped in frustration, stealing the eagerness from Drizzt's shining eyes.

Drizzt slumped back to consider the possibilities, and Zak could hardly bear to watch the confusion that twisted his young face.

"War with another city?" Drizzt asked somberly. "I did not know . . ."

Zak let it go at that. He turned and moved silently toward his private chamber. Let Malice or one of her lackeys destroy Drizzt's innocent logic. Behind him, Drizzt held his next line of questions in check, understanding that the conversation, and the lesson, was at an end. Understanding, too, that something important had just transpired.

⚔ ⚔ ⚔ ⚔ ⚔

The weapons master battled Drizzt through long hours as the days blended into tendays, and the tendays into months. Time became unimportant; they fought until exhaustion overwhelmed them, and went back to the training floor again as soon as they were able.

By the third year, at the age of nineteen, Drizzt was able to hold out for hours against the weapons master, even taking the offensive in many of their contests.

Zak enjoyed these days. For the first time in many years, he had met one with the potential to become his fighting equal. For the first time that Zak could ever remember, laughter often accompanied the clash of adamantine weapons in the training room.

He watched Drizzt grow tall and straight, attentive, eager, and intelligent. The masters of the Academy would be hard put just to hold a stalemate against Drizzt, even in his first year!

That thought thrilled the weapons master only as long as it took him to remember the principles of the Academy, the precepts of drow life, and what they would do to his wonderful student. How they would steal that smile from Drizzt's lavender eyes.

A pointed reminder of that drow world outside the practice room visited them one day in the person of Matron Malice.

"Address her with proper respect," Zak warned Drizzt when Maya announced the matron mother's entrance. The weapons master prudently moved out a few steps to greet the head of House Do'Urden privately.

"My greetings, Matron," he said with a low bow. "To what do I owe the honor of your presence?"

Matron Malice laughed at him, seeing through his facade.

"So much time do you and my son spend in here," she said. "I came to witness the benefit to the boy."

"He is a fine fighter," Zak assured her.

"He will have to be," Malice muttered. "He goes to the Academy in only a year."

Zak narrowed his eyes at her doubting words and growled, "The Academy has never seen a finer swordsman."

The matron walked away from him to stand before Drizzt. "I doubt not your prowess with the blade," she said to Drizzt, though she shot a sly gaze back at Zak as she spoke the words. "You have the proper blood. There are other qualities that make up a drow warrior—qualities of the heart. The attitude of a warrior!"

Drizzt didn't know how to respond to her. He had seen her only a few times in all of the last three years, and they had exchanged no words.

Zak saw the confusion on Drizzt's face and feared that the boy would slip up—precisely what Matron Malice wanted. Then Malice would have an excuse to pull Drizzt out of Zak's tutelage—dishonoring Zak in the process—and give him over to Dinin or some other passionless killer. Zak may have been the finest instructor with the blade, but now that Drizzt had learned the use of weapons, Malice wanted him emotionally hardened.

Zak couldn't risk it; he valued his time with young Drizzt too much. He pulled his swords from their jeweled scabbards and charged right by Matron Malice, yelling, "Show her, young warrior!"

Drizzt's eyes became burning flames at the approach of his wild instructor. His scimitars came into his hands as quickly as if he had willed them to appear.

It was a good thing they had! Zak came in on Drizzt with a fury that the young drow had never before seen, more so even than the time Zak had shown Drizzt the value of the cross-down parry. Sparks flew as sword rang against scimitar, and Drizzt found himself driven back, both of his arms already aching from the thudding force of the heavy blows.

"What are you . . ." Drizzt tried to ask.

"Show her," Zak growled, slamming in again and again.

Drizzt barely dodged one cut that surely would have killed him. Still, confusion kept his moves purely defensive.

Zak slapped one of Drizzt's scimitars, then the other, out wide, and used an unexpected weapon, bringing his foot straight up in front of him and slamming his heel into Drizzt's nose.

Drizzt heard the crackle of cartilage and felt the warmth of his own blood running freely down his face. He dived back into a roll, trying to keep a safe distance from his crazed opponent until he could realign his senses.

From his knees he saw Zak, a short distance away and approaching. "Show her!" Zak growled angrily with every determined step.

The purple flames of faerie fire limned Drizzt's skin, making him an easier target. He responded the only way he could; he dropped a globe of darkness over himself and Zak. Sensing the weapons master's next move, Drizzt dropped to his belly and scrambled out, keeping his head low—a wise choice.

At his first realization of the darkness, Zak had quickly levitated up about ten feet and rolled right over, sweeping his blades down to Drizzt's face level.

When Drizzt came clear of the other side of the darkened globe, he looked back and saw only the lower half of Zak's legs. He didn't need to watch anything more to understand the weapons master's deadly blind attacks. Zak would have cut him apart if he had not dropped low in the blackness.

Anger replaced confusion. When Zak dropped from his magical perch and came rushing back out the front of the globe, Drizzt let his rage lead him back into the fight. He spun a pirouette just before he reached Zak, his lead scimitar cutting a gracefully arcing line and his other following in a deceptively sharp stab straight over that line.

Zak dodged the thrusting point and put a backhand block on the other.

Drizzt wasn't finished. He set his thrusting blade into a series of short, wicked pokes that kept Zak on the retreat for a dozen steps and more, back into the conjured darkness. They now had to rely on their incredibly keen sense of hearing and their instincts. Zak finally managed to regain a foothold, but Drizzt immediately set his own feet into action, kicking away whenever the balance of his swinging blades allowed for it. One foot even slipped through Zak's defenses, blasting the breath from the weapons master's lungs.

They came back out the side of the globe, and Zak, too, glowed in the outline of faerie fire. The weapons master felt sickened by the hatred etched on his young student's face, but he realized that this time, neither he nor Drizzt had been given a choice in the matter. This fight had to be ugly, had to be real. Gradually, Zak settled into an easy rhythm, solely defensive, and let Drizzt, in his explosive fury, wear himself down.

Drizzt played on and on, relentless and tireless. Zak coaxed him by letting him see openings where there were none, and Drizzt was always quick to oblige, launching a thrust, cut, or kick.

Matron Malice watched the spectacle silently. She couldn't deny the measure of training Zak had given her son; Drizzt was—physically—more than ready for battle.

Zak knew that, to Matron Malice, sheer skill with weapons might not be enough. Zak had to keep Malice from conversing with Drizzt for any length of time. She would not approve of her son's attitudes.

Drizzt was tiring now, Zak could see, though he recognized the weariness in his student's arms to be partly deception.

"Go with it," he muttered silently, and he suddenly "twisted" his ankle, his right arm flailing out wide and low as he struggled for balance, opening a hole in his defenses that Drizzt could not resist.

The expected thrust came in a flash, and Zak's left arm streaked in a short crosscut that slapped the scimitar right out of Drizzt's hand.

"Ha!" Drizzt cried, having expected the move and launching his second ruse. His remaining scimitar knifed over Zak's left shoulder, inevitably dipping in the follow-through of the parry.

But by the time Drizzt even launched the second blow, Zak was already down to his knees. As Drizzt's blade cut harmlessly high, Zak sprang to his feet and launched a right cross, hilt first, that caught Drizzt squarely in the face. A stunned Drizzt leaped back a long step and stood perfectly still for a long moment. His remaining scimitar dropped to the ground, and his glossed eyes did not blink.

"A feint within a feint within a feint!" Zak calmly explained.

Drizzt slumped to the floor, unconscious.

Matron Malice nodded her approval as Zak walked back over to her. "He is ready for the Academy," she remarked.

Zak's face turned sour and he did not answer.

"Vierna is there already," Malice continued, "to teach as a mistress in Arach-Tinilith, the School of Lolth. It is a high honor."

A laurel for House Do'Urden, Zak knew, but he was smart enough to keep his thoughts silent.

"Dinin will leave soon," said the matron.

Zak was surprised. Two children serving as masters in the Academy at the same time? "You must have worked hard to get such accommodations," he dared to remark.

Matron Malice smiled. "Favors owed, favors called in."

"To what end?" asked Zak. "Protection for Drizzt?"

Malice laughed aloud. "From what I have just witnessed, Drizzt would more likely protect the other two!"

Zak bit his lip at the comment. Dinin was still twice the fighter and ten times the heartless killer as Drizzt. Zak knew that Malice had other motives.

"Three of the first eight houses will be represented by no fewer than four children in the Academy over the next two decades," Matron Malice admitted. "Matron Baenre's own son will begin in the same class as Drizzt."

"So you have aspirations," Zak said. "How high, then, will House Do'Urden climb under the guidance of Matron Malice?"

"Sarcasm will cost you your tongue," the matron mother warned. "We would be fools to let slip by such an opportunity to learn more of our rivals!"

"The first eight houses," Zak mused. "Be cautious, Matron Malice. Do not forget to watch for rivals among the lesser houses. There once was a house named DeVir that made such a mistake."

"No attack will come from behind," Malice sneered. "We are the ninth house but boast more power than but a handful of others. None will strike at our backs; there are easier targets higher up the line."

"And all to our gain," Zak put in.

"That is the point of it all, is it not?" Malice asked, her evil smile wide on her face.

Zak didn't need to respond; the matron knew his true feelings. That precisely was not the point.

⚔ ⚔ ⚔ ⚔ ⚔

"Speak less and your jaw will heal faster," Zak said later, when he again was alone with Drizzt.

Drizzt cast him a vile glance.

The weapons master shook his head. "We have become great friends," he said.

"So I had thought," mumbled Drizzt.

"Then think clearly," Zak scolded. "Do you believe that Matron Malice would approve of such a bonding between her weapons master and her youngest—her prized youngest—son? You are a drow, Drizzt Do'Urden, and of noble birth. You may have no friends!"

Drizzt straightened as if he had been slapped in the face.

"None openly, at least," Zak conceded, laying a comforting hand on the youngster's shoulder. "Friends equate to vulnerability, inexcusable vulnerability. Matron Malice would never accept . . ." He paused, realizing that he was browbeating his student. "Well," he admitted in quiet conclusion, "at least we two know who we are."

Somehow, to Drizzt, that just didn't seem enough.

# 9 Families

"Come quickly," Zak instructed Drizzt one evening after they had finished their sparring. By the urgency of the weapons master's tone, and by the fact that Zak didn't even pause to wait for Drizzt, Drizzt knew that something important was happening.

He finally caught up to Zak on the balcony of House Do'Urden, where Maya and Briza already stood.

"What is it?" Drizzt asked.

Zak pulled him close and pointed out across the great cavern, to the northeastern reaches of the city. Lights flashed and faded in sudden bursts, a pillar of fire rose into the air, then disappeared.

"A raid," Briza said of offhandedly. "Minor houses, and of no concern to us."

Zak saw that Drizzt did not understand.

"One house has attacked another," he explained. "Revenge, perhaps, but most likely an attempt to climb to a higher rank in the city."

"The battle has been long," Briza remarked, "and still the lights flash."

Zak continued to clarify the event for the confused secondboy of the house. "The attackers should have blocked the battle within rings of darkness. Their inability to do so might indicate that the defending house was ready for the raid."

"All cannot be going well for the attackers," Maya agreed.

Drizzt could hardly believe what he was hearing. Even more alarming than the news itself was the way his family talked about the event. They were so calm in their descriptions, as if this was an expected occurrence.

"The attackers must leave no witnesses," Zak explained to Drizzt, "else they will face the wrath of the ruling council."

"But we are witnesses," Drizzt reasoned.

"No," Zak replied. "We are onlookers; this battle is none of our affair. Only the nobles of the defending house are awarded the right to place accusations against their attackers."

"If any nobles are left alive," Briza added, obviously enjoying the drama.

At that moment, Drizzt wasn't sure if he liked this new revelation. However he might have felt, he found that he could not tear his gaze from the continuing spectacle of drow battle. All the Do'Urden compound was astir now, soldiers and slaves running about in search of a better vantage point and shouting out descriptions of the action and rumors of the perpetrators.

This was drow society in all its macabre play, and while it seemed ultimately wrong in the heart of the youngest member of House Do'Urden, Drizzt could not deny the excitement of the night. Nor could Drizzt deny the expressions of obvious pleasure stamped upon the faces of the three who shared the balcony with him.

⚔ ⚔ ⚔ ⚔ ⚔

Alton made his way through his private chambers one final time, to make certain that any artifacts or tomes that might seem even the least bit sacrilegious were safely hidden. He was expecting a visit from a matron mother, a rare occasion for a master of the Academy not connected with Arach-Tinilith, the School of Lolth. Alton was more than a little anxious about the motives of this particular visitor, Matron SiNafay Hun'ett, head of the city's fifth house and mother of Masoj, Alton's partner in conspiracy.

A bang on the stone door of the outermost chamber in his complex told Alton that his guest had arrived. He straightened his robes and took yet another glance around the room. The door swung open before Alton could get there, and Matron SiNafay swept into the room. How easily she made the transformation—walking from the absolute dark of the outside corridor into the candlelight of Alton's chamber—without so much as a flinch.

SiNafay was smaller than Alton had imagined, diminutive even by the standards of the drow. She stood barely more than four feet high and weighed, by Alton's estimation, no more than fifty pounds. She was a matron mother, though, and Alton reminded himself that she could strike him dead with a single spell.

Alton averted his gaze obediently and tried to convince himself that there was nothing unusual about this visit. He grew less at ease, however, when Masoj trotted in and to his mother's side, a smug smile on his face.

"Greetings from House Hun'ett, Gelroos," Matron SiNafay said. "Twenty-five years and more it has been since we last talked."

"Gelroos?" Alton mumbled under his breath. He cleared his throat to cover his surprise. "My greetings to you, Matron SiNafay," he managed to stammer. "Has it been so very long?"

"You should come to the house," the matron said. "Your chambers remain empty."

My chambers? Alton began to feel very sick.

SiNafay did not miss the look. A scowl crossed her face and her eyes narrowed evilly.

Alton suspected that his secret was out. If the Faceless One had been a member of the Hun'ett family, how could Alton hope to fool the matron mother of the house? He scanned for the best escape route, or for some way he could at least kill the traitorous Masoj before SiNafay struck him down.

When he looked back toward Matron SiNafay, she had already begun a quiet spell. Her eyes popped wide at its completion, her suspicions confirmed.

"Who are you?" she asked, her voice sounding more curious than concerned.

There was no escape, no way to get at Masoj, standing prudently close to his powerful mother's side.

"Who are you?" SiNafay asked again, taking a three-headed instrument from her belt, the dreaded snake-headed whip that injected the most painful and incapacitating poison known to drow.

"Alton," he stuttered, having no choice but to answer. He knew that since she now was on her guard, SiNafay would use simple magic to detect any lies he might concoct. "I am Alton DeVir."

"DeVir?" Matron SiNafay appeared at least intrigued. "Of the House DeVir that died some years ago?"

"I am the only survivor," Alton admitted.

"And you killed Gelroos—Gelroos Hun'ett—and took his place as master in Sorcere," the matron reasoned, her voice a snarl. Doom closed in all around Alton.

"I did not . . . I could not know his name . . . He would have killed me!" Alton stuttered.

"I killed Gelroos," came a voice from the side.

SiNafay and Alton turned to Masoj, who once again held his favorite two-handed crossbow.

"With this," the young Hun'ett explained. "On the night House DeVir fell. I found my excuse in Gelroos's battle with that one." He pointed to Alton.

"Gelroos was your brother," Matron SiNafay reminded Masoj.

"Damn his bones!" Masoj spat. "For four miserable years I served him—served him as if he were a matron mother! He would have kept me from Sorcere, would have forced me into the Melee-Magthere instead."

The matron looked from Masoj to Alton and back to her son. "And you let this one live," she reasoned, a smile again on her lips. "You killed your enemy and forged an alliance with a new master in a single move."

"As I was taught," Masoj said through clenched teeth, not knowing whether punishment or praise would follow.

"You were just a child," SiNafay remarked, suddenly realizing the timetable involved.

Masoj accepted the compliment silently.

Alton watched it all anxiously. "Then what of me?" he cried. "Is my life forfeit?"

SiNafay turned a glare on him. "Your life as Alton DeVir ended, so it would seem, on the night House DeVir fell. Thus you remain the Faceless One, Gelroos Hun'ett. I can use your eyes in the Academy—to watch over my son and my enemies."

Alton could hardly breathe. To so suddenly find himself allied with one of the most powerful houses in Menzoberranzan. A jumble of possibilities and questions flooded his mind, one in particular, which had haunted him for nearly two decades.

His adopted matron mother recognized his excitement. "Speak your thoughts," she commanded.

"You are a high priestess of Lolth," Alton said boldly, that one notion overpowering all caution. "It is within your power to grant me my fondest desire."

"You dare to ask a favor?" Matron SiNafay balked, though she saw the torment on Alton's face and was intrigued by the apparent importance of this mystery. "Very well"

"What house destroyed my family?" Alton growled. "Ask the nether world, I beg, Matron SiNafay."

SiNafay considered the question carefully, and the possibilities of Alton's apparent thirst for vengeance. Another benefit of allowing this one into the family? SiNafay wondered.

"This is known to me already," she replied. "Perhaps when you have proven your value, I will tell—"

"No!" Alton cried. He stopped short, realizing that he had interrupted a matron mother, a crime that could invoke a punishment of death.

SiNafay held back her angry urges. "This question must be very important for you to act so foolishly," she said.

"Please," Alton begged. "I must know. Kill me if you will, but tell me first who it was."

SiNafay liked his courage, and his obsession could only prove of value to her. "House Do'Urden," she said.

"Do'Urden?" Alton echoed, hardly believing that a house so far back in the city hierarchy could have defeated House DeVir.

"You will take no actions against them," Matron SiNafay warned. "And

I will forgive your insolence—this time. You are a son of House Hun'ett now; remember always your place!" She let it stay at that, knowing that one who had been clever enough to carry out such a deception for the better part of two decades would not be foolish enough to disobey the matron mother of his house.

"Come Masoj," SiNafay said to her son, "let us leave this one alone so that he may consider his new identity."

⚔ ⚔ ⚔ ⚔ ⚔

"I must tell you, Matron SiNafay," Masoj dared to say as he and his mother made their way out of Sorcere, "Alton DeVir is a buffoon. He might bring harm to House Hun'ett."

"He survived the fall of his own house," SiNafay replied, "and has played through the ruse as the Faceless One for nineteen years. A buffoon? Perhaps, but a resourceful buffoon at the least."

Masoj unconsciously rubbed the area of his eyebrow that had never grown back. "I have suffered the antics of Alton DeVir for all these years," he said. "He does have a fair share of luck, I admit, and can get himself out of trouble—though he is usually the one who puts himself into it!"

"Do not fear," SiNafay laughed. "Alton brings value to our house."

"What can we hope to gain?"

"He is a master of the Academy," SiNafay replied. "He gives me eyes where I now need them." She stopped her son and turned him to face her so that he might understand the implications of her every word. "Alton DeVir's claim against House Do'Urden may work in our favor. He was a noble of the house, with rights of accusation."

"You mean to use Alton DeVir's charge to rally the great houses into punishing House Do'Urden?" Masoj asked.

"The great houses would hardly be willing to strike out for an incident that occurred almost twenty years ago," SiNafay replied. "House Do'Urden executed House DeVir's destruction nearly to perfection—a clean kill. To so much as speak an open charge against the Do'Urdens now would be to invite the wrath of the great houses on ourselves."

"What good then is Alton DeVir?" Masoj asked. "His claim is useless to us."

The matron replied, "You are only a male and cannot understand the complexities of the ruling hierarchy. With Alton DeVir's charge whispered into the proper ears, the ruling council might look the other way if a single house took revenge on Alton's behalf."

"To what end?" Masoj remarked, not understanding the importance. "You would risk the losses of such a battle for the destruction of a lesser house?"

"So thought House DeVir of House Do'Urden," explained SiNafay. "In our world, we must be as concerned with the lower houses as with the higher ones. All of the great houses would be wise now to watch closely the moves of Daermon N'a'shezbaernon, the ninth house that is known as Do'Urden. It now has both a master and a mistress serving in the Academy and three high priestesses, with a fourth nearing the goal."

"Four high priestesses?" Masoj pondered. "In a single house." Only three of the top eight houses could claim more than that. Normally, sisters aspiring to such heights inspired rivalries that inevitably thinned the ranks.

"And the legions of House Do'Urden number more than three hundred fifty," SiNafay continued, "all of them trained by perhaps the finest weapons master in all the city."

"Zaknafein Do'Urden, of course!" Masoj recalled.

"You have heard of him?"

"His name is often spoken at the Academy, even in Sorcere."

"Good," SiNafay purred. "Then you will understand the full weight of the mission I have chosen for you."

An eager light came into Masoj's eyes.

"Another Do'Urden is soon to begin there," SiNafay explained. "Not a master, but a student. By the words of those few who have seen this boy, Drizzt, at training, he will be as fine a fighter as Zaknafein. We should not allow this."

"You want me to kill the boy?" Masoj asked eagerly.

"No," SiNafay replied, "not yet. I want you to learn of him, to understand the motivations of his every move. If the time to strike does come, you must be ready."

Masoj liked the devious assignment, but one thing still bothered him more than a little. "We still have Alton to consider," he said. "He is impatient and daring. What are the consequences to House Hun'ett if he strikes House Do'Urden before the proper time? Might we invoke open war in the city, with House Hun'ett viewed as the perpetrator?"

"Do not worry, my son," Matron SiNafay replied. "If Alton DeVir makes a grievous error while in the guise of Gelroos Hun'ett, we expose him as a murderous imposter and no member of our family. He will be an unhoused rogue with an executioner facing him from every direction."

Her casual explanation put Masoj at ease, but Matron SiNafay, so knowledgeable in the ways of drow society, had understood the risk she was taking from the moment she had accepted Alton DeVir into her house. Her plan seemed foolproof, and the possible gain—the elimination of this growing House Do'Urden—was a tempting piece of bait.

But the dangers, too, were very real. While it was perfectly acceptable for one house to covertly destroy another, the consequences of failure could not be ignored. Earlier that very night, a lesser house had struck out against a rival and, if the rumors held true, had failed. The illuminations of the next day would probably force the ruling council to enact a pretense of justice, to make an example of the unsuccessful attackers. In her long life, Matron SiNafay had witnessed this "justice" several times.

Not a single member of any of the aggressor houses—she was not even allowed to remember their names—had ever survived.

⚔ ⚔ ⚔ ⚔ ⚔

Zak awakened Drizzt early the next morning. "Come," he said. "We are bid to go out of the house this day."

All thoughts of sleep washed away from Drizzt at the news. "Outside the house?" he echoed. In all of his nineteen years, Drizzt had never once walked beyond the adamantine fence of the Do'Urden complex. He had only watched that outside world of Menzoberranzan from the balcony.

While Zak waited, Drizzt quickly collected his soft boots and his *piwafwi*. "Will there be no lesson this day?" Drizzt asked.

"We shall see," was all that Zak replied, but in his thoughts, the weapons master figured that Drizzt might be in for one of the most startling revelations of his life. A house had failed in a raid, and the ruling council had requested the presence of all the nobles of the city, to bear witness to the weight of justice.

Briza appeared in the corridor outside the practice room's door. "Hurry," she scolded. "Matron Malice does not wish our house to be among the last groups joining the gathering!"

The matron mother herself, floating atop a blue-glowing disk—for matron mothers rarely walked through the city—led the procession out of House Do'Urden's grand gate. Briza walked at her mother's side, with Maya and Rizzen in the second rank and Drizzt and Zak taking up the rear. Vierna and Dinin, attending to the duties of their positions in the Academy, had gone to the ruling council's summons with a different group.

All the city was astir this morning, rumbling in the rumors of the failed raid. Drizzt walked through the bustle wide-eyed, staring in wonderment at the close-up view of the decorated drow houses. Slaves of every inferior race—goblins, orcs, even giants—scrambled out of the way, recognizing Malice, riding her enchanted carriage, as a matron mother. Drow commoners halted conversations and remained respectfully silent as the noble family passed.

As they made their way toward the northwestern section, the location of the guilty house, they came into a lane blocked by a squabbling caravan of duergar, gray dwarves. A dozen carts had been overturned or locked together—apparently, two groups of duergar had come into the narrow lane together, neither relinquishing the right-of-way.

Briza pulled the snake-headed whip from her belt and chased off a few of the creatures, clearing the way for Malice to float up to the apparent leaders of the two groups.

The dwarves turned on her angrily—until they realized her station.

"Beggin' yer pardon, Madam," one of them stammered. "Un-fortunate accident is all."

Malice eyed the contents of one of the nearest carts, crates of giant crab legs and other delicacies.

"You have slowed my journey," Malice said calmly.

"We have come to your city in hopes of trade," the other duergar explained. He cast an angry glare at his counterpart, and Malice understood that the two were rivals, probably bartering the same goods to the same drow house.

"I will forgive your insolence . . ." she offered graciously, still eyeing the crates.

The two duergar suspected what was forthcoming. So did Zak. "We eat well tonight," he whispered to Drizzt with a sly wink. "Matron Malice would not let such an opportunity slip by without gain."

". . . if you can see your way to deliver half of these carts to the gate of House Do'Urden this night," Malice finished.

The duergar started to protest but quickly dismissed the foolish notion. How they hated dealing with drow elves!

"You will be compensated appropriately," Malice continued. "House Do'Urden is not a poor house. Between both of your caravans, you will still have enough goods to satisfy the house you came to see."

Neither of the duergar could refute the simple logic, but under these trading circumstances, where they had offended a matron mother, they knew the compensation for their valuable foods would hardly be appropriate. Still, the gray dwarves could only accept it all as a risk of doing business in Menzoberranzan. They bowed politely and set their troops to clearing the way for the drow procession.

⚔ ⚔ ⚔ ⚔ ⚔

House Teken'duis, the unsuccessful raiders of the previous night, had barricaded themselves within their two-stalagmite structure, fully expecting what was to come. Outside their gates, all of the nobles of Menzoberranzan, more than a thousand drow, had gathered, with Matron Baenre and the other seven matron mothers of the ruling council at their head. More disastrous for the guilty house, the entirety of the three schools of the Academy, students and instructors, had surrounded the Teken'duis compound.

Matron Malice led her group to the front line behind the ruling matrons. As she was matron of the ninth house, only one step from the council, other drow nobles readily stepped out of her way.

"House Teken'duis has angered the Spider Queen!" Matron Baenre proclaimed in a voice amplified by magical spells.

"Only because they failed," Zak whispered to Drizzt.

Briza cast both males an angry glare.

Matron Baenre bade three young drow, two females and a male, to her side. "These are all that remain of House Freth," she explained. "Can you tell us, orphans of House Freth," she asked of them, "who it was that attacked your home?"

"House Teken'duis!" they shouted together.

"Rehearsed," Zak commented.

Briza turned around again. "Silence!" she whispered harshly.

Zak slapped Drizzt on the back of the head. "Yes," he agreed. "Do be quiet!"

Drizzt started to protest, but Briza had already turned away and Zak's smile was too wide to argue against.

"Then it is the will of the ruling council," Matron Baenre was saying, "that House Teken'duis suffer the consequences of their actions!"

"What of the orphans of House Freth?" came a call from the crowd.

Matron Baenre stroked the head of the oldest female, a cleric recently finished in her studies at the Academy. "Nobles they were born, and nobles they remain," Baenre said. "House Baenre accepts them into its protection; they bear the name of Baenre now."

Disgruntled whispers filtered through the gathering. Three young nobles, two of them female, was quite a prize. Any house in the city gladly would have taken them in.

"Baenre," Briza whispered to Malice. "Just what the first house needs more clerics!"

"Sixteen high priestesses is not enough, it seems," Malice answered.

"And no doubt, Baenre will take any surviving soldiers of House Freth," Briza reasoned.

Malice was not so certain. Matron Baenre was walking a thin line by taking even the surviving nobles. If House Baenre got too powerful, Lolth surely would take exception. In situations such as this, where a house had been almost eradicated, surviving common soldiers were normally pooled out to bidding houses. Malice would have to watch for such an auction. Soldiers did not come cheaply, but at this time, Malice would welcome the opportunity to add to her forces, particularly if there were any magic-users to be had.

Matron Baenre addressed the guilty house. "House Teken'duis!" she called. "You have broken our laws and have been rightfully caught. Fight if you will, but know that you have brought this doom upon yourself!" With a wave of her hand, she set the Academy, the dispatcher of justice, into motion.

Great braziers had been placed in eight positions around House Teken'duis, attended by mistresses of Arach-Tinilith and the highest-ranking clerical students. Flames roared to life and shot into the air as the high priestesses opened gates to the lower planes. Drizzt watched closely, mesmerized and hoping to catch a glimpse of either Dinin or Vierna.

Denizens of the lower planes, huge, many-armed monsters, slime covered and spitting fire, stepped through the flames. Even the nearest high priestesses backed away from the grotesque horde. The creatures gladly accepted such servitude. When the signal from Matron Baenre came, they eagerly descended upon House Teken'duis.

Glyphs and wards exploded at every corner of the house's feeble gate, but these were mere inconveniences to the summoned creatures.

The wizards and students of Sorcere then went into action, slamming at the top of House Teken'duis with conjured lightning bolts, balls of acid, and fireballs.

Students and masters of Melee-Magthere, the school of fighters, rushed about with heavy crossbows, firing into windows where the doomed family might try to escape.

The horde of monsters bashed through the doors. Lightning flashed and thunder boomed.

Zak looked at Drizzt, and a frown replaced the master's smile. Caught up in the excitement—and it certainly was exciting—Drizzt bore an expression of awe.

The first screams of the doomed family rolled out from the house, screams so terrible and agonized that they stole any macabre pleasure that Drizzt might have been experiencing. He grabbed Zak's shoulder, spinning the weapons master to him, begging for an explanation.

One of the sons of House Teken'duis, fleeing a ten-armed giant monster, stepped out onto the balcony of a high window. A dozen crossbow quarrels struck him simultaneously, and before he even fell dead, three separate lightning bolts alternately lifted him from the balcony, then dropped him back onto it.

Scorched and mutilated, the drow corpse started to tumble from its high perch, but the grotesque monster reached out a huge, clawed hand from the window and pulled it back in to devour it.

"Drow justice," Zak said coldly. He didn't offer Drizzt any consolation; he wanted the brutality of this moment to stick in the young drow's mind for the rest of his life.

The siege went on for more than an hour, and when it was finished, when the denizens of the lower planes were dismissed through the braziers' gates and the students and instructors of the Academy started their march back to Tier Breche, House Teken'duis was no more than a glowing lump of lifeless, molten stone.

Drizzt watched it all, horrified, but too afraid of the consequences to run away. He did not notice the artistry of Menzoberranzan on the return trip to House Do'Urden.

# 10
# Stain of Blood

"Zaknafein is out of the house?" Malice asked.

"I sent him and Rizzen to the Academy to deliver a message to Vierna," Briza explained. "He shan't return for many hours, not before the light of Narbondel begins its descent."

"That is good," said Malice. "You both understand your duties in this farce?"

Briza and Maya nodded. "I have never heard of such a deception," Maya remarked. "Is it necessary?"

"It was planned for another of the house," Briza answered, looking to Matron Malice for confirmation. "Nearly four centuries ago."

"Yes," agreed Malice. "The same was to be done to Zaknafein, but the unexpected death of Matron Vartha, my mother, disrupted the plans."

"That was when you became the matron mother," Maya said.

"Yes," replied Malice, "though I had not passed my first century of life and was still training in Arach-Tinilith. It was not a pleasant time in the history of House Do'Urden."

"But we survived," said Briza. "With the death of Matron Vartha, Nalfein and I became nobles of the house."

"The test on Zaknafein was never attempted," Maya reasoned.

"Too many other duties preceded it," Malice answered.

"We will try it on Drizzt, though," said Maya.

"The punishment of House Teken'duis convinced me that this action had to be taken," said Malice.

"Yes," Briza agreed. "Did you notice Drizzt's expression throughout the execution?"

"I did," answered Maya. "He was revolted."

"Unfitting for a drow warrior," said Malice, "and so this duty is upon us. Drizzt will leave for the Academy in a short time; we must stain his hands with drow blood and steal his innocence."

"It seems a lot of trouble for a male child," Briza grumbled. "If Drizzt cannot adhere to our ways, then why do we not simply give him to Lolth?"

"I will bear no more children!" Malice growled in response. "Every member of this family is important if we are to gain prominence in the city!" Secretly Malice hoped for another gain in converting Drizzt to the evil ways of the drow. She hated Zaknafein as much as she desired him, and turning Drizzt into a drow warrior, a true heartless drow warrior, would distress the weapons master greatly.

"On with it, then," Malice proclaimed. She clapped her hands, and a large chest walked in, supported by eight animated spider legs. Behind it came a nervous goblin slave.

"Come, Byuchyuch," Malice said in a comforting tone. Anxious to please, the slave bounded up before Malice's throne and held perfectly still as the matron mother went through the incantation of a long and complicated spell.

Briza and Maya watched in admiration at their mother's skills; the little goblin's features bulged and twisted, and its skin darkened. A few minutes later, the slave had assumed the appearance of a male drow. Byuchyuch looked at its features happily, not understanding that the transformation was merely a prelude to death.

"You are a drow soldier now," Maya said to it, "and my champion. You must kill only a single, inferior fighter to take your place as a free commoner of House Do'Urden!"

After ten years as an indentured servant to the wicked dark elves, the goblin was more than eager.

Malice rose and started out of the anteroom. "Come," she ordered, and her two daughters, the goblin, and the animated chest fell in line behind her.

They came upon Drizzt in the practice room, polishing the razor edge of his scimitars. He leaped straight up to silent attention at the sight of the unexpected visitors.

"Greetings, my son," Malice said in a tone more motherly than Drizzt had ever heard. " We have a test for you this day, a simple task necessary for your acceptance into Melee-Magthere."

Maya moved before her brother. "I am the youngest, beside yourself," she declared. "Thus, I am granted the rights of challenge, which I now execute."

Drizzt stood confused. He had never heard of such a thing. Maya called the chest to her side and reverently opened the cover.

"You have your weapons and your *piwafwi*," she explained. "Now it is time for you to don the complete outfit of a noble of House Do'Urden." From the chest she pulled out a pair of high black boots and handed them to Drizzt.

Drizzt eagerly slipped out of his normal boots and put on the new ones. They were incredibly soft, and they magically shifted and adjusted to a perfect fit on his feet. Drizzt knew the magic within them: they would allow him to move in absolute silence. Before he had even finished admiring them, though, Maya gave him the next gift, even more magnificent.

Drizzt dropped his *piwafwi* to the floor as he took a set of silvery chain mail. In all the Realms, there was no armor as supple and finely crafted as drow chain mail. It weighed no more than a heavy shirt and would bend as easily as silken cloth, yet could deflect the tip of a spear as surely as dwarven-crafted plate mail.

"You fight with two weapons," Maya said, "and therefore need no shield. But put your scimitars in this; it is more fitting to a drow noble." She handed Drizzt a black leather belt, its clasp a huge emerald and its two scabbards richly decorated in jewels and gemstones.

"Prepare yourself," Malice said to Drizzt. "The gifts must be earned." As Drizzt started to don the outfit, Malice moved beside the altered goblin, which stood nervously in the growing realization that its fight would be no simple task.

"When you kill him, the items will be yours," Malice promised. The goblin's smile returned tenfold; it could not comprehend that it had no chance against Drizzt.

When Drizzt again fastened his *piwafwi* around his neck, Maya introduced the phony drow soldier. "This is Byuchyuch," she said, "my champion. You must defeat him to earn the gifts . . . and your proper place in the family."

Never doubting his abilities, and thinking the contest to be a simple sparring match, Drizzt readily agreed. "Let it begin, then," he said, drawing his scimitars from their lavish sheaths.

Malice gave Byuchyuch a comforting nod, and the goblin took up the sword and shield that Maya had provided and moved right in at Drizzt.

Drizzt began slowly, trying to take a measure of his opponent before attempting any daring offensive strikes. In only a moment, though, Drizzt realized how badly Byuchyuch handled the sword and shield. Not knowing the truth of the creature's identity, Drizzt could hardly believe that a drow would show such ineptitude with weapons. He wondered if Byuchyuch was baiting him, and with that thought, continued his cautious approach.

After a few more moments of Byuchyuch's wild and off balance swings, however, Drizzt felt compelled to take the initiative. He slapped one scimitar against Byuchyuch's shield. The goblin-drow responded with a lumbering thrust, and Drizzt slapped its sword from its hand with his free blade and executed a simple twist that brought the scimitar's tip to a halt against the hollow of Byuchyuch's chest.

"Too easy," Drizzt muttered under his breath.

But the true test had only begun.

On cue, Briza cast a mind-numbing spell on the goblin, freezing it in its helpless position. Still aware of its predicament, Byuchyuch tried to dive away, but Briza's spell held it still.

"Finish the strike," Malice said to Drizzt. Drizzt looked at his scimitar, then to Malice, unable to believe what he was hearing.

"Maya's champion must be killed," Briza snarled.

"I cannot—" Drizzt began.

"Kill!" Malice roared, and this time the word carried the weight of a magical command.

"Thrust!" Briza likewise commanded.

Drizzt felt their words compelling his hand to action. Thoroughly disgusted with the thought of murdering a helpless foe, he concentrated with all of his mental strength to resist. While he managed to deny the commands for a few seconds, Drizzt found that he could not pull the weapon away.

"Kill!" Malice screamed.

"Strike!" yelled Briza.

It went on for several more agonizing seconds. Sweat beaded on Drizzt's brow. Then the young drow's willpower broke. His scimitar slipped quickly between Byuchyuch's ribs and found the unfortunate creature's heart. Briza released Byuchyuch from her holding spell then, to let Drizzt see the agony on the phony drow's face and hear the gurgles as the dying Byuchyuch slipped to the floor.

Drizzt could not find his breath as he stared at his bloodstained weapon.

It was Maya's turn to act. She clipped Drizzt on the shoulder with her mace, knocking him to the floor.

"You killed my champion!" she growled. "Now you must fight me!"

Drizzt rolled back to his feet, away from the enraged female. He had no intention of fighting, but before he could even drop his weapons, Malice read his thoughts and warned, "If you do not fight, Maya will kill you!"

"This is not the way," Drizzt protested, but his words were lost in the ring of adamantine as he parried a heavy blow with one scimitar.

He was now into it, whether he liked it or not. Maya was a skilled fighter—all females spent many hours training with weapons—and she was stronger than Drizzt. But Drizzt was Zak's son, the prime student, and when he admitted to himself that he had no way out of this predicament, he came in at Maya's mace and shield with every cunning maneuver he had been taught.

Scimitars weaved and dipped in a dance that awed Briza and Maya. Malice hardly noticed, caught in the midst of yet another mighty spell.

Malice never doubted that Drizzt could defeat his sister, and she had incorporated her expectations into the plan.

Drizzt's moves were all defensive as he continued to hope for some semblance of sanity to come over his mother, and that this whole thing would be stopped. He wanted to back Maya up, cause her to stumble, and end the fight by putting her in a helpless position. Drizzt had to believe that Briza and Malice would not compel him to kill Maya as he had killed Byuchyuch.

Finally, Maya did slip. She threw her shield out to deflect an arcing scimitar but became overbalanced in the block, and her arm went wide. Drizzt's other blade knifed in, only to nick at Maya's breast and force her back.

Malice's spell caught the weapon in mid-thrust.

The bloodstained adamantine blade writhed to life and Drizzt found himself holding the tail of a serpent, a fanged viper that turned back against him!

The enchanted snake spat its venom in Drizzt's eyes, blinding him, then he felt the pain of Briza's whip. All six snake heads of the awful weapon bit into Drizzt's back, tearing through his new armor and jolting him in excruciating pain. He crumbled down into a curled position, helpless as Briza snapped the whip in, again and again.

"Never strike at a drow female!" she screamed as she beat Drizzt into unconsciousness.

An hour later, Drizzt opened his eyes. He was in his bed, Matron Malice standing over him. The high priestess had tended to his wounds, but the sting remained, a vivid reminder of the lesson. But it was not nearly as vivid as the blood that still stained Drizzt's scimitar.

"The armor will be replaced," Malice said to him. "You are a drow warrior now. You have earned it." She turned and walked out of the room, leaving Drizzt to his pain and his fallen innocence.

⚔ ⚔ ⚔ ⚔ ⚔

"Do not send him," Zak argued as emphatically as he dared. He stared up at Matron Malice, the smug queen on her high throne of stone and black velvet. As always, Briza and Maya stood obediently by her sides.

"He is a drow fighter," Malice replied, her tone still controlled. "He must go to the Academy. It is our way."

Zak looked around helplessly. He hated this place, the chapel anteroom, with its sculptures of the Spider Queen leering down at him from every angle, and with Malice sitting—towering—above him from her seat of power.

Zak shook the images away and regained his courage, reminding himself that this time he had something worth arguing about.

"Do not send him!" he growled. "They will ruin him!"

Matron Malice's hands clenched down on the rock arms of her great chair.

"Already Drizzt is more skilled than half of those in the Academy," Zak continued quickly, before the matron's anger burst forth. "Allow me two more years, and I will make him the finest swordsman in all of Menzoberranzan!"

Malice eased back on her seat. From what she had seen of her son's progress, she could not deny the possibilities of Zak's claim. "He goes," she said calmly. "There is more to the making of a drow warrior than skill with weapons. Drizzt has other lessons he must learn."

"Lessons of treachery?" Zak spat, too angry to care about the consequences. Drizzt had told him what Malice and her evil daughters had done that day, and Zak was wise enough to understand their actions. Their "lesson" had nearly broken the boy, and had, perhaps, forever stolen from Drizzt the ideals he held so dear. Drizzt would find his morals and principles harder to cling to now that the pedestal of purity had been knocked out from under him.

"Watch your tongue, Zaknafein," Matron Malice warned.

"I fight with passion!" the weapons master snapped. "That is why I win. Your son, too, fights with passion—do not let the conforming ways of the Academy take that from him!"

"Leave us," Malice instructed her daughters. Maya bowed and rushed out through the door. Briza followed more slowly, pausing to cast a suspicious eye upon Zak.

Zak didn't return the glare, but he entertained a fantasy concerning his sword and Briza's smug smile.

"Zaknafein," Malice began, again coming forward in her chair. "I have tolerated your blasphemous beliefs through these many years because of your skill with weapons. You have taught my soldiers well, and your love of killing drow, particularly clerics of the Spider Queen, has aided the ascent of House Do'Urden. I am not, and have not been, ungrateful.

"But I warn you now, one final time, that Drizzt is my son, not his sire's! He will go to the Academy and learn what he must to take his place as a prince of House Do'Urden. If you interfere with what must be, Zaknafein, I will no longer turn my eyes from your actions! Your heart will be given to Lolth."

Zak stamped his heels on the floor and snapped a short bow of his head, then spun about and departed, trying to find some option in this dark and hopeless picture.

As he made his way through the main corridor, he again heard in his mind the screams of the dying children of House DeVir, children who never got the chance to witness the evils of the drow Academy. Perhaps they were better off dead.

# II
# Grim Preference

Zak slid one of his swords from its scabbard and admired the weapon's wondrous detail. This sword, as with most of the drow weapons, had been forged by the gray dwarves, then traded to Menzoberranzan. The duergar workmanship was exquisite, but it was the work done on the weapon after the dark elves had acquired it that made it so very special. None of the races of the surface or Underdark could outdo the dark elves in the art of enchanting weapons. Imbued with the strange emanations of the Underdark, the magical power unique to the lightless world, and blessed by the unholy clerics of Lolth, no blade ever sat in a wielder's hand more ready to kill.

Other races, mostly dwarves and surface elves, also took pride in their crafted weapons. Fine swords and mighty hammers hung over mantles as showpieces, always with a bard nearby to spout the accompanying legend that most often began, "In the days of yore . . ."

Drow weapons were different, never showpieces. They were locked in the necessities of the present, never in reminiscences, and their purpose remained unchanged for as long as they held an edge fine enough for battle—fine enough to kill.

Zak brought the blade up before his eyes. In his hands, the sword had become more than an instrument of battle. It was an extension of his rage, his answer to an existence he could not accept.

It was his answer, too, perhaps, to another problem that seemed to have no resolution.

He walked into the training hall, where Drizzt was hard at work spinning attack routines against a practice dummy. Zak paused to watch the young drow at practice, wondering if Drizzt would ever again consider the dance of weapons a form of play. How the scimitars flowed in Drizzt's hands! Interweaving with uncanny precision, each blade seemed to anticipate the other's moves and whirred about in perfect complement.

This young drow might soon be an unrivaled fighter, a master beyond Zaknafein himself.

"Can you survive?" Zak whispered. "Have you the heart of a drow warrior?" Zak hoped that the answer would be an emphatic "no," but either way, Drizzt was surely doomed.

Zak looked down at his sword again and knew what he must do. He slid its sister blade from its sheath and started a determined walk toward Drizzt.

Drizzt saw him coming and turned at the ready. "A final fight before I leave for the Academy?" He laughed.

Zak paused to take note of Drizzt's smile. A facade? Or had the young drow really forgiven himself for his actions against Maya's champion. It did not matter, Zak reminded himself. Even if Drizzt had recovered from his mother's torments, the Academy would destroy him. The weapons master said nothing; he just came on in a flurry of cuts and stabs that put Drizzt immediately on the defensive. Drizzt took it in stride, not yet realizing that this final encounter with his mentor was much more than their customary sparring.

"I will remember everything you taught me," Drizzt promised, dodging a cut and launching a fierce counter of his own. "I will carve my name in the halls of Melee-Magthere and make you proud."

The scowl on Zak's face surprised Drizzt, and the young drow grew even more confused when the weapons master's next attack sent a sword knifing straight at his heart. Drizzt leaped aside, slapping at the blade in sheer desperation, and narrowly avoided impalement.

"Are you so very sure of yourself?" Zak growled, stubbornly pursuing Drizzt.

Drizzt set himself as their blades met in ringing fury. "I am a fighter," he declared. "A drow warrior!"

"You are a dancer!" Zak shot back in a derisive tone. He slammed his sword onto Drizzt's blocking scimitar so savagely that the young drow's arm tingled.

"An imposter!" Zak cried. "A pretender to a title you cannot begin to understand!"

Drizzt went on the offensive. Fires burned in his lavender eyes and new strength guided his scimitars' sure cuts.

But Zak was relentless. He fended the attacks and continued his lesson. "Do you know the emotions of murder?" he spat. "Have you reconciled yourself to the act you committed?"

Drizzt's only answers were a frustrated growl and a renewed attack.

"Ah, the pleasure of plunging your sword into the bosom of a high priestess," Zak taunted. "To see the light of warmth leave her body while her lips utter silent curses in your face! Or have you ever heard the screams of dying children?"

Drizzt let up his attack, but Zak would not allow a break. The weapons master came back on the offensive, each thrust aimed for a vital area.

"How loud, those screams," Zak continued. "They echo over the centuries in your mind; they chase you down the paths of your entire life."

Zak halted the action so that Drizzt might weigh his every word. "You have never heard them, have you, dancer?" The weapons master stretched his arms out wide, an invitation. "Come, then, and claim your second kill," he said, tapping his stomach. "In the belly, where the pain is greatest, so that my screams may echo in your mind. Prove to me that you are the drow warrior you claim to be."

The tips of Drizzt's scimitars slowly made their way to the stone floor. He wore no smile now.

"You hesitate," Zak laughed at him. "This is your chance to make your name. A single thrust, and you will send a reputation into the Academy before you. Other students, even masters, will whisper your name as you pass. 'Drizzt Do'Urden,' they will say. 'The boy who slew the most honored weapons master in all of Menzoberranzan!' Is this not what you desire?"

"Damn you," Drizzt spat back, but still he made no move to attack.

"Drow warrior?" Zak chided him. "Do not be so quick to claim a title you cannot begin to understand!"

Drizzt came on then, in a fury he had never before known. His purpose was not to kill, but to defeat his teacher, to steal the taunts from Zak's mouth with a fighting display too impressive to be derided.

Drizzt was brilliant. He followed every move with three others and worked Zak low and high, inside and out wide. Zak found his heels under him more often than the balls of his feet, too involved was he in staying away from his student's relentless thrusts to even think of taking the offensive. He allowed Drizzt to continue the initiative for many minutes, dreading its conclusion, the outcome he had already decided to be the most preferable.

Zak then found that he could stand the delay no longer. He sent one sword out in a lazy thrust, and Drizzt promptly slapped the weapon out of his hand.

Even as the young drow came on in anticipation of victory, Zak slipped his empty hand into a pouch and grabbed a magical little ceramic ball—one of those that so often had aided him in battle.

"Not this time, Zaknafein!" Drizzt proclaimed, keeping his attacks under control, remembering well the many occasions that Zak reversed feigned disadvantage into clear advantage.

Zak fingered the ball, unable to come to terms with what he must do.

Drizzt walked him through an attack sequence, then another, measuring the advantage he had gained in stealing a weapon. Confident of his position, Drizzt came in low and hard with a single thrust.

Though Zak was distracted at the time, he still managed to block the attack with his remaining sword. Drizzt's other scimitar slashed down on top of the sword, pinning its tip to the floor. In the same lightning movement, Drizzt slipped his first blade free of Zak's parry and brought it up and around, stopping the thrust barely an inch from Zak's throat.

"I have you!" the young drow cried.

Zak's answer came in an explosion of light beyond anything Drizzt had ever imagined.

Zak had prudently closed his eyes, but Drizzt, surprised, could not accept the sudden change. His head burned in agony, and he reeled backward, trying to get away from the light, away from the weapons master.

Keeping his eyes tightly shut, Zak had already divorced himself from the need of vision. He let his keen ears guide him now, and Drizzt, shuffling and stumbling, was an easy target to discern. In a single motion, the whip came off Zak's belt and he lashed out, catching Drizzt around the ankles and dropping him to the floor.

Methodically, the weapons master came on, dreading every step but knowing his chosen course of action to be correct.

Drizzt realized that he was being stalked, but he could not understand the motive. The light had stunned him, but he was more surprised by Zak's continuation of the battle. Drizzt set himself, unable to escape the trap, and tried to think his way around his loss of sight. He had to feel the flow of battle, to hear the sounds of his attacker and anticipate each coming strike.

He brought his scimitars up just in time to block a sword chop that would have split his skull.

Zak hadn't expected the parry. He recoiled and came in from a different angle. Again he was foiled.

Now more curious than wanting to kill Drizzt, the weapons master went through a series of attacks, sending his sword into motions that would have sliced through the defenses of many who could see him.

Blinded, Drizzt fought him off, putting a scimitar in line with each new thrust.

"Treachery!" Drizzt yelled, painful residual explosions from the bright light still bursting inside his head. He blocked another attack and tried to regain his footing, realizing that he had little chance of continuing to fend off the weapons master from a prone position.

The pain of the stinging light was too great, though, and Drizzt, barely holding the edge of consciousness, stumbled back to the stone, losing one scimitar in the process. He spun over wildly, knowing that Zak was closing in.

The other scimitar was knocked from his hand.

"Treachery," Drizzt growled again. "Do you so hate to lose?"

"Do you not understand?" Zak yelled back at him. "To lose is to die! You may win a thousand fights, but you can only lose one!" He put his sword in line with Drizzt's throat. It would be a single clean blow. He knew that he should do it, mercifully, before the masters of the Academy got hold of his charge.

Zak sent his sword spinning across the room, and he reached out with his empty hands, grabbed Drizzt by the front of his shirt, and hoisted him to his feet.

They stood face-to-face, neither seeing the other very well in the blinding glare, and neither able to break the tense silence. After a long and breathless moment, the dweomer of the enchanted pebble faded and the room became more comfortable. Truly, the two dark elves looked upon each other in a different light.

"A trick of Lolth's clerics," Zak explained. "Always they keep such a spell of light at the ready" A strained smile crossed his face as he tried to ease Drizzt's anger. "Though I daresay that I have turned such light against clerics, even high priestesses, more than a few times."

"Treachery," Drizzt spat a third time.

"It is our way," Zak replied. "You will learn."

"It is your way," snarled Drizzt. "You grin when you speak of murdering clerics of the Spider Queen. Do you so enjoy killing? Killing drow?"

Zak could not find an answer to the accusing question. Drizzt's words hurt him profoundly because they rang of truth, and because Zak had come to view his penchant for killing clerics of Lolth as a cowardly response to his own unanswerable frustrations.

"You would have killed me," Drizzt said bluntly.

"But I did not," Zak retorted. "And now you live to go to the Academy—to take a dagger in the back because you are blind to the realities of our world, because you refuse to acknowledge what your people are.

"Or you will become one of them," Zak growled. "Either way, the Drizzt Do'Urden I have known will surely die."

Drizzt's face twisted, and he couldn't even find the words to dispute the possibilities Zak was spitting at him. He felt the blood drain from his face, though his heart raged. He walked away, letting his glare linger on Zak for many steps.

"Go, then, Drizzt Do'Urden!" Zak cried after him. "Go to the Academy and bask in the glory of your prowess. Remember, though, the consequences of such skills. Always there are consequences!"

Zak retreated to the security of his private chamber. The door to the room closed behind the weapons master with such a sound of finality that it spun Zak back to face its empty stone.

"Go, then, Drizzt Do'Urden," he whispered in quiet lament. "Go to the Academy and learn who you really are."

⚔ ⚔ ⚔ ⚔ ⚔

Dinin came for his brother early the next morning. Drizzt slowly left the training room, looking back over his shoulder every few steps to see if Zak would come out and attack him again or bid him farewell.

He knew in his heart that Zak would not.

Drizzt had thought them friends, had believed that the bond he and Zaknafein had sown went far beyond the simple lessons and swordplay. The young drow had no answers to the many questions spinning in his mind, and the person who had been his teacher for the last five years had nothing left to offer him.

"The heat grows in Narbondel," Dinin remarked when they stepped out onto the balcony. "We must not be late for your first day in the Academy."

Drizzt looked out into the myriad colors and shapes that composed Menzoberranzan. "What is this place?" he whispered, realizing how little he knew of his homeland beyond the walls of his own house. Zak's words—Zak's rage—pressed in on Drizzt as he stood there, reminding him of his ignorance and hinting at a dark path ahead.

"This is the world," Dinin replied, though Drizzt's question had been rhetorical. "Do not worry, Secondboy," he laughed, moving up onto the railing. "You will learn of Menzoberranzan in the Academy. You will learn who you are and who your people are."

The declaration unsettled Drizzt. Perhaps—remembering his last bitter encounter with the drow he had most trusted—that knowledge was exactly what he was afraid of.

He shrugged in resignation and followed Dinin over the balcony in a magical descent to the compound floor: the first steps down that dark path.

Another set of eyes watched intently as Dinin and Drizzt started out from House Do'Urden.

Alton DeVir sat quietly against the side of a gigantic mushroom, as he had every day for the last tenday, staring at the Do'Urden complex.

Daermon N'a'shezbaernon, Ninth House of Menzoberranzan. The house that had murdered his matron, his sisters and brothers, and all there ever was of House DeVir . . . except for Alton.

Alton thought back to the days of House DeVir, when Matron Ginafae had gathered the family members together so that they might discuss their aspirations. Alton, just a student when House DeVir fell, now had a greater insight to those times. Twenty years had brought a wealth of experience.

Ginafae had been the youngest matron among the ruling families, and her potential had seemed unlimited. Then she had aided a gnomish patrol, had used her Lolth-given powers to hinder the drow elves that ambushed the little people in the caverns outside Menzoberranzan—all because Ginafae desired the death of a single member of that attacking drow party, a wizard son of the city's third house, the house labeled as House DeVir's next victim.

The Spider Queen took exception to Ginafae's choice of weapons; deep gnomes were the dark elves' worst enemy in the whole of the Underdark. With Ginafae fallen out of Lolth's favor, House DeVir had been doomed.

Alton had spent twenty years trying to learn of his enemies, trying to discover which drow family had taken advantage of his mother's mistake and had slaughtered his kin. Twenty long years, and his adopted matron, SiNafay Hun'ett, had ended his quest as abruptly as it had begun.

Now, as Alton sat watching the guilty house, he knew only one thing for certain: twenty years had done nothing to diminish his rage.

# Part Three

# The Academy

The Academy.

It is the propagation of the lies that bind drow society together, the ultimate perpetration of falsehoods repeated so many times that they ring true against any contrary evidence. The lessons young drow are taught of truth and justice are so blatantly refuted by everyday life in wicked Menzoberranzan that it is hard to understand how any could believe them. Still they do.

Even now, decades removed, the thought of the place frightens me, not for any physical pain or the ever-present sense of possible death—I have trod down many roads equally dangerous in that way. The Academy of Menzoberranzan frightens me when I think of the survivors, the graduates, existing—reveling—within the evil fabrications that shape their world.

They live with the belief that anything is acceptable if you can get away with it, that self-gratification is the most important aspect of existence, and that power comes only to she or he who is strong enough and cunning enough to snatch it from the failing hands of those who no longer deserve it. Compassion has no place in Menzoberranzan, and yet it is compassion, not fear, that brings harmony to most races. It is harmony, working toward shared goals, that precedes greatness.

Lies engulf the drow in fear and mistrust, refute friendship at the tip of a Lolth-blessed sword The hatred and ambition fostered by these amoral tenets are the doom of my people, a weakness that they perceive as strength. The result is a paralyzing, paranoid existence that the drow call the edge of readiness.

I do not know how I survived the Academy, how I discovered the falsehoods early enough to use them in contrast, and thus strengthen, those ideals I most cherish.

It was Zaknafein, I must believe, my teacher. Through the experiences of Zak's long years, which embittered him and cost him so much, I came to hear the screams: the screams of protest against murderous treachery; the screams of rage from the leaders of drow society, the high priestesses of the Spider Queen, echoing down the paths of my mind, ever to hold a place within my mind. The screams of dying children.

–Drizzt Do'Urden

# 12 This Enemy, "They"

Wearing the outfit of a noble son, and with a dagger concealed in one boot—a suggestion from Dinin—Drizzt ascended the wide stone stairway that led to Tier Breche, the Academy of the drow. Drizzt reached the top and moved between the giant pillars, under the impassive gazes of two guards, last-year students of Melee-Magthere.

Two dozen other young drow milled about the Academy compound, but Drizzt hardly noticed them. Three structures dominated his vision and his thoughts. To his left stood the pointed stalagmite tower of Sorcere, the school of wizardry. Drizzt would spend the first sixth months of his tenth and last year of study in there.

Before him, at the back of the level, loomed the most impressive structure, Arach-Tinilith, the school of Lolth, carved from the stone into the likeness of a giant spider. By drow reckoning, this was the Academy's most important building and thus was normally reserved for females. Male students were housed within Arach-Tinilith only during their last six months of study.

While Sorcere and Arach-Tinilith were the more graceful structures, the most important building for Drizzt at that tentative moment lined the wall to his right. The pyramidal structure of Melee-Magthere, the school of fighters. This building would be Drizzt's home for the next nine years. His companions, he now realized, were those other dark elves in the compound—fighters, like himself, about to begin their formal training. The class, at twenty-five, was unusually large for the school of fighters.

Even more unusual, several of the novice students were nobles. Drizzt wondered how his skills would measure up against theirs, how his sessions with Zaknafein compared to the battles these others had no doubt fought with the weapons masters of their respective families.

Those thoughts inevitably led Drizzt back to his last encounter with his mentor. He quickly dismissed the memories of that unpleasant duel, and, more pointedly, the disturbing questions Zak's observations had forced him to consider. There was no place for such doubts on this occasion. Melee-Magthere loomed before him, the greatest test and the greatest lesson of his young life.

"My greetings," came a voice behind him. Drizzt turned to face a fellow novice, who wore a sword and dirk uncomfortably on his belt and who appeared even more nervous than Drizzt—a comforting sight.

"Kelnozz of House Kenafin, fifteenth house," the novice said.

"Drizzt Do'Urden of Daermon N'a'shezbaernon, House Do'Urden, Ninth House of Menzoberranzan," Drizzt replied automatically, exactly as Matron Malice had instructed him.

"A noble," remarked Kelnozz, understanding the significance of Drizzt bearing the same surname as his house. Kelnozz dropped into a low bow. "I am honored by your presence."

Drizzt was starting to like this place already. With the treatment he normally received at home, he hardly thought of himself as a noble. Any self-important notions that might have occurred to him at Kelnozz's gracious greeting were dispelled a moment later, though, when the masters came out.

Drizzt saw his brother, Dinin, among them but pretended—as Dinin had warned him to—not to notice, nor to expect any special treatment. Drizzt rushed inside Melee-Magthere along with the rest of the students when the whips began to snap and the masters started shouting of the dire consequences if they tarried. They were herded down a few side corridors and into an oval room.

"Sit or stand as you will!" one of the masters growled. Noticing two of the students whispering off to the side, the master took his whip out and—crack!—took one of the offenders off his feet.

Drizzt couldn't believe how quickly the room then came to order.

"I am Hatch'net," the master began in a resounding voice, "the master of Lore. This room will be your hall of instruction for fifty cycles of Narbondel." He looked around at the adorned belts on every figure. "You will bring no weapons to this place!"

Hatch'net paced the perimeter of the room, making certain that every eye followed his movements attentively. "You are drow," he snapped suddenly. "Do you understand what that means? Do you know where you come from, and the history of our people? Menzoberranzan was not always our home, nor was any other cavern of the Underdark. Once we walked the surface of the world." He spun suddenly and came up right in Drizzt's face.

"Do you know of the surface?" Master Hatch'net snarled.

Drizzt recoiled and shook his head.

"An awful place," Hatch'net continued, turning back to the whole of the group. "Each day, as the glow begins its rise in Narbondel, a great ball of fire rises into the open sky above, bringing hours of a light greater than the punishing spells of the priestesses of Lolth!" He held his arms outstretched, with his eyes turned upward, and an unbelievable grimace spread across his face.

Students' gasps rose up all about him.

"Even in the night, when the ball of fire has gone below the far rim of the world," Hatch'net continued, weaving his words as if he were telling a horror tale, "one cannot escape the uncounted terrors of the surface. Reminders of what the next day will bring, dots of light—and sometimes a lesser ball of silvery fire—mar the sky's blessed darkness.

"Once our people walked the surface of the world," he repeated, his tone now one of lament, "in ages long past, even longer than the lines of the great houses. In that distant age, we walked beside the pale-skinned elves, the faeries!"

"It cannot be true!" one student cried from the side.

Hatch'net looked at him earnestly, considering whether more would be gained by beating the student for his unasked-for interruption or by allowing the group to participate. "It is!" he replied, choosing the latter course. "We thought the faeries our friends; we called them kin! We could not know, in our innocence, that they were the embodiments of deceit and evil. We could not know that they would turn on us suddenly and drive us from them, slaughtering our children and the eldest of our race!

"Without mercy the evil faeries pursued us across the surface world. Always we asked for peace, and always we were answered by swords and killing arrows!"

He paused, his face twisting into a widening, malicious smile. "Then we found the goddess!"

"Praise Lolth!" came one anonymous cry. Again Hatch'net let the slip of tongue go by unpunished, knowing that every accenting comment only drew his audience deeper into his web of rhetoric.

"Indeed," the master replied. "All praise to the Spider Queen. It was she who took our orphaned race to her side and helped us fight off our enemies. It was she who guided the fore-matrons of our race to the paradise of the Underdark. It is she," he roared, a clenched fist rising into the air, "who now gives us the strength and the magic to pay back our enemies.

"We are the drow!" Hatch'net cried. "You are the drow, never again to be downtrodden, rulers of all you desire, conquerors of lands you choose to inhabit!"

"The surface?" came a question.

"The surface?" echoed Hatch'net with a laugh. "Who would want to return to that vile place? Let the faeries have it! Let them burn under the fires of the open sky! We claim the Underdark, where we can feel the core of the world thrumming under our feet, and where the stones of the walls show the heat of the world's power!"

Drizzt sat silent, absorbing every word of the talented orator's often-rehearsed speech. Drizzt was caught, as were all the new students, in Hatch'net's hypnotic variations of inflection and rallying cries. Hatch'net had been the master of Lore at the Academy for more than two centuries, owning more prestige in Menzoberranzan than nearly any other male drow, and many of the females. The matrons of the ruling families understood well the value of his practiced tongue.

So it went every day, an endless stream of hate rhetoric directed against an enemy that none of the students had ever seen. The surface elves were not the only target of Hatch'net's sniping. Dwarves, gnomes, humans, halflings, and all of the surface races—and even subterranean races such as the duergar dwarves, which the drow often traded with and fought beside—each found an unpleasant spot in the master's ranting.

Drizzt came to understand why no weapons were permitted in the oval chamber. When he left his lesson each day, he found his hands clenched by his sides in rage, unconsciously grasping for a scimitar hilt. It was obvious from the commonplace fights among the students that others felt the same way. Always, though, the overriding factor that kept some measure of control was the master's lie of the horrors of the outside world and the comforting bond of the students' common heritage—a heritage, the students would soon come to believe, that gave them enough enemies to battle beyond each other.

⚔ ⚔ ⚔ ⚔ ⚔

The long, draining hours in the oval chamber left little time for the students to mingle. They shared common barracks, but their extensive duties outside of Hatch'net's lessons—serving the older students and masters, preparing meals, and cleaning the building—gave them barely enough time for rest. By the end of the first tenday, they walked on the edge of exhaustion, a condition, Drizzt realized, that only increased the stirring effect of Master Hatch'net's lessons.

Drizzt accepted the existence stoically, considering it far better than the six years he had served his mother and sisters as page prince. Still, there was one great disappointment to Drizzt in his first tendays at Melee-Magthere. He found himself longing for his practice sessions.

He sat on the edge of his bedroll late one night, holding a scimitar up before his shining eyes, remembering those many hours engaged in battle-play with Zaknafein.

"We go to the lesson in two hours," Kelnozz, in the next bunk, reminded him. "Get some rest."

"I feel the edge leaving my hands," Drizzt replied quietly. "The blade feels heavier, unbalanced."

"The grand melee is barely ten cycles of Narbondel away," Kelnozz said. "You will get all the practice you desire there! Fear not, whatever edge has been dulled by the days with the master of Lore will soon be regained. For the next nine years, that fine blade of yours will rarely leave your hands!"

Drizzt slid the scimitar back into its scabbard and reclined on his bunk. As with so many aspects of his life so far—and, he was beginning to fear, with so many aspects of his future in Menzoberranzan—he had no choice but to accept the circumstances of his existence.

⚔ ⚔ ⚔ ⚔ ⚔

"This segment of your training is at an end," Master Hatch'net announced on the morning of the fiftieth day. Another master, Dinin, entered the room, leading a magically suspended iron box filled with meagerly padded wooden poles of every length and design comparable to drow weapons.

"Choose the sparring pole that most resembles your own weapon of choice," Hatch'net explained as Dinin made his way around the room. He came to his brother, and Drizzt's eyes settled at once on his choice: two slightly curving poles about three-and-a-half feet long. Drizzt lifted them out and put them through a simple cut. Their weight and balance closely resembled the scimitars that had become so familiar to his hands.

"For the pride of Daermon N'a'shezbaernon," Dinin whispered, then moved along.

Drizzt twirled the mock weapons again. It was time to measure the value of his sessions with Zak.

"Your class must have an order," Hatch'net was saying as Drizzt turned his attention beyond the scope of his new weapons. "Thus the grand melee. Remember, there can be only one victor!"

Hatch'net and Dinin herded the students out of the oval chamber and out of Melee-Magthere altogether, down the tunnel between the two guardian spider statues at the back of Tier Breche. For all of the students, this was the first time they had ever been out of Menzoberranzan.

"What are the rules?" Drizzt asked Kelnozz, in line at his side.

"If a master calls you out, then you are out," Kelnozz replied.

"The rules of engagement?" asked Drizzt.

Kelnozz cast him an incredulous glance. "Win," he said simply, as though there could be no other answer.

A short time later they came into a fairly large cavern, the arena for the grand melee. Pointed stalactites leered down at them from the ceiling and stalagmite mounds broke the floor into a twisting maze filled with ambush holes and blind corners.

"Choose your strategies and find your starting point," Master Hatch'net said to them. "The grand melee begins in a count of one hundred!"

The twenty-five students set off into action, some pausing to consider the landscape laid out before them, others sprinting off into the gloom of the maze.

Drizzt decided to find a narrow corridor, to ensure that he would fight off one-against-one, and he just started off in his search when he was grabbed from behind.

"A team?" Kelnozz offered.

Drizzt did not respond, unsure of the other's fighting worth and the accepted practices of this traditional encounter.

"Others are forming into teams," Kelnozz pressed. "Some in threes. Together we might have a chance."

"The master said there could be only one victor," Drizzt reasoned.

"Who better than you, if not me," Kelnozz replied with a sly wink. "Let us defeat the others, then we can decide the issue between ourselves."

The reasoning seemed prudent, and with Hatch'net's count already approaching seventy-five, Drizzt had little time to ponder the possibilities. He clapped Kelnozz on the shoulder and led his new ally into the maze.

Catwalks had been constructed all around the room's perimeter, even crossing through the center of the chamber, to give the judging masters a good view of all the action below. A dozen of them were up there now, all eagerly awaiting the first battles so that they might measure the talent of this young class.

"One hundred!" cried Hatch'net from his high perch.

Kelnozz began to move, but Drizzt stopped him, keeping him back in the narrow corridor between two long stalagmite mounds.

"Let them come to us," Drizzt signaled in the silent hand and facial expression code. He crouched in battle readiness. "Let them fight each other to weariness. Patience is our ally!"

Kelnozz relaxed, thinking he had made a good choice in Drizzt.

Their patience was not tested severely, though, for a moment later, a tall and aggressive student burst into their defensive position, wielding a long spear-shaped pole. He came right in on Drizzt, slapping with the butt of his weapon, then spinning it over full in a brutal thrust designed for a quick kill, a strong move perfectly executed.

To Drizzt, though, it seemed the most basic of attack routines—too basic, almost, for Drizzt hardly believed that a trained student would attack another skilled fighter in such a straightforward manner. Drizzt convinced himself in time that this was indeed the chosen method of attack, and no feint, and he launched the proper parry. His scimitar poles spun counter-clockwise in front of him, striking the thrusting spear in succession and driving the weapon's tip harmlessly above the striking line of its wielder's shoulder.

The aggressive attacker, stunned by the advanced parry, found himself open and off balance. Barely a split second later, before the attacker could even begin to recover, Drizzt's counter poked one, then the other scimitar pole into his chest.

A soft blue light appeared on the stunned student's face, and he and Drizzt followed its line up to see a wand-wielding master looking down at them from the catwalk.

"You are defeated," the master said to the tall student. "Fall where you stand!"

The student shot an angry glare at Drizzt and obediently dropped to the stone.

"Come," Drizzt said to Kelnozz, casting a glance up at the master's revealing light. "Any others in the area will know of our position now. We must seek a new defensible area."

Kelnozz paused a moment to watch the graceful hunting strides of his comrade. He had indeed made a good choice in selecting Drizzt, but he knew already, after only a single quick encounter, that if he and this skilled swordsman were the last two standing—a distinct possibility—he would have no chance at all of claiming victory.

Together they rushed around a blind corner, right into two opponents. Kelnozz chased after one, who fled in fright, and Drizzt faced off against the other, who wielded sword and dirk poles.

A wide smile of growing confidence crossed Drizzt's face as his opponent took the offensive, launching routines similarly basic to those of the spear wielder that Drizzt had easily dispatched.

A few deft twists and turns of his scimitars, a few slaps on the inside edges of his opponent's weapons, had the sword and dirk flying wide. Drizzt's attack came right up the middle, where he executed another double-poke into his opponent's chest.

The expected blue light appeared. "You are defeated," came the master's call. "Fall where you stand."

Outraged, the stubborn student chopped viciously at Drizzt. Drizzt blocked with one weapon and snapped the other against his attacker's wrist, sending the sword pole flying to the floor.

The attacker clenched his bruised wrist, but that was the least of his troubles. A blinding flash of lightning exploded from the observing master's wand, catching him full in the chest and hurtling him ten feet backward to crash into a stalagmite mound. He crumpled to the floor, groaning in agony, and a line of glowing heat rose from his scorched body, which lay against the cool gray stone.

"You are defeated!" the master said again.

Drizzt started to the fallen drow's aid, but the master issued an emphatic, "No!"

Then Kelnozz was back at Drizzt's side. "He got away," Kelnozz began, but he broke into a laugh when he saw the downed student. "If a master calls you out, then you are out!" Kelnozz repeated into Drizzt's blank stare.

"Come," Kelnozz continued. "The battle is in full now. Let us find some fun!"

Drizzt thought his companion quite cocky for one who had yet to lift his weapons. He only shrugged and followed.

Their next encounter was not so easy. They came into a double passage turning in and out of several rock formations and found themselves faced off against a group of three—nobles from leading houses, both Drizzt and Kelnozz realized.

Drizzt rushed the two on his left, both of whom wielded single swords, while Kelnozz worked to fend off the third. Drizzt had little experience against multiple opponents, but Zak had taught him the techniques of such a battle quite well. His movements were solely defensive at first, then he settled into a comfortable rhythm and allowed his opponents to tire themselves out, and to make the critical mistakes.

These were cunning foes, though, and familiar with each other's movements. Their attacks complemented each other, slicing in at Drizzt from widely opposing angles.

"Two-hands," Zak had once called Drizzt, and now he lived up to the title. His scimitars worked independently, yet in perfect harmony, foiling every attack.

From a nearby perch on the catwalk, Masters Hatch'net and Dinin looked on, Hatch'net more than a little impressed, and Dinin swelling with pride.

Drizzt saw the frustration mounting on his opponents' faces, and he knew that his opportunity to strike would soon be at hand. Then they crossed up, coming in together with identical thrusts, their sword poles barely inches apart.

Drizzt spun to the side and launched a blinding uppercut slice with his left scimitar, deflecting both attacks. Then he reversed his body's momentum, dropped to one knee, back in line with his opponents, and thrust in low with two snaps of his free right arm. His jabbing scimitar pole caught the first, and the second, squarely in the groin.

They dropped their weapons in unison, clutched their bruised parts, and slumped to their knees. Drizzt leaped up before them, trying to find the words for an apology.

Hatch'net nodded his approval at Dinin as the two masters set their lights on the two losers.

"Help me! " Kelnozz cried from beyond the dividing wall of stalagmites.

Drizzt dived into a roll through a break in the wall, came up quickly, and downed a fourth opponent, who was concealed for a backstab surprise, with a backhand chop to the chest. Drizzt stopped to consider his latest victim. He hadn't even consciously known that the drow was there, but his aim had been perfect!

Hatch'net blew a low whistle as he shifted his light to the most recent loser's face. "He is good!" the master breathed.

Drizzt saw Kelnozz a short distance away, practically forced down to his back by his opponent's skilled maneuvers. Drizzt leaped between the two and deflected an attack that surely would have finished Kelnozz.

This newest opponent, wielding two sword poles, proved Drizzt's toughest challenge yet. He came at Drizzt with complicated feints and twists, forcing him on his heels more than once.

"Berg'inyon of House Baenre," Hatch'net whispered to Dinin. Dinin understood the significance and hoped that his young brother was up to the test.

Berg'inyon was not a disappointment to his distinguished kin. His moves came skilled and measured, and he and Drizzt danced about for many minutes with neither finding any advantage. The daring Berg'inyon then came in with the attack routine perhaps most familiar to Drizzt: the double-thrust low.

Drizzt executed the cross-down to perfection, the appropriate parry as Zaknafein had so pointedly proved to him. Never satisfied, though, Drizzt then reacted on an impulse, agilely snapping a foot up between the hilts of his crossed blades and into his opponent's face. The stunned son of House Baenre fell back against the wall.

"I knew the parry was wrong!" Drizzt cried, already savoring the next time he would get the opportunity to foil the double-thrust low in a session against Zak.

"He is good," Hatch'net gasped again to his glowing companion.

Dazed, Berg'inyon could not fight his way out of the disadvantage. He put a globe of darkness around himself, but Drizzt waded right in, more than willing to fight blindly.

Drizzt put the son of House Baenre through a quick series of attacks, ending with one of Drizzt's scimitar poles against Berg'inyon's exposed neck.

"I am defeated," the young Baenre conceded, feeling the pole. Hearing the call, Master Hatch'net dispelled the darkness. Berg'inyon set both his weapons on the stone and slumped down, and the blue light appeared on his face.

Drizzt couldn't hold back the widening grin. Were there any here that he could not defeat? he wondered.

Drizzt then felt an explosion on the back of his head that dropped him to his knees. He managed to look back in time to see Kelnozz walking away.

"A fool," Hatch'net chuckled, putting his light on Drizzt, then turning his gaze upon Dinin. "A good fool."

Dinin crossed his arms in front of his chest, his face glowing brightly now in a flush of embarrassment and anger.

Drizzt felt the cool stone against his cheek, but his only thoughts at that moment were rooted in the past, locked onto Zaknafein's sarcastic, but painfully accurate, statement: "It is our way!"

# 13
# The Price of Winning

"You deceived me," Drizzt said to Kelnozz that night in the barracks. The room was black around them and no other students stirred in their cots, exhausted from the day's fighting and from their endless duties serving the older students.

Kelnozz fully expected this encounter. He had guessed Drizzt's naiveté early on, when Drizzt had actually queried him about the rules of engagement. An experienced drow warrior, particularly a noble, should have known better, should have understood that the only rule of his existence was the pursuit of victory. Now, Kelnozz knew, this foolish young Do'Urden would not strike at him for his earlier actions—vengeance fueled by anger was not one of Drizzt's traits.

"Why?" Drizzt pressed, finding no answer forthcoming from the smug commoner of House Kenafin.

The volume of Drizzt's voice caused Kelnozz to glance around nervously. They were supposed to be sleeping; if a master heard them arguing . . .

"What is the mystery?" Kelnozz signaled back in the hand code, the warmth of his fingers glowing clearly to Drizzt's heat-sensing eyes. "I acted as I had to act, though I now believe I should have held off a bit longer. Perhaps, if you had defeated a few more, I might have finished higher than third in the class."

"If we had worked together, as we had agreed, you might have won, or finished second at the least," Drizzt signaled back, the sharp movements of his hands reflecting his anger.

"Most assuredly second," Kelnozz replied. "I knew from the beginning that I would be no match for you. You are the finest swordsman I have ever seen."

"Not by the masters standing," Drizzt grumbled aloud.

"Eighth is not so low," Kelnozz, whispered back. "Berg'inyon is only ranked tenth, and he is from the ruling house of Menzoberranzan. You should be glad that your standing is not to be envied by your classmates." A shuffle outside the room's door sent Kelnozz back into the silent code. "Holding a higher rank means only that I have more fighters eyeing my back as a convenient place to rest their daggers."

Drizzt let the implications of Kelnozz's statement slip by; he refused to consider such treachery in the Academy. "Berg'inyon was the finest fighter I saw in the grand melee," he signaled. "He had you beaten until I interceded on your behalf."

Kelnozz smiled the thought away. "Let Berg'inyon serve as a cook in some lowly house for all I care," he whispered even more quietly than before—for the son of House Baenre's bunk was only a few yards away. "He is tenth, yet I, Kelnozz of Kenafin, am third!"

"I am eighth," said Drizzt, an uncharacteristic edge on his voice, more anger than jealousy," but I could defeat you with any weapon."

Kelnozz shrugged, a strangely blurring movement to onlookers seeing in the infrared spectrum. "You did not," he signaled. "I won our encounter."

"Encounter?" Drizzt gasped. "You deceived me, that is all!"

"Who was left standing?" Kelnozz pointedly reminded him. "Who wore the blue light of a master's wand?"

"Honor demands that there be rules of engagement," growled Drizzt.

"There is a rule," Kelnozz snapped back at him. "You may do whatever you can get away with. I won our encounter, Drizzt Do'Urden, and I hold the higher rank! That is all that matters!"

In the heat of the argument, their voices had grown too loud. The door to the room swung wide, and a master stepped onto the threshold, his form vividly outlined by the hallway's blue lights. Both students promptly rolled over and closed their eyes—and their mouths.

The finality of Kelnozz's last statement rocked Drizzt to some prudent observations. He realized then that his friendship with Kelnozz had come to an end—and, perhaps, that he and Kelnozz had never been friends at all.

⚔ ⚔ ⚔ ⚔ ⚔

"You have seen him?" Alton asked, his fingers tapping anxiously on the small table in the highest chamber of his private quarters. Alton had set the younger students of Sorcere to work repairing the blasted place, but the scorch marks on the stone walls remained, a legacy of Alton's fireball.

"I have," replied Masoj. "I have heard of his skill with weapons."

"Eighth in his class after the grand melee," said Alton, "a fine achievement."

"By all accounts, he has the prowess to be first," said Masoj. "One day he will claim that title. I shall be careful around that one."

"He will never live to claim it!" Alton promised. "House Do'Urden puts great pride in this purple-eyed youth, and thus I have decided upon Drizzt as my first target for revenge. His death will bring pain to that treacherous Matron Malice!"

Masoj saw a problem here and decided to put it to rest once and for all. "You will not harm him," he warned Alton. "You will not even go near him."

Alton's tone became no less grim. "I have waited two decades—" he began.

"You can wait a few more," Masoj snapped back. "I remind you that you accepted Matron SiNafay's invitation into House Hun'ett. Such an alliance requires obedience. Matron SiNafay—our matron mother—has placed upon my shoulders the task of handling Drizzt Do'Urden, and I will execute her will."

Alton rested back in his seat across the table and put what was left of his acid-torn chin into a slender palm, carefully weighing the words of his secret partner.

"Matron SiNafay has plans that will bring you all the revenge you could possibly desire," Masoj continued. "I warn you now, Alton DeVir," he snarled, emphasizing the surname that was not Hun'ett, "that if you begin a war with House Do'Urden, or even put them on the defensive with any act of violence unsanctioned by Matron SiNafay, you will incur the wrath of House Hun'ett. Matron SiNafay will expose you as a murderous imposter and will exact every punishment allowable by the ruling council upon your pitiful bones!"

Alton had no way to refute the threat. He was a rogue, without family beyond the adopted Hun'etts. If SiNafay turned against him, he would find no allies. "What plan does SiNafay . . . Matron SiNafay . . . have for House Do'Urden?" he asked calmly. "Tell me of my revenge so that I may survive these torturous years of waiting."

Masoj knew that he had to act carefully at this point. His mother had not forbidden him to tell Alton of the future course of action, but if she had wanted the volatile DeVir to know, Masoj realized, she would have told him herself.

"Let us just say that House Do'Urden's power has grown, and continues to grow, to the point where it has become a very real threat to all the great houses," Masoj purred, loving the intrigue of positioning before a war. "Witness the fall of House DeVir, perfectly executed with no obvious trail. Many of Menzoberranzan's nobles would rest easier if . . ." He let it go at that, deciding that he probably had said too much already.

By the hot glimmer in Alton's eyes, Masoj could tell that the lure had been strong enough to buy Alton's patience.

⚔ ⚔ ⚔ ⚔ ⚔

The Academy held many disappointments for young Drizzt, particularly in that first year, when so many of the dark realities of drow society, realities that Zaknafein had barely hinted at, remained on the edges of Drizzt's cognizance with stubborn resilience. He weighed the masters' lectures of hatred and mistrust in both hands, one side holding the masters' views in the context of the lectures, the other bending those same words into the very different logic assumed by his old mentor. The truth seemed so ambiguous, so hard to define. Through all of the examination, Drizzt found that he could not escape one pervading fact: In his entire young life, the only treachery he had ever witnessed—and so often!—was at the hands of drow elves.

The physical training of the Academy, hours on end of dueling exercises and stealth techniques, was more to Drizzt's liking. Here, with his weapons so readily in his hands, he freed himself of the disturbing questions of truth and perceived truth.

Here he excelled. If Drizzt had come into the Academy with a higher level of training and expertise than that of his classmates, the gap grew only wider as the grueling months passed. He learned to look beyond the accepted defense and attack routines put forth by the masters and create his own methods, innovations that almost always at least equaled—and usually outdid—the standard techniques.

At first, Dinin listened with increasing pride as his peers exalted in his younger brother's fighting prowess. So glowing came the compliments that the eldest son of Matron Malice soon took on a nervous wariness. Dinin was the elderboy of House Do'Urden, a title he had gained by eliminating Nalfein. Drizzt, showing the potential to become one of the finest swordsmen in all of Menzoberranzan, was now the secondboy of the house, eyeing, perhaps, Dinin's title.

Similarly, Drizzt's fellow students did not miss the growing brilliance of his fighting dance. Often they viewed it too close for their liking! They looked upon Drizzt with seething jealousy, wondering if they could ever measure up against his whirling scimitars. Pragmatism was ever a strong trait in drow elves. These young students had spent the bulk of their years observing the elders of their families twisting every situation into a favorable light. Every one of them recognized the value of Drizzt Do'Urden as an ally, and thus, when the grand melee came around the next year, Drizzt was inundated with offers of partnership.

The most surprising query came from Kelnozz of House Kenafin, who had downed Drizzt through deceit the previous year. "Do we join again, this time to the very top of the class?" the haughty young fighter asked as he moved beside Drizzt down the tunnel to the prepared cavern. He moved around and stood before Drizzt easily, as if they were the best of friends, his forearms resting across the hilts of his belted weapons and an overly friendly smile spread across his face.

Drizzt could not even answer. He turned and walked away, pointedly keeping his eye over one shoulder as he left.

"Why are you so amazed?" Kelnozz pressed, stepping quickly to keep up.

Drizzt spun on him. "How could I join again with one who so deceived me?" he snarled. "I have not forgotten your trick!"

"That is the point," Kelnozz argued. "You are more wary this year; certainly I would be a fool to attempt such a move again!"

"How else could you win?" said Drizzt. "You cannot defeat me in open battle." His words were not a boast, just a fact that Kelnozz accepted as readily as Drizzt.

"Second rank is highly honored," Kelnozz reasoned.

Drizzt glared at him. He knew that Kelnozz would not settle for anything less than ultimate victory. "If we meet in the melee," he said with cold finality, "it will be as opponents." He walked off again, and this time Kelnozz did not follow.

⚔ ⚔ ⚔ ⚔ ⚔

Luck bestowed a measure of justice upon Drizzt that day, for his first opponent, and first victim, in the grand melee was none other than his former partner. Drizzt found Kelnozz in the same corridor they had used as a defensible starting point the previous year and took him down with his very first attack combination. Drizzt somehow managed to hold back on his winning thrust, though he truly wanted to jab his scimitar pole into Kelnozz's ribs with all his strength.

Then Drizzt was off into the shadows, picking his way carefully until the numbers of surviving students began to dwindle. With his reputation, Drizzt had to be extra wary, for his classmates recognized a common advantage in eliminating one of his prowess early in the competition. Working alone, Drizzt had to fully scope out every battle before he engaged, to ensure that each opponent had no secret companions lurking nearby.

This was Drizzt's arena, the place where he felt most comfortable, and he was up to the challenge. In two hours, only five competitors remained, and after another two hours of cat and mouse, it came down to only two: Drizzt and Berg'inyon Baenre.

Drizzt moved out into an open stretch of the cavern. "Come out, then, student Baenre!" he called. "Let us settle this challenge openly and with honor!"

Watching from the catwalk, Dinin shook his head in disbelief.

"He has relinquished all advantage," said Master Hatch'net, standing beside the elderboy of House Do'Urden. "As the better swordsman, he had Berg'inyon worried and unsure of his moves. Now your brother stands out in the open, showing his position."

"Still a fool," Dinin muttered.

Hatch'net spotted Berg'inyon slipping behind a stalagmite mound a few yards behind Drizzt. "It should be settled soon."

"Are you afraid?" Drizzt yelled into the gloom. "If you truly deserve the top rank, as you freely boast, then come out and face me openly. Prove your words, Berg'inyon Baenre, or never speak them again!"

The expected rush of motion from behind sent Drizzt into a sidelong roll.

"Fighting is more than swordplay!" the son of House Baenre cried as he came on, his eyes gleaming at the advantage he now seemed to hold.

Berg'inyon stumbled then, tripped up by a wire Drizzt had set out, and fell flat to his face. Drizzt was on him in a flash, scimitar pole tip in at Berg'inyon's throat.

"So I have learned," Drizzt replied grimly.

"Thus a Do'Urden becomes the champion," Hatch'net observed, putting his blue light on the face of House Baenre's defeated son. Hatch'net then stole Dinin's widening smile with a prudent reminder: "Elderboys should beware secondboys with such skills."

⚔ ⚔ ⚔ ⚔ ⚔

While Drizzt took little pride in his victory that second year, he took great satisfaction in the continued growth of his fighting skills. He practiced every waking hour when he was not busy in the many serving duties of a young student. Those duties were reduced as the years passed—the youngest students were worked the hardest—and Drizzt found more and more time in private training. He reveled in the dance of his blades and the harmony of his movements. His scimitars became his only friends, the only things he dared to trust.

He won the grand melee again the third year, and the year after that, despite the conspiracies of many others against him. To the masters, it became obvious that none in Drizzt's class would ever defeat him, and the next year they placed him into the grand melee of students three years his senior. He won that one, too.

The Academy, above anything else in Menzoberranzan, was a structured place, and though Drizzt's advanced skill defied that structure in terms of battle prowess, his tenure as a student would not be lessened. As a fighter, he would spend ten years in the Academy, not such a long time considering the thirty years of study a wizard endured in Sorcere, or the fifty years a budding priestess would spend in Arach-Tinilith. While fighters began their training at the young age of twenty, wizards could not start until their twenty-fifth birthday, and clerics had to wait until the age of forty.

The first four years in Melee-Magthere were devoted to singular combat, the handling of weapons. In this, the masters could teach Drizzt little that Zaknafein had not already shown him.

After that, though, the lessons became more involved. The young drow warriors spent two full years learning group fighting tactics with other warriors, and the subsequent three years incorporated those tactics into warfare techniques beside, and against, wizards and clerics.

The final year of the Academy rounded out the fighters' education. The first six months were spent in Sorcere, learning the basics of magic use, and the last six, the prelude to graduation, saw the fighters in tutelage under the priestesses of Arach-Tinilith.

All the while there remained the rhetoric, the hammering in of those precepts that the Spider Queen held so dear, those lies of hatred that held the drow in a state of controllable chaos.

To Drizzt, the Academy became a personal challenge, a private classroom within the impenetrable womb of his whirling scimitars. Inside the adamantine walls he formed with those blades, Drizzt found he could ignore the many injustices he observed all around him, and could somewhat insulate himself against words that would have poisoned his heart. The Academy was a place of constant ambition and deceit, a breeding ground for the ravenous, consuming hunger for power that marked the life of all the drow.

Drizzt would survive it unscathed, he promised himself.

As the years passed, though, as the battles began to take on the edge of brutal reality, Drizzt found himself caught up time and again in the heated throes of situations he could not so easily brush away.

# 14
# Proper Respect

They moved through the winding tunnels as quietly as a whispering breeze, each step measured in stealth and ending in an alert posture. They were ninth-year students working on their last year in Melee-Magthere, and they operated as often outside the cavern of Menzoberranzan as within. No longer did padded poles adorn their belts; adamantine weapons hung there now, finely forged and cruelly edged.

At times, the tunnels closed in around them, barely wide enough for one dark elf to squeeze through. Other times, the students found themselves in huge caverns with walls and ceilings beyond their sight. They were drow warriors, trained to operate in any type of Underdark landscape and learned in the ways of any foe they might encounter.

"Practice patrols," Master Hatch'net had called these drills, though he had warned the students that "practice patrols" often met monsters quite real and unfriendly.

Drizzt, still rated in the top of his class and in the point position, led this group, with Master Hatch'net and ten other students following in formation behind. Only twenty-two of the original twenty-five in Drizzt's class remained. One had been dismissed—and subsequently executed—for a foiled assassination attempt on a high-ranking student, a second had been killed in the practice arena, and a third had died in his bunk of natural causes—for a dagger in the heart quite naturally ends one's life.

In another tunnel a short distance away, Berg'inyon Baenre, holding the class's second rank, led Master Dinin and the other half of the class in a similar exercise.

Day after day, Drizzt and the others had struggled to keep the fine edge of readiness. In three months of these mock patrols, the group had encountered only one monster, a cave fisher, a nasty crablike denizen of the Underdark. Even that conflict had provided only brief excitement, and no practical experience, for the cave fisher had slipped out along the high ledges before the drow patrol could even get a strike at it.

This day, Drizzt sensed something different. Perhaps it was an unusual edge on Master Hatch'net's voice or a tingling in the stones of the cavern, a subtle vibration that hinted to Drizzt's subconscious of other creatures in the maze of tunnels. Whatever the reason, Drizzt knew enough to follow his instincts, and he was not surprised when the telltale glow of a heat source flitted down a side passage on the periphery of his vision. He signaled for the rest of the patrol to halt, then quickly climbed to a perch on a tiny ledge above the side passage's exit.

When the intruder emerged into the main tunnel, he found himself lying back down on the floor with two scimitar blades crossed over his neck. Drizzt backed away immediately when he recognized his victim as another drow student.

"What are you doing down here?" Master Hatch'net demanded of the intruder. "You know that the tunnels outside Menzoberranzan are not to be traveled by any but the patrols!"

"Your pardon, Master," the student pleaded. "I bring news of an alert."

All in the patrol crowded around, but Hatch'net backed them off with a glare and ordered Drizzt to set them out in defensive positions.

"A child is missing," the student went on, "a princess of House Baenre! Monsters have been spotted in the tunnels!"

"What sort of monsters?" Hatch'net asked. A loud clacking noise, like the sound of two stones being chipped together, answered his question.

"Hook horrors!" Hatch'net signaled to Drizzt at his side. Drizzt had never seen such beasts, but he had learned enough about them to understand why

Master Hatch'net had suddenly reverted to the silent hand code. Hook horrors hunted through a sense of hearing more acute than that of any other creature in all the Underdark. Drizzt immediately relayed the signal around to the others, and they held absolutely quiet for instructions from the master. This was the situation they had trained to handle for the last nine years of their lives, and only the sweat on their palms belied the calm readiness of these young drow warriors.

"Spells of darkness will not foil hook horrors," Hatch'net signaled to his troops. "Nor will these." He indicated the pistol crossbow in his hand and the poison-tipped dart it held, a common first-strike weapon of the dark elves. Hatch'net put the crossbow away and drew his slender sword.

"You must find a gap in the creature's bone armor," he reminded the others, "and slip your weapon through to the flesh." He tapped Drizzt on the shoulder, and they started off together, the other students falling into line behind them.

The clacking resounded clearly, but, echoing off the stone walls of the tunnels, it provided a confusing beacon for the hunting drow. Hatch'net let Drizzt steer their course and was impressed by the way the student soon discerned the pattern of the echo riddle. Drizzt's step came in confidence, though many of the others in the patrol glanced about anxiously, unsure of the peril's direction or distance.

Then a singular sound froze them all where they stood, cutting through the din of the clacking monsters and resounding again and again, surrounding the patrol in the echoing madness of a terrifying wail. It was the scream of a child.

"Princess of House Baenre!" Hatch'net signaled to Drizzt. The master started to order his troops into a battle formation, but Drizzt didn't wait to watch the commands. The scream had sent a shudder of revulsion through his spine, and when it sounded again, it lighted angry fires in his lavender eyes.

Drizzt sprinted off down the tunnel, the cold metal of his scimitars leading the way.

Hatch'net organized the patrol into quick pursuit. He hated the thought of losing a student as skilled as Drizzt, but he considered, too, the benefits of Drizzt's rash actions. If the others watched the finest of their class die in an act of stupidity, it would be a lesson they would not soon forget.

Drizzt cut around a sharp corner and down a straight expanse of narrow, broken walls. He heard no echoes now, just the ravenous clacking of the waiting monsters and the muffled cries of the child.

His keen ears caught the slight sounds of his patrol at his back, and he knew that if he was able to hear them, the hook horrors surely could. Drizzt would not relinquish the passion or the immediacy of his quest. He climbed to a ledge ten feet above the floor, hoping it would run the length of the corridor. When he slipped around a final bend, he could barely distinguish the heat of the monsters' forms through the blurring coolness of their bony exoskeletons, shells nearly equal in temperature to the surrounding stone.

He made out five of the giant beasts, two pressed against the stone and guarding the corridor and three others farther back, in a little cul-de-sac, toying with some—crying—object.

Drizzt mustered his nerve and continued along the ledge, using all the stealth he had ever learned to creep by the sentries. Then he saw the child princess, lying in a broken heap at the foot of one of the monstrous bipeds. Her sobs told Drizzt that she was alive. Drizzt had no intention of engaging the monsters if he could help it, hoping that he might perhaps slip in and steal the child away.

Then the patrol came headlong around the bend in the corridor, forcing Drizzt to action.

"Sentries!" he screamed in warning, probably saving the lives of the first four of the group. Drizzt's attention abruptly returned to the wounded child as one of the hook horrors raised its heavy, clawed foot to crush her.

The beast stood nearly twice Drizzt's height and outweighed him more than five times over. It was fully armored in the hard shell of its exoskeleton and adorned with gigantic clawed hands and a long and powerful beak. Three of the monsters stood between Drizzt and the child.

Drizzt couldn't care about any of those details at that horrible, critical moment. His fears for the child outweighed any concern for the danger looming before him. He was a drow warrior, a fighter trained and outfitted for battle, while the child was helpless and defenseless.

Two of the hook horrors rushed at the ledge, just the break Drizzt needed. He rose up to his feet and leaped out over them, coming down in a fighting blur onto the side of the remaining hook horror. The monster lost all thoughts of the child as Drizzt's scimitars snapped in at its beak relentlessly, cracking into its facial armor in a desperate search for an opening.

The hook horror fell back, overwhelmed by its opponent's fury and unable to catch up to the blades' blinding, stinging movements.

Drizzt knew that he had the advantage on this one, but he knew, as well, that two others would soon be at his back. He did not relent. He slid down from his perch on the monster's side and rolled around to block its retreat, dropping between its stalagmite-like legs and tripping it to the stone. Then he was on top of it, poking furiously as it floundered on its belly.

The hook horror desperately tried to respond, but its armored shell was too encumbering for it to twist out from under the assault.

Drizzt knew his own situation was even more desperate. Battle had been joined in the corridor, but Hatch'net and the others couldn't possibly get through the sentries in time to stop the two hook horrors undoubtedly charging his back. Prudence dictated that Drizzt relinquish his position over this one and spin away into a defensive posture.

The child's agonized scream, however, overruled prudence. Rage burned in Drizzt's eyes so blatantly that even the stupid hook horror knew its life was soon to end. Drizzt put the tips of his scimitars together in a V and plunged them down onto the back of the monster's skull with all his might. Seeing a slight crack in the creature's shell, Drizzt crossed the hilts of his weapons, reversed the points, and split a clear opening in the monster's defense. He then snapped the hilts together and plunged the blades straight down, through the soft flesh and into the monster's brain.

A heavy claw sliced a deep line across Drizzt's shoulders, tearing his *piwafwi* and drawing blood. He dived forward into a roll and came up with his wounded back to the far wall. Only one hook horror moved in at him; the other picked up the child.

"No!" Drizzt screamed in protest. He started forward, only to be slapped back by the attacking monster. Then, paralyzed, he watched in horror as the other hook horror put an end to the child's screams.

Rage replaced determination in Drizzt's eyes. The closest hook horror rushed at him, meaning to crush him against the stone. Drizzt recognized its intentions and didn't even try to dodge out of the way. Instead, he reversed his grip on his weapons and locked them against the wall, above his shoulders.

With the momentum of the monster's eight-hundred-pound bulk carrying it on, even the armor of its shell could not protect the hook horror from the adamantine scimitars. It slammed Drizzt up against the wall, but in doing so impaled itself through the belly.

The creature jumped back, trying to wriggle free, but it could not escape the fury of Drizzt Do'Urden. Savagely the young drow twisted the impaled blades. He then shoved off from the wall with the strength of anger, tumbling the giant monster backward.

Two of Drizzt's enemies were dead, and one of the hook horror sentries in the hallway was down, but Drizzt found no relief in those facts. The third hook horror towered over him as he desperately tried to get his blades free from his latest victim. Drizzt had no escape from this one.

The second patrol arrived then, and Dinin and Berg'inyon Baenre rushed into the cul-de-sac, along the same ledge Drizzt had taken. The hook horror turned away from Drizzt just as the two skilled fighters came at it.

Drizzt ignored the painful gash in his back and the cracks he had no doubt suffered in his slender ribs. Breathing came to him in labored gasps, but this, too, was of no consequence. He finally managed to free one of his blades, and he charged at the monster's back. Caught in the middle of the three skilled drow, the hook horror went down in seconds.

The corridor was finally cleared, and the dark elves rushed in all around the cul-de-sac. They had lost only one student in their battle against the monster sentries.

"A princess of House Barrison'del'armgo," remarked one of the students in Dinin's patrol, looking at the child's body.

"House Baenre, we were told," said another student, one from Hatch'net's group. Drizzt did not miss the discrepancy.

Berg'inyon Baenre rushed over to see if the victim was indeed his youngest sister.

"Not of my house," he said with obvious relief after a quick inspection. He then laughed as further examination revealed a few other details about the corpse. "Not even a princess!" he declared.

Drizzt watched it all curiously, noting the impassive, callous attitude of his companions most of all.

Another student confirmed Berg'inyon's observation. "A boy child!" he spouted. "But of what house?"

Master Hatch'net moved over to the tiny body and reached down to take the purse from around the child's neck. He emptied its contents into his hand, revealing the emblem of a lesser house.

"A lost waif," he laughed to his students, tossing the empty purse back to the ground and pocketing its contents," of no consequence."

"A fine fight," Dinin was quick to add, "with only one loss. Go back to Menzoberranzan proud of the work you have accomplished this day."

Drizzt slapped the blades of his scimitars together in a resounding ring of protest.

Master Hatch'net ignored him. "Form up and head back," he told the others. "You all performed well this day." He then glared at Drizzt, stopping the angry student in his tracks.

"Except for you!" Hatch'net snarled. "I cannot ignore the fact that you downed two of the beasts and helped with a third," Hatch'net scolded, "but you endangered the rest of us with your foolish bravado!"

"I warned of the sentries—" Drizzt stuttered.

"Damn your warning!" shouted the master. "You went off without command! You ignored the accepted methods of battle! You led us in here blindly! Look at the corpse of your fallen companion!" Hatch'net raged, pointing to the dead student in the corridor. "His blood is on your hands!"

"I meant to save the child," Drizzt argued.

"We all meant to save the child!" retorted Hatch'net.

Drizzt was not so certain. What would a child be doing out in these corridors all alone? How convenient that a group of hook horrors, a rarely seen beast in the region of Menzoberranzan, just happened by to provide training for this "practice patrol." Too convenient, Drizzt knew, considering that the passages farther from the city teemed with the true patrols of seasoned warriors, wizards, and even clerics.

"You knew what was around the bend in the tunnel," Drizzt said evenly, his eyes narrowing at the master.

The slap of a blade across the wound on his back made Drizzt lurch in pain, and he nearly lost his footing. He turned to find Dinin glaring down at him.

"Keep your foolish words unspoken," Dinin warned in a harsh whisper, "or I will cut out your tongue."

⚔ ⚔ ⚔ ⚔ ⚔

"The child was a plant," Drizzt insisted when he was alone with his brother in Dinin's room.

Dinin's response was a stinging smack across the face.

"They sacrificed him for the purpose of the drill," growled the unrelenting younger Do'Urden.

Dinin launched a second punch, but Drizzt caught it in mid-swing. "You know the truth of my words," Drizzt said. "You knew about it all along."

"Learn your place, Secondboy," Dinin replied in open threat, "in the Academy and in the family." He pulled away from his brother.

"To the Nine Hells with the Academy!" Drizzt spat at Dinin's face. "If the family holds similar . . ." He noticed that Dinin's hands now held sword and dirk.

Drizzt jumped back, his own scimitars coming out at the ready. "I have no desire to fight you, my brother," he said. "Know well that if you attack, I will defend. Only one of us will walk out of here."

Dinin considered his next move carefully. If he attacked and won, the threat to his position in the family would be at an end. Certainly no one, not even Matron Malice, would question the punishment he levied against his impertinent younger brother. Dinin had seen Drizzt in battle, though. Two hook horrors! Even Zaknafein would be hard pressed to attain such a victory. Still, Dinin knew that if he did not carry through with his threat, if he let Drizzt face him down, he might give Drizzt confidence in their future struggles, possibly inciting the treachery he had always expected from the secondboy.

"What is this, then?" came a voice from the room's door way. The brothers turned to see their sister Vierna, a mistress of Arach-Tinilith. "Put your weapons away," she scolded. "House Do'Urden cannot afford such infighting now!"

Realizing that he had been let off the hook, Dinin readily complied with the demands, and Drizzt did likewise.

"Consider yourselves fortunate," said Vierna, "for I'll not tell Matron Malice of this stupidity. She would not be merciful, I promise you."

"Why have you come unannounced to Melee-Magthere?" asked the elderboy, perturbed by his sister's attitude. He, too, was a master of the Academy, even if he was only a male, and deserved some respect.

Vierna glanced up and down the hallway, then closed the door behind her. "To warn my brothers," she explained quietly. "There are rumors of vengeance against our house."

"By what family?" Dinin pressed. Drizzt just stood back in confused silence and let the two continue. "For what deed?"

"For the elimination of House DeVir, I would presume," replied Vierna. "Little is known; the rumors are vague. I wanted to warn you both, though, so that you might keep your guard especially high in the coming months."

"House DeVir fell many years ago," said Dinin. "What penalty could still be enacted?"

Vierna shrugged. "They are just rumors," she said. "Rumors to be listened to!"

"We have been accused of a wrongful deed?" Drizzt asked. "Surely our family must call out this false accuser."

Vierna and Dinin exchanged smiles. "Wrongful?" Vierna laughed.

Drizzt's expression revealed his confusion.

"On the very night you were born," Dinin explained, "House DeVir ceased to exist. An excellent attack, thank you."

"House Do'Urden?" gasped Drizzt, unable to come to terms with the startling news. Of course, Drizzt knew of such battles, but he had held out hope that his own family was above that sort of murderous action.

"One of the finest eliminations ever carried out," Vierna boasted. "Not a witness left alive."

"You . . . our family . . . murdered another family?"

"Watch your words, Secondboy," Dinin warned. "The deed was perfectly executed. In the eyes of Menzoberranzan, therefore, it never happened."

"But House DeVir ceased to exist," said Drizzt.

"To a child," said Dinin with a laugh.

A thousand possibilities assaulted Drizzt at that awful moment, a thousand pressing questions that he needed answered. One in particular stood out vividly, welling like a lump of bile in his throat.

"Where was Zaknafein that night?" he asked.

"In the chapel of House DeVir's clerics, of course," replied Vierna "Zaknafein plays his part in such business so very well."

Drizzt rocked back on his heels, hardly able to believe what he was hearing. He knew that Zak had killed drow before, had killed clerics of Lolth before, but Drizzt had always assumed that the weapons master had acted out of necessity, in self-defense.

"You should show more respect to your brother," Vierna scolded him. "To draw weapons against Dinin! You owe him your life!"

"You know?" Dinin chuckled, casting Vierna a curious glance.

"You and I were melded that night," Vierna reminded him. "Of course I know."

"What are you talking about?" asked Drizzt, almost afraid to hear the reply.

"You were to be the third-born male in the family," Vierna explained, "the third living son."

"I have heard of my brother Nal—" The name stuck in Drizzt's throat as he began to understand. All he had ever been able to learn of Nalfein was that he had been killed by another drow.

"You will learn in your studies at Arach-Tinilith that third living sons are customarily sacrificed to Lolth," Vierna continued. "So were you promised. On the night that you were born, the night that House Do'Urden battled House DeVir, Dinin made his ascent to the position of elderboy." She cast a sly glance at her brother, standing with his arms proudly crossed over his chest.

"I can speak of it now," Vierna smiled at Dinin, who nodded his head in accord. "It happened too long ago for any punishment to be brought against Dinin."

"What are you talking about?" Drizzt demanded. Panic hovered all about him. "What did Dinin do?"

"He put his sword into Nalfein's back," Vierna said calmly.

Drizzt swam on the edge of nausea. Sacrifice? Murder? The annihilation of a family, even the children? What were his siblings talking about?

"Show respect to your brother!" Vierna demanded. "You owe him your life."

"I warn the both of you," she purred, her ominous glare shaking Drizzt and knocking Dinin from his confident pedestal. "House Do'Urden may be on a course of war. If either of you strike out against the other, you will bring the wrath of all your sisters and Matron Malice—four high priestesses—down upon your worthless soul!" Confident that her threat carried sufficient weight, she turned and left the room.

"I will go," Drizzt whispered, wanting only to skulk away to a dark corner.

"You will go when you are dismissed!" Dinin scolded. "Remember your place, Drizzt Do'Urden, in the Academy and in the family."

"As you remembered yours with Nalfein?"

"The battle against DeVir was won," Dinin replied, taking no offense. "The act brought no peril to the family."

Another wave of disgust swept over Drizzt. He felt as if the floor were climbing up to swallow him, and he almost hoped that it would.

"It is a difficult world we inhabit," Dinin said.

"We make it so," Drizzt retorted. He wanted to continue further, to implicate the Spider Queen and the whole amoral religion that would sanction such destructive and treacherous actions. Drizzt wisely held his tongue, though. Dinin wanted him dead; he understood that now. Drizzt understood as well that if he gave his scheming brother the opportunity to turn the females of the family against him, Dinin surely would.

"You must learn," Dinin said, again in a controlled tone, "to accept the realities of your surroundings. You must learn to recognize your enemies and defeat them."

"By whatever means are available," Drizzt concluded.

"The mark of a true warrior!" Dinin replied with a wicked laugh.

"Are our enemies drow elves?"

"We are drow warriors!" Dinin declared sternly. "We do what we must to survive,"

"As you did, on the night of my birth," Drizzt reasoned, though at this point, there was no remaining trace of outrage in his resigned tone. "You were cunning enough to get away cleanly with the deed."

Dinin's reply, though expected, stung the younger drow profoundly.

"It never happened."

# 15 On The Dark Side

I am Drizzt—"

"I know who you are," replied the student mage, Drizzt's appointed tutor in Sorcere. "Your reputation precedes you. Most in all the Academy have heard of you and of your prowess with weapons."

Drizzt bowed low, a bit embarrassed.

"That skill will be of little use to you here," the mage went on. "I am to tutor you in the wizardly arts, the dark side of magic, we call them. This is a test of your mind and your heart; meager metal weapons will play no part. Magic is the true power of our people!"

Drizzt accepted the berating without reply. He knew that the traits this young mage was boasting of were also necessary qualities of a true fighter. Physical attributes played only a minor role in Drizzt's style of battle. Strong will and calculated maneuvers, everything the mage apparently believed only wizards could handle, won the duels that Drizzt fought.

"I will show you many marvels in the next few months," the mage went on, "artifacts beyond your belief and spells of a power beyond your experience!"

"May I know your name?" Drizzt asked, trying to sound somewhat impressed by the student's continued stream of self-glorification. Drizzt had already learned quite a lot about wizardry from Zaknafein, mostly of the weaknesses inherent in the profession. Because of magic's usefulness in situations other than battle, drow wizards were accorded a high position in the society, second to the clerics of Lolth. It was a wizard, after all, who lighted the glowing Narbondel, timeclock of the city, and wizards who lighted faerie fires on the sculptures of the decorated houses.

Zaknafein had little respect for wizards. They could kill quickly and from a distance, he had warned Drizzt, but if one could get in close to them, they had little defense against a sword.

"Masoj," replied the mage. "Masoj Hun'ett of House Hun'ett, beginning my thirtieth and final year of study. Soon I will be recognized as a full wizard of Menzoberranzan, with all of the privileges accorded my station."

"Greetings, then, Masoj Hun'ett," Drizzt replied. "I, too, have but a year remaining in my training at the Academy, for a fighter spends only ten years."

"A lesser talent," Masoj was quick to remark. "Wizards study thirty years before they are even considered practiced enough to go out and perform their craft."

Again Drizzt accepted the insult graciously. He wanted to get this phase of his instruction over with, then finish out the year and be rid of the Academy altogether.

⚔ ⚔ ⚔ ⚔ ⚔

Drizzt found his six months under Masoj's tutelage actually the best of his stay at the Academy. Not that he came to care for Masoj; the budding wizard constantly sought ways to remind Drizzt of fighters' inferiority. Drizzt sensed a competition between himself and Masoj, almost as if the mage were setting him up for some future conflict. The young fighter shrugged his way through it, as he always had, and tried to get as much out of the lessons as he could.

Drizzt found that he was quite proficient in the ways of magic. Every drow, the fighters included, possessed a degree of magical talent and certain innate abilities. Even drow children could conjure a globe of darkness or edge their opponents in a glowing outline of harmless colored flames. Drizzt handled these tasks easily, and in a few tendays, he could manage several cantrips and a few lesser spells.

With the innate magical talents of the dark elves also came a resistance to magical attacks, and that is where Zaknafein had recognized the wizards' greatest weakness. A wizard could cast his most powerful spell to perfection, but if his intended victim was a drow elf, the wizard may well have found no results for his efforts. The surety of a well-aimed sword thrust always impressed Zaknafein, and Drizzt, after witnessing the drawbacks of drow magic during those first tendays with Masoj, began to appreciate the course of training he had been given.

He still found great enjoyment in many of the things Masoj showed him, particularly the enchanted items housed in the tower of Sorcere. Drizzt held wands and staves of incredible power and went through several attack routines with a sword so heavily enchanted that his hands tingled from its touch.

Masoj, too, watched Drizzt carefully through it all, studying the young warrior's every move, searching for some weakness that he might exploit if House Hun'ett and House Do'Urden ever did fall into the expected conflict. Several times, Masoj saw an opportunity to eliminate Drizzt, and he felt in his heart that it would be a prudent move. Matron SiNafay's instructions to him, though, had been explicit and unbending.

Masoj's mother had secretly arranged for him to be Drizzt's tutor. This was not an unusual situation; instruction for fighters during their six months in Sorcere was always handled one-on-one by higher-level Sorcere students. When she had told Masoj of the setup, SiNafay quickly reminded him that his sessions with the young Do'Urden remained no more than a scouting mission. He was not to do anything that might even hint of the planned conflict between the two houses. Masoj was not fool enough to disobey.

Still, there was one other wizard lurking in the shadows, who was so desperate that even the warnings of the matron mother did little to deter him.

⚔⚔⚔⚔⚔

"My student, Masoj, has informed me of your fine progress," Alton DeVir said to Drizzt one day.

"Thank you, Master Faceless One," Drizzt replied hesitantly, more than a little intimidated that a master of Sorcere had invited him to a private audience.

"How do you perceive magic, young warrior?" Alton asked. "Has Masoj impressed you?"

Drizzt didn't know how to respond. Truly, magic had not impressed him as a profession, but he did not want to insult a master of the craft. "I find the art beyond my abilities," he said tactfully. "For others, it seems a powerful course, but I believe my talents are more closely linked to the sword."

"Could your weapons defeat one of magical power?" Alton snarled. He quickly bit back the sneer, trying not to tip off his intent.

Drizzt shrugged. "Each has its place in battle," he replied. "Who could say which is the mightier? As with every combat, it would depend upon the individuals engaged."

"Well, what of yourself?" Alton teased. "First in your class, I have heard, year after year. The masters of Melee-Magthere speak highly of your talents."

Again Drizzt found himself flushed with embarrassment. More than that, though, he was curious as to why a master and student of Sorcere seemed to know so much about him.

"Could you stand against one of magical powers?" asked Alton. "Against a master of Sorcere, perhaps?"

"I do not—" Drizzt began, but Alton was too enmeshed in his own ranting to hear him.

"Let us learn!" the Faceless One cried. He drew out a thin wand and promptly loosed a bolt of lightning at Drizzt.

Drizzt was down into a dive before the wand even discharged. The lightning bolt sundered the door to Alton's highest chamber and bounced about the adjourning room, breaking items and scorching the walls.

Drizzt came rolling back to his feet at the side of the room, his scimitars drawn and ready. He still was unsure of this master's intent.

"How many can you dodge?" Alton teased, waving the wand in a threatening circle. "What of the other spells I have at my disposal—those that attack the mind, not the body?"

Drizzt tried to understand the purpose of this lesson and the part he was meant to play in it. Was he supposed to attack this master?

"These are not practice blades," he warned, holding his weapons out toward Alton.

Another bolt roared in, forcing Drizzt to dodge back to his original position. "Does this seem like practice to you, foolish Do'Urden?" Alton growled. "Do you know who I am?"

Alton's time of revenge had come—damn the orders of Matron SiNafay!

Just as Alton was about to reveal the truth to Drizzt, a dark form slammed into the master's back, knocking him to the floor. He tried to squirm away but found himself helplessly pinned by a huge black panther.

Drizzt lowered the tips of his blades; he was at a loss to understand any of this.

"Enough, Guenhwyvar!" came a call from behind Alton. Looking past the fallen master and the cat, Drizzt saw Masoj enter the room.

The panther sprang away from Alton obediently and moved to rejoin its master. It paused on its way, to consider Drizzt, who stood ready in the middle of the room.

So enchanted was Drizzt with the beast, the graceful flow of its rippling muscles and the intelligence in its saucer eyes, that he paid little attention to the master who had just attacked him, though Alton, unhurt, was back to his feet and obviously upset.

"My pet," Masoj explained. Drizzt watched in amazement as Masoj dismissed the cat back to its own plane of existence by sending its corporeal form back into the magical onyx statuette he held in his hand.

"Where did you get such a companion?" Drizzt asked.

"Never underestimate the powers of magic," Masoj replied, dropping the figurine into a deep pocket. His beaming smile became a scowl as he looked to Alton.

Drizzt, too, glanced at the faceless master. That a student had dared to attack a master seemed impossibly odd to the young fighter. This situation grew more puzzling each minute.

Alton knew that he had overstepped his bounds, and that he would have to pay a high price for his foolishness if he could not find some way out of this predicament.

"Have you learned your lesson this day?" Masoj asked Drizzt, though Alton realized that the question was also directed his way.

Drizzt shook his head. "I am not certain of the point of all this," he answered honestly.

"A display of the weakness of magic," Masoj explained, trying to disguise the truth of the encounter, "to show you the disadvantage caused by the necessary intensity of a casting wizard; to show you the vulnerability of a mage obsessed—" he eyed Alton directly at this point—"with spellcasting. The complete vulnerability when a wizard's intended prey becomes his overriding concern."

Drizzt recognized the lie for what it was, but he could not understand the motives behind this day's events. Why would a master of Sorcere attack him so? Why would Masoj, still just a student, risk so much to come to his defense?

"Let us bother the master no more," Masoj said, hoping to deflect Drizzt's curiosity further. "Come with me now to our practice hall. I will show you more of Guenhwyvar, my magical pet."

Drizzt looked to Alton, wondering what the unpredictable master would do next.

"Do go," Alton said calmly, knowing the facade Masoj had begun would be his only way around the wrath of his adopted matron mother. "I am confident that this day's lesson was learned," he said, his eyes on Masoj.

Drizzt glanced back to Masoj, then back to Alton again. He let it go at that. He wanted to learn more of Guenhwyvar.

⚔ ⚔ ⚔ ⚔ ⚔

When Masoj had Drizzt back in the privacy of the tutor's own room, he took out the polished onyx figurine in the form of a panther and called

Guenhwyvar back to his side. The mage breathed easier after he had introduced Drizzt to the cat, for Drizzt spoke no more about the incident with Alton.

Never before had Drizzt encountered such a wonderful magical item. He sensed a strength in Guenhwyvar, a dignity, that belied the beast's enchanted nature. Truly, the cat's sleek muscles and graceful moves epitomized the hunting qualities drow elves so dearly desired. Just by watching Guenhwyvar's movements, Drizzt believed, he could improve his own techniques.

Masoj let them play together and spar together for hours, grateful that Guenhwyvar could help him smooth over any damage that foolish Alton had done.

Drizzt had already put his meeting with the faceless master far behind him.

⚔ ⚔ ⚔ ⚔ ⚔

"Matron SiNafay would not understand," Masoj warned Alton when they were alone later that day.

"You will tell her," Alton reasoned matter-of-factly. So frustrated was he with his failure to kill Drizzt that he hardly cared.

Masoj shook his head. "She need not know."

A suspicious smile found its way across Alton's disfigured face. "What do you want?" he asked coyly. "Your tenure here is almost at its end. What more might a master do for Masoj?"

"Nothing," Masoj replied. "I want nothing from you."

"Then why?" Alton demanded. "I desire no debts following my paths. This incident is to be done with here and now!"

"It is done," Masoj replied. Alton didn't seem convinced.

"What could I gain from telling Matron SiNafay of your foolish actions?" Masoj reasoned. "Likely, she would kill you, and the coming war with House Do'Urden would have no basis. You are the link we need to justify the attack. I desire this battle; I'll not risk it for the little pleasure I might find in your tortured demise."

"I was foolish," Alton admitted, more somberly. "I had not planned to kill Drizzt when I summoned him here, just to watch him and learn of him, so that I might savor more when the time to kill him finally arrived. Seeing him before me, though, seeing a cursed Do'Urden standing unprotected before me . . . !"

"I understand," said Masoj sincerely. "I have had those same feelings when looking upon that one."

"You have no grudge against House Do'Urden."

"Not the house," Masoj explained, "that one! I have watched him for nearly a decade, studied his movements and his attitudes."

"You like not what you see?" Alton asked, a hopeful tone in his voice.

"He does not belong," Masoj replied grimly. "After six months by his side, I feel I know him less now than I ever did. He displays no ambition, yet has emerged victorious from his class's grand melee nine years in a row. It's unprecedented! His grasp of magic is strong; he could have been a wizard, a very powerful wizard, if he had chosen that course of study."

Masoj clenched his fist, searching for the words to convey his true emotions about Drizzt. "It is all too easy for him," he snarled. "There is no sacrifice in Drizzt's actions, no scars for the great gains he makes in his chosen profession."

"He is gifted," Alton remarked, "but he trains as hard as any I have ever seen, by all accounts."

"That is not the problem," Masoj groaned in frustration. There was something less tangible about Drizzt Do'Urden's character that truly irked the young Hun'ett. He couldn't recognize it now, because he had never witnessed it in any dark elf before, and because it was so very foreign to his own makeup. What bothered Masoj—and many other students and masters—was the fact that Drizzt excelled in all the fighting skills the drow elves most treasured but hadn't given up his passion in return. Drizzt had not paid the price that the rest of the drow children were made to sacrifice long before they had even entered the Academy.

"It is not important," Masoj said after several fruitless minutes of contemplation. "I will learn more of the young Do'Urden in time."

"His tutelage under you was finished, I had thought," said Alton. "He goes to Arach-Tinilith for the final six months of his training—quite inaccessible to you."

"We both graduate after those six months," Masoj explained. "We will share our indenture time in the patrol forces together."

"Many will share that time," Alton reminded him. "Dozens of groups patrol the corridors of the region. You may never even see Drizzt in all the years of your term."

"I already have arranged for us to serve in the same group," replied Masoj. He reached into his pocket and produced the onyx figurine of the magical panther.

"A mutual agreement between yourself and the young Do'Urden," Alton reasoned with a complimentary smile.

"It appears that Drizzt has become quite fond of my pet," Masoj chuckled.

"Too fond?" Alton warned. "You should watch your back for scimitars."

Masoj laughed aloud. "Perhaps our friend, Do'Urden, should watch his back for panther claws!"

# 16

# Sacrilege

"Last day," Drizzt breathed in relief as he donned his ceremonial robes. If the first six months of this final year, learning the subtleties of magic in Sorcere, had been the most enjoyable, these last six in the school of Lolth had been the least. Every day, Drizzt and his classmates had been subjected to endless eulogies to the Spider Queen, tales and prophecies of her power and of the rewards she bestowed upon loyal servants.

"Slaves" would have been a better word, Drizzt had come to realize, for nowhere in all this grand school to the drow deity had he heard anything synonymous with, or even hinting at, the word love. His people worshiped Lolth; the females of Menzoberranzan gave over their entire existence in her servitude. Their giving was wholly wrought of selfishness, though; a cleric of the Spider Queen aspired to the position of high priestess solely for the personal power that accompanied the title.

It all seemed so very wrong in Drizzt's heart.

Drizzt had drifted through the six months of Arach-Tinilith with his customary stoicism, keeping his eyes low and his mouth shut. Now, finally, he had come to the last day, the Ceremony of Graduation, an event most holy to the drow, and wherein, Vierna had promised him, he would come to understand the true glory of Lolth.

With tentative steps, Drizzt moved out from the shelter of his tiny, unadorned room. He worried that this ceremony had become his personal trial. Up to now, very little about the society around Drizzt had made any sense to him, and he wondered, despite his sister's assurances, whether the events of this day would allow him to see the world as his kin saw it. Drizzt's fears had taken a spiral twist, one rolling out from the other to surround him in a predicament be could not escape.

Perhaps, he worried, he truly feared that the day's events would fulfill Vierna's promise.

Drizzt shielded his eyes as he entered the circular ceremonial hall of Arach-Tinilith. A fire burned in the center of the room, in an eight-legged brazier that resembled, as everything in this place seemed to resemble, a spider. The headmistress of all the Academy, the matron mistress, and the other twelve high priestesses serving as instructors of Arach-Tinilith, including Drizzt's sister, sat cross-legged in a circle around the brazier. Drizzt and his classmates from the school of fighters stood along the wall behind them.

"*Ma ku!*" the matron mistress commanded, and all was silent save the crackle of the brazier's flames. The door to the room opened again, and a young cleric entered. She was to be the first graduate of Arach-Tinilith this year, Drizzt had been told, the finest student in the school of Lolth. Thus, she had been awarded the highest honors in this ceremony. She shrugged off her robes and walked naked through the ring of sitting priestesses to stand before the flames, her back to the matron mistress.

Drizzt bit his lip, embarrassed and a little excited. He had never seen a female in such a light before, and he suspected that the sweat on his brow was from more than the brazier's heat. A quick glance around the room told him that his classmates entertained similar ideas.

"*Bae-go si'n'ee calamay,*" the matron mistress whispered, and red smoke poured from the brazier, coloring the room in a hazy glow. It carried an aroma with it, rich and sickly sweet. As Drizzt breathed the scented air, he felt himself grow lighter and wondered if he soon would be floating off the floor.

The flames in the brazier suddenly roared higher, causing Drizzt to squint against the brightness and turn away. The clerics began a ritual chant, though the words were unfamiliar to Drizzt. He hardly paid them any heed, though, for he was too intent on holding his own thoughts in the overpowering swoon of the inebriating haze.

"*Glabrezu*," the matron mistress moaned, and Drizzt recognized the tone as a summons, the name of a denizen of the lower planes. He looked back to the events at hand and saw the matron mistress holding a single-tongued snake whip.

"Where did she get that?" Drizzt mumbled, then he realized that he had spoken aloud and hoped he hadn't disturbed the ceremony. He was comforted when he glanced around, for many of his classmates were mumbling to themselves, and some seemed hardly able to hold their balance.

"Call to it," the matron mistress instructed the naked student.

Tentatively, the young cleric spread her arms out wide and whispered, "*Glabrezu*."

The flames danced about the rim of the brazier. The smoke wafted into Drizzt's face, compelling him to inhale it. His legs tingled on the edge of numbness, yet they somehow felt more sensitive, more alive, than they ever had before.

"*Glabrezu*," he heard the student say again louder, and Drizzt heard, too, the roar of the flames. Brightness assaulted him, but somehow he didn't seem to care. His gaze roamed about the room, unable to find a focus, unable to place the strange, dancing sights in accord with the ritual's sounds.

He heard the high priestesses gasping and coaxing the student on, knowing the conjuring to be at hand. He heard the snap of the snake whip—another incentive?—and cries of "*Glabrezu!*" from the student. So primal, so powerful, were these screams that they cut through Drizzt and the other males in the room with an intensity they never would have believed possible.

The flames heard the call. They roared higher and higher and began to take shape. One sight caught the vision of all in the room now—caught it and held it fully. A giant head, a goat-horned dog, appeared within the flames, apparently studying this alluring young drow student who had dared to utter its name.

Somewhere beyond the other-planar form, the snake whip cracked again, and the female student repeated her call, her cry beckoning, praying.

The giant denizen of the lower planes stepped through the flames. The sheer unholy power of the creature stunned Drizzt. Glabrezu towered nine feet and seemed much more, with muscled arms ending in giant pincers instead of hands and a second set of smaller arms, normal arms, protruding from the front of its chest.

Drizzt's instincts told him to attack the monster and rescue the female student, but when he looked around for support, he found the matron mistress and the other teachers of the school back in their ritualistic chanting, this time with an excited edge permeating their every word.

Through all the haze and the daze, the tantalizing, dizzying aroma of the smoky red incense continued its assault on reality. Drizzt trembled, teetered on a narrow ledge of control, his gathering rage fighting the scented smoke's confusing allure. Instinctively, his hands went to the hilts of the scimitars on his belt.

Then a hand brushed against his leg.

He looked down to see a mistress, reclined and asking him to join her—a scene that had suddenly become general around the chamber.

The smoke continued its assault on him.

The mistress beckoned to him, her fingernails lightly scraping the skin of his leg.

Drizzt ran his fingers through his thick hair, trying to find some focal point in the dizziness. He did not like this loss of control, this mental numbness that stole the fine edge of his reflexes and alertness.

He liked even less the scene unfolding before him. The sheer wrongness of it assaulted his soul. He pulled away from the mistress's hopeful grasp and stumbled across the room, tripping over numerous entwined forms too engaged to take note of him. He made the exit as quickly as his wobbly legs could carry him, and he rushed out of the room, pointedly closing the door behind him.

Only the screams of the female student followed him. No stone or mental barricade could block them out.

Drizzt leaned heavily against the cool stone wall, grasping at his stomach.

He hadn't even paused to consider the implications of his actions; he knew only that he had to get out of that foul room.

Vierna then was beside him, her robe opened casually in the front. Drizzt, his head clearing, began to wonder about the price of his actions. The look on his sister's face, he noted with still more confusion, was not one of scorn.

"You prefer privacy," she said, her hand resting easily on Drizzt's shoulder. Vierna made no move to close her robe. "I understand," she said.

Drizzt grabbed her arm and pulled her away. "What insanity is this?" he demanded.

Vierna's face twisted as she came to understand her brother's true intentions in leaving the ceremony. "You refused a high priestess!" she snarled at him. "By the laws, she could kill you for your insolence."

"I do not even know her," Drizzt shot back. "I am expected to—"

"You are expected to do as you are instructed!"

"I care nothing for her," Drizzt stammered. He found he could not hold his hands steady.

"Do you think Zaknafein cared for Matron Malice?" Vierna replied, knowing that the reference to Drizzt's hero would surely sting him. Seeing that she had indeed wounded her brother, Vierna softened her expression and took his arm. "Come back," she purred, "into the room. There is still time."

Drizzt's cold glare stopped her as surely as the point of a scimitar.

"The Spider Queen is the deity of our people," Vierna sternly reminded him. "I am one of those who speaks her will."

"I would not be so proud of that," Drizzt retorted, clinging to his anger against the wave of very real fear that threatened to defeat his principled stand.

Vierna slapped him hard across the face. "Go back to the ceremony!" she demanded.

"Go kiss a spider," Drizzt replied. "And may its pincers tear your cursed tongue from your mouth."

It was Vierna now who could not hold her hands steady. "You should take care when you speak to a high priestess," she warned.

"Damn your Spider Queen!" Drizzt spat. "Though I am certain Lolth found damnation eons ago!"

"She brings us power!" Vierna shrieked.

"She steals everything that makes us worth more than the stone we walk upon!" Drizzt screamed back.

"Sacrilege!" Vierna sneered, the word rolling off her tongue like the whistle of the matron mistress's snake whip.

A climactic, anguished scream erupted from inside the room.

"Evil union," Drizzt muttered, looking away.

"There is a gain," Vierna replied, quickly back in control of her temper.

Drizzt cast an accusing glance her way. "Have you had a similar experience?"

"I am a high priestess," was her simple reply.

Darkness hovered all about Drizzt, outrage so intense that he nearly swooned. "Did it please you?" he spat.

"It brought me power," Vierna growled back. "You cannot understand the value."

"What did it cost you?"

Vierna's slap nearly knocked Drizzt from his feet. "Come with me," she said, grabbing the front of his robe. "There is a place I want to show to you."

They moved out from Arach-Tinilith and across the Academy's courtyard. Drizzt hesitated when they reached the pillars that marked the entrance to Tier Breche.

"l cannot pass between these," he reminded his sister. "I am not yet graduated from Melee-Magthere."

"A formality," Vierna replied, not slowing her pace at all. "I am a mistress of Arach-Tinilith; I have the power to graduate you."

Drizzt wasn't certain of the truth of Vierna's claim, but she was indeed a mistress of Arach-Tinilith. As much as Drizzt feared the edicts of the Academy, he didn't want to anger Vierna again.

He followed her down the wide stone stairs and out into the meandering roadways of the city proper.

"Home?" he dared to ask after a short while.

"Not yet," came the curt reply. Drizzt didn't press the point any further.

They veered off to the eastern end of the great cavern, across from the wall that held House Do'Urden, and came to the entrances of three small tunnels, all guarded by glowing statues of giant scorpions. Vierna paused for just a moment to consider which was the correct course, then led on again, down the smallest of the tunnels.

The minutes became an hour, and still they walked. The passage widened and soon led them into a twisting catacomb of crisscrossing corridors. Drizzt quickly lost track of the path behind them as they made their way through, but Vierna followed a predetermined course that she knew well.

Then, beyond a low archway, the floor suddenly dropped away and they found themselves on a narrow ledge overlooking a wide chasm. Drizzt looked at his sister curiously but held his question when he saw that she was deep in the concentration. She uttered a few simple commands, then tapped herself and Drizzt on the forehead.

"Come," she instructed, and she and Drizzt stepped off the ledge and levitated down to the chasm floor.

A thin mist, from some unseen hot pool or tar pit, hugged the stone. Drizzt could sense the danger here, and the evil. A brooding wickedness hung in the air as tangibly as the mist.

"Do not fear," Vierna signaled to him. "I have put a spell of masking upon us. They cannot see us."

"They?" Drizzt's hands asked, but even as he motioned in the code, he heard a scuttling off to the side. He followed Vierna's gaze down to a distant boulder and the wretched thing perched upon it.

At first, Drizzt thought it was a drow elf, and from the waist up, it was indeed, though bloated and pale. Its lower body, though, resembled a spider, with eight arachnid legs to support its frame. The creature held a bow ready in its hands but seemed confused, as though it could not discern what had entered its lair.

Vierna was pleased by the disgust on her brother's face as he viewed the thing. "Look upon it well, younger brother," she signaled. "Behold the fate of those who anger the Spider Queen."

"What is it?" Drizzt signaled back quickly.

"A drider," Vierna whispered in his ear. Then, back in the silent code, she added, "Lolth is not a merciful deity."

Drizzt watched, mesmerized, as the drider shifted its position on the boulder, searching for the intruders. Drizzt couldn't tell if it was a male or female, so bloated was its torso, but he knew that it didn't matter. The creature was not a natural creation and would leave no descendants behind, whatever its gender. It was a tormented body, nothing more, hating itself, in all probability, more than everything else around it.

"I am merciful," Vierna continued silently, though she knew her brother's attention was fully on the drider. She rested back flat against the stone wall.

Drizzt spun on her, suddenly realizing her intent.

Then Vierna sank into the stone. "Goodbye, little brother," came her final call. "This is a better fate than you deserve."

"No!" Drizzt growled, and he clawed at the empty wall until an arrow sliced into his leg. The scimitars flashed out in his hands as he spun back to face the danger. The drider took aim for a second shot.

Drizzt meant to dive to the side, to the protection of another boulder, but his wounded leg immediately fell numb and useless. Poison.

Drizzt just got one blade up in time to deflect the second arrow, and he dropped to one knee to clutch at his wound. He could feel the cold poison making its way through his limb, but he stubbornly snapped off the arrow shaft and turned his attention back to the attacker. He would have to worry about the wound later, would have to hope that he could tend to it in time. Right now, his only concern was to get out of the chasm.

He turned to flee, to seek a sheltered spot where he could levitate back up to the ledge, but he found himself face-to-face with another drider.

An axe sliced by his shoulder, barely missing its mark. Drizzt blocked the return blow and launched his second scimitar into a thrust, which the drider stopped with a second axe.

Drizzt was composed now, and was confident that he could defeat this foe, even with one leg limiting his mobility—until an arrow cracked into his back.

Drizzt lurched forward under the weight of the blow, but managed to parry another attack from the drider before him. Drizzt dropped to his knees and fell face-down.

When the axe-wielding drider, thinking Drizzt dead, started toward him, Drizzt kicked into a roll that put him squarely under the creature's bulbous belly. He plunged his scimitar up with all his strength, then curled back under the deluge of spidery fluids.

The wounded drider tried to scurry away but fell to the side, its insides draining out onto the stone floor. Still, Drizzt had no hope. His arms, too, were numb now, and when the other wretched creature descended upon him, he could not hope to fight it off. He struggled to cling to consciousness, searching for some way out, battling to the bitter end. His eyelids became heavy. . . .

Then Drizzt felt a hand grab his robe, and he was roughly lifted to his feet and slammed against the stone wall.

He opened his eyes to see his sister's face.

"He lives," Drizzt heard her say. "We must get him back quickly and tend to his wounds"

Another figure moved in front of him.

"I thought this the best way," Vierna apologized.

"We cannot afford to lose him," came an unemotional reply. Drizzt recognized the voice from his past. He fought through the blur and forced his eyes to focus.

"Malice," he whispered. "Mother."

Her enraged punch brought him into a clearer mindset.

"Matron Malice!" she growled, her angry scowl only an inch from Drizzt's face. "Do not ever forget that!"

To Drizzt, her coldness rivaled the poison's, and his relief at seeing her faded away as quickly as it had flooded through him.

"You must learn your place!" Malice roared, reiterating the command that had haunted Drizzt all of his young life. "Hear my words," she demanded, and Drizzt heard them keenly. "Vierna brought you to this place to have you killed. She showed you mercy." Malice cast a disappointed glance at her daughter.

"I understand the will of the Spider Queen better than she," the matron continued, her spittle spraying Drizzt with every word. "If ever you speak ill of Lolth, our goddess, again, I will take you back to this place myself! But not to kill you; that would be too easy." She jerked Drizzt's head to the side so that he could look upon the grotesque remains of the drider he had killed.

"You will come back here," Malice assured him, "to become a drider."

# Part Four

## Guenhwyvar

What eyes are these that see
The pain I know in my innermost soul?
What eyes are these that see
The twisted strides of my kindred,
Led on in the wake of
toys unbridled:
Arrow, bolt, and sword tip?

Yours . . . aye, yours,
Straight run and muscled spring,
Soft on padded paws, sheathed claws,
Weapons rested for their need,
Stained not by frivolous blood
Or murderous deceit.

Face to face, my mirror;
Reflection in a still pool by light.
Would that I might keep that image
Upon this face mine own.

Would that I might keep that heart
Within my breast untainted.

Hold tight to the proud honor of your spirit,
Mighty Guenhwyvar,
And hold tight to my side,
My dearest friend.

–Drizzt Do'Urden

# 17
# Homecoming

Drizzt was graduated—formally—on schedule and with the highest honors in his class. Perhaps Matron Malice had whispered into the right ears, smoothing over her son's indiscretions, but Drizzt suspected that more likely none of those present at the Ceremony of Graduation even remembered that he had left.

He moved through the decorated gate of House Do'Urden, drawing stares from the common soldiery, and over to the cavern floor below the balcony. "So I am home," he remarked under his breath, "for whatever that means." After what had happened in the drider lair, Drizzt wondered if he would ever view House Do'Urden as his home again. Matron Malice was expecting him. He didn't dare arrive late.

"It is good that you are home," Briza said to him when she saw him rise up over the balcony's railing.

Drizzt stepped tentatively through the entryway beside his oldest sister, trying to get a firm grasp on his surroundings. Home, Briza called it, but to Drizzt, House Do'Urden seemed as unfamiliar as the Academy had on his first day as a student. Ten years was not such a long time in the centuries of life a drow elf might know, but to Drizzt, more than the decade of absence now separated him from this place.

Maya joined them in the great corridor leading to the chapel anteroom.

"Greetings, Prince Drizzt," she said, and Drizzt couldn't tell if she was being sarcastic or not. "We have heard of the honors you achieved at Melee-Magthere. Your skill did House Do'Urden proud." In spite of her words, Maya could not hide a derisive chuckle as she finished the thought. "Glad, I am, that you did not become drider food."

Drizzt's glare stole the smile from her face.

Maya and Briza exchanged concerned glances. They knew of the punishment Vierna had put upon their younger brother, and of the vicious scolding he had received at the hands of Matron Malice. They each cautiously rested a hand on their snake whips, not knowing how foolish their dangerous young brother might have become.

It was not Matron Malice or Drizzt's sisters that now had Drizzt measuring every step before he took it. He knew where he stood with his mother and knew what he had to do to keep her appeased. There was another member of the family, though, that evoked both confusion and anger in Drizzt. Of all his kin, only Zaknafein pretended to be what he was not. As Drizzt made his way to the chapel, he glanced anxiously down every side passage, wondering when Zak would make his appearance.

"How long before you leave for patrol?" Maya asked, pulling Drizzt from his contemplations.

"Two days," Drizzt replied absently, his eyes still darting from shadow to shadow. Then he was at the anteroom door, with no sign of Zak. Perhaps the weapons master was within, standing beside Malice.

"We know of your indiscretions," Briza snapped, suddenly cold, as she placed her hand on the latch to the anteroom's door. Drizzt was not surprised by her outburst. He was beginning to expect such explosions from the high priestesses of the Spider Queen.

"Why could you not just enjoy the pleasures of the ceremony?" Maya added. "We are fortunate that the mistresses and the matron of the Academy were too involved in their own excitement to note your movements. You would have brought shame upon our entire house!"

"You might have placed Matron Malice in Lolth's disfavor," Briza was quick to add.

The best thing I could ever do for her, Drizzt thought. He quickly dismissed the notion, remembering Briza's uncanny proficiency at reading minds.

"Let us hope he did not," Maya said grimly to her sister. "The tides of war hang thick in the air."

"I have learned my place," Drizzt assured them. He bowed low. "Forgive me, my sisters, and know that the truth of the drow world is fast opening before my young eyes. Never will I disappoint House Do'Urden in such a way again."

So pleased were his sisters at the proclamation that the ambiguity of Drizzt's words slipped right past them. Then Drizzt, not wanting to push his luck too far, also slipped past them, making his way through the door, noting with relief that Zaknafein was not in attendance.

"All praises to the Spider Queen!" Briza yelled after him.

Drizzt paused and turned to meet her gaze. He bowed low a second time. "As it should be," he muttered.

⚔ ⚔ ⚔ ⚔ ⚔

Creeping behind the small group, Zak had studied Drizzt's every move, trying to measure the toll a decade at the Academy had exacted on the young fighter.

Gone now was the customary smile that lit Drizzt's face. Gone, too, Zak supposed, was the innocence that had kept this one apart from the rest of Menzoberranzan.

Zak leaned back heavily against the wall in a side passage. He had caught only portions of the conversation at the anteroom door. Most clearly he had heard Drizzt's heartfelt accord with Briza's honoring of Lolth.

"What have I done?" the weapons master asked himself. He looked back around the bend in the main corridor, but the door to the anteroom had already closed.

"Truly, when I look upon the drow—the drow warrior!—that was my most treasured, I shame for my cowardice," Zak lamented. "What has Drizzt lost that I might have saved?"

He drew his smooth sword from its scabbard, his sensitive fingers running the length of the razor edge. "A finer blade you would be had you tasted the blood of Drizzt Do'Urden, to deny this world, our world, another soul for its taking, to free that one from the unending torments of life!" He lowered the weapon's tip to the floor.

"But I am a coward," he said. "I have failed in the one act that could have brought meaning to my pitiful existence. The secondboy of House Do'Urden lives, it would appear, but Drizzt Do'Urden, my Two-hands, is long dead." Zak looked back to the emptiness where Drizzt had been standing, the weapons master's expression suddenly a grimace. "Yet this pretender lives.

"A drow warrior."

Zak's weapon clanged to the stone floor and his head slumped down to be caught by the embrace of his open palms, the only shield Zaknafein Do'Urden had ever found.

⚔ ⚔ ⚔ ⚔ ⚔

Drizzt spent the next day at rest, mostly in his room, trying to keep out of the way of the other members of his immediate family. Malice had dismissed him without a word in their initial meeting, but Drizzt did not want to confront her again. Likewise, he had little to say to Briza and Maya, fearing that sooner or later they would begin to understand the true connotations of his continuing stream of blasphemous responses. Most of all, though, Drizzt did not want to see Zaknafein, the mentor he had once thought of as his salvation against the realities around him, the one glowing light in the darkness that was Menzoberranzan.

That, too, Drizzt believed, had been only a lie.

On his second day home, when Narbondel, the timeclock of the city, had just begun its cycle of light, the door to Drizzt's small chamber swung open and Briza walked in. "An audience with Matron Malice," she said grimly.

A thousand thoughts rushed through Drizzt's mind as he grabbed his boots and followed his oldest sister down the passageways to the house chapel. Had Malice and the others discovered his true feelings toward their evil deity? What punishments did they now have waiting for him?

Unconsciously, Drizzt eyed the spider carvings on the chapel's arched entrance.

"You should be more familiar and more at ease with this place," Briza scolded, noting his discomfort. "It is the place of our people's highest glories."

Drizzt lowered his gaze and did not respond—and was careful not to even think of the many stinging retorts he felt in his heart.

His confusion doubled when they entered the chapel, for Rizzen, Maya, and Zaknafein stood before the matron mother, as expected. Beside them, though, stood Dinin and Vierna.

"We are all present," Briza said, taking her place at her mother's side.

"Kneel," Malice commanded, and the whole family fell to its knees. The matron mother paced slowly around them all, each pointedly dropping his or her eyes in reverence, or just in common sense, as the great lady walked by.

Malice stopped beside Drizzt. "You are confused by the presence of Dinin and Vierna," she said. Drizzt looked up at her. "Do you not yet understand the subtle methods of our survival?"

"I had thought that my brother and sister were to continue on at the Academy," Drizzt explained.

"That would not be to our advantage," Malice replied.

"Does it not bring a house strength to have mistresses and masters seated at the Academy?" Drizzt dared to ask.

"It does," replied Malice, "but it separates the power. You have heard tidings of war?"

"I have heard hinting of trouble," said Drizzt, looking over at Vierna, "though nothing more tangible."

"Hinting?" Malice huffed, angered that her son could not understand the importance. "They are more than most houses ever hear before the blade falls!" She spun away from Drizzt and addressed the whole group. "The rumors hold truth," she declared.

"Who?" asked Briza. "What house conspires against House Do'Urden?"

"None behind us in rank," Dinin replied, though the question had not been asked to him and it was not his place to speak unbidden.

"How do you know this?" Malice asked, letting the oversight pass. Malice understood Dinin's value and knew that his contributions to this discussion would be important.

"We are the ninth house of the city," Dinin reasoned, "but among our ranks we claim four high priestesses, two of them former mistresses of Arach-Tinilith." He looked at Zak. "We have, as well, two former masters of Melee-Magthere, and Drizzt was awarded the highest laurels from the school of fighters. Our soldiers number nearly four hundred, all skilled and battle-tested. Only a few houses claim more."

"What is your point?" Briza asked sharply.

"We are the ninth house," Dinin laughed, "but few above us could defeat us. . . ."

"And none behind," Matron Malice finished for him. "You show good judgment, Elderboy. I have come to the same conclusions."

"One of the great houses fears House Do'Urden," Vierna concluded. "It needs us gone to protect its own position."

"That is my belief," Malice answered. "An uncommon practice, for family wars usually are initiated by the lower-ranking house, desiring a better position within the city hierarchy."

"Then we must take great care," Briza said.

Drizzt listened carefully to their words, trying to make sense of it all. His eyes never left Zaknafein, though, who knelt impassively at the side. What did the callous weapons master think of all this? Drizzt wondered. Did the thought of such a war thrill him, that he might be able to kill more dark elves?

Whatever his feelings, Zak gave no outward clue. He sat quietly and by all appearances was not even listening to the conversation.

"It would not be Baenre," Briza said, her words sounding like a plea for confirmation. "Certainly we have not yet become a threat to them!"

"We must hope you are correct," Malice replied grimly, remembering vividly her tour of the ruling house. "Likely, it is one of the weaker houses above us, fearing its own unsteady position. I have not yet been able to learn any incriminating information against any in particular, so we must prepare for the worst. Thus, I have called Vierna and Dinin back to my side."

"If we learn of our enemies. . . ." Drizzt began impulsively. All eyes snapped upon him. It was bad enough for the elderboy to speak without being addressed, but for the secondboy, just graduated from the Academy, the act could be considered blasphemous.

Wanting all perspectives, Matron Malice again let the oversight pass. "Continue," she prompted.

"If we discover which house plots against us," Drizzt said quietly, "could we not expose it?"

"To what end?" Briza snarled at him. "Conspiracy without action is no crime."

"Then might we use reason?" Drizzt pressed, continuing against the barrage of incredulous glares that came at him from every face in the room—except from Zak's. "If we are the stronger, then let them submit without battle. Rank House Do'Urden as it should be and let the assumed threat to the weaker house be ended."

Malice grabbed Drizzt by the front of his cloak and heaved him to his feet. "I forgive your foolish thoughts," she growled, "this time!" She dropped him back to the floor, and the silent reprimands of his siblings descended upon him.

Again, though, Zak's expression did not match the others in the room. Indeed, Zak put a hand up over his mouth to hide his amusement. Perhaps there remained a bit of the Drizzt Do'Urden he had known, he dared to hope. Perhaps the Academy had not fully tainted the young fighter's spirit.

Malice whirled on the rest of the family, simmering fury and lust glowing in her eyes. "This is not the time to fear. This," she cried, a slender finger pointing out from in front of her face, "is the time to dream! We are House Do'Urden, Daermon N'a'shezbaernon, of power beyond the understanding of the great houses. We are the unknown entity of this war. We hold every advantage!

"Ninth house?" she laughed. "In short time, only seven houses will remain ahead of us!"

"What of the patrol?" Briza cut in. "Are we to allow the secondboy to go off alone, exposed?"

"The patrol will begin our advantage," the conniving matron explained. "Drizzt will go, and included in his group will be a member of at least four of the houses above us."

"One may strike at him," Briza reasoned.

"No," Malice assured her. "Our enemies in the coming war would not reveal themselves so clearly—not yet. The appointed assassin would have to defeat two Do'Urdens in such a confrontation."

"Two?" asked Vierna.

"Again, Lolth has shown us her favor," explained Malice. "Dinin will lead Drizzt's patrol group."

The elderboy's eyes lit up at the news. "Then Drizzt and I might become the assassins in this conflict," he purred.

The smile disappeared from the matron mother's face. "You will not strike without my consent," she warned in a tone so cold that Dinin fully understood the consequences of disobedience, "as you have done in the past."

Drizzt did not miss the reference to Nalfein, his murdered brother. His mother knew! Malice had done nothing to punish her murderous son. Now Drizzt's hand went up to his face, to hide an expression of horror that only could have brought him trouble in this setting.

"You are there to learn," Matron Malice said to Dinin, "to protect your brother, as Drizzt is there to protect you. Do not destroy our advantage for the gain of a single kill." An evil smile found its way back onto her bone-hued face. "But, if you learn of our enemy, . . ." she said.

"If the proper opportunity presents itself, . . ." Briza finished, guessing her mother's wicked thoughts and throwing an equally vile smile the matron's way.

Malice looked upon her eldest daughter with approval. Briza would prove a fine successor for the house!

Dinin's smile became wide and lascivious. Nothing pleased the elderboy of House Do'Urden more than the opportunity for an assassination.

"Go, then, my family," Malice said. "Remember that unfriendly eyes are upon us, watching our every move, waiting for the time to strike."

Zak was the first out of the chapel, as always, this time with an added spring in his step. It wasn't the prospect of fighting another war that guided his moves, though the thought of killing more clerics of the Spider Queen certainly pleased him. Rather, Drizzt's display of naiveté, his continued misconceptions of the common weal of drow existence, brought Zak hope.

Drizzt watched him go, thinking Zak's strides reflected his desire to kill. Drizzt didn't know whether to follow and confront the weapons master here and now or to let it pass, to shrug it away as readily as he had dismissed most of the cruel world around him. The decision was made for him when Matron Malice stepped in front of him and kept him in the chapel.

"To you, I say this," she began when they were alone. "You have heard the mission I placed upon your shoulders. I will not tolerate failure!"

Drizzt shrank back from the power of her voice.

"Protect your brother," came the grim warning, "or I shall give you to Lolth for judgment."

Drizzt understood the implications, but the matron took the pleasure to spell them out anyway.

"You would not enjoy your life as a drider."

⚔ ⚔ ⚔ ⚔ ⚔

A lightning blast cut across the still black waters of the underground lake, searing the heads of the approaching water trolls. Sounds of battle echoed through the cavern.

Drizzt had one monster—scrags, they were called—cornered on a small peninsula, blocking the wretched thing's path back to the water. Normally, a single drow faced off evenly against a water troll would not have the advantage, but as the others of his patrol group had come to see in the past few tendays, Drizzt was no ordinary young drow.

The scrag came on, oblivious to its peril. A single, blinding movement from Drizzt lopped off the creature's reaching arms. Drizzt moved in quickly for the kill, knowing too well the regenerative powers of trolls.

Then another scrag slipped out of the water at his back.

Drizzt had expected this, but he gave no outward indication that he saw the second scrag coming. He kept his concentration ahead of him, driving deep slashes into the maimed and all but defenseless troll's torso.

Just as the monster behind him was about to latch its claws onto him, Drizzt fell to his knees and cried, "Now!"

The concealed panther, crouched in the shadows at the peninsula's base, did not hesitate. One great stride brought Guenhwyvar into position, and it sprang, crashing heavily onto the unsuspecting scrag, tearing the life from the thing before it could respond to the attack.

Drizzt finished off his troll and turned to admire the panther's work. He extended his hand, and the great cat nuzzled it. How well the two fighters had come to know each other! thought Drizzt.

Another blast of lightning thundered in, this one close enough to steal Drizzt's sight.

"Guenhwyvar!" Masoj Hun'ett, the bolt's caster, cried. "To my side!"

The panther managed to brush against Drizzt's leg as it moved to obey. When his vision returned, Drizzt walked off in the other direction, not wanting to view the scolding that Guenhwyvar always seemed to receive when he and the cat worked together.

Masoj watched Drizzt's back as he went, wanting to put a third bolt right between the young Do'Urden's shoulder blades. The wizard of House Hun'ett did not miss the specter of Dinin Do'Urden, off to the side, watching with more than casual glances.

"Learn your loyalties!" Masoj snarled at Guenhwyvar. Too often, the panther left the wizard's side to join in combat with Drizzt. Masoj knew that the cat was better complemented by the moves of a fighter, but he knew, too, the vulnerability of a wizard involved in spellcasting. Masoj wanted Guenhwyvar at his side, protecting him from enemies—he shot another glance at Dinin—and "friends" alike.

He threw the statuette to the ground at his feet. "Begone!" he commanded.

In the distance, Drizzt had engaged another scrag and made short work of it as well. Masoj shook his head as he watched the display of swordsmanship. Every day, Drizzt grew stronger.

"Give the order to kill him soon, Matron SiNafay," Masoj whispered. The young wizard did not know how much longer he would be able to carry out the task. Masoj wondered whether he could win the fight even now.

⚔ ⚔ ⚔ ⚔ ⚔

Drizzt shielded his eyes as he struck a torch to seal a dead troll's wounds. Only fire ensured that trolls would not recuperate, even from the grave.

The other battles had died away as well, Drizzt noted, and he saw the flames of torches springing up all across the bank of the lake. He wondered if all of his twelve drow companions had survived, though he also wondered if he truly cared. Others were more than ready to take their places.

Drizzt knew that the only companion who really mattered—Guenhwyvar—was safely back in its home on the Astral Plane.

"Form a guard!" came Dinin's echoing command as the slaves, goblins, and orcs moved in to search for troll treasure, and to salvage whatever they might of the scrags.

When the fires had consumed the scrag he'd set ablaze, Drizzt dipped his torch in the black water, then paused for a moment to let his eyes readjust to the darkness. "Another day," he said softly, "another enemy defeated."

He liked the excitement of patrolling, the thrill of the edge of danger, and the knowledge that he was now putting his weapons to use against vile monsters.

Even here, though, Drizzt could not escape the lethargy that had come to pervade his life, the general resignation that marked his every step. For, though his battles these days were fought against the horrors of the Underdark, monsters killed of necessity, Drizzt had not forgotten the meeting in the chapel of House Do'Urden.

He knew that his scimitars soon would be put to use against the flesh of drow elves.

⚔ ⚔ ⚔ ⚔ ⚔

Zaknafein looked out over Menzoberranzan, as he so often did when Drizzt's patrol group was out of the city. Zak was torn between wanting to sneak out of the house to fight at Drizzt's side, and hoping that the patrol would return with the news that Drizzt had been slain.

Would Zak ever find the answer to the dilemma of the youngest Do'Urden? he wondered. Zak knew that he could not leave the house; Matron Malice was keeping a very close eye on him. She sensed his anguish over Drizzt, Zak knew, and she most definitely did not approve. Zak was often her lover, but they shared little other than that.

Zak thought back to the battles he and Malice had fought over Vierna, another child of common concern, centuries before. Vierna was a female, her fate sealed from the moment of her birth, and Zak could do nothing to halt the assault of the Spider Queen's overwhelming religion.

Did Malice fear that he might have better luck influencing the actions of a male child? Apparently the matron did, but even Zak was not so certain if her fears were justified; even he couldn't measure his influence over Drizzt.

He peered out over the city now, silently watching for the patrol group's return—waiting, as always, for Drizzt's safe return, but secretly hoping, that his dilemma would be ended by the claws and fangs of a lurking monster.

# 18
# The Back Room

"My greetings, Faceless One," the high priestess said, pushing past Alton into his private chambers in Sorcere.

"And mine to you, Mistress Vierna," Alton replied, trying to keep the fear out of his voice. Vierna Do'Urden coming to see him at this time had to be more than coincidence. "What act has brought me the honor of a visit from a mistress of Arach-Tinilith?"

"No longer a mistress," said Vierna. "I have returned to my home."

Alton paused to consider the news. He knew that Dinin Do'Urden had also resigned his position at the Academy.

"Matron Malice has brought her family back together," Vierna continued. "There are stirrings of war. You have heard them, no doubt?"

"Just rumors," Alton stuttered, now beginning to understand why Vierna had come to call on him. House Do'Urden had used the Faceless One before in its plotting—in its attempt to assassinate Alton! Now, with rumors of war whispered throughout Menzoberranzan, Matron Malice was reestablishing her network of spies and assassins.

"You know of them?" Vierna asked sharply.

"I have heard little," Alton breathed, careful now not to anger the powerful female. "Not enough to report to your house. I did not even suspect that House Do'Urden was involved until now, when you informed me." Alton could only hope that Vierna had no detection spell aimed at his words.

Vierna relaxed, apparently appeased by the explanation. "Listen more carefully to the rumors, Faceless One," she said. "My brother and I have left the Academy; you are to be the eyes and ears of House Do'Urden in this place."

"But . . ." Alton stuttered.

Vierna held up a hand to stop him. "We know of our failure in our last transaction," she said. She bowed low, something a high priestess rarely did to a male. "Matron Malice sends her deepest apologies that the unguent you received for the assassination of Alton DeVir did not restore the features to your face."

Alton nearly choked on the words, now understanding why an unknown messenger had delivered the jar of healing salve some thirty years before. The cloaked figure was an agent of House Do'Urden, come to repay the Faceless One for his assassination of Alton! Of course, Alton had never even tried the unguent. With his luck, it would have worked, and would have restored the features of Alton DeVir.

"This time, your payment cannot fail," Vierna went on, though Alton, too caught up in the irony of it all, hardly listened. "House Do'Urden possesses a wizard's staff but no wizard worthy to wield it. It belonged to Nalfein, my brother, who died in the victory over DeVir."

Alton wanted to strike out at her. Even he wasn't that stupid, though.

"If you can discern which house plots against House Do'Urden," Vierna promised, "the staff will be yours! A treasure indeed for such a small act."

"I will do what I can," Alton replied, having no other response to the incredible offer.

"That is all Matron Malice asks of you," said Vierna, and she left the wizard, quite certain that House Do'Urden had secured a capable agent within the Academy.

⚔ ⚔ ⚔ ⚔ ⚔

"Dinin and Vierna Do'Urden have resigned their positions," said Alton excitedly as the diminutive matron mother came to him later that same evening.

"This is already known to me," replied SiNafay Hun'ett.

She looked around disdainfully at the littered and scorched room, then took a seat at the small table.

"There is more," Alton said quickly, not wanting SiNafay to get upset about being disturbed over old news. "I have had a visitor this day, Mistress Vierna Do'Urden!"

"She suspects?" Matron SiNafay growled.

"No, no!" Alton replied. "Quite the opposite. House Do'Urden wishes to employ me as a spy, as it once employed the Faceless One to assassinate me!"

SiNafay paused for a moment, stunned, then issued a laugh straight from her belly. "Ah, the ironies of our lives!" she roared.

"I had heard that Dinin and Vierna were sent to the Academy only to oversee the education of their younger brother," remarked Alton.

"An excellent cover," SiNafay replied. "Vierna and Dinin were sent as spies for the ambitious Matron Malice. My compliments to her."

"Now they suspect trouble," Alton stated, sitting opposite his matron mother.

"They do," agreed SiNafay. "Masoj patrols with Drizzt, but House Do'Urden has also managed to plant Dinin in the group."

"Then Masoj is in danger," reasoned Alton.

"No," said SiNafay. "House Do'Urden does not know that House Hun'ett perpetrates the threat against it, else it would not have come to you for information. Matron Malice knows your identity."

A look of terror crossed Alton's face.

"Not your true identity," SiNafay laughed at him. "She knows the Faceless One as Gelroos Hun'ett, and she would not have come to a Hun'ett if she suspected our house."

"Then we have an excellent opportunity to throw House Do'Urden into chaos!" Alton cried. "If I implicate another house, even Baenre, perhaps, our position will be strengthened." He chuckled at the possibilities. "Malice will reward me with a staff of great power—a weapon I will turn against her at the proper moment!"

"Matron Malice!" SiNafay corrected sternly. Even though she and Malice were soon to be open enemies, SiNafay would not permit a male to show such disrespect to a matron mother. "Do you really believe that you could carry out such a deception?"

"When Mistress Vierna returns . . ."

"You will not deal with a lesser priestess with such valued information, foolish DeVir. You will face Matron Malice herself, a formidable foe. If she sees through your lies, do you know what she will do to your body?"

Alton gulped audibly. "I am willing to take the risk," he said, crossing his arms resolutely on the table.

"What of House Hun'ett when the biggest lie is revealed?" SiNafay asked. "What advantage will we enjoy when Matron Malice knows the Faceless One's true identity?"

"I understand," Alton answered, crestfallen but unable to refute SiNafay's logic. "Then what are we to do? What am I to do?"

Matron SiNafay was already considering their next moves. "You will resign your tenure," she said at length. "Return to House Hun'ett, within my protection."

"Such an act might also implicate House Hun'ett to Matron Malice," Alton reasoned.

"It may," replied SiNafay, "but it is the safest route. I will go to Matron Malice in feigned anger, telling her to leave House Hun'ett out of her troubles. If she wishes to make an informant of a member of my family, then she should come to me for permission—though I'll not grant it this time!"

SiNafay smiled at the possibilities of such an encounter. "My anger, my fear, alone could implicate a greater house against House Do'Urden, even a conspiracy between more than one house," she said, obviously enjoying the added benefits. "Matron Malice will certainly have much to think about, and much to worry about!"

Alton hadn't even heard SiNafay's last comments. The words about granting her permission "this time" had brought a disturbing notion into his mind. "And did she?" he dared to ask, though his words were barely audible.

"What do you mean?" asked SiNafay, not following his thoughts.

"Did Matron Malice come to you?" Alton continued, frightened but needing an answer. "Thirty years ago. Did Matron SiNafay grant her permission for Gelroos Hun'ett to become an agent, an assassin to complete House DeVir's elimination?"

A wide smile spread across SiNafay's face, but it vanished in the blink of an eye as she threw the table across the room, grabbed Alton by the front of his robes, and pulled him roughly to within an inch of her scowling visage.

"Never confuse personal feelings with politics!" the tiny but obviously strong matron growled, her tone carrying the unmistakable weight of an open threat. "And never ask me such a question again!"

She threw Alton to the floor but didn't release him from her penetrating glare.

Alton had known all along that he was merely a pawn in the intrigue between House Hun'ett and House Do'Urden, a necessary link for Matron SiNafay to carry out her treacherous plans. Every now and, though, Alton's personal grudge against House Do'Urden caused him to forget his lowly place in this conflict. Looking up now at SiNafay's bared power, he realized that he had overstepped the bounds of his position.

⚔ ⚔ ⚔ ⚔ ⚔

At the back end of the mushroom grove, the southern wall of the cavern that housed Menzoberranzan, was a small, heavily guarded cave. Beyond the ironbound doors stood a single room, used only for gatherings of the city's eight ruling matron mothers.

The smoke of a hundred sweet-smelling candles permeated the air; the matron mothers liked it that way. After almost half a century of studying scrolls in the candlelight of Sorcere, Alton did not mind the light, but he was indeed uncomfortable in the chamber. He sat at the back end of a spider-shaped table, in a small, unadorned chair reserved for guests of the council. Between the table's eight hairy legs were the ruling matron mothers' thrones, all jeweled and dazzling in the candlelight.

The matrons filed in, pompous and wicked, casting belittling glares at the male. SiNafay, at Alton's side, put a hand on his knee and gave him a reassuring wink. She would not have dared to request a gathering of the ruling council if she was not certain of the worthiness of her news. The ruling matron mothers viewed their seats as honorary in nature and did not appreciate being brought together except in times of crisis.

At the head of the spider table sat Matron Baenre, the most powerful figure in all of Menzoberranzan, an ancient and withered female with malicious eyes and a mouth unaccustomed to smiles.

"We are gathered, SiNafay," Baenre said when all eight members had found their appointed chairs. "For what reason have you summoned the council?"

"To discuss a punishment," SiNafay replied.

"Punishment?" Matron Baenre echoed, confused. The recent years had been unusually quiet in the drow city, without an incident since the Teken'duis Freth conflict. To the First Matron's knowledge, no acts had been committed that might require a punishment, certainly none so blatant as to force the ruling council to action. "What individual deserves this?"

"Not an individual," explained Matron SiNafay. She glanced around at her peers, measuring their interest. "A house," she said bluntly. "Daermon N'a'shezbaernon, House Do'Urden." Several gasps of disbelief came in reply, as SiNafay had expected.

"House Do'Urden?" Matron Baenre questioned, surprised that any would implicate Matron Malice. By all of Baenre's knowledge, Malice remained in high regard with the Spider Queen, and House Do'Urden had recently placed two instructors in the Academy.

"For what crime do you dare to charge House Do'Urden?" asked one of the other matrons.

"Are these words of fear, SiNafay?" Matron Baenre had to ask. Several of the ruling matrons had expressed concern about House Do'Urden. It was well known that Matron Malice desired a seat on the ruling council, and, by all measures of the power of her house, she seemed destined to get it.

"I have appropriate cause," SiNafay insisted.

"The others seem to doubt you," replied Matron Baenre. "You should explain your accusation—quickly, if you value your reputation."

SiNafay knew that more than her reputation was at stake; in

Menzoberranzan, a false accusation was a crime on par with murder. "We all remember the fall of House DeVir," SiNafay began. "Seven of us now gathered sat upon the ruling council beside Matron Ginafae DeVir."

"House DeVir is no more," Matron Baenre reminded her.

"Because of House Do'Urden," SiNafay said bluntly.

This time the gasps came out as open anger.

"How dare you speak such words?" came one reply.

"Thirty years!" came another. "The issue has been forgotten!"

Matron Baenre quieted them all before the clamor rose into violent action—a not uncommon occurrence in the council chamber. "SiNafay," she said through the dry sneer on her lips. "One cannot make such an accusation; one cannot discuss such beliefs openly so long after the event! You know our ways. If House Do'Urden did indeed commit this act, as you insist, it deserves our compliments, not our punishment, for it carried it through to perfection. House DeVir is no more, I say. It does not exist!"

Alton shifted uneasily, caught somewhere between rage and despair. SiNafay was far from dismayed, though; this was going exactly as she had envisioned and hoped.

"Oh, but it does!" she responded, rising to her feet. She pulled the hood from Alton's head. "In this person!"

"Gelroos?" asked Matron Baenre, not understanding.

"Not Gelroos," SiNafay replied. "Gelroos Hun'ett died the night House DeVir died. This male, Alton DeVir, assumed Gelroos's identity and position, hiding from further attacks by House Do'Urden!"

Baenre whispered some instructions to the matron at her right side, then waited as she went through the semantics of a spell. Baenre motioned for SiNafay to return to her seat then faced Alton.

"Speak your name," Baenre commanded.

"I am Alton DeVir," Alton said, gaining strength from the identity he had waited so very long to proclaim, "son of Matron Ginafae and a student of Sorcere on the night House Do'Urden attacked."

Baenre looked to the matron at her side.

"He speaks the truth," the matron assured her. Whispers sprang up all around the spider table, of amusement more than anything else.

"That is why I summoned the ruling council," SiNafay quickly explained.

"Very well, SiNafay," said Matron Baenre. "My compliments to you, Alton DeVir, on your resourcefulness and ability to survive. For a male, you have shown great courage and wisdom. Surely you both know that the council cannot exact punishment upon a house for a deed committed so long ago. Why would we so desire? Matron Malice Do'Urden sits in the favor of the Spider Queen; her house shows great promise. You must reveal to us greater need if you wish any punishment against House Do'Urden."

"I do not wish such a thing," SiNafay quickly replied. "This matter, thirty years removed, is no longer in the realm of the ruling council. House Do'Urden does indeed show promise, my peers, with four high priestesses and a host of other weapons, not the least of which being their secondboy, Drizzt, first graduate of his class." She had purposely mentioned Drizzt, knowing that the name would strike a wound in Matron Baenre. Baenre's own prized son, Berg'inyon, had spent the last nine years ranked behind the wonderful young Do'Urden.

"Then why have you bothered us?" Matron Baenre demanded, an unmistakable edge in her voice.

"To ask you to close your eyes," SiNafay purred. "Alton is a Hun'ett now, under my protection. He demands vengeance for the act committed against his family, and, as a surviving member of the attacked family, he has the right of accusation."

"House Hun'ett will stand beside him?" Matron Baenre asked, turning curious and amused.

"Indeed," replied SiNafay. "Thus is House Hun'ett bound!"

"Vengeance?" another matron quipped, also now more amused than angered. "Or fear? It would seem to my ears that the matron of House Hun'ett uses this pitiful DeVir creature for her own gain. House Do'Urden aspires to higher ranking, and Matron Malice desires to sit upon the ruling council, a threat to House Hun'ett, perhaps?"

"Be it vengeance or prudence, my claim—Alton DeVir's claim—must be deemed as legitimate," replied SiNafay, "to our mutual gain." She smiled wickedly and looked straight to the First Matron. "To the gain of our sons, perhaps, in their quest for recognition."

"Indeed," replied Matron Baenre in a chuckle that sounded more like a cough. A war between Hun'ett and Do'Urden might be to everyone's gain, but not, Baenre suspected, as SiNafay believed. Malice was a powerful matron, and her family truly deserved a ranking higher than ninth. If the fight did come, Malice probably would get her seat on the council, replacing SiNafay.

Matron Baenre looked around at the other matrons, and guessed from their hopeful expressions that they shared her thoughts. Let Hun'ett and Do'Urden fight it out; whatever the outcome, the threat of Matron Malice would be ended. Perhaps, Baenre hoped, a certain young Do'Urden male would fall in battle, propelling her own son into the position he deserved.

Then the First Matron spoke the words SiNafay had come to hear, the silent permission of Menzoberranzan's ruling council.

"This matter is settled, my sisters," Matron Baenre declared, to the accepting nods of all at the table. "It is good that we never met this day."

# 19
# Promises of Glory

"Have you found the trail?" Drizzt whispered, moving up beside the great panther. He gave Guenhwyvar a pat on the side and knew from the slackness of the cat's muscles that no danger was nearby.

"Gone, then," Drizzt said, staring off into the emptiness of the corridor in front of them. "'Wicked gnomes, my brother called them when we found the tracks by the pool. Wicked and stupid." He sheathed his scimitar and knelt beside the panther, his arm comfortable draped across Guenhwyvar's back. "They're smart enough to elude our patrol."

The cat looked up as if it had understood his every word, and Drizzt rubbed a hand roughly over Guenhwyvar's, his finest friend's, head. Drizzt remembered clearly his elation on the day, a tenday before, when Dinin had announced—to Masoj Hun'ett's outrage—that Guenhwyvar would be deployed at the patrol's point position beside Drizzt.

"The cat is mine!" Masoj had reminded Dinin.

"You are mine!" Dinin, the patrol leader, had replied, ending any further debate. Whenever the figurine's magic would permit, Masoj summoned Guenhwyvar from the Astral Plane and bid the cat to run up in front, bringing Drizzt an added degree of safety and a valued companion.

Drizzt knew from the unfamiliar heat patterns on the wall that they had gone the limit of their patrol route. He had purposely put a lot of ground, more than was advised, between himself and the rest of the patrol. Drizzt had confidence that he and Guenhwyvar could take care of themselves, and with the others far behind, he could relax and enjoy the wait. The minutes Drizzt spent in solitude gave him the time he needed in his endless effort to sort through his confused emotions. Guenhwyvar, seemingly non-judgmental and always approving, offered Drizzt a perfect audience for his audible contemplations.

"I begin to wonder the worth of it all," Drizzt whispered to the cat. "I do not doubt the value of these patrols—this tenday alone, we have defeated a dozen monsters that might have brought great harm to the city—but to what end?"

He looked deeply into the panther's saucer eyes and found sympathy there, and Drizzt knew that Guenhwyvar somehow understood his dilemma.

"Perhaps I still do not know who I am," Drizzt mused, "or who my people are. Every time I find a clue to the truth, it leads me down a path that I dare not continue upon, to conclusions I cannot accept."

"You are drow," came a reply behind them. Drizzt turned abruptly to see Dinin a few feet away, a look of grave concern on his face.

"The gnomes have fled beyond our reach," Drizzt said, trying to deflect his brother's concerns.

"Have you not learned what it means to be a drow?" Dinin asked. "Have you not come to understand the course of our history and the promise of our future?"

"I know of our history as it was taught at the Academy," Drizzt replied. "They were the very first lessons we received. Of our future, and more so of the place we now reside, though, I do not understand."

"You know of our enemies," Dinin prompted.

"Countless enemies," replied Drizzt with a heavy sigh. "They fill the holes of the Underdark, always waiting for us to let down our guard. We will not, and our enemies will fall to our power."

"Ah, but our true enemies do not reside in the lightless caverns of our world," said Dinin with a sly smile. "Theirs is a world strange and evil." Drizzt knew who Dinin was referring to, but he suspected that his brother was hiding something.

"The faeries," Drizzt whispered, and the word prompted a jumble of emotions within him. All of his life, he had been told of his evil cousins, of how they had forced the drow into the bowels of the world. Busily engaged in the duties of his everyday life, Drizzt did not think of them often, but whenever they came to mind, he used their name as a litany against everything he hated in his life. If Drizzt could somehow blame the surface elves—as every other drow seemed to blame them—for the injustices of drow society, he could find hope for the future of his people. Rationally, Drizzt had to dismiss the stirring legends of the elven war as another of the endless stream of lies, but in his heart and hopes, Drizzt clung desperately to those words.

He looked back to Dinin. "The faeries," he said again, "whatever they may be."

Dinin chuckled at his brother's relentless sarcasm; it had become so commonplace. "They are as you have learned," he assured Drizzt. "Without worth and vile beyond your imagination, the tormentors of our people, who banished us in eons past; who forced—"

"I know the tales," Drizzt interrupted, alarmed at the increasing volume of his excited brother's voice. Drizzt glanced over his shoulder. "If the patrol is ended, let us meet the others closer to the city. This place is too dangerous for such discussions." He rose to his feet and started back, Guenhwyvar at his side.

"Not as dangerous as the place I soon will lead you," Dinin replied with that same sly smile.

Drizzt stopped and looked at him curiously.

"I suppose you should know," Dinin teased. "We were selected because we are the finest of the patrol groups, and you have certainly played an important role in our attaining that honor."

"Chosen for what?"

"In a fortnight, we will leave Menzoberranzan," explained Dinin. "Our trail will take us many days and many miles from the city."

"How long?" Drizzt asked, suddenly very curious.

"Two tendays, maybe three," replied Dinin, "but well worth the time. We shall be the ones, my young brother, who enact a measure of revenge upon our most hated foes, who strike a glorious blow for the Spider Queen!"

Drizzt thought that he understood, but the notion was too outrageous for him to be certain.

"The elves!" Dinin beamed. "We have been chosen for a surface raid!"

Drizzt was not as openly excited as his brother, unsure of the implications of such a mission. At last he would get to view the surface elves and face the truth of his heart and hopes. Something more real to Drizzt, the disappointment he had known for so many years, tempered his elation, reminded him that while the truth of the elves might bring an excuse to the dark world of his kin, it might instead take away something more important. He was unsure how to feel.

⚔ ⚔ ⚔ ⚔ ⚔

"The surface," Alton mused. "My sister went there once—on a raid. A most marvelous experience, so she said!" He looked at Masoj, not knowing how to figure the forlorn expression on the young Hun'ett's face. "Now your patrol makes the journey. I envy you."

"I am not going," Masoj declared.

"Why?" Alton gasped. "This is a rare opportunity indeed. Menzoberranzan—to the anger of Lolth, I am certain—has not staged a surface raid in two decades. It may be twenty more years before the next, and by then you will no longer be among the patrols."

Masoj looked out from the small window of Alton's room in House Hun'ett, surveying the compound.

"Besides," Alton continued quietly, "up there, so far from prying eyes, you might find the chance to dispose of two Do'Urden's. Why would you not go?"

"Have you forgotten a ruling that you played a part in?" Masoj asked, whirling on Alton accusingly. "Two decades ago, the masters of Sorcere decided that no wizards are to travel anywhere near the surface!"

"Of course," Alton replied, remembering the meeting. Sorcere seemed so distant to him now, though he had been within the Hun'ett house for only a few tendays. "We concluded that drow magic may work differently—unexpectedly—under the open sky," he explained. "On that raid twenty years ago—"

"I know the story," Masoj growled, and he finished the sentence for Alton. "A wizard's fireball expanded beyond its normal dimensions, killing several drow. Dangerous side effects, you masters called it, though I've a belief that the wizard conveniently disposed of some enemies under the guise of an accident!"

"Yes," Alton agreed. "So said the rumors. In the absence of evidence . . ." He let the thought go, seeing that he was doing little to comfort Masoj. "That was so long ago," he said, trying to offer some hope. "Have you no recourse?"

"None," Masoj replied. "Things move so very slowly in Menzoberranzan; I doubt that the masters have even begun their investigation into the matter."

"A pity," Alton said. "It would have been the perfect opportunity."

"No more of that!" Masoj scolded. "Matron SiNafay has not given me her command to eliminate Drizzt Do'Urden or his brother. You have already been warned to keep your personal desires to yourself. When the matron bids me to strike, I will not fail her. Opportunities can be created."

"You speak as if you already know how Drizzt Do'Urden will die," Alton said.

An smile spread over Masoj's face as he reached into the pocket of his robe and produced the onyx figurine, his unthinking magical slave, which the foolish Drizzt had come to trust so dearly. "Oh, I do," he replied, giving the statuette of Guenhwyvar an easy toss, then catching it and holding it out on display.

"I do."

⚔ ⚔ ⚔ ⚔ ⚔

The members of the chosen raiding party quickly came to realize that this would be no ordinary mission. They did not go out on patrol from Menzoberranzan at all during the next tenday. Rather, they remained, day and night, sequestered within a barrack of Melee-Magthere. Through nearly every waking hour, the raiders huddled around an oval table in a conference room, hearing the detailed plans of their pending adventure, and, over and over again, Master Hatch'net, the master of Lore, spinning his tales of the vile elves.

Drizzt listened intently to the stories, allowing himself, forcing himself, to fall within Hatch'net's hypnotic web. The tales had to be true; Drizzt did not know what he would hold onto to preserve his principles if they were not.

Dinin presided over the raid's tactical preparations, displaying maps of the long tunnels the group would travel, grilling them over and over until they had memorized the route perfectly.

To this, as well, the eager raiders—except for Drizzt—listened intently, all the while fighting to keep their excitement from bursting out in a wild cheer. As the tenday of preparations neared its end, Drizzt took note that one member of the patrol group had not been attending. At first, Drizzt had reasoned that Masoj was learning his duties in the raid in Sorcere, with his old masters. With the departure time fast approaching and the battle plans clearly taking shape, though, Drizzt began to understand that Masoj would not be joining them.

"Where is our wizard?" Drizzt dared to ask in the late hours of one session.

Dinin, not appreciating the interruption, glared at his brother. "Masoj will not be joining us," he answered, knowing that others might now share Drizzt's concern, a distraction they could not afford at such a critical time.

"Sorcere has decreed that no wizards may travel to the surface," Master Hatch'net explained. "Masoj Hun'ett will await your return in the city. It is a great loss to you indeed, for Masoj has proven his worth many times over. Fear not, though, for a cleric of Arach-Tinilith shall accompany you."

"What of . . ." Drizzt began above the approving whispers of the other raiders.

Dinin cut his brother's thoughts short, easily guessing the question. "The cat belongs to Masoj," he said flatly. "The cat stays behind."

"I could talk to Masoj," Drizzt pleaded.

Dinin's stern glance answered the question without the need for words. "Our tactics will be different on the surface," he said to all the group, silencing their whispers. "The surface is a world of distance, not the blind enclosures of bending tunnels. Once our enemies are spotted, our task will be to surround them, to close off the distances." He looked straight at his young brother. "We will have no need of a point guard, and in such a conflict, a spirited cat could well prove more trouble than aid."

Drizzt had to be satisfied with the answer. Arguing would not help, even if he could get Masoj to let him take the panther—which he knew in his heart he could not. He shook the brooding desires out of his head and forced himself to hear his brother's words. This was to be the greatest challenge of Drizzt's young life, and the greatest danger.

Over the final two days, as the battle plan became ingrained into every thought, Drizzt found himself growing more and more agitated. Nervous energy kept his palms moist with sweat, and his eyes darted about, too alert.

Despite his disappointment over Guenhwyvar, Drizzt could not deny the excitement that bubbled within him. This was the adventure he had always wanted, the answer to his questions of the truth of his people. Up there, in the vast strangeness of that foreign world, lurked the surface elves, the unseen nightmare that had become the common enemy, and thus the common bond, of all the drow. Drizzt would discover the glory of battle, exacting proper revenge upon his people's most hated foes. Always before, Drizzt had fought out of necessity, in training gyms or against the stupid monsters that ventured too near his home.

Drizzt knew that this encounter would be different. This time his thrusts and cuts would be carried by the strength of deeper emotions, guided by the honor of his people and their common courage and resolve to strike back against their oppressors. He had to believe that.

Drizzt lay back in his cot the night before the raiding party's departure and brought his scimitars through some slow-motion maneuvers above him.

"This time," he whispered aloud to the blades while marveling at their intricate dance even at such a slow speed. "This time your ring will sound out in the song of justice!"

He placed the scimitars down at the side of his cot and rolled over to find some needed sleep. "This time," he said again, teeth clenched and eyes shining with determination.

Were his proclamations his belief or his hope? Drizzt had dismissed the disturbing question the very first time it had entered his thoughts, having no more room for doubts than he had for brooding. He no longer considered the possibility of disappointment; it had no place in the heart of a drow warrior.

To Dinin, though, studying Drizzt curiously from the shadows of the doorway, it sounded as if his younger brother was trying to convince himself of the truth of his own words.

# 20
# That Foreign World

The fourteen members of the patrol group made their way through twisting tunnels and giant caverns that suddenly opened wide before them. Silent on magical boots and nearly invisible behind their *piwafwis*, they communicated only in their hand code. For the most part, the ground's slope was barely perceptible, though at times the group climbed straight up rocky chimneys, every step and every handhold drawing them nearer their goal. They crossed through the boundaries of claimed territories, of monsters and the other races, but the hated gnomes and even the duergar dwarves wisely kept their heads hidden. Few in all the Underdark would purposely intercept a drow raiding party.

By the end of a tenday, all the drow could sense the difference in their surroundings. The depth still would have seemed stifling to a surface dweller, but the dark elves were accustomed to the constant oppression of a thousand thousand tons of rock hanging over their heads. They turned every corner expecting the stone ceiling to fly away into the vast openness of the surface world.

Breezes wafted past them—not the sulfur-smelling hot winds rising off the magma of deep earth, but moist air, scented with a hundred aromas unknown to the drow. It was springtime above, though the dark elves, in their seasonless environs, knew nothing of that, and the air was full of the scents of new-blossomed flowers and budding trees. In the seductive allure of those tantalizing aromas, Drizzt had to remind himself again and again that the place they approached was wholly evil and dangerous. Perhaps, he thought, the scents were merely a diabolical lure, a bait to an unsuspecting creature to bring it into the surface world's murderous grip.

The cleric of Arach-Tinilith who was traveling with the raiding party walked near to one wall and pressed her face against every crack she encountered. "This one will suffice," she said a short time later. She cast a spell of seeing and looked into the tiny crack, no more than a finger's width, a second time.

"How are we to get through that?" one of the patrol members signaled to another. Dinin caught the gestures and ended the silent conversation with a scowl.

"It is daylight above," the cleric announced. "We shall have to wait here."

"For how long?" Dinin asked, knowing his patrol to be on the edge of readiness with their long-awaited goal so very near.

"I cannot know," the cleric replied. "No more than half a cycle of Narbondel. Let us remove our packs and rest while we may."

Dinin would have preferred to continue, just to keep his troops busy, but he did not dare speak against the priestess. The break did not prove a long one, though, for a couple of hours later, the cleric checked through the crack once more and announced that the time had come.

"You first," Dinin said to Drizzt. Drizzt looked at his brother incredulously, having no idea of how he could pass through such a tiny crack.

"Come," instructed the cleric, who now held a many-holed orb. "Walk past me and continue through."

As Drizzt passed the cleric, she spoke the orb's command word and held it over Drizzt's head. Black flakes, blacker than Drizzt's ebony skin, drifted over him, and he felt a tremendous shudder ripple across his spine.

The others looked on in amazement as Drizzt's body narrowed to the width of a hair and he became a two-dimensional image, a shadow of his former self.

Drizzt did not understand what was happening, but the crack suddenly widened before him. He slipped into it, found movement in his present form merely an enactment of will, and, drifted through the twists, turns, and bends of the tiny channel like a shadow on the broken face of a rocky cliff. He then was in a long cave, standing across from its single exit.

A moonless night had fallen, but even this seemed bright to the deep-dwelling drow. Drizzt felt himself pulled toward the exit, toward the surface world's openness. The other raiders began slipping through the crack and into the cavern then, one by one with the cleric coming in last. Drizzt was the first to feel the shudder as his body resumed its natural state. In a few moments, they all were eagerly checking their weapons.

"I will remain here," the cleric told Dinin. "Hunt well. The Spider Queen is watching."

Dinin warned his troops once again of the dangers of the surface, then he moved to the front of the cave, a small hole on the side of a rocky spur of a tall mountain. "For the Spider Queen," Dinin proclaimed. He took a steadying breath and led them through the exit, under the open sky.

Under the stars! While the others seemed nervous under those revealing lights, Drizzt found his gaze pulled heavenward to the countless points of mystical twinkling. Bathed in the starlight, he felt his heart lift and didn't even notice the joyful singing that rode on the night wind, so fitting it seemed.

Dinin heard the song, and he was experienced enough to recognize it as the eldritch calling of the surface elves. He crouched and surveyed the horizon, picking out the light of a single fire down in the distant expanse of a wooded valley. He nudged his troops to action—and pointedly nudged the wonderment from his brother's eyes—and started them off.

Drizzt could see the anxiety on his companions' faces, so contrasted by his own inexplicable sense of serenity. He suspected at once that something was very wrong with the whole situation. In his heart Drizzt had known from the minute he had stepped out of the tunnel that this was not the vile world the masters at the Academy had taken such pains to describe. He did feel unusual with no stone ceiling above him, but not uncomfortable. If the stars, calling to his heartstrings, were indeed reminders of what the next day might bring, as Master Hatch'net had said, then surely the next day would not be so terrible.

Only confusion dampened the feeling of freedom that Drizzt felt, for either he had somehow fallen into a trap of perception, or his companions, his brother included, viewed their surroundings through tainted eyes.

It fell on Drizzt as another unanswered burden: were his feelings of comfort here weakness or truth of heart?

"They are akin to the mushroom groves of our home," Dinin assured the others as they tentatively moved under the perimeter boughs of a small forest, "neither sentient nor harmful."

Still, the younger dark elves flinched and brought their weapons to the ready whenever a squirrel skipped across a branch overheard or an unseen bird called out to the night. The dark elves' was a silent world, far different from the chattering life of a springtime forest, and in the Underdark, nearly every living thing could, and most certainly would, try to harm anything invading its lair. Even a cricket's chirp sounded ominous to the alert ears of the drow.

Dinin's course was true, and soon the faerie song drowned out every other sound and the light of a fire became visible through the boughs. Surface elves were the most alert of the races, and a human—or even a sneaky halfling—would have had little chance of catching them unawares.

The raiders this night were drow, more skilled in stealth than the most proficient alley thief. Their footfalls went unheard, even across beds of dry, fallen leaves, and their crafted armor, shaped perfectly to the contours of their slender bodies, bent with their movements without a rustle. Unnoticed, they lined the perimeter of the small glade, where a score of faeries danced and sang.

Transfixed by the sheer joy of the elves' play, Drizzt hardly noticed the commands his brother issued then in the silent code. Several children danced among the gathering, marked only by the size of their bodies, and were no freer in spirit than the adults they accompanied. So innocent they all seemed, so full of life and wistfulness, and obviously bonded to each other by friendship more profound than Drizzt had ever known in Menzoberranzan. So unlike the stories Hatch'net had spun of them, tales of vile, hating wretches.

Drizzt sensed more than saw that his group was on the move, fanning out to gain a greater advantage. Still he did not take his eyes from the spectacle before him. Dinin tapped him on the shoulder and pointed to the small crossbow that hung from his belt, then slipped off into position in the brush off to the side.

Drizzt wanted to stop his brother and the others, wanted to make them wait and observe the surface elves that they were so quick to name enemies. Drizzt found his feet rooted to the earth and his tongue weighted heavily in the sudden dryness that had come into his mouth. He looked to Dinin and could only hope that his brother mistakenly thought his labored breaths the exaltations of battlelust.

Then Drizzt's keen ears heard the soft thrum of a dozen tiny bowstrings. The elven song carried on a moment longer, until several of the group dropped to the earth.

"No!" Drizzt screamed in protest, the words torn from his body by a profound rage even he did not understand. The denial sounded like just another war cry to the drow raiders, and before the surface elves could even begin to react, Dinin and the others were upon them.

Drizzt, too, leaped into the glade's lighted ring, his weapons in hand, though he had given no thought to his next move. He wanted only to stop the battle, to put an end to the scene unfolding before him.

Quite at ease in their woodland home, the surface elves weren't even armed. The drow warriors sliced through their ranks mercilessly, cutting them down and hacking at their bodies long after the light of life had flown from their eyes.

One terrified female, dodging this way and that, came before Drizzt. He dipped the tips of his weapons to the earth, searching for some way to give a measure of comfort.

The female then jerked straight as a sword dived into her back, its tip thrusting right through her slender form. Drizzt watched, mesmerized and horrified, as the drow warrior behind her grasped the weapon hilt in both hands and twisted it savagely. The female elf looked straight at Drizzt in the last fleeting seconds of her life, her eyes crying for mercy. Her voice was no more than the sickening gurgle of blood.

His face the exultation of ecstacy, the drow warrior tore his sword free and sliced it across, taking the head from the elven female's shoulders.

"Vengeance!" he cried at Drizzt, his face contorted in furious glee, his eyes burning with a light that shone demonic to the stunned Drizzt. The warrior hacked at the lifeless body one more time, then spun away in search of another kill.

Only a moment later, another elf, this one a young girl, broke free of the massacre and rushed in Drizzt's direction, screaming a single word over and over. Her cry was in the tongue of the surface elves, a dialect foreign to Drizzt, but when he looked upon her fair face, streaked with tears, he understood what she was saying. Her eyes were on the mutilated corpse at his feet; her anguish outweighed even the terror of her own impending doom. She could only be crying, "Mother!"

Rage, horror, anguish, and a dozen other emotions racked Drizzt at that horrible moment. He wanted to escape his feelings, to lose himself in the blind frenzy of his kin and accept the ugly reality. How easy it would have been to throw away the conscience that pained him so.

The elven child rushed up before Drizzt but hardly saw him, her gaze locked upon her dead mother, the back of the child's neck open to a single, clean blow. Drizzt raised his scimitar, unable to distinguish between mercy and murder.

"Yes, my brother!" Dinin cried out to him, a call that cut through his comrades," screams and whoops and echoed in Drizzt's ears like an accusation. Drizzt looked up to see Dinin, covered from head to foot in blood and standing amid a hacked cluster of dead elves.

"Today you know the glory it is to be a drow!" Dinin cried, and he punched a victorious fist into the air. "Today we appease the Spider Queen!"

Drizzt responded in kind, then snarled and reared back for a killing blow.

He almost did it. In his unfocused outrage, Drizzt Do'Urden almost became as his kin. He almost stole the life from that beautiful child's sparkling eyes.

At the last moment, she looked up at him, her eyes shining as a dark mirror into Drizzt's blackening heart. In that reflection, that reverse image of the rage that guided his hand, Drizzt Do'Urden found himself.

He brought the scimitar down in a mighty sweep, watching Dinin out of the corner of his eye as it whisked harmlessly past the child. In the same motion, Drizzt followed with his other hand, catching the girl by the front of her tunic and pulling her face-down to the ground.

She screamed, unharmed but terrified, and Drizzt saw Dinin thrust his fist into the air again and spin away.

Drizzt had to work quickly; the battle was almost at its gruesome end. He sliced his scimitars expertly above the huddled child's back, cuffing her clothing but not so much as scratching her tender skin. Then he used the blood of the headless corpse to mask the trick, taking grim satisfaction that the elven mother would be pleased to know that, in dying, she had saved the life of her daughter.

"Stay down," he whispered in the child's ear. Drizzt knew that she could not understand his language, but he tried to keep his tone comforting enough for her to guess at the deception. He could only hope he had done an adequate job a moment later, when Dinin and several others came over to him.

"Well done!" Dinin said exuberantly, trembling with sheer excitement. "A score of the orc-bait dead and not a one of us even injured! The matrons of Menzoberranzan will be pleased indeed, though we'll get no plunder from this pitiful lot!" He looked down at the pile at Drizzt's feet, then clapped his brother on the shoulder.

"Did they think they could get away?" Dinin roared.

Drizzt fought hard to sublimate his disgust, but Dinin was so entranced by the blood-bath that he wouldn't have noticed anyway.

"Not with you here!" Dinin continued. "Two kills for Drizzt!"

"One kill!" protested another, stepping beside Dinin. Drizzt set his hands firmly on the hilts of his weapons and gathered up his courage. If this approaching drow had guessed the deception, Drizzt would fight to save the elven child. He would kill his companions, even his brother, to save the little girl with the sparkling eyes—until he himself was slain. At least then Drizzt would not have to witness their slaughter of the child.

Luckily, the problem never came up. "Drizzt got the child," the drow said to Dinin, "but I got the elder female. I put my sword right through her back before your brother ever brought his scimitars to bear!"

It came as a reflex, an unconscious strike against the evil all about him. Drizzt didn't even realize the act as it happened, but a moment later, he saw the boasting drow lying on his back, clutching at his face and groaning in agony. Only then did Drizzt notice the burning pain in his hand, and he looked down to see his knuckles, and the scimitar hilt they clutched, spattered with blood.

"What are you about?" Dinin demanded.

Thinking quickly, Drizzt did not even reply to his brother. He looked past Dinin, to the squirming form on the ground, and transferred all the rage in his heart into a curse that the others would accept and respect. "If ever you steal a kill from me again," he spat, sincerity dripping from his false words, "I will replace the head lost from its shoulders with your own!"

Drizzt knew that the elven child at his feet, though doing her best, had begun a slight shudder of sobbing, and he decided not to press his luck. "Come, then," he growled. "Let us leave this place. The stench of the surface world fills my mouth with bile!"

He stormed away, and the others, laughing, picked up their dazed comrade and followed.

"Finally," Dinin whispered as he watched his brother's tense strides. "Finally you have learned what it is to be a drow warrior!"

Dinin, in his blindness, would never understand the irony of his words.

⚔ ⚔ ⚔ ⚔ ⚔

"We have one more duty before we return home," the cleric explained to the group when it reached the cave's entrance. She alone knew of the raid's second purpose. "The matrons of Menzoberranzan have bid us to witness the ultimate horror of the surface world, that we might warn our kindred."

Our kindred? Drizzt mused, his thoughts black with sarcasm. As far as he could see, the raiders had already witnessed the horror of the surface world: themselves!

"There!" Dinin cried, pointing to the eastern horizon.

The tiniest shading of light limned the dark outline of distant mountains. A surface dweller would not even have noticed it, but the dark elves saw it clearly, and all of them, even Drizzt, recoiled instinctively.

"It is beautiful," Drizzt dared to remark after taking a moment to consider the spectacle.

Dinin's glare came at him icy cold, but no colder than the look the cleric cast Drizzt's way. "Remove your cloaks and equipment, even your armor," she instructed the group. "Quickly. Place them within the shadows of the cave so that they will not be affected by the light."

When the task was completed, the cleric led them out into the growing light. "Watch," was her grim command.

The eastern sky assumed a hue of purplish pink, then pink altogether, its brightening causing the dark elves to squint uncomfortably. Drizzt wanted to deny the event, to put it into the same pile of anger that denied the master of Lore's words concerning the surface elves.

Then it happened; the top rim of the sun crested the eastern horizon. The surface world awakened to its warmth, its life-giving energy. Those same rays assaulted the drow elves' eyes with the fury of fire, tearing into orbs unaccustomed to such sights.

"Watch!" the cleric cried at them. "Witness the depth of the horror!"

One by one, the raiders cried out in pain and fell into the cave's darkness, until Drizzt stood alone beside the cleric in the growing daylight. Truly the light assaulted Drizzt as keenly as it had his kin, but he basked in it, accepting it as his purgatory, exposing him for all to view while its stinging fires cleansed his soul.

"Come," the cleric said to him at length, not understanding his actions. "We have borne witness. We may now return to our homeland."

"Homeland?" Drizzt replied, subdued.

"Menzoberranzan!" the cleric cried, thinking the male confused beyond reason. "Come, before the inferno burns the skin from your bones. Let our surface cousins suffer the flames, a fitting punishment for their evil hearts!"

Drizzt chuckled hopelessly. A fitting punishment? He wished that he could pluck a thousand such suns from the sky and set them in every chapel in Menzoberranzan, to shine eternally.

Then Drizzt could take the light no more. He scrambled dizzily back into the cave and donned his outfit. The cleric had the orb in hand, and Drizzt again was the first through the tiny crack. When all the group rejoined in the tunnel beyond, Drizzt took his position at the point and led them back into the descending path's deepening gloom—back down into the darkness of their existence.

# 21

# May It Please the Goddess

Did you please the goddess?" Matron Malice asked, her question as much a threat as an inquiry. At her side, the other females of House Do'Urden, Briza, Vierna, and Maya, looked on impassively, hiding their jealousy.

"Not a single drow was slain," Dinin replied, his voice thick with the sweetness of drow evil. "We cut them and slashed them!" He drooled as his recounting of the elven slaughter brought back the lust of the moment. "Bit them and ripped them!"

"What of you?" the matron mother interrupted, more concerned with the consequences to her own family's standing than with the raid's general success.

"Five," Dinin answered proudly. "I killed five, all of them females!"

The matron's smile thrilled Dinin. Then Malice scowled as she turned her gaze on Drizzt. "And him?" she inquired, not expecting to be pleased with the answer. Malice did not doubt her youngest son's prowess with weapons, but she had come to suspect that Drizzt had too much of Zaknafein's emotional makeup to ever be an attribute in such situations.

Dinin's smile confused her. He walked over to Drizzt and draped an arm comfortably across his brother's shoulders. "Drizzt got only one kill," Dinin began, "but it was a female child."

"Only one?" Malice growled.

From the shadows off to the side, Zaknafein listened in dismay. He wanted to shut out the elderboy Do'Urden's damning words, but they held Zak in their grip. Of all the evils Zak had ever encountered in Menzoberranzan, this surely had to be the most disappointing. Drizzt had killed a child.

"But the way he did it!" Dinin exclaimed. "He hacked her apart; sent all of Lolth's fury slicing into her twitching body! The Spider Queen must have treasured that kill above all the others."

"Only one," Matron Malice said again, her scowl hardly softening.

"He would have had two," Dinin continued. "Shar Nadal of House Maevret stole one from his blade—another female."

"Then Lolth will look with favor on House Maevret," Briza reasoned.

"No," Dinin replied. "Drizzt punished Shar Nadal for his actions. The son of House Maevret would not respond to the challenge."

The memory stuck in Drizzt's thoughts. He wished that Shar Nadal had come back at him, so he could have vented his rage more fully. Even that wish sent pangs of guilt coursing through Drizzt.

"Well done, my children," Malice beamed, now satisfied that both of them had acted properly in the raid. "The Spider Queen will look upon House Do'Urden with favor for this event. She will guide us to victory over this unknown house that seeks to destroy us."

⚔ ⚔ ⚔ ⚔ ⚔

Zaknafein left the audience hall with his eyes down and one hand nervously rubbing his sword's hilt. Zak remembered the time he had deceived Drizzt with the light bomb, when he had Drizzt defenseless and beaten. He could have spared the young innocent from his horrid fate. He could have killed Drizzt then and there, mercifully, and released him from the inevitable circumstances of life in Menzoberranzan.

Zak paused in the long corridor and turned back to watch the chamber. Drizzt and Dinin came out then, Drizzt casting Zak a single, accusatory look and pointedly turning away down a side passage.

The gaze cut through the weapons master. "So it has come to this," Zak murmured to himself. "The youngest warrior of House Do'Urden, so full of the hate that embodies our race, has learned to despise me for what I am."

Zak thought again of that moment in the training gym, that fateful second when Drizzt's life teetered on the edge of a poised sword. It indeed would have been a merciful act to kill Drizzt at that time.

With the sting of the young drow warrior's gaze still cutting so keenly into his heart, Zak couldn't decide whether the deed would have been more merciful to Drizzt or to himself.

⚔ ⚔ ⚔ ⚔ ⚔

"Leave us," Matron SiNafay commanded as she swept into the small room lighted by a candle's glow. Alton gawked at the request; it was, after all, his personal room! Alton prudently reminded himself that SiNafay was the matron mother of the family, the absolute ruler of House Hun'ett. With a few awkward bows and apologies for his hesitation, he backed out of the room.

Masoj watched his mother cautiously as she waited for Alton to move away. From SiNafay's agitated tone, Masoj understood the significance of her visit. Had he done something to anger his mother? Or, more likely, had Alton? When SiNafay spun back on him, her face twisted in evil glee, Masoj realized that her agitation was really excitement.

"House Do'Urden has erred!" she snarled. "It has lost the Spider Queen's favor!"

"How?" Masoj replied. He knew that Dinin and Drizzt had returned from a successful raid, an assault that all of the city was talking about in tones of high praise.

"I do not know the details," Matron SiNafay replied, finding a measure of calmness in her voice. "One of them, perhaps one of the sons, did something to displease Lolth. This was told to me by a handmaiden of the Spider Queen. It must be true!"

"Matron Malice will work quickly to correct the situation," Masoj reasoned. "How long do we have?"

"Lolth's displeasure will not be revealed to Matron Malice," SiNafay replied. "Not soon. The Spider Queen knows all. She knows that we plan to attack House Do'Urden, and only an unfortunate accident will inform Matron Malice of her desperate situation before her house is crushed!

"We must move quickly," Matron SiNafay went on. "Within ten cycles of Narbondel, the first strike must fall! The full battle will begin soon after, before House Do'Urden can link its loss to our wrongdoing."

"What is to be their sudden loss?" Masoj prompted, thinking, hoping, he had already guessed the answer.

His mother's words were like sweet music to his ears. "Drizzt Do'Urden," she purred, "the favored son. Kill him."

Masoj rested back and clasped his slender fingers behind his head, considering the command.

"You will not fail me," SiNafay warned.

"I will not," Masoj assured her. "Drizzt, though young, is already a powerful foe. His brother, a former master of Melee-Magthere, is never far from his side." He looked up at his matron mother, his eyes gleaming. "May I kill the brother, too?"

"Be cautious, my son," SiNafay replied. "Drizzt Do'Urden is your target. Concentrate your efforts toward his death."

"As you command," Masoj replied, bowing low.

SiNafay liked the way her young son heeded to her desires without question. She started out of the room, confident in Masoj's ability to perform the task.

"If Dinin Do'Urden somehow gets in the way," she said, turning back to throw Masoj a gift for his obedience, "you may kill him, too."

Masoj's expression revealed too much eagerness for the second task.

"You will not fail me!" SiNafay said again, this time in an open threat that stole some of the wind out of Masoj's filling sails. "Drizzt Do'Urden must die within ten days!"

Masoj forced any distracting thoughts of Dinin out of his mind. "Drizzt must die," he whispered over and over, long after his mother had gone. He already knew how he wanted to do it. He only had to hope that the opportunity would come soon.

⚔ ⚔ ⚔ ⚔ ⚔

The awful memory of the surface raid followed Drizzt, haunted him, as he wandered the halls of Daermon N'a'shezbaernon. He had rushed from the audience chamber as soon as Matron Malice had dismissed him, and had slipped away from his brother at the first opportunity, wanting only to be alone.

The images remained: the broken sparkle in the young elven girl's eyes as she knelt over her murdered mother's corpse; the elven woman's horrified expression, twisting in agony as Shar Nadal ripped the life from her body. The surface elves were there in Drizzt's thoughts; he could not dismiss them. They walked beside Drizzt as he wandered, as real as they had been when Drizzt's raiding group had descended upon their joyful song.

Drizzt wondered if he would ever be alone again.

Eyes down, consumed by his empty sense of loss, Drizzt did not mark the path before him. He jumped back, startled, when he turned a corner and bumped into somebody.

He stood facing Zaknafein.

"You are home," the weapons master said absently, his blank face revealing none of the tumultuous emotions swirling through his mind.

Drizzt wondered if he could properly hide his own grimace. "For a day," he replied, equally nonchalant, though his rage with Zaknafein was no less intense. Now that Drizzt had witnessed the wrath of drow elves firsthand, Zak's reputed deeds rang out to Drizzt as even more evil. "My patrol group goes back out at Narbondel's first light."

"So soon?" asked Zak, genuinely surprised.

"We are summoned," Drizzt replied, starting past. Zak caught him by the arm.

"General patrol?" he asked.

"Focused," Drizzt replied. "Activity in the eastern tunnels."

"So the heroes are summoned," chuckled Zak.

Drizzt did not immediately respond. Was there sarcasm in Zak's voice? Jealousy, perhaps, that Drizzt and Dinin were allowed to go out to fight, while Zak had to remain within the House Do'Urden's confines to fulfill his role as the family's fighting instructor? Was Zak's hunger for blood so great that he could not accept the duties thrust upon them all? Zak had trained Drizzt and Dinin, had he not? And hundreds of others; he'd transformed them into living weapons, into murderers.

"How long will you be out?" Zak pressed, more interested in Drizzt's whereabouts.

Drizzt shrugged. "A tenday at the longest."

"And?"

"Home."

"That is good," said Zak. "I will be pleased to see you back within the walls of House Do'Urden." Drizzt didn't believe a word of it.

Zak then slapped him on the shoulder in a sudden, unexpected movement designed to test Drizzt's reflexes. More surprised than threatened, Drizzt accepted the pat without response, not sure of his uncle's intent.

"The gym, perhaps?" asked Zak. "You and I, as it once was."

Impossible! Drizzt wanted to shout. Never again would it be as it once was. Drizzt held those thoughts to himself and nodded his assent. "I would enjoy that," he replied, secretly wondering how much satisfaction he would gain by cutting Zaknafein down. Drizzt knew the truth of his people now, and knew that he was powerless to change anything. Maybe he could make a change in his private life, though. Maybe by destroying Zaknafein, his greatest disappointment, Drizzt could remove himself from the wrongness around him.

"As would I," Zak said, the friendliness of his tone hiding his private thoughts—thoughts identical to Drizzt's.

"In a tenday, then," Drizzt said, and he pulled away, unable to continue the encounter with the drow who once had been his dearest friend, and who, Drizzt had come to learn, was truly as devious and evil as the rest of his kin.

⚔ ⚔ ⚔ ⚔ ⚔

"Please, my matron," Alton whimpered, "it is my right. I beg of you!"

"Rest easy, foolish DeVir," SiNafay replied, and there was pity in her voice, an emotion seldom felt and almost never revealed.

"I have waited—"

"The time is almost upon you," SiNafay countered, her tone growing more threatening. "You have tried for this one before."

Alton's grotesque gawk brought a smile to SiNafay's face.

"Yes," she said, "I know of your bungled attempt on Drizzt Do'Urden's life. If Masoj had not arrived, the young warrior would probably have slain you."

"I would have destroyed him!" Alton growled.

SiNafay did not argue the point. "Perhaps you would have won," she said, "only to be exposed as a murderous imposter, with the wrath of all of Menzoberranzan hanging over your head!"

"I did not care."

"You would have cared, I promise you!" Matron SiNafay sneered. "You would have forfeited your chance to claim a greater revenge. Trust in me, Alton DeVir. Your—our—victory is at hand."

"Masoj will kill Drizzt, and maybe Dinin," Alton grumbled.

"There are other Do'Urdens awaiting the fell hand of Alton DeVir," Matron SiNafay promised. "High priestesses."

Alton could not dismiss the disappointment he felt at not being allowed to go after Drizzt. He badly wanted to kill that one. Drizzt had brought him embarrassment that day in his chambers at Sorcere; the young drow should have died quickly and quietly. Alton wanted to make up for that mistake.

Alton also could not ignore the promise that Matron SiNafay had just made to him. The thought of killing one or more of the high priestesses of House Do'Urden did not displease him at all.

⚔ ⚔ ⚔ ⚔ ⚔

The pillowy softness of the plush bed, so different from the rest of the hard stone world of Menzoberranzan, offered Drizzt no relief from the pain. Another ghost had reared up to overwhelm even the images of carnage on the surface: the specter of Zaknafein.

Dinin and Vierna had told Drizzt the truth of the weapons master, of Zak's role in the fall of House DeVir, and of how Zak so enjoyed slaughtering other drow—other drow who had done nothing to wrong him or deserve his wrath.

So Zaknafein, too, took part in this evil game of drow life, the endless quest to please the Spider Queen.

"As I so pleased her on the surface?" Drizzt couldn't help but mumble, the sarcasm of the spoken words bringing him some small measure of comfort.

The comfort Drizzt felt in saving the life of the elven child seemed such a minor act against the overwhelming wrongs his raiding group had exacted on her people. Matron Malice, his mother, had so enjoyed hearing the bloody recounting. Drizzt remembered the elven child's horror at the sight of her dead mother. Would he, or any dark elf, be so devastated if they looked upon such a sight. Unlikely, he thought. Drizzt hardly shared a loving bond with Malice, and most drow would be too engaged in measuring the consequences of their mother's death to their own station to feel any sense of loss.

Would Malice have cared if either Drizzt or Dinin had fallen in the raid? Again Drizzt knew the answer. All that Malice cared about was how the raid affected her own base of power. She had reveled in the notion that her children had pleased her evil goddess.

What favor would Lolth show to House Do'Urden if she knew the truth of Drizzt's actions? Drizzt had no way to measure how much, if any, interest the Spider Queen had taken in the raid. Lolth remained a mystery to him, one he had no desire to explore. Would she be enraged if she knew the truth of the raid? Or if she knew the truth of Drizzt's thoughts at this moment?

Drizzt shuddered to think of the punishments he might be bringing upon himself, but he had already firmly decided upon his course of action, whatever the consequences. He would return to House Do'Urden in a tenday. He would go then to the practice gym for a reunion with his old teacher.

He would kill Zaknafein in a tenday.

⚔ ⚔ ⚔ ⚔ ⚔

Caught up in the emotions of a dangerous and heartfelt decision, Zaknafein hardly heard the biting scrape as he ran the whetstone along his sword's gleaming edge.

The weapon had to be perfect, with no jags or burrs. This deed had to be executed without malice or anger.

A clean blow, and Zak would rid himself of the demons of his own failures, hide himself once again within the sanctuary of his private chambers, his secret world. A clean blow, and he would do what he should have done a decade before.

"If only I had found the strength then," he lamented. "How much grief might I have spared Drizzt? How much pain did his days at the Academy bring to him, that he is so very changed?" The words rang hollow in the empty room. They were just words, useless now, for Zak had already decided that Drizzt was out of reason's reach. Drizzt was a drow warrior, with all of the wicked connotations carried in such a title.

The choice was gone to Zaknafein if he wished to hold any pretense of value to his wretched existence. This time, he could not stay his sword. He had to kill Drizzt.

# 22
# Gnomes, Wicked Gnomes

Among the twists and turns of the tunnel mazes of the Underdark, slipping about their silent way, went the svirfnebli, the deep gnomes. Neither kind nor evil, and so out of place in this world of pervading wickedness, the deep gnomes survived and thrived. Haughty fighters, skilled in crafting weapons and armor, and more in tune to the songs of the stone than even the evil gray dwarves, the svirfnebli continued their business of plucking gems and precious metals in spite of the perils awaiting them at every turn.

When the news came back to Blingdenstone, the cluster of tunnels and caverns that composed the deep gnomes' city, that a rich vein of gemstones had been discovered twenty miles to the east—as the rockworm, the thoqqua, burrowed—Burrow-warden Belwar Dissengulp had to climb over a dozen others of his rank to be awarded the privilege of leading the mining expedition. Belwar and all of the others knew well that forty miles east—as the rockworm burrowed—would put the expedition dangerously close to Menzoberranzan, and that even getting there would mean a tenday of hiking, probably through the territories of a hundred other enemies. Fear was no measure against the love svirfnebli had for gems, though, and every day in the Underdark was a risk.

When Belwar and his forty miners arrived in the small cavern described by the advance scouts and inscribed with the gnomes' mark of treasure, they found that the claims had not been exaggerated. The burrow-warden took care not to get overly excited, though. He knew that twenty thousand drow elves, the svirfnebli's most hated and feared enemy, lived less than five miles away.

Escape tunnels became the first order of business, winding constructions high enough for a three-foot gnome but not for a taller pursuer. All along the course of these the gnomes placed breaker walls, designed to deflect a lightning bolt or offer some protection from the expanding flames of a fireball.

Then, when the true mining at last began, Belwar kept fully a third of his crew on guard at all times and walked the area of the work with one hand always clutching the magical emerald, the summoning stone, he kept on a chain around his neck.

⚔ ⚔ ⚔ ⚔ ⚔

"Three full patrol groups," Drizzt remarked to Dinin when they arrived at the open "field" on the eastern side of Menzoberranzan. Few stalagmites lined this region of the city, but it did not seem so open now, with dozens of anxious drow milling about.

"Gnomes are not to be taken lightly," Dinin replied. "They are wicked and powerful—"

"As wicked as surface elves?" Drizzt had to interrupt, covering his sarcasm with false exuberance.

"Almost," his brother warned grimly, missing the connotations of Drizzt's question. Dinin pointed off to the side, where a contingent of female drow was coming in to join the group. "Clerics," he said, "and one of them a high priestess. The rumors of activity must have been confirmed."

A shudder coursed through Drizzt, a tingle of prebattle excitement. That excitement was altered and lessened, though, by fear, not of physical harm, or even of the gnomes. Drizzt feared that this encounter might be a repeat of the surface tragedy.

He shook the black thoughts away and reminded himself that this time, unlike the surface expedition, his home was being invaded. The gnomes had crossed the boundaries of the drow realm. If they were as evil as Dinin and all the others claimed, Menzoberranzan had no choice but to respond with force. If.

Drizzt's patrol, the most celebrated group among the males, was selected to lead, and Drizzt, as always, took the point position. Still unsure, he wasn't thrilled with the assignment, and as they started out, Drizzt even contemplated leading the group astray. Or perhaps, Drizzt thought, he could contact the gnomes privately before the others arrived and warn them to flee.

Drizzt realized the absurdity of the notion. He couldn't stop the wheels of Menzoberranzan from turning along their designated course, and he couldn't do anything to hinder the two score drow warriors, excited and impatient, at his back. Again he was trapped and on the edge of despair.

Masoj Hun'ett appeared then and made everything better.

"Guenhwyvar!" the young wizard called, and the great panther came bounding. Masoj left the cat beside Drizzt and headed back toward his place in the line.

Guenhwyvar could no more hide its elation at seeing Drizzt than Drizzt could contain his own smile. With the interruption of the surface raid, and his time back home, he hadn't seen Guenhwyvar in more than a month. Guenhwyvar thumped against Drizzt's side as it passed, nearly knocking the slender drow from his feet. Drizzt responded with a heavy pat, vigorously rubbing a hand over the cat's ear.

They both turned back together, suddenly conscious of the unhappy glare boring into them. There stood Masoj, arms crossed over his chest and a visible scowl heating up his face.

"I shan't use the cat to kill Drizzt," the young wizard muttered to himself. "I want the pleasure for myself!"

Drizzt wondered if jealousy prompted that scowl. Jealousy of Drizzt and the cat, or of everything in general? Masoj had been left behind when Drizzt had gone to the surface. Masoj had been no more than a spectator when the victorious raiding party returned in glory. Drizzt backed away from Guenhwyvar, sensitive to the wizard's pain.

As soon as Masoj had moved away to take his position farther down the line, Drizzt dropped to one knee and threw a headlock on Guenhwyvar.

⚔ ⚔ ⚔ ⚔ ⚔

Drizzt found himself even gladder for Guenhwyvar's companionship when they passed beyond the familiar tunnels of the normal patrol routes. It was a saying in Menzoberranzan that "no one is as alone as the point of a drow patrol," and Drizzt had come to understand this keenly in the last few months. He stopped at the far end of a wide way and held perfectly still, focusing his ears and eyes to the trails behind him. He knew that more than forty drow were approaching his position, fully arrayed for battle and agitated. Still, not a sound could Drizzt detect, and not a motion was discernible in the eerie shadows of cool stone. Drizzt looked down at Guenhwyvar, waiting patiently by his side, and started off again.

He could sense the hot presence of the war party at his back. That intangible sensation was the only thing that disproved Drizzt's feelings that he and Guenhwyvar were quite alone.

Near the end of that day, Drizzt heard the first signs of trouble. As he neared an intersection in the tunnel, cautiously pressed close to one wall, he felt a subtle vibration in the stone. It came again a second later, and then again, and Drizzt recognized it as the rhythmic tapping of a pick or hammer.

He took a magically heated sheet, a small square that fit into the palm of his hand, out of his pack. One side of the item was shielded in heavy leather, but the other shone brightly to eyes seeing in the infrared spectrum. Drizzt flashed it down the tunnel behind him, and a few seconds later Dinin came up to his side.

"Hammer," Drizzt signaled in the silent code, pointing to the wall. Dinin pressed against the stone and nodded in confirmation.

"Fifty yards?" Dinin's hand motions asked.

"Less than one hundred," Drizzt confirmed.

With his own prepared sheet, Dinin flashed the get-ready signal into the gloom behind him, then moved with Drizzt and Guenhwyvar around the intersection toward the tapping.

Only a moment later, Drizzt looked upon svirfnebli gnomes for the very first time. Two guards stood barely twenty feet away, chest-high to a drow and hairless, with skin strangely akin to the stone in both texture and heat radiations. The gnomes' eyes glowed brightly in the telltale red of infravision. One glance at those eyes reminded Drizzt and Dinin that deep gnomes were as much at home in the darkness as were the drow, and they both prudently ducked behind a rocky outcropping in the tunnel.

Dinin promptly signaled to the next drow in line, and so on, until the entire party was alerted. Then he crouched low and peeked out around the bottom of the outcropping. The tunnel continued another thirty feet beyond the gnome guards and around a slight bend, ending in some larger chamber. Dinin couldn't clearly see this area, but the glow of it, from the heat of the work and a cluster of bodies, spilled out into the corridor.

Again Dinin signaled back to his hidden comrades, and then he turned to Drizzt. "Stay here with the cat," he instructed, and he darted back down around the intersection to formulate plans with the other leaders.

Masoj, a few places back in the line, noted Dinin's movements and wondered if the opportunity to deal with Drizzt had suddenly come upon him. If the patrol was discovered with Drizzt all alone in front, was there some way Masoj could secretly blast the young Do'Urden? The opportunity, if ever it was truly there, passed quickly, though, as other drow soldiers came up beside the plotting wizard. Dinin soon returned from the back of the line and headed back to join his brother.

"The chamber has many exits," Dinin signaled to Drizzt when they were together. "The other patrols are moving into position around the gnomes."

"Might we parley with the gnomes?" Drizzt's hands asked in reply, almost subconsciously. He recognized the expression spreading across Dinin's face, but knew that he had already plunged in. "Send them away without conflict?"

Dinin grabbed Drizzt by the front of his *piwafwi* and pulled him close, too close, to that terrible scowl. "I will forget that you asked that question," he whispered, and he dropped Drizzt back to the stone, considering the issue closed.

"You start the fight," Dinin signaled. "When you see the sign from behind, darken the corridor and rush past the guards. Get to the gnome leader; he is the key to their strength with the stone."

Drizzt didn't fully understand what gnomish power his brother hinted at, but the instructions seemed simple enough, if somewhat suicidal.

"Take the cat if the cat will go," Dinin continued. "The entire patrol will be by your side in moments. The remaining groups will come in from the other passages."

Guenhwyvar nuzzled up to Drizzt, more than ready to follow him into battle. Drizzt took comfort in that when Dinin departed, leaving him alone again at the front. Only a few seconds later came the command to attack. Drizzt shook his head in disbelief when he saw the signal; how fast drow warriors found their positions!

He peeked around at the gnomish guards, still holding their silent vigil, completely unaware. Drizzt drew his blades and patted Guenhwyvar for luck, then called upon the innate magic of his race and dropped a globe of darkness in the corridor.

Squeals of alarm sounded throughout the tunnels, and Drizzt charged in, diving right into the darkness between the unseen guards and rolling back to his feet on the other side of his spell, only two running strides from the small chamber. He saw a dozen gnomes scrambling about, trying to prepare their defenses. Few of them paid Drizzt any attention, though, as the sounds of battle erupted from various side corridors.

One gnome chopped a heavy pick at Drizzt's shoulder. Drizzt got a blade up to block the blow but was amazed at the strength in the diminutive gnome's arms. Still, Drizzt could then have killed his attacker with the other scimitar. Too many doubts, and too many memories, though, haunted his actions. He brought a leg up into the gnome's belly, sending the little creature sprawling.

Belwar Dissengulp, next in line for Drizzt, noted how easily the young drow had dispatched one of his finest fighters and knew that the time had already come to use his most powerful magic. He pulled the emerald summoning stone from his neck and threw it to the ground at Drizzt's feet.

Drizzt jumped back, sensing the emanations of magic. Behind him,

Drizzt heard the approach of his companions, overpowering the shocked gnome guards and rushing to join him in the chamber. Then Drizzt's attentions went squarely to the heat patterns of the stone floor in front of him. The grayish lines wavered and swam, as if the stone was somehow coming alive.

The other drow fighters roared in past Drizzt, bearing down on the gnome leader and his charges. Drizzt didn't follow, guessing that the event unfolding at his feet was more critical than the general battle now echoing throughout the complex.

Fifteen feet tall and seven wide, an angry, towering humanoid monster of living stone rose before Drizzt.

"Elemental!" came a scream to the side. Drizzt glanced over to see Masoj, Guenhwyvar at his side, fumbling through a spellbook, apparently in search of some dweomer to battle this unexpected monster. To Drizzt's dismay, the frightened wizard mumbled a couple of words and vanished.

Drizzt set his feet under him, and took a measure of the monster, ready to spring aside in an instant. He could sense the thing's power, the raw strength of the earth embodied in living arms and legs.

A lumbering arm swung out in a wide arc, whooshing above Drizzt's ducking head and slamming into the cavern wall, crushing rocks into dust.

"Do not let it hit me," Drizzt instructed himself in a whisper that came out as a disbelieving gasp. As the elemental recoiled its arm, Drizzt poked a scimitar at it, chipping away a small chunk, barely a scratch. The elemental grimaced in pain—apparently Drizzt could indeed hurt it with his enchanted weapons.

Still standing in the same spot off to the side, the invisible Masoj held his next spell in check, watching the spectacle and waiting for the combatants to weaken each other. Perhaps the elemental would destroy Drizzt altogether. Invisible shoulders gave a resigned shrug. Masoj decided to let the gnomish power do his dirty work for him.

The monster launched another blow, and another, and Drizzt dived forward and scrambled through the thing's stone pillar legs. The elemental reacted quickly and stomped heavily with one foot, barely missing the agile drow, and sending branching cracks in the floor for many feet in either direction.

Drizzt was up in a flash, slicing and thrusting with both his blades into the elemental's backside, then springing back out of reach as the monster swung about, leading with another ferocious blow.

The sounds of battle grew more distant. The gnomes had taken flight—those that were still alive—but the drow warriors were in full pursuit, leaving Drizzt to face the elemental.

The monster stomped again, the thunder of its foot nearly knocking Drizzt from his feet, and it came in hard, falling down at Drizzt, using the tonnage of its body as a weapon. If Drizzt had been even slightly surprised, or if his reflexes had not been honed to such perfection, he surely would have been crushed flat. He managed to get to the side of the monster's bulk, while taking only a glancing blow from a swinging arm.

Dust rushed up from the terrific impact; cavern walls and ceiling cracked and dropped flecks and stones to the floor. As the elemental regained its feet, Drizzt backed away, overwhelmed by such unconquerable strength.

He was all alone against it, or so Drizzt thought. A sudden ball of hot fury enveloped the elemental's head, claws raking deep scratches into its face.

"Guenhwyvar!" Drizzt and Masoj shouted in unison, Drizzt in elation that an ally had been found, and Masoj in rage. The wizard did not want Drizzt to survive this battle, and he dared not launch any magical attacks, at Drizzt or the elemental, with his precious Guenhwyvar in the way.

"Do something, wizard!" Drizzt cried, recognizing the shout and understanding now that Masoj was still around.

The elemental bellowed in pain, its cry sounding as the rumble of huge boulders crashing down a rocky mountain. Even as Drizzt moved back in to help his feline friend, the monster spun, impossibly quick, and dived headfirst to the floor.

"No!" Drizzt cried, realizing that Guenhwyvar would be crushed. Then the cat and the elemental, instead of slamming against the stone, sank down into it!

⚔⚔⚔⚔⚔

The purple flames of faerie fire outlined the figures of the gnomes, showing the way for drow arrows and swords. The gnomes countered with magic of their own, illusionists' tricks mostly. "Down here!" one drow soldier cried, only to slam face first into the stone of a wall that had appeared as the entrance to a corridor.

Even though the gnome magic managed to keep the dark elves somewhat confused, Belwar Dissengulp grew frightened. His elemental, his strongest magic and only hope, was taking too long with the single drow warrior far back in the main chamber. The burrow-warden wanted the monster by his side when the main combat began. He ordered his forces into tight defensive formations, hoping that they could hold out.

Then the drow warriors, detained no more by gnomish tricks, were upon them, and fury stole Belwar's fear. He lashed out with his heavy pickaxe, smiling grimly as he felt the mighty weapon bite into drow flesh.

All magic was aside now, all formations and carefully laid battle plans dissolved into the wild frenzy of the brawl. Nothing mattered, except to hit the enemy, to feel the pick head or blade sinking into flesh. Above all others, deep gnomes hated the drow, and in all the Underdark there was nothing a dark elf enjoyed more than slicing a svirfnebli into littler pieces.

⚔⚔⚔⚔⚔

Drizzt rushed to the spot, but only the unbroken section of floor remained. "Masoj?" he gasped, looking for some answers from the one schooled in such strange magic.

Before the wizard could answer, the floor erupted behind Drizzt. He spun, weapons ready, to face the towering elemental.

Then Drizzt watched in helpless agony as the broken mist that was the great panther, his dearest companion, rolled off the elemental's shoulders and broke apart as it neared the floor.

Drizzt ducked another blow, though his eyes never left the dissipating dust-and-mist cloud. Was Guenhwyvar no more? Was his only friend gone from him forever? A new light grew in Drizzt lavender eyes, a primal rage that simmered throughout his body. He looked back to the elemental, unafraid.

"You are dead," he promised, and he walked in.

The elemental seemed confused, though of course it could not understand Drizzt's words. It dropped a heavy arm straight down to squash its foolish opponent. Drizzt did not even raise his blades to parry, knowing that every ounce of his strength could not possibly deflect such a blow. Just as the falling arm was about to reach him, he dashed forward, within its range.

The quickness of his move surprised the elemental, and the ensuing flurry of swordplay took Masoj's breath away. The wizard had never seen such grace in battle, such fluidity of motion. Drizzt climbed up and down the elemental's body, hacking and slashing, digging the points of his weapons home and flicking off pieces of the monster's stone skin.

The elemental howled its avalanche howl and spun in circles, trying to catch up to Drizzt and squash him once and for all. Blind anger brought new levels of expertise to the magnificent young swordsman, though, and the elemental caught nothing but air or its own stony body under its heavy slaps.

"Impossible," Masoj muttered when he found his breath. Could the young Do'Urden actually defeat an elemental? Masoj scanned the rest of the area. Several drow and many gnomes lay dead or grievously wounded, but the main fighting was moving even farther away as the gnomes found their tiny escape tunnels and the drow, enraged beyond good sense, followed them.

Guenhwyvar was gone. In this chamber, only Masoj, the elemental, and Drizzt remained as witnesses. The invisible wizard felt his mouth draw up in a smile. Now was the time to strike.

Drizzt had the elemental lurching to one side, nearly beaten, when the bolt roared in, a blast of lightning that blinded the young drow and sent him flying into the chamber's back wall. Drizzt watched the twitch of his hands, the wild dance of his stark white hair before his unmoving eyes. He felt nothing—no pain, no reviving draw of air into his lungs—and heard nothing, as if his life force had been some how suspended.

The attack dispelled Masoj's dweomer of invisibility, and he came back in view, laughing wickedly. The elemental, down in a broken, crumbled mass, slowly slipped back into the security of the stone floor.

"Are you dead?" the wizard asked Drizzt, the voice breaking the hush of Drizzt's deafness in dramatic booms. Drizzt could not answer, didn't really know the answer anyway. "Too easy," he heard Masoj say, and he suspected that the wizard was referring to him and not the elemental.

Then Drizzt felt a tingling in his fingers and bones and his lungs heaved suddenly, grabbing a volume of air. He gasped in rapid succession, then found control of his body and realized that he would survive.

Masoj glanced around for returning witnesses and saw none. "Good," he muttered as he watched Drizzt regain his senses. The wizard was truly glad that Drizzt's death had not been so very painless. He thought of another spell that would make the moment more fun.

A hand—a gigantic stone hand—reached out of the floor just then and grasped Masoj's leg, pulling his feet right into the stone.

The wizard's face twisted in a silent scream.

Drizzt's enemy saved his life. Drizzt snatched up one of the scimitars from the ground and hacked at the elemental's arm. The weapon sliced in, and the monster, its head reappearing between Drizzt and Masoj, howled in rage and pain and pulled the trapped wizard deeper into the stone.

With both hands on the scimitar's hilt, Drizzt struck as hard as he could, splitting the elemental's head right in half. This time the rubble did not sink back into its earthen plane; this time the elemental was destroyed.

"Get me out of here!" Masoj demanded. Drizzt looked at him, hardly believing that Masoj was still alive, for he was waist deep in solid stone.

"How?" Drizzt gasped. "You . . ." He couldn't even find the words to express his amazement.

"Just get me out!" the wizard cried.

Drizzt fumbled about, not knowing where to begin.

"Elementals travel between planes," Masoj explained, knowing that he had to calm Drizzt down if he ever wanted to get out of the floor. Masoj knew, too, that the conversation could go a long way in deflecting Drizzt's obvious suspicions that the lightning bolt had been aimed at him. "The ground an earth elemental traverses becomes a gate between the Plane of Earth and our plane, the Material Plane. The stone parted around me as the monster pulled me in, but it is quite uncomfortable." He twitched in pain as the stone tightened around one foot. "The gate is closing fast!"

"Then Guenhwyvar might be . . ." Drizzt started to reason.

He plucked the statuette right out of Masoj's front pocket and carefully inspected it for any flaws in its perfect design.

"Give me that!" Masoj demanded, embarrassed and angry.

Reluctantly, Drizzt handed the figurine over. Masoj glanced at it quickly and dropped it back into the pocket.

"Is Guenhwyvar unharmed?" Drizzt had to ask.

"It is not your concern," Masoj snapped back. The wizard, too, was worried about the cat, but at this moment, Guenhwyvar was the least of his troubles. "The gate is closing," he said again. "Go get the clerics!"

Before Drizzt could start off, a slab of stone in the wall behind him slid away, and the rock-hard fist of Belwar Dissengulp slammed into the back of his head.

# 23
# A Single Clean Blow

"The gnomes took him," Masoj said to Dinin when the patrol leader returned to the cavern. The wizard lifted his arms over his head to give the high priestess and her assistants a better view of his predicament.

"Where?" Dinin demanded. "Why did they let you live?"

Masoj shrugged. "A secret door," he explained, "somewhere on the wall behind you. I suspect that they would have taken me as well, except . . ." Masoj looked down at the floor, still holding him tightly up to the waist. "The gnomes would have killed me, but for your arrival."

"You are fortunate, wizard," the high priestess said to Masoj. "I have memorized a spell this day that will release the stone's hold on you." She whispered some instructions to her assistants and they took out water skins and pouches of clay and began tracing a ten foot square on the floor around the trapped wizard. The high priestess moved over to the wall of the chamber and prepared for her prayers.

"Some have escaped," Dinin said to her.

The high priestess understood. She whispered a quick detection spell and studied the wall. "Right there," she said. Dinin and another male rushed over to the spot and soon found the almost imperceptible outline to the secret door.

As the high priestess began her incantation, one of her cleric assistants threw the end of a rope to Masoj. "Hold on," the assistant teased, "and hold your breath!"

"Wait—" Masoj began, but the stone floor all around him transformed into mud and the wizard slipped under.

Two clerics, laughing, pulled Masoj out a moment later.

"Nice spell," the wizard remarked, spitting mud.

"It has its purposes," replied the high priestess. "Especially when we fight against the gnomes and their tricks with the stone. I carried it as a safeguard against earth elementals." She looked at a piece of rubble at her feet, unmistakably one eye and the nose of such a creature. "I see that my spell was not needed in that manner."

"I destroyed that one," Masoj lied.

"Indeed," said the high priestess, unconvinced. She could tell by the cut of the rubble that a blade had made the wound. She let the issue drop when the scrape of sliding stone turned them all to the wall.

"A maze," moaned the fighter beside Dinin when he peered into the tunnel. "How will we find them?"

Dinin thought for a moment, then spun on Masoj. "They have my brother," he said, an idea coming to mind. "Where is your cat?"

"About," Masoj stalled, guessing Dinin's plan and not really wanting Drizzt rescued.

"Bring it to me," Dinin ordered. "The cat can smell Drizzt."

"I cannot . . . I mean," Masoj stuttered.

"Now, wizard!" Dinin commanded. "Unless you wish me to tell the ruling council that some of the gnomes escaped because you refused to help!"

Masoj tossed the figurine to the ground and called for Guenhwyvar, not really knowing what would happen next. Had the earth elemental really destroyed Guenhwyvar? The mist appeared, in seconds transforming into the panther's corporeal body.

"Well," Dinin prompted, indicating the tunnel.

"Go find Drizzt!" Masoj commanded the cat. Guenhwyvar sniffed around the area for a moment, then bounded off down the small tunnel, the drow patrol in silent pursuit.

⚔ ⚔ ⚔ ⚔ ⚔

"Where . . ." Drizzt started when he finally began the long climb from the depths of unconsciousness. He understood that he was sitting, and knew, too, that his hands were bound in front of him.

A small but undeniably strong hand caught him by the back of the hair and pulled his head back roughly.

"Quiet!" Belwar whispered harshly, and Drizzt was surprised that the creature could speak his language. Belwar let go of Drizzt and turned to join other svirfnebli.

From the chamber's low height and the gnomes' nervous movements, Drizzt realized that this group had taken flight.

The gnomes began a quiet conversation in their own tongue, which Drizzt could not begin to understand. One of them asked the gnome who had ordered Drizzt to be quiet, apparently the leader, a heated question. Another grunted his accord and spoke some harsh words, turning on Drizzt with a dangerous look in his eyes.

The leader slapped the other gnome hard on the back and sent him off through one of the two low exits in the chamber, then put the others into defensive positions. He walked over to Drizzt. "You come with us to Blingdenstone," he said in hesitant words.

"Then?" Drizzt asked.

Belwar shrugged. "The king'll decide. If you cause me no trouble, I'll tell him to let you go."

Drizzt laughed cynically.

"Well, then," said Belwar, "if the king says to kill you, I'll make sure it comes in a single clean blow."

Again Drizzt laughed. "Do you believe that I believe?" he asked. "Torture me now and have your fun. That is your evil way!"

Belwar started to slap him but held his hand in check. "Svirfnebli don't torture!" he declared, louder than he should have. "Drow elves torture!" He turned away but spun back, reiterating his promise. "A single clean blow."

Drizzt found that he believed the sincerity in the gnome's voice, and he had to accept that promise as a measure of mercy far greater than the gnome would have received if Dinin's patrol had captured him. Belwar turned to walk away, but Drizzt, intrigued, had to learn more of the curious creature.

"How have you learned my language?" he asked.

"Gnomes are not stupid," Belwar retorted, unsure of what Drizzt was leading to.

"Nor are drow," Drizzt replied earnestly, "but I have never heard the language of the svirfnebli spoken in my city."

"There once was a drow in Blingdenstone," Belwar explained, now nearly as curious about Drizzt as Drizzt was about him.

"Slave," Drizzt reasoned.

"Guest!" Belwar snapped. "Svirfnebli keep no slaves!"

Again Drizzt found that he could not refute the sincerity in Belwar's voice. "What is your name?" he asked.

The gnome laughed at him. "Do you think me stupid?" Belwar asked. "You desire my name that you might use its power in some dark magic against me!"

"No," Drizzt protested.

"I should kill you now for thinking me stupid!" Belwar growled, ominously lifting his heavy pick. Drizzt shifted uncomfortably, not knowing what the gnome would do next.

"My offer remains," Belwar said, lowering the pick. "No trouble, and I tell the king to let you go." Belwar didn't believe that would happen any more than did Drizzt, so the svirfneblin, with a helpless shrug, offered Drizzt the next best thing. "Or else, a single clean blow."

A commotion from one of the tunnels turned Belwar away. "Belwar," called one of the other gnomes, rushing back into the small chamber. The gnome leader turned a wary eye on Drizzt to see if the drow had caught the mention of his name.

Drizzt wisely kept his head turned away, pretending not to listen. He had indeed heard the name of the gnome leader who had shown him mercy. Belwar, the other svirfneblin had said. Belwar, a name that Drizzt would never forget.

Fighting from down the passageway caught everyone's attention, then, and several svirfnebli scrambled back into the chamber. Drizzt knew from their excitement that the drow patrol was close behind.

Belwar started barking out commands, mostly organizing the retreat down the chamber's other tunnel. Drizzt wondered where he would fit into the gnome's thinking. Certainly Belwar couldn't hope to outrun the drow patrol dragging along a prisoner.

Then the gnome leader suddenly stopped talking and stopped moving. Too suddenly.

The drow clerics had led the way in with their insidious, paralyzing spells. Belwar and another gnome were held fast by the dweomer, and the rest of the gnomes, realizing this, broke into a wild scramble for the rear exit.

The drow warriors, Guenhwyvar leading the way, charged into the room. Any relief Drizzt might have felt at seeing his feline friend unharmed was buried under the ensuing slaughter. Dinin and his troops cut into the disorganized gnomes with typical drow savagery.

In seconds—horrible seconds that seemed like hours to Drizzt—only Belwar and the other gnome caught in the clerical spell remained alive in the chamber. Several of the svirfnebli had managed to flee down the back corridor, but most of the drow patrol was off in pursuit.

Masoj came into the chamber last, looking thoroughly wretched in his mud-covered clothing. He remained at the tunnel exit and did not even look Drizzt's way, except to note that his panther was standing protectively beside the secondboy of House Do'Urden.

"Again you have found your measure of luck, and more," Dinin said to Drizzt as he cut his brother's bonds.

Looking around at the carnage in the chamber, Drizzt wasn't so sure.

Dinin handed him back his scimitars, then turned to the drow standing watch over the two paralyzed gnomes. "Finish them," Dinin instructed.

A wide smile spread over the other drow's face, and he pulled a jagged knife from his belt. He held it up in front of a gnome's face, teasing the helpless creature. "Can they see it?" he asked the high priestess.

"That is the fun of the spell," the high priestess replied. "The svirfneblin understands what is about to happen. Even now he is struggling to break out of the hold."

"Prisoners!" Drizzt blurted.

Dinin and the others turned to him, the drow with the dagger wearing a scowl both angry and disappointed.

"For House Do'Urden?" Drizzt asked Dinin hopefully. "We could benefit from—"

"Svirfnebli do not make good slaves," Dinin replied.

"No," agreed the high priestess, moving beside the dagger-wielding fighter. She nodded to the warrior and his smile returned tenfold. He struck hard. Only Belwar remained.

The warrior waved his bloodstained dagger ominously and moved in front of the gnome leader.

"Not that one!" Drizzt protested, unable to bear anymore. "Let him live!" Drizzt wanted to say that Belwar could do them no harm, and that killing the defenseless gnome would be a cowardly and vile act. Drizzt knew that appealing to his kin for mercy would be a waste of time.

Dinin's expression was more a look of anger than curiosity this time.

"If you kill him, then no gnomes will remain to return to their city and tell of our strength," Drizzt reasoned, grasping at the one slim hope he could find. "We should send him back to his people, send him back to tell them of their folly in entering the domain of the drow!"

Dinin looked back to the high priestess for advice.

"It seems proper reasoning," she said with a nod.

Dinin was not so certain of his brother's motives. Not taking his eyes off Drizzt, he said to the warrior, "Then cut off the gnome's hands."

Drizzt didn't flinch, realizing that if he did, Dinin would surely slaughter Belwar.

The warrior replaced the dagger on his belt and took out his heavy sword.

"Wait," said Dinin, still eyeing Drizzt. "Release him from the spell first; I want to hear his screams."

Several drow moved over to put the tips of their swords at Belwar's neck as the high priestess released her magical hold. Belwar made no moves.

The appointed drow warrior grasped his sword in both hands, and Belwar, brave Belwar, held his arms straight out and motionless in front of him.

Drizzt averted his gaze, unable to watch and awaiting, fearing, the gnome's cry.

Belwar noted Drizzt's reaction. Was it compassion?

The drow warrior then swung his sword. Belwar never took his stare off Drizzt as the sword cut across his wrists, lighting a million fires of agony in his arms.

Neither did Belwar scream. He wouldn't give Dinin the satisfaction. The gnome leader looked back to Drizzt one final time as two drow fighters ushered him out of the chamber, and he recognized the true anguish, and the apology, behind the young drow's feigned impassive facade.

Even as Belwar was leaving, the dark elves who had chased off after the fleeing gnomes returned from the other tunnel. "We could not catch them in these tiny passage ways," one of them complained.

"Damn!" Dinin growled. Sending a handless gnome victim back to Blingdenstone was one thing, but letting healthy members of the gnome expedition escape was quite an other. "I want them caught!"

"Guenhwyvar can catch them," Masoj proclaimed, then he called the cat to his side and eyed Drizzt all the while.

Drizzt's heart raced as the wizard patted the great cat.

"Come, my pet," Masoj said. "There is hunting left to be done!" The wizard watched Drizzt squirm at the words, knowing that Drizzt did not approve of Guenhwyvar engaging in such tactics.

"They are gone?" Drizzt asked Dinin, his voice on the edge of desperation.

"Running all the way back to Blingdenstone," Dinin replied calmly. "If we let them."

"And will they return?"

Dinin's sour scowl reflected the absurdity of his brother's question. "Would you?"

"Our task is complete, then," Drizzt reasoned, trying vainly to find some way out of Masoj's ignoble designs for the panther.

"We have won the day," Dinin agreed, "though our own losses have been great. We may find still more fun, with the help of the wizard's pet."

"Fun," Masoj echoed pointedly at Drizzt. "Be gone, Guenhwyvar, into the tunnels. Let us learn how fast a frightened gnome may run!"

Only a few minutes later, Guenhwyvar came back into the chamber, dragging a dead gnome in its mouth.

"Return!" Masoj commanded as Guenhwyvar dropped the body at his feet. "Bring me more!"

Drizzt's heart dropped at the sound of the corpse flopping to the stone floor. He looked into Guenhwyvar's eyes and saw a sadness as profound as his own. The panther was a hunter, as honorable in its own way as was Drizzt. To the evil Masoj, though, Guenhwyvar was a toy and nothing more, an instrument for his perverted pleasures, killing for no reason other than his master's joy of killing.

In the hands of the wizard, Guenhwyvar was no more than a murderer.

Guenhwyvar paused at the entrance to the small tunnel and looked to Drizzt almost apologetically.

"Return!" Masoj screamed, and he kicked the cat in the rear. Then Masoj, too, turned an eye back on Drizzt, a vindictive eye. Masoj had missed his chance to kill the young Do'Urden; he would have to be careful how he explained such a mistake to his unforgiving mother. Masoj decided to worry about that unpleasant encounter later. For now, at least, he had the satisfaction of watching Drizzt suffer.

Dinin and the others were oblivious to the unfolding drama between Masoj and Drizzt; too engaged in their wait for Guenhwyvar's return; too engaged in their speculations of the expressions of terror the gnomes would cast back at such a perfect killer; too caught up in the macabre humor of the moment, that perverted drow humor that brought laughter when tears were needed.

# Part Five

## Zaknafein

Zaknafein Do'Urden: mentor, teacher, friend. I, in the blind agony of my own frustrations, more than once came to recognize Zaknafein as none of these. Did I ask of him more than he could give? Did I expect perfection of a tormented soul; hold Zaknafein up to standards beyond his experiences, or standards impossible in the face of his experiences?

I might have been him. I might have lived, trapped within the helpless rage, buried under the daily assault of the wickedness that is Menzoberranzan and the pervading evil that is my own family, never in life to find escape.

It seems a logical assumption that we learn from the mistakes of our elders. This, I believe, was my salvation. Without the example of Zaknafein, I, too, would have found no escape—not in life.

Is this course I have chosen a better way than the life Zaknafein knew? I think, yes, though I find despair often enough sometimes to long for that other way. It would have been easier. Truth, though, is nothing in the face of self-falsehood, and principles are of no value if the idealist cannot live up to his own standards.

This, then, is a better way.

I live with many laments, for my people, for myself, but mostly for that weapons master, lost to me now, who showed me how—and why—to use a blade.

There is no pain greater than this; not the cut of a jagged-edged dagger nor the fire of a dragon's breath. Nothing burns in your heart like the emptiness of losing something, someone, before you truly have learned of its value. Often now I lift my cup in a futile toast, an apology to ears that cannot hear:

To Zak, the one who inspired my courage.

—Drizzt Do'Urden

# 24
# To Know Our Enemies

Eight drow dead, and one a cleric," Briza said to Matron Malice on the balcony of House Do'Urden. Briza had rushed back to the compound with the first reports of the encounter, leaving her sisters at the central plaza of Menzoberranzan with the gathered throng, awaiting further information. "But nearly two score of the gnomes died, a clear victory."

"What of your brothers?" asked Malice. "How did House Do'Urden fare in this encounter?"

"As with the surface elves, Dinin's hand slew five," replied Briza. "They say that he led the main assault fearlessly, and he killed the most gnomes."

Matron Malice beamed with the news, though she suspected that Briza, standing patiently behind a smug smile, was holding something dramatic back from her. "What of Drizzt?" the matron demanded, having no patience for her daughter's games. "How many svirfnebli fell at his feet?"

"None," Briza replied, but still the smile remained. "Still the day belonged to Drizzt!" she added quickly, seeing an angry scowl spreading across her volatile mother's face. Malice did not seem amused.

"Drizzt defeated an earth elemental," Briza cried, "all alone, almost, with only minor help from a wizard! The high priestess of the patrol named the kill his!"

Matron Malice gasped and turned away. Drizzt had ever been an enigma to her, as fine with the blade as any but lacking the proper attitude and the proper respect. Now this: an earth elemental! Malice herself had seen such a monster ravage an entire drow raiding party, killing a dozen seasoned warriors before wandering off on its way. Yet her son, her confusing son, had defeated one single-handedly!

"Lolth will favor us this day," Briza commented, not quite understanding her mother's reaction.

Briza's words struck an idea in Malice. "Gather your sisters," she commanded. "We shall meet in the chapel. If House Do'Urden so fully won the day out in the tunnels, perhaps the Spider Queen will grace us with some information."

"Vierna and Maya await the forthcoming news in the city plaza," Briza explained, mistakenly believing her mother to be referring to information about the battle. "Surely we will know the entire story within an hour."

"I care nothing for a battle against gnomes!" Malice scolded. "You have told everything that is important to our family; the rest does not matter. We must parlay your brothers' heroics into gain."

"To learn of our enemies!" Briza blurted as she realized what her mother had in mind.

"Exactly," replied Malice. "To learn which house it is that threatens House Do'Urden. If the Spider Queen truly finds favor with us this day, she may grace us with the knowledge we need to defeat our enemies!"

A short while later, the four high priestesses of House Do'Urden gathered around the spider idol in the chapel anteroom. Before them, in a bowl of the deepest onyx, burned the sacred incense—sweet, deathlike, and favored by the yochlol, the handmaidens of Lolth.

The flame moved through a variety of colors, from orange to green to brilliant red. It then took shape, heard the beckons of the four priestesses and the urgency in the voice of Matron Malice. The top of the fire, no longer dancing, smoothed and rounded, assumed the form of a hairless head, then stretched upward, growing. The flame disappeared, consumed by the yochlol's image, a half melted pile of wax with grotesquely elongated eyes and a drooping mouth.

"Who has summoned me?" the small figure demanded telepathically.

The yochlol's thoughts, too powerful for its diminutive stature, boomed within the heads of the gathered drow.

"I have, handmaiden," Malice replied aloud, wanting her daughters to hear. The matron bowed her head. "I am Malice, loyal servant of the Spider Queen."

In a puff of smoke, the yochlol disappeared, leaving only glowing incense embers in the onyx bowl. A moment later, the handmaiden reappeared, full size, standing behind Matron Malice. Briza, Vierna, and Maya held their breath as the being laid two sickly tentacles on their mother's shoulders.

Matron Malice accepted the tentacles without reply, confident in her cause for summoning the yochlol.

"Explain to me why you dare to disturb me," came the yochlol's insidious thoughts.

"To ask a simple question," Malice replied silently, for no words were necessary to communicate with a handmaiden. "One whose answer you know."

"Does this question interest you so greatly?" the yochlol asked. "You risk such dire consequences."

"It is imperative that I learn the answer," replied Matron Malice. Her three daughters watched curiously, hearing the yochlol's thoughts but only guessing at their mother's unspoken replies.

"If the answer is so important, and it is known to the handmaidens, and thus to the Spider Queen, do you not believe that Lolth would have given it to you if she so chose?"

"Perhaps, before this day, the Spider Queen did not deem me worthy to know," Malice responded. "Things have changed."

The handmaiden paused and rolled its elongated eyes back into its head as if communicating with some distant plane.

"Greetings, Matron Malice Do'Urden," the yochlol said aloud after a few tense moments. The creature's spoken voice was calm and overly smooth for the thing's grotesque appearance.

"My greetings to you, and to your mistress, Queen of Spiders," replied Malice. She shot a wry smile at her daughters and still didn't turn to face the creature behind her. Apparently Malice's guess of Lolth's favor had been correct.

"Daermon N'a'shezbaernon has pleased Lolth," the handmaiden said. "The males of your house have won the day, even above the females that journeyed with them. I must accept Matron Malice Do'Urden's summons." The tentacles slid off Malice's shoulders, and the yochlol stood rigid behind her, awaiting her commands.

"Glad I am to please the Spider Queen," Malice began. She sought the proper way to phrase her question. "For the summons, as I have said, I beg only the answer to a simple question."

"Ask it," prompted the yochlol, and the mocking tone told Malice and her daughters that the monster already knew the question.

"My house is threatened, say the rumors," said Malice.

"Rumors?" The yochlol laughed an evil, grating sound.

"I trust in my sources," Malice replied defensively. "I would not have called upon you if I did not believe the threat."

"Continue," said the yochlol, amused by the whole affair. "They are more than rumors, Matron Malice Do'Urden. Another house plans war upon you."

Maya's immature gasp brought scornful eyes upon her from her mother and her sisters.

"Name this house to me," Malice pleaded. "If Daermon N'a'shezbaernon truly has pleased the Spider Queen this day, then I bid Lolth to reveal our enemies, that we might destroy them!"

"And if this other house also has pleased the Spider Queen?" the handmaiden mused. "Would Lolth then betray it to you?"

"Our enemies hold every advantage," Malice protested. "They know of House Do'Urden. No doubt they watch us every day, laying their plans. We ask Lolth only to give us knowledge equal to that of our enemies. Reveal them and let us prove which house is more worthy of victory."

"What if your enemies are greater than you?" asked the handmaiden. "Would Matron Malice Do'Urden then call upon Lolth to intervene and save her pitiful house?"

"No!" cried Malice. "We would call upon those powers that Lolth has given us to fight our foes. Even if our enemies are the more powerful, let Lolth be assured that they will suffer great pain for their attack on House Do'Urden!"

Again the handmaiden sank back within itself, finding the link to its home plane, a place darker than Menzoberranzan. Malice clenched tightly to Briza's hand, to her right, and Vierna's, to her left. They in turn passed along the confirmation of their bond to Maya, at the foot of the circle.

"The Spider Queen is pleased, Matron Malice Do'Urden," the handmaiden said at length. "Trust that she will favor House Do'Urden more than your enemies when battle rings out—perhaps . . ." Malice flinched at the ambiguity of that final word, grudgingly accepting that Lolth never made any promises, at any time.

"What of my question," Malice dared to protest, "the reason for the summons?"

There came a bright flash that stole the four clerics' vision. When their eyesight returned to them, they saw the yochlol, tiny again, and glaring out at them from the flames of the onyx bowl.

"The Spider Queen does not give an answer that is already known!" The handmaiden proclaimed, the sheer power of its otherworldly voice cutting into the drow ears. The fire erupted in another blinding flash, and the yochlol disappeared, leaving the precious bowl sundered into a dozen pieces.

Matron Malice grabbed a large piece of the shattered onyx and threw it against a wall. "Already known?" she cried in rage. "Known to whom? Who in my family keeps this secret from me?"

"Perhaps the one who knows does not know that she knows," Briza put in, trying to calm her mother. "Or perhaps the information is newly found, and she has not yet had the chance to come to you with it."

"She?" growled Matron Malice. "What 'she' do you speak of, Briza? We are all here. Are any of my daughters stupid enough to miss such an obvious threat to our family?"

"No, Matron!" Vierna and Maya cried together, terrified of Malice's growing wrath, rising beyond control.

"Never have I seen any sign!" said Vierna.

"Nor l! " added Maya. "By your side I have been these many tendays, and I have seen no more than you!"

"Are you implying that I have missed something?" Malice growled, her knuckles white at her sides.

"No, Matron!" Briza shouted above the commotion, loud enough to settle her mother for the moment and turn Malice's attention fully upon her eldest daughter.

"Not she, then," Briza reasoned. "He. One of your sons may have the answer, or Zaknafein or Rizzen, perhaps."

"Yes," agreed Vierna. "They are only males, too stupid to understand the importance of minor details."

"Drizzt and Dinin have been out of the house," added Briza, "out of the city. In their patrol group are children of every powerful house, every house that would dare to threaten us!"

The fires in Malice's eyes glowed, but she relaxed at the reasoning. "Bring them to me when they return to Menzoberranzan," she instructed Vierna and Maya. "You," she said to Briza, "bring Rizzen and Zaknafein. All the family must be present, so that we may learn what we may learn!"

"The cousins, and the soldiers, too?" asked Briza. "Perhaps one beyond the immediate family knows the answer."

"Should we bring them together, as well?" offered Vierna, her voice edged with the rising excitement of the moment. "A gathering of the whole clan, a general war party of House Do'Urden?"

"No," Malice replied, "not the soldiers or the cousins. I do not believe they are involved in this; the handmaiden would have told us the answer if one of my direct family did not know it. It is my embarrassment to ask a question whose answer should be known to me, whose answer someone within the circle of my family knows." She gritted her teeth as she spat out the rest of her thoughts.

"I do not enjoy being embarrassed!"

⚔ ⚔ ⚔ ⚔ ⚔

Drizzt and Dinin came into the house a short while later, exhausted and glad the adventure was over. They had barely passed the entrance and turned down the wide corridor that led to their rooms when they bumped into Zaknafein, coming the other way.

"So the hero has returned," Zak remarked, eyeing Drizzt directly. Drizzt did not miss the sarcasm in his voice.

"We've completed our job—successfully," Dinin shot back, more than a little perturbed at being excluded from Zak's greeting. "I led—"

"I know of the battle," Zak assured him. "It has been endlessly recounted throughout the city. Now leave us, Elderboy. I have unfinished business with your brother."

"I leave when I choose to leave!" Dinin growled.

Zak snapped a glare upon him. "I wish to speak to Drizzt, only to Drizzt, so leave."

Dinin's hand went to his sword hilt, not a smart move. Before he even moved the weapon hilt an inch from the scabbard, Zak had slapped him twice in the face with one hand. The other had somehow produced a dagger and put its tip at Dinin's throat.

Drizzt watched in amazement, certain that Zak would kill Dinin if this continued.

"Leave," Zak said again, "on your life."

Dinin threw his hands up and slowly backed away. "Matron Malice will hear of this!" he warned.

"I will tell her myself," Zak laughed at him. "Do you think she will trouble herself on your behalf, fool? As far as Matron Malice cares, the family males determine their own hierarchy. Go away, Elderboy. Come back when you have found the courage to challenge me."

"Come with me, brother," Dinin said to Drizzt.

"We have business," Zak reminded Drizzt.

Drizzt looked to both of them, once and back again, stunned by their open willingness to kill each other. "I will stay," he decided. "I do indeed have unfinished business with the weapons master."

"As you choose, hero," Dinin spat, and he turned on his heel and stormed away.

"You have made an enemy," Drizzt remarked to Zak.

"I have made many," Zak laughed, "and I will make many more before my day ends! But no mind. Your actions have inspired jealousy in your brother—your older brother. You are the one who should be wary."

"He hates you openly," reasoned Drizzt.

"But would gain nothing from my death," Zak replied. "I am no threat to Dinin, but you . . ." He let the word hang in the air.

"Why would I threaten him?" Drizzt protested. "Dinin has nothing I desire."

"He has power," Zak explained. "He is the elderboy now but was not always."

"He killed Nalfein, the brother I never met."

"You know of this?" said Zak. "Perhaps Dinin suspects that another secondboy will follow the same course he took to become the elderboy of House Do'Urden."

"Enough," Drizzt growled, tired of the whole stupid system of ascension. How well you know it, Zaknafein, he thought. How many did you murder to attain your position?

"An earth elemental," Zak said, blowing a low whistle with the words. "It is a powerful foe that you defeated this day." He bowed low, showing Drizzt mockery beyond any doubt. "What is next for the young hero? A daemon, perhaps? A demigod? Surely there is nothing that can—"

"Never have I heard such senseless words stream from your mouth," Drizzt retorted. Now it was time for some sarcasm of his own. "Is it that I have inspired jealousy in another besides my brother?"

"Jealousy?" Zak cried. "Wipe your nose, sniveling little boy! A dozen earth elementals have fallen to my blade! Daemons, too! Do not overestimate your deeds or your abilities. You are one warrior among a race of warriors. To forget that surely will prove fatal." He ended the line with pointed emphasis, almost in a sneer, and Drizzt began to consider again just how real their appointed "practice" in the gym would become.

"I know my abilities," Drizzt replied, "and my limitations. I have learned to survive."

"As have I," Zak shot back, "for so many centuries!"

"The gym awaits," Drizzt said calmly.

"Your mother awaits," Zak corrected. "She bids us all to the chapel. Fear not, though. There will be time for our meeting."

Drizzt walked past Zak without another word, suspecting that his and Zak's blades would finish the conversation for them. What had become of

Zaknafein? Drizzt wondered. Was this the same teacher who had trained him those years before the Academy? Drizzt could not sort through his feelings. Was he seeing Zak differently because of the things he had learned of Zak's exploits, or was there truly something different, something harder, about the weapons master's demeanor since Drizzt had returned from the Academy?

The sound of a whip brought Drizzt from his contemplations.

"I am your patron!" he heard Rizzen say.

"That's of no consequence!" retorted a female voice, the voice of Briza. Drizzt slipped to the corner of the next intersection and peeked around. Briza and Rizzen faced off, Rizzen unarmed, but Briza holding her snake-headed whip.

"Patron," Briza laughed, "a meaningless title. You are a male lending your seed to the matron and of no more importance."

"Four I have sired," Rizzen said indignantly.

"Three!" Briza corrected, snapping the whip to accentuate the point. "Vierna is Zaknafein's, not yours! Nalfein is dead, leaving only two. One of those is female and above you. Only Dinin is truly under your rank!"

Drizzt sank back against the wall and looked behind him to the empty corridor he had just walked. He had always suspected that Rizzen was not his true father. The male had never paid him any mind, had never scolded him or praised him or offered to him any advice or training. To hear Briza say it, though, . . . and Rizzen not deny it!

Rizzen fumbled about for some retort to Briza's stinging words. "Does Matron Malice know of your desires?" he snarled. "Does she know that her eldest daughter seeks her title?"

"Every eldest daughter seeks the title of matron mother," Briza laughed at him. "Matron Malice would be a fool to suspect otherwise. I assure you that she is not, nor am I. I will get the title from her when she is weak with age. She knows and accepts this as fact."

"You admit that you will kill her?"

"If not I, then Vierna. If not Vierna, then Maya. It is our way, stupid male. It is the word of Lolth."

Rage burned in Drizzt as he heard the evil proclamations, but he remained silent at the corner.

"Briza will not wait for age to steal her mother's power," Rizzen snarled, "not when a dagger will expedite the transfer. Briza hungers for the throne of the house!"

Rizzen's next words came out as an indecipherable scream as the six-headed whip went to work again and again.

Drizzt wanted to intervene, to rush out and cut them both down, but, of course, he could not. Briza acted now as she had been taught, followed the words of the Spider Queen in asserting her dominance over Rizzen. She wouldn't kill him, Drizzt knew.

But what if Briza got carried away in the frenzy? What if she did kill Rizzen? In the empty void that was beginning to grow in his heart, Drizzt wondered if he even cared.

⚔ ⚔ ⚔ ⚔ ⚔

"You let him escape!" Matron SiNafay roared at her son. "You will learn not to disappoint me!"

"No, my matron!" Masoj protested. "I hit him squarely with a lightning bolt. He never even suspected the blow to be aimed at him! I could not finish the deed; the monster had me caught in the gate to its own plane!"

SiNafay bit her lip, forced to accept her son's reasoning. She knew that she had given Masoj a difficult mission. Drizzt was a powerful foe, and to kill him without leaving an obvious trail would not be easy.

"I will get him," Masoj promised, determination showing on his face. "I have the weapon readied; Drizzt will be dead before the tenth cycle, as you commanded."

"Why should I grant you another chance?" SiNafay asked him. "Why should I believe that you will fare better the next time you try?"

"Because I want him dead!" Masoj cried. "More than even you, my matron. I want to tear the life from Drizzt Do'Urden! When he is dead, I want to rip out his heart and display it as a trophy!"

SiNafay could not deny her son's obsession. "Granted," she said. "Get him, Masoj Hun'ett. On your life, strike the first blow against House Do'Urden and kill its secondboy."

Masoj bowed, the grimace never leaving his face, and swept out of the room.

"You heard everything," SiNafay signaled when the door had closed behind her son. She knew that Masoj might well have his ear to the door, and she did not want him to know of this conversation.

"I did," Alton replied in the silent code, stepping out from behind a curtain.

"Do you concur with my decision?" SiNafay's hands asked.

Alton was at a loss. He had no choice but to abide by his matron mother's decisions, but he did not think that SiNafay had been wise in sending Masoj back out after Drizzt. His silence grew long.

"You do not approve," Matron SiNafay bluntly motioned.

"Please, Matron Mother," Alton replied quickly. "I would not . . ."

"You are forgiven," SiNafay assured him. "I am not so certain that I should have allowed Masoj a second opportunity. Too much could go wrong."

"Then why?" Alton dared to ask. "You did not grant me a second chance, though I desire Drizzt Do'Urden's death as fiercely as any."

SiNafay cast him a scornful glare, sending him back on his courageous heels. "You doubt my judgment?"

"No!" Alton cried aloud. He slipped a hand over his mouth and dropped to his knees in terror. "Never, my matron," he signaled silently. "I just do not understand the problem as clearly as you. Forgive me my ignorance."

SiNafay's laughter sounded like the hiss of a hundred angry snakes. "We see together in this matter," she assured Alton. "I would no more give Masoj a second chance than I gave you."

"But—" Alton started to protest.

"Masoj will go back after Drizzt, but this time he will not be alone," SiNafay explained. "You will follow him, Alton DeVir. Keep him safe and finish the deed, on your life."

Alton beamed at the news that he would finally find some taste of vengeance. SiNafay's final threat didn't even concern him. "Could it ever be any other way?" his hands asked casually.

⚔⚔⚔⚔⚔

"Think!" Malice growled, her face close, her breath hot on Drizzt's face. "You know something!"

Drizzt slumped back from the overpowering figure and glanced nervously around at his gathered family. Dinin, similarly grilled just a moment ago, kneeled with his chin in hand. He tried vainly to come up with an answer before Matron Malice upped the level of the interrogation techniques. Dinin did not miss Briza's motions toward her snake whip, and the unnerving sight did little to aid his memory.

Malice slapped Drizzt hard across the face and stepped away. "One of you has learned the identity of our enemies," she snapped at her sons. "Out there, on patrol, one of you has seen some hint, some sign."

"Perhaps we saw it but did not know it for what it was," Dinin offered.

"Silence!" Malice screamed, her face bright with rage. "When you know the answer to my question, you may speak! Only then!" She turned to Briza. "Help Dinin find his memory!"

Dinin dropped his head to his arms, folded on the floor in front of him, and arched his back to accept the torture. To do otherwise would only enrage Malice more.

Drizzt closed his eyes and recounted the events of his many patrols. He jerked involuntarily when he heard the snake whip's crack and his brother's soft groan.

"Masoj," Drizzt whispered, almost unconsciously. He looked up at his mother, who held her hand out to halt Briza's attacks—to Briza's dismay.

"Masoj Hun'ett," Drizzt said more loudly. "In the fight against the gnomes, he tried to kill me."

All the family, particularly Malice and Dinin, leaned forward toward Drizzt, hanging on his every word.

"When I battled the elemental," Drizzt explained, spitting out the last word as a curse upon Zaknafein. He cast an angry glare at the weapons master and continued, "Masoj Hun'ett struck me down with a bolt of lightning."

"He may have been shooting for the monster," Vierna insisted. "Masoj insisted that it was he who killed the elemental, but the high priestess of the patrol denied his claim."

"Masoj waited," Drizzt replied. "He did nothing until I began to gain the advantage over the monster. Then he loosed his magic, as much at me as at the elemental. I think he hoped to destroy us both."

"House Hun'ett," Matron Malice whispered.

"Fifth House," Briza remarked, "under Matron SiNafay."

"So that is our enemy," said Malice.

"Perhaps not," said Dinin, wondering even as he spoke the words why he hadn't left well enough alone. To disprove the theory only invited more whipping.

Matron Malice did not like his hesitation as he reconsidered the argument. "Explain!" she commanded.

"Masoj Hun'ett was angry at being excluded from the surface raid," said Dinin. "We left him in the city, only to witness our triumphant return." Dinin fixed his eyes straight on his brother. "Masoj has ever been jealous of Drizzt and all the glories that my brother has found, rightly or wrongly. Many are jealous of Drizzt and would see him dead."

Drizzt shifted uncomfortably in his seat, knowing the last words to be an open threat. He glanced over to Zaknafein and marked the weapons master's smug smile.

"Are you certain of your words?" Malice said to Drizzt, shaking him from his private thoughts.

"There is the cat," Dinin interrupted, "Masoj Hun'ett's magical pet, though it holds closer to Drizzt's side than to the wizard's."

"Guenhwyvar walks the point beside me," Drizzt protested, "a position that you ordered."

"Masoj does not like it," Dinin retorted.

Perhaps that is why you put the cat there, Drizzt thought, but he kept the words to himself. Was he seeing conspiracies in coincidence? Or was his world so truly filled with devious schemes and silent struggles for power?

"Are you certain of your words?" Malice asked Drizzt again, pulling him from his pondering.

"Masoj Hun'ett tried to kill me," he asserted. "I do not know his reasons, but his intent I do not doubt!"

"House Hun'ett, then," Briza remarked, "a mighty foe."

"We must learn of them," Malice said. "Dispatch the scouts! I will know the count of House Hun'ett's soldiers, its wizards, and, particularly, its clerics."

"If we are wrong," Dinin said. "If House Hun'ett is not the conspiring house—"

"We are not wrong!" Malice screamed at him.

"The yochlol said that one of us knows the identity of our enemy," reasoned Vierna. "All we have is Drizzt's tale of Masoj."

"Unless you are hiding something," Matron Malice growled at Dinin, a threat so cold and wicked that it stole the blood from the elderboy's face.

Dinin shook his head emphatically and slumped back, having nothing more to add to the conversation.

"Prepare a communion," Malice said to Briza. "Let us learn of Matron SiNafay's standing with the Spider Queen."

Drizzt watched incredulously as the preparations began at a frantic pace, each command from Matron Malice following a practiced defensive course. It wasn't the precision of Drizzt's family's battle planning that amazed him—he would expect nothing less from this group. It was the eager gleam in every eye.

# 25
# THE WEAPONS MASTERS

"Impudent!" growled the yochlol. The fire in the brazier puffed, and the creature again stood behind Malice, again draped dangerous tentacles over the matron mother. "You dare to summon me again?"

Malice and her daughters glanced around, on the edge of panic. They knew that the mighty being was not toying with them; the handmaiden truly was enraged this time.

"House Do'Urden pleased the Spider Queen, it is true," the yochlol answered their unspoken thoughts, "but that one act does not dispel the displeasure your family brought upon Lolth in the recent past. Do not think that all is forgiven, Matron Malice Do'Urden!"

How small and vulnerable Matron Malice felt now. Her power paled in the face of the wrath of one of Lolth's personal servants.

"Displeasure?" she dared to whisper. "How has my family brought displeasure to the Spider Queen? By what act?"

The handmaiden's laughter erupted in a spout of flames and flying spiders, but the high priestesses held their positions. They accepted the heat and the crawling things as part of their penance.

"I have told you before, Matron Malice Do'Urden," the yochlol snarled with its droopy mouth, "and I shall tell you one final time. The Spider Queen does not reply to questions whose answers are already known!" In a blast of explosive energy that sent the four females of House Do'Urden tumbling to the floor, the handmaiden was gone.

Briza was the first to recover. She prudently rushed over to the brazier and smothered the remaining flames, thus closing the gate to the Abyss, the yochlol's home plane.

"Who?" screamed Malice, the powerful matriarch once again. "Who in my family has invoked the wrath of Lolth?" Malice appeared small again then, as the implications of the yochlol's warning became all too clear. House Do'Urden was about to go to war with a powerful family. Without Lolth's favor, House Do'Urden likely would cease to exist.

"We must find the perpetrator," Malice instructed her daughters, certain that none of them was involved. They were high priestesses, one and all. If any of them had done some misdeed in the eyes of the Spider Queen, the summoned yochlol surely would have exacted punishment on the spot. By itself, the handmaiden could have leveled House Do'Urden.

Briza pulled the snake whip from her belt. "I will get the information we require!" she promised.

"No!" said Matron Malice. "We must not reveal our search. Be it a soldier or a member of House Do'Urden, the guilty one is trained and hardened against pain. We cannot hope that torture will pull the confession from his lips; not when he knows the consequences of his actions. We must discover the cause of Lolth's displeasure immediately and properly punish the criminal. The Spider Queen must stand behind us in our struggles!"

"How, then, are we to discern the perpetrator?" the eldest daughter complained, reluctantly replacing the snake whip on her belt.

"Vierna and Maya, leave us," Matron Malice instructed. "Say nothing of these revelations and do nothing to hint at our purpose."

The two younger daughters bowed and scurried away, not happy with their secondary roles but unable to do anything about them.

"First we will look," Malice said to Briza. "We will see if we can learn of the guilty one from afar."

Briza understood. "The scrying bowl," she said. She rushed from the anteroom and into the chapel proper. In the central altar she found the valuable item, a wide golden bowl laced throughout with black pearls. Hands trembling,

Briza placed the bowl atop the altar and reached into the most sacred of the many compartments. This was the holding bin for the prized possession of House Do'Urden, a great onyx chalice.

Malice then joined Briza in the chapel proper and took the chalice from her. Moving to the large font at the entrance to the great room, Malice dipped the chalice into a sticky fluid, the unholy water of her religion. She then chanted, "*Spiderae aught icor ven.*" The ritual complete, Malice moved back to the altar and poured the unholy water into the golden bowl.

She and Briza sat down to watch.

⚔ ⚔ ⚔ ⚔ ⚔

Drizzt stepped onto the floor of Zaknafein's training gym for the first time in more than a decade and felt as if he had come home. He'd spent the best years of his young life here—almost wholly here. For all the disappointments he had encountered since—and no doubt would continue to experience throughout his life—Drizzt would never forget that brief sparkle of innocence, that joy, he had known when he was a student in Zaknafein's gym.

Zaknafein entered and walked over to face his former student. Drizzt saw nothing familiar or comforting in the weapons master's face. A perpetual scowl now replaced the once common smile. It was an angry demeanor that hated everything around it, perhaps Drizzt most of all. Or had Zaknafein always worn such a grimace? Drizzt had to wonder. Had nostalgia glossed over Drizzt's memories of those years of early training? Was this mentor, who had so often warmed Drizzt's heart with a lighthearted chuckle, actually the cold, lurking monster that Drizzt now saw before him?

"Which has changed, Zaknafein," Drizzt asked aloud, "you, my memories, or my perceptions?"

Zak seemed not even to hear the whispered question. "Ah, the young hero has returned," he said, "the warrior with exploits beyond his years."

"Why do you mock me?" Drizzt protested.

"He who killed the hook horrors," Zak continued. His swords were out in his hands now, and Drizzt responded by drawing his scimitars. There was no need to ask the rules of engagement in this contest, or the choice of weapons.

Drizzt knew, had known before he had ever come here, that there would be no rules this time. The weapons would be their weapons of preference, the blades that each of them had used to kill so many foes.

"He who killed the earth elemental," Zak snarled derisively. He launched a measured attack, a simple lunge with one blade. Drizzt batted it aside without even thinking of the parry.

Sudden fires erupted in Zak's eyes, as if the first contact had sundered all the emotional bonds that had tempered his thrust. "He who killed the girl child of the surface elves!" he cried, an accusation and no compliment. Now came the second attack, vicious and powerful, an arcing swipe descending at Drizzt's head. "Who cut her apart to appease his own thirst for blood!"

Zak's words knocked Drizzt off his guard emotionally,. wrapped his heart in confusion like some devious mental whip. Drizzt was a seasoned warrior, though, and his reflexes did not register the emotional distraction. A scimitar came up to catch the descending sword and deflected it harmlessly aside.

"Murderer! " Zak snarled openly. "Did you enjoy the dying child's screams?" He came at Drizzt in a furious whirl, swords dipping and diving, slicing at every angle.

Drizzt, enraged by the hypocrite's accusations, matched the fury, screaming out for no better reason than to hear the anger of his own voice.

Any watching the battle would have found no breath in the next few blurring moments. Never had the Underdark witnessed such a vicious fight as when these two masters of the blade each attacked the demon possessing the other—and himself.

Adamantine sparked and nicked, droplets of blood spattered both the combatants, though neither felt any pain, and neither knew if he'd injured the other.

Drizzt came with a two blade sidelong swipe that drove Zak's swords out wide. Zak followed the motion quickly, turned a complete circle, and slammed back into Drizzt's thrusting scimitars with enough force to knock the young warrior from his feet. Drizzt fell into a roll and came back up to meet his charging adversary.

A thought came over him.

Drizzt came up high, too high, and Zak drove him back on his heels. Drizzt knew what would soon be coming; he invited it openly. Zak kept Drizzt's weapons high through several combined maneuvers. He then went with the move that had defeated Drizzt in the past, expecting that the best Drizzt could attain would be equal footing: double-thrust low.

Drizzt executed the appropriate cross-down parry, as he had to, and Zak tensed, waiting for his eager opponent to try to improve the move. "Child killer!" he growled, goading on Drizzt.

He didn't know that Drizzt had found the solution.

With all the anger he had ever known, all the disappointments of his young life gathering within his foot, Drizzt focused on Zak. That smug face, feigning smiles and drooling for blood.

Between the hilts, between the eyes, Drizzt kicked, blowing out every ounce of rage in a single blow.

Zak's nose crunched flat. His eyes lolled upward, and blood exploded over his hollow cheeks. Zak knew that he was falling, that the devilish young warrior would be on him in a flash, gaining an advantage that Zak could not hope to overcome.

"What of you, Zaknafein Do'Urden?" he heard Drizzt snarl, distantly, as though he were falling far away. "I have heard of the exploits of House Do'Urden's weapons master! How he so enjoys killing!" The voice was closer now, as Drizzt stalked in, and as the rebounding rage of Zaknafein sent him spiraling back to the battle.

"I have heard how murder comes so very easily to Zaknafein!" Drizzt spat derisively. "The murder of clerics, of other drow! Do you so enjoy it all?" He ended the question with a blow from each scimitar, attacks meant to kill Zak, to kill the demon in them both.

But Zaknafein was now fully back to consciousness, hating himself and Drizzt equally. At the last moment, his swords came up and crossed, lightning fast, throwing Drizzt's arms wide. Then Zak finished with a kick of his own, not so strong from the prone position but accurate in its search for Drizzt's groin.

Drizzt sucked in his breath and twirled away, forcing himself back into composure when he saw Zaknafein, still dazed, rising to his feet. "Do you so enjoy it all?" he managed to ask again.

"Enjoy?" the weapons master echoed.

"Does it bring you pleasure?" Drizzt grimaced.

"Satisfaction!" Zak corrected. "I kill. Yes, I kill."

"You teach others to kill!"

"To kill drow!" Zak roared, and he was back in Drizzt's face, his weapons up but waiting for Drizzt to make the next move.

Zak's words again entwined Drizzt in a mesh of confusion. Who was this drow standing before him?

"Do you think that your mother would let me live if I did not serve her evil designs?" Zak cried.

Drizzt did not understand.

"She hates me," Zak said, more in control as he began to understand Drizzt's confusion, "despises me for what I know." Drizzt cocked his head.

"Are you so blind to the evil around you?" Zak yelled in his face. "Or has it consumed you, as it consumes all of them, in this murderous frenzy that we call life?"

"The frenzy that holds you?" Drizzt retorted, but there was little conviction in his voice now. If he understood Zak's words correctly—if Zak played the killing game simply because of his hatred for the perverted drow—the most Drizzt could blame him for was cowardice.

"No frenzy holds me," Zak replied. "I live as best I can. I survive in a world that is not my own, not my heart." The lament in his words, the droop of his head as he admitted his helplessness, struck a familiar chord in Drizzt. "I kill, kill drow, to serve Matron Malice—to placate the rage, the frustration, that I know in my soul. When I hear the children scream . . ." His gaze snapped up on Drizzt and he rushed in all of a sudden, his fury returned tenfold.

Drizzt tried to get his scimitars up, but Zak knocked one of them across the room and drove the other aside. He rushed in step with Drizzt's awkward retreat until he had Drizzt pinned against a wall. The tip of Zak's sword drew a droplet of blood from Drizzt's throat.

"The child lives!" Drizzt gasped. "I swear, I did not kill the elven child!"

Zak relaxed a bit but still held Drizzt, sword to throat. "Dinin said—"

"Dinin was mistaken," Drizzt replied frantically. "Fooled by me. I knocked the child down—only to spare her—and covered her with the blood of her murdered mother to mask my own cowardice!"

Zak leaped back, overwhelmed.

"I killed no elves that day," Drizzt said to him. "The only ones I desired to kill were my own companions!"

⚔ ⚔ ⚔ ⚔ ⚔

"So now we know," said Briza, staring into the scrying bowl, watching the conclusion of the battle between Drizzt and Zaknafein and hearing their every word. "It was Drizzt who angered the Spider Queen."

"You suspected him all along, as did I," Matron Malice replied, "though we both hoped differently."

"So much promise!" Briza lamented. "How I wish that one had learned his place, his values. Perhaps . . ."

"Mercy?" Matron Malice snapped at her. "Do you show mercy that would further invoke the Spider Queen's displeasure?"

"No, Matron," Briza replied. "I had only hoped that Drizzt could be used in the future, as you have used Zaknafein all these years. Zaknafein is growing older."

"We are about to fight a war, my daughter," Malice reminded her. "Lolth must be appeased. Your brother has brought his fate upon himself; his actions were his own to decide."

"He decided wrongly."

⚔ ⚔ ⚔ ⚔ ⚔

The words hit Zaknafein harder than Drizzt's boot had. The weapons master threw his swords to the ends of the room and rushed in on Drizzt. He buried him in a hug so intense that it took the young drow a long moment to even realize what had happened.

"You have survived!" Zak said, his voice broken by muffled tears. "Survived the Academy, where all the others died!"

Drizzt returned the embrace, tentatively, still not guessing the depth of Zak's elation.

"My son!"

Drizzt nearly fainted, overwhelmed by the admission of what he had always suspected, and even more so by the knowledge that he was not the only one in his dark world angered by the ways of the drow. He was not alone.

"Why?" Drizzt asked, pushing Zak out to arm's length. "Why have you stayed?"

Zak looked at him incredulously. "Where would I go? No one, not even a drow weapons master would survive for long out in the caverns of the Underdark. Too many monsters, and other races, hunger for the sweet blood of dark elves."

"Surely you had options."

"The surface?" Zak replied. "To face the painful inferno every day? No, my son, I am trapped, as you are trapped."

Drizzt had feared that statement, had feared that he would find no solution from his newfound father to the dilemma that was his life. Perhaps there were no answers.

"You will do well in Menzoberranzan," Zak said to comfort him. "You are strong, and Matron Malice will find an appropriate place for your talents, whatever your heart may desire."

"To live a life of assassinations, as you have?" Drizzt asked, trying futilely to keep the rage out of his words.

"What choice is before us?" Zak answered, his eyes seeking the unjudging stone of the floor.

"I will not kill drow," Drizzt declared flatly.

Zak's eyes snapped back on him. "You will," he assured his son. "In Menzoberranzan, you will kill or be killed."

Drizzt looked away, but Zak's words pursued him, could not be blocked out.

"There is no other way," the weapons master continued softly. "Such is our world. Such is our life. You have escaped this long, but you will find that your luck soon will change." He grabbed Drizzt's chin firmly and forced his son to look at him directly.

"I wish that it could be different," Zak said honestly, "but it is not such a bad life. I do not lament killing dark elves. I perceive their deaths as their salvation from this wicked existence. If they care so dearly for their Spider Queen, then let them go and visit her!"

Zak's growing smile washed away suddenly. "Except for the children," he whispered. "Often have I heard the cries of dying children, though never, I promise you, have I caused them. I have always wondered if they, too, are evil, born evil. Or if the weight of our dark world bends them to fit our foul ways."

"The ways of the demon Lolth," Drizzt agreed.

They both paused for many heartbeats, each privately weighing the realities of his own personal dilemma. Zak was next to speak, having long ago come to terms with the life that was offered to him.

"Lolth," he chuckled. "She is a vicious queen, that one. I would sacrifice everything for a chance at her ugly face!"

"I almost believe you would," Drizzt whispered, finding his smile.

Zak jumped back from him. "I would indeed," he laughed heartily. "So would you!"

Drizzt flipped his lone scimitar up into the air, letting it spin over twice before catching it again by the hilt. "True enough!" he cried. "But no longer would I be alone!"

# 26

# Angler of The Underdark

Drizzt wandered alone through the maze of Menzoberranzan, drifting past the stalagmite mounds, under the leering points of the great stone spears that hung from the cavern's high ceiling. Matron Malice had specifically ordered all of the family to remain within the house, fearing an assassination attempt by House Hun'ett. Too much had happened to Drizzt this day for him to obey. He had to think, and contemplating such blasphemous thoughts, even silently, in a house full of nervous clerics might get him into serious trouble.

This was the quiet time of the city; the heat-light of Narbondel was only a sliver at the stone's base, and most of the drow comfortably slept within their stone houses. Soon after he slipped through the adamantine gate of the House Do'Urden compound, Drizzt began to understand the wisdom of Matron Malice's command. The city's quiet now seemed to him like the crouched hush of a predator. It was poised to drop upon him from behind every one of the many blind corners he faced on this trek.

He would find no solace here in which he might truly contemplate the day's events, the revelations of Zaknafein, kindred in more than blood. Drizzt decided to break all the rules—that was the way of the drow, after all—and head out of the city, down the tunnels he knew so well from his tendays of patrol.

An hour later, he was still walking, lost in thought and feeling safe enough, for he was well within the boundaries of the patrol region.

He entered a high corridor, ten paces wide and with broken walls lined in loose rubble and crossed by many ledges. It seemed as though the passage once had been much wider. The ceiling was far beyond sight, but Drizzt had been through here a dozen times, up on the many ledges, and he gave the place no thought.

He envisioned the future, the times that he and Zaknafein, his father, would share now that no secrets separated them. Together they would be unbeatable, a team of weapons masters, bonded by steel and emotions. Did House Hun'ett truly understand what it would be facing? The smile on Drizzt's face disappeared as soon as he considered the implications: he and Zak, together, cutting through House Hun'ett's ranks with deadly ease, through the ranks of drow elves—killing their own people.

Drizzt leaned against the wall for support, understanding firsthand the frustration that had racked his father for many centuries. Drizzt did not want to be like Zaknafein, living only to kill, existing in a protective sphere of violence, but what choices lay before him? Leave the city?

Zak had balked when Drizzt asked him why he had not left. "Where would I go?" Drizzt whispered now, echoing Zak's words. His father had proclaimed them trapped, and so it seemed to Drizzt.

"Where would I go?" he asked again. "Travel the Underdark, where our people are so despised and a single drow would become a target for everything he passed? Or to the surface, perhaps, and let that ball of fire in the sky burn out my eyes so that I may not witness my own death when the elven folk descend upon me?"

The logic of the reasoning trapped Drizzt as it had trapped Zak. Where could a drow elf go? Nowhere in all the Realms would an elf of dark skin be accepted.

Was the choice then to kill? To kill drow?

Drizzt rolled over against the wall, his physical movement an unconscious act, for his mind whirled down the maze of his future. It took him a moment to realize that his back was against something other than stone.

He tried to leap away, alert again now that his surroundings were not as they should be. When he pushed out, his feet came up from the ground and he landed back in his original position. Frantically, before he took the time to consider his predicament, Drizzt reached behind his neck with both hands.

They, too, stuck fast to the translucent cord that held him. Drizzt knew his folly then, and all the tugging in the world would not free his hands from the line of the angler of the Underdark, a cave fisher.

"Fool!" he scolded himself as he felt himself lifted from the ground. He should have suspected this, should have been more careful alone in the caverns. But to reach out barehanded! He looked down at the hilts of his scimitars, useless in their sheaths.

The cave fisher reeled him in, pulled him up the long wall toward its waiting maw.

⚔ ⚔ ⚔ ⚔ ⚔

Masoj Hun'ett smiled smugly to himself as he watched Drizzt depart the city. Time was running short for him, and Matron SiNafay would not be pleased if he failed again in his mission to destroy the secondboy of House Do'Urden. Now Masoj's patience had apparently paid off, for Drizzt had come out alone, had left the city! There were no witnesses. It was too easy.

Eagerly the wizard pulled the onyx figurine from his pouch and dropped it to the ground. "Guenhwyvar!" he called as loudly as he dared, glancing around at the nearest stalagmite house for signs of activity.

The dark smoke appeared and transformed a moment later into Masoj's magical panther. Masoj rubbed his hands together, thinking himself marvelous for having concocted such a devious and ironic end to the heroics of Drizzt Do'Urden.

"I have a job for you," he told the cat, "one that you'll not enjoy!"

Guenhwyvar slumped casually and yawned as though the wizard's words were hardly a revelation.

"Your point companion has gone out on patrol," Masoj explained as he pointed down the tunnel, "by himself. It's too dangerous."

Guenhwyvar stood back up, suddenly very interested.

"Drizzt should not be out there alone," Masoj continued. "He could get killed."

The evil inflections of his voice told the panther his intent before he ever spoke the words.

"Go to him, my pet," Masoj purred. "Find him out there in the gloom and kill him!" He studied Guenhwyvar's reaction, measured the horror he had laid on the cat. Guenhwyvar stood rigid, as unmoving as the statue used to summon it.

"Go!" Masoj ordered. "You cannot resist your master's commands! I am your master, unthinking beast! You seem to forget that fact too often!"

Guenhwyvar resisted for a long moment, a heroic act in itself, but the magic's urges, the incessant pull of the master's command, outweighed any instinctive feelings the great panther might have had. Reluctantly at first, but then pulled by the primordial desires of the hunt, Guenhwyvar sped off between the enchanted statues guarding the tunnel and easily found Drizzt's scent.

⚔ ⚔ ⚔ ⚔ ⚔

Alton DeVir slumped back behind the largest of the stalagmite mounds, disappointed at Masoj's tactics. Masoj would let the cat do his work for him; Alton would not even witness Drizzt Do'Urden's death!

Alton fingered the powerful wand that Matron SiNafay had given to him when he set out after Masoj that night. It seemed that the item would play no role in Drizzt's demise.

Alton took comfort in the item, knowing that he would have ample opportunity to put it to proper use against the remainder of House Do'Urden.

⚔ ⚔ ⚔ ⚔ ⚔

Drizzt fought for the first half of his ascent, kicking and spinning, ducking his shoulders under any outcrop he passed in a futile effort to hold back the pull of the cave fisher. He knew from the outset, though, against those warrior instincts that refused to surrender, that he had no chance to halt the incessant pull.

Halfway up, one shoulder bloodied, the other bruised, and with the floor nearly thirty feet below him, Drizzt resigned himself to his fate. If he would find a chance against the crablike monster that waited at the top of the line, it would be in the last instant of the ascent. For now, he could only watch and wait.

Perhaps death was not so bad an alternative to the life he would find among the drow, trapped within the evil framework of their dark society. Even Zaknafein, so strong and powerful and wise with age, had never been able to come to terms with his existence in Menzoberranzan; what chance did Drizzt have?

When Drizzt had passed through his small bout with self pity, when the angle of his ascent changed, showing him the lip of the final ledge, the fighting spirit within him took over once again. The cave fisher might have him, he decided then, but he'd put a boot or two into the thing's eyes before it got its meal!

He could hear the clacking of the anxious monster's eight crablike legs. Drizzt had seen a cave fisher before, though it had scrambled away before he and his patrol could catch up to it. He had imagined it then, and could imagine it now, in battle. Two of its legs ended in wicked claws, pincers that snipped up prey to fit into the maw.

Drizzt turned himself face-in to the cliff, wanting to view the thing as soon as his head crested the ledge. The anxious clacking grew louder, resounding alongside the thumping of Drizzt's heart. He reached the ledge.

Drizzt peeked over, only a foot or two from the monster's long proboscis, with the maw just inches behind. Pincers reached out to grab him before he could get his footing; he would get no chance to kick out at the thing.

He closed his eyes, hoping again that death would be preferable to his life in Menzoberranzan.

A familiar growl then brought him from his thoughts.

Slipping through the maze of ledges, Guenhwyvar came in sight of the cave fisher and Drizzt just before Drizzt had reached the final ledge. This was a moment of salvation or death for the cat as surely as for Drizzt. Guenhwyvar had traveled here under Masoj's direct command, giving no consideration to its duty and acting only on its own instincts in accord with the compelling magic. Guenhwyvar could not go against that edict, that premise for the cat's very existence . . . until now.

The scene before the panther, with Drizzt only seconds from death, brought to Guenhwyvar a strength unknown to the cat, and unforeseen to the creator of the magical figurine. That instant of terror gave a life to Guenhwyvar beyond the scope of the magic.

By the time Drizzt had opened his eyes, the battle was in full fury. Guenhwyvar leaped atop the cave fisher but nearly went right over, for the monster's six remaining legs were rooted to the stone by the same goo that held Drizzt fast to the long filament. Undaunted, the cat raked and bit, a ball of frenzy trying to find a break in the fisher's armored shell.

The monster retaliated with his pincers, flipping them over its back with surprising agility and finding one of Guenhwyvar's forelegs.

Drizzt was no longer being pulled in; the monster had other business to attend to.

Pincers cut through Guenhwyvar's soft flesh, but the cat's blood was not the only dark fluid staining the cave fisher's back. Powerful feline claws tore up a section of the shell armor, and great teeth plunged beneath it. As the cave fisher's blood splattered to the stone, its legs began to slip.

Watching the goo under the crablike legs dissolve as the blood of the monster struck it, Drizzt understood what would happen as a line of that same blood made its way down the filament, toward him. He would have to strike fast if the opportunity came; he would have to be ready to help Guenhwyvar.

The fisher stumbled to the side, rolling Guenhwyvar away and spinning Drizzt over in a complete bumping circuit.

Still the blood oozed down the line, and Drizzt felt the filament's hold loosen from his top hand as the liquid came in contact.

Guenhwyvar was up again, facing the fisher, looking for an attack route through the waiting pincers.

Drizzt's hand was free. He snapped up a scimitar and dived straight ahead, sinking the tip into the fisher's side. The monster reeled about, the jolt and the continuing blood flow shaking Drizzt from the filament altogether. The drow was agile enough to find a handhold before he had fallen far, though his drawn scimitar tumbled down to the floor.

Drizzt's diversion opened the fisher's defenses for just a moment, and Guenhwyvar did not hesitate. The cat barreled into its foe, teeth finding the same fleshy hold they had already ripped. They went deeper, under the skin, crushing organs as Guenhwyvar's raking claws kept the pincers at bay.

By the time Drizzt climbed back to the level of the battle, the cave fisher shuddered in the throes of death. Drizzt pulled himself up and rushed to his friend's side.

Guenhwyvar retreated step for step, its ears flattened and teeth bared.

At first, Drizzt thought that the pain of a wound blinded the cat, but a quick survey dispelled that theory. Guenhwyvar had only one injury, and that was not serious. Drizzt had seen the cat with worse.

Guenhwyvar continued to retreat, continued to growl, as the incessant pounding of Masoj's command, back again after the instant of terror, hammered at its heart. The cat fought the urges, tried to see Drizzt as an ally, not as prey, but the urges . . .

"What is wrong, my friend?" Drizzt asked softly, resisting the urge to draw his remaining blade in defense. He dropped to one knee. "Do you not recognize me? How often we have fought together!"

Guenhwyvar crouched low and tamped down its hind legs, preparing, Drizzt knew, to spring. Still Drizzt did not draw his weapon, did nothing to threaten the cat. He had to trust that Guenhwyvar was true to his perceptions, that the panther was everything he believed it to be. What now could be guiding these unfamiliar reactions? What had brought Guenhwyvar out here at this late hour?

Drizzt found his answers when he remembered Matron Malice's warnings about leaving House Do'Urden.

"Masoj sent you to kill me!" he said bluntly. His tone confused the cat, and it relaxed a bit, not yet ready to spring. "You saved me, Guenhwyvar. You resisted the command."

Guenhwyvar's growl sounded in protest.

"You could have let the cave fisher do the deed for you," Drizzt retorted, "but you did not! You charged in and saved my life! Fight the urges,

Guenhwyvar! Remember me as your friend, a better companion than Masoj Hun'ett could ever be!"

Guenhwyvar backed away another step, caught in a pull that it could not yet resolve. Drizzt watched the cat's ears come up from its head and knew that he was winning the contest.

"Masoj claims ownership," he went on, confident that the cat, through some intelligence Drizzt could not know, understood the meaning of his words. "I claim friendship. I am your friend, Guenhwyvar, and I'll not fight against you."

He leaped forward, arms unthreateningly wide, face and chest fully exposed. "Even at the cost of my own life!"

Guenhwyvar did not strike. Emotions pulled at the cat stronger than any magical spell, those same emotions that had put Guenhwyvar into action when it first saw Drizzt in the cave fisher's clutches.

Guenhwyvar reared up and leaped out, crashing into Drizzt and knocking him to his back, then burying him in a rush of playful slaps and mock bites.

The two friends had won again; they had defeated two foes this day.

When Drizzt paused from the greeting to consider all that had transpired, though, he realized that one of the victories was not yet complete. Guenhwyvar was his in spirit now but still held by another, one who did not deserve the cat, who enslaved the cat in a life that Drizzt could no longer witness.

None of the confusion that had followed Drizzt Do'Urden out of Menzoberranzan that night remained. For the first time in his life, he saw the road he must follow, the path to his own freedom.

He remembered Zaknafein's warnings, and the same impossible alternatives that he had contemplated, to no resolution.

Where, indeed, could a drow elf go?

"Worse to be trapped within a lie," he whispered absently. The panther cocked its head to the side, sensing again that Drizzt's words carried great importance. Drizzt returned the curious stare with one that came suddenly grim.

"Take me to your master," he demanded, "your false master."

# 27

# UNTROUBLED DREAMS

Zaknafein sank down into his bed in an easy sleep, the most comfortable rest he had ever known. Dreams did come to him this night, a rush of dreams. Far from tumultuous, they only enhanced his comfort. Zak was free now of his secret, of the lie that had dominated every day of his adult life.

Drizzt had survived! Even the dreaded Academy of Menzoberranzan could not daunt the youth's indomitable spirit and sense of morality. Zaknafein Do'Urden was no longer alone. The dreams that played in his mind showed him the same wonderful possibilities that had followed Drizzt out of the city.

Side by side they would stand, unbeatable, two as one against the perverted foundations of Menzoberranzan.

A stinging pain in his foot brought Zak from his slumbers. He saw Briza immediately, at the bottom of his bed, her snake whip in hand. Instinctively, Zak reached over the side to fetch his sword.

The weapon was gone. Vierna stood at the side of the room, holding it. On the opposite side, Maya held Zak's other sword.

How had they come in so stealthily? Zak wondered. Magical silence, no doubt, but Zak was still surprised that he had not sensed their presence in time. Nothing had ever caught him unawares, awake or asleep.

Never before had he slept so soundly, so peacefully. Perhaps, in Menzoberranzan, such pleasant dreams were dangerous.

"Matron Malice will see you," Briza announced.

"I am not properly dressed," Zak replied casually. "My belt and weapons, if you please."

"We do not please!" Briza snapped, more at her sisters than at Zak. "You will not need the weapons."

Zak thought otherwise.

"Come, now," Briza commanded, and she raised the whip.

"I should be certain of Matron Malice's intentions before I acted so boldly, were I you," Zak warned. Briza, reminded of the power of the male she now threatened, lowered her weapon.

Zak rolled out of bed, putting the same intense glare alternately on Maya and Vierna, watching their reactions to better conclude Malice's reasons for summoning him.

They surrounded him as he left his room, keeping a cautious but ready distance from the deadly weapons master. "Must be serious," Zak remarked quietly, so that only Briza, in front of the troupe, could hear. Briza turned and flashed him a wicked smile that did nothing to dispel his suspicions.

Neither did Matron Malice, who leaned forward in her throne in anticipation even before they entered the room.

"Matron," Zak offered, dipping into a bow and pulling the side of his nightshirt out wide to draw attention to his inappropriate dress. He wanted to let Malice know his feelings of being ridiculed at such a late hour.

The matron offered no return greeting. She rested back in her throne. One slender hand rubbed her sharp chin, while her eyes locked upon Zaknafein.

"Perhaps you could tell me why you've summoned me," Zak dared to say, his voice still holding an edge of sarcasm. "I would prefer to return to my slumbers. We should not give House Hun'ett the advantage of a tired weapons master."

"Drizzt has gone," growled Malice.

The news slapped Zak like a wet rag. He straightened, and the teasing smile disappeared from his face.

"He left the house against my commands," Malice went on. Zak relaxed visibly; when Malice announced that Drizzt was gone, Zak had first thought that she and her devious cohorts had driven him out or killed him.

"A spirited boy," Zak remarked. "Surely he will return soon."

"Spirited," Malice echoed, and her tone did not put the description in a positive light.

"He will return," Zak said again. "There's no need for our alarm, for such extreme measures." He glared at Briza, though he knew well that the matron mother had called him to audience to do more than tell him of Drizzt's departure.

"The secondboy disobeyed the matron mother," Briza snarled, a rehearsed interruption.

"Spirited," Zak said again, trying not to chuckle. "A minor indiscretion."

"How often he seems to have those," Malice commented. "Like another spirited male of House Do'Urden."

Zak bowed again, taking her words as a compliment. Malice already had his punishment decided, if she meant to punish him at all, His actions now, at this trial—if that's what it was—would be of little consequence.

"The boy has displeased the Spider Queen!" Malice growled, openly enraged and tired of Zak's sarcasm. "Even you were not foolish enough to do that!"

A dark cloud passed across Zak's face. This meeting was indeed serious; Drizzt's life could be at stake.

"But you know of his crime," Malice continued, easing back again. She liked that she had Zak concerned and on the defensive. She had found his vulnerable spot. It was her turn to tease.

"Leaving the house?" Zak protested. "A minor error in judgment. Lolth would not be concerned with such a trifle issue."

"Do not feign ignorance, Zaknafein. You know that the elven child lives!"

Zak lost his breath in a sharp gasp. Malice knew! Damn it all, Lolth knew!

"We are about to go to war," Malice continued calmly, "we are not in

Lolth's favor, and we must correct the situation."

She eyed Zak directly. "You are aware of our ways and know that we must do this."

Zak nodded, trapped. Anything he did now to disagree would only make matters worse for Drizzt—if matters could be worse for Drizzt.

"The secondboy must be punished," Briza said.

Another rehearsed interruption, Zak knew. He wondered how many times Briza and Malice had practiced this encounter.

"Am I to punish him, then?" Zak asked. "I'll not whip the boy; that is not my place."

"His punishment is none of your concern," Malice said.

"Then why disturb my slumber?" Zak asked, trying to detach himself from Drizzt's predicament, more for Drizzt's sake than his own.

"I thought that you would wish to know," Malice replied. "You and Drizzt became so close this day in the gym. Father and son."

She saw! Zak realized. Malice, and probably that wretched Briza, had watched the whole encounter! Zak's head drooped as he came to know that he had unwittingly played a part in Drizzt's predicament.

"An elven child lives," Malice began slowly, rolling out each word in dramatic clarity, "and a young drow must die."

"No!" The word came out of Zak before he realized he was speaking. He tried to find some escape. "Drizzt was young. He did not understand . . ."

"He knew exactly what he was doing!" Malice screamed back at him. "He does not regret his actions! He is so like you, Zaknafein! Too like you."

"Then he can learn," Zak reasoned. "I have not been a burden to you, Mali—Matron Malice. You have profited by my presence. Drizzt is no less skilled than I; he can be valuable to us."

"Dangerous to us," Matron Malice corrected. "You and he standing together? The thought does not please me."

"His death will aid House Hun'ett," Zak warned, grabbing at anything he could find to defeat the matron's intent.

"The Spider Queen demands his death," Malice replied sternly. "She must be appeased if Daermon N'a'shezbaernon is to have any hope in its struggles against House Hun'ett."

"I beg you, do not kill the boy."

"Sympathy?" Malice mused. "It does not become a drow warrior, Zaknafein. Have you lost your fighting will?"

"I am old, Malice."

"Matron Malice!" Briza protested, but Zak put a look on her so cold that she lowered her snake whip before she had even begun to put it to use.

"Older still will I become if Drizzt is put to his death."

"I do not desire this either," Malice agreed, but Zak recognized her lie. She didn't care about Drizzt, or about anything else, beyond gaining the Spider Queen's favor.

"Yet I see no alternative. Drizzt has angered Lolth, and she must be appeased before our war."

Zak began to understand. This meeting wasn't about Drizzt at all. "Take me in the boy's stead," he said.

Malice's narrow grin could not hide her feigned surprise. This was what she had desired from the very beginning.

"You are a proven fighter," the matron argued. "Your value, as you yourself have already admitted, cannot be underestimated. To sacrifice you to the Spider Queen would appease her, but what void will be left in House Do'Urden in the wake of your passing?"

"A void that Drizzt can fill," Zak replied. He secretly hoped that Drizzt, unlike he, would find some escape from it all, some way around Matron Malice's evil plots.

"You are certain of this?"

"He is my equal in battle," Zak assured her. "He will grow stronger, too, beyond what Zaknafein has ever attained."

"You are willing to do this for him?" Malice sneered, eager drool edging her mouth.

"You know that I am," Zak replied.

"Ever the fool," Malice put in.

"To your dismay," Zak continued, undaunted, "you know that Drizzt would do the same for me."

"He is young," Malice purred. "He will be taught better."

"As you taught me?" snapped Zak.

Malice's victorious grin became a grimace. "I warn you, Zaknafein," she growled in all her vile rage. "If you do anything to disrupt the ceremony to appease the Spider Queen, if, in the end of your wasted life, you choose to anger me one final time, I will give Drizzt to Briza. She and her torturous toys will give him to Lolth!"

Unafraid, Zak held his head high. "I have offered myself, Malice," he spat. "Have your fun while you may. In the end, Zaknafein will be at peace; Matron Malice Do'Urden will ever be at war!"

Shaking in anger, the moment of triumph stolen by a few simple words, Malice could only whisper, "Take him!"

Zak offered no resistance as Vierna and Maya tied him to the spider-shaped altar in the chapel. He watched Vierna mostly, seeing an edge of sympathy rimming her quiet eyes. She, too, might have been like him, but whatever hope he had for that possibility had been buried long ago under the relentless preaching of the Spider Queen.

"You are sad," Zak remarked to her.

Vierna straightened and tugged tightly on one of Zak's bonds, causing him to grimace in pain. "A pity," she replied as coldly as she could. "House Do'Urden must give much to repay Drizzt's foolish deed. I would have enjoyed watching the two of you together in battle."

"House Hun'ett would not have enjoyed the sight," Zak replied with a wink. "Cry not . . . my daughter."

Vierna slapped him across the face. "Take your lies to your grave!"

"Deny it as you choose, Vierna," was all that Zak cared to reply.

Vierna and Maya backed away from the altar. Vierna fought to hold her scowl and Maya bit back an amused chuckle, as Matron Malice and Briza entered the room. The matron mother wore her greatest ceremonial robe, black and weblike, clinging and floating about her all at once, and Briza carried a sacred coffer.

Zak paid them no heed as they began their ritual, chanting for the Spider Queen, offering their hopes for appeasement. Zak had his own hopes at that moment.

"Beat them all," he whispered under his breath. "Do more than survive, my son, as I have survived. Live! Be true to the callings in your heart."

Braziers roared to life; the room glowed. Zak felt the heat, knew that contact to that darker plane had been achieved.

"Take this . . ." he heard Matron Malice chant, but he put the words out of his thoughts and continued the final prayers of his life.

The spider-shaped dagger hovered over his chest. Malice clenched the instrument in her bony hands, the sheen of her sweat-soaked skin catching the orange reflection of the fires in a surrealistic glow.

Surreal, like the transition from life to death.

# 28
# Rightful Owner

How long had it been? An hour? Two? Masoj paced the length of the gap between the two stalagmite mounds just a few feet from the entrance to the tunnel that Drizzt, and Guenhwyvar, had taken. "The cat should have returned by now," the wizard grumbled, at the end of his patience.

Relief flooded through his face a moment later, when Guenhwyvar's great black head peered around the edge of the tunnel, behind one of the displacer beast statue guardians. The fur around the cat's maw was conspicuously wet with fresh blood.

"It is done?" Masoj asked, barely able to contain a shout of elation. "Drizzt Do'Urden is dead?"

"Hardly," came the reply. Drizzt, for all his idealism, had to admit a tinge of pleasure as a cloud of dread cooled the elated fires in the sinister wizard's cheeks.

"What is this, Guenhwyvar?" Masoj demanded. "Do as I bid you! Kill him now!"

Guenhwyvar stared blankly at Masoj, then lay at Drizzt's feet.

"You admit your attempt on my life?" Drizzt asked.

Masoj measured the distance to his adversary—ten feet. He might be able to get off one spell. Perhaps. Masoj had seen Drizzt move, quick and sure, and had little desire to chance the attack if he could find another way out of this predicament. Drizzt had not yet drawn a weapon, though the young warrior's hands rested easily across the hilts of his deadly blades.

"I understand," Drizzt continued calmly. "House Hun'ett and House Do'Urden are to battle."

"How did you know?" Masoj blurted without thinking, too shocked by the revelation to consider that Drizzt might merely be goading him into a larger admission.

"I know much but care little," Drizzt replied. "House Hun'ett wishes to wage war against my family. For what reason, I cannot guess."

"For the vengeance of House DeVir!" came a reply from a different direction.

Alton, standing on the side of a stalagmite mound, looked down at Drizzt.

A smile spread over Masoj's face. The odds had so quickly changed.

"House Hun'ett cares not at all for House DeVir," Drizzt replied, still composed in the face of this new development. "I have learned enough of the ways of our people to know that the fate of one house is not the concern of another."

"But it is my concern!" Alton cried, and he threw back the cowl of his hood, revealing the hideous face, scarred by acid for the sake of a disguise. "I am Alton DeVir, lone survivor of House DeVir! House Do'Urden will die for its crimes against my family, starting with you."

"I was not even born when the battle took place," Drizzt protested.

"Of little consequence!" Alton snarled. "You are a Do'Urden, a filthy Do'Urden. That is all that matters."

Masoj tossed the onyx figurine to the ground. "Guenhwyvar!" he commanded. "Be gone!"

The cat looked over its shoulder to Drizzt, who nodded his approval.

"Be gone!" Masoj cried again. "I am your master! You cannot disobey me!"

"You do not own the cat," Drizzt said calmly.

"Who does, then?" Masoj snapped. "You?"

"Guenhwyvar," Drizzt replied. "Only Guenhwyvar. I would think that a wizard would have a better understanding of the magic around him."

With a low growl that might have been a mocking laugh, Guenhwyvar loped across the stone to the figurine and dissipated into smoky nothingness.

The cat walked down the length of the planar tunnel, toward its home in the Astral Plane. Ever before had Guenhwyvar been anxious to make this journey, to escape the foul commands of its drow masters. This time, though, the cat hesitated with every stride, looking back over its shoulder to the dot of darkness that was Menzoberranzan.

"Will you deal?" Drizzt offered.

"You are in no position to bargain," Alton laughed, drawing out the slender wand that Matron SiNafay had given him.

Masoj cut him short. "Wait," he said. "Perhaps Drizzt will prove valuable to our struggle against House Do'Urden." He eyed the young warrior directly. "You will betray your family?"

"Hardly," Drizzt snickered. "As I have already said to you, I care little for the coming conflict. Let House Hun'ett and House Do'Urden both be damned, as surely they will! My concerns are personal."

"You must have something to offer us in exchange for your gain," Masoj explained. "Otherwise, what bargain can you hope to make?"

"I do have something to give to you in return," Drizzt replied, his voice calm, "your lives."

Masoj and Alton looked to each other and laughed aloud, but there was a trace of nervousness in their chuckles.

"Give me the figurine, Masoj," Drizzt continued, undaunted. "Guenhwyvar never belonged to you and will serve you no more."

Masoj stopped laughing.

"In return," Drizzt went on before the wizard could reply, "I will leave House Do'Urden and not take part in the battle."

"Corpses do not fight." Alton sneered.

"I will take another Do'Urden with me," Drizzt spat at him. "A weapons master. Surely House Hun'ett will have gained an advantage if both Drizzt and Zaknafein—"

"Silence!" Masoj screamed. "The cat is mine! I do not need any bargains from a pitiful Do'Urden! You are dead, fool, and House Do'Urden's weapons master will follow you to your grave!"

"Guenhwyvar is free!" Drizzt growled.

The scimitars came out in Drizzt's hands. He had never really fought a wizard before, let alone two, but he remembered vividly from past encounters the sting of their spells. Masoj had already begun to cast, but of more concern was Alton, out of quick reach and pointing that slender wand.

Before Drizzt ever decided his course of action, the issue was settled for him. A cloud of smoke engulfed Masoj and he fell back, his spell disrupted with the shock.

Guenhwyvar was back.

Alton was out of Drizzt's reach. Drizzt could not hope to get to the wizard before the wand went off, but to Guenhwyvar's streamlined feline muscles, the distance was not so great. Hind legs tamped a footing and snapped, launching the hunting panther through the air.

Alton brought the wand to bear on this new nemesis in time and released a mighty bolt, scorching Guenhwyvar's chest. Greater strength than a single bolt, though, would be needed to deter the ferocious panther. Stunned but still fighting, Guenhwyvar slammed into the faceless wizard, dropping him off the back side of the stalagmite mound.

The lightning bolt's flash stunned Drizzt as well, but he continued to pursue Masoj and could only hope that Guenhwyvar had survived. He rushed around the base of the other stalagmite mound and came face-to-face with Masoj, once again in the act of spellcasting. Drizzt didn't slow; he ducked his head and barreled into his opponent, his scimitars leading the way.

He slipped right through his opponent—right through the image of his opponent!

Drizzt crashed heavily into the stone and rolled aside, trying to escape the magical attack he knew was coming.

This time, Masoj, standing fully thirty feet behind the projection of his image, was taking no chances with a miss. He launched a volley of magical missiles of energy that veered unerringly to intercept the dodging fighter. They slammed into Drizzt, jolting him, bruising him under his skin.

But Drizzt was able to shake away the numbing pain and regain his footing. He knew where the real Masoj was standing now and had no intention of letting the trickster out of sight again.

A dagger in his hand, Masoj watched Drizzt's stalking approach.

Drizzt didn't understand. Why wasn't the wizard preparing another spell? The fall had reopened the wound in Drizzt's shoulder, and the magical bolts had torn his side and one leg. The wounds were not serious, though, and Masoj had no chance against him in physical combat.

The wizard stood before him, unconcerned, dagger drawn and a wicked smile on his face.

Face down on the hard stone, Alton felt the warmth of his own blood running freely between the melted holes that were his eyes. The cat was higher up the side of the mound, not yet fully recovered from the lightning bolt.

Alton forced himself up and raised his wand for a second strike . . . but the wand had snapped in half.

Frantically Alton recovered the other piece and held it up before his melted, disbelieving eyes. Guenhwyvar was coming again, but Alton didn't notice.

The glowing ends of the wand, a power building within the magical stick, enthralled him. "You cannot do that," Alton whispered in protest.

Guenhwyvar leaped just as the broken wand exploded.

A ball of fire roared up into Menzoberranzan's night, chunks of rubble rocketed off the great cavern's eastern wall and ceiling, and both Drizzt and Masoj were knocked from their feet.

"Now Guenhwyvar belongs to no one," Masoj sneered, tossing the figurine to the ground.

"No DeVir remains to claim vengeance on House Do'Urden," Drizzt growled back, his anger holding off his despair. Masoj became the focus of that anger, and the wizard's mocking laughter led Drizzt toward him in a furious rush. Just as Drizzt got in range, Masoj snapped his fingers and was gone.

"Invisible," Drizzt roared, slicing futilely at the empty air before him. His exertions took the edge from his blind rage and he realized that Masoj was no longer in front of him. How foolish he must seem to the wizard. How vulnerable!

Drizzt crouched to listen. He sensed a distant chanting from up above, on the cavern wall.

Drizzt's instincts told him to dive to the side, but his new understanding of wizards told him that Masoj would anticipate such a move. Drizzt feigned to the left and heard the climactic words of the building spell. As the lightning blast thundered harmlessly to the side, Drizzt sprinted straight ahead, hoping his vision would return in time for him to get to the wizard.

"Damn you!" Masoj cried, understanding the feint as soon as he had errantly fired. Rage became terror in the next instant, as Masoj caught sight of Drizzt, sprinting across the stone, leaping the rubble, and crossing the sides of the mounds with all the grace of a hunting cat.

Masoj fumbled in his pockets for the components to his next spell. He had to be quick. He was fully twenty feet from the cavern floor, perched on a narrow ledge, but Drizzt was moving fast, impossibly fast!

The ground beneath him did not register in Drizzt's conscious thoughts. The cavern wall would have seemed unclimbable to him in a more rational state, but now he gave it not a care. Guenhwyvar was lost to him. Guenhwyvar was gone.

That wicked wizard on the ledge, that embodiment of demonic evil, had caused it. Drizzt sprang to the wall, found one hand free—he must have discarded one scimitar—and caught a tenuous hold. It wasn't enough for a rational drow, but Drizzt's mind ignored the protests of the muscles in his straining fingers. He had only ten feet to go.

Another volley of energy bolts thudded into Drizzt, hammering the top of his head in rapid succession.

"How many spells remain, wizard?" he heard himself defiantly cry as he ignored the pain.

Masoj fell back when Drizzt looked up at him, when the burning light of those lavender orbs fell upon him like a pronouncement of doom. He had seen Drizzt in battle many times, and the sight of the fighting young warrior had haunted him through all the planning of this assassination.

But Masoj had never seen Drizzt enraged before. If he had, he never would have agreed to try to kill Drizzt. If he had, he would have told

Matron SiNafay to go sit on a stalagmite.

What spell was next? What spell could slow the monster that was Drizzt Do'Urden?

A hand, glowing with the heat of anger, grabbed the lip of the ledge. Masoj stomped on it with the heel of his boot. The fingers were broken—the wizard knew that the fingers were broken—but Drizzt, impossibly, was up beside him and the blade of a scimitar was through the wizard's ribs.

"The fingers are broken!" the dying mage gasped in protest.

Drizzt looked down at his hand and realized the pain for the first time. "Perhaps," he said absently, "but they will heal."

⚔ ⚔ ⚔ ⚔ ⚔

Drizzt, limping, found his other scimitar and cautiously picked his way over the rubble of one of the mounds. Fighting the fear within his broken heart, he forced himself to peer over the crest at the destruction. The back side of the mound glowed eerily in the residual heat, a beacon for the awakening city.

So much for stealth.

Pieces of Alton DeVir lay scattered at the bottom, around the wizard's smoldering robes. "Have you found peace, Faceless One?" Drizzt whispered, exhaling the last of his anger. He remembered the assault Alton had launched against him those years ago in the Academy. The faceless master and Masoj had explained it away as a test for a budding warrior.

"How long you have carried your hate," Drizzt muttered at the blasted bits of corpse.

But Alton DeVir was not his concern now. He scanned the rest of the rubble, looking for some clue to Guenhwyvar's fate, not certain how a magical creature would fare in such a disaster. Not a sign of the cat remained, nothing that would even hint that Guenhwyvar had ever been there.

Drizzt consciously reminded himself that there was no hope, but the anxious spring in his steps mocked his stern visage. He rushed back down the mound and around the other stalagmite, where Masoj and he had been when the wand exploded. He spotted the onyx figurine immediately.

He lifted it gently in his hands. It was warm, as though it, too, had been caught in the blast, and Drizzt could sense that its magic had diminished. Drizzt wanted to call the cat, then, but he didn't dare, knowing that the travel between the planes heavily taxed Guenhwyvar. If the cat had been injured, Drizzt figured that it would be better to give it some time to recuperate.

"Oh, Guenhwyvar," he moaned, "my friend, my brave friend." He dropped the figurine into his pocket.

He could only hope that Guenhwyvar had survived.

# 29

# Alone

Drizzt walked back around the stalagmite, back to the body of Masoj Hun'ett. He had had no choice but to kill his adversary; Masoj had drawn the battle lines.

That fact did little to dispel the guilt in Drizzt as he looked upon the corpse. He had killed another drow, had taken the life of one of his own people. Was he trapped, as Zaknafein had been trapped for so very many years, in a cycle of violence that would know no end?

"Never again," Drizzt vowed to the corpse. "Never again will I kill a drow elf."

He turned away, disgusted, and knew as soon as he looked back to the silent, sinister mounds of the vast drow city that he would not survive long in Menzoberranzan if he held to that promise.

A thousand possibilities whirled in Drizzt's mind as he made his way through the winding ways of Menzoberranzan. He pushed the thoughts aside, stopped them from dulling his alertness. The light was general now in Narbondel; the drow day was beginning, and activity had started from every corner of the city. In the world of the surface-dwellers, the day was the safer time, when light exposed assassins. In Menzoberranzan's eternal darkness, the daytime of the dark elves was even more dangerous than the night.

Drizzt picked his way carefully, rolling wide from the mushroom fence of the noblest houses, wherein lay House Hun'ett. He encountered no more adversaries and made the safety of the Do'Urden compound a short time later. He rushed through the gate and by the surprised soldiers without a word of explanation and shoved aside the guards below the balcony.

The house was strangely quiet; Drizzt would have expected them all to be up and about with battle imminent. He gave the eerie stillness no more thought, and he cut a straight line to the training gym and Zaknafein's private quarters.

Drizzt paused outside the gym's stone door, his hand tightly clenched on the handle of the portal. What would he propose to his father? That they leave? He and Zaknafein on the perilous trails of the Underdark, fighting when they must and escaping the burdensome guilt of their existence under drow rule? Drizzt liked the thought, but he wasn't so certain now, standing before the door, that he could convince Zak to follow such a course. Zak could have left before, at any time during the centuries of his life, but when Drizzt had asked him why he had remained, the heat had drained from the weapons master's face. Were they indeed trapped in the life offered to them by Matron Malice and her evil cohorts?

Drizzt grimaced away the worries; no sense in arguing to himself with Zak only a few steps away.

The training gym was as quiet as the rest of the house. Too quiet. Drizzt hadn't expected Zak to be there, but something more than his father was absent. The father's presence, too, was gone.

Drizzt knew that something was wrong, and each step he took toward Zak's private door quickened until he was in full flight. He burst in without a knock, not surprised to find the bed empty.

"Malice must have sent him out in search of me," Drizzt reasoned. "Damn, I have caused him trouble!" He turned to leave, but something caught his eye and held him in the room—Zak's sword belt.

Never would the weapons master have left his room, not even for functions within the safety of House Do'Urden, without his swords. "Your weapon is your most trusted companion," Zak had told Drizzt a thousand times. "Keep it ever at your side!"

"House Hun'ett?" Drizzt whispered, wondering if the rival house had magically attacked in the night, while he was out battling Alton and Masoj. The compound, though, was serene; surely the soldiers would have known if anything like that had occurred.

Drizzt picked up the belt for inspection. No blood, and the clasp neatly unbuckled. No enemy had torn this from Zak. The weapons master's pouch lay beside it, also intact.

"What, then?" Drizzt asked aloud. He replaced the sword belt beside the bed, but slung the pouch across his neck, and turned, not knowing where he should go next.

He had to see about the rest of the family, he realized before he had even stepped through the door. Perhaps then this riddle about Zak would become more clear.

Dread grew out of that thought as Drizzt headed down the long and decorated corridor to the chapel anteroom. Had Malice, or any of them, brought Zak harm? For what purpose? The notion seemed illogical to Drizzt, but it nagged him every step, as if some sixth sense were warning him.

There still was no sign of anyone.

The anteroom's ornate doors swung in, magically and silently, even as Drizzt raised his hand to knock on them. He saw the matron mother first, sitting smugly on her throne at the rear of the room, her smile inviting.

Drizzt's discomfort did not diminish when he entered. The whole family was there: Briza, Vierna, and Maya to the sides of their matron, Rizzen and Dinin unobtrusively standing beside the left wall. The whole family. Except for Zak.

Matron Malice studied her son carefully, noting his many wounds. "I instructed you not to leave the house," she said to Drizzt, but she was not scolding him. "Where did your travels take you?"

"Where is Zaknafein?" Drizzt asked in reply.

"Answer the matron mother!" Briza yelled at him, her snake whip prominently displayed on her belt.

Drizzt glared at her and she recoiled, feeling the same bitter chill that Zaknafein had cast over her earlier in the night.

"I instructed you not to leave the house," Malice said again, still holding calm. "Why did you disobey me?"

"I had matters to attend," Drizzt replied, "urgent matters. I did not wish to bother you with them."

"War is upon us, my son," Matron Malice explained. "You are vulnerable out in the city by yourself. House Do'Urden cannot afford to lose you now."

"My business had to be handled alone," Drizzt answered.

"Is it completed?"

"It is."

"Then I trust that you will not disobey me again." The words came calm and even, but Drizzt understood at once the severity of the threat behind them.

"To other matters, then," Malice went on.

"Where is Zaknafein?" Drizzt dared to ask again.

Briza mumbled some curse under her breath and pulled the whip from her belt. Matron Malice threw an outstretched hand in her direction to stay her. They needed tact, not brutality, to bring Drizzt under control at this critical time. There would be ample opportunities for punishment after House Hun'ett was properly defeated.

"Concern yourself not with the fate of the weapons master," Malice replied. "He works for the good of House Do'Urden even as we speak—on a personal mission."

Drizzt didn't believe a word of it. Zak would never have left without his weapons. The truth hovered about Drizzt's thoughts, but he wouldn't let it in.

"Our concern is House Hun'ett," Malice went on, addressing them all. "The war's first strikes may fall this day."

"The first strikes already have fallen," Drizzt interrupted. All eyes came back to him, to his wounds. He wanted to continue the discussion about Zak but knew that he would only get himself, and Zak, if Zak was still alive, into further trouble. Perhaps the conversation would bring him more clues.

"You have seen battle?" Malice asked.

"You know of the Faceless One?" Drizzt asked.

"Master of the Academy," Dinin answered, "of Sorcere. We have dealt with him often."

"He has been of use to us in the past," said Malice, "but no more, I believe. He is a Hun'ett, Gelroos Hun'ett."

"No," Drizzt replied. "Once he may have been, but Alton DeVir is his name . . . was his name."

"The link!" Dinin growled, suddenly comprehending. "Gelroos was to kill Alton on the night of House DeVir's fall!"

"It would seem that Alton DeVir proved the stronger," mused Malice, and all became clear to her. "Matron SiNafay Hun'ett accepted him, used him to her gain," she explained to her family. She looked back to Drizzt. "You battled with him?"

"He is dead," Drizzt answered.

Matron Malice cackled with delight.

"One less wizard to deal with," Briza remarked, replacing the whip on her belt.

"Two," Drizzt corrected, but there was no boasting in his voice. He was not proud of his actions. "Masoj Hun'ett is no more."

"My son!" Matron Malice cried. "You have brought us a great edge in this war!" She glanced all about her family, infecting them, except Drizzt, with her elation. "House Hun'ett may not even choose to strike us now, knowing its disadvantage. We will not let them get away! We will destroy them this day and become the Eighth House of Menzoberranzan! Woe to the enemies of Daermon N'a'shezbaernon!

"We must move at once, my family," Malice reasoned, her hands rubbing over each other in excitement. "We cannot wait for an attack. We must take the offensive! Alton DeVir is gone now; the link that justifies this war is no more. Surely the ruling council knew of Hun'ett's intentions, and with both her wizards dead and the element of surprise lost, Matron SiNafay will move quickly to stop the battle."

Drizzt's hand unconsciously slipped into Zak's pouch as the others joined Malice in her plotting.

"Where is Zak?" Drizzt demanded again, above the chorus.

Silence dropped as quickly as the tumult had begun.

"He is of no concern to you, my son," Malice said to him, still keeping to her tact despite Drizzt's impudence. "You are the weapons master of House Do'Urden now. Lolth has forgiven your insolence; you have no crimes weighing against you. Your career may begin anew, to glorious heights!"

Her words cut through Drizzt as surely as his own scimitar might. "You killed him," he whispered aloud, the truth too awful to be contained in silent thought.

The matron's face suddenly gleamed, hot with rage. "You killed him!" she shot back at Drizzt. "Your insolence demanded repayment to the Spider Queen!"

Drizzt's tongue got all tangled up behind his teeth.

"But you live," Malice went on, relaxing again in her chair, "as the elven child lives."

Dinin was not the only one in the room to gasp audibly.

"Yes, we know of your deception," Malice sneered. "The Spider Queen always knew. She demanded restitution."

"You sacrificed Zaknafein?" Drizzt breathed, hardly able to get the words out of his mouth. "You gave him to that damned Spider Queen?"

"I would watch how I spoke of Queen Lolth," Malice warned. "Forget Zaknafein. He is not your concern. Look to your own life, my warrior son. All glories are offered to you, a station of honor."

Drizzt was indeed looking to his own life at that moment; at the proposed path that offered him a life of battle, a life of killing drow.

"You have no options," Malice said to him, seeing his inward struggle. "I offer to you now your life. In exchange, you must do as I bid, as Zaknafein once did."

"You kept your bargain with him," Drizzt spat sarcastically.

"I did!" Matron Malice protested. "Zaknafein went willingly to the altar, for your sake!"

Her words stung Drizzt for only a moment. He would not accept the guilt for Zaknafein's death! He had followed the only course he could, on the surface against the elves and here in the evil city.

"My offer is a good one," Malice said. "I give it here, before all the family.

Both of us will benefit from the agreement . . . Weapons Master?"

A smile spread across Drizzt's face when he looked into Matron Malice's cold eyes, a grin that Malice took as acceptance.

"Weapons Master?" Drizzt echoed. "Not likely."

Again Malice misunderstood. "I have seen you in battle," she argued. "Two wizards! You underestimate yourself."

Drizzt nearly laughed aloud at the irony of her words. She thought he would fail where Zaknafein had failed, would fall into her trap as the former weapons master had fallen, never to climb back out. "It is you who underestimate me, Malice," Drizzt said with threatening calm.

"Matron!" Briza demanded, but she held back, seeing that Drizzt and everyone else was ignoring her as the drama played out.

"You ask me to serve your evil designs," Drizzt continued. He knew but didn't care that all of them were nervously fingering weapons or preparing spells, were waiting for the proper moment to strike the blasphemous fool dead. Those childhood memories of the agony of snake whips reminded him of the punishment for his actions. Drizzt's fingers closed around a circular object, adding to his courage, though he would have continued in any case.

"They are a lie, as our—no, your—people are a lie!"

"Your skin is as dark as mine," Malice reminded him. "You are a drow, though you have never learned what that means!"

"Oh, I do know what it means."

"Then act by the rules!" Matron Malice demanded.

"Your rules?" Drizzt growled back. "But your rules are a damned lie as well, as great a lie as that filthy spider you claim as a deity!"

"Insolent slug," Briza cried, raising her snake whip.

Drizzt struck first. He pulled the object, the tiny ceramic globe, from Zaknafein's pouch.

"A true god damn you all!" he cried as he slammed the ball to the stone floor. He snapped his eyes shut as the pebble within the ball, enchanted by a powerful light-emanating dweomer, exploded into the room and erupted into his kin's sensitive eyes. "And damn that Spider Queen as well!"

Malice reeled backward, taking her great throne right over in a heavy crash to the hard stone. Cries of agony and rage came from every corner of the room as the sudden light bored into the stunned drow. Finally Vierna managed to launch a countering spell and returned the room to its customary gloom.

"Get him!" Malice growled, still trying to shake off the heavy fall. "I want him dead!"

The others had hardly recovered enough to heed to her commands, and Drizzt was already out of the house.

⚔ ⚔ ⚔ ⚔ ⚔

Carried on the silent winds of the Astral Plane, the call came. The entity of the panther stood up, ignoring its pains, and took note of the voice, a familiar, comforting voice.

The cat was off, then, running with all its heart and strength to answer the summons of its new master.

⚔ ⚔ ⚔ ⚔ ⚔

A short while later, Drizzt crept out of a little tunnel, Guenhwyvar at his side, and moved through the courtyard of the Academy to look down upon Menzoberranzan for the last time.

"What place is this," Drizzt asked the cat quietly, "that I call home? These are my people, by skin and by heritage, but I am no kin to them. They are lost and ever will be.

"How many others are like me, I wonder?" Drizzt whispered, taking one final look. "Doomed souls, as was Zaknafein, poor Zak. I do this for him, Guenhwyvar; I leave as he could not. His life has been my lesson, a dark scroll etched by the heavy price exacted by Matron Malice's evil promises.

"Goodbye, Zak!" he cried, his voice rising in final defiance. "My father. Take heart, as do I, that when we meet again, in a life after this, it will surely not be in the hellfire our kin are doomed to endure!"

Drizzt motioned the cat back into the tunnel, the entrance to the untamed Underdark. Watching the cat's easy movements, Drizzt realized again how fortunate he was to have found a companion of like spirit, a true friend. The way would not be easy for him and Guenhwyvar beyond the guarded borders of Menzoberranzan. They would be unprotected and alone—though better off, by Drizzt's estimation—more than they ever could be amid the evilness of the drow.

Drizzt stepped into the tunnel behind Guenhwyvar and left Menzoberranzan behind.

EXILE
THE LEGEND OF DRIZZT BOOK II

# PRELUDE

The monster lumbered along the quiet corridors of the Underdark, its eight scaly legs occasionally scuffing the stone. It did not recoil at its own echoing sounds, fearing the revealing noise. Nor did it scurry for cover, expecting the rush of another predator. For even in the dangers of the Underdark, this creature knew only security, confident of its ability to defeat any foe. Its breath reeked of deadly poison, the hard edges of its claws dug deep gouges into solid stone, and the rows of spearlike teeth that lined its wicked maw could tear through the thickest of hides. But worst of all was the monster's gaze, the gaze of a basilisk, which could transmutate into solid stone any living thing it fell upon.

This creature, huge and terrible, was among the greatest of its kind. It did not know fear.

The hunter watched the basilisk pass as he had watched it earlier that same day. The eight-legged monster was the intruder here, coming into the hunter's domain. He had witnessed the basilisk kill several of his rothé—the small, cattlelike creatures that enhanced his table—with its poison breath, and the rest of the herd had fled blindly down the endless tunnels, perhaps never to return.

The hunter was angry.

He watched now as the monster trudged down the narrow passageway, just the route the hunter had suspected it would take. He slid his weapons from their sheaths, gaining confidence, as always, as soon as he felt their fine balance. The hunter had owned them since his childhood, and even after nearly three decades of almost constant use, they bore only the slightest hints of wear. Now they would be tested again.

The hunter replaced his weapons and waited for the sound that would spur him to motion.

A throaty growl stopped the basilisk in its tracks. The monster peered ahead curiously, though its poor eyes could distinguish little beyond a few feet. Again came the growl, and the basilisk hunched down, waiting for the challenger, its next victim, to spring out and die.

Far behind, the hunter came out of his cubby, running impossibly fast along the tiny cracks and spurs in the corridor walls. In his magical cloak, his *piwafwi*, he was invisible against the stone, and with his agile and practiced movements, he made not a sound.

He came impossibly silent, impossibly fast.

The growl issued again from ahead of the basilisk but had not come any closer. The impatient monster shuffled forward, anxious to get on with the killing. When the basilisk crossed under a low archway, an impenetrable globe of absolute darkness enveloped its head and the monster stopped suddenly and took a step back, as the hunter knew it would.

The hunter was upon it then. He leaped from the passage wall, executing three separate actions before he ever reached his mark. First he cast a simple spell, which lined the basilisk's head in glowing blue and purple flames. Next he pulled his hood down over his face, for he did not need his eyes in battle, and against a basilisk a stray gaze could only bring him doom. Then, drawing his deadly scimitars, he landed on the monster's back and ran up its scales to get to its head.

The basilisk reacted as soon as the dancing flames outlined its head. They did not burn, but their outline made the monster an easy target. The basilisk spun back, but before its head had turned halfway, the first scimitar had dived into one of its eyes. The creature reared and thrashed, trying to get at the hunter. It breathed its noxious fumes and whipped its head about.

The hunter was the faster. He kept behind the maw, out of death's way. His second scimitar found the basilisk's other eye, then the hunter unleashed his fury.

The basilisk was the intruder; it had killed his rothé! Blow after savage blow bashed into the monster's armored head, flecked off scales, and dived for the flesh beneath.

The basilisk understood its peril but still believed that it would win. It had always won. If it could only get its poisonous breath in line with the furious hunter.

The second foe, the growling feline foe, was upon the basilisk then, having sprung toward the flame-lined maw without fear. The great cat latched on and took no notice of the poisonous fumes, for it was a magical beast, impervious to such attacks. Panther claws dug deep lines into the basilisk's gums, letting the monster drink of its own blood.

Behind the huge head, the hunter struck again and

again, a hundred times and more. Savagely, viciously, the scimitars slammed through the scaly armor, through the flesh, and through the skull, battering the basilisk down into the blackness of death.

Long after the monster lay still, the pounding of the bloodied scimitars slowed.

The hunter removed his hood and inspected the broken pile of gore at his feet and the hot stains of blood on his blades. He raised the dripping scimitars into the air and proclaimed his victory with a scream of primal exultation.

He was the hunter and this was his home!

When he had thrown all of his rage out in that scream, though, the hunter looked upon his companion and was ashamed. The panther's saucer eyes judged him, even if the panther did not. The cat was the hunter's only link to the past, to the civilized existence the hunter once had known.

"Come, Guenhwyvar," he whispered as he slid the scimitars back into their sheaths. He reveled in the sound of the words as he spoke them. It was the only voice he had heard for a decade. But every time he spoke now, the words seemed more foreign and came to him with difficulty.

Would he lose that ability, too, as he had lost every other aspect of his former existence? This the hunter feared greatly, for without his voice, he could not summon the panther.

He then truly would be alone.

Down the quiet corridors of the Underdark went the hunter and his cat, making not a sound, disturbing no rubble. Together they had come to know the dangers of this hushed world. Together they had learned to survive. Despite the victory, though, the hunter wore no smile this day. He feared no foes, but was no longer certain whether his courage came from confidence or from apathy about living.

Perhaps survival was not enough.

# Part One

# The Hunter

I remember vividly the day I walked away from the city of my birth, the city of my people. All the Underdark lay before me, a life of adventure and excitement, with possibilities that lifted my heart. More than that, though, I left Menzoberranzan with the belief that I could now live my life in accordance with my principles. I had Guenhwyvar at my side and my scimitars belted on my hips. My future was my own to determine.

But that drow, the young Drizzt Do'Urden who walked out of Menzoberranzan on that fated day, barely into my fourth decade of life, could not begin to understand the truth of time, of how its passage seemed to slow when the moments were not shared with others. In my youthful exuberance, I looked forward to several centuries of life.

How do you measure centuries when a single hour seems a day and a single day seems a year?

Beyond the cities of the Underdark, there is food for those who know how to find it and safety for those who know how to hide. More than anything else, though, beyond the teeming cities of the Underdark, there is solitude.

As I became a creature of the empty tunnels, survival became easier and more difficult all at once. I gained in the physical skills and experience necessary to live on. I could defeat almost anything that wandered into my chosen domain, and those few monsters that I could not defeat, I could surely flee or hide from. It did not take me long, however, to discover one nemesis that I could neither defeat nor flee. It followed me wherever I went–indeed, the farther I ran, the more it closed in around me. My enemy was solitude, the interminable, incessant silence of hushed corridors.

Looking back on it these many years later, I find myself amazed and appalled at the changes I endured under such an existence. The very identity of every reasoning being is defined by the language, the communication, between that being and others around it. Without that link, I was lost. When I left Menzoberranzan, I determined that my life would be based on principles, my strength adhering to unbending beliefs. Yet after only a few months alone in the Underdark, the only purpose for my survival was my survival. I had become a creature of instinct, calculating and cunning but not thinking, not using my mind for anything more than directing the newest kill.

Guenhwyvar saved me, I believe. The same companion that had pulled me from certain death in the clutches of monsters unnumbered rescued me from a death of emptiness—less dramatic, perhaps, but no less fatal. I found myself living for those moments when the cat could walk by my side, when I had another living creature to hear my words, strained though they had become. In addition to every other value, Guenhwyvar became my time clock, for I knew that the cat could come forth from the Astral Plane for a half-day every other day.

Only after my ordeal had ended did I realize how critical that one-quarter of my time actually was. Without Guenhwyvar, I would not have found the resolve to continue. I would never have maintained the strength to survive.

Even when Guenhwyvar stood beside me, I found myself growing more and more ambivalent toward the fighting. I was secretly hoping that some denizen of the Underdark would prove stronger than I. Could the pain of tooth or talon be greater than the emptiness and the silence?

I think not.

—Drizzt Do'Urden

# ANNIVERSARY PRESENT

Matron Malice Do'Urden shifted uneasily on the stone throne in the small and darkened anteroom to the great chapel of House Do'Urden. To the dark elves, who measured time's passage in decades, this was a day to be marked in the annals of Malice's house, the tenth anniversary of the ongoing covert conflict between the Do'Urden family and House Hun'ett. Matron Malice, never one to miss a celebration, had a special present prepared for her enemies.

Briza Do'Urden, Malice's eldest daughter, a large and powerful drow female, paced about the anteroom anxiously, a not uncommon sight. "It should be finished by now," she grumbled as she kicked a small three-legged stool. It skidded and tumbled, chipping away a piece of mushroom-stem seat.

"Patience, my daughter," Malice replied somewhat recriminatory, though she shared Briza's sentiments. "Jarlaxle is a careful one." Briza turned away at the mention of the outrageous mercenary and moved to the room's ornately carved stone doors. Malice did not miss the significance of her daughter's actions.

"You do not approve of Jarlaxle and his band," the matron mother stated flatly.

"They are houseless rogues," Briza spat in response, still not turning to face her mother. "There is no place in Menzoberranzan for houseless rogues. They disrupt the natural order of our society. And they are males!"

"They serve us well," Malice reminded her. Briza wanted to argue about the extreme cost of hiring the mercenary band, but she wisely held her tongue. She and Malice had been at odds almost continually since the start of the Do'Urden-Hun'ett war.

"Without Bregan D'aerthe, we could not take action against our enemies," Malice continued. "Using the mercenaries, the houseless rogues, as you have named them, allows us to wage war without implicating our house as the perpetrator."

"Then why not be done with it?" Briza demanded, spinning back toward the throne. "We kill a few of Hun'ett's soldiers, they kill a few of ours. And all the while, both houses continue to recruit replacements! It will not end! The only winners in the conflict are the mercenaries of Bregan D'aerthe—and whatever band Matron SiNafay Hun'ett has hired—feeding off the coffers of both houses!"

"Watch your tone, my daughter," Malice growled as an angry reminder. "You are addressing a matron mother."

Briza turned away again. "We should have attacked House Hun'ett immediately, on the night Zaknafein was sacrificed," she dared to grumble.

"You forget the actions of your youngest brother on that night," Malice replied evenly.

But the matron mother was wrong. If she lived a thousand more years, Briza would not forget Drizzt's actions on the night he had forsaken his family. Trained by Zaknafein, Malice's favorite lover and reputably the finest weapon master in all of Menzoberranzan, Drizzt had achieved a level of fighting ability far beyond the drow norm. But Zak had also given Drizzt the troublesome and blasphemous attitudes that Lolth, the Spider Queen deity of the dark elves, would not tolerate. Finally, Drizzt's sacrilegious ways had invoked Lolth's wrath, and the Spider Queen, in turn, had demanded his death.

Matron Malice, impressed by Drizzt's potential as a warrior, had acted boldly on Drizzt's behalf and had given Zaknafein's heart to Lolth to compensate for Drizzt's sins. She forgave Drizzt in the hope that without

Zaknafein's influences he would amend his ways and replace the deposed weapon master.

In return, though, the ungrateful Drizzt had betrayed them all, had run off into the Underdark—an act that had not only robbed House Do'Urden of its only potential remaining weapon master, but also had placed Matron Malice and the rest of the Do'Urden family out of Lolth's favor. In the disastrous end of all their efforts, House Do'Urden had lost its premier weapon master, the favor of Lolth, and its would-be weapon master. It had not been a good day.

Luckily, House Hun'ett had suffered similar woes on that same day, losing both its wizards in a botched attempt to assassinate Drizzt. With both houses weakened and in Lolth's disfavor, the expected war had been turned into a calculated series of covert raids.

Briza would never forget.

A knock on the anteroom door startled Briza and her mother from their private memories of that fateful time. The door swung open, and Dinin, the elderboy of the house, walked in.

"Greetings, Matron Mother," he said in appropriate manner and dipping into a low bow. Dinin wanted his news to be a surprise, but the grin that found its way onto his face revealed everything.

"Jarlaxle has returned!" Malice snarled in glee. Dinin turned toward the open door, and the mercenary, waiting patiently in the corridor, strode in. Briza, ever amazed at the rogue's unusual mannerisms, shook her head as Jarlaxle walked past her. Nearly every dark elf in Menzoberranzan dressed in a quiet and practical manner, in robes adorned with the symbols of the Spider Queen or in supple chain-link armor under the folds of a magical and camouflaging *piwafwi* cloak.

Jarlaxle, arrogant and brash, followed few of the customs of Menzoberranzan's inhabitants. He was most certainly not the norm of drow society and he flaunted the differences openly, brazenly. He wore not a cloak nor a robe, but a shimmering cape that showed every color of the spectrum both in the glow of light and in the infrared spectrum of heat-sensing eyes. The cape's magic could only be guessed, but those closest to the mercenary leader indicated that it was very valuable indeed.

Jarlaxle's vest was sleeveless and cut so high that his slender and tightly muscled stomach was open for all to view. He kept a patch over one eye, though careful observers would understand it as ornamental, for Jarlaxle often shifted it from one eye to the other.

"My dear Briza," Jarlaxle said over his shoulder, noting the high priestess's disdainful interest in his appearance. He spun about and bowed low, sweeping off the wide-brimmed hat—another oddity, and even more so since the hat was overly plumed in the monstrous feathers of a diatryma, a gigantic Underdark bird—as he stooped.

Briza huffed and turned away at the sight of the mercenary's dipping head. Drow elves wore their thick white hair as a mantle of their station, each cut designed to reveal rank and house affiliation. Jarlaxle the rogue wore no hair at all, and from Briza's angle, his clean-shaven head appeared as a ball of pressed onyx.

Jarlaxle laughed quietly at the continuing disapproval of the eldest Do'Urden daughter and turned back toward Matron Malice, his ample jewelry tinkling and his hard and shiny boots clumping with every step. Briza took note of this as well, for she knew that those boots, and that jewelry, only seemed to make noise when Jarlaxle wished them to do so.

"It is done?" Matron Malice asked before the mercenary could even begin to offer a proper greeting.

"My dear Matron Malice," Jarlaxle replied with a pained sigh, knowing that he could get away with the informalities in light of his grand news. "Did you doubt me? Surely I am wounded to my heart."

Malice leaped from her throne, her fist clenched in victory. "Dipree Hun'ett is dead!" she proclaimed. "The first noble victim of the war!"

"You forget Masoj Hun'ett," remarked Briza, "slain by Drizzt ten years ago. And Zaknafein Do'Urden," Briza had to add, against her better judgment, "killed by your own hand."

"Zaknafein was not noble by birth," Malice sneered at her impertinent daughter. Briza's words stung Malice nonetheless. Malice had decided to sacrifice Zaknafein in Drizzt's stead against Briza's recommendations.

Jarlaxle cleared his throat to deflect the growing tension. The mercenary knew that he had to finish his business and be out of House Do'Urden as quickly as possible. Already he knew—though the Do'Urdens did not—that the appointed hour drew near. "There is the matter of my payment," he reminded Malice.

"Dinin will see to it," Malice replied with a wave of her hand, not turning her eyes from her daughter's pernicious stare.

"I will take my leave," Jarlaxle said, nodding to the elderboy.

Before the mercenary had taken his first step toward the door, Vierna, Malice's second daughter, burst into the room, her face glowing brightly in the infrared spectrum, heated with obvious excitement.

"Damn," Jarlaxle whispered under his breath.

"What is it?" Matron Malice demanded.

"House Hun'ett," Vierna cried. "Soldiers in the compound! We are under attack!"

Out in the courtyard, beyond the cavern complex, nearly five hundred soldiers of House Hun'ett—fully a hundred more than the house reportedly possessed—followed the blast of a lightning bolt through House Do'Urden's adamantite gates. The three hundred fifty soldiers of the Do'Urden household swarmed out of the shaped stalagmite mounds that served as their quarters to meet the attack.

Outnumbered but trained by Zaknafein, the Do'Urden troops formed into proper defensive positions, shielding their wizards and clerics so that they might cast their spells.

An entire contingent of Hun'ett soldiers, empowered with enchantments of flying, swooped down the cavern wall that housed the royal chambers of House Do'Urden. Tiny hand-held crossbows clicked and thinned the ranks of the aerial force with deadly, poison-tipped darts. The aerial invaders' surprise had been achieved, though, and the Do'Urden troops were quickly put into a precarious position.

"Hun'ett has not the favor of Lolth!" Malice screamed. "It would not dare to openly attack!" She flinched at the refuting, thunderous sounds of another, and then still another, bolt of lightning.

"Oh?" Briza snapped.

Malice cast her daughter a threatening glare but didn't have time to continue the argument. The normal method of attack by a drow house would involve the rush of soldiers combined with a mental barrage by the house's highest-ranking clerics. Malice, though, felt no mental attack, which told her beyond any doubt that it was indeed House Hun'ett that had come to her gates. The clerics of Hun'ett, out of the Spider Queen's favor, apparently could not use their Lolth-given powers to launch the mental assault. If they had, Malice and her daughters, also out of the Spider Queen's favor, could not have hoped to counter.

"Why would they dare to attack?" Malice wondered aloud.

Briza understood her mother's reasoning. "They are bold indeed," she said, "to hope that their soldiers alone can eliminate every member of our house." Everyone in the room, every drow in Menzoberranzan, understood the brutal, absolute punishments exacted upon any house that failed to eradicate another house. Such attacks were not frowned upon, but getting caught at the deed most certainly was.

Rizzen, the present patron of House Do'Urden, came into the anteroom then, his face grim. "We are outnumbered and outpositioned," he said. "Our defeat will be swift, I fear."

Malice would not accept the news. She struck Rizzen with a blow that knocked the patron halfway across the floor, then she spun on Jarlaxle. "You must summon your band!" Malice cried at the mercenary. "Quickly!"

"Matron," Jarlaxle stuttered, obviously at a loss. "Bregan D'aerthe is a secretive group. We do not engage in open warfare. To do so could invoke the wrath of the ruling council!"

"I will pay you whatever you desire," the desperate matron mother promised.

"But the cost—"

"Whatever you desire!" Malice snarled again.

"Such action—" Jarlaxle began.

Again, Malice did not let him finish his argument. "Save my house, mercenary," she growled. "Your profits will be great, but I warn you, the cost of your failure will be far greater!"

Jarlaxle did not appreciate being threatened, especially by a lame matron mother whose entire world was fast crumbling around her. But in the mercenary's ears the sweet ring of the word "profits" outweighed the threat a thousand times over. After ten straight years of exorbitant rewards in the Do'Urden-Hun'ett conflict, Jarlaxle did not doubt Malice's willingness or ability to pay as promised, nor did he doubt that this deal would prove even more lucrative than the agreement he had struck with Matron SiNafay Hun'ett earlier that same tenday.

"As you wish," he said to Matron Malice with a bow and a sweep of his garish hat. "I will see what I can do." A wink at Dinin set the elderboy on his heels as he exited the room.

When the two got out on the balcony overlooking the Do'Urden compound, they saw that the situation was even more desperate than Rizzen had described. The soldiers of House Do'Urden—those still alive—were trapped in and around one of the huge stalagmite mounds anchoring the front gate.

One of Hun'ett's flying soldiers dropped onto the balcony at the sight of a Do'Urden noble, but Dinin dispatched the intruder with a single, blurring attack routine.

"Well done," Jarlaxle commented, giving Dinin an approving nod. He moved to pat the elderboy Do'Urden on the shoulder, but Dinin slipped out of reach.

"We have other business," he pointedly reminded Jarlaxle. "Call your troops, and quickly, else I fear that House Hun'ett will win the day."

"Be at ease, my friend Dinin," Jarlaxle laughed. He pulled a small whistle from around his neck and blew into it. Dinin heard not a sound, for the instrument was magically tuned exclusively for the ears of members of Bregan D'aerthe.

The elderboy Do'Urden watched in amazement as Jarlaxle calmly puffed out a specific cadence, then he watched in even greater amazement as more than a hundred of House Hun'ett's soldiers turned against their comrades.

Bregan D'aerthe owed allegiance only to Bregan D'aerthe.

⚔ ⚔ ⚔ ⚔ ⚔

"They could not attack us," Malice said stubbornly, pacing about the chamber. "The Spider Queen would not aid them in their venture."

"They are winning without the Spider Queen's aid," Rizzen reminded her, prudently ducking into the room's farthest corner even as he spoke the unwanted words.

"You said that they would never attack!" Briza growled at her mother. "Even as you explained why we could not dare to attack them!" Briza remembered that conversation vividly, for it was she who had suggested the open attack on House Hun'ett. Malice had scolded her harshly and publicly, and now Briza meant to return the humiliation. Her voice dripped of angry sarcasm as she aimed each word at her mother. "Could it be that Matron Malice Do'Urden has erred?"

Malice's reply came in the form of a glare that wavered somewhere between rage and terror. Briza returned the threatening look without ambiguity and suddenly the matron mother of House Do'Urden did not feel so very invincible and sure of her actions. She started forward nervously a moment later when Maya, the youngest of the Do'Urden daughters, entered the room.

"They have breached the house!" Briza cried, assuming the worst. She grabbed at her snake-headed whip. "And we have not even begun our preparations for defense!"

"No!" Maya quickly corrected. "No enemies have crossed the balcony. The battle has turned against House Hun'ett!"

"As I knew it would," Malice observed, pulling herself straight and speaking pointedly at Briza. "Foolish is the house that moves without the favor of Lolth!" Despite her proclamation, though, Malice guessed that more than the judgment of the Spider Queen had come into play out in the courtyard. Her reasoning led her inescapably to Jarlaxle and his untrustworthy band of rogues.

⚔ ⚔ ⚔ ⚔ ⚔

Jarlaxle stepped off the balcony and used his innate drow abilities to levitate down to the cavern floor. Seeing no need to involve himself in a battle that was obviously under control, Dinin rested back and watched the mercenary go, considering all that had just transpired. Jarlaxle had played both sides off against the other, and once again the mercenary and his band had been the only true winners. Bregan D'aerthe was undeniably unscrupulous, but Dinin had to admit, undeniably effective.

Dinin found that he liked the renegade.

⚔ ⚔ ⚔ ⚔ ⚔

"The accusation has been properly delivered to Matron Baenre?" Malice asked Briza when the light of Narbondel, the magically heated stalagmite mound that served as the time clock of Menzoberranzan, began its steady climb, marking the dawn of the next day.

"The ruling house expected the visit," Briza replied with a smirk. "All of the city whispers of the attack, and of how House Do'Urden repelled the invaders of House Hun'ett."

Malice futilely tried to hide her vain smile. She enjoyed the attention and the glory that she knew would be lavished upon her house.

"The ruling council will be convened this very day," Briza went on. "No doubt to the dismay of Matron SiNafay Hun'ett and her doomed children."

Malice nodded her agreement. To eradicate a rival house in Menzoberranzan was a perfectly acceptable practice among the drow. But to fail in the attempt, to leave even one witness of noble blood alive to make an accusation, invited the judgment of the ruling council, a wrath that wrought absolute destruction in its wake.

A knock turned them both toward the room's ornate door.

"You are summoned, Matron," Rizzen said as he entered. "Matron Baenre has sent a chariot for you."

Malice and Briza exchanged hopeful but nervous glances. When punishment fell upon House Hun'ett, House Do'Urden would move into the eighth rank of the city hierarchy, a most desirable position. Only the matron mothers of the top eight houses were accorded a seat on the city's ruling council.

"Already?" Briza asked her mother.

Malice only shrugged in reply and followed Rizzen out of the room and down to the house's balcony. Rizzen offered her a hand of assistance, which she promptly and stubbornly slapped away. Her pride apparent with every move, Malice stepped over the railing and floated down to the courtyard, where the bulk of her remaining soldiery was gathered. The floating, blue-glowing disk bearing the insignia of House Baenre hovered just outside the blasted adamantite gate of the Do'Urden compound.

Malice proudly strode through the gathered crowd; dark elves fell over each other trying to get out of her way. This was her day, she decided, the day she achieved the seat on the ruling council, the position she so greatly deserved.

"Matron Mother, I will accompany you through the city," offered Dinin, standing at the gate.

"You will remain here with the rest of the family," Malice corrected. "The summons is for me alone."

"How can you know?" Dinin questioned, but he realized he had overstepped his rank as soon as the words had left his mouth.

By the time Malice turned her reprimanding glare toward him, he had already disappeared into the mob of soldiers.

"Proper respect," Malice muttered under her breath, and she instructed the nearest soldiers to remove a section of the propped and tied gate. With a final, victorious glance at her subjects, Malice stepped out and took a seat on the floating disk.

This was not the first time that Malice had accepted such an invitation from Matron Baenre, so she was not the least bit surprised when several Baenre clerics moved out from the shadows to encircle the floating disk in a protective guard. The last time Malice had made this trip, she had been tentative, not really understanding Baenre's intent in summoning her. This time, though, Malice folded her arms defiantly across her chest and let the curious onlookers view her in all the splendor of her victory.

Malice accepted the stares proudly, feeling positively superior. Even when the disk reached the fabulous weblike fence of House Baenre, with its thousand marching guards and towering stalagmite and stalactite structures, Malice's pride had not diminished.

She was of the ruling council now, or soon would be; no longer did she have to feel intimidated anywhere in the city.

Or so she thought.

"Your presence is requested in the chapel," one of Baenre's clerics said to her when the disk came to a stop at the base of the great domed building's sweeping stairs.

Malice stepped down and ascended the polished stones. As soon as she entered, she noticed a figure sitting on one of the chairs atop the raised central altar. The seated drow, the only other person visible in the chapel, apparently did not notice that Malice had entered. She sat back comfortably, watching the huge illusionary image at the top of the dome shift through its forms, first appearing as a gigantic spider, then a beautiful drow female.

As she moved closer, Malice recognized the robes of a matron mother, and she assumed, as she had all along, that it was Matron Baenre herself, the most powerful figure in all of Menzoberranzan, awaiting her. Malice made her way up the altar's stairs, coming up behind the seated drow. Not waiting for an invitation, she boldly walked around to greet the other matron mother.

It was not, however, the ancient and emaciated form of Matron Baenre that Malice Do'Urden encountered on the dais of the Baenre chapel. The seated matron mother was not old beyond the years of a drow and as withered and dried as some bloodless corpse. Indeed, this drow was no older than Malice and quite diminutive. Malice recognized her all too well.

"SiNafay!" she cried, nearly toppling.

"Malice," the other replied calmly.

A thousand troublesome possibilities rolled through Malice's mind. SiNafay Hun'ett should have been huddling in fear in her doomed house, awaiting the annihilation of her family. Yet here SiNafay sat, comfortably, in the hallowed quarters of Menzoberranzan's most important family!

"You do not belong in this place!" Malice protested, her slender fists clenched at her side. She considered the possibilities of attacking her rival there and then, of throttling SiNafay with her own hands.

"Be at ease, Malice," SiNafay remarked casually. "I am here by the invitation of Matron Baenre, as are you."

The mention of Matron Baenre and the reminder of where they were calmed Malice considerably. One did not act out of sorts in the chapel of House Baenre! Malice moved to the opposite end of the circular dais and took a seat, her gaze never leaving the smugly smiling face of SiNafay Hun'ett.

After a few interminable moments of silence, Malice had to speak her mind. "It was House Hun'ett that attacked my family in the last dark of Narbondel," she said. "I have many witnesses to the fact. There can be no doubt!"

"None," SiNafay replied, her agreement catching Malice off her guard.

"You admit the deed?" she balked.

"Indeed," said SiNafay. "Never have I denied it."

"Yet you live," Malice sneered. "The laws of Menzoberranzan demand justice upon you and your house."

"Justice?" SiNafay laughed at the absurd notion. Justice had never been more than a facade and a means of keeping the pretense of order in chaotic Menzoberranzan. "I acted as the Spider Queen demanded of me."

"If the Spider Queen approved of your methods, you would have been victorious," Malice reasoned.

"Not so," interrupted another voice. Malice and SiNafay turned about just as Matron Baenre magically appeared, sitting comfortably in the chair farthest back on the dais.

Malice wanted to scream out at the withered matron mother, both for spying on her conversation and for apparently refuting her claims against SiNafay. Malice had managed to survive the dangers of Menzoberranzan for five hundred years, though, primarily because she understood the implications of angering one such as Matron Baenre.

"I claim the rights of accusation against House Hun'ett," she said calmly.

"Granted," replied Matron Baenre. "As you have said, and as SiNafay agreed, there can be no doubt."

Malice turned triumphantly on SiNafay, but the matron mother of House Hun'ett still sat relaxed and unconcerned.

"Then why is she here?" Malice cried, her tone edged in explosive violence. "SiNafay is an outlaw. She—"

"We have not argued against your words," Matron Baenre interrupted. "House Hun'ett attacked and failed. The penalties for such a deed are well known and agreed upon, and the ruling council will convene this very day to see that justice is carried through."

"Then why is SiNafay here?" Malice demanded.

"Do you doubt the wisdom of my attack?" SiNafay asked Malice, trying to keep a chuckle under her breath.

"You were defeated," Malice reminded her matter-of-factly. "That alone should provide your answer."

"Lolth demanded the attack," said Matron Baenre.

"Why, then, was House Hun'ett defeated?" Malice asked stubbornly. "If the Spider Queen—"

"I did not say that the Spider Queen had imbued her blessings upon House Hun'ett," Matron Baenre interrupted, somewhat crossly. Malice shifted back in her seat, remembering her place and her predicament.

"I said only that Lolth demanded the attack," Matron Baenre continued. "For ten years all of Menzoberranzan has suffered the spectacle of your private war. The intrigue and excitement wore away long ago, let me assure you both. It had to be decided."

"And it was," declared Malice, rising from her seat. "House Do'Urden has proven victorious, and I claim the rights of accusation against SiNafay Hun'ett and her family!"

"Sit down, Malice," SiNafay said. "There is more to this than your simple rights of accusation."

Malice looked to Matron Baenre for confirmation, though, considering the present situation, she could not doubt SiNafay's words.

"It is done," Matron Baenre said to her. "House Do'Urden has won, and House Hun'ett will be no more."

Malice fell back into her seat, smiling smugly at SiNafay. Still, though, the matron mother of House Hun'ett did not seem the least bit concerned.

"I will watch the destruction of your house with great pleasure," Malice assured her rival. She turned to Baenre. "When will punishment be exacted?"

"It is already done," Matron Baenre replied mysteriously.

"SiNafay lives!" Malice cried.

"No," the withered matron mother corrected. "She who was SiNafay Hun'ett lives."

Now Malice was beginning to understand. House Baenre had always been opportunistic. Could it be that Matron Baenre was stealing the high priestesses of House Hun'ett to add to her own collection?

"You will shelter her?" Malice dared to ask.

"No," Matron Baenre replied evenly. "That task will fall to you."

Malice's eyes went wide. Of all the many duties she had ever been appointed in her days as a high priestess of Lolth, she could think of none more distasteful. "She is my enemy! You ask that I give her shelter?"

"She is your daughter," Matron Baenre shot back. Her tone softened and a wry smile cracked her thin lips. "Your oldest daughter, returned from travels to Ched Nasad, or some other city of our kin."

"Why are you doing this?" Malice demanded. "It is unprecedented!"

"Not completely correct," replied Matron Baenre. Her fingers tapped together out in front of her while she sank back within her thoughts, remembering some of the strange consequences of the endless line of battles within the drow city.

"Outwardly, your observations are correct," she continued to explain to Malice. "But surely you are wise enough to know that many things occur behind the appearances in Menzoberranzan. House Hun'ett must be destroyed—that cannot be changed—and all of the nobles of House Hun'ett must be slaughtered. It is, after all, the civilized thing to do." She paused a moment to ensure that Malice was fully comprehending the meaning of her next statement. "They must appear, at least, to be slaughtered."

"And you will arrange this?" Malice asked.

"I already have," Matron Baenre assured her.

"But what is the purpose?"

"When House Hun'ett initiated its attack against you, did you call upon the Spider Queen in your struggles?" Matron Baenre asked bluntly.

The question startled Malice, and the expected answer upset her more than a little.

"And when House Hun'ett was repelled," Matron Baenre went on coldly, "did you give praise to the Spider Queen? Did you call upon a handmaiden of Lolth in your moment of victory, Malice Do'Urden?"

"Am I on trial here?" Malice cried. "You know the answer, Matron Baenre." She looked at SiNafay uncomfortably as she replied, fearing that she might be giving some valued information away. "You are aware of my situation concerning the Spider Queen. I dare not summon a yochlol until I have seen some sign that I have regained Lolth's favor."

"And you have seen no sign," SiNafay remarked.

"None other than the defeat of my rival," Malice growled back at her.

"That was not a sign from the Spider Queen," Matron Baenre assured them both. "Lolth did not involve herself in your struggles. She only demanded that they be finished!"

"Is she pleased at the outcome?" Malice asked bluntly.

"That is yet to be determined," replied Matron Baenre. "Many years ago, Lolth made clear her desires that Malice Do'Urden sit upon the ruling council. Beginning with the next light of Narbondel, it shall be so."

Malice's chin rose with pride.

"But understand your dilemma," Matron Baenre scolded her, rising up out of her chair. Malice slumped back immediately.

"You have lost more than half of your soldiers," Baenre explained. "And you do not have a large family surrounding and supporting you. You rule the eighth house of the city, yet it is known by all that you are not in the Spider Queen's favor. How long do you believe House Do'Urden will hold its position? Your seat on the ruling council is in jeopardy even before you have assumed it!"

Malice could not refute the ancient matron's logic. They both knew the ways of Menzoberranzan. With House Do'Urden so obviously crippled, some lesser house would soon take advantage of the opportunity to better its station. The attack by House Hun'ett would not be the last battle fought in the Do'Urden compound.

"So I give to you SiNafay Hun'ett . . . Shi'nayne Do'Urden . . . a new daughter, a new high priestess," said Matron Baenre. She turned then to SiNafay to continue her explanation, but Malice found herself suddenly distracted as a voice called out to her in her thoughts, a telepathic message.

*Keep her only as long as you need her, Malice Do'Urden,* it said. Malice looked around, guessing the source of the communication. On a previous visit to House Baenre, she had met Matron Baenre's mind flayer, a telepathic beast. The creature was nowhere in sight, but neither had Matron Baenre been when Malice had first entered the chapel. Malice looked around alternately at the remaining empty seats atop the dais, but the stone furniture showed no signs of any occupants.

A second telepathic message left her no doubts.

*You will know when the time is right.*

". . . and the remaining fifty of House Hun'ett's soldiers," Matron Baenre was saying. "Do you agree, Matron Malice?"

Malice looked at SiNafay, an expression that might have been acceptance or wicked irony. "I do," she replied.

"Go, then, Shi'nayne Do'Urden," Matron Baenre instructed SiNafay. "Join your remaining soldiers in the courtyard. My wizards will get you to House Do'Urden in secrecy."

SiNafay cast a suspicious glance Malice's way, then moved out of the great chapel.

"I understand," Malice said to her hostess when SiNafay had gone.

"You understand nothing!" Matron Baenre yelled back at her, suddenly enraged. "I have done all that I may for you, Malice Do'Urden! It was Lolth's wish that you sit upon the ruling council, and I have arranged, at great personal cost, for that to be so."

Malice knew then, beyond any doubt, that House Baenre had prompted House Hun'ett to action. How deep did Matron Baenre's influence go, Malice wondered? Perhaps the withered matron mother also had anticipated, and possibly arranged, the actions of Jarlaxle and the soldiers of Bregan D'aerthe, ultimately the deciding factor in the battle.

She would have to find out about that possibility, Malice promised herself. Jarlaxle had dipped his greedy fingers quite deeply into her purse.

"No more," Matron Baenre continued. "Now you are left to your own wiles. You have not found the favor of Lolth, and that is the only way you, and House Do'Urden, will survive!"

Malice's fist clenched the arm of her chair so tightly that she almost expected to hear the stone cracking beneath it. She had hoped, with the defeat of House Hun'ett, that she had put the blasphemous deeds of her youngest son behind her.

"You know what must be done," said Matron Baenre. "Correct the wrong, Malice. I have put myself forward on your behalf. I will not tolerate continued failure!"

⚔ ⚔ ⚔ ⚔ ⚔

"The arrangements have been explained to us, Matron Mother," Dinin said to Malice when she returned to the adamantite gate of House Do'Urden. He followed Malice across the compound and then levitated up beside her to the balcony outside the noble quarters of the house.

"All of the family is gathered in the anteroom," Dinin went on. "Even the newest member," he added with a wink.

Malice did not respond to her son's feeble attempt at humor. She pushed Dinin aside roughly and stormed down the central corridor, commanding the anteroom door to open with a single powerful word. The family scrambled out of her way as she crossed to her throne, on the far side of the spider-shaped table.

They had anticipated a long meeting, to learn the new situation confronting them and the challenges they must overcome. What they got instead was a brief glimpse at the rage burning within Matron Malice. She glared at them alternately, letting each of them know beyond any doubt that she would not accept anything less than she demanded. Her voice grating as though her mouth were filled with pebbles, she growled, "Find Drizzt and bring him to me!"

Briza started to protest, but Malice shot her a glare so utterly cold and threatening that it stole the words away. The eldest daughter, as stubborn as her mother and always ready for an argument, averted her eyes. And no one else in the anteroom, though they shared Briza's unspoken concerns, made any motion to argue.

Malice then left them to sort out the specifics of how they would accomplish the task. Details were not at all important to Malice.

The only part she meant to play in all of this was the thrust of the ceremonial dagger into her youngest son's chest.

# 2
# Voices in the Dark

Drizzt stretched away his weariness and forced himself to his feet. The efforts of his battle against the basilisk the night before, of slipping fully into that primal state so necessary for survival, had drained him thoroughly. Yet Drizzt knew that he could afford no more rest; his rothé herd, the guaranteed food supply, had been scattered among the maze of tunnels and had to be retrieved.

Drizzt quickly surveyed the small and unremarkable cave that served as his home, ensuring that all was as it should be. His eyes lingered on the onyx statuette of the panther. He was held by a profound longing for Guenhwyvar's companionship. In his ambush of the basilisk, Drizzt had kept the panther by his side for a long period—nearly the entire night—and Guenhwyvar would need to rest back on the Astral Plane. More than a full day would pass before Drizzt could bring a rested Guenhwyvar forth again, and to attempt to use the figurine before then in any but a desperate situation would be foolish. With a resigned shrug, Drizzt dropped the statuette into his pocket and tried vainly to dismiss his loneliness.

After a quick inspection of the rock barricade blocking the entrance to the main corridor, Drizzt moved to the smaller crawl tunnel at the back of the cave. He noticed the scratches on the wall by the tunnel, the notches he had scrawled to mark the passage of the days. Drizzt absently scraped another one now, but realized that it was not important. How many times had he forgotten to scratch the mark? How many days had slipped past him unnoticed, between the hundreds of scratches on that wall?

Somehow, it no longer seemed to matter. Day and night were one, and all the days were one, in the life of the hunter. Drizzt hauled himself up into the tunnel and crawled for many minutes toward the dim light source at the other end. Though the presence of light, the result of the glow of an unusual type of fungus, normally would have been uncomfortable to a dark elf's eyes, Drizzt felt a sincere sense of security as he crossed through the crawl tunnel into the long chamber.

Its floor was broken into two levels, the lower being a moss-filled bed crossed by a small stream, and the upper being a grove of towering mushrooms. Drizzt headed for the grove, though he was not normally welcomed there. He knew that the myconids, the fungus-men, a weird cross between humanoid and toadstool, were watching him anxiously. The basilisk had come in here in its first travels to the region, and the myconids had suffered a great loss. Now they were no doubt scared and dangerous, but Drizzt suspected that they knew, as well, that it was he who had slain the monster. Myconids were not stupid beings; if Drizzt kept his weapons sheathed and made no unexpected moves, the fungus-men probably would accept his passage through their tended grove.

The wall to the upper tier was more than ten feet high and nearly sheer, but Drizzt scaled it as easily and as quickly as if it had sported a wide and flat staircase. A group of myconids fanned out around him as he reached the top, some only half Drizzt's height, but most twice as tall as the drow. Drizzt crossed his arms over his chest, a commonly accepted Underdark signal of peace.

The fungus-men found Drizzt's appearance disgusting—as disgusting as he considered them—but they did indeed understand that Drizzt had destroyed the basilisk. For many years the myconids had lived beside the rogue drow, each protecting the life-filled chamber that served as their mutual sanctuary. An oasis such as this place, with edible plants, a stream full of fish, and a herd of rothé, was not common in the harsh and empty stone caverns of the Underdark, and predators wandering along the outer tunnels invariably found their way in. Then it was left to the fungus-men, and to Drizzt, to defend their domain.

The largest of the myconids moved forward to stand before the dark elf. Drizzt made no move, understanding the importance of establishing an acceptance between himself and the new king of the fungus-man colony. Still, Drizzt tensed his muscles, preparing a spring to the side if things did not go as he expected.

The myconid spewed forth a cloud of spores. Drizzt studied them in the split-second it took them to descend over him, knowing that the mature myconids could emit many different types of spore, some quite dangerous. But Drizzt recognized the hue of this particular cloud and accepted it wholly.

*King dead. Me king,* came the myconid's thoughts through the telepathic bond inspired by the spore cloud.

*You are king,* Drizzt responded mentally. How he wished these fungoids could speak aloud! *As it was?*

*Bottom for dark elf, grove for myconid,* replied the fungus-man.

*Agreed.*

*Grove for myconid!* the fungus-man thought again, this time emphatically.

Drizzt silently dropped down off the ledge. He had accomplished his mission with the fungoid; neither he nor the new king had any desire to continue the meeting.

Off at a swift pace, Drizzt leaped the five-foot-wide stream and padded out across the thick moss. The chamber was longer than it was wide and it rolled back for many yards, turning a slight bend before it reached the larger exit to the twisting maze of Underdark tunnels. Around that bend, Drizzt looked again upon the destruction wreaked by the basilisk. Several half-eaten rothé lay about—Drizzt would have to dispose of those corpses before their stench attracted even more unwelcome visitors—and other rothé stood perfectly still, petrified by the gaze of the dreaded monster. Directly in front of the chamber exit stood the former myconid king, a twelve-foot giant, now no more than an ornamental statue.

Drizzt paused to regard it. He had never learned the fungoid's name, and had never given it his, but Drizzt supposed that the thing had been his ally at least, perhaps even his friend. They had lived side by side for several years, though they had rarely encountered each other, and both had realized a bit more security just by the other's presence. All told, though, Drizzt felt no remorse at the sight of his petrified ally. In the Underdark, only the strongest survived, and this time the myconid king had not been strong enough.

In the wilds of the Underdark, failure allowed for no second chance.

Out in the tunnels again, Drizzt felt his rage beginning to build. He welcomed it fully, focusing his thoughts on the carnage in his domain and accepting the anger as an ally in the wilds. He came through a series of tunnels and turned into the one where he had placed his darkness spell the night before, where Guenhwyvar had crouched, ready to spring upon the basilisk. Drizzt's spell was long gone now and using his infravision, he could make out several warm-glowing forms crawling over the cooling mound that Drizzt knew to be the dead monster.

The sight of the thing only heightened the hunter's rage.

Instinctively, he grasped the hilt of one of his scimitars. As though it moved of its own accord, the weapon shot out as Drizzt passed the basilisk's head, splatting sickeningly into the exposed brains. Several blind cave rats took flight at the sound and Drizzt, again without thinking, snapped off a thrust with his second blade, pinning one to the stone. Without even slowing his pace, he scooped the rat up and dropped it into his pouch. Finding the rothé could be a tedious process, and the hunter would need to eat.

For the remainder of that day and half of the next, the hunter moved out away from his domain. The cave rat was not a particularly enjoyable meal, but it sustained Drizzt, allowing him to continue, allowing him to survive. To the hunter in the Underdark, nothing else mattered.

That second day out, the hunter knew he was closing in on a group of his lost beasts. He summoned Guenhwyvar to his side and with the panther's help, had little trouble finding the rothé. Drizzt had hoped that all of the herd would still be together, but he found only a half-dozen in the area. Six were better than none, though, and Drizzt set Guenhwyvar into motion, herding the rothé back toward the moss cave. Drizzt set a brutal pace, knowing that the task would be much easier and safer with Guenhwyvar by his side. By the time the panther tired and had to return to its home plane, the rothé were comfortably grazing by the familiar stream.

The drow set out again immediately, this time taking two dead rats along for the ride. He called Guenhwyvar again when he was able and dismissed the panther when he had to, then again after that, as the days rolled by without further sign. But the hunter did not surrender his search. Frightened rothé could cover an incredible amount of ground, and in the maze of twisting tunnels and huge caverns, the hunter knew that many more days could pass before he caught up to the beasts.

Drizzt found his food where he could, taking down a bat with a perfect throw of a dagger—after tossing up a deceptive screen of pebbles—and dropping a boulder onto the back of a giant Underdark crab. Eventually, Drizzt grew weary of the search and longed for the security of his small cave. Doubting that the rothé, running blind, could have survived this long out in the tunnels, so far from their water and food, he accepted his herd's loss and decided to return home via a route that would bring him back to the region of the moss cavern from a different direction.

Only the clear tracks of his lost herd would detour him from his set course, Drizzt decided, but as he rounded a bend halfway home, a strange sound caught his attention and held it.

Drizzt pressed his hands against the stone, feeling the subtle, rhythmical vibrations. A short distance away, something banged the stone in succession. Measured hammering.

The hunter drew his scimitars and crept along, using the continuing vibrations to guide him through the winding passageways.

The flickering light of a fire dropped him into a crouch, but he did not flee, drawn by the knowledge that an intelligent being was nearby. Quite possibly the stranger would prove to be a threat, but perhaps, Drizzt hoped in the back of his mind, it could be something more than that.

Then Drizzt saw them, two banging at the stone with crafted pickaxes, another collecting rubble in a wheelbarrow, and two more standing guard. The hunter knew at once that more guards would be about; he probably had penetrated their defenses without even seeing them. Drizzt summoned one of the abilities of his heritage and drifted slowly up into the air, guiding his levitation with his hands along the stone. Luckily, the tunnel was high at this point, so the hunter could observe the mining creatures in relative safety.

They were shorter that Drizzt and hairless, with squat and muscled torsos perfectly designed for the mining that was their calling in life. Drizzt had encountered this race before and had learned much of them during his years at the Academy back in Menzoberranzan. These were svirfnebli, deep gnomes, the most hated enemies of the drow in all the Underdark.

Once, long ago, Drizzt had led a drow patrol into battle against a group of svirfnebli and personally had defeated an earth elemental that the deep gnome leader had summoned. Drizzt remembered that time now, and like all of the memories of his existence, the thoughts pained him. He had been captured by the deep gnomes, roughly tied, and held prisoner in a secret chamber. The svirfnebli had not mistreated him, though they suspected—and explained to Drizzt—that they would eventually have to kill him. The group's leader had promised Drizzt as much mercy as the situation allowed.

Drizzt's comrades, though, led by Dinin, his own brother, had stormed in, showing the deep gnomes no mercy at all. Drizzt had managed to convince his brother to spare the svirfneblin leader's life, but Dinin, showing typical drow cruelty, had ordered the deep gnome's hands severed before releasing him to flee to his homeland.

Drizzt shook himself from the anguishing memories and forced his thoughts back to the situation at hand. Deep gnomes could be formidable adversaries, he reminded himself, and they would not likely welcome a drow elf to their mining operations. He had to keep alert.

The miners apparently had struck a rich vein, for they began talking in excited tones. Drizzt reveled in the sound of those words, though he could not begin to understand the strange gnomish language. A smile not inspired by victory in battle found its way onto Drizzt's face for the first time in years as the svirfnebli scrambled about the stone, tossing huge chunks into their wheelbarrows and calling for other nearby companions to come and join in the fun. As Drizzt had suspected, more than a dozen unseen svirfnebli came in from every direction.

Drizzt found a high perch against the wall and watched the miners long after his levitation spell had expired. When at last their wheelbarrows were overfilled, the deep gnomes formed a column and started away. Drizzt realized that his prudent course at that time would be to let them get far away, then slip back to his home.

But, against the simple logic that guided his survival, Drizzt found that he could not so easily let the sound of the voices get away. He picked his way down the high wall and fell into pace behind the svirfneblin caravan, wondering where it would lead.

For many days Drizzt followed the deep gnomes. He resisted the temptation to summon Guenhwyvar, knowing that the panther could use the extended rest and himself satisfied in the company, however distant, of the deep gnomes' chatter. Every instinct warned the hunter against continuing in his actions, but for the first time in a very long time, Drizzt overruled the instincts of his more primal self. He needed to hear the gnomish voices more than he needed the simple necessities of survival.

The corridors became more worked, less natural, around him, and Drizzt knew that he was approaching the svirfneblin homeland. Again the potential dangers loomed up before him, and again he dismissed them as secondary. He quickened his pace and put the mining caravan in sight, suspecting that the svirfnebli would have some cunning traps set about.

The deep gnomes measured their steps at this point, taking care to avoid certain areas. Drizzt carefully mimicked their movements and nodded knowingly as he noticed a loose stone here and a low trip-wire there. Then Drizzt ducked back behind an outcropping as new voices joined the sound of the miners.

The mining troupe had come to a long and wide stairway, ascending between two walls of absolutely sheer and uncracked stone. To the side of the stair was an opening barely high and wide enough for the wheelbarrows, and Drizzt watched with sincere admiration as the deep gnome miners moved the carts to this opening and fastened the lead one to a chain. A series of taps on the stone sent a signal to an unseen operator, and the chain creaked, drawing the wheelbarrow into the hole. One by one the carts disappeared, and the svirfneblin band thinned as well, taking to the stairs as their load lessened.

As the two remaining deep gnomes hitched the last cart to the chain and tapped out the signal, Drizzt took a gamble borne of desperation. He waited for the deep gnomes to turn their backs and darted to the cart, catching it just as it disappeared into the low tunnel. Drizzt understood the depth of his foolishness when the last deep gnome, still apparently unaware of his presence, replaced a stone at the bottom of the passage, blocking any possible retreat.

The chain pulled on and the cart rolled up at an angle as steep as the paralleling staircase. Drizzt could see nothing ahead, for the wheelbarrow, designed for a perfect fit, took up the entire height and width of the tunnel. Drizzt noticed then that the cart had little wheels along its sides as well, aiding in its passage. It felt so good to be in the presence of such intelligence again, but Drizzt could not ignore the danger surrounding him. The svirfnebli would not take well to an intruding drow elf; it was likely they would strike out with weapons, not questions.

After several minutes, the passage leveled off and widened. A single svirfneblin was there, effortlessly turning the crank that hauled up the wheelbarrows. Intent on his business, the deep gnome did not notice Drizzt's dark form dart from behind the last cart and silently slip through the room's side door.

Drizzt heard voices as soon as he opened the door. He continued ahead, though, having nowhere else to go, and dropped to his belly on a narrow ledge. The deep gnomes, guards and miners, were below him, talking on a landing at the top of the wide stairway. At least a score stood there now, the miners recounting the tales of their rich find.

At the back end of the landing, through two immense and partly ajar metal-bound stone doors, Drizzt caught a glimpse of the svirfneblin city. The drow could see but a fraction of the place, and that not very well from his position on the ledge, but he guessed that the cavern beyond those massive doors was not nearly as large as the chamber housing Menzoberranzan.

Drizzt wanted to go in there! He wanted to jump up and rush through those doors, give himself over to the deep gnomes for whatever judgment they deemed fair. Perhaps they would accept him; perhaps they would see

Drizzt Do'Urden for who he truly was.

The svirfnebli on the landing, laughing and chatting, made their way into the city.

Drizzt had to go now, had to spring up and follow them beyond the massive doors.

But the hunter, the being who had survived a decade in the savage wilds of the Underdark, could not move from the ledge. The hunter, the being who had defeated a basilisk and countless other of this dangerous world's monsters, could not give himself over in the hopes of civilized mercy. The hunter did not understand such concepts.

The massive stone doors closed—and the moment of flickering light in Drizzt's darkening heart died—with a resounding crash.

After a long and tormented moment, Drizzt Do'Urden rolled off the ledge and dropped to the landing at the top of the stairs. His vision blurred suddenly as he made his way down, the path away from the teeming life beyond the doors, and it was only the primal instincts of the hunter that sensed the presence of still more svirfneblin guards. The hunter leaped wildly over the startled deep gnomes and rushed out again into the freedom offered by the wild Underdark's open passageways.

When he had put the svirfneblin city far behind, Drizzt reached into his pocket and took out the statuette, the summons to his only companion. A moment later, though, Drizzt dropped the figurine back, refusing to call the cat, punishing himself for his weakness on the ledge. If he had been stronger on the ledge beside the immense doors, he could have put an end to his torment, one way or another.

The instincts of hunter battled Drizzt for control as he made his way along the passages that would take him back to the moss-filled cavern. As the Underdark and the press of undeniable danger continued to close in around him, those primal, alert instincts took command, denying any further distracting thoughts of the svirfnebli and their city.

Those primal instincts were the salvation and the damnation of Drizzt Do'Urden.

# 3

# Snakes and Swords

"How many tendays has it been?" Dinin signaled to Briza in the silent hand code of the drow. "How many tendays have we hunted through these tunnels for our renegade brother?"

Dinin's expression revealed his sarcasm as he motioned the thoughts. Briza scowled at him and did not reply. She cared for this tedious duty even less than he. She was a high priestess of Lolth and had been the eldest daughter, accorded a high place of honor within the family structure. Never before would Briza have been sent off on such a hunt. But now, for some unexplained reason, SiNafay Hun'ett had joined the family, relegating Briza to a lesser position.

"Five?" Dinin continued, his anger growing with each darting movement of his slender fingers. "Six? How long has it been, sister?" he pressed. "How long has SiNaf—Shi'nayne . . . been sitting at Matron Malice's side?"

Briza's snake-headed whip came off her belt, and she spun angrily on her brother. Dinin, realizing that he had gone too far with his sarcastic prodding, defensively drew his sword, and tried to duck away. Briza's strike came faster, easily defeating Dinin's pitiful attempt at a parry, and three of the six heads connected squarely on the elderboy Do'Urden's chest and shoulder. Cold pain spread through Dinin's body, leaving only a helpless numbness in its wake. His sword arm drooped and he started to topple forward.

Briza's powerful hand shot out and caught him by the throat as he swooned, easily lifting him onto his toes. Then, looking around at the other five members of the hunting party to ensure that none were moving in Dinin's favor, Briza slammed her stunned brother roughly into the stone wall. The high priestess leaned heavily on Dinin, one hand tight against his throat.

"A wise male would measure his gestures more carefully," Briza snarled aloud, though she and the others had been explicitly instructed by Matron Malice not to communicate in any method other than the silent code once they were beyond Menzoberranzan's borders.

It took Dinin a long while to fully appreciate his predicament. As the numbness wore away, he realized that he could not draw breath, and though his hand still held his sword, Briza, outweighing him by a score of pounds, had it pinned close to his side. Even more distressing, his sister's free hand held the dreaded snake-whip aloft. Unlike ordinary whips, that evil instrument needed little room to work its snap. The animated snake heads could coil and strike from close range simply as an extension of their wielder's will.

"Matron Malice would not question your death," Briza whispered harshly. "Her sons have ever been trouble to her!"

Dinin looked past his hulking captor to the common soldiers of the patrol.

"Witnesses?" Briza laughed, guessing his thoughts. "Do you really believe they will speak against a high priestess for the sake of a mere male?" Briza's eyes narrowed and she moved her face right up to Dinin's. "A mere male corpse?" She cackled once again and released Dinin suddenly, and he dropped to his knees, struggling to regain a normal rhythm to his breathing.

"Come," Briza signaled in the silent code to the rest of the patrol. "I sense that my youngest brother is not in this area. We shall return to the city and restock our packs."

Dinin watched his sister's back as she made the preparations for their departure. He wanted nothing more than to put his sword between her shoulder blades. Dinin was smarter than to try such a move, though. Briza had been a high priestess of the Spider Queen for more than three centuries and was now in the favor of Lolth, even if Matron Malice and the rest of House Do'Urden was not. Even if her evil goddess had not been looking over her, Briza was a formidable foe, skilled in spells and with that cruel whip always ready at her side.

"My sister," Dinin called after her as she started away. Briza spun on him, surprised that he would dare to speak aloud to her.

"Accept my apologies," Dinin said. He motioned for the other soldiers to keep moving, then returned to using the hand code, so that the commoners would not know his further conversation with Briza.

"I am not pleased by the addition of SiNafay Hun'ett to the family," Dinin explained.

Briza's lips curled up in one of her typically ambiguous smiles; Dinin couldn't be sure if she was agreeing with him or mocking him. "You think yourself wise enough to question the decisions of Matron Malice?" her fingers asked.

"No!" Dinin signaled back emphatically. "Matron Malice does as she must, and always for the welfare of House Do'Urden. But I do not trust the displaced Hun'ett. SiNafay watched her house smashed into bits of heated rock by the judgment of the ruling council. All of her treasured children were slain; and most of her commoners as well. Can she truly be loyal to House Do'Urden after such a loss?"

"Foolish male," Briza signaled in reply. "Priestesses understand that loyalty is owed only to Lolth. SiNafay's house is no more, thus SiNafay is no more. She is Shi'nayne Do'Urden now, and by the order of the Spider Queen, she will fully accept all of the responsibilities that accompany the name."

"I do not trust her," Dinin reiterated. "Nor am I pleased to see my sisters, the true Do'Urdens, moved down the hierarchy to make room for her. Shi'nayne should have been placed beneath Maya, or housed among the commoners."

Briza snarled at him, though she wholeheartedly agreed. "Shi'nayne's rank in the family is of no concern to you. House Do'Urden is stronger for the addition of another high priestess. That is all a male need care about!"

Dinin nodded his acceptance of her logic and wisely sheathed his sword before beginning to rise from his knees. Briza likewise replaced the snake-whip on her belt but continued to watch her volatile brother out of the corner of her eye.

Dinin would be more careful around Briza now. He knew that his survival depended on his ability to walk beside his sister, for Malice would continue to send Briza out on these hunting patrols beside him. Briza was the strongest of the Do'Urden daughters, with the best chance of finding and capturing Drizzt. And Dinin, having been a patrol leader for the city for more than a decade, was the most familiar of anyone in the house with the tunnels beyond Menzoberranzan.

Dinin shrugged at his rotten luck and followed his sister back down the tunnels to the city. A short respite, no more than a day, and they would be back on the march again, back on the prowl for their elusive and dangerous brother, whom Dinin truly had no desire to find.

⚔ ⚔ ⚔ ⚔ ⚔

Guenhwyvar's head turned abruptly and the great panther froze perfectly still, one paw cocked and ready to move.

"You heard it, too," Drizzt whispered, moving tightly to the panther's side. "Come, my friend. Let us see what new enemy has entered our domain."

They sped off together, equally silent, down corridors they knew so very well. Drizzt stopped suddenly, and Guenhwyvar did likewise, at the echo of a scuffle. It was made by a boot, Drizzt knew, and not by some natural monster of the Underdark. Drizzt pointed up to a broken pile of rubble overlooking a wide and many-tiered cavern on its other side. Guenhwyvar led him there, where they could find a better vantage point.

The drow patrol came into view only a few moments later, a group of seven, though they were too far away for Drizzt to make out any particulars. Drizzt was amazed that he had heard them so easily, for he remembered those days when he had taken the point position on such patrols. How alone he had felt then, up at the lead of more than a dozen dark elves, for they made not a whisper with their practiced movements and they kept to the shadows so well that even Drizzt's keen eyes could not begin to locate them.

And yet, this hunter that Drizzt had become, this primal, instinctive self, had found this group easily.

⚔ ⚔ ⚔ ⚔ ⚔

Briza stopped suddenly and closed her eyes, concentrating on the emanations of her spell of location.

"What is it?" Dinin's fingers asked her when she looked back to him. Her startled and obviously excited expression revealed much.

"Drizzt?" Dinin breathed aloud, hardly able to believe.

"Silence!" Briza's hands cried out at him. She glanced around to survey her surroundings, then signaled to the patrol to follow her to the shadows of the wall in the immense, and exposed, cavern.

Briza nodded her confirmation to Dinin then, confident that their mission would at last be completed.

"Can you be sure it is Drizzt?" Dinin's fingers asked. In his excitement, he could barely keep the movements precise enough to convey his thoughts. "Perhaps some scavenger—"

"We know that our brother lives," Briza motioned quickly. "Matron Malice would no longer be out of Lolth's favor if it were otherwise. And if Drizzt lives, then we can assume that he possesses the item!"

⚔ ⚔ ⚔ ⚔ ⚔

The sudden evasive movement of the patrol caught Drizzt by surprise. The group could not possibly have seen him under the cover of the jutting rocks, and he held faith in the silence of his footfalls, and of Guenhwyvar's. Yet Drizzt felt certain that it was he the patrol was hiding from. Something felt out of place in this whole encounter. Dark elves were rare this far from Menzoberranzan. Perhaps it was no more than the paranoia necessary to survive in the wilds of the Underdark, Drizzt told himself. Still, he

suspected that more than chance had brought this group to his domain.

"Go, Guenhwyvar," he whispered to the cat. "View our guests and return to me." The panther sped away through the shadows circumventing the large cavern. Drizzt sank low into the rubble, listened, and waited.

Guenhwyvar returned to him only a minute later, though it seemed an eternity to Drizzt.

"Did you know them?" Drizzt asked. The cat scratched a paw across the stone.

"Of our old patrol?" Drizzt wondered aloud. "The fighters you and I walked beside?"

Guenhwyvar seemed uncertain and made no definite movements.

"A Hun'ett then," Drizzt said, thinking he had solved the riddle. House Hun'ett had at last come looking for him to repay him for the deaths of Alton and Masoj, the two Hun'ett wizards who had died trying to kill Drizzt. Or perhaps the Hun'etts had come in search of Guenhwyvar, the magical item that Masoj once had possessed.

When Drizzt took a moment from his pondering to study Guenhwyvar's reaction, he realized that his assumptions were wrong. The panther had backed away from him a step and seemed agitated by his stream of suppositions.

"Then who?" Drizzt asked. Guenhwyvar reared up on its hind legs and straddled Drizzt's shoulders, one great paw patting Drizzt's neck-purse. Not understanding, Drizzt slipped the item off his neck and emptied its contents into a palm, revealing a few gold coins, a small gemstone, and the emblem of his house, a silvery token engraved with the initials of Daermon N'a'shezbaernon, House Do'Urden. Drizzt realized at once what Guenhwyvar was hinting at.

"My family," he whispered harshly. Guenhwyvar backed away from him and again scratched a paw excitedly across the stone.

A thousand memories flooded through Drizzt at that moment, but all of them, good and bad, led him inescapably to one possibility: Matron Malice had neither forgiven nor forgotten his actions on that fated day. Drizzt had abandoned her and the ways of the Spider Queen, and he knew well enough the ways of Lolth to realize that his actions had not left his mother in good standing.

Drizzt looked back into the gloom of the wide cavern. "Come," he panted to Guenhwyvar, and he ran off down the tunnels. His decision to leave Menzoberranzan had been painful and uncertain, and now Drizzt had no desire to encounter his kin and rekindle all of the doubts and fears.

He and Guenhwyvar ran on for more than an hour, turning down secret passageways and crossing into the most confusing sections of the area's tunnels. Drizzt knew the region intimately and felt certain that he could leave the patrol group far behind with little effort.

But when at last he paused to catch his breath, Drizzt sensed—and he only had to look at Guenhwyvar to confirm his suspicions—that the patrol was still on his trail, perhaps even closer than before.

Drizzt knew then that he was being magically tracked; there could be no other explanation. "But how?" he asked the panther. "I am hardly the drow they knew as a brother, in appearance or in thought. What could they be sensing that would be familiar enough for their magical spells to hold on to?" Drizzt surveyed himself quickly, his eyes first falling upon his crafted weapons.

The scimitars were indeed wondrous, but so were the majority of the drow weapons in Menzoberranzan. And these particular blades had not even been crafted in House Do'Urden and were not of any design favored by Drizzt's family. His cloak then, he wondered? The *piwafwi* was a signpost of a house, bearing the stitch patterns and designs of a single family.

But Drizzt's *piwafwi* had been tattered and torn beyond recognition and he could hardly believe that a location spell would recognize it as belonging to House Do'Urden.

"Belonging to House Do'Urden," Drizzt whispered aloud. He looked at Guenhwyvar and nodded suddenly—he had his answer. He again removed his neck pouch and took out the token, the emblem of Daermon N'a'shezbaernon. Created by magic, it possessed its own magic, a dweomer distinct to that one house. Only a noble of House Do'Urden would carry one.

Drizzt thought for a moment, then replaced the token and slipped the neck-purse over Guenhwyvar's head. "Time for the hunted to become the hunter," he purred to the great cat.

* * * * *

"He knows he is being followed," Dinin's hands flashed to Briza. Briza didn't justify the statement with a reply. Of course Drizzt knew of the pursuit; it was obvious that he was trying to evade them. Briza remained unconcerned. Drizzt's house emblem burned as a distinct directional beacon in her magically enhanced thoughts.

Briza stopped, though, when the party came to a fork in the passage. The signal came from beyond the fork, but not in any definitive way to either side. "Left," Briza signaled to three of the commoner soldiers, then, "Right," to the remaining two. She held her brother back, signaling that she and Dinin would hold their position at the fork to serve as a reserve for both groups.

High above the scattering patrol, hovering in the shadows of the stalactite-covered ceiling, Drizzt smiled at his cunning. The patrol might have kept pace with him, but it would have no chance at all of catching Guenhwyvar.

The plan had been executed and completed to perfection, for Drizzt had only meant to lead the patrol on until it was far from his domain and weary of the hopeless search. But as Drizzt floated there, looking down upon his brother and eldest sister, he found himself longing for something more. A few moments passed, and Drizzt was certain that the dispatched soldiers were a good distance away. He drew out his scimitars, thinking then that a meeting with his siblings might not be so bad after all.

"He moves farther away," Briza spoke to Dinin, not fearing the sound of her own voice, since she felt certain of her renegade brother's distant position. "At great speed."

"Drizzt was always adept in the Underdark," Dinin replied, nodding. "He will prove a difficult catch."

Briza snickered. "He will tire long before my spells expire. We will find him breathless in a dark hole." But Briza's cockiness turned to blank amazement a second later when a dark form dropped right between her and Dinin.

Dinin, too, hardly even registered the shock of it all. He saw Drizzt for just a split second, then his eyes crisscrossed, following the descending arc of a scimitar's rushing hilt. Dinin went down heavily, with the smooth stone of the floor pressing against his cheek, a sensation to which Dinin was oblivious.

Even as one hand did its work on Dinin, Drizzt's other hand shot a scimitar tip close to Briza's throat, meaning to force her surrender. Briza was not as surprised as Dinin, though, and she always kept a hand close to her whip. She danced back from Drizzt's attack, and six snake heads shot up into the air, coiled and searching for an opening.

Drizzt turned full to face her, weaving his scimitars into defensive patterns to keep the stinging vipers at bay. He remembered the bite of those dreaded whips; like every drow male, he had been taught it many times during his childhood.

"Brother Drizzt," Briza said loudly, hoping the patrol would hear her and understand the call back to her side. "Lower your weapons. It does not have to be like this."

The sound of familiar words, of drow words, overwhelmed Drizzt. How good it was to hear them again, to remember that he was more than a single-minded hunter, that his life was more than mere survival.

"Lower your weapons," Briza said again, more pointedly.

"Wh—why are you here?" Drizzt stammered at her.

"For you, of course, my brother," Briza replied, too kindly. "The war with House Hun'ett is, at long last, ended. It is time for you to come home."

A part of Drizzt wanted to believe her, wanted to forget those facts of drow life that had forced him out of the city of his birth. A part of Drizzt wanted to drop the scimitars to the stone and return to the shelter—and the companionship—of his former life. Briza's smile was so inviting.

Briza recognized his weakening resolve. "Come home, dear Drizzt," she purred, her words holding the bindings of a minor magical spell. "You are needed. You are the weapon master of House Do'Urden now."

The sudden change in Drizzt's expression told Briza that she had erred. Zaknafein, Drizzt's mentor and dearest friend, had been the weapon master of House Do'Urden, and Zaknafein had been sacrificed to the Spider

Queen. Drizzt would never forget that fact.

Indeed, Drizzt remembered much more than the comforts of home at that moment. He remembered even more clearly the wrongs of his past life, the wickedness that his principles simply could not tolerate.

"You should not have come," Drizzt said, his voice sounding like a growl. "You must never come this way again!"

"Dear brother," Briza replied, more to buy time than to correct her obvious error. She stood still, her face frozen in that double-edged smile of hers.

Drizzt looked behind Briza's lips, which were thick and full by drow standards. The priestess spoke no words, but Drizzt could clearly see that her mouth was moving behind that frozen smile.

A spell!

Briza had always been skilled at such deceptions. "Go home!" Drizzt cried at her, and he launched an attack.

Briza ducked away from the blow easily enough, for it was not meant to strike, only to disrupt her spellcasting.

"Damn you, Drizzt the rogue," she spat, all pretense of friendship gone. "Lower your weapons at once, on pain of death!" Her snake-whip came up in open threat.

Drizzt set his feet wide apart. Fires burned in his lavender eyes as the hunter within him rose to meet the challenge.

Briza hesitated, taken aback by the sudden ferocity brewing in her brother. This was no ordinary drow warrior standing before her, she knew beyond doubt. Drizzt had become something more than that, something more formidable.

But Briza was a high priestess of Lolth, near the top of the drow hierarchy. She would not be frightened away by a mere male.

"Surrender!" she demanded. Drizzt couldn't even decipher her words, for the hunter standing against Briza was no longer Drizzt Do'Urden. The savage, primal warrior that memories of dead Zaknafein had invoked was impervious to words and lies.

Briza's arm pumped, and the whip's six viper heads whirled in, twisting and weaving of their own volition to gain the best angles of attack.

The hunter's scimitars responded in an indistinguishable blur. Briza couldn't begin to follow their lightning-quick motions, and when her attack routine was ended, she knew only that none of the snakeheads had found a mark, but that only five of the heads remained attached to the whip.

Now in rage that nearly matched her opponent's, Briza charged in, flailing away with her damaged weapon. Snakes and scimitars and slender drow limbs intertwined in a deadly ballet.

A head bit into the hunter's leg, sending a burst of cold pain coursing through his veins. A scimitar defeated another deceptive attack, splitting a head down the middle, right between the fangs.

Another head bit into the hunter. Another head fell free to the stone.

The opponents separated, taking measure of each other. Briza's breath came hard after the few furious minutes, but the hunter's chest moved easily and rhythmically. Briza had not been struck, but Drizzt had taken two hits.

The hunter had learned long ago to ignore pain, though. He stood ready to continue, and Briza, her whip now sporting only three heads, stubbornly came in on him. She hesitated for a split-second when she noticed Dinin still prone on the floor but with his senses apparently returning. Might her brother rise to her aid?

Dinin squirmed and tried to stand but found no strength in his legs to lift him.

"Damn you," Briza growled, her venom aimed at Dinin, or at Drizzt—it didn't matter. Calling on the power of her Spider Queen deity, the high priestess of Lolth lashed out with all of her strength.

Three snake heads dropped to the floor after a single cross of the hunter's blades.

"Damn you!" Briza screamed again, this time pointedly at Drizzt. She grasped the mace from her belt and swung a vicious overhand chop at her defiant brother's head.

Crossed scimitars caught the clumsy blow long before it found its mark, and the hunter's foot came up and kicked once, twice, and then a third time into Briza's face before it went back to the floor.

Briza staggered backward, blood in her eyes and running freely from her nose. She made out the lines of her brother's form beyond the blurring heat of her own blood, and she launched a desperate, wide-arcing hook.

The hunter set one scimitar to parry the mace, turning its blade so that Briza's hand ran down its cruel edge even as the mace swept wide of its mark. Briza screamed in agony and dropped her weapon.

The mace fell to the floor beside two of her fingers.

Dinin was up then, behind Drizzt, with his sword in his hand. Using all of her discipline, Briza kept her eyes locked on Drizzt, holding his attention. If she could distract him long enough . . .

The hunter sensed the danger and spun on Dinin.

All that Dinin saw in his brother's lavender eyes was his own death. He threw his sword to the ground and crossed his arms over his chest in surrender.

The hunter issued a growling command, hardly intelligible, but Dinin fathomed its meaning well enough, and he ran away as fast as his legs could carry him.

Briza started to slip around, meaning to follow Dinin, but a scimitar blade cut her off, locking under her chin and forcing her head so far back that all she could see was the dark stone of the ceiling.

Pain burned in the hunter's limbs, pain inflicted by this one and her evil whip. Now the hunter meant to end the pain and the threat. This was his domain!

Briza uttered a final prayer to Lolth as she felt the razor-sharp edge begin its cut. But then, in the instant of a black blur, she was free. She looked down to see Drizzt pinned to the floor by a huge black panther. Not taking the time to ask questions, Briza sped off down the tunnel after Dinin.

The hunter squirmed away from Guenhwyvar and leaped to his feet. "Guenhwyvar!" he cried, pushing the panther away. "Get her! Kill . . . !"

Guenhwyvar replied by falling into a sitting position and issuing a wide and drawn out yawn. With one lazy movement, the panther brought a paw under the string of the neck-purse and snapped it off to the ground.

The hunter burned with rage. "What are you doing?" he screamed, snatching up the purse. Had Guenhwyvar sided against him? Drizzt backed away a step, hesitantly bringing his scimitars up between him and the panther. Guenhwyvar made no move, but just sat there staring at Drizzt.

A moment later, the click of a crossbow told Drizzt of the absolute absurdity of his line of thinking. The dart would have found him, no doubt, but Guenhwyvar sprang up suddenly and intercepted its flight. Drow poison had no effect on the likes of a magical cat.

Three drow fighters appeared on one side of the fork, two more on the other. All thoughts of revenge on Briza flew from Drizzt then, and he followed Guenhwyvar in full flight down the twisting passageways. Without the guidance of the high priestess and her magic, the commoner fighters did not even attempt to follow.

A long while later, Drizzt and Guenhwyvar turned into a side passage and paused in their flight, listening for any sounds of pursuit.

"Come," Drizzt instructed, and he started slowly away, certain that the threat of Dinin and Briza had been successfully repelled.

Again Guenhwyvar dropped to a sitting position.

Drizzt looked curiously at the panther. "I told you to come," he growled. Guenhwyvar fixed a stare upon him, a look that filled the renegade drow with guilt. Then the cat rose and walked slowly toward its master.

Drizzt nodded his accord, thinking that Guenhwyvar meant to obey him. He turned and started again to walk off, but the panther circled around him, stopping his progress. Guenhwyvar continued the circular pacing and slowly the telltale mist began to appear.

"What are you doing?" Drizzt demanded.

Guenhwyvar did not slow.

"I did not dismiss you!" Drizzt shouted as the panther's corporeal form melted away. Drizzt spun about frantically, trying to catch hold of something.

"I did not dismiss you!" he cried again, helplessly.

Guenhwyvar had gone.

It was a long walk back to Drizzt's sheltered cave. That last image of Guenhwyvar followed his every step, the cat's saucer eyes boring into his back. Guenhwyvar had judged him, he realized beyond any doubt. In his blind rage, Drizzt had almost killed his sister; he surely would have slain Briza if Guenhwyvar had not pounced upon him.

At last, Drizzt crawled into the little stone cubby that served as his bedroom.

His contemplations crawled in with him. A decade before, Drizzt had killed Masoj Hun'ett, and on that occasion had vowed never to kill a drow again. To Drizzt, his word was the core of his principles, those very same principles that had forced him to give up so very much.

Drizzt surely would have forsaken his word this day had it not been for Guenhwyvar's actions. How much better, then, was he from those dark elves he had left behind?

Drizzt clearly had won the encounter against his siblings and was confident that he could continue to hide from Briza—and from all the other enemies that Matron Malice sent against him. But alone in that tiny cave, Drizzt realized something that distressed him greatly.

He couldn't hide from himself.

# 4

# Flight from the Hunter

Drizzt gave no thought at all to his actions as he went about his daily routines over the next few days. He would survive, he knew. The hunter would have it no other way. But the rising price of that survival struck a deep and discordant note in the heart of Drizzt Do'Urden.

If the constant rituals of the day warded away the pain, Drizzt found himself unprotected at day's end. The encounter with his siblings haunted him, stayed in his thoughts as vividly as if it were recurring every night. Inevitably, Drizzt awoke terrified and alone, engulfed by the monsters of his dreams. He understood—and the knowledge heightened his helplessness—that no swordplay, however dazzling, could hope to defeat them.

Drizzt did not fear that his mother would continue her quest to capture and punish him, though he knew beyond any doubt that she certainly would. This was his world, far different from Menzoberranzan's winding avenues, with ways that the drow living in the city could not begin to understand. Out in the wilds, Drizzt held confidence that he could survive against whatever nemeses Matron Malice sent after him.

Drizzt also had managed to release himself from the overwhelming guilt of his actions against Briza. He rationalized that it was his siblings who had forced the dangerous encounter, and it was Briza, in trying to cast a spell, who had initiated the combat. Still, Drizzt realized that he would spend many days finding answers to the questions his actions had raised concerning the nature of his character.

Had he become this savage and merciless hunter because of the harsh conditions imposed on him? Or was this hunter an expression of the being Drizzt had been all along? They were not questions that Drizzt would easily answer, but at this time, they were not foremost among his thoughts.

The thing that Drizzt could not dismiss about the encounter with his siblings was the sound of their voices, the melody of spoken words that he could understand and respond to. In all of his recollections of those few moments with Briza and Dinin, the words, not the blows, stood out most clearly. Drizzt clung to them desperately, listening to them over and over again in his mind and dreading the day when they would fade away. Then, though he might remember them, he would no longer hear them.

He would be alone again.

Drizzt pulled the onyx figurine out of his pocket for the first time since Guenhwyvar had drifted away from him. He placed it on the stone before him and looked at his wall scratches to determine just how long it had been since he had last summoned the panther. Immediately, Drizzt realized the futility of that approach. When was the last time he had scratched that wall? And what use were the markings anyway? How could Drizzt be certain of his count even if he dutifully notched the mark after every one of his sleep periods?

"Time is something of that other world," Drizzt mumbled, his tone clearly a lament. He lifted his dagger toward the stone, an act of denial against his own proclamation.

"What does it matter?" Drizzt asked rhetorically, and he dropped the dagger to the ground. The ring as it struck the stone sent a shiver along Drizzt's spine, as though it was a bell signaling his surrender.

His breathing came hard. Sweat beaded on his ebony brow, and his hands felt suddenly cold. All around him, the walls of his cave, the close stone that had sheltered him for years against the ever-encroaching dangers of the Underdark, now pressed in on him. He imagined leering faces in the lines of cracks and the shapes of rocks. The faces mocked him and laughed at him, belittling his stubborn pride.

He turned to flee but stumbled on a stone and fell to the ground. He scraped a knee in the process and tore yet another hole in his tattered *piwafwi*. Drizzt hardly cared for his knee or his cloak when he looked back to the stumbling stone, for another fact assailed him, leaving him in utter confusion.

The hunter had tripped. For the first time in more than a decade, the hunter had tripped.

"Guenhwyvar!" Drizzt cried frantically. "Come to me! Oh, please, my Guenhwyvar!"

He didn't know if the panther would respond. After their last less-than-friendly parting, Drizzt couldn't be certain that Guenhwyvar would ever walk by his side again. Drizzt clawed his way toward the figurine, every inch seeming a tedious fight in the weakness of his despair.

Presently the swirling mist appeared. The panther would not desert its master, would not hold lasting judgment against the drow who had been its friend.

Drizzt relaxed as the mist took form, using the sight of it to block the evil hallucinations in the stones. Soon Guenhwyvar was sitting beside him and casually licking at one great paw. Drizzt locked the panther's saucer eyes in a stare and saw no judgment there. It was just Guenhwyvar, his friend and his salvation.

Drizzt curled his legs under him, sprang out to the cat, and wrapped the muscled neck in a tight and desperate embrace. Guenhwyvar accepted the hold without response, wiggling loose only enough to continue the paw-licking. If the cat, in its otherworldly intelligence, understood the importance of that hug, it offered no outward signs.

⚔ ⚔ ⚔ ⚔ ⚔

Restlessness marked Drizzt's next days. He kept on the move, running the circuits of the tunnels around his sanctuary. Matron Malice was after him, he continually reminded himself. He could not afford any holes in his defenses.

Deep inside himself, beyond the rationalizations, Drizzt knew the truth of his movements. He could offer himself the excuse of patrolling, but he had, in fact, taken flight. He ran from the voices and the walls of his small cave. He ran from Drizzt Do'Urden and back toward the hunter.

Gradually, his routes took a wider course, often keeping him from his cave for many days at a stretch. Secretly, Drizzt hoped for an encounter with a powerful foe. He needed a tangible reminder of the necessity of his primal existence, a battle against some horrid monster that would place him in a mode of purely instinctive survival.

What Drizzt found instead one day was the vibration of a distant tapping on the wall, the rhythmical, measured tap of a miner's pick.

Drizzt leaned back against the wall and carefully considered his next move. He knew where the sound would lead him; he was in the same tunnels that he had wandered when he went in search of his lost rothé, the same tunnels where he had encountered the svirfneblin mining party a few tendays before. At that time, Drizzt could not admit it to himself, but it was no simple coincidence that he had happened into this region again. His subconscious had brought him to hear the tapping of the svirfneblin hammers, and more particularly, to hear the laughter and chatter of the deep gnomes' voices.

Now Drizzt, leaning heavily against a wall, truly was torn. He knew that going to spy on the svirfneblin miners would only bring him more torment, that in hearing their voices he would become even more vulnerable to the pangs of loneliness. The deep gnomes surely would go back to their city, and Drizzt again would be left empty and alone.

But Drizzt had come to hear the tapping, and now it vibrated in the stone, beckoning him with a pull too great to ignore. His better judgment fought the urges that pulled him toward that sound, but his decision had been made even as he had taken the first steps into this region. He berated himself for his foolishness, shook his head in denial. In spite of his conscious reasoning, his legs were moving, carrying him toward the rhythmic sound of the tapping pickaxes.

The alert instincts of the hunter argued against remaining near the miners even as Drizzt looked down from a high ledge upon the group of svirfnebli. But Drizzt did not leave. For several days, as far as he could measure, he stayed in the vicinity of the deep gnome miners, catching bits of their conversations wherever he could, watching them at work and at play.

When the inevitable day came that the miners began to pack up their wagons, Drizzt understood the depth of his folly. He had been weak in coming to the deep gnomes; he had denied the brutal truth of his existence. Now he would have to go back to his dark and empty hole, all the more lonely for the memories of the last few days.

The wagons rolled out of sight down the tunnels toward the svirfneblin city. Drizzt took the first steps back toward his sanctuary, the moss-covered cave with the fast-running stream and the myconid-tended mushroom grove.

In all the centuries of life he had left to live, Drizzt Do'Urden would never look upon that place again.

He did not later remember when his direction had turned; it had not been a conscious decision. Something pulled at him—the lingering rumble of the ore-filled wagons perhaps—and only when Drizzt heard the slam of Blingdenstone's great outer doors did he realize what he meant to do.

"Guenhwyvar," Drizzt whispered to the figurine, and he flinched at the disturbing volume of his own voice. The svirfneblin guards on the wide staircase were engaged in a conversation of their own, though, and Drizzt was quite safe.

The gray mist swirled around the statuette and the panther came to its master's call. Guenhwyvar's ears flattened and the panther sniffed around cautiously, trying to resolve the unfamiliar setting.

Drizzt took a deep breath and forced the words from his mouth. "I wanted to say good-bye to you, my friend," he whispered. Guenhwyvar's ears came up straight, and the pupils of the cat's shining yellow eyes widened then narrowed again as Guenhwyvar took a quick study of Drizzt.

"In case . . ." Drizzt continued. "I cannot live out there anymore, Guenhwyvar. I fear I am losing everything that gives meaning to life. I fear I am losing my self." He glanced back over his shoulder at the ascending stairway to Blingdenstone. "And that is more precious to me than my life. Can you understand, Guenhwyvar? I need more, more than simple survival. I need a life defined by more than the savage instincts of this creature I have become."

Drizzt slumped back against the passageway's stone wall. His words sounded so logical and simple, yet he knew that every step up that stair to the deep gnome city would be a trial of his courage and his convictions. He remembered the day he'd stood on the ledge outside Blingdenstone's great doors. As much as he wanted to, Drizzt could not bring himself to follow the deep gnomes in. He was fully caught in a very real paralysis that had gripped him and held him firmly when he thought of rushing through the portals into the deep gnome city.

"You have rarely judged me, my friend," Drizzt said to the panther. "And in those times, always you have judged me fairly. Can you understand, Guenhwyvar? In the next few moments, we may become lost from each other forever. Can you understand why I must do this?"

Guenhwyvar padded over to Drizzt's side and nuzzled its great feline head into the drow's ribs.

"My friend," Drizzt whispered into the cat's ear. "Go back now before I lose my courage. Go back to your home and hope that we shall meet again."

Guenhwyvar turned away obediently and paced to the figurine. The transition seemed too fast to Drizzt this time, then only the figurine remained. Drizzt scooped it up and considered it. He considered again the risk before him. Then, driven by the same subconscious needs that had brought him this far, Drizzt rushed to the stair and started up. Above him, the deep gnome conversation had ceased; apparently the guards sensed that someone or something was approaching.

But the svirfnebli guards' surprise was no less when a drow elf walked over the top of the staircase and onto the landing before the doors of their city.

Drizzt crossed his arms over his chest, a defenseless gesture that the drow elves took as a signal of truce. Drizzt could only hope that the svirfnebli were familiar with the motion, for his mere appearance had absolutely unnerved the guards. They fell over each other, scrambling around the small landing, some rushing to protect the doors to the city, others surrounding Drizzt within a ring of weapon tips, and still others rushing frantically to the stairs and down a few, trying to see if this dark elf was just the first of an entire drow war party.

One svirfneblin, the leader of the guard contingent and apparently looking for some explanation, barked out a series of pointed demands at Drizzt. Drizzt shrugged helplessly, and the half-dozen deep gnomes around him jumped back a cautious step at his innocuous movement.

The svirfneblin spoke again, more loudly, and jabbed the very sharp point of his iron spear in Drizzt's direction. Drizzt could not begin to understand or respond to the foreign tongue. Very slowly and in obvious view, he slid one hand down over his stomach to the clasp of his belt buckle. The deep gnome leader's hands wrung tightly over the shaft of his weapon as he watched the dark elf's every movement.

A flick of Drizzt's wrist released the clasp and his scimitars clanged loudly on the stone floor.

The svirfnebli jumped in unison, then recovered quickly and came in on him. On a single word from the leader of the group, two of the guards dropped their weapons and began a complete, and not overly gentle, search of the intruder. Drizzt flinched when they found the dagger he had kept in his boot. He thought himself stupid for forgetting the weapon and not revealing it openly from the beginning.

A moment later, when one of the svirfnebli reached into the deepest pocket of Drizzt's *piwafwi* and pulled out the onyx figurine, Drizzt flinched even more.

Instinctively, Drizzt reached for the panther, a pleading expression on his face.

He received the butt end of a spear in the back for his efforts. Deep gnomes were not an evil race, but they held no love for dark elves. The svirfnebli had survived for centuries untold in the Underdark with few allies but many enemies, and they ever ranked the drow elves as foremost among the latter. Since the founding of the ancient city of Blingdenstone, the majority of all of the many svirfnebli who had been killed in the wilds had fallen at the ends of drow weapons.

Now, inexplicably, one of these same dark elves had walked right up to their city doors and willingly surrendered his weapons.

The deep gnomes bound Drizzt's hands tightly behind his back, and four of the guards kept their weapon tips resting on him, ready to drive them home at Drizzt's slightest threatening movement. The remaining guards returned from their search of the stairway, reporting no other drow elves anywhere in the vicinity. The leader remained suspicious, though, and he posted guards at various strategic positions, then motioned to the two deep gnomes waiting at the city's doors.

The massive portals parted, and Drizzt was led in. He could only hope in that moment of fear and excitement that he had left the hunter out in the wilds of the Underdark.

# 5 Unholy Ally

In no hurry to stand before his outraged mother, Dinin wandered slowly toward the anteroom to House Do'Urden's chapel. Matron Malice had called for him, and he could not refuse the summons. He found Vierna and Maya in the corridor beyond the ornate doors, similarly tentative.

"What is it about?" Dinin asked his sisters in the silent hand code.

"Matron Malice has been with Briza and Shi'nayne all the day," Vierna's hands replied.

"Planning another expedition in search of Drizzt," Dinin motioned half heartedly, not liking the idea that he would no doubt be included in such plans.

The two females did not miss their brother's disdainful scowl. "Was it really so terrible?" Maya asked. "Briza would say little about it."

"Her severed fingers and torn whip revealed much," Vierna put in, a wry smile crossing her face as she motioned. Vierna, like every other sibling of House Do'Urden, had little love for her eldest sister.

No agreeing smile spread on Dinin's face as he remembered his encounter with Drizzt. "You witnessed our brother's prowess when he lived among us," Dinin's hands replied. "His skills have improved tenfold in his years outside the city."

"But what was he like?" Vierna asked, obviously intrigued by Drizzt's ability to survive. Ever since the patrol had returned with the report that Drizzt was still alive, Vierna had secretly hoped that she would see her younger brother again. They had shared a father, so it was said, and Vierna held more sympathy for Drizzt than was wise, given Malice's feelings for him.

Noticing her excited expression, and remembering his own humiliation at Drizzt's hands, Dinin cast a disapproving scowl at her. "Fear not, dear sister," Dinin's hands said quickly. "If Malice sends you out into the wilds this time, as I suspect she will, you will see all of Drizzt you wish to see, and more!" Dinin clapped his hands together for emphasis as he ended, and he strode right between the two females and through the anteroom's door.

"Your brother has forgotten how to knock," Matron Malice said to Briza and Shi'nayne, who stood at her sides.

Rizzen, kneeling before the throne, looked up over his shoulder to see Dinin.

"I did not give you permission to lift your eyes!" Malice screamed at the patron. She pounded her fist on the arm of her great throne, and Rizzen fell down to his belly in fear. Malice's next words carried the strength of a spell.

"Grovel!" she commanded, and Rizzen crawled to her feet. Malice extended her hand to the male, all the while looking straight at Dinin. The elderboy did not miss his mother's point.

"Kiss," she said to Rizzen, and he quickly began lavishing kisses onto her extended hand. "Stand," Malice issued her third command.

Rizzen got about halfway to his feet before the matron punched him squarely in the face, dropping him in a heap to the stone floor.

"If you move, I shall kill you," Malice promised, and Rizzen lay perfectly still, not doubting her in the least.

Dinin knew that the continued show had been more for his benefit than for Rizzen's. Still, unblinking, Malice eyed him.

"You have failed me," she said at length. Dinin accepted the berating without argument, without even daring to breathe until Malice turned sharply on Briza.

"And you!" Malice shouted. "Six trained drow warriors beside you, and you, a high priestess, could not bring Drizzt back to me."

Briza clenched and unclenched the weakened fingers that Malice had magically restored to her hand.

"Seven against one," Malice ranted, "and you come running back here with tales of doom!"

"I will get him, Matron Mother," Maya promised as she took her place beside Shi'nayne. Malice looked to Vierna, but the second daughter was more reluctant to make such grand claims.

"You speak boldly," Dinin said to Maya. Immediately, Malice's disbelieving grimace fell upon him in a harsh reminder that it was not his place to speak.

But Briza promptly completed Dinin's thought. "Too boldly," she growled. Malice's gaze descended upon her on cue, but Briza was a high priestess in the favor of the Spider Queen and was well within her rights to speak. "You know nothing of our young brother," Briza went on, speaking as much to Malice as to Maya.

"He is only a male," Maya retorted. "I would—"

"You would be cut down!" Briza yelled. "Hold your foolish words and empty promises, youngest sister. Out in the tunnels beyond Menzoberranzan, Drizzt would kill you with little effort."

Malice listened intently to it all. She had heard Briza's account of the meeting with Drizzt several times, and she knew enough about her oldest daughter's courage and powers to understand that Briza did not speak falsely.

Maya backed down from the confrontation, not wanting any part of a feud with Briza.

"Could you defeat him?" Malice asked Briza, "now that you better understand what he has become?"

In response, Briza flexed her wounded hand again. It would be several tendays before she regained full use of the replaced fingers.

"Or you?" Malice asked Dinin, understanding Briza's pointed gesture as a conclusive answer.

Dinin fidgeted about, not knowing how to respond to his volatile mother.

The truth might put him at odds with Malice, but a lie surely would land him back in the tunnels against his brother.

"Speak truly with me!" Malice roared. "Do you wish another hunt for Drizzt, so that you may regain my favor?"

"I . . ." Dinin stuttered, then he lowered his eyes defensively. Malice had put a detection spell on his reply, Dinin realized. She would know if he tried to lie to her. "No," he said flatly. "Even at the cost of your favor, Matron Mother, I do not wish to go out after Drizzt again."

Maya and Vierna—even Shi'nayne—started in surprise at the honest response, thinking nothing could be worse than a matron mother's wrath. Briza, though, nodded in agreement, for she, too, had seen as much of Drizzt as she cared to see. Malice did not miss the significance of her daughter's motion.

"Your pardon, Matron Mother," Dinin went on, trying desperately to heal any ill feelings he had stirred. "I have seen Drizzt in combat. He took me down too easily—as I believed that no foe ever could. He defeated Briza fairly, and I have never seen her beaten! I do not wish to hunt my brother again, for I fear that the result would only bring more anger to you and more trouble to House Do'Urden."

"You are afraid?" Malice asked slyly.

Dinin nodded. "And I know that I would only disappoint you again, Matron Mother. In the tunnels that he names as home, Drizzt is beyond my skills. I cannot hope to outdo him."

"I can accept such cowardice in a male," Malice said coldly. Dinin, with no recourse, accepted the insult stoically.

"But you are a high priestess of Lolth!" Malice taunted Briza. "Certainly a rogue male is not beyond the powers that the Spider Queen has given to you!"

"Hear Dinin's words, my matron," Briza replied.

"Lolth is with you!" Shi'nayne shouted at her.

"But Drizzt is beyond the Spider Queen," Briza snapped back. "I fear that Dinin speaks the truth—for all of us. We cannot catch Drizzt out there. The wilds of the Underdark are his domain, where we are only strangers."

"Then what are we to do?" Maya grumbled.

Malice rested back in her throne and put her sharp chin in her palm. She had coaxed Dinin under the weight of a threat, and yet he still declared that he would not willingly venture after Drizzt. Briza, ambitious and powerful, and in the favor of Lolth even if House Do'Urden and Matron Malice were not, came back without her prized whip and the fingers of one hand.

"Jarlaxle and his band of rogues?" Vierna offered, seeing her mother's dilemma. "Bregan D'aerthe has been of value to us for many years."

"The mercenary leader will not agree," Malice replied, for she had tried to hire the soldier of fortune for the endeavor years before. "Every member of Bregan D'aerthe abides by the decisions of Jarlaxle, and all the wealth we possess will not tempt him. I suspect that Jarlaxle is under the strict orders of Matron Baenre. Drizzt is our problem, and we are charged by the Spider Queen with correcting that problem."

"If you command me to go, I shall," Dinin spoke out. "I fear only that I will disappoint you, Matron Mother. I do not fear Drizzt's blades, or death itself if it is in service to you." Dinin had read his mother's dark mood well enough to know that she had no intention of sending him back out after Drizzt, and he thought himself wise in being so generous when it didn't cost him anything.

"I thank you, my son," Malice beamed at him. Dinin had to hold his snicker when he noticed all three of his sisters glaring at him. "Now leave us," Malice continued condescendingly, stealing Dinin's moment. "We have business that does not concern a male."

Dinin bowed low and swept toward the door. His sisters took note of how easily Malice had stolen the proud spring from his step.

"I will remember your words," Malice said wryly, enjoying the power play and the silent applause. Dinin paused, his hand on the handle of the ornate door. "One day you will prove your loyalty to me, do not doubt."

All five of the high priestesses laughed at Dinin's back as he rushed out of the room.

On the floor, Rizzen found himself in quite a dangerous dilemma. Malice had sent Dinin away, saying in essence that males had no right to remain in the room. Yet Malice had not given Rizzen permission to move. He planted his feet and fingers against the stone, ready to spring away in an instant.

"Are you still here?" Malice shrieked at him. Rizzen bolted for the door.

"Hold!" Malice cried at him, her words once again empowered by a magical spell.

Rizzen stopped suddenly, against his better judgment and unable to resist the dweomer of Matron Malice's spell.

"I did not give you permission to move!" Malice screamed behind him.

"But—" Rizzen started to protest.

"Take him!" Malice commanded her two youngest daughters, and Vierna and Maya rushed over and roughly grabbed Rizzen.

"Put him in a dungeon cell," Malice instructed them. "Keep him alive. We will need him later."

Vierna and Maya hauled the trembling male out of the anteroom. Rizzen did not dare offer any resistance.

"You have a plan," Shi'nayne said to Malice. As SiNafay, the matron mother of House Hun'ett, the newest Do'Urden had learned to see purpose in every action. She knew the duties of a matron mother well and understood that Malice's outburst against Rizzen, who had in fact done nothing wrong, was more of calculated design than of true outrage.

"I agree with your assessment," Malice said to Briza. "Drizzt has gone beyond us."

"But by the words of Matron Baenre herself, we must not fail," Briza reminded her mother. "Your seat on the ruling council must be strengthened at all cost."

"We shall not fail," Shi'nayne said to Briza, eyeing Malice all the while. Another wry look came across Malice's face as Shi'nayne continued. "In ten years of battle against House Do'Urden," she said, "I have come to understand the methods of Matron Malice. Your mother will find a way to catch Drizzt." She paused, noting her mother's widening smile. "Or has she, perhaps, already found a way?"

"We shall see," Malice purred, her confidence growing in her former rival's decree of respect. "We shall see."

⚔ ⚔ ⚔ ⚔ ⚔

More than two hundred commoners of House Do'Urden milled about the great chapel, excitedly exchanging rumors of the coming events. Commoners were rarely allowed in this sacred place, only on the high holidays of Lolth or in communal prayer before a battle. Yet there were no expectations among them of any impending war, and this was no holy day on the drow calendar.

Dinin Do'Urden, also anxious and excited, moved about the crowd, settling dark elves into the rows of seats encircling the raised central dais. Being only a male, Dinin would not partake of the ceremony at the altar and Matron Malice had told him nothing of her plans. From the instructions she had given him, though, Dinin knew that the results of this day's events would prove critical to the future of his family. He was the chant leader; he would continually move throughout the assembly, leading the commoners in the appropriate verses to the Spider Queen.

Dinin had played this role often before, but this time Matron Malice had warned him that if a single voice called out incorrectly, Dinin's life would be forfeit. Still another fact disturbed the elderboy of House Do'Urden. He was normally accompanied in his chapel duties by the other male noble of the house, Malice's present mate. Rizzen had not been seen since that day when the whole family had gathered in the anteroom. Dinin suspected that Rizzen's reign as patron soon would come to a crashing end. It was no secret that Matron Malice had given previous mates to Lolth.

When all of the commoners were seated, magical red lights began to glow softly all about the room. The illumination increased gradually, allowing the gathered dark elves to comfortably shift their dual-purpose eyes from the infrared spectrum into the realm of light.

Misty vapors rolled out from under the seats, hugged the floor, and rose in curling wisps. Dinin led the crowd in a low hum, the calling of Matron Malice.

Malice appeared at the top of the room's domed ceiling, her arms outstretched and the folds of her spider-emblazoned black robes whipping

about in an enchanted breeze. She descended slowly, turning complete circuits to survey the gathering—and to let them look upon the splendor that was their matron mother.

When Malice alighted on the central dais, Briza and Shi'nayne appeared on the ceiling, floating down in similar fashion. They landed and took their places, Briza at the cloth-covered case off to the side of the spider-shaped sacrificial table and Shi'nayne behind Matron Malice.

Malice clapped her hands and the humming stopped abruptly. Eight braziers lining the central dais roared to life, their flames' brightness less painful to the sensitive drow eyes in the red, mist-enshrouded glow.

"Enter, my daughters!" Malice cried, and all heads turned to the chapel's main doors. Vierna and Maya came in, with Rizzen, sluggish and apparently drugged, supported between them and a casket floating in the air behind them.

Dinin, among others, thought this an odd arrangement. He could assume, he supposed, that Rizzen was to be sacrificed, but he had never heard of a coffin being brought in to the ceremony.

The younger Do'Urden daughters moved up to the central dais and quickly strapped Rizzen down to the sacrificial table. Shi'nayne intercepted the floating casket and guided it to a position off to the side opposite Briza.

"Call to the handmaiden!" Malice cried, and Dinin immediately sent the gathering into the desired chant. The braziers roared higher; Malice and the other high priestesses prodded the crowd on with magically enhanced shouts of key words in the summoning. A sudden wind came up from nowhere, it seemed, and whipped the mist into a frenzied dance.

The flames of all eight braziers shot out in high lines over Malice and the others, joining in a furious burst above the center of the circular platform. The braziers puffed once in a unified explosion, throwing the last of their flames into the summoning, then burned low as the lines of fire rolled together in a gathered ball and became a singular pillar of flame.

The commoners gasped but continued their chanting as the pillar rolled through the colors of the spectrum, gradually cooling until the flames were no more. In their place stood a tentacled creature, taller than a drow elf and resembling a half-melted candle with elongated, drooping facial features. All the crowd recognized the being, though few commoners had ever actually seen one before, except perhaps in illustrations in the clerical books. All in attendance knew well enough the importance of this gathering at that moment, for no drow could possibly miss the significance of the presence of a yochlol, a personal handmaiden of Lolth.

"Greetings, Handmaiden," Malice said loudly. "Blessed is Daermon N'a'shezbaernon for your presence."

The yochlol surveyed the gathering for a long while, surprised that House Do'Urden had issued such a summons. Matron Malice was not in the favor of Lolth.

Only the high priestesses felt the telepathic question. *Why dare you call to me?*

"To right our wrongs!" Malice cried out aloud, drawing the whole of the gathering into the tense moment. "To regain the favor of your Mistress, the favor that is the only purpose of our existence!" Malice looked pointedly at Dinin, and he began the correct song, the highest song of praise to the Spider Queen.

*I am pleased by your display, Matron Malice,* came the yochlol's thoughts, this time directed solely at Malice. *But you know that this gathering does nothing to aid in your peril!*

*This is but the beginning,* Malice answered mentally, confident that the handmaiden could read her every thought. The matron took comfort in that knowledge, for she held faith that her desires to regain the favor of Lolth were sincere. *My youngest son has wronged the Spider Queen. He must pay for his deeds.*

The other high priestesses, excluded from the telepathic conversation, joined in the song to Lolth.

*Drizzt Do'Urden lives,* the yochlol reminded Malice. *And he is not in your custody.*

*That shall soon be corrected,* Malice promised.

*What do you desire of me?*

"Zin-carla!" Malice cried aloud.

The yochlol swayed backward, momentarily stunned by the boldness of the request. Malice held her ground, determined that her plan would not fail. Around her, the other priestesses held their breath, fully realizing that the moment of triumph or disaster was upon them all.

*It is our highest gift,* came the yochlol's thoughts, *given rarely even to matrons in the favor of the Spider Queen. And you, who have not pleased Lolth, dare to ask for Zin-carla?*

*It is right and fitting,* Malice replied. Then aloud, needing the support of her family, she cried, "Let my youngest son learn the folly of his ways and the power of the enemies he has made. Let my son witness the horrible glory of Lolth revealed, so that he will fall to his knees and beg forgiveness!" Malice reverted to telepathic communication. *Only then shall the spirit-wraith drive a sword into his heart!*

The yochlol's eyes went blank as the creature fell into itself, seeking guidance from its home plane of existence. Many minutes—agonizing minutes to Matron Malice and all of the hushed gathering—passed before the yochlol's thoughts came back.

*Have you the corpse?*

Malice signaled to Maya and Vierna, and they rushed over to the casket and removed the stone lid. Dinin understood then that the box was not brought for Rizzen, but was already occupied. An animated corpse crawled out of it and staggered over to Malice's side. It was badly decomposed and many of its features had rotted away altogether, but Dinin and most of the others in the great chapel recognized it immediately: Zaknafein Do'Urden, the legendary weapon master.

*Zin-carla,* the yochlol asked, *so that the weapon master you gave to the Spider Queen might correct the wrongs of your youngest son?*

*It is appropriate,* Malice replied. She sensed that the yochlol was pleased, as she had expected. Zaknafein, Drizzt's tutor, had helped to inspire the blasphemous attitudes that had ruined Drizzt. Lolth, the queen of chaos, enjoyed ironies, and to have this same Zaknafein serve as executioner would inevitably please her.

*Zin-carla requires great sacrifice,* came the yochlol's demand.

The creature looked over to the spider-shaped table, where Rizzen lay oblivious to his surroundings. The yochlol seemed to frown, if such creatures could frown, at the sight of such a pitiful sacrifice. The creature then turned back to Matron Malice and read her thoughts.

*Do continue,* the yochlol prompted, suddenly very interested.

Malice lifted her arms, beginning yet another song to Lolth. She motioned to Shi'nayne, who walked to the case beside Briza and took out the ceremonial dagger, the most precious possession of House Do'Urden. Briza flinched when she saw her newest "sister" handle the item, its hilt the body of a spider with eight blade-like legs reaching down under it. For centuries it had been Briza's place to drive the ceremonial dagger into the hearts of gifts to the Spider Queen.

Shi'nayne smirked at the eldest daughter as she walked away, sensing Briza's anger. She joined Malice at the table beside Rizzen and moved the dagger out over the doomed patron's heart.

Malice grabbed her hands to stop her. "This time I must do it," Malice explained, to Shi'nayne's dismay. Shi'nayne looked back over her shoulder to see Briza returning her smirk tenfold.

Malice waited until the song had ended, and the gathering remained absolutely silent as Malice alone began the proper chant. "*Takken bres duis bres,*" she began, both her hands wringing over the hilt of the deadly instrument.

A moment later, Malice's chant neared completion and the dagger went up high. All the house tensed, awaiting the moment of ecstacy, the savage giving to the foul Spider Queen.

The dagger came down, but Malice turned it abruptly to the side and drove it instead into the heart of Shi'nayne, Matron SiNafay Hun'ett, her most hated rival.

"No!" gasped SiNafay, but the deed was done. Eight blade-legs grasped at her heart. SiNafay tried to speak, to cast a spell of healing on herself or a curse upon Malice, but only blood came out of her mouth. Gasping her last breaths, she fell forward over Rizzen.

All the house erupted in screams of shock and joy as Malice tore the dagger out from under SiNafay Hun'ett, and her enemy's heart along with it.

"Devious!" Briza screamed above the tumult, for even she had not known Malice's plans. Once again, Briza was the eldest daughter of House Do'Urden, back in the position of honor that she so dearly craved.

*Devious!* the yochlol echoed in Malice's mind. *Know that we are pleased!*

Behind the gruesome scene, the animated corpse fell limply to the floor. Malice looked at the handmaiden and understood. "Put Zaknafein on the table! Quickly!" she instructed her younger daughters. They scrambled about, roughly displacing Rizzen and SiNafay and getting Zaknafein's body in place.

Briza, too, went into motion, carefully lining up the many jars of unguents that had been painstakingly prepared for this moment. Matron Malice's reputation as the finest salve maker in the city would be put to the test in this effort.

Malice looked at the yochlol. "Zin-carla?" she asked aloud.

*You have not regained the favor of Lolth!* came the telepathic reply, so powerfully that Malice was driven to her knees. Malice clutched at her head, thinking it would explode from the building pressure.

Gradually the pain eased away. But you have pleased the Spider Queen this day, Malice Do'Urden, the yochlol explained. *And it is agreed that your plans for your sacrilegious son are appropriate. Zin-carla is granted, but know it as your final chance, Matron Malice Do'Urden! Your greatest fears cannot begin to approach the truth of the consequences of failure!*

The yochlol disappeared in an explosive fireball that rocked the chapel of House Do'Urden. Those gathered only rose to a higher frenzy at the bared power of the evil deity, and Dinin led them again in a song of praise to Lolth.

"Ten tendays!" came the final cry of the handmaiden, a voice so mighty that the lesser drow covered their ears and cowered on the floor.

And so for ten tendays, for seventy cycles of Narbondel, the daily time clock of Menzoberranzan, all of House Do'Urden gathered in the great chapel, Dinin and Rizzen leading the commoners in songs to the Spider Queen, while Malice and her daughters worked over Zaknafein's corpse with magical salves and combinations of powerful spells.

The animation of a corpse was a simple spell for a priestess, but Zin-carla went far beyond that feat. Spirit-wraith, the undead result would be called, a zombie imbued with the skills of its former life and controlled by the matron mother appointed by Lolth. It was the most precious of Lolth's gifts, rarely asked for and even more rarely granted, for Zin-carla—returning the spirit to the body—was a risky practice indeed. Only through the sheer willpower of the enchanting priestess were the undead being's desired skills kept separate from the unwanted memories and emotions. The edge of consciousness and control was a fine line to walk, even considering the mental discipline required of a high priestess. Furthermore, Lolth only granted Zin-carla for the completion of specific tasks, and stumbling from that fine line of discipline inevitably would result in failure.

Lolth was not merciful in the face of failure.

# 6

# Blingdenstone

Blingdenstone was different from anything that Drizzt had ever seen. When the svirfneblin guards ushered him in through the immense stone and iron doors, he had expected a sight not unlike Menzoberranzan, though on a lesser scale. His expectations could not have been further from the truth.

While Menzoberranzan sprawled in a single huge cavern, Blingdenstone was composed of a series of chambers interconnected by low tunnels. The largest cavern of the complex, just beyond the iron doors, was the first section Drizzt entered. The city guard was housed there, and the chamber had been shaped and designed solely for defense. Dozens of tiers and twice that number of smooth stairways rose and fell, so that while an attacker might be only ten feet from a defender, he would possibly have to climb down several levels and up several others to get close enough to strike. Low walls of perfectly fitted piled stone defined the walkways and weaved around higher, thicker walls that could keep an invading army bottled up for a painfully long time in the chamber's exposed sections.

Scores of svirfnebli rushed about their posts to confirm the whispers that a drow elf had been brought in through the doors. They leered down at Drizzt from every perch, and he couldn't be certain if their expressions signified curiosity or outrage. In either case, the deep gnomes were certainly prepared against anything he might attempt; every one of them clutched darts or heavy crossbows, cocked and ready.

The svirfnebli led Drizzt through the chamber, up as many stairs as they went down, always within the defined walkways and always with several other deep gnome guards nearby. The path turned and dropped, rose up quickly, and cut back on itself many times, and the only way that Drizzt could keep his bearing was by watching the ceiling, which was visible even from the lowest levels of the chamber. The drow smirked inwardly but dared not show a smile at the thought that even if no deep gnome soldiers were present, an invading army would likely spend hours trying to find its way through this single chamber.

Down at the end of a low and narrow corridor, where the deep gnomes had to travel single file and Drizzt had to crouch with every step, the troupe entered the city proper. Wider but not nearly as long as the first room, this chamber, too, was tiered, though with far fewer levels. Dozens of cave entrances lined the walls to all sides and fires burned in several areas, a rare sight in the Underdark, for fuel was not easily found. Blingdenstone was bright and warm by Underdark standards but not uncomfortable in either case.

Drizzt felt at ease, despite his obvious predicament, as he watched the svirfnebli go about their daily routines all around him. Curious gazes fell on him but did not linger, for the deep gnomes of Blingdenstone were an industrious lot with hardly the time to stand idly and watch.

Again Drizzt was led down clearly defined roadways. These in the city proper were not as twisting and difficult as the ones in the entrance cavern. Here the roads rolled out smoothly and straight, and all apparently led to a large, central stone building.

The leader of the group escorting Drizzt rushed ahead to speak with two pick-wielding guards at this central structure. One of the guards bolted inside, while the other held the iron door open for the patrol and its prisoner. Moving with urgency for the first time since they had entered the city, the svirfnebli rushed Drizzt through a series of bending corridors ending in a circular chamber no more than eight feet in diameter and with an uncomfortably low ceiling. The room was empty except for a single stone chair. As soon as he was placed in this, Drizzt understood its purpose. Iron shackles were built into the chair, and Drizzt was belted down tightly at every joint. The svirfnebli were not overly gentle, but when Drizzt flinched as the chain around his waist doubled up and pinched him, one of the deep gnomes quickly released then reset it, firmly but smoothly.

They left Drizzt alone in the dark and empty room. The stone door closed with a dull thud of finality, and Drizzt could hear not a sound from beyond.

The hours passed.

Drizzt flexed his muscles, seeking some give in the tight shackles. One hand wiggled and pulled, and only the pain of the iron biting into his wrist alerted him to his actions. He was reverting to the hunter again, acting to survive and desiring only to escape.

"No!" Drizzt yelled. He tensed every muscle and forced them back under his rational control. Had the hunter gained that much of a place? Drizzt had come here willingly, and thus far, the meeting had proceeded better than he had expected. This was not the time for desperate action, but was the hunter strong enough to overrule even Drizzt's rational decisions?

Drizzt didn't find the time to answer those questions, for a second later, the stone door banged open and a group of seven elderly—judging from the extraordinary number of wrinkles crossing their faces—svirfnebli entered and fanned out around the stone chair. Drizzt recognized the apparent importance of this group, for where the guards had worn leather jacks set with mithral rings, these deep gnomes wore robes of fine material. They bustled about, inspecting Drizzt closely and chattering in their undecipherable tongue.

One svirfneblin held up Drizzt's house emblem, which had been taken from his neck purse, and uttered, "Menzoberranzan?"

Drizzt nodded as much as his iron collar would allow, eager to strike up some kind of communication with his captors. The deep gnomes had other intentions, however. They went back to their private—and now even more excited—conversation.

It went on for many minutes, and Drizzt could tell by the inflections of their voices that a couple of the svirfnebli were less than thrilled at having a dark elf prisoner from the city of their closest and most-hated enemies. By the angry tone of their arguing, Drizzt almost expected one of them to turn at any moment and slice his throat.

It didn't happen like that, of course; deep gnomes were neither rash nor cruel creatures. One of the group did turn from the others and walk over to face Drizzt squarely. He asked, in halting but unmistakably drow language, "By the stones, dark elf, why have you come?"

Drizzt did not know how to answer that simple question. How could he even begin to explain his years of loneliness in the Underdark? Or the decision to forsake his evil people and live in accordance with his principles?

"Friend," he replied simply, and then he shifted uncomfortably, thinking his response absurd and inadequate.

The svirfneblin, though, apparently thought otherwise. He scratched his hairless chin and considered the answer deeply. "You . . . you came in to us from Menzoberranzan?" he asked, his hawklike nose crinkling as he uttered each word.

"I did," Drizzt replied, gaining confidence.

The deep gnome tilted his head, waiting for Drizzt to extrapolate.

"I left Menzoberranzan many years ago," Drizzt tried to explain. His eyes stared away into the past as he remembered the life he had deserted. "It was never my home."

"Ah, but you lie, dark elf!" the svirfneblin shrieked, holding up the emblem of House Do'Urden and missing the private connotations of Drizzt's words.

"I lived for many years in the city of the drow," he replied quickly. "I am Drizzt Do'Urden, once the secondboy of House Do'Urden." He looked at the emblem the svirfneblin held, stamped with the insignia of his family, and tried to explain. "Daermon N'a'shezbaernon."

The deep gnome turned to his comrades, who began talking all at once. One of them nodded excitedly, apparently recognizing the drow house's ancient name, which surprised Drizzt.

The deep gnome who had been questioning Drizzt tapped his fingers over his wrinkled lips, making annoying little smacking sounds while he contemplating the interrogation's direction. "By all of our information,

House Do'Urden survives," he remarked casually, noting Drizzt's reactions. When Drizzt did not immediately respond, the deep gnome snapped at him accusingly, "You are no rogue!"

How could the svirfnebli know that? Drizzt wondered. "I am a rogue by choice . . ." he started to explain.

"Ah, dark elf," the deep gnome replied, again calmly. "You are here by choice, that much I can believe. But a rogue? By the stones, dark elf—" the deep gnome's face contorted suddenly and fearfully—"you are a spy!" Then, suddenly, the deep gnome once again calmed and relaxed into a comfortable posture.

Drizzt eyed him carefully. Was this svirfneblin adept at such abrupt attitude changes, designed to keep a prisoner off guard? Or was such unpredictability the norm for this race? Drizzt struggled with it for a moment, trying to remember his one previous encounter with deep gnomes. But then his questioner reached into an impossibly deep pocket in his thick robes and produced a familiar figurine.

"Tell me, now tell me true, dark elf, and spare yourself much torment. What is this?" the deep gnome asked quietly.

Drizzt felt his muscles twitching again. The hunter wanted to call to Guenhwyvar, to bring the panther in so that it could tear these wrinkled old svirfnebli apart. One of them might hold the keys to Drizzt's chains—then he would be free . . .

Drizzt shook the thoughts from his head and drove the hunter out of his mind. He knew the desperation of his situation and had known it from the moment he had decided to come to Blingdenstone. If the svirfnebli truly believed him a spy, they surely would execute him. Even if they were not certain of his intent, could they dare to keep him alive?

"It was folly to come here," Drizzt whispered under his breath, realizing the dilemma he had placed upon himself and upon the deep gnomes. The hunter tried to get back into his thoughts. A single word, and the panther would appear.

"No!" Drizzt cried for the second time that day, dismissing that darker side of himself. The deep gnomes jumped back, fearing that the drow was casting a spell. A dart nicked into Drizzt's chest, releasing a puff of gas on impact.

Drizzt swooned as the gas filled his nostrils. He heard the svirfnebli shuffling about him, discussing his fate in their foreign tongue. He saw the form of one, only a shadow, close in on him and grasp at his fingers, searching his hands for possible magical components.

When Drizzt's thoughts and vision had at last cleared, all was as it had been. The onyx figurine came up before his eyes. "What is this?" the same deep gnome asked him again, this time a bit more insistently.

"A companion," Drizzt whispered. "My only friend." Drizzt thought hard about his next actions for a long moment. He really couldn't blame the svirfnebli if they killed him, and Guenhwyvar should be more than a statuette adorning some unknowing deep gnome's mantle.

"Its name is Guenhwyvar," Drizzt explained to the deep gnome. "Call to the panther and it will come, an ally and friend. Keep it safe, for it is very precious and very powerful."

The svirfneblin looked to the figurine and then back to Drizzt, curiously and cautiously. He handed the figurine to one of his companions and sent him out of the room with it, not trusting the drow. If the drow had spoken truly, and the deep gnome did not doubt that he had, Drizzt had just given away the secret to a very valuable magical item. Even more startling, if Drizzt had spoken truly, he might have relinquished his single chance of escape. This svirfneblin had lived for nearly two centuries and was as knowledgeable in the ways of the dark elves as any of his people. When a drow elf acted unpredictably, as this one surely had, it troubled the svirfneblin deeply. Dark elves were cruel and evil by well-earned reputation, and when an individual drow fit that usual pattern, he could be dealt with efficiently and without remorse. But what might the deep gnomes do with a drow who showed a measure of unexpected morals?

The svirfnebli went back to their private conversation, ignoring Drizzt altogether. Then they left, with the exception of the one who could speak the dark elf tongue.

"What will you do?" Drizzt dared to ask.

"Judgment is reserved for the king alone," the deep gnome replied soberly. "He will rule on your fate in several days perhaps, based on the observations of his advising council, the group you have met." The deep gnome bowed low, then looked Drizzt in the eye as he rose and said bluntly, "I suspect, dark elf, that you will be executed."

Drizzt nodded, resigned to the logic that would call for his death.

"But I believe you are different, dark elf," the deep gnome went on. "I suspect, as well, that I will recommend leniency, or at least mercy, in the execution." With a quick shrug of his heavyset shoulders, the svirfneblin turned about and headed for the door.

The tone of the deep gnome's words struck a familiar chord in Drizzt. Another svirfneblin had spoken to Drizzt in a similar manner, with strikingly similar words, many years before.

"Wait," Drizzt called. The svirfneblin paused and turned, and Drizzt fumbled with his thoughts, trying to remember the name of the deep gnome he had saved on that past occasion.

"What is it?" the svirfneblin asked, growing impatient.

"A deep gnome," Drizzt sputtered. "From your city, I believe. Yes, he had to be."

"You know one of my people, dark elf?" the svirfneblin prompted, stepping back to the stone chair. "Name him."

"I do not know," Drizzt replied. "I was a member of a hunting party, years ago, a decade perhaps. We battled a group of svirfnebli that had come into our region." He flinched at the deep gnome's frown but continued on, knowing that the single svirfneblin survivor of that encounter might be his only hope. "Only one deep gnome survived, I think, and returned to Blingdenstone."

"What was this survivor's name?" the svirfneblin demanded angrily, his arms crossed tightly over his chest and his heavy boot tapping on the stone floor.

"I do not remember," Drizzt admitted.

"Why do you tell me this?" the svirfneblin growled. "I had thought you different from—"

"He lost his hands in the battle," Drizzt went on stubbornly. "Please, you must know of him."

"Belwar?" the svirfneblin replied immediately. The name rekindled even more memories in Drizzt.

"Belwar Dissengulp," Drizzt spouted. "Then he is alive! He might remember—"

"He will never forget that evil day, dark elf!" the svirfneblin declared through clenched teeth, an angry edge evident in his voice. "None in Blingdenstone will ever forget that evil day!"

"Get him. Get Belwar Dissengulp," Drizzt pleaded.

The deep gnome backed out of the room, shaking his head at the dark elf's continued surprises.

The stone door slammed shut, leaving Drizzt alone to contemplate his mortality and to push aside hopes he dared not hope.

⚔ ⚔ ⚔ ⚔ ⚔

"Did you think that I would let you go away from me?" Malice was saying to Rizzen when Dinin entered the chapel's anteroom. "It was but a ploy to keep SiNafay Hun'ett's suspicions at ease."

"Thank you, Matron Mother," Rizzen replied in honest relief. Bowing with every step, he backed away from Malice's throne.

Malice looked around at her gathered family. "Our tendays of toil are ended," she proclaimed. "Zin-carla is complete!"

Dinin wrung his hands in anticipation. Only the females of the family had seen the product of their work. On cue from Malice, Vierna moved to a curtain on the side of the room and pulled it away. There stood Zaknafein, the weapon master, no longer a rotting corpse, but showing the vitality he had possessed in life.

Dinin rocked back on his heels as the weapon master came forward to stand before Matron Malice.

"As handsome as you always were, my dear Zaknafein," Malice purred to the spirit-wraith. The undead thing made no response.

"And more obedient," Briza added, drawing chuckles from all the females.

"This . . . he . . . will go after Drizzt?" Dinin dared to ask, though he fully understood that it was not his place to speak. Malice and the others were too absorbed by the spectacle of Zaknafein to punish the elderboy's oversight.

"Zaknafein will exact the punishment that your brother so deeply deserves," Malice promised, her eyes sparkling at the notion.

"But wait," Malice said coyly, looking from the spirit-wraith to Rizzen. "He is too pretty to inspire fear in my impudent son." The others exchanged confused glances, wondering if Malice was further trying to placate Rizzen for the ordeal she had put him through.

"Come, my husband," Malice said to Rizzen. "Take your blade and mark your dead rival's face. It will feel good to you, and it will inspire terror in Drizzt when he looks upon his old mentor!"

Rizzen moved tentatively at first, then gained confidence as he closed on the spirit-wraith. Zaknafein stood perfectly still, not breathing or blinking, seemingly oblivious to the events around him. Rizzen put a hand to his sword, looking back to Malice one final time for confirmation.

Malice nodded. With a snarl, Rizzen brought his sword out of its sheath and thrust it at Zaknafein's face.

But it never got close.

Quicker than the others could follow, the spirit-wraith exploded into motion. Two swords came out and cut away, diving and crossing with perfect precision. The sword went flying from Rizzen's hand and before the doomed patron of House Do'Urden could even speak a word of protest, one of Zaknafein's swords crossed over his throat and the other plunged deep into his heart.

Rizzen was dead before he hit the floor, but the spirit-wraith was not so quickly and cleanly finished with him. Zaknafein's weapons continued their assault, hacking and slicing into Rizzen a dozen times until Malice, satisfied with the display, called him off.

"That one bores me," Malice explained to the disbelieving stares of her children. "I have another patron already selected from among the commoners."

It was not, however, Rizzen's death that inspired the awestruck expressions of Malice's children; they cared nothing for any of the mates that their mother chose as patron of the house, always a temporary position. It was the speed and skill of the spirit-wraith that had stolen their breath.

"As good as in life," Dinin remarked.

"Better!" Malice replied. "Zaknafein is all that he was as a warrior, and now that fighting skill holds his every thought. He will view no distractions from his chosen course. Look upon him, my children. Zin-carla, the gift of Lolth." She turned to Dinin and smiled wickedly.

"I'll not approach the thing," Dinin gasped, thinking his macabre mother might desire a second display.

Malice laughed at him. "Fear not, Elderboy. I have no cause to harm you."

Dinin hardly relaxed at her words. Malice needed no cause; the hacked body of Rizzen showed that fact all too clearly.

"You will lead the spirit-wraith out," Malice said.

"Out?" Dinin replied tentatively.

"Into the region where you encountered your brother," Malice explained.

"I am to stay beside the thing?" Dinin gasped.

"Lead him out and leave him," Malice replied. "Zaknafein knows his prey. He has been imbued with spells to aid him in his hunt."

Off to the side, Briza seemed concerned.

"What is it?" Malice demanded of her, seeing her frown.

"I do not question the spirit-wraith's power, or the magic that you have placed upon it," Briza began tentatively, knowing that Malice would accept no discord regarding this all-important matter.

"You still fear your youngest brother?" Malice asked her.

Briza didn't know how to answer.

"Allay your fears, as valid as you may think them," Malice said calmly. "All of you. Zaknafein is the gift of our queen. Nothing in all the Underdark will stop him!" She looked at the undead monster. "You will not fail me, will you my weapon master?"

Zaknafein stood impassive, bloodied swords back in their scabbards, hands at his sides, and eyes unblinking. A statue, he seemed, not breathing. Unalive.

But any who thought Zaknafein inanimate needed only to look at the spirit-wraith's feet, to the mutilated lump of gore that had been the patron of House Do'Urden.

# Part Two

## Belwar

Friendship: The word has come to mean many different things among the various races and cultures of both the Underdark and the surface of the Realms. In Menzoberranzan, friendship is generally born out of mutual profit. While both parties are better off for the union, it remains secure. But loyalty is not a tenet of drow life, and as soon as a friend believes that he will gain more without the other, the union—and likely the other's life—will come to a swift end.

I have had few friends in my life, and if I live a thousand years, I suspect that this will remain true. There is little to lament in this fact, though, for those who have called me friend have been persons of great character and have enriched my existence, given it worth. First there was Zaknafein, my father and mentor, who showed me that I was not alone and that

I was not incorrect in holding to my beliefs. Zaknafein saved me, from both the blade and the chaotic, evil, fanatic religion that damns my people.

Yet I was no less lost when a handless deep gnome came into my life, a svirfneblin that I had rescued from certain death, many years before, at my brother Dinin's merciless blade. My deed was repaid in full, for when the svirfneblin and I again met, this time in the clutches of his people, I would have been killed—truly would have preferred death—were it not for Belwar Dissengulp.

My time in Blingdenstone, the city of the deep gnomes, was such a short span in the measure of my years. I remember well Belwar's city and his people, and I always shall. Theirs was the first society I came to know that was based on the strengths of community, not the paranoia of selfish individualism. Together the deep gnomes survive against the perils of the hostile Underdark, labor in their endless toils of mining the stone, and play games that are hardly distinguishable from every other aspect of their rich lives.

Greater indeed are pleasures that are shared.

—Drizzt Do'Urden

# 7
# Most Honored Burrow-Warden

"Our thanks for your coming, Most Honored Burrow-Warden," said one of the deep gnomes gathered outside the small room holding the drow prisoner. The entire group of svirfneblin elders bowed low at the burrow-warden's approach.

Belwar Dissengulp flinched at the gracious greeting. He had never come to terms with the many laurels his people had mantled upon him since that disastrous day more than a decade before, when the drow elves had discovered his mining troupe in the corridors east of Blingdenstone, near Menzoberranzan. Horribly maimed and nearly dead from loss of blood, Belwar had limped back to Blingdenstone as the only survivor of the expedition.

The gathered svirfnebli parted for Belwar, giving him a clear view of the room and the drow. To prisoners strapped in the chair, the circular chamber seemed solid, unremarkable stone with no opening other than the heavy iron-bound door. There was, however, a single window in the chamber, covered by illusions of both sight and sound, that allowed the svirfneblin captors to view the prisoner at all times.

Belwar studied Drizzt for several moments. "He is a drow," the burrow-warden huffed in his resonant voice, sounding a bit perturbed. Belwar still could not understand why he had been summoned.

"Appearing as any other drow."

"The prisoner claims he met you out in the Underdark," an ancient svirfneblin said to Belwar. His voice was barely a whisper, and he dropped his gaze to the floor as he completed the thought. "On that day of great loss."

Belwar flinched again at the mention of that day. How many times must he relive it?

"He may have," Belwar said with a noncommittal shrug. "Not much can I distinguish between the appearances of drow elves, and not much do I wish to try!"

"Agreed," said the other. "They all look alike."

As the deep gnome spoke, Drizzt turned his face to the side and faced them directly, though he could not see or hear anything beyond the illusion of stone.

"Perhaps you may remember his name, Burrow-Warden," another svirfneblin offered. The speaker paused, seeing Belwar's sudden interest in the drow.

The circular chamber was lightless, and under such conditions, the eyes of a creature seeing in the infrared spectrum shone clearly. Normally, these eyes appeared as dots of red light, but that was not the case with Drizzt Do'Urden. Even in the infrared spectrum, this drow's eyes showed clearly as lavender.

Belwar remembered those eyes.

"*Magga cammara,*" Belwar breathed. "Drizzt," he mumbled in reply to the other deep gnome.

"You do know him!" several of the svirfnebli cried together.

Belwar held up the handless stumps of his arms, one capped with the mithral head of a pickaxe, the other with the head of a hammer. "This drow, this Drizzt," he stammered, trying to explain. "Responsible for my condition, he was!"

Some of the others murmured prayers for the doomed drow, thinking the burrow-warden was angered by the memory. "Then King Schnicktick's decision stands," one of them said. "The drow is to be executed immediately."

"But he, this Drizzt, he saved my life," Belwar interjected loudly. The others, incredulous, turned on him.

"Never was it Drizzt's decision that my hands be severed," the burrow-warden went on. "It was his offering that I be allowed to return to Blingdenstone. 'As an example,' this Drizzt said, but I understood even then that the words were uttered only to placate his cruel kin. The truth behind those words, I know, and that truth was mercy!"

⚔ ⚔ ⚔ ⚔ ⚔

An hour later, a single svirfneblin councilor, the one who had spoken to Drizzt earlier, came to the prisoner. "It was the decision of the king that you be executed," the deep gnome said bluntly as he approached the stone chair.

"I understand," Drizzt replied as calmly as he could. "I will offer no resistance to your verdict." Drizzt considered his shackles for a moment. "Not that I could."

The svirfneblin stopped and considered the unpredictable prisoner, fully believing in Drizzt's sincerity. Before he continued, meaning to expand on the events of the day, Drizzt completed his thought.

"I ask only one favor," Drizzt said. The svirfneblin let him finish, curious of the unusual drow's reasoning.

"The panther," Drizzt went on. "You will find Guenhwyvar to be a valued companion and a dear friend indeed. When I am no more, you must see to it that the panther is given to a deserving master—Belwar Dissengulp perhaps. Promise me this, good gnome, I beg."

The svirfneblin shook his hairless head, not to deny Drizzt's plea, but in simple disbelief. "The king, with much remorse, simply could not allow the risks of keeping you alive," he said somberly. The deep gnome's wide mouth turned up in a smile as he quickly added, "But the situation has changed!"

Drizzt cocked his head, hardly daring to hope.

"The burrow-warden remembers you, dark elf," the svirfneblin proclaimed. "Most Honored Burrow-Warden Belwar Dissengulp has spoken for you and will accept the responsibility of keeping you!"

"Then . . . I am not to die?"

"Not unless you bring death upon yourself."

Drizzt could barely utter the words. "And I am to be allowed to live among your people? In Blingdenstone?"

"That is yet to be determined," replied the svirfneblin. "Belwar Dissengulp has spoken for you, and that is a very great thing. You will go to live with him. Whether the situation will be continued or expanded . . ." He let it hang at that, giving an unanswering shrug.

Following his release, the walk through the caverns of Blingdenstone was truly an exercise in hope for the beleaguered drow. Drizzt saw every sight in the deep gnome city as a contrast to Menzoberranzan. The dark elves had worked the great cavern of their city into shaped artwork, undeniably beautiful. The deep gnome city, too, was beautiful, but its features remained the natural traits of the stone. Where the drow had taken their cavern as their own, cutting it to their designs and tastes, the svirfnebli had fitted themselves into the native designs of their complex.

Menzoberranzan held a vastness, with a ceiling up beyond sight, that Blingdenstone could not approach. The drow city was a series of individual family castles, each a closed fortress and a house unto itself. In the deep gnome city was a general sense of home, as if the entire complex within the mammoth stone-and-metal doors was a singular structure, a community shelter from the ever-present dangers of the Underdark.

The angles of the svirfneblin city, too, were different. Like the features of the diminutive race, Blingdenstone's buttresses and tiers were rounded, smooth, and gracefully curving. Conversely, Menzoberranzan was an angular place, as sharp as the point of a stalactite, a place of alleyways and leering terraces. Drizzt considered the two cities distinctive of the races they housed, sharp and soft like the features—and the hearts, Drizzt dared to imagine—of their respective inhabitants.

Tucked away in a remote corner of one of the outer chambers sat Belwar's dwelling, a tiny structure of stone built around the opening of an even smaller cave. Unlike most of the open-faced svirfneblin dwellings, Belwar's house had a front door.

One of the five guards escorting Drizzt tapped on the door with the butt of his mace. "Greetings, Most Honored Burrow-Warden!" he called. "By orders of King Schnicktick, we have delivered the drow."

Drizzt took note of the respectful tone of the guard's voice. He had feared for Belwar on that day a decade and more ago, and had wondered if Dinin's cutting off the deep gnome's hands wasn't more cruel than simply killing the unfortunate creature. Cripples did not fare well in the savage Underdark.

The stone door swung open and Belwar greeted his guests. Immediately his gaze locked with Drizzt's in a look they had shared ten years before, when they had last parted.

Drizzt saw a somberness in the burrow-warden's eyes, but the stout pride remained, if a bit diminished. Drizzt did not want to look upon the svirfnebli's disfigurement; too many unpleasant memories were tied up in that long-ago deed. But inevitably, the drow's gaze dropped, down Belwar's barrel-like torso to the ends of his arms, which hung by his side.

Far from his fears, Drizzt's eyes widened in wonderment when he looked upon Belwar's "hands." On the right side, wondrously fitted to cap the stub of his arm, was the blocked head of a hammer crafted of mithral and etched with intricate, fabulous runes and carvings of an earth elemental and some other creatures that Drizzt did not know.

Belwar's left appendage was no less spectacular. There the deep gnome wielded a two-headed pickaxe, also of mithral and equally crafted in runes and carvings, most notably a dragon taking flight across the flat surface of the instrument's wider end. Drizzt could sense the magic in Belwar's hands, and he realized that many other svirfnebli, both artisans and magic-users, had played a part in perfecting the items.

"Useful," Belwar remarked after allowing Drizzt to study his mithral hands for a few moments.

"Beautiful," Drizzt whispered in reply, and he was thinking of more than the hammer and pick. The hands themselves were indeed marvelous, but the implications of their crafting seemed even more so to Drizzt. If a dark elf, particularly a drow male, had crawled back into Menzoberranzan in such a disfigured state, he would have been rejected and put out by his family to wander about as a helpless rogue until some slave or other drow finally put an end to his misery. There was no room for apparent weakness in the drow culture. Here, obviously, the svirfnebli had accepted Belwar and had cared for him in the best way they knew how.

Drizzt politely returned his stare to the burrow-warden's eyes. "You remembered me," he said. "I had feared—"

"Later we shall talk, Drizzt Do'Urden," Belwar interrupted. Using the svirfneblin tongue, which Drizzt did not know, the burrow-warden said to the guards, "If your business is completed, then take your leave."

"We are at your command, Most Honored Burrow-Warden," one of the guards replied. Drizzt noticed Belwar's slight shudder at the mention of the title. "The king has sent us as escorts and guards, to remain by your side until the truth of this drow is revealed."

"Be gone, then," Belwar replied, his booming voice rising in obvious ire. He looked directly at Drizzt as he finished. "I know the truth of this one already. I am in no danger."

"Your pardon, Most Honor—"

"You are excused," Belwar said abruptly, seeing that the guard meant to argue. "Be gone. I have spoken for this one. He is in my care, and I fear him not at all."

The svirfneblin guards bowed low and slowly moved away. Belwar took Drizzt inside the door, then turned him back to slyly point out that two of the guards had taken up cautious positions beside nearby structures. "Too much do they worry for my health," he remarked dryly in the drow tongue.

"You should be grateful for such care," Drizzt replied.

"I am not ungrateful!" Belwar shot back, an angry flush coming to his face.

Drizzt read the truth behind those words. Belwar was not ungrateful, that much was correct, but the burrow-warden did not believe that he deserved such attention. Drizzt kept his suspicions private, not wanting to further embarrass the proud svirfneblin.

The inside of Belwar's house was sparsely furnished with a stone table and single stool, several shelves of pots and jugs, and a fire pit with an iron cooking grate. Beyond the rough-hewn entrance to the back room, the room within the small cave, was the deep gnome's sleeping quarters, empty except for a hammock strung from wall to wall. Another hammock, newly acquired for Drizzt, lay in a heap on the floor, and a leather, mithral-ringed jack hung on the back wall, with a pile of sacks and pouches underneath it.

"In the entry room we shall string it," Belwar said, pointing with his hammer-hand to the second hammock. Drizzt moved to get the item, but Belwar caught him with his pick-hand and spun him about.

"Later," the svirfneblin explained. "First you must tell me why you have come." He studied Drizzt's battered clothing and scuffed and dirty face. It was obvious that the drow had been out in the wilds for some time. "And tell me, too, you must, where you have come from."

Drizzt flopped down on the stone floor and put his back against the wall. "I came because I had nowhere else to go," he answered honestly.

"How long have you been out of your city, Drizzt Do'Urden?" Belwar asked him softly. Even in quieter tones, the solid deep gnome's voice rang out with the clarity of a finely tuned bell. Drizzt marveled at its emotive range and how it could convey sincere compassion or inspire fear with subtle changes of volume.

Drizzt shrugged and let his head roll back so that his gaze was raised to the ceiling. His mind already looked down a road to his past. "Years—I have lost count of the time." He looked back to the svirfneblin. "Time has little meaning in the open passages of the Underdark."

From Drizzt's ragged appearance, Belwar could not doubt the truth of his words, but the deep gnome was surprised nonetheless. He moved over to the table in the center of the room and took a seat on a stool. Belwar had witnessed Drizzt in battle, had once seen the drow defeat an earth elemental—no easy feat! But if Drizzt was indeed speaking the truth, if he had survived alone out in the wilds of the Underdark for years, then the burrow-warden's respect for him would be even more considerable.

"Of your adventures, you must tell me, Drizzt Do'Urden," Belwar prompted. "I wish to know everything about you, so that I may better understand your purpose in coming to a city of your racial enemies."

Drizzt paused for a long time, wondering where and how to begin. He trusted Belwar—what other choice did he have?—but he wasn't sure if the svirfneblin could begin to understand the dilemma that had forced him out of the security of Menzoberranzan. Could Belwar, living in a community of such obvious friendship and cooperation, understand the tragedy that was Menzoberranzan? Drizzt doubted it, but again, what choice did he have?

Drizzt quietly recounted to Belwar the story of the last decade of his life; of the impending war between House Do'Urden and House Hun'ett; of his meeting with Masoj and Alton, when he acquired Guenhwyvar; of the sacrifice of Zaknafein, Drizzt's mentor, father, and friend; and of his subsequent decision to forsake his kin and their evil deity, Lolth. Belwar realized that Drizzt was talking about the dark goddess the deep gnomes called Lolth, but he calmly let the regionalism pass. If Belwar had any suspicions at all, not really knowing Drizzt's true intent on that day when they had met many years before, the burrow-warden soon came to believe that his guesses about this drow had been accurate. Belwar found himself shuddering and trembling as Drizzt told of life in the Underdark, of his encounter with the basilisk, and the battle with his brother and sister.

Before Drizzt even mentioned his reason for seeking the svirfnebli—the agony of his loneliness and the fear that he was losing his very identity in the savagery necessary to survive in the wilds—Belwar had guessed it all. When Drizzt came to the final days of his life outside of Blingdenstone, he picked his words carefully. Drizzt had not yet come to terms with his feelings and fears of who he truly was, and he was not yet ready to divulge his thoughts, however much he trusted his new companion.

The burrow-warden sat silently, just looking at Drizzt when the drow had finished his tale. Belwar understood the pain of the recounting. He did not prod for more information or ask for details of personal anguish that Drizzt had not openly shared.

"*Magga cammara,*" the deep gnome whispered soberly.

Drizzt cocked his head.

"By the stones," Belwar explained. "*Magga cammara.*"

"By the stones indeed," Drizzt agreed. A long and uncomfortable silence ensued.

"A fine tale, it is," Belwar said quietly. He patted Drizzt once on the shoulder, then walked into the cave-room to retrieve the spare hammock. Before Drizzt even rose to assist, Belwar had set the hammock in place between hooks on the walls.

"Sleep in peace, Drizzt Do'Urden," Belwar said, as he turned to retire. "No enemies have you here. No monsters lurk beyond the stone of my door."

Then Belwar was gone into the other room and Drizzt was left alone in the undecipherable swirl of his thoughts and emotions. He remained uncomfortable, but surely, his was hope renewed.

# 8
# Strangers

Drizzt looked out Belwar's open door at the daily routines of the svirfneblin city, as he had every day for the last few tendays. Drizzt felt as though his life was in a state of limbo, as though everything had been put into stasis. He had not seen or heard of Guenhwyvar since he had come to Belwar's house, nor had he any expectations of getting his *piwafwi* or his weapons and armor back anytime soon. Drizzt accepted it all stoically, figuring that he, and Guenhwyvar, were better off now than they had been in many years and confident that the svirfnebli would not harm the statuette or any of his other possessions. The drow sat and watched, letting events take their due course.

Belwar had gone out this day, one of the rare occasions that the reclusive burrow-warden left his house. Despite the fact that the deep gnome and Drizzt rarely conversed—Belwar was not the type who spoke simply for the sake of hearing his own voice—Drizzt found that he missed the burrow-warden. Their friendship had grown, even if the substance of their conversations had not.

A group of young svirfnebli walked past and shouted a few quick words at the drow within. This had happened many times before, particularly in the first days after Drizzt had entered the city. On those previous occasions, Drizzt had been left wondering if he had been greeted or insulted. This time, though, Drizzt understood the basic friendly meaning of the words, for Belwar had taken the time to instruct him in the basics of the svirfneblin tongue.

The burrow-warden returned hours later to find Drizzt sitting on the stone stool, watching the world slip past.

"Tell me, dark elf," the deep gnome asked in his hearty, melodic voice, "what do you see when you look upon us? Are we so foreign to your ways?"

"I see hope," Drizzt replied. "And I see despair."

Belwar understood. He knew that the svirfneblin society was better suited to the drow's principles, but watching the bustle of Blingdenstone from afar could only evoke painful memories in his new friend.

"King Schnicktick and I met this day," the burrow-warden said. "I tell you in truth that he is very interested in you."

"Curious would seem a better word," Drizzt replied, but he smiled as he did so, and Belwar wondered how much pain was hidden behind the grin.

The burrow-warden dipped into a short, apologetic bow, surrendering to Drizzt's blunt honesty. "Curious, then, as you wish. You must know that you are not as we have come to regard drow elves. I beg that you take no offense."

"None," Drizzt answered honestly. "You and your people have given me more than I dared hope. If I had been killed that first day in the city, I would have accepted the fate without placing blame on the svirfnebli."

Belwar followed Drizzt's gaze out across the cavern, to the group of gathered youngsters. "You should go among them," Belwar offered.

Drizzt looked at him, surprised. In all the time he had spent in Belwar's house, the svirfneblin had never suggested such a thing. Drizzt had assumed that he was to remain the burrow-warden's guest, and that Belwar had been made personally responsible for curtailing his movements.

Belwar nodded toward the door, silently reiterating his suggestion. Drizzt looked out again. Across the cavern, the group of young svirfnebli, a dozen or so, had begun a contest of heaving rather large stones at an effigy of a basilisk, a life-sized likeness built of stones and old suits of armor. Svirfnebli were highly skilled in the magical crafts of illusion, and one such illusionist had placed minor enchantments upon the likeness to smooth out the rough spots and make the effigy appear even more lifelike.

"Dark elf, you must go out sometime," Belwar reasoned. "How long will you find my home's blank walls fulfilling?"

"They suit you," Drizzt retorted, a bit more sharply than he had intended.

Belwar nodded and slowly turned about to survey the room. "So they do," he said quietly, and Drizzt could clearly see his great pain. When Belwar turned back to the drow, his round-featured face held an unmistakably resigned expression. "*Magga cammara*, dark elf. Let that be your lesson."

"Why?" Drizzt asked him. "Why does Belwar Dissengulp, the Most Honored Burrow-Warden—" Belwar flinched again at the title—"remain within the shadows of his own door?"

Belwar's jaw firmed up and his dark eyes narrowed. "Go out," he said in a resonating growl. "Young you are, dark elf, and all the world is before you. Old I am. My day is long past."

"Not so old," Drizzt started to argue, determined this time to press the burrow-warden into revealing what it was that troubled him so. But Belwar simply turned and walked silently into his cave-room, pulling closed behind him the blanket he had strung up as a door.

Drizzt shook his head and banged his fist into his palm in frustration. Belwar had done so much for him, first by saving him from the svirfneblin king's judgment, then by befriending him over the last few tendays and teaching him the svirfneblin tongue and the deep gnomes' ways. Drizzt had been unable to return the favor, though he clearly saw that Belwar carried some great burden. Drizzt wanted to rush through the blanket now, go to the burrow-warden, and make him speak his gloomy thoughts.

Drizzt would not yet be so bold with his new friend, however. He would find the key to the burrow-warden's pain in time, he vowed, but right now he had his own dilemma to overcome. Belwar had given him permission to go out into Blingdenstone!

Drizzt looked back to the group across the cavern. Three of them stood perfectly still before the effigy, as if turned to stone. Curious, Drizzt moved to the doorway, and then, before he realized what he was doing, he was outside and approaching the young deep gnomes.

The game ended as the drow neared, the svirfnebli being more interested in meeting the dark elf they had rumored about for so many tendays. They rushed over to Drizzt and surrounded him, whispering curiously.

Drizzt felt his muscles tense involuntarily as the svirfnebli moved all about him. The primal instincts of the hunter sensed a vulnerability that could not be tolerated. Drizzt fought hard to sublimate his alter ego, silently but firmly reminding himself that the svirfnebli were not his enemies.

"Greetings, drow friend of Belwar Dissengulp," one of the youngsters offered. "I am Seldig, fledgling and pledgling, and to be an expedition miner in but three years hence."

It took Drizzt a long moment to sort out the deep gnome's rapid speech patterns. He did understand the significance of Seldig's future occupation, though, for Belwar had told him that expedition miners, those svirfnebli who went out into the Underdark in search of precious minerals and gems, were among the highest ranking deep gnomes in all the city.

"Greetings, Seldig," Drizzt answered at length. "I am Drizzt Do'Urden." Not really knowing what he should do next, Drizzt crossed his arms over his chest. To the dark elves, this was a gesture of peace, though Drizzt was not certain if the motion was universally accepted throughout the Underdark.

The svirfnebli looked around at each other, returned the gesture, then smiled in unison at the sound of Drizzt's relieved sigh.

"You have been in the Underdark, so it is said," Seldig went on, motioning for Drizzt to follow him back to the area of their game.

"For many years," Drizzt replied, falling into step beside the young svirfneblin. The hunting ego within the drow grew ill at ease at the following deep gnomes' proximity, but Drizzt was in full control of his reflexive paranoia. When the group reached the fabricated basilisk's side, Seldig sat on the stone and bid Drizzt to give them a tale or two of his adventures.

Drizzt hesitated, doubting that his command of the svirfneblin tongue would be sufficient for such a task, but Seldig and the others pressed him. At length, Drizzt nodded and stood. He spent a moment in thought, trying to remember some tale that might interest the youngsters. His gaze unconsciously roamed the cavern, searching for some clue. It fell upon, and locked upon, the illusion-heightened basilisk effigy.

"Basilisk," Seldig explained.

"I know," Drizzt replied. "I have met such a creature." He turned casually back to the group and was startled by its appearance. Seldig and every one of his companions had rocked forward, their mouths hanging open in a mixture of expressed intrigue, terror, and delight.

"Dark elf! You have seen a basilisk?" one of them asked incredulously. "A real, living basilisk?"

Drizzt smiled as he came to decipher their amazement. The svirfnebli, unlike the dark elves, sheltered the younger members of their community. Though these deep gnomes were probably as old as Drizzt, they had rarely, if ever, been out of Blingdenstone. By their age, drow elves would have spent years patrolling the corridors beyond Menzoberranzan. Drizzt's recognition of the basilisk would not have been so unbelievable to the deep gnomes then, though the formidable monsters were rare even in the Underdark.

"You said that basilisks were not real!" one of the svirfnebli shouted to another, and he pushed him hard on the shoulder.

"Never I did!" the other protested, returning the shove.

"My uncle saw one once," offered another.

"Scrapings in the stone was all your uncle saw!" Seldig laughed. "They were the tracks of a basilisk, by his own proclamation."

Drizzt's smile widened. Basilisks were magical creatures, more common on other planes of existence. While drow, particularly the high priestesses, often opened gates to other planes, such monsters obviously were beyond the norm of svirfneblin life. Few were the deep gnomes who had ever looked upon a basilisk. Drizzt chuckled aloud. Fewer still, no doubt, were the deep gnomes who ever returned to tell that they had seen one!

"If your uncle followed the trail and found the monster," Seldig continued, "he would sit to this day as a pile of stone in a passageway! I say to you now that rocks do not tell such tales!"

The berated deep gnome looked around for some rebuttal. "Drizzt Do'Urden has seen one!" he protested. "He is not so much a pile of stone!" All eyes turned back to Drizzt.

"Have you really seen one, dark elf?" Seldig asked. "Answer only in truth, I beg."

"One," Drizzt replied.

"And you escaped from it before it could return the gaze?" Seldig asked, a question he and the other svirfnebli considered rhetorical.

"Escaped?" Drizzt echoed the gnomish word, unsure of its meaning.

"Escape . . . err . . . run away," Seldig explained. He looked to one of the other svirfnebli, who promptly feigned a look of sheer horror, then stumbled and scrambled frantically a few steps away. The other deep gnomes applauded the performance, and Drizzt joined in their laughter.

"You ran from the basilisk before it could return your gaze," Seldig reasoned.

Drizzt shrugged, a bit embarrassed, and Seldig guessed that he was withholding something.

"You did not run away?"

"I could not . . . escape," Drizzt explained. "The basilisk had invaded my home and had killed many of my rothé. Homes," he paused, searching for the correct svirfneblin word. "Sanctuaries," he explained at length, "are not commonplace in the wilds of the Underdark. Once found and secured, they must be defended at all costs."

"You fought it?" came an anonymous cry from the rear of the svirfneblin group.

"With stones from afar?" asked Seldig. "That is the accepted method."

Drizzt looked over at the pile of boulders the deep gnomes had been hurling at the effigy, then considered his own slender frame. "My arms could not even lift such stones." He laughed.

"Then how?" asked Seldig. "You must tell us."

Drizzt now had his story. He paused for a few moments, collecting his thoughts. He realized that his limited skills with his new language would not allow him to weave much of an intricate tale, so he decided to illustrate his words. He found two poles that the svirfnebli had been carrying, explained them as scimitars, then examined the effigy's construction to ensure that it would hold his weight.

The young deep gnomes huddled around anxiously as Drizzt set up the situation, detailing his darkness spell—actually placing one just beyond the basilisk's head—and the positioning of Guenhwyvar, his feline companion. The svirfnebli sat on their hands and leaned forward, gasping at every word. The effigy seemed to come alive in their minds, a lumbering monster, with Drizzt, this stranger to their world, lurking in the shadows behind it.

The drama played out and the time came for Drizzt to enact his movements in the battle. He heard the svirfnebli gasp in unison as he sprang lightly onto the basilisk's back, carefully picking his steps up toward the thing's head. Drizzt became caught up in their excitement, and this only heightened his memories.

It all became so real.

The deep gnomes moved in close, anticipating a dazzling display of swordsmanship from this remarkable drow who had come to them from the wilds of the Underdark.

Then something terrible happened.

One moment he was Drizzt the showman, entertaining his new friends with a tale of courage and weaponry. The next moment, as the drow lifted one of his pole props to strike at the phony monster, he was Drizzt no longer. The hunter stood atop the basilisk, just as he had that day back in the tunnels outside the moss filled cave.

Poles jabbed at the monster's eyes; poles slammed viciously into the stone head.

The svirfnebli backed away, some in fear, others in simple caution. The hunter pounded away, and the stone chipped and cracked. The slab that served as the creature's head broke away and fell, the dark elf tumbling behind. The hunter went down in a precise roll, came back to his feet, and charged right back in, slamming away furiously with his poles. The wooden weapons snapped apart and Drizzt's hands bled, but he—the hunter—would not yield.

Strong deep gnome hands grabbed the drow by the arms, trying to calm him. The hunter spun on his newest adversaries. They were stronger than he, and two held him tightly, but a few deft twists had the svirfnebli off balance. The hunter kicked at their knees and dropped to his own, turning about as he fell and launching the two svirfnebli into headlong rolls.

The hunter was up at once, broken scimitars at the ready as a single foe moved in at him.

Belwar showed no fear, held his arms defenselessly out wide. "Drizzt!" he called over and over. "Drizzt Do'Urden!"

The hunter eyed the svirfnebli's hammer and pick, and the sight of the mithral hands invoked soothing memories. Suddenly, he was Drizzt again. Stunned and ashamed, he dropped the poles and eyed his scraped hands.

Belwar caught the drow as he swooned, hoisted him up in his arms and carried him back to his hammock.

⚔ ⚔ ⚔ ⚔ ⚔

Troubled dreams invaded Drizzt's sleep, memories of the Underdark and of that other, darker self that he could not escape.

"How can I explain?" he asked Belwar when the burrow-warden found him sitting on the edge of the stone table later that night. "How can I possibly offer an apology?"

"None is needed," Belwar said to him.

Drizzt looked at him incredulously. "You do not understand," Drizzt began, wondering how he could possibly make the burrow-warden comprehend the depth of what had come over him.

"Many years you have lived out in the Underdark," Belwar said, "surviving where others could not."

"But have I survived?" Drizzt wondered aloud.

Belwar's hammer-hand patted the drow's shoulder gently, and the burrow-warden sat down on the table beside him. There they remained throughout the night. Drizzt said no more, and Belwar didn't press him. The burrow-warden knew his role that night: a silent support.

Neither knew how many hours had passed when Seldig's voice came in from beyond the door. "Come, Drizzt Do'Urden," the young deep gnome called. "Come and tell us more tales of the Underdark."

Drizzt looked at Belwar curiously, wondering if the request was part of some devious trick or ironic joke.

Belwar's smile dispelled that notion. "*Magga cammara*, dark elf," the deep gnome chuckled. "They'll not let you hide."

"Send them away," Drizzt insisted.

"So willing are you to surrender?" Belwar retorted, a distinct edge to his normally round-toned voice. "You who have survived the trials of the wilds?"

"Too dangerous," Drizzt explained desperately, searching for the words. "I cannot control . . . cannot be rid of . . ."

"Go with them, dark elf," Belwar said. "They will be more cautious this time."

"This . . . beast . . . follows me," Drizzt tried to explain.

"Perhaps for a while," the burrow-warden replied casually. "*Magga cammara*, Drizzt Do'Urden! Five tendays is not such a long time, not measured against the trials you have endured over the last ten years. Your freedom will be gained from this . . . beast."

Drizzt's lavender eyes found only sincerity in Belwar Dissengulp's dark gray orbs.

"But only if you seek it," the burrow-warden finished.

"Come out, Drizzt Do'Urden," Seldig called again from beyond the stone door.

This time, and every time in the days to come, Drizzt, and only Drizzt, answered the call.

⚔ ⚔ ⚔ ⚔ ⚔

The myconid king watched the dark elf prowl across the cavern's moss-covered lower level. It was not the same drow that had left, the fungoid knew, but Drizzt, an ally, had been the king's only previous contact with the dark elves. Oblivious to its peril, the eleven-foot giant crept down to intercept the stranger.

The spirit-wraith of Zaknafein did not even attempt to flee or hide as the animated mushroom-man closed in. Zaknafein's swords were comfortably set in his hands. The myconid king puffed a cloud of spores, seeking a telepathic conversation with the newcomer.

But undead monsters existed on two distinct planes, and their minds were impervious to such attempts. Zaknafein's material body faced the myconid, but the spirit-wraith's mind was far distant, linked to his corporeal form by Matron Malice's will. The spirit-wraith closed over the last few feet to his adversary.

The myconid puffed a second cloud, this one of spores designed to pacify an opponent, and this cloud was equally futile. The spirit-wraith came on steadily, and the giant raised its powerful arms to strike it down.

Zaknafein blocked the swings with quick cuts of his razor-edged swords, severing the myconid's hands. Too fast to follow, the spirit-wraith's weapons slashed at the king's mushroomlike torso, and dug deep wounds that drove the fungoid backward and to the ground.

From the top level, dozens of the older and stronger myconids lumbered down to rescue their injured king. The spirit-wraith saw their approach but did not know fear. Zaknafein finished his business with the giant, then turned calmly to meet the assault.

Fungus-men came on, blasting their various spores. Zaknafein ignored the clouds, none of which could possibly affect him, and concentrated fully on the clubbing arms. Myconids came charging in all around him.

And they died all around him.

They had tended their grove for centuries untold, living in peace and going about their own way. But when the spirit-wraith returned from the crawl-tunnel that led to the now-abandoned small cave that once had served as Drizzt's home, Zak's fury would tolerate no semblance of peace. Zaknafein rushed up the wall to the mushroom grove, hacking at everything in his path.

Giant mushrooms tumbled like cut trees. Below, the small rothé herd, nervous by nature, broke into a frenzied stampede and rushed out into the tunnels of the open Underdark. The few remaining fungus-men, having witnessed the power of this dark elf, scrambled to get out of his thrashing way. But myconids were not fast-moving creatures, and Zaknafein relentlessly chased them down.

Their reign in the moss-covered cave, and the mushroom grove they had tended for so very long, came to a sudden and final end.

# 9

# Whispers in the Tunnels

The svirfneblin patrol inched its way around the bends of the broken and twisting tunnel, war hammers and pickaxes held at the ready. The deep gnomes were not far from Blingdenstone—less than a day out—but they had gone into their practiced battle formations usually reserved for the deep Underdark.

The tunnel reeked of death.

The lead deep gnome, knowing that the carnage lay just beyond, gingerly peeked over a boulder. *Goblins!* his senses cried out to his companions, a clear voice in the racial empathy of the svirfnebli. When the dangers of the Underdark closed in on the deep gnomes, they rarely spoke aloud, reverting to a communal empathic bond that could convey basic thoughts.

The other svirfnebli clutched their weapons and began deciphering a battle plan from the excited jumble of their mental communications. The leader, still the only one who had peered over the boulder, halted them with an overriding notion. *Dead goblins!*

The others followed him around the boulder to the grisly scene. A score of goblins lay about, hacked and torn.

"Drow," one of the svirfneblin party whispered, after seeing the precision of the wounds and the obvious ease with which the blades had cut through the unfortunate creatures' hides. Among the Underdark races, only the drow wielded such slender and wicked-edged blades.

*Too close,* another deep gnome responded empathetically, punching the speaker on the shoulder.

"These have been dead for a day and more," another said aloud, refuting his companion's caution. "The dark elves would not lie in wait in the area. It is not their way."

"Nor is it their way to slaughter bands of goblins," the one who had insisted on the silent communications replied. "Not when there are prisoners to be taken!"

"They would take prisoners only if they meant to return directly to Menzoberranzan," remarked the first. He turned to the leader. "Burrow-Warden Krieger, at once we must go back to Blingdenstone and report this carnage!"

"A thin report it would be," Krieger replied. "Dead goblins in the tunnels? It is not such an uncommon sight."

"This is not the first sign of drow activity in the region," the other remarked. The burrow-warden could deny neither the truth of his companion's words nor the wisdom of the suggestion. Two other patrols had returned to Blingdenstone recently with tales of dead monsters—most probably slain by drow elves—lying in the corridors of the Underdark.

"And look," the other deep gnome continued, bending low to scoop a pouch off one of the goblins. He opened it to reveal a handful of gold and silver coins. "What dark elf would be so impatient as to leave such booty behind?"

"Can we be sure that this was the doings of the drow?" Krieger asked, though he himself did not doubt the fact. "Perhaps some other creature has come to our realm. Or possibly some lesser foe, goblin or orc, has found drow weapons."

*Drow!* the thoughts of several of the others agreed immediately.

"The cuts were swift and precise," said one. "And I see nothing to indicate any wounds beyond those suffered by the goblins. Who else but dark elves are so efficient in their killing?"

Burrow-Warden Krieger walked off alone a bit farther down the passage, searching the stone for some clue to this mystery. Deep gnomes possessed an affinity to the rock beyond that of most creatures, but this passage's stone walls told the burrow-warden nothing. The goblins had been killed by weapons, not the clawed hands of monsters, yet they hadn't been looted. All of the kills were confined to a small area, showing that the unfortunate goblins hadn't even found the time to flee. That twenty goblins were cut down so quickly implicated a drow patrol of some size, and even if there had been only a handful of the dark elves, one of them, at least, would have pillaged the bodies.

"Where shall we go, Burrow-Warden?" one of the deep gnomes asked at Krieger's back. "Onward to scout out the reported mineral cache or back to Blingdenstone to report this?"

Krieger was a wily old svirfneblin who thought that he knew every trick of the Underdark. He wasn't fond of mysteries, but this scene had him scratching his bald head without a clue. Back, he relayed to the others, reverting to the silent empathic method. He found no arguments among his kin; deep gnomes always took great care to avoid drow elves whenever possible.

The patrol promptly shifted into a tight defensive formation and began its trek back home.

Levitating off to the side, in the shadows of the high ceiling's stalactites, the spirit-wraith of Zaknafein Do'Urden watched their progress and marked well their path.

⚔ ⚔ ⚔ ⚔ ⚔

King Schnicktick leaned forward in his stone throne and considered the burrow-warden's words carefully. Schnicktick's councilors, seated around him, were equally curious and nervous, for this report only confirmed the two previous tales of potential drow activity in the eastern tunnels.

"Why would Menzoberranzan be edging in on our borders?" one of the councilors asked when Krieger had finished. "Our agents have made no mention of any intent of war. Surely we would have had some indications if Menzoberranzan's ruling council planned something dramatic."

"We would," King Schnicktick agreed, to silence the nervous chatter that sprang up in the wake of the councilor's grim words. "To all of you I offer the reminder that we do not know if the perpetrators of these reported kills were drow elves at all."

"Your pardon, my King," Krieger began tentatively.

"Yes, Burrow-Warden," Schnicktick replied immediately, slowly waving one stubby hand before his craggy face to prevent any protests. "You are quite certain of your observations. And well enough do I know you to trust in your judgments. Until this drow patrol has been seen, however, no assumptions will I make."

"Then we may agree only that something dangerous has invaded our eastern region," another of the councilors put in.

"Yes," answered the svirfneblin king. "We must set about discovering the truth of the matter. The eastern tunnels are therefore sealed from further mining expeditions." Schnicktick again waved his hands to calm the ensuing groans. "I know that several promising veins of ore have been reported—we will get to them as soon as we may. But for the present, the east, northeast, and southeast regions are hereby declared war patrol exclusive. The patrols will be doubled, both in the number of groups and in the size of each, and their range will be extended to encompass all the region within a three-day march of Blingdenstone. Quickly must this mystery be resolved."

"What of our agents in the drow city?" asked a councilor. "Should we make contact?"

Schnicktick held his palms out. "Be at ease," he explained. "We will keep our ears open wide, but let us not inform our enemies that we suspect their movements." The svirfneblin king did not have to express his concerns that their agents within Menzoberranzan could not be entirely relied upon. The informants might readily accept svirfneblin gemstones in exchange for minor information, but if the powers of Menzoberranzan were planning something drastic in Blingdenstone's direction, agents would quite likely work double-deals against the deep gnomes.

"If we hear any unusual reports from Menzoberranzan," the king continued, "or if we discover that the intruders are indeed drow elves, then we will increase our network's actions. Until then, let the patrols learn what they may."

The king dismissed his council then, preferring to remain alone in his throne room to consider the grim news. Earlier that same tenday, Schnicktick had heard of Drizzt's savage attack on the basilisk effigy.

Lately, it seemed, King Schnicktick of Blingdenstone had heard too much of dark elves' exploits.

⚔ ⚔ ⚔ ⚔ ⚔

The svirfneblin scouting patrols moved farther out into the eastern tunnels. Even those groups that found nothing came back to Blingdenstone full of suspicions, for they had sensed a stillness in the Underdark beyond the quiet norm. Not a single svirfneblin had been injured so far, but none seemed anxious to travel out on the patrols. There was something evil in the tunnels, they knew instinctively, something that killed without question and without mercy.

One patrol found the moss-covered cavern that once had served as Drizzt's sanctuary. King Schnicktick was saddened when he heard that the peaceable myconids and their treasured mushroom grove were destroyed.

Yet, for all of the endless hours the svirfnebli spent wandering the tunnels, not an enemy did they spot. They continued with their assumption that dark elves, so secretive and brutal, were involved.

"And we now have a drow living in our city," a deep gnome councilor reminded the king during one of their daily sessions.

"Has he caused any trouble?" Schnicktick asked.

"Minor," replied the councilor. "And Belwar Dissengulp, the Most Honored Burrow-Warden, speaks for him still and keeps him in his house as guest, not prisoner. Burrow-Warden Dissengulp will accept no guards around the drow."

"Have the drow watched," the king said after a moment of consideration. "But from a distance. If he is a friend, as Master Dissengulp most obviously believes, then he should not suffer our intrusions."

"And what of the patrols?" asked another councilor, this one a representative from the entrance cavern that housed the city guard. "My soldiers grow weary. They have seen nothing beyond a few signs of battle, have heard nothing but the scrape of their own tired feet."

"We must be alert," King Schnicktick reminded him. "If the dark elves are massing . . ."

"They are not," the councilor replied firmly. "We have found no camp, nor any trace of a camp. This patrol from Menzoberranzan, if it is a patrol, attacks and then retreats to some sanctuary we cannot locate, possibly magically inspired."

"And if the dark elves truly meant to attack Blingdenstone," offered another, "would they leave so many signs of their activity? The first slaughter, the goblins found by Burrow-Warden Krieger's expedition, occurred nearly a tenday ago, and the tragedy of the myconids was some time before that. I have never heard of dark elves wandering about an enemy city, and leaving signs such as slaughtered goblins, for days before they execute their full attack."

The king had been thinking along the same lines for some time. When he awoke each day and found Blingdenstone intact, the threat of a war with Menzoberranzan seemed more distant. but though Schnicktick took comfort in the similar reasoning of his councilor, he could not ignore the gruesome scenes his soldiers had been finding in the eastern tunnels. Something, probably drow, was down there, too close for his liking.

"Let us assume that Menzoberranzan does not plan war against us at this time," Schnicktick offered. "Then why are drow elves so close to our doorway? Why would drow elves haunt the eastern tunnels of Blingdenstone, so far from home?"

"Expansion?" replied one councilor.

"Renegade raiders?" questioned another. Neither possibility seemed very likely. Then a third councilor chirped in a suggestion, so simple that it caught the others off guard.

"They are looking for something."

The king of the svirfnebli dropped his dimpled chin heavily into his hands, thinking he had just heard a possible solution to the puzzle and feeling foolish that he had not thought of it before.

"But what?" asked one of the councilors, obviously feeling the same. "Dark elves rarely mine the stone—they do not do it very well when they try, I must add—and they would not have to go so far from Menzoberranzan to find precious minerals. What, so near to Blingdenstone, might the dark elves be looking for?"

"Something they have lost," replied the king. Immediately his thoughts went to the drow that had come to live among his people. It all seemed too much of a coincidence to be ignored. "Or someone," Schnicktick added, and the others did not miss his point.

"Perhaps we should invite our drow guest to sit with us in council?"

"No," the king replied. "But perhaps our distant surveillance of this Drizzt is not enough. Get orders to Belwar Dissengulp that the drow is to be monitored every minute. and Firble," he said to the councilor nearest him. "Since we have reasonably concluded that no war is imminent with the dark elves, set the spy network into motion. Get me information from Menzoberranzan, and quickly. I like not the prospect of dark elves wandering about my front door. It does so diminish the neighborhood."

Councilor Firble, the chief of covert security in Blingdenstone, nodded in agreement, though he wasn't pleased by the request. Information from Menzoberranzan was not cheaply gained, and it as often turned out to be a calculated deception as the truth. Firble did not like dealing with anyone or anything that could outsmart him, and he numbered dark elves as first on that ill-favored list.

⚔ ⚔ ⚔ ⚔ ⚔

The spirit-wraith watched as yet another svirfneblin patrol made its way down the twisting tunnel. The tactical wisdom of the being that once had been the finest weapon master in all of Menzoberranzan had kept the undead monster and his anxious sword arm in check for the last few days. Zaknafein did not truly understand the significance of the increasing number of deep gnome patrols, but he sensed that his mission would be put into jeopardy if he struck out against one of them. At the very least, his attack against so organized a foe would send alarms ringing throughout the corridors, alarms that the elusive Drizzt surely would hear.

Similarly, the spirit-wraith had sublimated his vicious urges against other living things and had left the svirfneblin patrols nothing to find in the last few days, purposely avoiding conflicts with the many denizens of the region. Matron Malice Do'Urden's evil will followed Zaknafein's every move, pounding relentlessly at his thoughts, urging him on with a great vengeance. Any killing that Zaknafein did sated that insidious will temporarily, but the undead thing's tactical wisdom overruled the savage summons. The slight flicker that was Zaknafein's remaining reasoning knew that he would only find his return to the peace of death when Drizzt Do'Urden joined him in his eternal sleep.

The spirit-wraith kept his swords in their sheaths as he watched the deep gnomes pass by.

Then, as still another group of weary svirfnebli made its way back to the west, another flicker of cognition stirred within the spirit-wraith. If these deep gnomes were so prominent in this region, it seemed likely that Drizzt Do'Urden would have encountered them.

This time, Zaknafein did not let the deep gnomes wander out beyond his sight. He floated down from the concealment of the stalactite-strewn ceiling and fell into pace behind the patrol. The name of Blingdenstone bobbed at the edge of his conscious grasp, a memory of his past life.

"Blingdenstone," the spirit-wraith tried to speak aloud, the first word Matron Malice's undead monster had tried to utter. But the name came out as no more than an undecipherable snarl.

# 10
# Belwar's Guilt

Drizzt went out with Seldig and his new friends many times during the passing days. The young deep gnomes, on advice from Belwar, kept their time with the drow elf in calm and unobtrusive games; no more did they press Drizzt for re-enactments of exciting battles he had fought in the wilds.

For the first few times Drizzt went out, Belwar watched him from the door. The burrow-warden did trust Drizzt, but he also understood the trials the drow had endured. A life of savagery and brutality such as the one Drizzt had known could not so easily be dismissed.

Soon, though, it became apparent to Belwar, and to all the others who observed Drizzt, that the drow had settled into a comfortable rhythm with the young deep gnomes and posed little threat to any of the svirfnebli of Blingdenstone. Even King Schnicktick, worried of the events beyond the city's borders, came to agree that Drizzt could be trusted.

"You have a visitor," Belwar said to Drizzt one morning. Drizzt followed the burrow-warden's movements to the stone door, thinking Seldig had come to call on him early this day. When Belwar opened the door, though, Drizzt nearly toppled over in surprise, for it was no svirfneblin that bounded into the stone structure. Rather, it was a huge and black feline form.

"Guenhwyvar!" Drizzt cried out, dropping into a low crouch to catch the rushing panther. Guenhwyvar bowled him over, playfully swatting him with a great paw.

When at last Drizzt managed to get out from under the panther and into a sitting position, Belwar walked over to him and handed him the onyx figurine. "Surely the councilor charged with examining the panther was sorry to part with it," the burrow-warden said. "But Guenhwyvar is your friend, first and most."

Drizzt could not find the words to reply. Even before the panther's return, the deep gnomes of Blingdenstone had treated him better than he deserved, or so he believed. Now for the svirfnebli to return so powerful a magical item, to show him such absolute trust, touched him deeply.

"At your leisure you may return to the House Center, the building in which you were detained when first you came to us," Belwar went on, "and retrieve your weapons and armor."

Drizzt was a bit tentative at the notion, remembering the incident at the mock-up of the basilisk. What damage might he have wrought that day if he had been armed, not with poles, but with fine drow scimitars?

"We will keep them here and keep them safe," Belwar said, understanding his friend's sudden distress. "If you need them, you will have them."

"I am in your debt," Drizzt replied. "In the debt of all Blingdenstone."

"We do not consider friendship a debt," the burrow-warden replied with a wink. He left Drizzt and Guenhwyvar then and went back into the cave-room of his house, allowing the two dear friends a private reunion.

Seldig and the other young deep gnomes were in for quite a treat that day when Drizzt came out to join them with Guenhwyvar by his side. Seeing the cat at play with the svirfnebli, Drizzt could not help but remember that tragic day, a decade before, when Masoj had used Guenhwyvar to hunt down the last of Belwar's fleeing miners. Apparently, Guenhwyvar had dismissed that awful memory altogether, for the panther and the young deep gnomes frolicked together for the entire day.

Drizzt wished only that he could so readily dismiss the errors of his past.

⚔ ⚔ ⚔ ⚔ ⚔

"Most Honored Burrow-Warden," came a call a couple of days later, while Belwar and Drizzt were enjoying their morning meal. Belwar paused and sat perfectly still, and Drizzt did not miss the unexpected cloud of pain that crossed his host's broad features. Drizzt had come to know the svirfneblin so very well, and when Belwar's long, hawklike nose turned up in a certain way, it inevitably signaled the burrow-warden's distress.

"The king has reopened the eastern tunnels," the voice continued. "There are rumors of a thick vein of ore only a day's march. It would do honor to my expedition if Belwar Dissengulp would find his way to accompany us."

A hopeful smile widened on Drizzt's face, not for any thoughts he had of venturing out, but because he had noticed that Belwar seemed a bit too reclusive in the otherwise open svirfneblin community.

"Burrow-Warden Brickers," Belwar explained to Drizzt grimly, not sharing the drow's budding enthusiasm in the least. "One of those who comes to my door before every expedition, bidding me to join in the journey."

"And you never go," Drizzt reasoned.

Belwar shrugged. "A courtesy call, nothing more," he said, his nose twitching and his wide teeth grating together.

"You are not worthy to march beside them," Drizzt added, his tone dripping with sarcasm. At last, he believed, he had found the source of his friend's frustration.

Again Belwar shrugged.

Drizzt scowled at him. "I have seen you at work with your mithral hands," he said. "You would be no detriment to any party! Indeed, far more! Do you so quickly consider yourself crippled, when those about you do not?"

Belwar slammed his hammer-hand down on the table, sending a fair-sized crack running through the stone. "I can cut rock faster than the lot of them!" the burrow-warden growled fiercely. "And if monsters descended upon us . . ." He waved his pickaxe-hand in a menacing way, and Drizzt did not doubt that the barrel-chested deep gnome could put the instrument to good use.

"Enjoy the day, Most Honored Burrow-Warden," came a final cry from outside the door. "As ever, we shall respect your decision, but as ever, we also shall lament your absence."

Drizzt stared curiously at Belwar. "Why, then?" he asked at length. "If you are as competent as all—yourself included—agree, why do you remain behind? I know the love svirfnebli have for such expeditions, yet you are not interested. Nor do you ever speak of your own adventures outside Blingdenstone. Is it my presence that holds you at home? Are you bound to watch over me?"

"No," Belwar replied, his booming voice echoing back several times in Drizzt's keen ears. "You have been granted the return of your weapons, dark elf. Do not doubt our trust."

"But . . ." Drizzt began, but he stopped short, suddenly realizing the truth of the deep gnome's reluctance. "The fight," he said softly, almost apologetically. "That evil day more than a decade ago."

Belwar's nose verily rolled up over itself, and he briskly turned away.

"You blame yourself for the loss of your kin!" Drizzt continued, gaining volume as he gained confidence in his reasoning. Still, the drow could hardly believe his words as he spoke them.

But when Belwar turned back on him, the burrow-warden's eyes were rimmed with wetness and Drizzt knew that the words had struck home.

Drizzt ran a hand through his thick white mane, not really knowing how to respond to Belwar's dilemma. Drizzt personally had led the drow party against the svirfnebli mining group, and he knew that no blame for the disaster could rightly be placed on any of the deep gnomes. Yet, how could Drizzt possibly explain that to Belwar?

"I remember that fated day," Drizzt began tentatively. "Vividly I remember it, as if that evil moment will be frozen in my thoughts, never to recede."

"No more than in mine," the burrow-warden whispered. Drizzt nodded his accord. "Equally, though," he said, "for I find myself caught within the very same web of guilt that entraps you."

Belwar looked at him curiously, not really understanding.

"It was I who led the drow patrol," Drizzt explained. "I found your troupe, errantly believing you to be marauders intending to descend upon Menzoberranzan."

"If not you, then another," Belwar replied.

"But none could have led them as well as I," Drizzt said. "Out there—" he glanced at the door—"in the wilds, I was at home. That was my domain."

Belwar was listening to his every word now, just as Drizzt had hoped.

"And it was I who defeated the earth elemental," Drizzt continued, speaking matter-of-factly, not cockily. "Had it not been for my presence, the battle would have proved equal. Many svirfnebli would have survived to return to Blingdenstone."

Belwar could not hide his smile. There was a measure of truth in Drizzt's words, for Drizzt had indeed been a major factor in the drow attack's success. But Belwar found Drizzt's attempt to dispel his guilt a bit of a stretch of the truth.

"I do not understand how you can blame yourself," Drizzt said, now smiling and hoping that his levity would bring some measure of comfort to his friend. "With Drizzt Do'Urden at the lead of the drow party, you never had a chance"

"*Magga cammara*! It is a painful subject to jest of," Belwar replied, though he chuckled in spite of himself even as he spoke the words.

"Agreed," said Drizzt, his tone suddenly serious. "But dismissing the tragedy in a jest is no more ridiculous than living mired in guilt for a blameless incident. No, not blameless," Drizzt quickly corrected himself. "The blame lies on the shoulders of Menzoberranzan and its inhabitants. It is the way of the drow that caused the tragedy. It is the wicked existence they live, every day, that doomed your expedition's peaceable miners."

"Charged with the responsibility of his group is a burrow-warden," Belwar retorted. "Only a burrow-warden may call an expedition. He must then accept the responsibility of his decision."

"You chose to lead the deep gnomes so close to Menzoberranzan?" Drizzt asked.

"I did."

"Of your own volition?" Drizzt pressed. He believed that he understood the ways of the deep gnomes well enough to know that most, if not all, of their important decisions were democratically resolved. "Without the word of Belwar Dissengulp, the mining party would never have come into that region?"

"We knew of the find," Belwar explained. "A rich cache of ore. It was decided in council that we should risk the nearness to Menzoberranzan. I led the appointed party."

"If not you, then another," Drizzt said pointedly, mimicking Belwar's earlier words.

"A burrow-warden must accept the respons—" Belwar began, his gaze drifting away from Drizzt.

"They do not blame you," Drizzt said, following Belwar's empty stare to the blank stone door. "They honor you and care for you."

"They pity me!" Belwar snarled.

"Do you need their pity?" Drizzt cried back. "Are you less than they? A helpless cripple?"

"Never I was!"

"Then go out with them!" Drizzt yelled at him. "See if they truly pity you. I do not believe that at all, but if your assumptions prove true, if your people do pity their 'Most Honored Burrow-Warden,' then show them the truth of Belwar Dissengulp! If your companions mantle upon you neither pity nor blame, then do not place either burden upon your own shoulders!"

Belwar stared at his friend for a very long moment, but he did not reply.

"All the miners who accompanied you knew the risk of venturing so close to Menzoberranzan," Drizzt reminded him. A smile widened on Drizzt's face. "None of them, yourself included, knew that Drizzt Do'Urden would lead your drow opponents against you. If you had, you certainly would have stayed at home."

"*Magga cammara*," Belwar mumbled. He shook his head in disbelief, both at Drizzt's joking attitude and at the fact that, for the first time in over a decade, he did feel better about those tragic memories. He rose up from the stone table, flashed a grin at Drizzt, and headed for the inner room of his house.

"Where are you going?" Drizzt asked.

"To rest," replied the burrow-warden. "The events of this day have already wearied me."

"The mining expedition will depart without you."

Belwar turned back and cast an incredulous stare at Drizzt. Did the drow really expect that Belwar would so easily refute years of guilt and just go bounding off with the miners?

"I had thought Belwar Dissengulp possessed more courage," Drizzt said to him. The scowl that crossed the burrow-warden's face was genuine, and Drizzt knew that he had found a weakness in Belwar's armor of self-pity.

"Boldly do you speak," Belwar growled through a grimace.

"Boldly to a coward," Drizzt replied. The mithral-handed svirfneblin stalked in, his breathing coming in great heaves of his densely muscled chest.

"If you do not like the title, then cast it away!" Drizzt growled in his face. "Go with the miners. Show them the truth of Belwar Dissengulp, and learn it for yourself!"

Belwar banged his mithral hands together. "Run out then and get your weapons!" he commanded. Drizzt hesitated. Had he just been challenged? Had he gone too far in his attempt to shake the burrow-warden loose of his guilty bonds?

"Get your weapons, Drizzt Do'Urden," Belwar growled again, "for if I am to go with the miners, then so are you!"

Elated, Drizzt clasped the deep gnome's head between his long, slender hands and banged his forehead softly into Belwar's, the two exchanging stares of deep admiration and affection. In an instant, Drizzt rushed away, scrambling to the House Central to retrieve his suit of finely meshed chain mail, his *piwafwi*, and his scimitars.

Belwar just banged a hand against his head in disbelief, nearly knocking himself from his feet, and watched Drizzt's wild dash out of the front door.

It would prove an interesting trip.

⚔⚔⚔⚔⚔

Burrow-Warden Brickers accepted Belwar and Drizzt readily, though he gave Belwar a curious look behind Drizzt's back, inquiring as to the drow's respectability. Even the doubting burrow-warden could not deny the value of a dark elf ally out in the wilds of the Underdark, particularly if the whispers of drow activity in the eastern tunnels proved to be true.

But the patrol saw no activity, or carnage, as they proceeded to the region named by the scouts. The rumors of a thick vein of ore were not exaggerated in the least, and the twenty-five miners of the expedition went to work with an eagerness unlike any the drow had ever witnessed. Drizzt was especially pleased for Belwar, for the burrow-warden's hammer and pickaxe hands chopped away at the stone with a precision and power that outdid any of the others. It didn't take long for Belwar to realize that he was not being pitied by his comrades in any way. He was a member of the expedition—an honored member and no detriment—who filled the wagons with more ore than any of his companions.

Through the days they spent in the twisting tunnels, Drizzt, and Guenhwyvar, when the cat was available, kept a watchful guard around the camp. After the first day of mining, Burrow-Warden Brickers assigned a third companion guard for the drow and panther, and Drizzt suspected correctly that his new svirfneblin companion had been appointed as much to watch him as to look for dangers from beyond. As the time passed, though, and the svirfneblin troupe became more accustomed to their ebon-skinned companion, Drizzt was left to roam about as he chose.

It was an uneventful and profitable trip, just the way the svirfnebli liked it, and soon, having encountered not a single monster, their wagons were filled with precious minerals. Clapping each other on the backs—Belwar being careful not to pat too hard—they gathered up their equipment, formed their pull-carts into a line, and set off for home, a journey that would take them two days bearing the heavy wagons.

After only a few hours of travel, one of the scouts ahead of the caravan returned, his face grim.

"What is it?" Burrow-Warden Brickers prompted, suspecting that their good fortune had ended.

"Goblin tribe," the svirfneblin scout replied. "Two score at the least. They have put up in a small chamber ahead—to the west and up a sloping passage."

Burrow-Warden Brickers banged a fist into a wagon. He did not doubt that his miners could handle the goblin band, but he wanted no trouble. Yet with the heavy wagons rumbling along noisily, avoiding the goblins would be no easy feat. "Pass the word back that we sit quiet," he decided at length. "If a fight there will be, let the goblins come to us."

"What is the trouble?" Drizzt asked Belwar as he came in at the back of the caravan. He had kept a rear guard since the troupe had broken camp.

"Band of goblins," Belwar replied. "Brickers says we stay low and hope they pass us by."

"And if they do not?" Drizzt had to ask.

Belwar tapped his hands together. "They're only goblins," he muttered grimly, "but I, and all my kin, wish the path had stayed clear."

It pleased Drizzt that his new companions were not so anxious for battle, even against an enemy they knew they could easily defeat. If Drizzt had been traveling beside a drow party, the whole of the goblin tribe probably would be dead or captured already.

"Come with me," Drizzt said to Belwar. "I need you to help Burrow-Warden Brickers understand me. I have a plan, but I fear that my limited command of your language will not allow me to explain its subtleties."

Belwar hooked Drizzt with his pickaxe-hand, spinning the slender drow about more roughly than he had intended. "No conflicts do we desire," he explained. "Better that the goblins go their own way."

"I wish for no fight," Drizzt assured him with a wink. Satisfied, the deep gnome fell into step behind Drizzt.

Brickers smiled widely as Belwar translated Drizzt's plan. "The expressions on the goblins' faces will be well worth seeing," Brickers laughed to Drizzt. "I should like to accompany you myself!"

"Better left for me," Belwar said. "Both the goblin and drow languages are known to me, and you have responsibilities back here, in case things do not go as we hope."

"The goblin tongue is known to me as well," Brickers replied. "And I can understand our dark elf companion well enough. As for my duties with the caravan, they are not as great as you believe, for another burrow-warden accompanies us this day."

"One who has not seen the wilds of the Underdark for many years," Belwar reminded him.

"Ah, but he was the finest of his trade," retorted Brickers. "The caravan is under your command, Burrow-Warden Belwar. I choose to go and meet with the goblins beside the drow."

Drizzt had understood enough of the words to fathom Brickers's general course of action. Before Belwar could argue, Drizzt put a hand on his shoulder and nodded. "If the goblins are not fooled and we need you, come in fast and hard," he said.

Then Brickers removed his gear and weapons, and Drizzt led him away. Belwar turned to the others cautiously, not knowing how they would feel about the decision. His first glance at the caravan's miners told him that they stood firmly behind him, every one, waiting and willing to carry out his commands.

Burrow-Warden Brickers was not the least disappointed with the expressions on the goblins' toothy and twisted faces when he and Drizzt walked into their midst. One goblin let out a shriek and lifted a spear to throw, but Drizzt, using his innate magical abilities, dropped a globe of darkness over its head, blinding it fully. The spear came out anyway and Drizzt snapped out a scimitar and sliced it from the air as it flew by.

Brickers, his hands bound, for he was emulating a prisoner in this farce, dropped his jaw open at the speed and ease with which the drow took down the flying spear. The svirfneblin then looked to the band of goblins and saw that they were similarly impressed.

"One more step and they are dead," Drizzt promised in the goblin tongue, a guttural language of grunts and whimpers. Brickers came to understand a moment later when he heard a wild shuffle of boots and a whimper from behind. The deep gnome turned to see two goblins, limned by the dancing purplish flames of the drow's faerie fire, scrambling away as fast as their floppy feet could carry them.

Again the svirfneblin looked at Drizzt in amazement. How had Drizzt even known that the sneaky goblins were back there?

Brickers, of course, could not know of the hunter, that other self of Drizzt Do'Urden that gave this drow a distinct edge in encounters such as this. Nor could the burrow-warden know that at that moment Drizzt was engaged in yet another struggle to control that dangerous alter ego.

Drizzt looked at the scimitar in his hand and back to the crowd of goblins. At least three dozen of them stood ready, yet the hunter beckoned Drizzt to attack, to bite hard into the cowardly monsters and send them fleeing down every passageway leading out of the room. One look at his bound svirfneblin companion, though, reminded Drizzt of his plan in coming here and allowed him to put the hunter to rest.

"Who is the leader?" he asked in guttural goblin.

The goblin chieftain was not so anxious to single itself out to a drow elf, but a dozen of its subordinates, showing typical goblin courage and loyalty, spun on their heels and poked their stubby fingers in its direction.

With no other choice, the goblin chieftain puffed out its chest, straightened its bony shoulders, and strode forward to face the drow. "Bruck!" the chieftain named itself, thumping a fist into its chest.

"Why are you here?" Drizzt sneered as he said it.

Bruck simply did not know how to answer such a question. Never before had the goblin thought to ask permission for its tribe's movements.

"This region belongs to the drow!" Drizzt growled. "You do not belong here!"

"Drow city many walks," Bruck complained, pointing over Drizzt's head—the wrong way to Menzoberranzan, Drizzt noted, but he let the error pass. "This svirfneblin land."

"For now," replied Drizzt, prodding Brickers with the butt of his scimitar. "But my people have decided to claim the region as our own." A small flame flickered in Drizzt's lavender eyes and a devious smile spread across his face. "Will Bruck and the goblin tribe oppose us?"

Bruck held its long-fingered hands out helplessly.

"Be gone!" Drizzt demanded. "We have no need of slaves now, nor do we wish the revealing sound of battle echoing down the tunnels! Name yourself as lucky, Bruck. Your tribe will flee and live . . . this time!"

Bruck turned to the others, looking for some assistance. Only one drow elf had come against them, while more than three dozen goblins stood ready with their weapons. The odds were promising if not overwhelming.

"Be gone!" Drizzt commanded, pointing his scimitar at a side passage. "Run until your feet grow too weary to carry you!"

The goblin chieftain defiantly hooked its fingers into the piece of rope holding up its loincloth.

A cacophonous banging sounded all around the small chamber then, showing the tempo of purposeful drumming on the stone. Bruck and the other goblins looked around nervously, and Drizzt did not miss the opportunity.

"You dare defy us?" the drow cried, causing Bruck to be edged by the purple-glowing flames. "Then let stupid Bruck be the first to die!"

Before Drizzt even finished the sentence, the goblin chieftain was gone, running with all speed down the passage Drizzt had indicated. Justifying the flight as loyalty to their chieftain, the whole lot of the goblin tribe set off in quick pursuit. The swiftest even passed Bruck by.

A few moments later, Belwar and the other svirfneblin miners appeared at every passage. "Thought you might need some support," the mithral-handed burrow-warden explained, tapping his hammer hand on the stone.

"Perfect was your timing and your judgment, Most Honored Burrow-Warden," Brickers said to his peer when he managed to stop laughing. "Perfect, as we have come to expect from Belwar Dissengulp!"

A short while later, the svirfneblin caravan started on its way again, the whole troupe excited and elated by the events of the last few days. The deep gnomes thought themselves very clever in the way they had avoided trouble. The gaiety turned into a full-fledged party when they arrived in Blingdenstone—and svirfnebli, though usually a serious, work-minded people, threw parties as well as any race in all the Realms.

Drizzt Do'Urden, for all of his physical differences with the svirfnebli, felt more at home and at ease than he had ever felt in all the four decades of his life.

And never again did Belwar Dissengulp flinch when a fellow svirfneblin addressed him as "Most Honored Burrow-Warden."

The spirit-wraith was confused. Just as Zaknafein had begun to believe that his prey was within the svirfneblin city, the magical spells that Malice had placed upon him sensed Drizzt's presence in the tunnels. Luckily for Drizzt and the svirfneblin miners, the spirit-wraith had been far away when he caught the scent. Zaknafein worked his way back through the tunnels, dodging deep gnome patrols. Every potential encounter he avoided proved a struggle for Zaknafein, for Matron Malice, back on her throne in Menzoberranzan, grew increasingly impatient and agitated.

Malice wanted the taste of blood, but Zaknafein kept to his purpose, closing in on Drizzt. But then, suddenly, the scent was gone.

⚔ ⚔ ⚔ ⚔ ⚔

Bruck groaned aloud when another solitary dark elf wandered into his encampment the next day. No spears were hoisted and no goblins even attempted to sneak up behind this one.

"We went as we were ordered!" Bruck complained, moving to the front of the group before he was called upon. The goblin chieftain knew now that his underlings would point him out anyway.

If the spirit-wraith even understood the goblin's words, he did not show it in any way. Zaknafein kept walking straight at the goblin chieftain, his swords in his hands.

"But we—" Bruck began, but the rest of his words came out as gurgles of blood. Zaknafein tore his sword out of the goblin's throat and rushed at the rest of the group.

Goblins scattered in all directions. A few, trapped between the crazed drow and the stone wall, raised crude spears in defense. The spirit wraith waded through them, hacking away weapons and limbs with every slice. One goblin poked through the spinning swords, the tip of its spear burying deep into Zaknafein's hip.

The undead monster didn't even flinch. Zak turned on the goblin and struck it with a series of lightning-fast, perfectly aimed blows that took its head and both of its arms from its body.

In the end, fifteen goblins lay dead in the chamber and the tribe was scattered and still running down every passage in the region. The spirit-wraith, covered in the blood of his enemies, exited the chamber through the passage opposite from the one in which he had entered, continuing his frustrated search for the elusive Drizzt Do'Urden.

⚔ ⚔ ⚔ ⚔ ⚔

Back in Menzoberranzan, in the anteroom to the chapel of House Do'Urden, Matron Malice rested, thoroughly exhausted and momentarily sated. She had felt every kill as Zaknafein made it, had felt a burst of ecstacy every time her spirit-wraith's sword had plunged into another victim.

Malice pushed away her frustrations and her impatience, her confidence renewed by the pleasures of Zaknafein's cruel slaughter. How great Malice's ecstacy would be when the spirit-wraith at last encountered her traitorous son!

# II
# THE INFORMANT

Councilor Firble of Blingdenstone moved tentatively into the small rough-hewn cavern, the appointed meeting place. An army of svirfnebli, including several deep gnome enchanters holding stones that could summon earth elemental allies, moved into defensive positions all along the corridors to the west of the room. Despite this, Firble was not at ease. He looked down the eastern tunnel, the only other entrance into the chamber, wondering what information his agent would have for him and worrying over how much it would cost.

Then the drow made his swaggering entrance, his high black boots kicking loudly on the stone. His gaze darted about quickly to ensure that Firble was the only svirfneblin in the chamber—their usual deal—then strode up to the deep gnome councilor and dropped into a low bow.

"Greetings, little friend with the big purse," the drow said with a laugh. His command of the svirfneblin language and dialect, with the perfect inflections and pauses of a deep gnome who had lived a century in Blingdenstone, always amazed Firble.

"You could exercise some caution," Firble retorted, again glancing around anxiously.

"Bah," the drow snorted, clicking the hard heels of his boots together. "You have an army of deep gnome fighters and wizards behind you, and I . . . well, let us just agree that I am well protected as well."

"That fact I do not doubt, Jarlaxle," Firble replied. "Still, I would prefer that our business remain as private and as secretive as possible."

"All of the business of Bregan D'aerthe is private, my dear Firble," Jarlaxle answered, and again he bowed low, sweeping his wide-brimmed hat in a long and graceful arc.

"Enough of that," said Firble. "Let us be done with our business, so that I may return to my home."

"Then ask," said Jarlaxle.

"There has been an increase in drow activity near Blingdenstone," explained the deep gnome.

"Has there?" Jarlaxle asked, appearing surprised. The drow's smirk revealed his true emotions, though. This would be an easy profit for Jarlaxle, for the very same matron mother in Menzoberranzan who had recently employed him was undoubtedly connected with the Blingdenstone's distress. Jarlaxle liked coincidences that made the profits come easy.

Firble knew the ploy of feigned surprise all too well. "There has," he said firmly.

"And you wish to know why?" Jarlaxle reasoned, still holding a facade of ignorance.

"It would seem prudent, from our vantage point," huffed the councilor, tired of Jarlaxle's unending game. Firble knew without any doubts that Jarlaxle was aware of the drow activity near Blingdenstone, and of the purpose behind it. Jarlaxle was a rogue without house, normally an unhealthy position in the world of the dark elves. Yet this resourceful mercenary survived—even thrived—in his renegade position. Through it all, Jarlaxle's greatest advantage was knowledge—knowledge of every stirring within Menzoberranzan and the regions surrounding the city.

"How long will you require?" Firble asked. "My king wishes to complete this business as swiftly as possible."

"Have you my payment?" the drow asked, holding out a hand.

"Payment when you bring me the information," Firble protested. "That has always been our agreement."

"So it has," agreed Jarlaxle. "This time, though, I need no time to gather your information. If you have my gems, we can be done with our business right now."

Firble pulled the pouch of gems from his belt and tossed them to the drow. "Fifty agates, finely cut," he said with a growl, never pleased by the price. He had hoped to avoid using Jarlaxle this time; like any deep gnome, Firble did not easily part with such sums.

Jarlaxle quickly glanced into the pouch, then dropped it into a deep pocket. "Rest easy, little deep gnome," he began, "for the powers who rule Menzoberranzan plan no actions against your city. A single drow house has an interest in the region, nothing more."

"Why?" Firble asked after a long moment of silence had passed. The svirfneblin hated having to ask, knowing the inevitable consequence.

Jarlaxle held out his hand. Ten more finely cut agates passed over.

"The house searches for one of its own," Jarlaxle explained. "A renegade whose actions have put his family out of the favor of the Spider Queen."

Again a few interminable moments of silence passed. Firble could guess easily enough the identity of this hunted drow, but King Schnicktick would roar until the ceiling fell in if he didn't make certain. He pulled ten more gemstones from his belt pouch. "Name the house," he said.

"Daermon N'a'shezbaernon," replied Jarlaxle, casually dropping the gems into his deep pocket. Firble crossed his arms over his chest and scowled. The unscrupulous drow had caught him once again.

"Not the ancestral name!" the councilor growled, grudgingly pulling out another ten gems.

"Really, Firble," Jarlaxle teased. "You must learn to be more specific in your questioning. Such errors do cost you so much!"

"Name the house in terms that I might understand," Firble instructed. "And name the hunted renegade. No more will I pay you this day, Jarlaxle."

Jarlaxle held his hand up and smiled to silence the deep gnome. "Agreed," he laughed, more than satisfied with his take. "House Do'Urden, Eighth House of Menzoberranzan searches for its secondboy." The mercenary noted a hint of recognition in Firble's expression. Might this little meeting provide Jarlaxle with information that he could turn into further profit at the coffers of Matron Malice?

"Drizzt is his name," the drow continued, carefully studying the svirfneblin's reaction. Slyly, he added, "Information of his whereabouts would bring a high profit in Menzoberranzan."

Firble stared at the brash drow for a long time. Had he given away too much when the renegade's identity had been revealed? If Jarlaxle had guessed that Drizzt was in the deep gnome city, the implications could be grim. Now Firble was in a predicament. Should he admit his mistake and try to correct it? But how much would it cost Firble to buy Jarlaxle's promise of silence? And no matter how great the payment, could Firble really trust the unscrupulous mercenary?

"Our business is at its end," Firble announced, deciding to trust that Jarlaxle had not guessed enough to bargain with House Do'Urden. The councilor turned on his heel and started out of the chamber.

Jarlaxle secretly applauded Firble's decision. He had always believed the svirfneblin councilor a worthy bargaining adversary and was not now disappointed. Firble had revealed little information, too little to take to Matron Malice, and if the deep gnome had more to give, his decision to abruptly end the meeting was a wise one. In spite of their racial differences, Jarlaxle had to admit that he actually liked Firble. "Little gnome," he called out after the departing figure. "I offer you a warning."

Firble spun back, his hand defensively covering his closed gem pouch.

"Free of charge," Jarlaxle said with a laugh and a shake of his bald head. But then the mercenary's visage turned suddenly serious, even grim. "If you know of Drizzt Do'Urden," Jarlaxle continued, "keep him far away. Lolth herself has charged Matron Malice Do'Urden with Drizzt's death, and Malice will do whatever she must to accomplish the task. And even if Malice fails, others will take up the hunt, knowing that the Do'Urden's death will bring great pleasure to the Spider Queen. He is doomed, Firble, and so doomed will be any foolish enough to stand beside him."

"An unnecessary warning," Firble replied, trying to keep his expression calm. "For none in Blingdenstone know or care anything for this renegade dark elf. Nor, I assure you, do any in Blingdenstone hold any desire to find the favor of the dark elves' Spider Queen deity!"

Jarlaxle smiled knowingly at the svirfneblin's bluff. "Of course," he replied, and he swept off his grand hat, dropping into yet another bow.

Firble paused a moment to consider the words and the bow, wondering again if he should try to buy the mercenary's silence.

Before he came to any decision, though, Jarlaxle was gone, clomping his hard boots loudly with every departing step. Poor Firble was left to wonder.

He needn't have. Jarlaxle did indeed like little Firble, the mercenary admitted to himself as he departed, and he would not divulge his suspicions of Drizzt's whereabouts to Matron Malice.

Unless, of course, the offer was simply too tempting.

Firble just stood and watched the empty chamber for many minutes, wondering and worrying.

For Drizzt, the days had been filled with friendship and fun. He was somewhat of a hero with the svirfneblin miners who had gone out into the tunnels beside him, and the story of his clever deception against the goblin tribe grew with every telling. Drizzt and Belwar went out often, now, and whenever they entered a tavern or meeting house, they were greeted by cheers and offers of free food and drink. Both the friends were glad for the other, for together they had found their place and their peace.

Already Burrow-Warden Brickers and Belwar were busily planning another mining expedition. Their biggest task was narrowing the list of volunteers, for svirfnebli from every corner of the city had contacted them, eager to travel beside the dark elf and the most honored burrow-warden.

When a loud and insistent knock came one morning on Belwar's door, both Drizzt and the deep gnome figured it to be more recruits looking for a place in the expedition. They were indeed surprised to find the city guard waiting for them, bidding Drizzt, at the point of a dozen spears, to go with them to an audience with the king.

Belwar appeared unconcerned. "A precaution," he assured Drizzt, pushing away his breakfast plate of mushrooms and moss sauce. Belwar went to the wall to grab his cloak, and if Drizzt, concentrating on the spears, had noticed Belwar's jerking and unsure movements, the drow most certainly would not have been assured.

The journey through the deep gnome city was quick indeed, with the anxious guards prodding the drow and the burrow-warden along. Belwar continued to brush the whole thing off as a "precaution" with every step, and in truth, Belwar did a fine job keeping a measure of calm in his round-toned voice. But Drizzt carried no illusions with him into the king's chambers. All of his life had been filled with crashing ends to promising beginnings.

King Schnicktick sat uncomfortably on his stone throne, his councilors standing equally ill at ease around him. He did not like this duty that had been placed upon his shoulders—the svirfnebli considered themselves loyal friends—but in light of councilor Firble's revelations, the threat to Blingdenstone could not be ignored.

Especially not for the likes of a dark elf.

Drizzt and Belwar moved to stand before the king, Drizzt curious, though ready to accept whatever might come of this, but Belwar on the edge of anger.

"My thanks in your prompt arrival," King Schnicktick greeted them, and he cleared his throat and looked around to his councilors for support.

"Spears do keep one in motion," Belwar snarled sarcastically.

The svirfneblin king cleared his throat again, noticeably uncomfortable, and shifted in his seat. "My guard does get a bit excited," he apologized. "Please take no offense."

"None taken," Drizzt assured him.

"Your time in our city you have enjoyed?" Schnicktick asked, managing a bit of a smile.

Drizzt nodded. "Your people have been gracious beyond anything I could have asked for or expected," he replied.

"And you have proven yourself a worthy friend, Drizzt Do'Urden," Schnicktick said. "Truly our lives have been enriched by your presence."

Drizzt bowed low, full of gratitude for the svirfneblin king's kind words. But Belwar narrowed his dark gray eyes and crinkled his hooked nose, beginning to understand what the king was leading up to.

"Unfortunately," King Schnicktick began, looking around pleadingly to his councilors, and not directly at Drizzt, "a situation has come upon us . . ."

"*Magga cammara*!" shouted Belwar, startling everyone in attendance. "No!" King Schnicktick and Drizzt looked at the burrow-warden in disbelief.

"You mean to put him out," Belwar snarled accusingly at Schnicktick.

"Belwar!" Drizzt began to protest.

"Most Honored Burrow-Warden," the svirfneblin king said sternly. "It is not your place to interrupt. If again you do so, I will be forced to have you removed from this chamber."

"It is true then," Belwar groaned softly. He looked away.

Drizzt glanced from the king to Belwar and back again, confused as to the purpose behind this whole encounter.

"You have heard of the suspected drow activity in the tunnels near our eastern borders?" the king asked Drizzt.

Drizzt nodded.

"We have learned the purpose of this activity," Schnicktick explained. The pause as the svirfneblin king looked yet another time to his councilors sent shivers through Drizzt's spine. He knew beyond any doubts what was coming next, but the words wounded him deeply anyway. "You, Drizzt Do'Urden, are that purpose."

"My mother searches for me," Drizzt replied flatly.

"But she will not find you!" Belwar snarled in defiance aimed at both Schnicktick and this unknown mother of his new friend. "Not while you remain a guest of the deep gnomes of Blingdenstone!"

"Belwar, hold!" King Schnicktick scolded. He looked back to Drizzt and his visage softened. "Please, friend Drizzt, you must understand. I cannot risk war with Menzoberranzan."

"I do understand," Drizzt assured him with sincerity. "I will gather my things."

"No!" Belwar protested. He rushed up to the throne. "We are svirfnebli. We do not put out friends in the face of any danger!" The burrow-warden ran from councilor to councilor, pleading for justice. "Only friendship has Drizzt Do'Urden shown us, and we would put him out! *Magga cammara*! If our loyalties are so fragile, are we any better than the drow of Menzoberranzan?"

"Enough, Most Honored Burrow-Warden!" King Schnicktick cried out in a tone of finality that even stubborn Belwar could not ignore. "Our decision did not come easily to us, but it is final! I will not put Blingdenstone in jeopardy for the sake of a dark elf, no matter that he has shown himself to be a friend." Schnicktick looked to Drizzt. "I am truly sorry."

"Do not be," Drizzt replied. "You do only as you must, as I did on that long-ago day when I chose to forsake my people. That decision I made alone, and I have never asked any for approval or aid. You, good svirfneblin king, and your people have given me back so much that I had lost. Believe that I have no desire to invoke the wrath of Menzoberranzan against Blingdenstone. I would never forgive myself if I played any part in that tragedy. I will be gone from your fair city within the hour. And in parting I offer only gratitude."

The svirfneblin king was touched by the words, but his position remained unbending. He motioned for his guardsmen to accompany Drizzt, who accepted the armed escort with a resigned sigh. He looked once to Belwar, standing helplessly beside the svirfneblin councilors, then left the king's halls.

⚔ ⚔ ⚔ ⚔ ⚔

A hundred deep gnomes, particularly Burrow-Warden Krieger and the other miners of the single expedition Drizzt had accompanied, said their farewells to the drow as he walked out of Blingdenstone's huge doors. Conspicuously absent was Belwar Dissengulp; Drizzt had not seen the burrow-warden at all in the hour since he had left the throne room. Still, Drizzt was grateful for the send-off these svirfnebli gave him. Their kind words comforted him and gave him the strength that he knew he would need in the trials of the coming years. Of all the memories Drizzt would take out of Blingdenstone, he vowed to hold onto those parting words.

Still, when Drizzt moved away from the gathering, across the small platform and down the wide staircase, he heard only the resounding echoes of the enormous doors slamming shut behind him. Drizzt trembled as he looked down the tunnels of the wild Underdark, wondering how he could possibly survive the trials this time. Blingdenstone had been his salvation from the hunter; how long would it take that darker side to rear up again and steal his identity?

But what choice did Drizzt have? Leaving Menzoberranzan had been his decision, the right decision. Now, though, knowing better the consequences of his choice, Drizzt wondered about his resolve. Given the opportunity to do it all over again, would he now find the strength to walk away from his life among his people?

He hoped that he would.

A shuffle off to the side brought Drizzt alert. He crouched and drew his scimitars, thinking that Matron Malice had agents waiting for him who had expected him to be expelled from Blingdenstone. A shadow moved a moment later, but it was no drow assassin that came in at Drizzt.

"Belwar!" he cried in relief. "I feared that you would not say farewell."

"And so I will not," replied the svirfneblin.

Drizzt studied the burrow-warden, noticing the full pack that Belwar wore. "No, Belwar, I cannot allow—"

"I do not remember asking for your permission," the deep gnome interrupted. "I have been looking for some excitement in my life. Thought I might venture out and see what the wide world has to offer."

"It is not as grand as you expect," Drizzt replied grimly. "You have your people, Belwar. They accept you and care for you. That is a greater gift than anything you can imagine."

"Agreed," replied the burrow-warden. "And you, Drizzt Do'Urden, have your friend, who accepts you and cares for you. And stands beside you. Now, are we going to be on with this adventure, or are we going to stand here and wait for that wicked mother of yours to walk up and cut us down?"

"You cannot begin to imagine the dangers," Drizzt warned, but Belwar could see that the drow's resolve was already starting to wear away.

Belwar banged his mithral hands together. "And you, dark elf cannot begin to imagine the ways I can deal with such dangers! I am not letting you walk off alone into the wilds. Understand that as fact—*magga cammara*—and we can get on with things."

Drizzt shrugged helplessly, looked once more to the stubborn determination stamped openly on Belwar's face, and started off down the tunnel, the deep gnome falling into step at his side. This time, at least, Drizzt had a companion he could talk to, a weapon against the intrusions of the hunter. He put his hand in his pocket and fingered the Guenhwyvar's onyx figurine. Perhaps, Drizzt dared to hope, the three of them would have a chance to find more than simple survival in the Underdark.

For a long time afterward, Drizzt wondered if he had acted selfishly in giving in so easily to Belwar. Whatever guilt he felt, however, could not begin to compare with the profound sense of relief Drizzt knew whenever he looked down at his side, to the most honored burrow-warden's bald, bobbing head.

# Part Three

## Friends and Foes

To live or to survive? Until my second time out in the wilds of the Underdark, after my stay in Blingdenstone, I never would have understood the significance of such a simple question.

When first I left Menzoberranzan, I thought survival enough; I thought that I could fall within myself, within my principles, and be satisfied that I had followed the only course open to me. The alternative was the grim reality of Menzoberranzan and compliance with the wicked ways that guided my people. If that was life, I believed, simply surviving would be far preferable.

And yet, that "simple survival" nearly killed me. Worse, it nearly stole everything that I held dear.

The svirfnebli of Blingdenstone showed me a different way. Svirfneblin society, structured

**and nurtured on communal values and unity, proved to be everything that I had always hoped Menzoberranzan would be. The svirfnebli did much more than merely survive. They lived and laughed and worked, and the gains they made were shared by the whole, as was the pain of the losses they inevitably suffered in the hostile subsurface world.**

**Joy multiplies when it is shared among friends, but grief diminishes with every division. That is life.**

**And so, when I walked back out of Blingdenstone, back into the empty Underdark's lonely chambers, I walked with hope. At my side went Belwar, my new friend, and in my pocket went the magical figurine that could summon Guenhwyvar, my proven friend. In my brief stay with the deep gnomes, I had witnessed life as I always had hoped it would be—I could not return to simply surviving.**

**With my friends beside me, I dared to believe that I would not have to.**

**—Drizzt Do'Urden**

# 12 Wilds, Wilds, Wilds

"Did you set it?" Drizzt asked Belwar when the burrow-warden returned to his side in the winding passage.

"The fire pit is cut," Belwar replied, tapping his mithral hands triumphantly—but not too loudly—together. "And I rumpled the extra bedroll off in a corner. Scraped my boots all over the stone and put your neck-purse in a place where it will be easily found. I even left a few silver coins under the blanket—I figure I'll not be needing them anytime soon, anyway." Belwar managed a chuckle, but despite the disclaimer, Drizzt could see that the svirfneblin did not so easily part with valuables.

"A fine deception," Drizzt offered, to take away the sting of the cost.

"And what of you, dark elf?" Belwar asked. "Have you seen or heard anything?"

"Nothing," Drizzt replied. He pointed down a side corridor. "I sent Guenhwyvar away on a wide circuit. If anyone is near, we will soon know."

Belwar nodded. "Good plan," he remarked. "Setting the false camp this far from Blingdenstone should keep your troublesome mother from my kinfolk."

"And perhaps it will lead my family to believe that I am still in the region and plan to remain," Drizzt added hopefully. "Have you given any thought to our destination?"

"One way is as good as another," remarked Belwar, hoisting his hands out wide. "No cities are there, beyond our own, anywhere close. None to my knowledge, at least."

"West, then," offered Drizzt. "Around Blingdenstone and off into the wilds, straight away from Menzoberranzan."

"A wise course, it would seem," agreed the burrow-warden. Belwar closed his eyes and attuned his thoughts to the emanations of the stone. Like many Underdark races, deep gnomes possessed the ability to recognize magnetic variations in the rock, an ability that allowed them to judge direction as accurately as a surface dweller might follow the sun's trail. A moment later, Belwar nodded and pointed down the appropriate tunnel.

"West," Belwar said. "And quickly. The more distance you put between yourself and that mother of yours, the safer we all shall be." He paused to consider Drizzt for a long moment, wondering if he might be prodding his new friend a bit too deeply with his next question.

"What is it?" Drizzt asked him, recognizing his apprehension.

Belwar decided to risk it, to see just how close he and Drizzt had become. "When first you learned that you were the reason for the drow activity in the eastern tunnels," the deep gnome began bluntly, "you seemed a bit weak in the knees, if you understand me. They are your family, dark elf. Are they so terrible?"

Drizzt's chuckle put Belwar at ease, told the deep gnome that he had not pressed too far. "Come," Drizzt said, seeing Guenhwyvar return from the scouting trek. "If the deception of the camp is complete, then let us take our first steps into our new life. Our road should be long enough for tales of my home and family."

"Hold," said Belwar. He reached into his pouch and produced a small coffer. "A gift from King Schnicktick," he explained as he lifted the lid and removed a glowing brooch, its quiet illumination bathing the area around them.

Drizzt stared at the burrow-warden in disbelief. "It will mark you as a fine target," the drow remarked.

Belwar corrected him. "It will mark us as fine targets," he said with a sly snort. "But fear not, dark elf, the light will keep more enemies at bay than it will bring. I am not so fond of tripping on crags and chips in the floor!"

"How long will it glow?" Drizzt asked, and Belwar gathered from his tone that the drow hoped it would fade soon.

"Forever is the dweomer," Belwar replied with a wide smirk. "Unless some priest or wizard counters it. Stop your worrying. What creatures of the Underdark would willingly walk into an illuminated area?"

Drizzt shrugged and trusted in the experienced burrow-warden's judgment. "Very well," he said, shaking his white mane helplessly. "Then off for the road."

"The road and the tales," replied Belwar, falling into step beside Drizzt, his stout little legs rolling along to keep up with the drow's long and graceful strides.

They walked for many hours, stopped for a meal, then walked for many more. Sometimes Belwar used his illuminating brooch; other times the friends walked in darkness, depending on whether or not they perceived danger in the area. Guenhwyvar was frequently about yet rarely seen, the panther eagerly taking up its appointed duties as a perimeter guard.

For a tenday straight, the companions stopped only when weariness or hunger forced a break in the march, for they were anxious to be as far from Blingdenstone—and from those hunting Drizzt—as possible. Still, another full tenday would pass before the companions moved out into tunnels that Belwar did not know. The deep gnome had been a burrow-warden for almost fifty years, and he had led many of Blingdenstone's farthest-reaching mining expeditions.

"This place is known to me," Belwar often remarked when they entered a cavern. "Took a wagon of iron," he would say, or mithral, or a multitude of other precious minerals that Drizzt had never even heard of. And though the burrow-warden's extended tales of those mining expeditions all ran in basically the same direction—how many ways can a deep gnome chop stone?—Drizzt always listened intently, savoring every word.

He knew the alternative.

For his part in the storytelling, Drizzt recounted his adventures in Menzoberranzan's Academy and his many fond memories of Zaknafein and the training gym. He showed Belwar the double-thrust low and how the pupil had discovered a parry to counter the attack, to his mentor's surprise and pain. Drizzt displayed the intricate hand and facial combinations of the silent drow code, and he briefly entertained the notion of teaching the language to Belwar. The deep gnome promptly burst into loud and rolling laughter. His dark eyes looked incredulously at Drizzt, and he led the drow's gaze down to the ends of his arms. With a hammer and pickaxe for hands, the svirfneblin could hardly muster enough gestures to make the effort worthwhile. Still, Belwar appreciated that Drizzt had offered to teach him the silent code. The absurdity of it all gave them both a fine laugh.

Guenhwyvar and the deep gnome also became friends during those first couple of tendays on the trail. Often, Belwar would fall into a deep slumber only to be awakened by prickling in his legs, fast asleep under the weight of six hundred pounds of panther. Belwar always grumbled and swatted Guenhwyvar on the rump with his hammer-hand—it became a game between the two—but Belwar truly didn't mind the panther being so close. In fact, Guenhwyvar's mere presence made sleep—which always left one so vulnerable in the wilds—much easier to come by.

"Do you understand?" Drizzt whispered to Guenhwyvar one day. Off to the side, Belwar was fast asleep, flat on his back on the stone, using a rock for a pillow. Drizzt shook his head in continued amazement when he studied the little figure. He was beginning to suspect that the deep gnomes carried their affinity with the earth a bit too far.

"Go get him," he prompted the cat

Guenhwyvar lumbered over and plopped across the burrow-warden's legs. Drizzt moved away into the shielding entrance of a tunnel to watch.

Only a few minutes later, Belwar awoke with a snarl. "*Magga cammara*, panther!" the deep gnome growled. "Why must you always bed down on me, instead of beside me?" Guenhwyvar shifted slightly but let out only a deep sigh in response.

"*Magga cammara*, cat!" Belwar roared again. He wiggled his toes frantically, trying futilely to keep the circulation going and dismiss the tingles that had already begun. "Away with you!" The burrow-warden propped himself up on one elbow and swung his hammer-hand at Guenhwyvar's backside.

Guenhwyvar sprang away in feigned flight, quicker than Belwar's swat. But just as the burrow-warden relaxed, the panther cut back on its tracks, pivoted completely, and leaped atop Belwar, burying him and pinning him flat to the stone.

After a few moments of struggling, Belwar managed to get his face out from under Guenhwyvar's muscled chest.

"Get yourself off me or suffer the consequences!" the deep gnome growled, obviously an empty threat. Guenhwyvar shifted, getting a bit more comfortable in its perch.

"Dark elf!" Belwar called as loudly as he dared. "Dark elf, take your panther away. Dark elf!"

"Greetings," Drizzt answered, walking in from the tunnel as though he had only just arrived. "Are you two playing again? I had thought my time as sentry near to its end."

"Your time has passed," replied Belwar, but the svirfneblin's words were mulled by thick black fur as Guenhwyvar shifted again. Drizzt could see Belwar's long, hooked nose, though, crinkle up in irritation.

"Oh, no, no," said Drizzt. "I am not so tired. I would not think of interrupting your game. I know that you both enjoy it so." He walked by, giving Guenhwyvar a complimentary pat on the head and a sly wink as he passed.

"Dark elf!" Belwar grumbled at his back as Drizzt departed. But the drow kept going, and Guenhwyvar, with Drizzt's blessings, soon fell fast asleep.

⚔ ⚔ ⚔ ⚔ ⚔

Drizzt crouched low and held very still, letting his eyes go through the dramatic shift from infravision—viewing the heat of objects in the infrared spectrum—to normal vision in the realm of light. Even before the transformation was completed, Drizzt could tell that his guess had been correct. Ahead, beyond a low natural archway, came a red glow. The drow held his position, deciding to let Belwar catch up to him before he went to investigate. Only a moment later, the dimmer glow of the deep gnome's enchanted brooch came into view.

"Put out the light," Drizzt whispered, and the brooch's glow disappeared.

Belwar crept along the tunnel to join his companion. He, too, saw the red glow beyond the archway and understood Drizzt's caution. "Can you bring the panther?" the burrow-warden asked quietly.

Drizzt shook his head. "The magic is limited by spans of time. Walking the material plane tires Guenhwyvar. The panther needs to rest."

"Back the way we came, we could go," Belwar suggested. "Perhaps there is another tunnel around."

"Five miles," replied Drizzt, considering the length of the unbroken passageway behind them. "Too long."

"Then let us see what is ahead," the burrow-warden reasoned, and he started boldly off. Drizzt liked Belwar's straightforward attitude and quickly joined him.

Beyond the archway, which Drizzt had to crouch nearly double to get under, they found a wide and high cavern, its floor and walls covered in a mosslike growth that emitted the red light. Drizzt pulled up short, at a loss, but Belwar recognized the stuff well enough.

"Baruchies!" the burrow-warden blurted, the word turning into a chuckle. He turned to Drizzt and not seeing any reaction to his smile, explained. "Crimson spitters, dark elf. Not for decades have I seen such a patch of the stuff. Quite a rare sight they are, you know."

Drizzt, still at a loss, shook the tenseness out of his muscles and shrugged, then started forward. Belwar's pick hand hooked him under the arm, and the powerful deep gnome spun him back abruptly.

"Crimson spitters," the burrow-warden said again, pointedly emphasizing the latter of the words. "*Magga cammara*, dark elf, how did you get along through the years?"

Belwar turned to the side and slammed his hammer-hand into the wall of the archway, taking off a fair-sized chunk of stone. He scooped this up in the flat of his pick-hand and flipped it off to the side of the cavern. The stone hit the red-glowing fungus with a soft thud, then a burst of smoke and spores blasted into the air.

"Spit," explained Belwar, "and choke you to death will the spore! If you plan to cross here, walk lightly, my brave, foolish friend."

Drizzt scratched his unkempt white locks and considered the predicament. He had no desire to return the five miles down the tunnel, but neither did he plan to go plodding through this field of red death. He stood tall just inside the archway and looked around for some solution. Several stones, a possible walkway, rose up out of the baruchies, and beyond them lay a trail of clear stone about ten feet wide running perpendicular to the archway across the chasm.

"We can make it through," he told Belwar. "There is a clear path."

"There always is in a field of baruchies," the burrow-warden replied under his breath.

Drizzt's keen ears caught the comment. "What do you mean?" he asked, springing agilely out to the first of the raised stones.

"A grubber is about," the deep gnome explained. "Or has been."

"A grubber?" Drizzt prudently hopped back to stand beside the burrow-warden.

"Big caterpillar," Belwar explained. "Grubbers love baruchies. They are the only things the crimson spitters do not seem to bother."

"How big?"

"How wide was the clear path?" Belwar asked him.

"Ten feet, perhaps," Drizzt answered, hopping back out to the first stepping stone to view it again.

Belwar considered the answer for a moment. "One pass for a big grubber, two for most."

Drizzt hopped back to the side of the burrow-warden again, giving a cautious look over his shoulder. "Big caterpillar," he remarked.

"But with a little mouth," Belwar explained. "Grubbers eat only moss and molds—and baruchies, if they can find them. Peaceful enough creatures, all in all."

For the third time, Drizzt sprang out to the stone. "Is there anything else I should know before I continue?" he asked in exasperation.

Belwar shook his head.

Drizzt led the way across the stones, and soon the two companions stood in the middle of the ten-foot path. It traversed the cavern and ended with the entrance to a passage on either side. Drizzt pointed both ways, wondering which direction Belwar would prefer.

The deep gnome started to the left, then stopped abruptly and peered ahead. Drizzt understood Belwar's hesitation, for he, too, felt the vibrations in the stone under his feet.

"Grubber," said Belwar. "Stand quiet and watch, my friend. They are quite a sight."

Drizzt smiled wide and crouched low, eager for the entertainment. When he heard a quick shuffle behind him, though, Drizzt began to suspect that something was out of sorts.

"Where . . ." Drizzt began to ask when he turned about and saw Belwar in full flight toward the other exit.

Drizzt stopped speaking abruptly when an explosion like the crash of a cave-in erupted from the other way, the way he had been watching.

"Quite a sight!" he heard Belwar call, and he couldn't deny the truth of the deep gnome's words when the grubber made its appearance. It was huge—bigger than the basilisk Drizzt had killed—and looked like a gigantic pale gray worm, except for the multitude of little feet pumping along beside its massive torso. Drizzt saw that Belwar had not lied, for the thing had no mouth to speak of, and no talons or other apparent weapons. But the giant was coming straight at Drizzt with a vengeance now, and Drizzt couldn't get the image of a flattened dark elf, stretched from one end of the cavern to the other, out of his mind. He reached for his scimitars, then realized the absurdity of that plan. Where would he hit the thing to slow it? Throwing his hands helplessly out wide, Drizzt spun on his heel and fled after the departing burrow-warden.

The ground shook under Drizzt's feet so violently that he wondered if he might topple to the side and be blasted by the baruchies. But then the tunnel entrance was just ahead and Drizzt could see a smaller side passage, too small for the grubber, just outside the baruchie cavern. He darted ahead the last few strides, then cut swiftly into the small tunnel, diving into a roll to break his momentum. Still, he ricocheted hard off the wall, then the grubber slammed in behind, smashing at the tunnel entrance and dropping pieces of stone all about.

When the dust finally cleared, the grubber remained outside the passage, humming a low, growling moan and every so often, banging its head against the stone. Belwar stood just a few feet farther in than Drizzt, the deep gnome's arms crossed over his chest and a satisfied grin on his face.

"Peaceful enough?" Drizzt asked him, rising to his feet and shaking off the dust.

"They are indeed," replied Belwar with a nod. "But grubbers do love their baruchies and have no mind to share the things!"

"You almost got me crushed!" Drizzt snarled at him.

Again Belwar nodded. "Mark it well, dark elf, for the next time you set your panther to sleep on me, I will surely do worse!"

Drizzt fought hard to hide his smile. His heart still pumped wildly under the influence of the adrenaline burst, but Drizzt held no anger toward his companion. He thought back to encounters he had suffered just a few months before, when he was out alone in the wilds. How different life would be with Belwar Dissengulp by his side! How much more enjoyable! Drizzt glanced back over his shoulder to the angry and stubborn grubber.

And how much more interesting!

"Come along," the smug svirfneblin continued, starting off down the passage. "We are only making the grubber angrier by loitering in its sight."

The passageway narrowed and turned a sharp bend just a few feet farther in. Around the bend, the companions found even more trouble, for the corridor ended in a blank stone wall. Belwar moved right up to inspect it, and it was Drizzt's turn to cross his arms over his chest and gloat.

"You have put us in a dangerous spot, little friend" the drow said. "An angry grubber behind, trapping us in a box corridor!"

Pressing his ear to the stone, Belwar waved Drizzt off with his hammer-hand. "Merely an inconvenience," the deep gnome assured him. "There is another tunnel beyond—not more than seven feet."

"Seven feet of stone," Drizzt reminded him.

But Belwar didn't seem concerned. "A day," he said. "Perhaps two." Belwar held his arms out wide and began a chant too low for Drizzt to hear clearly, though the drow realized that Belwar was engaged in some sort of spellcasting.

*"Bivrip!"* Belwar cried.

Nothing happened.

The burrow-warden turned back on Drizzt and did not seem disappointed. "A day," he proclaimed again.

"What did you do?" Drizzt asked him.

"Set my hands a humming," replied the deep gnome. Seeing that Drizzt was completely at a loss, Belwar turned on his heel and slammed his hammer hand into the wall. An explosion of sparks brightened the small passage, blinding Drizzt. By the time the drow's eyes could adjust to the continuing burst of Belwar's punching and hacking, he saw that his svirfneblin companion already had ground several inches of rock into fine dust at his feet.

"*Magga cammara*, dark elf," Belwar cried with a wink. "You did not believe that my people would go to all the trouble of crafting such fine hands for me without puffing a bit of magic into them, did you?"

Drizzt moved to the side of the passage and sat. "You are full of surprises, little friend," he answered with a sigh of surrender.

"I am indeed!" Belwar roared, and he pounded the stone again, sending flecks flying in every direction.

They were out of the box corridor in a day, as Belwar had promised, and they set off again, traveling now—by the deep gnome's estimation—generally north. Luck had followed them so far, and they both knew it, for they had spent two tendays in the wilds and had encountered nothing more hostile than a grubber protecting its baruchies.

A few days later, their luck changed.

"Summon the panther," Belwar bade Drizzt as they crouched in the wide tunnel they had been traveling. Drizzt did not argue the wisdom of the burrow-warden's request; he didn't like the green glow ahead any more than Belwar did. A moment later, the black mist swirled and took shape, and Guenhwyvar stood beside them.

"I go first," Drizzt said. "You both follow together, twenty steps behind." Belwar nodded and Drizzt turned and started away. Drizzt almost expected the movement when the svirfneblin's pickaxe-hand hooked him and turned him about.

"Be careful," Belwar said. Drizzt only smiled in reply, touched at the sincerity in his friend's voice and thinking again how much better it was to have a companion by his side. Then Drizzt dismissed his thoughts and moved away, letting his instincts and experience guide him.

He found the glow to be emanating from a hole in the corridor floor. Beyond it, the corridor continued but bent sharply, nearly doubling back on itself. Drizzt fell to his belly and peered down the hole. Another passage, about ten feet below him, ran perpendicular to the one he was in, opening a short way ahead into what appeared to be a large cavern.

"What is it?" Belwar whispered, coming up behind.

"Another corridor to a chamber," Drizzt replied. "The glow comes from there." He lifted his head and looked down into the ensuing darkness of the higher corridor. "Our tunnel continues," Drizzt reasoned. "We can go right by it."

Belwar looked down the passageway they had been traveling, noting the turn. "Doubles back," he reasoned. "And probably comes right out at that side passage we passed an hour ago." The deep gnome dropped to the dirt and looked into the hole.

"What would make such a glow?" Drizzt asked him, easily guessing that Belwar's curiosity was as keen as his own. "Another form of moss?"

"None that I know," Belwar replied.

"Shall we find out?"

Belwar smiled at him, then hooked his pick-hand on the ledge and swung over and in, dropping down to the lower tunnel. Drizzt and Guenhwyvar followed silently, the drow, scimitars in hand, again taking the lead as they moved toward the glow.

They came into a wide and high chamber, its ceiling far beyond their sight and a lake of green-glowing foul-smelling liquid bubbling and hissing twenty feet below them. Dozens of interconnected narrow stone walkways, varying from one to ten feet wide, crisscrossed the gorge, most ending at exits leading into more side corridors.

"*Magga cammara*," whispered the stunned svirfneblin, and Drizzt shared that thought.

"It appears as though the floor was blasted away," Drizzt remarked when he again found his voice.

"Melted away," replied Belwar, guessing the liquid's nature. He hacked off a chunk of stone at his side and tapping Drizzt to get his attention, dropped it into the green lake. The liquid hissed as if in anger where the rock hit, eating away at the stone before it even sank from sight.

"Acid," Belwar explained.

Drizzt looked at him curiously. He knew of acid from his days of training under the wizards of Sorcere in the Academy. Wizards often concocted such vile liquids for use in their magical experiments, but Drizzt did not figure that acid would appear naturally, or in such quantities.

"Some wizard's working, I would guess," said Belwar. "An experiment out of control. It has probably been here for a hundred years, eating away at the floor, sinking down inch by inch."

"But what remains of the floor seems secure enough," observed Drizzt, pointing to the walkways. "And we have a score of tunnels to choose from."

"Then let us begin at once," said Belwar. "I do not like this place. We are exposed in the light, and I would not care to take quick flight along such narrow bridges—not with a lake of acid below me!"

Drizzt agreed and took a cautious step out on the walkway, but Guenhwyvar quickly moved past him. Drizzt understood the panther's logic and wholeheartedly agreed. "Guenhwyvar will lead us," he explained to Belwar. "The panther is the heaviest and quick enough to spring away if a section begins to fall."

The burrow-warden was not completely satisfied. "What if Guenhwyvar does not make it to safety?" he asked, truly concerned. "What will the acid do to a magical creature?"

Drizzt wasn't certain of the answer. "Guenhwyvar should be safe," he reasoned, pulling the onyx figurine from his pocket. "I hold the gateway to the panther's home plane."

Guenhwyvar was a dozen strides away by then—the walkway seemed sturdy enough—and Drizzt set out to follow. "*Magga cammara*, I pray you are right," he heard Belwar mumble at his back as he took the first steps out from the ledge.

The chamber was huge, several hundred feet across even to the nearest exit. The companions neared the halfway point—Guenhwyvar had already passed it—when they heard a strange chanting sound. They stopped and glanced about, searching for the source.

A weird-looking creature stepped out from one of the numerous side passages. It was bipedal and black skinned, with a beaked bird's head and the torso of a man, featherless and wingless. Both of its powerful-looking arms ended in hooked, wicked claws, and its legs ended in three-toed feet. Another creature stepped out from behind it, and another from behind them.

"Relatives?" Belwar asked Drizzt, for the creatures did indeed resemble some weird cross between a dark elf and a bird.

"Hardly," Drizzt replied. "In all of my life, I have never heard of such creatures."

"Doom! Doom!" came the continuing chant, and the friends looked around to see more of the bird-men stepping out from other passages. They were dire corbies, an ancient race more common to the southern reaches of the Underdark—though rare even there—and almost unknown in this part of the world. Corbies had never been of much concern to any of the Underdark races, for the bird-men's methods were crude and their numbers were small. To a passing band of adventurers, however, a flock of savage dire corbies meant trouble indeed.

"Nor have I ever encountered such creatures," Belwar agreed. "But I do not believe that they are pleased to see us."

The chant became a series of horrifying shrieks as the corbies began to disperse out onto the walkways, walking at first, but occasionally breaking into quick trots, their anxiety obviously increasing.

"You are wrong, my little friend," Drizzt remarked. "I believe that they are quite pleased to have their dinner delivered to them."

Belwar looked around helplessly. Nearly all of their escape routes were already cut off, and they couldn't hope to get out without a fight. "Dark elf, I can think of a thousand places I would rather do battle," the burrow-warden said with a resigned shrug and a shudder as he took another look down into the acid lake. Taking a deep breath to calm himself, Belwar began his ritual to enchant his magical hands.

"Move while you chant," Drizzt instructed him, leading him on. "Let us get as close to an exit as we can before the fighting begins."

One group of corbies closed rapidly at the party's side, but Guenhwyvar, with a mighty spring that spanned two of the walkways, cut the bird-men off.

*"Bivrip!"* Belwar cried, completing his spell, and he turned toward the impending battle.

"Guenhwyvar can take care of that group," Drizzt assured him, quickening his steps toward the nearest wall. Belwar saw the drow's reasoning; still another group of enemies had come out of the exit they were making for.

The momentum of Guenhwyvar's leap carried the panther straight into the pack of corbies, bowling two of them right off the walkway. The bird men shrieked horribly as they fell to their deaths, but their remaining companions seemed unbothered by the loss. Drooling and chanting, "Doom! Doom!" they tore in at Guenhwyvar with their sharp talons.

The panther had formidable weapons of its own. Each swat of a great claw tore the life from a corby or sent it tumbling from the walkway to the acid lake. But while the cat continued to slash into the birdmen's ranks, the fearless corbies continued to fight back, and more rushed in eagerly to join. A second group came from the opposite direction and surrounded Guenhwyvar.

⚔ ⚔ ⚔ ⚔ ⚔

Belwar set himself on a narrow section of the walkway and let the line of corbies come to him. Drizzt, taking a parallel route along a walkway fifteen feet to his friend's side, did likewise, drawing his scimitars somewhat reluctantly. The drow could feel the savage instincts of the hunter welling up within him as the battle drew near, and he fought back with all of his willpower to sublimate the wild urges. He was Drizzt Do'Urden, no more the hunter, and he would face his foes fully in control of his every movement.

Then the corbies were upon him, flailing away, shrieking their frenzied chants. Drizzt did little more than parry in those first seconds, the flats of his blades working marvelously to deflect each attempted strike. The scimitars spun and whirled, but the drow, refusing to loose the killer within him, made little headway in his fight. After several minutes, he still faced off against the first corby that had come at him.

Belwar was not so reserved. Corby after corby rushed in at the little svirfneblin, only to be pounded to a sudden halt by the burrow-warden's explosive hammer-hand. The electrical jolt and the sheer force of the blow often killed the corby where it stood, but Belwar never waited long enough to find out. Following each hammer blow, the deep gnome's pickaxe-hand came across in a roundhouse arc, sweeping the latest victim from the walkway.

The svirfneblin had dropped a half-dozen of the bird-men before he got the chance to look over at Drizzt. He recognized at once the inner struggle the drow was fighting.

"*Magga cammara*!" Belwar screamed. "Fight them, dark elf, and fight to win! They will show no mercy! There can be no truce! Kill them—cut them down—or surely they shall kill you!"

Drizzt hardly heard Belwar's words. Tears rimmed his lavender eyes, though even in that blur, the almost magical rhythm of his weaving blades did not slow. He caught his opponent off balance and reversed the motion of a thrust, slamming the bird-man in the head with the pommel of his scimitar. The corby dropped like a stone and rolled. It would have fallen from the ledge, but Drizzt stepped across it and held it in place.

Belwar shook his head and belted another adversary. The corby hopped backward, its chest smoking and charred by the jarring impact of the enchanted hammer-hand. The corby looked at Belwar in blank disbelief, but uttered not a sound, nor made any move at all, as the pickaxe hooked in, catching it in the shoulder and launching it out over the acid lake.

⚔ ⚔ ⚔ ⚔ ⚔

Guenhwyvar flustered the hungry attackers. As the corbies closed in on the panther's back, thinking the kill at hand, Guenhwyvar crouched and sprang. The panther soared through the green light as though it had taken flight, landing on yet another of the walkways fully thirty feet away. Skidding on the smooth stone, Guenhwyvar just managed to halt before toppling over the ledge into the acid pool.

The corbies glanced around in stunned amazement for just a moment, then took up their shrieks and wails and set off along the walkways in pursuit.

A single corby, near where Guenhwyvar had landed, ran fearlessly to battle the cat. Guenhwyvar's teeth found its neck in an instant and squeezed the life from it.

But while the panther was so engaged, the corbies' devilish trap showed another twist. From far above in the high-ceilinged cavern, a corby at last saw a victim in position. The bird-man wrapped its arms around the heavy boulder on the ledge beside it and pushed out, dropping with the stone.

At the last second, Guenhwyvar saw the plummeting monster and scrambled out of its path. The corby, in its suicidal ecstacy, didn't even care. The bird-man slammed into the walkway, the momentum of the heavy boulder shattering the narrow bridge to pieces.

The great panther tried to spring out again, but the stone underneath Guenhwyvar's feet disintegrated before they could set and spring. Claws scratching futilely at the crumbling bridge, Guenhwyvar followed the corby and its boulder down into the acid lake.

Hearing the elated shouts of the bird-men behind him, Belwar spun about just in time to see Guenhwyvar's fall. Drizzt, too engaged at the time—for another corby flailed away at him and the one he had dropped was stirring back to consciousness between his feet—did not see. But the drow did not have to see. The figurine in Drizzt's pocket heated suddenly, wisps of smoke rising ominously from Drizzt's *piwafwi* cloak. Drizzt could guess easily enough what had happened to his dear Guenhwyvar. The drow's eyes narrowed, their sudden fire melting away his tears.

He welcomed the hunter.

Corbies fought with fury. The highest honor of their existence was to die in battle. And those closest to Drizzt Do'Urden soon realized that the moment of their highest honor was upon them.

The drow thrust both his scimitars straight out, each finding an eye of the corby facing him. The hunter pulled out the blades, spun them over in his hands, and plunged them down into the bird-man at his feet. He snapped the scimitars up immediately and plunged them down again, taking grim satisfaction in the sound of their smooth cut.

Then the drow dived headlong into the corbies ahead of him, his blades cutting in from every possible angle.

Hit a dozen times before it ever launched a single swing, the first corby was quite dead before it even fell. Then the second, then the third. Drizzt backed them up to a wider section of the walkway. They came at him three at a time.

They died at his feet three at a time.

"Get them, dark elf," mumbled Belwar, seeing his friend explode into action. The corby coming to meet the burrow-warden turned its head to see what had caught Belwar's attention. When it turned back, it was met squarely in the face by the deep gnome's hammer-hand. Pieces of beak flew in every direction, and that unfortunate corby was the first of its species to take flight in several millennium of evolution. Its short airborne excursion pushed its companions back from the deep gnome, and the corby landed, dead on its back, many feet from Belwar.

The enraged deep gnome wasn't finished with this one. He raced up, bowling from the walkway the single corby who managed to get back to intercept him. When he arrived at last at his beakless victim, Belwar drove his pickaxe-hand deep into its chest. With that single muscled arm, the burrow-warden hoisted the dead corby high into the air and let out a horrifying shriek of his own.

The other corbies hesitated. Belwar looked to Drizzt and was dismayed.

A score of corbies crowded in on the wide section of the walkway where the drow made his stand. Another dozen lay dead at Drizzt feet, their blood running off the ledge and dripping into the acid lake in rhythmic hissing *plops*. But it wasn't the odds that Belwar feared; with his precise movements and measured thrusts, Drizzt was undeniably winning. High above the drow, though, another suicidal corby and his pet rock took a dive.

Belwar believed that Drizzt's life had come to a crashing end.

But the hunter sensed the peril.

A corby reached for Drizzt. With a flash of the drow's scimitars, both its arms flew free of their respective shoulders. In the same dazzling movement, Drizzt snapped his bloodied scimitars into their sheaths and bolted for the edge of the platform. He reached the lip and leaped out toward Belwar just as the suicidal boulder-riding corby crashed down, taking the platform and a score of its kin with it into the acid pool.

Belwar heaved his beakless trophy into the corbies facing him and dropped to his knees, reaching out with his pickaxe-hand to try to aid his soaring friend. Drizzt caught the burrow-warden's hand and the ledge at the same time, slamming his face into the stone but finding a hold.

The jolt ripped the drow's *piwafwi*, though, and Belwar watched helplessly as the onyx figurine rolled out and dropped toward the acid.

Drizzt caught it between his feet.

Belwar nearly laughed aloud at the futility and hopelessness of it all. He looked over his shoulder to see the corbies resuming their advance.

"Dark elf, surely it has been fun," the svirfneblin said resignedly to Drizzt, but the drow's response stole the levity from Belwar as surely as it stole the blood from the deep gnome's face.

"Swing me!" Drizzt growled so powerfully that Belwar obeyed before he even realized what he was doing.

Drizzt rolled out and came swinging back toward the walkway, and when he bounced into the stone, every muscle in his body jerked violently to aid his momentum.

He rolled right around the bottom of the walkway, scrambling and clawing with his arms and legs to gain a footing back up behind the crouching deep gnome. By the time Belwar realized what Drizzt had done and thought to turn around, Drizzt had his scimitars out and slicing across the face of the first approaching corby.

"Hold this," Drizzt bade his friend, flicking the onyx figurine to Belwar with his toe. Belwar caught the item between his arms and fumbled it into a pocket. Then the deep gnome stood back and watched, taking up a rear guard, as Drizzt cut a devastating path to the nearest exit.

Five minutes later, to Belwar's absolute amazement, they were running free down a darkened tunnel, the frustrated shrieks of "Doom! Doom!" fast fading behind them.

# 13

# A Little Place to Call Home

Enough. Enough!" the winded burrow-warden gasped at Drizzt, trying to slow his companion. "*Magga cammara*, dark elf. We have left them far behind."

Drizzt spun on the burrow-warden, scimitars ready in hand and angry fires burning still in his lavender eyes. Belwar backed away quickly and cautiously.

"Calm, my friend," the svirfneblin said quietly, but despite the reassurance, the burrow-warden's mithral hands came defensively in front of him. "The threat to us is ended."

Drizzt breathed deeply to steady himself, then, realizing that he had not put his scimitars away, promptly slipped them into their sheaths.

"Are you all right?" Belwar asked, moving back to Drizzt's side. Blood smeared the drow's face from where he had slammed into the side of the walkway.

Drizzt nodded. "It was the fight," he tried vainly to explain. "The excitement. I had to let go of—"

"You need not explain," Belwar cut him short. "You did fine, dark elf. Better than fine. Had it not been for your actions, we, all three, surely would have fallen."

"It came back to me," Drizzt groaned, searching for the words that could explain. "That darker part of me. I had thought it gone."

"It is," the burrow-warden said.

"No," argued Drizzt. "That cruel beast that I have become possessed me fully against those bird-men. It guided my blades, savagely and without mercy."

"You guided your own blades," Belwar assured him.

"But the rage," replied Drizzt. "The unthinking rage. All I wanted to do was kill them and hack them down."

"If that was the truth, we would be there still," reasoned the svirfneblin. "By your actions, we escaped. There are many more of the bird-men back there to be killed, yet you led the way from the chamber. Rage? Perhaps, but surely not unthinking rage. You did as you had to do, and you did it well, dark elf. Better than anyone I have ever seen. Do not apologize, to me or to yourself!"

Drizzt leaned back against the wall to consider the words. He was comforted by the deep gnome's reasoning and appreciated Belwar's efforts. Still, though, the burning fires of rage he had felt when Guenhwyvar fell into the acid lake haunted him, an emotion so overwhelming that Drizzt had not yet come to terms with it. He wondered if he ever would.

In spite of his uneasiness, though, Drizzt felt comforted by the presence of his svirfneblin friend. He remembered other encounters of the last years, battles he had been forced to fight alone. Then, like now, the hunter had welled within him, had come to the fore and guided the deadly strikes of his blades. But there was a difference this time that Drizzt could not deny. Before, when he was alone, the hunter did not so readily depart. Now, with Belwar by his side, Drizzt was fully back in control.

Drizzt shook his thick white mane, trying to dismiss any last remnants of the hunter. He thought himself foolish now for the way he had begun the battle against the bird-men, slapping with the flat of his blades. He and Belwar might be in the cavern still if Drizzt's instinctive side had not emerged, if he had not learned of Guenhwyvar's fall.

He looked at Belwar suddenly, remembering the inspiration of his anger. "The statuette!" he cried. "You have it."

Belwar scooped the item out of his pocket. "*Magga cammara*!" Belwar exclaimed, his round toned voice edged with panic. "Might the panther be wounded? What effect would the acid have against Guenhwyvar? Might the panther have escaped to the Astral Plane?"

Drizzt took the figurine and examined it in trembling hands, taking comfort in the fact that it was not marred in any way. Drizzt believed that he should wait before calling Guenhwyvar; if the panther was injured, it surely would heal better at rest in its own plane of existence. But Drizzt could not wait to learn of Guenhwyvar's fate. He placed the figurine down on the ground at his feet and called out softly.

Both the drow and the svirfneblin sighed audibly when the mist began to swirl around the onyx statue. Belwar took out his enchanted brooch to better observe the cat.

A dreadful sight awaited them. Obediently, faithfully, Guenhwyvar came to Drizzt's summons, but as soon as the drow saw the panther, he knew that he should have left Guenhwyvar alone so that it might lick its wounds. Guenhwyvar's silken black coat was burned and showing more patches of scalded skin than fur. Once-sleek muscles hung ragged, burned from the bone, and one eye remained closed and horribly scarred.

Guenhwyvar stumbled, trying to get to Drizzt's side. Drizzt rushed to Guenhwyvar instead, dropping to his knees and throwing a gentle hug around the panther's huge neck.

"Guen," he mumbled.

"Will it heal?" Belwar asked softly, his voice nearly breaking apart on every word.

Drizzt shook his head, at a loss. Truly, he knew very little about the panther beyond its abilities as his companion. Drizzt had seen Guenhwyvar wounded before, but never seriously. Now he could only hope that the magical extra-planar properties would allow Guenhwyvar to recover fully.

"Go back home," Drizzt said. "Rest and get well, my friend. I will call for you in a few days."

"Perhaps we can give some aid now," Belwar offered.

Drizzt knew the futility of that suggestion. "Guenhwyvar will better heal at rest," he explained as the cat dissipated into the mist again. "We can do nothing for Guenhwyvar that will carry over to the other plane. Being here in our world taxes the panther's strength. Every minute takes a toll."

Guenhwyvar was gone and only the figurine remained. Drizzt picked it up and studied it for a very long time before he could bear to drop it back into a pocket.

⚔ ⚔ ⚔ ⚔ ⚔

A sword flicked the bedroll up into the air, then slashed and cut beside its sister blade until the blanket was no more than a tattered rag. Zaknafein glanced down at the silver coins on the floor. Such an obvious dupe, but the camp, and the prospect of Drizzt returning to it, had kept Zaknafein at bay for several days!

Drizzt Do'Urden was gone, and he had taken great pains to announce his departure from Blingdenstone. The spirit-wraith paused to consider this new bit of information, and the necessity of thought, of tapping into the rational being that Zaknafein had been on more than an instinctive level, brought the inevitable conflict between this undead animation and the spirit of the being it held captive.

⚔ ⚔ ⚔ ⚔ ⚔

Back in her anteroom, Matron Malice Do'Urden felt the struggle within her creation. In Zin-carla, control of the spirit-wraith remained the responsibility of the matron mother that the Spider Queen graced with the gift. Malice had to work hard at the appointed task, had to spit off a succession of chants and spells to insinuate herself between the thought processes of the spirit wraith and the emotions and soul of Zaknafein Do'Urden.

⚔ ⚔ ⚔ ⚔ ⚔

The spirit-wraith lurched as he felt the intrusions of Malice's powerful will. It proved to be no contest; in barely a second, the spirit-wraith was studying the small chamber Drizzt and one other being, probably a deep gnome, had disguised as a campsite. They were gone now, tendays out, and no doubt moving away from Blingdenstone with all speed. Probably, the spirit-wraith reasoned, moving away from Menzoberranzan as well.

Zaknafein moved outside the chamber into the main tunnel. He sniffed one way, back east toward Menzoberranzan, then turned and dropped to a crouch and sniffed again. The location spells Malice had imbued upon Zaknafein could not cover such distances, but the minute sensations the spirit wraith received from his inspection only confirmed his suspicions. Drizzt had gone west.

Zaknafein walked off down the tunnel, not the slightest limp evident from the wound he had received at the end of a goblin's spear, a wound that would have crippled a mortal being. He was more than a tenday behind Drizzt, maybe two, but the spirit-wraith was not concerned. His prey had to sleep, had to rest and eat. His prey was flesh, and mortal—and weak.

⚔ ⚔ ⚔ ⚔ ⚔

"What manner of being is it?" Drizzt whispered to Belwar as they watched the curious bipedal creature filling buckets in a fast-running stream. This entire area of the tunnels was magically lighted, but Drizzt and Belwar felt safe enough in the shadows of a rocky outcropping a few dozen yards from the stooping robed figure.

"A man," Belwar replied. "Human, from the surface."

"He is a long way from home," Drizzt remarked. "Yet he seems comfortable in his surroundings. I would not believe that a surface-dweller could survive in the Underdark. It goes against the teachings I received in the Academy."

"Probably a wizard," Belwar reasoned. "That would account for the light in this region. And it would account for his being here."

Drizzt looked at the svirfneblin curiously.

"A strange lot are wizards," Belwar explained, as though the truth was self-evident. "Human wizards, even more than any others, so I've heard tell. Drow wizards practice for power. Svirfneblin wizards practice the arts to better know the stone. But human wizards," the deep gnome went on, obvious disdain in his tone. "*Magga cammara*, dark elf, human wizards are a different lot altogether!"

"Why do human wizards practice the art of magic at all?" Drizzt asked.

Belwar shook his head. "I do not believe that any scholars have yet discovered the reason," he replied in all sincerity. "A strange and dangerously unpredictable race are the humans, and better to be left alone."

"You have met some?"

"A few." Belwar shuddered, as though the memory was not a pleasant one. "Traders from the surface. Ugly things, and arrogant. The whole of the world is only for them, by their thinking."

The resonant voice rang out a bit more loudly than Belwar had intended, and the robed figure by the stream cocked his head in the companions' direction.

"Comen out, leetle rodents," the human called in a language that the companions could not understand. The wizard reiterated the request in another tongue, then in drow, and then in two more unknown tongues, and then in svirfneblin. He continued on for many minutes, Drizzt and Belwar looking at each other in disbelief.

"He is a learned man," Drizzt whispered to the deep gnome.

"Rats, probibably," the human muttered to himself. He glanced around, seeking some way to flush out the unseen noisemakers, thinking that the creatures might provide a fine meal.

"Let us learn if he is friend or foe," Drizzt whispered, and he started to move out from the concealment. Belwar stopped him and looked at him doubtfully, but then, with no recourse other than his own instincts, he shrugged and let Drizzt move on.

"Greetings, human so far from home," Drizzt said in his native language, stepping out from behind the outcropping.

The human's eyes went hysterically wide and he pulled roughly on his scraggly white beard. "You ist notten a rat!" he shrieked in strained but understandable drow.

"No," Drizzt said. He looked back to Belwar, who was moving out to join him.

"Thieves!" the human cried. "Comen to shteal my home, ist you?"

"No," Drizzt said again.

"Go avay!" the human yelled, waving his hands as a farmer would to shoo chickens. "Getten. Go on, qvickly now!"

Drizzt and Belwar exchanged curious glances.

"No," Drizzt said a third time.

"Thees ist my home, stupit dark elven!" the human spat. "Did I asket you to comen here? Did I sent a letter invititing you to join me in my home? Or perhapst you and your oogly little friend simply consider it your duty to velcome me to the neighborhood!"

"Careful, drow," Belwar whispered as the human rambled on. "He's a wizard, for sure, and a shaky one, even by human standards."

"Oren maybe bot the drow ant deep gnome races fear of me?" the human mused, more to himself than to the intruders. "Yes, of course. They have heard that I, Brister Fendlestick, decided to take to the corridors of the Underdark and have joined forces to protecket themselvens against me! Yes, yes, it all seems so clear, and so pititiful, to me now!"

"I have fought wizards before," Drizzt replied to Belwar under his breath. "Let us hope that we can settle this without blows. Whatever must happen, though, know that I have no desire to return the way we came." Belwar nodded his grim agreement as Drizzt turned back to the human. "Perhaps we can convince him simply to let us pass," Drizzt whispered.

The human trembled on the verge of an explosion. "Fine!" he screamed suddenly. "Then do not getten away!" Drizzt saw his error in thinking that he might reason with this one. The drow started forward, meaning to close in before the wizard could launch any attacks.

But the human had learned to survive in the Underdark, and his defenses were in place long before Drizzt and Belwar ever appeared around the rocky outcropping. He waved his hands and uttered a single word that the companions could not understand. A ring on his finger glowed brightly and loosed a tiny ball of fire up into the air between him and the intruders.

"Velcome to my home, then!" the wizard yelled triumphantly. "Play with this!" He snapped his fingers and vanished.

Drizzt and Belwar could feel the explosive energy gathering around the glowing orb.

"Run!" the burrow-warden cried, and he turned to flee. In Blingdenstone, most of the magic was illusionary, designed for defense. But in Menzoberranzan, where Drizzt had learned of magic, the spells were undeniably offensive. Drizzt knew the wizard's attack, and he knew that in these narrow and low corridors, flight would not be an option.

"No!" he cried, and he grabbed the back of Belwar's leather jack and pulled the deep gnome along, straight toward the glowing orb. Belwar knew to trust in Drizzt, and he turned and ran willingly beside his friend. The burrow-warden understood the drow's plan as soon as his eyes managed to tear away from the spectacle of the orb. Drizzt was making for the stream.

The friends dived headlong into the water, bouncing and scraping on the stones, just as the fireball exploded.

A moment later, they rose up from the steaming water, wisps of smoke rising from the back of their clothing, which had not been submerged. They coughed and sputtered, for the flames had temporarily stolen the air from the chamber, and the residual heat from the glowing stones nearly overwhelmed them.

"Humans," Belwar muttered grimly. He pulled himself from the water and shook vigorously. Drizzt came out beside him and couldn't hide his laughter.

The deep gnome, though, found no levity at all in the situation. "The wizard," he pointedly reminded Drizzt. Drizzt dropped into a crouch and glanced nervously all around. They set off at once.

⚔ ⚔ ⚔ ⚔ ⚔

"Home!" Belwar proclaimed a couple of days later. The two friends looked down from a narrow ledge at a wide and high cavern that housed an underground lake. Behind them was a three-chambered cave with only a single tiny entrance, easily defensible.

Drizzt climbed the ten or so feet to stand by his friend on the topmost ledge. "Possibly," he tentatively agreed, "though we left the wizard only a few days' walk from here."

"Forget the human," Belwar snarled, glancing over at the burn mark on his precious jack.

"And I am not so fond of having so large a pool only a few feet from our door," Drizzt continued.

"With fish it is filled!" the burrow-warden argued. "And with mosses and plants that will keep our bellies full, and water that seems clean enough!"

"But such an oasis will attract visitors," reasoned Drizzt. We would find little rest, I fear."

Belwar looked down the sheer wall to the floor of the large cavern. "Never a problem," he said with a snicker. "The bigger ones cannot get up here, and the smaller ones . . . well, I have seen the cut of your blades, and you have seen the strength of my hands. About the smaller ones I shall not worry!"

Drizzt liked the svirfneblin's confidence, and he had to agree that they had found no other place suitable for use as a dwelling. Water, hard to find and more often than not, undrinkable, was a precious commodity in the dry Underdark. With the lake and the growth about it, Drizzt and Belwar would never have to travel far to find a meal.

Drizzt was about to agree, but then a movement down by the water caught his and Belwar's attention.

"And crabs!" spouted the svirfneblin, obviously not having the same reaction to the sight as the drow. "*Magga cammara*, dark elf! Crabs! As fine a meal as ever you will find!"

Indeed it was a crab that had slipped out of the lake, a gigantic, twelve-foot monster with pincers that could snap a human—or an elf or a gnome—fully in half. Drizzt looked at Belwar incredulously. "A meal?" he asked.

Belwar's smile rolled right up around his crinkled nose as he banged his hammer and pick hands together.

They ate crab meat that night, and the day after that, and the day after that, and the day after that, and Drizzt soon was quite willing to agree that the three-chambered cave by the underground lake made a fine home.

⚔ ⚔ ⚔ ⚔ ⚔

The spirit-wraith paused to consider the red-glowing field. In life, Zaknafein Do'Urden would have avoided such a patch, respecting the inherent dangers of odd-glowing rooms and luminous mosses. But to the spirit-wraith the trail was clear; Drizzt had come this way.

The spirit-wraith waded in, ignoring the noxious puffs of deadly spores that shot up at him with every step, choking spores that filled the lungs of unfortunate creatures.

But Zaknafein did not draw breath.

Then came the rumbling as the grubber rushed to protect its domain. Zaknafein fell into a defensive crouch, the instincts of the being he once had been sensing the danger. The grubber rolled into the glowing moss patch but noticed no intruder to chase away. It moved in anyway, thinking that a meal of baruchies might not be such a bad thing.

When the grubber reached the center of the chamber, the spirit-wraith let his levitation spell dissipate. Zaknafein landed on the monster's back, locking his legs fast. The grubber thrashed and thundered about the room, but Zaknafein's balance did not waver.

The grubber's hide was thick and tough, able to repel all but the finest of weapons, which Zaknafein possessed.

⚔ ⚔ ⚔ ⚔ ⚔

"What was that?" Belwar asked one day, stopping his work on the new door blocking their cave opening. Down by the pool, Drizzt apparently had heard the sound as well, for he had dropped the helmet he was using to fetch some water and had drawn both scimitars. He held a hand up to keep the burrow-warden silent, then picked his way back to the ledge for a quiet conversation.

The sound, a loud clacking noise, came again.

"You know it, dark elf?" Belwar asked softly.

Drizzt nodded. "Hook horrors," he replied, "possessing the keenest hearing in all the Underdark." Drizzt kept his recollections of his sole encounter with this type of monster to himself. It had occurred during a patrol exercise, with Drizzt leading his Academy class through the tunnels outside Menzoberranzan. The patrol came upon a group of the giant, bipedal creatures with exoskeletons as hard as plated metal armor and powerful beaks and claws. The drow patrol, mostly through Drizzt's exploits, had won the day, but what Drizzt remembered most keenly was his belief that the encounter had been an exercise planned by the masters of the Academy, and that they had sacrificed an innocent drow child to the hook horrors for the sake of realism.

"Let us find them," Drizzt said quietly but grimly. Belwar paused to catch his breath when he saw the dangerous simmer in the drow's lavender eyes.

"Hook horrors are dangerous rivals," Drizzt explained, noticing the deep gnome's hesitation. "We cannot allow them to roam the region."

Following the clacking noises, Drizzt had little trouble closing in. He silently picked his way around a final bend with Belwar close by his side. In a wider section of the corridor stood a single hook horror, banging its heavy claws rhythmically against the stone as a svirfneblin miner might use his pickaxe.

Drizzt held Belwar back, indicating that he could dispatch the monster quickly if he could sneak in on it without being noticed. Belwar agreed but remained poised to join in at the first opportunity or need.

The hook horror, obviously engaged in its game with the stone wall, did not hear or see the approaching stealthy drow. Drizzt came right in beside the monster, looking for the easiest and fastest way to dispatch it. He saw only one opening in the exoskeleton, a slit between the creature's breastplate and its wide neck. Getting a blade in there could be a bit of a problem, though, for the hook horror was nearly ten feet tall.

But the hunter found the solution. He came in hard and fast at the hook horror's knee, butting with both his shoulders and bringing his blades up into the creature's crotch. The hook horror's legs buckled, and it tumbled back over the drow. As agile as any cat, Drizzt rolled out and sprang on top of the felled monster, both his blades coming tip in at the slit in the armor.

He could have finished the hook horror at once; his scimitars easily could have slipped through the bony defenses. But Drizzt saw something—terror?—on the hook horror's face, something in the creature's expression that should not have been there. He forced the hunter back inside, took control of his swords, and hesitated for just a second—long enough for the hook horror, to Drizzt's absolute amazement, to speak in clear and proper drow language, "Please . . . do . . . not . . . kill . . . me!"

# 14
# Clacker

The scimitars slowly eased away from the hook horror's neck.

"Not . . . as I . . . ap-appear," the monster tried to explain in its halting speech. With each uttered word, the hook horror seemed to become more comfortable with the language. "I am . . . pech."

"Pech?" Belwar gawked, moving up to Drizzt's side. The svirfneblin looked down at the trapped monster with understandable confusion. "A bit big you are for a pech," he remarked.

Drizzt looked from the monster to Belwar, seeking some explanation. The drow had never heard the word before.

"Rock children," Belwar explained to him. "Strange little creatures. Hard as the stone and living for no other reason than to work it."

"Sounds like a svirfneblin," Drizzt replied.

Belwar paused a moment to figure out if he had been complimented or insulted. Unable to discern, the burrow-warden continued somewhat cautiously. "There are not many pech about, and fewer still that look like this one!" He cast a doubting eye at the hook horror, then gave Drizzt a look that told the drow to keep his scimitars at the ready.

"Pech . . . n-n-no more," the hook horror stammered, clear remorse evident in its throaty voice. "Pech no more."

"What is your name?" Drizzt asked it, hoping to find some clues to the truth.

The hook horror thought for a long moment, then shook its great head helplessly. "Pech . . . n-n-no more," the monster said again, and it purposely tilted its beaked face backward, widening the crack in its exoskeleton armor and inviting Drizzt to finish the strike.

"You cannot remember your name?" Drizzt asked, not so anxious to kill the creature. The hook horror neither moved nor replied. Drizzt looked to Belwar for advice, but the burrow-warden only shrugged helplessly.

"What happened?" Drizzt pressed the monster. "You must tell me what happened to you."

"W-w-w . . ." The hook horror struggled to reply. "W-wi-wizard. Evil wi-zard."

Somewhat schooled in the ways of magic and in the unscrupulous uses its practitioners often put it to, Drizzt began to understand the possibilities and began to believe this strange creature. "A wizard changed you?" he asked, already guessing the answer. He and Belwar exchanging amazed expressions. "I have heard of such spells."

"As have I," agreed the burrow-warden. "*Magga cammara*, dark elf, I have seen the wizards of Blingdenstone use similar magic when we needed to infiltrate . . ." The deep gnome paused suddenly, remembering the heritage of the elf he was addressing.

"Menzoberranzan," Drizzt finished with a chuckle.

Belwar cleared his throat, a bit embarrassed, and turned back to the monster. "A pech you once were," he said, needing to hear the whole explanation spelled out in one clear thought, "and some wizard changed you into a hook horror."

"True," the monster replied. "Pech no more."

"Where are your companions?" the svirfneblin asked. "If what I have heard of your people is true, pech do not often travel alone."

"D-d-d-dead," said the monster. "Evil w-w-w—"

"Human wizard?" Drizzt prompted.

The great beak bobbed in an excited nod. "Yes, m-m-man."

"And the wizard then left you to your pains as a hook horror," Belwar said. He and Drizzt looked long and hard at each other, and then the drow stepped away, allowing the hook horror to rise.

"I w-w-w-wish you w-w-w-would k-k-kill me," the monster then said, twisting up into a sitting position. It looked at its clawed hands with obvious disgust. "The s-stone, the stone . . . lost to me."

Belwar raised his own crafted hands in response. "So had I once believed," he said. "You are alive, and no longer are you alone. Come with us to the lake, where we can talk some more."

Presently the hook horror agreed and began, with much effort, to raise its quarter-ton bulk from the floor. Amid the scraping and shuffling of the creature's hard exoskeleton, Belwar prudently whispered to Drizzt, "Keep your blades at the ready!"

The hook horror finally stood, towering to its imposing ten-foot height, and the drow did not argue Belwar's logic.

For many hours, the hook horror recounted its adventures to the two friends. As amazing as the story was the monster's growing acclimation to the use of language. This fact, and the monster's descriptions of its previous existence—of a life tapping and shaping the stone in an almost holy reverence—further convinced Belwar and Drizzt of the truth of its bizarre tale.

"It feels g-g-good to speak again, though the language is not my own," the creature said after a while. "It feels as if I have f-found again a part of what I once w-w-was."

With his own similar experiences so clear in his mind, Drizzt understood the sentiments completely.

"How long have you been this way?" Belwar asked.

The hook horror shrugged, its huge chest and shoulders rattling through the movement. "Tendays, m-months," it said. "I cannot remember. The time is l-lost to me."

Drizzt put his face in his hands and exhaled a deep sigh, in full empathy and sympathy with the unfortunate creature. Drizzt, too, had felt so lost and alone out in the wilds. He, too, knew the grim truth of such a fate. Belwar patted the drow softly with his hammer-hand.

"And where now are you going?" the burrow-warden asked the hook horror. "Or where were you coming from?"

"Chasing the w-w-w—" the hook horror replied, fumbling helplessly over that last word as though the mere mention of the evil wizard pained the creature greatly. "But so much is l-lost to me. I would find him with l-little effort if I was still p-p-pech. The stones would tell me where to l-look. But I cannot talk to them very often anymore." The monster rose from its seat on the stone. "I will go," it said determinedly. "You are not safe with me around."

"You will stay," Drizzt said suddenly and with a tone of finality that could not be denied.

"I c-cannot control," the hook horror tried to explain.

"You've no need to worry," said Belwar. He pointed to the doorway up on the ledge at the side of the cavern. "Our home is up there, with a door too small for you to get through. Down here by the lake you must rest until we all decide our best course of action."

The hook horror was exhausted, and the svirfneblin's reasoning seemed sound enough. The monster dropped heavily back to the stone and curled up as much as its bulky body would allow. Drizzt and Belwar took their leave, glancing back at their strange new companion with every step.

"Clacker," Belwar said suddenly, stopping Drizzt beside him. With great effort, the hook horror rolled over to consider the deep gnome, understanding that Belwar had uttered the word in its direction.

"That is what we shall call you, if you have no objections," the svirfneblin explained to the creature and to Drizzt. "Clacker!"

"A fitting name," Drizzt remarked.

"It is a g-good name," agreed the hook horror, but silently the creature wished that it could remember its pech name, the name that rolled on and on like a rounded boulder in a sloping passage and spoke prayers to the stone with each growling syllable.

"We will widen the door," Drizzt said when he and Belwar got inside their cave complex. "So that Clacker may enter and rest beside us in safety."

"No, dark elf," argued the burrow-warden. "That we shall not do."

"He is not safe out there beside the water," Drizzt replied. "Monsters will find him."

"Safe enough he is!" snorted Belwar. "What monster would willingly attack a hook horror?" Belwar understood Drizzt's sincere concern, but he understood, too, the danger in Drizzt's suggestion. "I have witnessed such spells," the svirfneblin said somberly. "They are called polymorph. Immediately comes the change of the body, but the change of the mind can take time."

"What are you saying?" Drizzt's voice edged on panic.

"Clacker is still a pech," replied Belwar, "trapped though he is in the body of a hook horror. But soon, I fear, Clacker will be a pech no more. A hook horror he will become, mind and body, and however friendly we might be, Clacker will come to think of us as no more than another meal."

Drizzt started to argue, but Belwar silenced him with one sobering thought. "Would you enjoy having to kill him, dark elf?"

Drizzt turned away. "His tale is familiar to me."

"Not as much as you believe," replied Belwar.

"I, too, was lost," Drizzt reminded the burrow-warden.

"So you believe," Belwar answered. "But that which was essentially Drizzt Do'Urden remained within you, my friend. You were as you had to be, as the situation around you forced you to be. This is different. Not just in body, but in very essence will Clacker become a hook horror. His thoughts will be the thoughts of a hook horror and *Magga cammara*, he will not return your grant of mercy when you are the one on the ground."

Drizzt could not be satisfied, though he could not refute the deep gnome's blunt logic. He moved into the complex's left-hand chamber, the one he had claimed as his bedroom, and fell into his hammock.

"Alas for you, Drizzt Do'Urden," Belwar mumbled under his breath as he watched the drow's heavy movements, laden with sorrow. "And alas for our doomed pech friend." The burrow-warden went into his own chamber and crawled into his hammock, feeling terrible about the whole situation but determined to remain coldly logical and practical, whatever the pain. For Belwar understood that Drizzt felt a kinship to the unfortunate creature, a potentially fatal bond founded in empathy for Clacker's loss of self.

Later that night, an excited Drizzt shook the svirfneblin from his slumber. "We must help him," Drizzt whispered harshly.

Belwar wiped an arm across his face and tried to orient himself. His sleep had been uneasy, filled with dreams in which he had cried *"Bivrip!"*

in an impossibly loud voice, then had proceeded to bash the life out of his newest companion.

"We must help him!" Drizzt said again, even more forcefully. Belwar could tell by the drow's haggard appearance that Drizzt had found no sleep this night.

"I am no wizard," the burrow-warden said. "Neither are—"

"Then we will find one." Drizzt growled. "We will find the human who cursed Clacker and force him to reverse the dweomer! We saw him by the stream only a few days ago. He cannot be so far away!"

"A mage capable of such magic will prove no easy foe," Belwar was quick to reply. "Have you so quickly forgotten the fireball?" Belwar glanced to the wall, to where his scorched leather jack hung on a peg, as if to convince himself. "The wizard is beyond us, I fear," Belwar mumbled, but Drizzt could see the lack of conviction in the burrow-warden's expression as he spoke the words.

"Are you so quick to condemn Clacker?" Drizzt asked bluntly. A wide smile began to spread over Drizzt's face as he saw the svirfneblin weakening. "Is this the same Belwar Dissengulp who took in a lost drow? That most honored burrow-warden who would not give up hope for a dark elf that everyone else considered dangerous and beyond help?"

"Go to sleep, dark elf," Belwar retorted, pushing Drizzt away with his hammer-hand.

"Wise advice, my friend," said Drizzt. "And you sleep well. We may have a long road ahead of us."

"*Magga cammara*," huffed the taciturn svirfneblin, stubbornly holding to his facade of gruff practicality. He rolled away from Drizzt and soon was snoring.

Drizzt noted that Belwar's snores now sounded from the depths of a deep and contented sleep.

⚔⚔⚔⚔⚔

Clacker beat against the wall with his clawed hands, tap- tapping the stone relentlessly.

"Not again," a flustered Belwar whispered to Drizzt. "Not out here!"

Drizzt sped along the winding corridor, homing in on the monotonous sound. "Clacker!" he called softly when the hook horror was in sight.

The hook horror turned to face the approaching drow, clawed hands wide and ready and a growing hiss slipping through his great beak. A moment later, Clacker realized what he was doing and abruptly stopped.

"Why must you continue that banging?" Drizzt asked him, trying to pretend, even to himself, that he had not seen Clacker's battle stance. "We are out in the wilds, my friend. Such sounds invite visitors."

The giant monster's head drooped. "You should not have c-c-come out with m-me," Clacker said. "I c-c-cannot—t-too many things will happen that I cannot c-control."

Drizzt reached up and put a comforting hand on Clacker's bony elbow. "It was my fault," the drow said, understanding the hook horror's meaning. Clacker had apologized for turning dangerously on Drizzt. "We should not have gone off in different directions," Drizzt continued, "and I should not have approached you so quickly and without warning. We will all stay together now, though our search may prove longer, and Belwar and I will help you to maintain control."

Clacker's beaked face brightened. "It does feel so very g-good to t-t-tap the stone," he proclaimed. Clacker banged a claw on the rock as if to jolt his memory. His voice and his gaze trailed away as he thought of his past life, the one that the wizard had stolen from him. All the pech's days had been spent tapping the stone, shaping the stone, talking to the precious stone.

"You will be pech again," Drizzt promised.

Belwar, approaching from the tunnel, heard the drow's words and was not so certain. They had been out in the tunnels for more than a tenday and had found not a sign of the wizard. The burrow-warden took some comfort in the fact that Clacker seemed to be winning back part of himself from his monstrous state, seemed to be regaining a measure of his pech personality. Belwar had watched the same transformation in Drizzt just a few tendays before, and beneath the survivalistic barriers of the hunter that Drizzt had become, Belwar had discovered his closest friend.

But the burrow-warden took care not to assume the same results with

Clacker. The hook horror's condition was the result of powerful magic, and no amount of friendship could reverse the workings of the wizard's dweomer. In finding Drizzt and Belwar, Clacker had been granted a temporary—and only temporary—reprieve from a miserable and undeniable fate.

They moved on through the tunnels of the Underdark for several more days without any luck. Clacker's personality still did not deteriorate, but even Drizzt, who had left the cave complex beside the lake so full of hope, began to feel the weight of increasing reality.

Then, just as Drizzt and Belwar had begun discussing returning to their home, the group came into a fair-sized cavern littered with rubble from a recent collapse of the ceiling.

"He has been here!" Clacker cried, and he offhandedly lifted a huge boulder and tossed it against a distant wall, where it shattered into so much rubble. "He has been here!" The hook horror rushed about, smashing stone and throwing boulders with growing, explosive rage.

"How can you know?" Belwar demanded, trying to stop his giant friend's tirade.

Clacker pointed up at the ceiling. "He d-did this. The w-w-w—he did this!"

Drizzt and Belwar exchanged concerned glances. The chamber's ceiling, which had been about fifteen feet up, was gouged and blasted, and in its center loomed a massive hole that extended up to twice the ceiling's former height. If magic had caused that devastation, it was powerful magic indeed!

"The wizard did this?" Belwar echoed. He cast that stubbornly practical look he had perfected toward Drizzt one more time.

"His t-t-tower," Clacker replied, and rushed off about the chamber to see if he could discern which exit the wizard had taken.

Now Drizzt and Belwar were completely at a loss, and Clacker, when he finally took the time to look at them, realized their confusion.

"The w-w-w—"

"Wizard," Belwar put in impatiently.

Clacker took no offense, even appreciated the assistance. "The w-wizard has a t-tower," the excited hook horror tried to explain. "A g-great iron t-tower that he takes with him, setting it up wherever it is c-c-convenient." Clacker looked up at the ruined ceiling. "Even if it does not always fit."

"He carries a tower?" Belwar asked, his long nose crinkling right up over itself.

Clacker nodded excitedly, but then didn't take the time to explain further, for he had found the wizard's trail, a clear boot print in a bed of moss leading down another of the corridors.

Drizzt and Belwar had to be satisfied with their friend's incomplete explanation, for the chase was on. Drizzt took up the lead, using all the skills he had learned in the drow Academy and had heightened during his decade alone in the Underdark. Belwar, with his innate racial understanding of the Underdark and his magically lighted brooch, kept track of their direction, and Clacker, in those instances when he fell more completely back into his former self, asked the stones for guidance. The three of them passed another blasted chamber, and another chamber that showed clear signs of the tower's presence, though its ceiling was high enough to accommodate the structure.

A few days later, the three companions turned into a wide and high cavern, and far back from them, beside a rushing stream, loomed the wizard's home. Again Drizzt and Belwar looked at each other helplessly, for the tower stood fully thirty feet high and twenty across, its smooth metallic walls mocking their plans. They took separate and cautious routes to the structure and were even more amazed, for the tower's walls were pure adamantite, the hardest metal in all the world.

They found only a single door, small and barely showing its outline in the perfection of the tower's craftsmanship. They didn't have to test it to know that it was secure against unwelcome visitors.

"The w-w-w—he is in there," Clacker snarled, running his claws over the door in desperation.

"Then he will have to come out," Drizzt reasoned. "And when he does, we will be waiting for him."

The plan did not satisfy the pech. With a rumbling roar that echoed throughout the region, Clacker threw his huge body against the tower door, then jumped back and slammed it again. The door didn't even shudder under the pounding, and it quickly became obvious to the deep gnome and the drow that Clacker's body would certainly lose the battle.

Drizzt tried vainly to calm his giant friend, while Belwar moved off to the side and began a familiar chant.

Finally, Clacker tumbled down in a heap, sobbing in exhaustion and pain and helpless rage. Then Belwar, his mithral hands sparking whenever they touched, waded in.

"Move aside!" the burrow-warden demanded. "I have come too far to be stopped by a single door!" Belwar moved directly in front of the small door and slammed his enchanted hammer-hand at it with all his strength. A blinding flash of blue sparks burst out in every direction. The deep gnome's muscled arms worked furiously, scraping and bashing, but when Belwar had exhausted his energy, the tower door showed only the slightest of scratches and superficial burns.

Belwar banged his hands together in disgust, showering himself in harmless sparks, and Clacker agreed wholeheartedly with his frustrated sentiments. Drizzt, though, was more angry and concerned than his friends. Not only had the wizard's tower stopped them, but the wizard inside undoubtedly knew of their presence. Drizzt moved about the structure cautiously, noting the many arrow slits. Creeping below one, he heard a soft chant, and though he couldn't understand the wizard's words, he could guess easily enough the human's intent.

"Run!" he yelled to his companions, and then, in sheer desperation, he grabbed a nearby stone and hauled it up into the opening of the arrow slit. Luck was with the drow, for the wizard completed his spell just as the rock slammed against the opening. A lightning bolt roared out, shattered the stone, and sent Drizzt flying, but it reflected back into the tower.

"Damnation! Damnation!" came a squeal from inside the tower. "I hate vhen that hoppens!"

Belwar and Clacker rushed over to help their fallen friend. The drow was only stunned, and he was up and ready before they ever got there.

"Oh, you ist going to pay dearly for that one, yest you ist!" came a cry from within.

"Run away!" cried the burrow-warden, and even the outraged hook horror was in full agreement. But as soon as Belwar looked into the drow's lavender eyes, he knew that Drizzt would not flee. Clacker, too, backed away a step from the fires gathering within Drizzt Do'Urden.

"*Magga cammara*, dark elf, we cannot get in," the svirfneblin prudently reminded Drizzt.

Drizzt pulled out the onyx figurine and held it against the arrow slit, blocking it with his body. "We shall see," he growled, and then he called to Guenhwyvar.

The black mist swirled about and found only one empty path clear from the figurine.

"I vill keell you all!" cried the unseen wizard.

The next sound from within the tower was a low panther's growl, and then the wizard's voice rang out again. "I cood be wrong!"

"Open the door!" Drizzt screamed. "On your life, foul wizard!"

"Never!"

Guenhwyvar roared again, then the wizard screamed and the door swung wide.

Drizzt led the way. They entered a circular room, the tower's bottom level. An iron ladder ran up its center to a trap door, the wizard's attempted escape route. The human hadn't quite made it, however, and he hung upside-down off the back side of the ladder, one leg hooked at the knee through a rung. Guenhwyvar, appearing fully healed from the ordeal in the acid lake and looking again like the most magnificent of panthers, perched on the other side of the ladder, casually mouthing the wizard's calf and foot.

"Do come een!" the wizard cried, throwing his arms out wide, then drawing them back to pull his drooping robe up from his face. Wisps of smoke rose from the remaining tatters of the lightning-blackened robe. "I am Brister Fendlestick. Velcome to my hoomble home!"

Belwar kept Clacker at the door, holding his dangerous friend back with his hammer-hand, while Drizzt moved up to take charge of the prisoner. The drow paused long enough to regard his dear feline companion, for he hadn't summoned Guenhwyvar since that day when he had sent the panther away to heal.

"You speak drow," Drizzt remarked, grabbing the wizard by the collar and agilely spinning him down to his feet. Drizzt eyed the man suspiciously; he had never seen a human before the encounter in the corridor by the stream. To this point, the drow wasn't overly impressed.

"Many tongues ist known to me," replied the wizard, brushing himself off. And then, as if his proclamation was meant to carry some great importance, he added, "I am Brister Fendlestick!"

"Do you name pech among your languages?" Belwar growled from the door.

"Pech?" the wizard replied, spitting the word with apparent distaste.

"Pech," Drizzt snarled, emphasizing his response by snapping the edge of a scimitar to within an inch of the wizard's neck.

Clacker took a step forward, easily sliding the blocking svirfneblin across the smooth floor.

"My large friend was once a pech," Drizzt explained. "You should know that."

"Pech," the wizard spat. "Useless leetle things, and always they ist in the way" Clacker took another long stride forward.

"Be on with it, drow," Belwar begged, futilely leaning against the huge hook horror.

"Give him back his identity," Drizzt demanded. "Make our friend a pech again. And be quick about it."

"Bah!" snorted the wizard. "He ist better off as he ist!" the unpredictable human replied. "Why would anyone weesh to remain a pech?"

Clacker's breath came in a loud gasp. The sheer strength of his third stride sent Belwar skidding off to the side.

"Now, wizard," Drizzt warned. From the ladder, Guenhwyvar issued a long and hungry growl.

"Oh, very vell, very vell!" the wizard spouted, throwing up his hands in disgust. "Wretched pech!" He pulled an immense book from of a pocket much too small to hold it. Drizzt and Belwar smiled to each other, thinking victory at hand. But then the wizard made a fatal mistake.

"I shood have killed him as I killed the others," he mumbled under his breath, too low for even Drizzt, standing right beside him, to make out the words.

But hook horrors had the keenest hearing of any creature in the Underdark.

A swipe of Clacker's enormous claw sent Belwar spiraling across the room. Drizzt, spinning about at the sound of heavy steps, was thrown aside by the momentum of the rushing giant, the drow's scimitars flying from his hands. And the wizard, the foolish wizard, padded Clacker's impact with the iron ladder, a jolt so vicious that it bowed the ladder and sent Guenhwyvar flying off the other side.

Whether the initial crushing blow of the hook horror's five-hundred-pound body had killed the wizard was academic by the time either Drizzt or Belwar had recovered enough to call out to their friend. Clacker's hooks and beak slashed and snapped relentlessly, tearing and crushing. Every now and then came a sudden flash and a puff of smoke as another of the many magical items that the wizard carried snapped apart.

And when the hook horror had played out his rage and looked around at his three companions, surrounding him in battle-ready stances, the lump of gore at Clacker's feet was no longer recognizable.

Belwar started to remark that the wizard had agreed to change Clacker back, but he didn't see the point. Clacker fell to his knees and dropped his face into his claws, hardly believing what he had done.

"Let us be gone from this place," Drizzt said, sheathing his blades.

"Search it," Belwar suggested, thinking that marvelous treasures might be hidden within. But Drizzt could not remain for another moment. He had seen too much of himself in the unbridled rage of his giant companion, and the smell of the bloodied heap filled him with frustrations and fears that he could not tolerate. With Guenhwyvar in tow, he walked from the tower.

Belwar moved over and helped Clacker to his feet, then guided the trembling giant from the structure. Stubbornly practical, though, the burrow-warden made his companions wait around while he scoured the tower, searching for items that might aid them, or for the command word that would allow him to carry the tower along. But either the wizard was a poor man—which Belwar doubted—or he had his treasures safely hidden away, possibly in some other plane of existence, for the svirfneblin found nothing beyond a simple water skin and a pair of worn boots. If the marvelous adamantite tower had a command word, it had gone to the grave with the wizard.

Their journey home was a quiet one, lost in private concerns, regrets, and memories. Drizzt and Belwar did not have to speak their most pressing fear. In their discussions with Clacker, they both had learned enough of the normally peaceable race of pech to know that Clacker's murderous outburst was far removed from the creature he once had been.

But, the deep gnome and the drow had to admit to themselves, Clacker's actions were not so far removed from the creature he was fast becoming.

# 15 Pointed Reminders

"What do you know?" Matron Malice demanded of Jarlaxle, walking at her side across the compound of House Do'Urden. Malice normally would not have been so conspicuous with the infamous mercenary, but she was worried and impatient. Reported stirring within the hierarchy of Menzoberranzan's ruling families did not bode well for House Do'Urden.

"Know?" Jarlaxle echoed, feigning surprise.

Malice scowled at him, as did Briza, walking on the other side of the brash mercenary.

Jarlaxle cleared his throat, though it sounded more like a laugh. He couldn't supply Malice with the details of the rumblings; he was not so foolish as to betray the more powerful houses of the city. But Jarlaxle could tease Malice with a simple statement of logic that only confirmed what she already had assumed. "Zin-carla, the spirit-wraith, has been in use for a very long time."

Malice struggled to keep her breathing inconspicuously smooth. She realized that Jarlaxle knew more than he would say, and the fact that the calculating mercenary had so coolly stated the obvious told her that her fears were justified. The spirit-wraith of Zaknafein had indeed been searching for Drizzt for a very long time. Malice did not need to be reminded that the Spider Queen was not known for her patience.

"Have you any more to tell me?" Malice asked.

Jarlaxle shrugged noncommittally.

"Then be gone from my house," the matron mother snarled.

Jarlaxle hesitated for a moment, wondering if he should demand payment for the little information he had provided. Then he dipped into one of his well-known low, hat-sweeping bows and turned for the gate.

He would find his payment soon enough.

In the anteroom to the house chapel an hour later, Matron Malice rested back in her throne and let her thoughts roll out into the winding tunnels of the wild Underdark. Her telepathy with the spirit-wraith was limited, usually a passing of strong emotions, nothing more. But from those internal struggles of Zaknafein, who had been Drizzt's father and closest friend in life and was now Drizzt's deadliest enemy, Malice could learn much of her spirit-wraith's progress. Anxieties caused by Zaknafein's inner struggle inevitably would increase whenever the spirit-wraith got close to Drizzt.

Now, after the disturbing meeting with Jarlaxle, Malice had to learn of Zaknafein's progress. A short time later, her efforts were rewarded.

⚔ ⚔ ⚔ ⚔ ⚔

"Matron Malice insists that the spirit-wraith has gone west, beyond the svirfneblin city," Jarlaxle explained to Matron Baenre. The mercenary had set out straight from House Do'Urden to the mushroom grove in the southern end of Menzoberranzan, to where the greatest of the drow families were housed.

"The spirit-wraith keeps to the trail," Matron Baenre mused, more to herself than to her informant. "That is good."

"But Matron Malice believes that Drizzt has a lead of many days, even tendays," Jarlaxle went on.

"She told you this?" Matron Baenre asked incredulously, amazed that Malice would reveal such damaging information.

"Some information can be gathered without words," the mercenary replied slyly. "Matron Malice's tone inferred much that she did not wish me to know."

Matron Baenre nodded and closed her wrinkled eyes, wearied by the whole experience. She had played a role in getting Matron Malice onto the ruling council, but now she could only sit and wait to see if Malice would remain.

"We must trust in Matron Malice," Matron Baenre said at length.

Across the room from Baenre and Jarlaxle, El-viddinvelp, Matron Baenre's companion mind flayer, turned its thoughts away from the conversation. The drow mercenary had reported that Drizzt had gone west, far out from Blingdenstone, and that news carried potential importance that could not be ignored.

The mind flayer projected its thoughts far out to the west, issued a clear warning down the corridors that were not as empty as they might appear.

⚔ ⚔ ⚔ ⚔ ⚔

Zaknafein knew as soon as he looked upon the still lake that he had caught up to his quarry. He dropped low into the crooks and crags along the wide cavern's wall and made his way about. Then he found the unnatural door and the cave complex beyond.

Old feelings stirred within the spirit-wraith, feelings of the kinship he once had known with Drizzt. New, savage emotions were quick to overwhelm them, though, as Matron Malice came into Zaknafein's mind in a wild fury. The spirit-wraith burst through the door, swords drawn, and tore through the complex. A blanket flew into the air and came down in pieces as Zaknafein's swords sliced across it a dozen times.

When the fit of rage had played itself out, Matron Malice's monster settled back into a crouch to examine the situation.

Drizzt was not at home.

It took the hunting spirit-wraith only a short time to determine that Drizzt, and a companion, or perhaps even two, had set out from the cavern a few days before. Zaknafein's tactical instincts told him to lie in wait, for surely this was no phony campsite, as had been the one outside the deep gnome city. Surely Zaknafein's prey meant to return.

The spirit-wraith sensed that Matron Malice, back on her throne in the drow city, would endure no delays. Time was running short for her—the dangerous whispers were growing louder every day—and Malice's fears and impatience cost her dearly this time.

⚔ ⚔ ⚔ ⚔ ⚔

Only a few hours after Malice had driven the spirit-wraith into the tunnels in pursuit of her renegade son, Drizzt, Belwar, and Clacker returned to the cavern by a different route.

Drizzt sensed at once that something was very wrong. He drew his blades and rushed across to the ledge, springing up to the door of the cave complex before Belwar and Clacker could even begin to question him.

When they arrived at the cave, they understood Drizzt's alarm. The place was destroyed, hammocks and bedrolls torn apart, bowls and a small box that had been stuffed with gathered foods smashed and thrown to every corner. Clacker, who could not fit inside the complex, spun from the door and moved away, ensuring that no enemy was lurking in the far reaches of the large cavern.

"*Magga cammara*!" Belwar roared. "What monster did this?"

Drizzt held up a blanket and pointed out the clean cuts in the fabric. Belwar did not miss the drow's meaning.

"Blades," the burrow-warden said grimly. "Fine and crafted blades."

"The blades of a drow," Drizzt finished for him.

"Far are we from Menzoberranzan," Belwar reminded him. "Far out in the wilds, beyond the knowledge and sight of your kin."

Drizzt knew better than to agree with such an assumption. For the bulk of his young life, Drizzt had witnessed the fanaticism that guided the lives of Lolth's foul priestesses. Drizzt himself had traveled on a raid many miles to the surface of the Realms, a raid that suited no better purpose than to give the Spider Queen a sweet taste of the blood of surface elves. "Do not underestimate Matron Malice," he said grimly.

"If it is indeed your mother come to call," Belwar growled, clapping his hands together, "she will find more than she expected waiting for her. We shall lie for her," the svirfneblin promised, "the three of us."

"Do not underestimate Matron Malice," Drizzt said again. "This encounter was no coincidence, and Matron Malice will be prepared for whatever we have to offer."

"You cannot know that," Belwar reasoned, but when the burrow-warden recognized the sincere dread in the drow's lavender eyes, all conviction drifted out of his voice.

They gathered what few usable items remained and set out only a short while later, again going west to put even more distance between themselves and Menzoberranzan.

Clacker took up the lead, for few monsters would willingly put themselves in the path of a hook horror. Belwar walked in the middle, the solid anchor of the party, and Drizzt floated along silently far to the rear, taking it upon himself to protect his friends if his mother's agents should catch up to them. Belwar had reasoned that they might have a good lead on whoever ruined their home. If the perpetrators had set off in pursuit of them from the cave complex, following their trail to the tower of the dead wizard, many days would pass before the enemy even returned to the cavern of the lake. Drizzt was not so secure in the burrow-warden's reasoning.

He knew his mother too well.

After several interminable days, the troupe came into a region of broken floors, jagged walls, and ceilings filled with stalactites that leered down at them like poised monsters. They closed in their ranks, needing the comfort of companionship. Despite the attention it might draw, Belwar took out his magically lighted brooch and pinned it on his leather jack. Even in the glow, the shadows thrown by sharp-edged mounds promised only peril.

This region seemed more hushed than the Underdark's usual stillness. Rarely did travelers in the subterranean world of the Realms hear the sounds of other creatures, but here the quiet felt more profound, as though all life somehow had been stolen from the place. Clacker's heavy steps and the scrape of Belwar's boots echoed unnervingly off the many stone faces.

Belwar was the first to sense approaching danger. Subtle vibrations in the stone called out to the svirfneblin that he and his friends were not alone. He stopped Clacker with his pick-hand, then looked back to Drizzt to see if the drow shared his uneasy feelings.

Drizzt signaled to the ceiling, then levitated up into the darkness, seeking an ambush spot among the many stalactites. The drow drew one of his scimitars as he ascended and put his other hand on the onyx figurine in his pocket.

Belwar and Clacker set up behind a ridge of stone, the deep gnome mumbling through the refrain that would enchant his mithral hands. Both felt better in the knowledge that the drow warrior was above them, looking over them.

But Drizzt was not the only one who figured the stalactites as an ambush spot. As soon as he entered the layer of jagged, spearlike stones, the drow knew he was not alone.

A form, slightly larger than Drizzt but obviously humanoid, drifted out around a nearby stalactite. Drizzt kicked off a stone to propel himself at it, drawing his other scimitar as he went. He knew his peril a moment later, for his enemy's head resembled a four-tentacled octopus. Drizzt had never actually viewed such a creature before, but he knew what it was: an illithid, a mind flayer, the most evil and most feared monster in all the Underdark.

The mind flayer struck first, long before Drizzt had closed within his scimitar's limited range. The monster's tentacles wiggled and waved, and—*fwoop!*—a cone of mental energy rolled over Drizzt. The drow fought back against the impending blackness with all of his willpower. He tried to concentrate on his target, tried to focus his anger, but the illithid blasted again. Another mind flayer appeared and fired its stunning force at Drizzt from the side.

Belwar and Clacker could see nothing of the encounter, for Drizzt was above the radius of the deep gnome's illuminating brooch. Both sensed that something was going on above them, though, and the burrow-warden risked a whispered call to his friend.

"Drizzt?"

His answer came only a moment later, when two scimitars clanged to the stone. Belwar and Clacker started toward the weapons in surprise, then fell back. Before them the air shimmered and wavered, as if an invisible door to some other plane of existence was being opened.

An illithid stepped through, appearing right before the surprised friends and letting out its mental blast before either of them even had time to cry out. Belwar reeled and stumbled to the floor, but Clacker, his mind already in conflict between hook horror and pech, was not so adversely affected.

The mind flayer loosed its force again, but the hook horror stepped right through the stunning cone and smashed the illithid with a single blow of his enormous clawed hand.

Clacker looked all around, and then up. Other mind flayers were drifting down from the ceiling, two holding Drizzt by the ankles. More invisible doors opened. In an instant, blast after blast came at Clacker from every angle, and the defense of his dual personalities' inner turmoil quickly began to wear away. Desperation and welling outrage took over Clacker's actions.

Clacker was solely a hook horror at that moment, acting on the instinctive rage and ferocity of the monstrous breed.

But even the hard shell of a hook horror proved no defense against the mind flayers' continuing insidious blasts. Clacker rushed at the two holding Drizzt.

The darkness caught him halfway there.

He was kneeling on the stone—he knew that much. Clacker crawled on, refusing to surrender, refusing to relinquish the sheer anger.

Then he lay on the floor, with no thoughts of Drizzt or Belwar or rage.

There was only darkness.

# Part Four

## Helpless

There have been many times in my life when I have felt helpless. It is perhaps the most acute pain a person can know, founded in frustration and ventless rage. The nick of a sword upon a battling soldier's arm cannot compare to the anguish a prisoner feels at the crack of a whip. Even if the whip does not strike the helpless prisoner's body, it surely cuts deeply at his soul.

We all are prisoners at one time or another in our lives, prisoners to ourselves or to the expectations of those around us. It is a burden that all people endure, that all people despise, and that few people ever learn to escape. I consider myself fortunate in this respect, for my life has traveled along a fairly straight-running path of improvement. Beginning in Menzoberranzan, under the relentless scrutiny of the evil Spider Queen's high priestesses, I suppose that my situation could only have improved.

In my stubborn youth, I believed that I could stand alone, that I was strong enough to conquer my enemies with sword and with principles. Arrogance convinced me that by sheer determination, I could conquer helplessness itself. Stubborn and foolish youth, I must admit, for when I look back on those years now, I see quite clearly that rarely did I stand alone and rarely did I have to stand alone. Always there were friends, true and dear, lending me support even when I believed I did not want it, and even when I did not realize they were doing it.

Zaknafein, Belwar, Clacker, Mooshie, Bruenor, Regis, Catti-brie, Wulfgar, and of course, Guenhwyvar, dear Guenhwyvar. These were the companions who justified my principles, who gave me the strength to continue against any foe, real or imagined. These were the companions who fought the helplessness, the rage, and frustration.

These were the friends who gave me my life.

–Drizzt Do'Urden

# 16
# Insidious Chains

Clacker looked down to the far end of the long and narrow cavern, to the many-towered structure that served as a castle to the illithid community. Though his vision was poor, the hook horror could make out the squat forms crawling about on the rock castle, and he could plainly hear the chiming of their tools. They were slaves, Clacker knew—duergar, goblins, deep gnomes, and several other races that Clacker did not know—serving their illithid masters with their skills in stonework, helping to continue the improvement and design on the huge lump of rock that the mind flayers had claimed as their home.

Perhaps Belwar, so obviously suited to such endeavors, was already at work on the massive building.

The thoughts fluttered through Clacker's mind and were forgotten, replaced by the hook horror's less involved instincts. The mind flayers' stunning blasts had reduced Clacker's mental resistance and the wizard's polymorph spell had taken more of him, so much so that he could not even realize the lapse. Now his twin identities battled evenly, leaving poor Clacker in a state of simple confusion.

If he understood his dilemma, and if he had known the fate of his friends, he might have considered himself fortunate.

The mind flayers suspected that there was more to Clacker than his hook horror body would indicate. The illithid community's survival was based on knowledge and by reading thoughts, and though they could not penetrate the jumble that was Clacker's mind, they saw clearly that the mental workings within the bony exoskeleton were decidedly unlike those expected from a simple Underdark monster.

The mind flayers were not foolish masters, and they knew, too, the dangers of trying to decipher and control an armed and armored quarter-ton killing monster. Clacker was simply too dangerous and unpredictable to be kept in close quarters. In the illithids' slave society, however, there was a place for everyone.

Clacker stood upon an island of stone, a slab of rock perhaps fifty yards in diameter and surrounded by a deep and wide chasm. With him were assorted other creatures, including a small herd of rothé and several battered duergar who obviously had spent too long under the illithids' mind-melting influences. The gray dwarves sat or stood, blank-faced, staring out at nothing at all and awaiting, Clacker soon came to understand, their turn on the supper table of their cruel masters.

Clacker paced the island's perimeter, searching for some escape, though the pech part of him would have recognized the futility of it all. Only a single bridge spanned the warding chasm, a magical and mechanical thing that recoiled tightly against the chasm's other side when not in use.

A group of mind flayers with a single burly ogre slave approached the lever that controlled the bridge. Immediately, Clacker was assaulted by their telepathic suggestions. A single course of action cut through the jumble of his thoughts, and at that moment, he learned of his purpose on the island. He was to be the shepherd for the mind flayers' flock. They wanted a gray dwarf and a rothé, and the shepherd slave obediently went to work.

Neither victim offered any resistance. Clacker neatly twisted the gray dwarf's neck, then, not so neatly, bashed in the rothé's skull. He sensed that the illithids were pleased, and this notion brought some curious emotions to him, satisfaction being the most prevalent.

Hoisting both creatures, Clacker moved to the gorge to stand opposite the group of illithids.

An illithid pulled back on the bridge's waist-high lever. Clacker noted that the action of the trigger was away from him; an important fact, though the hook horror did not exactly understand why at that time. The stone-and-metal bridge grumbled and shook and shot out from the cliff opposite Clacker. It rolled out toward the island until it caught securely on the stone at Clacker's feet.

*Come to me,* came one illithid's command. Clacker might have managed to resist the command if he had seen any point in it. He stepped out onto the bridge, which groaned considerably under his bulk.

*Halt! Drop the kills,* came another suggestion when the hook horror was halfway across. *Drop the kills!* the telepathic voice cried again. *And get back to your island!*

Clacker considered his alternatives. The rage of the hook horror welled within him, and his thoughts that were pech, angered by the loss of his friends, were in complete agreement. A few strides would take him to his enemies.

On command from the mind flayers, the ogre moved up to the lip of the bridge. It stood a bit taller than Clacker and was nearly as wide, but it was unarmed and would not be able to stop him. Off to the side of the burly guard, though, Clacker recognized a more serious defense. The illithid who had pulled the lever to activate the bridge stood by it still, one hand, a curious four-fingered appendage, eagerly clenching and unclenching it.

Clacker would not get across the remaining portion and past the blocking ogre before the bridge rolled away from under him, dropping him into the depths of the chasm. Reluctantly, the hook horror placed his kills on the bridge and stepped back to his stone island. The ogre came out immediately and retrieved the dead dwarf and rothé for its masters.

The illithid then pulled the lever, and in the blink of an eye, the magical bridge snapped back across the gorge, leaving Clacker stranded once more.

*Eat,* one of the illithids instructed. An unfortunate rothé wandered by the hook horror as the command came surging into his thoughts, and Clacker absently dropped a heavy claw onto its head.

As the illithids departed, Clacker sat down to his meal, reveling in the taste of blood and meat. His hook horror side won over completely during the raw feast, but every time Clacker looked back across the gorge and down the narrow cavern to the illithid castle, a tiny pech voice within him piped out its concern for a svirfneblin and a drow.

⚔ ⚔ ⚔ ⚔ ⚔

Of all the slaves recently captured in the tunnels outside the illithid castle, Belwar Dissengulp was the most sought after. Aside from the curiosity factor of the svirfneblin's mithral hands, Belwar was perfectly suited for the two duties most desired in an illithid slave: working the stone and fighting in the gladiatorial arena.

The illithid slave auction went into an uproar when the deep gnome was marched forward. Bids of gold and magic items, private spells and tomes of knowledge, were thrown about with abandon. In the end, the burrow-warden was sold to a group of three mind flayers, the three who had led the party that had captured him. Belwar, of course, had no knowledge of the transaction; before it was ever completed, the deep gnome was ushered away down a dark and narrow tunnel and placed in a small, unremarkable room.

A short while later, three voices echoed in his mind, three unique telepathic voices that the deep gnome understood and would not forget—the voices of his new masters.

An iron portcullis rose before Belwar, revealing a well-lighted circular room with high walls and rows of audience seats above them.

*Do come out,* one of the masters bade him, and the burrow-warden, fully desiring only to please his master, did not hesitate. When he exited the short passageway, he saw that several dozen mind flayers had gathered all about on stone benches. Those strange four-fingered illithid hands pointed down at him from every direction, all backed by the same expressionless octopus face. Following the telepathic link, though, Belwar had no trouble finding his master among the crowd, busily arguing odds and antes with a small group.

Across the way, a similar portcullis opened and a huge ogre stepped out. Immediately the creature's eyes went up into the crowd as it sought its own master, the focal point of its existence.

*This evil ogre beast has threatened me, my brave svirfneblin champion,* came the telepathic encouragement of Belwar's master a short while later, after all of the betting had been settled. *Do destroy it for me.*

Belwar needed no further prompting, nor did the ogre, having received a similar message from its master. The gladiators rushed each other furiously, but while the ogre was young and rather stupid, Belwar was a crafty old veteran. He slowed at the last moment and rolled to the side.

The ogre, trying desperately to kick at him as it ended its charge, stumbled for just a moment.

Too long.

Belwar's hammer-hand crunched into the ogre's knee with a crack that resounded as powerfully as a wizard's lightning bolt. The ogre lurched forward, nearly doubling over, and Belwar drove his pickaxe-hand into the ogre's meaty backside. As the giant monster stumbled off balance to the side, Belwar threw himself at its feet, tripping it to the stone.

The burrow-warden was up in an instant, leaping onto the prone giant and running right up it toward its head. The ogre recovered quickly enough to catch the svirfneblin by the front of his jack, but even as the monster started to hurl the nasty little opponent away, Belwar dug his pickaxe-hand deep into its chest. Howling in rage and pain, the stupid ogre continued its throw, and Belwar was jerked out straight.

The sharp tip of the pickaxe held its grip and the deep gnome's momentum tore a wide gash in the ogre's chest. The ogre rolled and flailed, finally freeing itself from the cruel mithral hand. A huge knee caught Belwar in the rump, launching him to the stone many feet away. The burrow-warden came back up to his feet after a few short bounces, dazed and smarting but still desiring nothing but to please his master.

He heard the silent cheering and telepathic shouting of every illithid in the room, but one call cut through the mental din with precise clarity.

*Kill it!* Belwar's master commanded.

Belwar didn't hesitate. Still flat on its back, the ogre clutched at its chest, trying vainly to stop its lifeblood from flowing away. The wounds it already had suffered probably would have proved fatal, but Belwar was far from satisfied. This wretched thing had threatened his master! The burrow-warden charged straight at the top of the ogre's head, his hammer-hand leading the way. Three quick punches softened the monster's skull, then the pickaxe dived in for the killing blow.

The doomed ogre jerked wildly in the last spasms of its life, but Belwar felt no pity. He had pleased his master; nothing else in all the world mattered to the burrow-warden at that moment.

Up in the stands, the proud owner of the svirfneblin champion collected his due of gold and potion bottles. Contented that it had done well in selecting this one, the illithid looked back to Belwar, who still chopped and bashed at the corpse. Though it enjoyed watching its new champion at savage play, the illithid quickly sent out a message to cease. The dead ogre, after all, was also part of the bet.

No sense in ruining dinner.

⚔ ⚔ ⚔ ⚔ ⚔

At the heart of the illithid castle stood a huge tower, a gigantic stalagmite hollowed and sculpted to house the most important members of the strange community. The inside of the giant stone structure was ringed by balconies and spiraling stairways, each level housing several of the mind flayers. But it was the bottom chamber, unadorned and circular, that held the most important being of all, the central brain.

Fully twenty feet in diameter, this boneless lump of pulsating flesh tied the mind flayer community together in telepathic symbiosis. The central brain was the composite of their knowledge, the mental eye that guarded their outside chambers and which had heard the warning cries of the illithid from the drow city many miles to the east. To the illithids of the community, the central brain was the coordinator of their entire existence and nothing short of their god. Thus, only a very few slaves were allowed within this special tower, captives with sensitive and delicate fingers that could massage the illithid god-thing and soothe it with tender brushes and warm fluids.

Drizzt Do'Urden was among this group.

The drow knelt on the wide walkway that ringed the room, reaching out to stroke the amorphous mass, feeling keenly its pleasures and displeasures. When the brain became upset, Drizzt felt the sharp tingles and the tenseness in the veined tissues. He would massage more forcefully, easing his beloved master back to serenity.

When the brain was pleased, Drizzt was pleased. Nothing else in all the world mattered; the renegade drow had found his purpose in life. Drizzt Do'Urden had come home.

⚔ ⚔ ⚔ ⚔ ⚔

"A most profitable capture, that one," said the mind flayer in its watery, otherworldly voice. The creature held up the potions it had won in the arena.

The other two illithids wiggled their four-fingered hands, indicating their agreement.

*Arena champion,* one of them remarked telepathically.

"And tooled to dig," the third added aloud. A notion entered its mind and thus, the minds of the others. *Perhaps to carve?*

The three illithids looked over to the far side of the chamber, where the work had begun on a new cubby area.

The first illithid wiggled its fingers and gurgled, "In time the svirfneblin will be put to such menial tasks. Now he must win for me more potions, more gold. A most profitable capture!"

"As were all taken in the ambush," said the second.

"The hook horror tends the herd," explained the third.

"And the drow tends the brain," gurgled the first. "I noticed him as I ascended to our chamber. That one will prove a proficient masseuse, to the pleasure of the brain and to the benefit of us all."

"And there is this," said the second, one of its tentacles snapping out to nudge the third. The third illithid held up an onyx figurine.

*Magic?* wondered the first.

Indeed, the second mentally responded. *Linked to the Astral Plane. An entity stone, I believe.*

"Have you called to it?" the first asked aloud.

Together, the other illithids clenched their hands, the mind flayer signal for no. "A dangerous foe, mayhaps," explained the third. "We thought it prudent to observe the beast on its own plane before summoning it."

"A wise choice," agreed the first. "When will you be going?"

"At once," said the second. "And will you accompany us?"

The first illithid clenched its fists, then held out the potion bottle. "Profits to be won," it explained.

The other two wiggled their fingers excitedly. Then, as their companion retired to another room to count its winnings, they sat down in comfortable, overstuffed chairs and prepared themselves for their journey.

They floated together, leaving their corporeal bodies at rest on the chairs. They ascended beside the figurine's link to the Astral Plane, visible to them in their astral state as a thin silvery cord. They were beyond their companions' cavern now, beyond the stones and noises of the Material Plane, floating into the vast serenity of the astral world. Here, there were few sounds other than the continuous chanting of the astral wind. Here, too, there was no solid structure—none in terms of the material world—with matter being defined in gradations of light.

The illithids veered away from the figurine's silver cord as they neared the completion of their astral ascent. They would come into the plane near to the entity of the great panther, but not so close as to make it aware of their presence. Illithids were not normally welcome guests, being despised by nearly every creature on every plane they traveled.

They came fully into their astral state without incident and had little trouble locating the entity represented by the figurine.

Guenhwyvar romped through a forest of starlight in pursuit of the entity of the elk, continuing the endless cycle. The elk, no less magnificent than the panther, leaped and sprang in perfect balance and unmistakable grace. The elk and Guenhwyvar had played out this scenario a million times and would play it out a million, million more. This was the order and harmony that ruled the panther's existence, that ultimately ruled the planes of all the universe.

Some creatures, though, like the denizens of the lower planes, and like the mind flayers that now observed the panther from afar, could not accept the simple perfection of this harmony and could not recognize the beauty of this eternal hunt. As they watched the wondrous panther in its life's play, the illithids' only thoughts centered on how they might use the cat to their best advantage.

# 17
# A Delicate Balance

Belwar studied his latest foe carefully, sensing some familiarity with the armored beast's appearance. Had he befriended such a creature before? he wondered. Whatever doubts the svirfneblin gladiator might have had, though, could not break into the deep gnome's consciousness, for Belwar's illithid master continued its insidious stream of telepathic deceptions.

*Kill it, my brave champion,* the illithid pleaded from its perch in the stands. *It is your enemy, most assuredly, and it shall bring harm to me if you do not kill it!*

The hook horror, much larger than Belwar's lost friend, charged the svirfneblin, having no reservations about making a meal of the deep gnome.

Belwar coiled his stubby legs under him and waited for the precise moment. As the hook horror bore down on him, its clawed hands wide to prevent him from dodging to the side, Belwar sprang straight ahead, his hammer-hand leading the way right up into the monster's chest. Cracks ran all through the hook horror's exoskeleton from the sheer force of the blow, and the monster swooned as it continued forward.

Belwar's flight made a quick reversal, for the hook horror's weight and momentum was much greater than the svirfneblin's. He felt his shoulder snap out of joint, and he, too, nearly fainted from the sudden agony. Again the callings of Belwar's illithid master overruled his thoughts, and even the pain.

The gladiators crashed together in a heap, Belwar buried beneath the monster's bulk. The hook horror's encumbering size prevented it from getting its arms at the burrow-warden, but it had other weapons. A wicked beak dived at Belwar. The deep gnome managed to get his pickaxe-hand in its path, but still the hook horror's giant head pushed on, twisting Belwar's arm backward. The hungry beak snapped and twisted barely an inch from the burrow-warden's face.

Throughout the stands of the large arena, illithids jumped about and chatted excitedly, both in their telepathic mode and in their gurgling, watery voices. Fingers wiggled in opposition to clenched fists as the mind flayers prematurely tried to collect on bets.

Belwar's master, fearing the loss of its champion, called out to the hook horror's master. *Do you yield?* it asked, trying to make the thoughts appear confident.

The other illithid turned away smugly and shut down its telepathic receptacles. Belwar's master could only watch.

The hook horror could not drive any closer; the svirfneblin's arm was locked against the stone at the elbow, the mithral pickaxe firmly holding back the monster's deadly beak. The hook horror reverted to a different tactic, raising its head free of Belwar's hand in a sudden jerking movement.

Belwar's warrior intuition saved him at that moment, for the hook horror reversed suddenly and the deadly beak dived back in. The normal reaction and expected defense would have been to swipe the monster's head to the side with the pickaxe-hand. The hook horror anticipated such a counter, and Belwar anticipated that it would.

Belwar threw his arm across in front of him, but shortened his reach so that the pickaxe passed well below the hook horror's plunging beak. The monster, meanwhile, believing that Belwar was attempting to strike a blow, stopped its dive exactly as it had planned.

But the mithral pickaxe reversed its direction much quicker than the monster anticipated. Belwar's backhand caught the hook horror right behind the beak and snapped its head to the side. Then, ignoring the searing pain from his injured shoulder, Belwar curled his other arm at the elbow and punched out. There was no strength behind the blow, but at that moment, the hook horror came back around the pickaxe and opened its beak for a bite at the deep gnome's exposed face.

Just in time to catch a mithral hammer instead.

Belwar's hand wedged far back in the hook horror's mouth, opening the beak more than it was designed to open. The monster jerked wildly, trying to free itself, each sudden twist sending waves of pain down the burrow-warden's wounded arm.

Belwar responded with equal fury, whacking again and again at the side of the hook horror's head with his free hand. Blood oozed down the giant beak as the pickaxe dug in.

"Do you yield?" Belwar's master now shouted in its watery voice at the hook horror's master.

The question was premature again, however, for down in the arena, the armored hook horror was far from defeated. It used another weapon: its sheer weight. The monster ground its chest into the lying deep gnome, trying simply to crush the life out of him.

"Do *you* yield?" the hook horror's master retorted, seeing the unexpected turn of events.

Belwar's pickaxe caught the hook horror's eye, and the monster howled in agony. Illithids jumped and pointed, wiggling their fingers and clenching and unclenching their fists.

Both masters of the gladiators understood how much they had to lose. Would either participant ever be fit to fight again if the battle was allowed to continue?

*Mayhaps we should consider a draw?* Belwar's master offered telepathically. The other illithid readily agreed. Both masters sent messages down to their champions. It took several brutal moments to calm the fires of rage and end the contest, but eventually, the illithid suggestions overruled the gladiators' savage instincts of survival. Suddenly, both the deep gnome and the hook horror felt an affinity for each other, and when the hook horror rose, it lent a claw to the svirfneblin to help him to his feet.

A short while later, Belwar sat on the single stone bench in his tiny, unadorned cell, just inside the tunnel to the circular arena. The burrow-warden's hammer-wielding arm had gone completely numb and a gruesome purplish blue bruise covered his entire shoulder. Many days would pass before Belwar would be able to compete in the arena again, and it troubled him deeply that he would not soon please his master.

The illithid came to him to inspect the damage. It had potions that could help heal the wound, but even with the magical aid, Belwar obviously needed time to rest. The mind flayer had other uses for the svirfneblin, though. A cubby in its private quarters needed completing.

*Come,* the illithid bade Belwar, and the burrow-warden jumped to his feet and rushed out, respectfully remaining a stride behind his master.

A kneeling drow caught Belwar's attention as the mind flayer led him through the bottom level of the central tower. How fortunate the dark elf was to be able to touch and bring pleasure to the central brain of the community! Belwar then thought no more of it, though, as he made the ascent to the structure's third level and to the suite of rooms that his three masters shared.

The other two illithids sat in their chairs, motionless and apparently lifeless. Belwar's master paid little heed to the spectacle; it knew that its companions were far away in their astral travels and that their corporeal bodies were quite safe. The mind flayer did pause to wonder, for just a moment, how its companions fared in that distant plane. Like all illithids, Belwar's master enjoyed astral travel, but pragmatism, a definite illithid trait, kept the creature's thoughts on the business at hand. It had made a large investment in buying Belwar, an investment it was not willing to lose.

The mind flayer led Belwar into a back room and sat him down on an unremarkable stone table. Then, suddenly, the illithid bombarded Belwar with telepathic suggestions and questions, probing as it roughly set the injured shoulder and applied wrappings. Mind flayers could invade a creature's thoughts on first contact, either with their stunning blow or with telepathic communications, but it could take tendays, even months, for an illithid to fully dominate its slave. Each encounter broke down more of the slave's natural resistance to the illithid's mental insinuations, revealed more of the slave's memories and emotions.

Belwar's master was determined to know everything about this curious svirfneblin, about his strange, crafted hands and about the unusual company he chose to keep. This time during the telepathic exchange, the illithid focused on the mithral hands, for it sensed that Belwar was not performing up to his capabilities.

The illithid's thoughts probed and prodded, and sometime later fell into a deep corner of Belwar's mind and learned a curious chant.

*Bivrip?* it questioned Belwar. Simply on reflex, the burrow-warden banged his hands together, then winced in pain from the shock of the blow.

The illithid's fingers and tentacles wiggled eagerly. It had touched upon something important, it knew, something that could make its champion stronger. If the mind flayer allowed Belwar the memory of the chant, however, it would give back to the svirfneblin a part of himself, a conscious memory of his days before slavery.

The illithid handed Belwar still another healing potion, then glanced around to inspect its wares. If Belwar was to continue as a gladiator, he would have to face the hook horror again in the arena; by illithid rules, a rematch was required after a draw. Belwar's master doubted that the svirfneblin would survive another battle against that armored champion.

Unless . . .

---

Dinin Do'Urden paced his lizard mount through the region of Menzoberranzan's lesser houses, the most congested section of the city. He kept the cowl of his *piwafwi* pulled low about his face and bore no insignia revealing him as a noble of a ruling house. Secrecy was Dinin's ally, both from the watching eyes of this dangerous section of the city, and from the disapproving glares of his mother and sister. Dinin had survived long enough to understand the dangers of complacency. He lived in a state that bordered on paranoia; he never knew when Malice and Briza might be watching.

A group of bugbears sauntered out of the walking lizard's way. Fury swept through the proud elderboy of House Do'Urden at the slaves' casual manner. Dinin's hand went instinctively to the whip on his belt.

Dinin wisely checked his rage, though, reminding himself of the possible consequences of being revealed. He turned another of the many sharp corners and moved down through a row of connected stalagmite mounds.

"So you have found me," came a familiar voice from behind and to the side. Surprised and afraid, Dinin stopped his mount and froze in his saddle. He knew that a dozen tiny crossbows—at least—were trained on him.

Slowly, Dinin turned his head to watch Jarlaxle's approach. Out here in the shadows, the mercenary seemed much different from the overly polite and compliant drow Dinin had known in House Do'Urden. Or perhaps it was just the specter of the two sword-wielding drow guards standing by Jarlaxle's sides and Dinin's own realization that he didn't have Matron Malice around to protect him.

"One should ask permission before entering another's house," Jarlaxle said calmly but with definite threatening undertones. "Common courtesy."

"I am out in the open streets," Dinin reminded him.

Jarlaxle's smile denied the logic. "My house."

Dinin remembered his station, and the thoughts inspired some courage. "Should a noble of a ruling house, then, ask Jarlaxle's permission before leaving his front gate?" the elderboy growled. "And what of Matron Baenre, who would not enter the least of Menzoberranzan's houses without seeking permission from the appropriate matron mother? Should Matron Baenre, too, ask permission of Jarlaxle, the houseless rogue?" Dinin realized that he might be carrying the insult a bit too far, but his pride demanded the words.

Jarlaxle relaxed visibly and the smile that came to his face almost appeared sincere. "So you have found me," he said again, this time dipping into his customary bow. "State your purpose and be done with it."

Dinin crossed his arms over his chest belligerently, gaining confidence at the mercenary's apparent concessions. "Are you so certain that I was looking for you?"

Jarlaxle exchanged grins with his two guards. Snickers from unseen soldiers in the shadows of the lane stole a good measure of Dinin's budding confidence.

"State your business, Elderboy," Jarlaxle said more pointedly, "and be done with it."

Dinin was more than willing to complete this encounter as quickly as possible. "I require information concerning Zin-carla," he said bluntly. "The spirit-wraith of Zaknafein has walked the Underdark for many days. Too many, perhaps?"

Jarlaxle's eyes narrowed as he followed the elderboy's reasoning. "Matron Malice sent you to me?" he stated as much as asked.

Dinin shook his head and Jarlaxle did not doubt his sincerity. "You are as wise as you are skilled in the blade," the mercenary offered graciously, slipping into a second bow, one that seemed somehow ambiguous out here in Jarlaxle's dark world.

"I have come of my own initiative," Dinin said firmly. "I must find some answers."

"Are you afraid, Elderboy?"

"Concerned," Dinin replied sincerely, ignoring the mercenary's taunting tone. "I never make the error of underestimating my enemies, or my allies."

Jarlaxle cast him a confused glance.

"I know what my brother has become," Dinin explained. "And I know who Zaknafein once was."

"Zaknafein is a spirit-wraith now," Jarlaxle replied, "under the control of Matron Malice."

"Many days," Dinin said quietly, believing the implications of his words spoke loudly enough.

"Your mother asked for Zin-carla," Jarlaxle retorted, a bit sharply. "It is Lolth's greatest gift, given only so that the Spider Queen is pleased in return. Matron Malice knew the risk when she requested Zin-carla. Surely you understand, Elderboy, that spirit-wraiths are given for the completion of a specific task."

"And what are the consequences of failure?" Dinin asked bluntly, matching Jarlaxle's perturbed attitude.

The mercenary's incredulous stare was all the answer Dinin needed. "How long does Zaknafein have?" Dinin asked.

Jarlaxle shrugged noncommittally and answered with a question of his own. "Who can guess at Lolth's plans?" he asked. "The Spider Queen can be a patient one—if the gain is great enough to justify the wait. Is Drizzt's value such?" Again the mercenary shrugged. "That is for Lolth, and for Lolth alone, to decide."

Dinin studied Jarlaxle for a long moment, until he was certain that the mercenary had nothing left to offer him. Then he turned back to his lizard mount and pulled the cowl of his *piwafwi* low. When he regained his saddle, Dinin spun about, thinking to issue one final comment, but the mercenary and his guards were nowhere to be found.

⚔ ⚔ ⚔ ⚔ ⚔

*"Bivrip!"* Belwar cried, completing the spell. The burrow-warden banged his hands together again, and this time did not wince, for the pain was not so intense. Sparks flew when the mithral hands crashed together, and Belwar's master clapped its four-fingered hands in absolute glee.

The illithid simply had to see its gladiator in action now. It looked about for a target and spotted the partially cut cubby. A whole set of telepathic instructions roared into the burrow-warden's mind as the illithid imparted mental images of the design and depth it wanted for the cubby.

Belwar moved right in. Unsure of the strength in his wounded shoulder, the one guiding the hammer-hand, he led with the pickaxe. The stone exploded into dust under the enchanted hand's blow, and the illithid sent a clear message of its pleasure flooding into Belwar's thoughts. Even the armor of a hook horror would not stand against such a blow!

Belwar's master reinforced the instructions it had given to the deep gnome, then moved into an adjoining chamber to study. Left alone to his work, so very similar to the tasks he had worked at for all of his century of life, Belwar found himself wondering.

Nothing in particular crossed the burrow-warden's few coherent thoughts; the need to please his illithid master remained the foremost guidance of his movements. For the first time since his capture, though, Belwar wondered.

Identity? Purpose?

The enchanting spell-song of his mithral hands ran through his mind again, became a focus of his unconscious determination to sort through the blur of his captors' insinuations. *"Bivrip?"* he muttered again, and the word triggered a more recent memory, an image of a drow elf, kneeling and massaging the god-thing of the illithid community.

"Drizzt?" Belwar muttered under his breath, but the name was forgotten in the next bang of his pick-hand, obliterated by the svirfneblin's continuing desire to please his illithid master.

The cubby had to be perfect.

⚔ ⚔ ⚔ ⚔ ⚔

A lump of flesh rippled under an ebon-skinned hand and a wave of anxiety flooded through Drizzt, imparted by the central brain of the mind flayer community. The drow's only emotional response was sadness, for he could not bear to see the brain in distress. Slender fingers kneaded and rubbed; Drizzt lifted a bowl of warm water and poured it slowly over the flesh. Then Drizzt was happy, for the flesh smoothed out under his skilled touch, and the brain's anxious emotions soon were replaced by a teasing hint of gratitude.

Behind the kneeling drow, across the wide walkway, two illithids watched it all and nodded approvingly. Drow elves always had proved skilled at this task, and this latest captive was one of the finest so far.

The illithids wiggled their fingers eagerly at the implications of that shared thought. The central brain had detected another drow intruder in the illithid webs that were the tunnels beyond the long and narrow cavern—another slave to massage and sooth.

So the central brain believed.

Four illithids moved out from the cavern, guided by the images imparted by the central brain. A single drow had entered their domain, an easy capture for four illithids.

So the mind flayers believed.

# 18
# The Element of Surprise

The spirit-wraith picked his silent way through the broken and twisting corridors, traveling with the light and practiced steps of a veteran drow warrior. But the mind flayers, guided by their central brain, anticipated Zaknafein's course perfectly and were waiting for him.

As Zaknafein came beside the same stone ridge where Belwar and Clacker had fallen, an illithid jumped out at him and—*fwoop!*—blasted its stunning energy.

At that close range, few creatures could have resisted such a powerful blow, but Zaknafein was an undead thing, a being not of this world. The proximity of Zaknafein's mind, linked to another plane of existence, could not be measured in steps. Impervious to such mental attacks, the spirit-wraith's swords dived straight in, each taking the startled illithid in one of its milky, pupil-less eyes.

The three other mind flayers floated down from the ceiling, loosing their stunning blasts as they came. Swords in hand, Zaknafein waited confidently for them, but the mind flayers continued their descent. Never before had their mental attacks failed them; they could not believe that the incapacitating cones of energy would prove futile now.

*Fwoop!* A dozen times the illithids fired, but the spirit-wraith seemed not to notice. The illithids, beginning to worry, tried to reach inside Zaknafein's thoughts to understand how he had possibly avoided the effects. What they found was a barrier beyond their penetrating capabilities, a barrier that transcended their present plane of existence.

They had witnessed Zaknafein's swordplay against their unfortunate companion and had no intention of engaging this skilled drow in melee combat. Telepathically, they promptly agreed to reverse their direction.

But they had descended too far.

Zaknafein cared nothing for the illithids and would have walked contentedly off on his way. To the illithid's misfortune, though, the spirit-wraith's instincts, and Zaknafein's past-life knowledge of mind flayers, led him to a simple conclusion: If Drizzt had traveled this way—and Zaknafein knew that he had—he most likely had encountered the mind flayers. An undead being could defeat them, but a mortal drow, even Drizzt, would find himself at a sorry disadvantage.

Zaknafein sheathed one sword and sprang up to the ridge of stone. In the blur of a second fast leap, the spirit-wraith caught one of the rising illithids by the ankle.

*Fwoop!* The creature blasted again, but it was a doomed thing with little defense against Zaknafein's slashing sword. With incredible strength, the spirit-wraith heaved himself straight up, his sword leading the way. The illithid slapped down at the blade vainly, but its empty hands could not defeat the spirit-wraith's aim. Zaknafein's sword sliced up through the mind flayer's belly and into its heart and lungs.

Gasping and clutching at the huge wound, the illithid could only watch helplessly as Zaknafein found his footing and kicked off the mind flayer's chest. The dying illithid tumbled away, head over heels, and slammed into the wall, then hung grotesquely in midair even after death, its blood spattering the floor below.

Zaknafein's leap sent him crashing into the next floating illithid, and the momentum took both of them into the last of the group. Arms flailed and tentacles waved wildly, seeking some hold on the drow warrior's flesh. More deadly, though, was the blade, and a moment later, the spirit-wraith pulled free of his latest two victims, enacted a levitation spell of his own, and floated gently back to the stone floor. Zaknafein walked calmly away, leaving three illithids hanging dead in the air for the duration of their levitation spells, and a fourth dead on the floor.

The spirit-wraith did not bother to wipe the blood from his swords; he realized that very soon there would be more killing.

⚔ ⚔ ⚔ ⚔ ⚔

The two mind flayers continued observing the panther's entity. They did not know it, but Guenhwyvar was aware of their presence. In the Astral Plane, where material senses such as smell and taste had no meaning, the panther substituted other subtle senses. Here, Guenhwyvar hunted through a sense that translated the emanations of energy into clear mental images, and the panther could readily distinguish between the aura of an elk and a rabbit without ever seeing the particular creature. Illithids were not so uncommon on the Astral Plane, and Guenhwyvar recognized their emanations.

The panther had not yet decided whether their presence was mere coincidence or was in some way connected to the fact that Drizzt had not called in many days. The apparent interest the mind flayers showed in Guenhwyvar suggested the latter, a most disturbing notion to the panther.

Still, Guenhwyvar did not want to make the first move against so dangerous an enemy. The panther continued its daily routines, keeping a wary eye on the unwanted audience.

Guenhwyvar noticed the shift in the mind flayers' emanations as the creatures began a rapid descent back to the Material Plane. The panther could wait no longer.

Springing through the stars, Guenhwyvar charged upon the mind flayers. Occupied in their efforts to begin their return journey, the illithids did not react until it was too late. The panther dived in below one, catching its silvery cord in fangs of sharp light. Guenhwyvar's neck flexed and twisted, and the silvery cord snapped. The helpless illithid drifted away, a castaway on the Astral Plane.

The other mind flayer, more concerned with saving itself, ignored its companion's frenzied pleas and continued its descent toward the planar tunnel that would return it to its corporeal body. The illithid almost slipped beyond Guenhwyvar's reach, but the panther's claws latched on firmly just as it entered the planar tunnel. Guenhwyvar rode along.

From his little stone island, Clacker saw the commotion growing all through the long and narrow cavern. Illithids rushed all about, telepathically commanding slaves into defensive formations. Lookouts disappeared through every exit, while other mind flayers floated up into the air to keep a general watch on the situation.

Clacker recognized that some crisis had come upon the community, and a single logical thought forced its way through the hook horror's base thinking: If the mind flayers became preoccupied with some new enemy, this might be his chance to escape. With a new focus to his thinking, Clacker's pech side found a firm footing. His largest problem would be the chasm, for he certainly could not leap across it. He figured that he could toss a gray dwarf or a rothé the distance, but that would hardly aid his own escape.

Clacker's gaze fell on the lever of the bridge, then back to his companions on the stone island. The bridge was retracted; the high lever leaned toward the island. A well-aimed projectile might push it back. Clacker banged his huge claws together—an action that reminded him of Belwar—and hoisted a gray dwarf high into the air. The unfortunate creature soared toward the lever but came up short, instead slamming into the chasm wall and plummeting to its death.

Clacker stamped an angry foot and turned to find another missile. He had no idea of how he would get to Drizzt and Belwar, and at that moment, he didn't pause to worry about them. Clacker's problem right now was getting off his prison island.

This time a young rothé went high into the air.

There was no subtlety, no secrecy, to Zaknafein's entrance. Having no fear of the mind flayers' primary attack methods, the spirit-wraith walked straight into the long and narrow cavern, right out into the open. A group of three illithids descended on him immediately, loosing their stunning blasts.

Again the spirit-wraith walked through the mental energy without a flinch, and the three illithids found the same fate as the four that had stood against Zaknafein out in the tunnels.

Then came the slaves. Desiring only to please their masters, goblins, gray dwarves, orcs, and even a few ogres, charged at the drow invader. Some brandished weapons, but most had only their hands and teeth, thinking to bury the lone drow under their sheer numbers.

Zaknafein's swords and feet were too quick for such straightforward tactics. The spirit-wraith danced and slashed, darting in one direction then reversing his motion suddenly and hacking down his closest pursuers.

Behind the action, the illithids formed their own defensive lines, reconsidering the wisdom of their tactics. Their tentacles wiggled wildly as their mental communications flooded forth, trying to make some sense of this unexpected turn. They had not trusted enough in their slaves to hand them all weapons, but as slave after slave fell to the stone, clawing at mortal wounds, the mind flayers came to regret their mounting losses. Still, the illithids believed they would win out. Behind them, more groups of slaves were being herded down to join the fray. The lone invader would tire, his steps would slow, and their horde would crush him.

The mind flayers could not know the truth of Zaknafein. They could not know that he was an undead thing, a magically animated thing that would not tire and would not slow.

⚔ ⚔ ⚔ ⚔ ⚔

Belwar and his master watched the spasmodic jerking of one of the illithid bodies, a telltale sign that the host spirit was returning from its astral journey. Belwar did not understand the implications of the convulsive movements, but he sensed that his master was glad, and that, in turn, pleased him.

But Belwar's master was also a bit concerned that only one of its companions was returning, for the central brain's summons took the highest priority and could not be ignored. The mind flayer watched as its companion's spasms settled into a pattern, and then was even more confused, for a dark mist appeared around the body.

At the same instant the illithid returned to the Material Plane, Belwar's master telepathically shared in its pain and terror. Before Belwar's master could begin to react, though, Guenhwyvar materialized atop the seated illithid, tearing and slashing at the body.

Belwar froze as a flicker of recognition coursed through him. *"Bivrip?"* he whispered under his breath, and then, "Drizzt?" and the image of the kneeling drow came clearly into his mind.

*Kill it my brave champion! Do kill it!* Belwar's master implored, but it was already too late for the illithid's unfortunate companion. The seated mind flayer flailed away frantically; its tentacles wiggled and latched onto the cat in an attempt to get at Guenhwyvar's brain. Guenhwyvar swiped across with a mighty claw, a single blow that tore the illithid's octopus head from its shoulders.

Belwar, his hands still enchanted from his work on the cubby, advanced slowly toward the panther, his steps bound not by fear, but by confusion. The burrow-warden turned to his master and asked, "Guenhwyvar?"

The mind flayer knew that it had given too much back to the svirfneblin. The recall of the enchanting spell had inspired other, dangerous memories in this slave. No longer could Belwar be relied upon.

Guenhwyvar sensed the illithid's intent and sprang out from the dead mind flayer only an instant before the remaining creature blasted at Belwar.

Guenhwyvar hit the burrow-warden squarely, sending him sprawling to the floor. Feline muscles flexed and strained as the cat landed, turning Guenhwyvar on the spot at an angle for the room's exit.

*Fwoop!* The mind flayer's assault clipped Belwar as he tumbled, but the deep gnome's confusion and his mounting rage held off the insidious attack. For that one moment, Belwar was free, and he rolled to his feet, viewing the illithid as the wretched and evil thing that it was.

"Go, Guenhwyvar!" the burrow-warden cried, and the cat needed no prodding. As an astral being, Guenhwyvar understood much about illithid society and knew the key to any battle against a lair of such creatures. The panther flew against the door with all its weight, bursting out onto the balcony high above the chamber that held the central brain.

Belwar's master, fearing for its god-thing, tried to follow, but the deep gnome's strength had returned tenfold with his anger, and his wounded arm felt no pain as he smashed his enchanted hammer-hand into the squishy flesh of the illithid's head. Sparks flew and scorched the illithid's face, and the creature slammed back into the wall, its milky, pupil-less eyes staring at Belwar in disbelief.

Then it slid, ever so slowly, to the floor, down into the darkness of death.

Forty feet below the room, the kneeling drow sensed his revered master's fear and outrage and looked up just as the black panther sprang out into the air. Fully entranced by the central brain, Drizzt did not recognize Guenhwyvar as his former companion and dearest friend; he saw at that moment only a threat to the being he most loved. But Drizzt and the other massaging slaves could only watch helplessly as the mighty panther, teeth bared and paws wide, plummeted down onto the middle of the bulbous mass of veined flesh that ruled the illithid community.

# 19
# Headaches

Approximately one hundred twenty illithids resided in and around the stone castle in the long and narrow cavern, and every one of them felt the same searing headache when Guenhwyvar dived into the community's central brain.

Guenhwyvar plowed through the mass of defenseless flesh, the cat's great claws tearing and slashing a path through the gore. The central brain imparted emotions of absolute terror, trying to inspire its servants. Understanding that help would not soon arrive, the thing reverted to pleading with the panther.

Guenhwyvar's primal ferocity, however, allowed for no mental intrusions. The panther dug on savagely and was buried in the spurting slime.

Drizzt shouted in outrage and ran all about the walkway, trying to find some way to get at the intruding panther. Drizzt felt his beloved master's anguish keenly and pleaded for somebody—anybody—to do something. Other slaves jumped and cried, and mind flayers ran about in a frenzy, but Guenhwyvar was out in the center of the huge mass, beyond the reach of any weapons the mind flayers could use.

A few moments later, Drizzt stopped his jumping and shouting. He wondered where and who he was, and what in the Nine Hells this great disgusting lump in front of him possibly could be. He looked around the walkway and caught similar confused expressions on the faces of several duergar dwarves, another dark elf, two goblins, and a tall and wickedly scarred bugbear. The mind flayers still rushed about, looking for some attack angle on the panther, the primary threat, and paid no heed to the confused slaves. Guenhwyvar made a sudden appearance from behind the folds of brain. The cat came up over a fleshy ridge for just a moment, then disappeared back into the gore. Several mind flayers fired their mind blasts at the fleeting target, but Guenhwyvar was out of sight too quickly for their energy cones to strike—but not too quickly for Drizzt to catch a glimpse.

"Guenhwyvar?" the drow cried as a multitude of thoughts rushed back into his mind. The last thing he remembered was floating up among the stalactites in a broken corridor, up to where other sinister shapes lurked.

An illithid moved right beside the drow, too intent on the action within the brain to realize that Drizzt was a slave no longer. Drizzt had no weapons other than his own body, but he hardly cared in that moment of sheer anger. He leaped high into the air behind the unsuspecting monster and kicked his foot into the back of the thing's octopus head. The illithid tumbled forward onto the central brain and bounced along the rubbery folds several times before it could find any hold.

All about the walkway, the slaves realized their freedom. The gray dwarves banded together immediately and took down two illithids in a wild rush, pummeling the creatures and stomping on them with their heavy boots.

*Fwoop!* A blast came from the side, and Drizzt turned to see the other dark elf reeling from the stunning blow. A mind flayer rushed in on the drow and grabbed him in a tight hug. Four tentacles latched on to the doomed dark elf's face, clamping on, then digging in toward his brain.

Drizzt wanted to go to the drow's aid, but a second illithid moved between them and took aim. Drizzt dived to the side as another attack sounded. *Fwoop!* He came up running, desperately trying to put more ground between himself and the illithid. The other drow's scream held Drizzt for a moment, though, and he glanced back over his shoulder.

Grotesque, bulging lines crossed up the drow's face, a visage contorted by more anguish than Drizzt had ever before witnessed. Drizzt saw the illithid's head jerk, and the tentacles, buried beneath the drow's skin and reaching and sucking at his brain, pulsed and bulged. The doomed drow screamed again, one final time, then he fell limp in the illithid's arms and the creature finished its gruesome feast.

The scarred bugbear unwittingly saved Drizzt from a similar fate. In its flight, the seven-foot-tall creature crossed right between Drizzt and the pursuing mind flayer just as the illithid fired again. The blow stunned the bugbear for the moment it took the illithid to close in. As the mind flayer reached for its supposedly helpless victim, the bugbear swung a huge arm and knocked the pursuer to the stone.

More mind flayers rushed out onto the balconies overlooking the circular chamber. Drizzt had no idea where his friends might be, or how he might escape, but the single door he spotted beside the walkway seemed his only chance. He charged straight at it, but it burst open just before he arrived.

Drizzt crashed into the waiting arms of yet another illithid.

⚔ ⚔ ⚔ ⚔ ⚔

If the inside of the stone castle was a tumult of confusion, the outside was chaos. No slaves charged at Zaknafein now. The wounding of the central brain had freed them from the mind flayers' suggestions, and now the goblins, gray dwarves, and all the others were more concerned with their own escape. Those closest to the cavern exits rushed out; others ran about wildly, trying to keep out of range of the continuing illithid mind blasts.

Hardly giving his actions a thought, Zaknafein whipped across with a sword, taking out a goblin as it ran screaming past. Then the spirit-wraith closed in on the creature that had been pursuing the goblin. Walking through yet another stunning blast, Zaknafein chopped the mind flayer down.

In the stone castle, Drizzt had regained his identity, and the magical spells imbued upon the spirit-wraith honed in on the target's thought patterns. With a gutteral growl, Zaknafein made a straight course toward the castle, leaving a host of dead and wounded, slave and illithid alike, in his wake.

⚔ ⚔ ⚔ ⚔ ⚔

Another rothé bleated out in surprise as it soared through the air. Three of the beasts limped about across the way; a fourth had followed the duergar to the bottom of the chasm. This time, though, Clacker's aim was true, and the small cowlike creature slammed into the lever, throwing it back. At once, the enchanted bridge rolled out and secured itself at Clacker's feet. The hook horror scooped up another gray dwarf, just for luck, and started out across the bridge.

He was nearly halfway across when the first mind flayer appeared, rushing toward the lever. Clacker knew that he couldn't possibly get all the way across before the illithid disengaged the bridge.

He had only one shot.

The gray dwarf, oblivious to its surroundings, went high into the air above the hook horror's head. Clacker held his throw and continued across, letting the illithid close in as much as possible. As the mind flayer reached a four-fingered hand toward the lever, the duergar missile crashed into its chest, throwing it to the stone.

Clacker ran for his life. The illithid recovered and pushed the lever forward. The bridge snapped back, opening the deep chasm.

A final leap just as the metal-and-stone bridge zipped out from under his feet sent Clacker crashing into the side of the chasm. He got his arms and shoulders over the lip of the gorge and kept enough wits about him to quickly scramble over to the side.

The illithid pulled back on the lever, and the bridge shot out again, clipping Clacker. The hook horror had moved far enough to the side, though, and Clacker's grip was strong enough to hold against the force as the rushing bridge scraped across his armored chest.

The illithid cursed and pulled the lever back, then rushed to meet the hook horror. Weary and wounded, Clacker had not yet begun to pull himself up when the illithid arrived. Waves of stunning energy rolled over him. His head drooped and he slid back several inches before his claws found another hold.

The mind flayer's greed cost it dearly. Instead of simply blasting and kicking Clacker from the ledge, it thought it could make a quick meal of the helpless hook horror's brain. It knelt before Clacker, four tentacles diving in eagerly to find an opening in his facial armor.

Clacker's dual entities had resisted the illithid blasts out in the tunnels, and now, too, the stunning mental energy had only a minimal effect. When the illithid's octopus head appeared right in front of his face, it shocked Clacker back to awareness.

A snap of a beak removed two of the probing tentacles, then a desperate lunge of a claw caught the illithid's knee. Bones crushed into dust under the mighty grip, and the illithid cried in agony, both telepathically and in its watery, otherworldly voice.

A moment later, its cries faded as it plummeted down the deep chasm. A levitation spell might have saved the falling illithid, but such spellcasting required concentration and the pain of a torn face and crushed knee delayed such actions. The illithid thought of levitating at the same moment that the point of a stalagmite drove through its backbone.

⚔ ⚔ ⚔ ⚔ ⚔

The hammer-hand crashed through the door of another stone chest. "Damn!" Belwar spat, seeing that this one, too, contained nothing more than illithid clothing. The burrow-warden was certain that his equipment would be nearby, but already half of his former masters' rooms lay in ruin with nothing to show for the effort.

Belwar moved back into the main chamber and over to the stone seats. Between the two chairs, he spotted the figurine of the panther. He scooped it into a pouch, then squashed the head of the remaining illithid, the astral castaway, with his pickaxe-hand almost as an afterthought; in the confusion, the svirfneblin had nearly forgotten that one monster remained. Belwar heaved the body away, sending it down in a heap on the floor.

"*Magga cammara*," the svirfneblin muttered when he looked back to the stone chair and saw the outline of a trap door where the creature had been sitting. Never putting finesse above efficiency, Belwar's hammer-hand quickly reduced the door to rubble, and the burrow-warden looked upon the welcome sight of familiar backpacks.

Belwar shrugged and followed the course of the logic, swiping across at the other illithid, the one Guenhwyvar had decapitated. The headless monster fell away, revealing another trap door.

"The drow shall find need of these," Belwar remarked when he cleared away the chunks of broken stone and lifted out a belt that held two sheathed scimitars. He darted for the exit and met an illithid right in the doorway.

More particularly, Belwar's humming hammer-hand met the illithid's chest. The monster flew backward, spinning over the balcony's metal railing.

Belwar rushed out and charged to the side, having no time to check if the illithid had somehow caught a handhold and having no time to stay and play in any case. He could hear the commotion below, the mental attacks and the screams, and the continuing growls of a panther that sounded like music in the burrow-warden's ears.

⚔ ⚔ ⚔ ⚔ ⚔

His arms pinned to his sides by the illithid's unexpectedly powerful hug, Drizzt could only twist and jerk his head about to slow the tentacles' progress. One found a hold, then another, and began burrowing under the drow's ebony skin.

Drizzt knew little of mind flayer anatomy, but it was a bipedal creature and he allowed himself some assumptions. Wiggling a bit to the side, so that he was not directly facing the horrid thing, he brought a knee slamming up into the creature's groin. By the sudden loosening of the illithid's grip, and by the way its milky eyes seemed to widen, Drizzt guessed that his assumptions had been correct. His knee slammed up again, then a third time.

Drizzt heaved with all his strength and broke free of the weakened illithid's hug. The stubborn tentacles continued their climb up the sides of Drizzt's face, though, reaching for his brain. Explosions of burning pain racked Drizzt and he nearly fainted, his head drooping forward limply.

But the hunter would not surrender.

When Drizzt looked up again, the fire in his lavender eyes fell upon the illithid like a damning curse. The hunter grasped the tentacles and tore them out savagely, pulling them straight down to bow the illithid's head.

The monster fired its mind blast, but the angle was wrong and the energy did nothing to slow the hunter. One hand held tightly to the tentacles while the other slammed in with the frenzy of a dwarven hammer at a mithral strike on the monster's soft head.

Blue-black bruises welled in the fleshy skin; one pupil-less eye swelled and closed. A tentacle dug into the drow's wrist; the frantic illithid raked and punched with its arms, but the hunter didn't notice. He pounded away at the head, pounded the creature down to the stone floor. Drizzt tore his arm away from the tentacle's grasp, then both fists flailed away until the illithid's eyes closed forever.

The ring of metal spun the drow about. Lying on the floor just a few feet away was a familiar and welcome sight.

⚔ ⚔ ⚔ ⚔ ⚔

Satisfied that the scimitars had landed near his friend, Belwar charged down a stone stairway at the nearest illithid. The monster turned and loosed its blast. Belwar answered with a scream of sheer rage—a scream that partially blocked the stunning effect—and he hurled himself through the air, meeting the waves of energy head on.

Though dazed from the mental assault, the deep gnome crashed into the illithid and they fell over into a second monster that had been rushing up to help. Belwar could hardly find his bearings, but he clearly understood that the jumble of arms and legs all about him were not the limbs of friends. The burrow-warden's mithral hands slashed and punched, and he scrambled away along the second balcony in search of another stair. By the time the two wounded illithids recovered enough to respond, the wild svirfneblin was long gone.

Belwar caught another illithid by surprise, splatting its fleshy head flat against the wall as he came down onto the next level. A dozen other mind flayers roamed all about this balcony, though, most of them guarding the two stairways down to the tower's bottom chamber. Belwar took a quick detour by springing up to the top of the metal railing, then dropping the fifteen feet to the floor.

⚔ ⚔ ⚔ ⚔ ⚔

A blast of stunning energy rolled over Drizzt as he reached for his weapons. The hunter resisted, though, his thoughts simply too primitive for such a sophisticated attack form. In a single movement too quick for his latest adversary to respond to, he snapped one scimitar from its sheath and spun about, slicing the blade at an upward angle. The scimitar buried itself halfway through the pursuing mind flayer's head.

The hunter knew that the monster was already dead, but he tore out the scimitar and whacked the illithid one more time as it fell, for no particular reason at all.

Then the drow was up and running, both blades drawn, one dripping illithid blood and the other hungry for more. Drizzt should have been looking for an escape route—that part that was Drizzt Do'Urden *would* have looked—but the hunter wanted more. His hunter-self demanded revenge on the brain mass that had enslaved him.

A single cry saved the drow then, brought him back from the spiraling depths of his blind, instinctive rage.

"Drizzt!" Belwar shouted, limping over to his friend. "Help me, dark elf! My ankle twisted in the fall!" All thoughts of revenge suddenly thrown away, Drizzt Do'Urden rushed to his svirfneblin companion's side.

Arm in arm, the two friends left the circular chamber. A moment later, Guenhwyvar, sleek from the blood and gore of the central brain, bounded up to join them.

"Lead us out," Drizzt begged the panther, and Guenhwyvar willingly took up a point position.

They ran down winding, rough-hewn corridors. "Not made by any svirfneblin," Belwar was quick to point out, throwing his friend a wink.

"I believe they were," Drizzt retorted easily, returning the wink. "Under the charms of a mind flayer, I mean," he quickly added.

"Never!" Belwar insisted. "Never the work of a svirfneblin is this, not even if his mind had been melted away!" In spite of their dire peril, the deep gnome managed a belly laugh, and Drizzt joined him.

Sounds of battle sounded from the side passages of every intersection they crossed. Guenhwyvar's keen senses kept them along the clearest route, though the panther had no way of knowing which way was out. Still, whatever lay in any direction could only be an improvement over the horrors they had left.

A mind flayer jumped out into their corridor just after Guenhwyvar crossed an intersection. The creature hadn't seen the panther and faced Drizzt and Belwar fully. Drizzt threw the svirfneblin down and dived into a headlong roll toward his adversary, expecting to be blasted before he ever got close.

But when the drow came out of the roll and looked up, his breath came back in a profound sigh of relief. The mind flayer lay face down on the stone, Guenhwyvar comfortably perched atop its back.

Drizzt moved to his feline companion as Guenhwyvar casually finished the grim business, and Belwar soon joined them.

"Anger, dark elf," the svirfneblin remarked. Drizzt looked at him curiously.

"I believe anger can fight back against their blasts," Belwar explained. "One got me up on the stairs, but I was so mad, I hardly noticed. Perhaps I am mistaken, but—"

"No," Drizzt interrupted, remembering how little he had been affected, even at close range, when he had gone to retrieve his scimitars. He had been in the thralls of his alter ego then, that darker, maniacal side he so desperately had tried to leave behind. The illithid's mental assault had been all but useless against the hunter. "You are not mistaken," Drizzt assured his friend. "Anger can beat them, or at least slow the effects of their mind assaults."

"Then get mad!" Belwar growled as he signaled Guenhwyvar ahead.

Drizzt threw his supporting arm back under the burrow-warden's shoulder and nodded his agreement with Belwar's suggestion. The drow realized, though, that blind rage such as Belwar was speaking of could not be consciously created. Instinctive fear and anger might defeat the illithids, but Drizzt, from his experiences with his alter ego, knew those were emotions brought on by nothing short of desperation and panic.

The small party crossed through several more corridors, through a large, empty room, and down yet another passage. Slowed by the limping svirfneblin, they soon heard heavy footsteps closing in from behind.

"Too heavy for illithids," Drizzt remarked, looking back over his shoulder.

"Slaves," Belwar reasoned.

*Fwoop!* An attack sounded behind them. *Fwoop! Fwoop!* The sounds came to them, followed by several thuds and groans.

"Slaves once again," Drizzt said grimly. The pursuing footsteps came on again, this time sounding more like a light shuffle.

"Faster!" Drizzt cried, and Belwar needed no prompting. They ran on, thankful for every turn in the passage, for they feared that the illithids were only steps behind.

They then came into a large and high hall. Several possible exits came into view, but one, a set of large iron doors, held their attention keenly. Between them and the doors was a spiraling iron stairway, and on a balcony not so far above loomed a mind flayer.

"He'll cut us off!" Belwar reasoned. The footsteps came louder from behind. Belwar looked back toward the waiting illithid curiously when he saw a wide smile cross the drow's face. The deep gnome, too, grinned widely.

Guenhwyvar took the spiraling stairs in three mighty bounds. The illithid wisely fled along the balcony and off into the shadows of adjoining corridors. The panther did not pursue, but held a high, guarding position above Drizzt and Belwar.

Both the drow and the svirfneblin called their thanks as they passed, but their elation turned sour when they arrived at the doors. Drizzt pushed hard, but the portals would not budge.

"Locked!" he cried.

"Not for long!" growled Belwar. The enchantment had expired in the deep gnome's mithral hands, but he charged ahead anyway, pounding his hammer-hand against the metal.

Drizzt moved behind the deep gnome, keeping a rear guard and expecting the illithids to enter the hall at any moment. "Hurry, Belwar," he begged.

Both mithral hands worked furiously on the doors. Gradually, the lock began to loosen and the doors opened just an inch. "*Magga cammara*, dark elf!" the burrow-warden cried. "A bar it is that holds them! On the other side!"

"Damn!" Drizzt spat, and across the way, a group of several mind flayers entered the hall.

Belwar didn't relent. His hammer-hand smashed at the door again and again.

The illithids crossed the stairway and Guenhwyvar sprang into their midst, bringing the whole group tumbling down. At that horrible moment, Drizzt realized that he did not have the onyx figurine.

The hammer-hand banged the metal in rapid succession, widening the gap between the doors. Belwar pushed his pickaxe-hand through in an uppercut motion and lifted the bar from its locking clasps. The doors swung wide.

"Come quickly!" the deep gnome yelled to Drizzt. He hooked his pickaxe-hand under the drow's shoulder to pull him along, but Drizzt shrugged away the hold.

"Guenhwyvar!" Drizzt cried.

*Fwoop!* The evil sound came repeatedly from the pile of bodies. Guenhwyvar's reply came as more of a helpless wail than a growl.

Drizzt's lavender eyes burned with rage. He took a single stride back toward the stairway before Belwar figured out a solution.

"Wait!" the svirfneblin called, and he was truly relieved when Drizzt turned about to hear him. Belwar thrust his hip toward the drow and tore open his belt pouch. "Use this!"

Drizzt pulled out the onyx figurine and dropped it at his feet. "Be gone, Guenhwyvar!" he shouted. "Go back to the safety of your home!"

Drizzt and Belwar couldn't even see the panther amid the throng of illithids, but they sensed the mind flayers' sudden distress even before the telltale black mist appeared around the onyx figurine.

As a group, the illithids spun toward them and charged.

"Get the other door!" Belwar cried. Drizzt had grabbed the figurine and was already moving in that direction. The iron portals slammed shut and Drizzt worked to replace the locking bar. Several clasps on the outside of the door had been broken under the burrow-warden's ferocious assault, and the bar was bent, but Drizzt managed to set it in place securely enough to at least slow the illithids.

"The other slaves are trapped," Drizzt remarked.

"Goblins and gray dwarves mostly," Belwar replied.

"And Clacker?"

Belwar threw his arms out helplessly.

"I pity them all," groaned Drizzt, sincerely horrified at the prospect. "Nothing in all the world can torture more than the mental clutches of mind flayers."

"Aye, dark elf," whispered Belwar.

The illithids slammed into the doors, and Drizzt pushed back, further securing the lock.

"Where do we go?" Belwar asked behind him, and when Drizzt turned and surveyed the long and narrow cavern, he certainly understood the burrow-warden's confusion. They spotted at least a dozen exits, but between them and every one rushed a crowd of terrified slaves or a group of illithids.

Behind them came another heavy thud, and the doors creaked open several inches.

"Just go!" Drizzt shouted, pushing Belwar along. They charged down a wide stairway, then out across the broken floor, picking a route that would get them as far from the stone castle as possible.

"Ware danger on all sides!" Belwar cried. "Slave and flayer alike!"

"Let them beware!" Drizzt retorted, his scimitars leading the way. He slammed a goblin down with the hilt of one blade as it stumbled into his way, and a moment later, sliced the tentacles from the face of an illithid as it began to suck the brain from a recaptured duergar.

Then another former slave, a bigger one, jumped in front of Drizzt. The drow rushed it headlong, but this time he stayed his scimitars.

"Clacker!" Belwar yelled behind Drizzt.

"B-b-back of . . . the . . . cavern," the hook horror panted, its grumbled words barely decipherable. "The b-b-best exit."

"Lead on," Belwar replied excitedly, his hopes returning. Nothing would stand against the three of them united. When the burrow-warden started after his giant hook horror friend, however, he noticed that Drizzt wasn't following. At first Belwar feared that a mind blast had caught the drow, but when he returned to Drizzt's side, he realized otherwise.

Atop another of the many wide stairways that ran through the many-tiered cavern, a single slender figure mowed through a group of slaves and illithids alike.

"By the gods," Belwar muttered in disbelief, for the devastating movements of this single figure truly frightened the deep gnome.

The precise cuts and deft twists of the twin swords were not at all frightening to Drizzt Do'Urden. Indeed, to the young dark elf, they rang with a familiarity that brought an old ache to his heart. He looked at Belwar blankly and spoke the name of the single warrior who could fit those maneuvers, the only name that could accompany such magnificent swordplay.

"Zaknafein."

# 20

# Father, My Father

How many lies had Matron Malice told him? What truth could Drizzt ever find in the web of deceptions that marked drow society? His father had not been sacrificed to the Spider Queen! Zaknafein was here, fighting before him, wielding his swords as finely as Drizzt had ever seen.

"What is it?" Belwar demanded.

"The drow warrior," Drizzt was barely able to whisper.

"From your city, dark elf?" Belwar asked." Sent after you?"

"From Menzoberranzan," Drizzt replied. Belwar waited for more information, but Drizzt was too enthralled by Zak's appearance to go into much detail.

"We must go," the burrow-warden said at length.

"Quickly," agreed Clacker, returning to his friends. The hook horror's voice sounded more controlled now, as though the mere appearance of Clacker's friends had aided his pech side in its continuing internal struggle. "The mind flayers are organizing defenses. Many slaves are down."

Drizzt spun out of the reach of Belwar's pick-hand. "No," he said firmly. "I'll not leave him!"

"*Magga cammara*, dark elf!" Belwar shouted at him. "Who is it?"

"Zaknafein Do'Urden," Drizzt yelled back, more than matching the burrow-warden's rising ire. Drizzt's volume dropped considerably as he finished the thought, though, and he nearly choked on the words, "My father."

By the time Belwar and Clacker exchanged disbelieving stares, Drizzt was gone, running to and then up the wide stairway. Atop it, the spirit-wraith stood among a mound of victims, mind flayers and slaves alike, who had found the great misfortune of getting in his way. Farther along the higher tier, several illithids had taken flight from the undead monster.

Zaknafein started to pursue them, for they were running toward the stone castle, following the course the spirit-wraith had determined from the beginning. A thousand magical alarms sounded within the spirit-wraith, though, and abruptly turned him back to the stair.

Drizzt was coming. Zin-carla's moment of fulfillment, the purpose of Zaknafein's animation, at last had arrived!

"Weapon master!" Drizzt cried, springing up lightly to stand by his father's side. The younger drow bubbled with elation, not realizing the truth of the monster standing before him. When Drizzt got near Zak, though, he sensed that something was wrong. Perhaps it was the strange light in the spirit-wraith's eyes that slowed Drizzt's rush. Perhaps it was the fact that Zaknafein did not return his joyful call.

A moment later, it was the downward slice of a sword.

Drizzt somehow managed to get a blocking scimitar up in time. Confused, he still believed that Zaknafein simply had not recognized him.

"Father!" he shouted. "I am Drizzt!"

One sword dived ahead, while the second started in a wide slice, then rushed suddenly toward Drizzt's side. Matching the spirit-wraith's speed, Drizzt came down with one scimitar to parry the first attack and sliced across with the other to foil the second.

"Who are you?" Drizzt demanded desperately, furiously.

A flurry of blows came straight in. Drizzt worked frantically to keep them at bay, but then Zaknafein came across with a backhand and managed to sweep both of Drizzt's blades out to the same side. The spirit-wraith's second sword followed closely, a cut aimed straight at Drizzt's heart, one that Drizzt could not possibly block.

Back down at the bottom of the stairway, Belwar and Clacker cried out, thinking their friend doomed.

Zaknafein's moment of victory was stolen from him, though, by the instincts of the hunter. Drizzt sprang to the side ahead of the plunging blade, then twisted and ducked under Zaknafein's deadly cut. The sword nicked him under his jawbone, leaving a painful gash. When Drizzt completed his roll and found his footing despite the angles of the stair, he showed no sign of acknowledging the injury. When Drizzt again faced his father's imposter, simmering fires burned in his lavender eyes.

Drizzt's agility amazed even his friends, who had seen him before in battle. Zaknafein rushed out immediately after completing his swing, but Drizzt was up and ready before the spirit-wraith caught up to him.

"Who are you?" Drizzt demanded again. This time his voice was deathly calm. "What are you?"

The spirit-wraith snarled and charged recklessly. Believing beyond any doubt that this was not Zaknafein, Drizzt did not miss the opening. He rushed back toward his original position, knocked a sword aside, and slipped a scimitar through as he passed his charging adversary. Drizzt's blade cut through the fine mesh armor and dug deeply into Zaknafein's lung, a wound that would have stopped any mortal opponent.

But Zaknafein did not stop. The spirit-wraith did not draw breath and did not feel pain. Zak turned back on Drizzt and flashed a smile so evil that it would have made Matron Malice stand up and applaud.

Back now on the top step of the stairway, Drizzt stood wide-eyed in amazement. He saw the gruesome wound and saw, against all possibility, Zaknafein steadily advancing, not even flinching.

"Get away!" Belwar cried from the bottom of the stairs. An ogre rushed at the deep gnome, but Clacker intercepted and immediately crushed the thing's head in a claw.

"We must leave," Clacker said to Belwar, the clarity of his voice turning the burrow-warden on his heel.

Belwar could see it clearly in the hook horror's eyes; in that critical moment, Clacker was more a pech than he had been since before the wizard's polymorph spell.

"The stones tell me of illithids gathering within the castle," Clacker explained, and the deep gnome was not surprised that Clacker had heard the voices of the stones. "The illithids will rush out soon," Clacker continued, "to the certain demise of every slave left in the cavern!"

Belwar did not doubt a word of it, but to the svirfneblin, loyalty far outweighed personal safety. "We cannot leave the drow," he replied through clenched teeth.

Clacker nodded in full agreement and charged out to chase away a group of gray dwarves that had come too close.

"Run, dark elf!" Belwar cried. "We have no time!"

Drizzt didn't hear his svirfneblin friend. He focused on the approaching weapon master, the monster impersonating his father, even as Zaknafein focused on him. Of all the many evils perpetrated by Matron Malice, none, by Drizzt's estimation, were greater than this abomination. Malice somehow had perverted the one thing in Drizzt's world that had given him pleasure. Drizzt had believed Zaknafein dead, and that thought was painful enough.

But now this.

It was more than the young drow could bear. He wanted to fight this monster with all his heart and soul, and the spirit-wraith, created for no other reason than this very battle, wholly concurred.

Neither noticed the illithid descending from the darkness above, farther back on the platform, behind Zaknafein.

"Come, monster of Matron Malice," Drizzt growled, sliding his weapons together. "Come and feel my blades."

Zaknafein paused only a few steps away and flashed his wicked smile again. The swords came up; the spirit-wraith took another step.

*Fwoop!*

The illithid's blast rolled over both of them. Zaknafein remained unaffected, but Drizzt caught the force fully. Darkness rolled over him; his eyelids drooped with undeniable weight. He heard his scimitars fall to the stone, but he was beyond any other comprehension.

Zaknafein snarled in gleeful victory, banged his swords together, and stepped toward the falling drow.

Belwar screamed, but it was Clacker's monstrous cry of protest that sounded loudest, rising above the din of the battle-filled cavern. Everything Clacker had ever known as a pech rushed back to him when he saw the drow who had befriended him fall, doomed. That pech identity surged back more keenly, perhaps, than Clacker had even known in his former life.

Zaknafein lunged, seeing his helpless victim in range, but then smashed headfirst into a stone wall that had appeared from nothingness. The spirit-wraith bounced back, his eyes wide in frustration. He clawed at the wall and pounded on it, but it was quite real and sturdy. The stone blocked Zaknafein fully from the stairway and his intended prey.

Back down the stairway, Belwar turned his stunned gaze on Clacker. The svirfneblin had heard that some pech could conjure such stone walls. "Did you . . . ?" the burrow-warden gasped.

The pech in a hook horror's body did not pause long enough to answer. Clacker leaped the stairs four at a stride and gently hoisted Drizzt in his huge arms. He even thought to retrieve the drow's scimitars, then came pounding back down the flight.

"Run!" Clacker commanded the burrow-warden. "For all of your life, run, Belwar Dissengulp!"

The deep gnome, scratching his head with his pickaxe-hand, did indeed run. Clacker cleared a wide path to the cavern's rear exit—none dared stand before his enraged charge—and the burrow-warden, with his short svirfneblin legs, one of which was sprained, had a difficult time keeping up.

Back up the stairs, behind the wall, Zaknafein could only assume that the floating illithid, the same one that had blasted Drizzt, had blocked his charge. Zaknafein whirled about on the monster and screamed in sheer hatred.

*Fwoop!* Another blast came.

Zaknafein leaped up and sliced off both of the illithid's feet with a single stroke. The illithid levitated higher, sending mental cries of anguish and distress to its companions.

Zaknafein couldn't reach the thing, and with other illithids rushing in from every angle, the spirit-wraith didn't have time to enact his own levitation spell. Zaknafein blamed this illithid for his failure; he would not let it escape. He hurled a sword as precisely as any spear.

The illithid looked down at Zaknafein in disbelief, then to the blade buried half to the hilt in its chest and knew that its life was at an end.

Mind flayers rushed toward Zaknafein, firing their stunning blasts as they came. The spirit-wraith had only one sword remaining, but he smashed his opponents down anyway, venting his frustrations on their ugly octopus heads.

Drizzt had escaped . . . for now.

# 21
# Lost and Found

"Praise Lolth," Matron Malice stammered, sensing the distant elation of her spirit-wraith. "He has Drizzt!" The matron mother snapped her gaze to one side, then the other, and her three daughters backed away at the sheer power of the emotions contorting her visage.

"Zaknafein has found your brother!"

Maya and Vierna smiled at each other, glad that this whole ordeal might finally be coming to a conclusion. Since the enactment of Zin-carla, the normal and necessary routines of House Do'Urden had virtually ceased, and every day their nervous mother had turned further and further inward, absorbed by the spirit-wraith's hunt.

Across the anteroom, Briza's smile would have shown a different light to any who took the time to notice, an almost disappointed light.

Fortunately for the first-born daughter, Matron Malice was too absorbed by distant events to take note. The matron mother fell deeper into her meditative trance, savoring every morsel of rage the spirit-wraith threw out, in the knowledge that her blasphemous son was on the receiving end of that anger. Malice's breathing came in excited gasps as Zaknafein and Drizzt played through their sword fight, then the matron mother nearly lost her breath altogether.

Something had stopped Zaknafein.

"No!" Malice screamed, leaping out of her decorated throne. She glanced around, looking for someone to strike or something to throw. "No!" she cried again. "It cannot be!"

"Drizzt has escaped?" Briza asked, trying to keep the smugness out of her voice. Malice's subsequent glare told Briza that her tone might have revealed too much of her thoughts.

"Is the spirit-wraith destroyed?" Maya cried in sincere distress.

"Not destroyed," Malice replied, an obvious tremor in her usually firm voice. "But once more, your brother runs free!"

"Zin-carla has not yet failed," Vierna reasoned, trying to console her excited mother.

"The spirit-wraith is very close," Maya added, picking up Vierna's cue.

Malice dropped back into her seat and wiped the sweat out of her eyes. "Leave me," she commanded her daughters, not wanting them to observe her in such a sorry state. Zin-carla was stealing her life away, Malice knew, for every thought, every hope, of her existence hinged on the spirit-wraith's success.

When the others had gone, Malice lit a candle and took out a tiny, precious mirror. What a wretched thing she had become in the last few tendays. She had hardly eaten, and deep lines of worry creased her formerly glass-smooth, ebony skin. By appearances, Matron Malice had aged more in the last few tendays than in the century before that.

"I will become as Matron Baenre," she whispered in disgust, "withered and ugly." For perhaps the very first time in her long life, Malice began to wonder of the value of her continual quest for power and the merciless Spider Queen's favor. The thoughts disappeared as quickly as they had come, though. Matron Malice had gone too far for such silly regrets. By her strength and devotion, Malice had taken her house to the status of a ruling family and had secured a seat for herself on the prestigious ruling council.

She remained on the verge of despair, though, nearly broken by the strains of the last years. Again she wiped the sweat from her eyes and looked into the little mirror.

What a wretched thing she had become.

Drizzt had done this to her, she reminded herself. Her youngest son's actions had angered the Spider Queen; his sacrilege had put Malice on the edge of doom.

"Get him, my spirit-wraith," Malice whispered with a sneer. At that moment of anger, she hardly cared what future the Spider Queen would lay out for her.

More than anything else in all the world, Matron Malice Do'Urden wanted Drizzt dead.

⚔ ⚔ ⚔ ⚔ ⚔

They ran through the winding tunnels blindly, hoping that no monsters would rear up suddenly before them. With the danger so very real at their backs, the three companions could not afford the usual caution.

Hours passed and still they ran. Belwar, older than his friends and with little legs working two strides for every one of Drizzt's and three strides for each of Clacker's, tired first, but that didn't slow the group. Clacker hoisted the burrow-warden onto a shoulder and ran on.

How many miles they had covered they could not know when they at last broke for their first rest. Drizzt, silent and melancholy through all the trek, took up a guard position at the entrance to the small alcove they had chosen as a temporary camp. Recognizing his drow friend's deep pain, Belwar moved over to offer comfort.

"Not what you expected, dark elf?" the burrow-warden asked softly. With no answer forthcoming, but with Drizzt obviously needing to talk, Belwar pressed on. "The drow in the cavern you knew. Did you claim that he was your father?"

Drizzt snapped an angry glare on the svirfneblin, but his visage softened considerably when he took the moment to realize Belwar's concern.

"Zaknafein," Drizzt explained. "Zaknafein Do'Urden, my father and mentor. It was he who trained me with the blade and who instructed me in all my life. Zaknafein was my only friend in Menzoberranzan, the only drow I have ever known who shared my beliefs."

"He meant to kill you," Belwar stated flatly. Drizzt winced, and the burrow-warden quickly tried to offer him some hope. "Did he not recognize you, perhaps?"

"He was my father," Drizzt said again, "my closest companion for two decades."

"Then why, dark elf?"

"That was not Zaknafein," replied Drizzt. "Zaknafein is dead, sacrificed by my mother to the Spider Queen."

"*Magga cammara*," Belwar whispered, horrified at the revelation concerning Drizzt's parents. The straightforwardness with which Drizzt explained the heinous deed led the burrow-warden to believe that Malice's sacrifice was not so very unusual in the drow city. A shudder coursed through Belwar's spine, but he sublimated his revulsion for the sake of his tormented friend.

"I do not yet know what monster Matron Malice has put in Zaknafein's guise," Drizzt went on, not even noticing Belwar's discomfort.

"A formidable foe, whatever it may be," the deep gnome remarked.

That was exactly what troubled Drizzt. The drow warrior he had battled in the illithid cavern moved with the precision and unmistakable style of Zaknafein Do'Urden. Drizzt's rationale could deny that Zaknafein would turn against him, but his heart told him that the monster he had crossed swords with was indeed his father.

"How did it end?" Drizzt asked after a long pause.

Belwar looked at him curiously.

"The fight," Drizzt explained. "I remember the illithid but nothing more."

Belwar shrugged and looked to Clacker. "Ask him," the burrow-warden replied. "A stone wall appeared between you and your enemies, but how it got there I can only guess."

Clacker heard the conversation and moved over to his friends. "I put it there," he said, his voice still perfectly clear.

"Powers of a pech?" Belwar asked. The deep gnome knew the reputation of pech powers with the stone, but not in enough detail to fully understand what Clacker had done.

"We are a peaceful race," Clacker began, realizing that this might be his only chance to tell his friends of his people. He remained more pechlike than he had since the polymorph, but already he felt the base urges of a hook horror creeping back in. "We desire only to work the stone. It is our calling and our love. And with this symbiosis with the earth comes a measure of power. The stones speak to us and aid us in our toils."

Drizzt looked wryly at Belwar. "Like the earth elemental you once raised against me."

Belwar snorted an embarrassed laugh.

"No," Clacker said soberly, determined not to get sidetracked. "Deep gnomes, too, can call upon the powers of the earth, but theirs is a different relationship. The svirfnebli's love of the earth is only one of their varied definitions of happiness." Clacker looked away from his companions, to the rock wall. "Pech are brothers with the earth. It aids us as we aid it, out of affection."

"You speak of the earth as though it is some sentient being," Drizzt remarked, not sarcastically, just out of curiosity.

"It is, dark elf," replied Belwar, imagining Clacker as he must have appeared before his encounter with the wizard, "for those who can hear it."

Clacker's huge beaked head nodded in accord. "Svirfnebli can hear the earth's distant song," he said. "Pech can speak to it directly."

This was all quite beyond Drizzt's understanding. He knew the sincerity in his companions' words, but drow elves were not nearly as connected to the rocks of the Underdark as the svirfnebli and the pech. Still, if Drizzt needed any proof of what Belwar and Clacker were hinting at, he had only to recall his battle against Belwar's earth elemental that decade ago, or imagine the wall that had somehow appeared out of nowhere to block his enemies in the illithid cavern.

"What do the stones tell you now?" Drizzt asked Clacker. "Have we outdistanced our enemies?"

Clacker moved over and put his ear to the wall. "The words are vague now," he said with obvious lament in his voice. His companions understood the connotation of his tone. The earth was speaking no less clearly; it was Clacker's hearing, impeded by the impending return of the hook horror, that had begun to fade.

"I hear no others in pursuit," Clacker went on, "but I am not so sure as to trust my ears." He snarled suddenly, spun away, and walked back to the far side of the alcove.

Drizzt and Belwar exchanged concerned looks, then moved to follow.

"What is it?" the burrow-warden dared to ask the hook horror, though he could guess readily enough.

"I am falling," Clacker replied, and the grating that had returned to his voice only emphasized the point. "In the illithid cavern, I was pech—more pech than ever before. I was pech in narrow focus. I was the earth." Belwar and Drizzt seemed not to understand.

"The w-w-wall," Clacker tried to explain. "Bringing up such a wall is a task that only a g-g-group of pech elders could accomplish, working together through painstaking rituals." Clacker paused and shook his head violently, as though he was trying to throw out the hook horror side. He slammed a heavy claw into the wall and forced himself to continue. "Yet I did it. I became the stone and merely lifted my hand to block Drizzt's enemies!"

"And now it is leaving," Drizzt said softly. "The pech is falling away from your grasp once again, buried under the instincts of a hook horror."

Clacker looked away and again banged a hook against the wall in reply. Something in the motion brought him comfort, and he repeated it, over and over, rhythmically tap-tapping as if trying to hold on to a piece of his former self.

Drizzt and Belwar walked out of the alcove and back into the corridor to give their giant friend his privacy. A short time later, they noticed that the tapping had ceased, and Clacker stuck his head out, his huge, birdlike eyes filled with sorrow. His stuttered words sent shivers through the spines of his friends, for they found that they could not deny his logic or his desire.

"P-please k-k-kill me."

# Part Five

## Spirit

Spirit. It cannot be broken and it cannot be stolen away. A victim in the throes of despair might feel otherwise, and certainly the victim's "master" would like to believe it so. But in truth, the spirit remains, sometimes buried but never fully removed.

That is the false assumption of Zin-carla and the danger of such sentient animation. The priestesses, I have come to learn, claim it as the highest gift of the Spider Queen deity who rules the drow. I think not. Better to call Zin-carla Lolth's greatest lie.

The physical powers of the body cannot be separated from the rationale of the mind and the emotions of the heart. They are one and the same, a compilation of a singular being. It is in the harmony of these three—body, mind, and heart—that we find spirit.

How many tyrants have tried? How many

rulers have sought to reduce their subjects to simple, unthinking instruments of profit and gain? They steal the loves, the religions, of their people; they seek to steal the spirit.

Ultimately and inevitably, they fail. This I must believe. If the flame of the spirit's candle is extinguished, there is only death, and the tyrant finds no gain in a kingdom littered with corpses.

But it is a resilient thing, this flame of spirit, indomitable and ever-striving. In some, at least, it will survive, to the tyrant's demise.

Where, then, was Zaknafein, my father, when he set out purposefully to destroy me? Where was I in my years alone in the wilds, when this hunter that I had become blinded my heart and guided my sword hand often against my conscious wishes?

We both were there all along, I came to know, buried but never stolen.

Spirit. In every language in all the Realms, surface and Underdark, in every time and every place, the word has a ring of strength and determination. It is the hero's strength, the mother's resilience, and the poor man's armor. It cannot be broken, and it cannot be taken away.

This I must believe.

–Drizzt Do'Urden

# 22
# Without Direction

The sword cut came too swiftly for the goblin slave to even cry out in terror. It toppled forward, quite dead before it ever hit the floor. Zaknafein stepped on its back and continued on; the path to the narrow cavern's rear exit lay open before the spirit-wraith, barely ten yards away.

Even as the undead warrior moved beyond his latest kill, a group of illithids came into the cavern in front of him. Zaknafein snarled and did not turn away or slow in the least. His logic and his strides were direct; Drizzt had gone through this exit, and he would follow.

Anything in his way would fall to his blade.

*Let this one go on its way!* came a telepathic cry from several points in the cavern, from other mind flayers who had witnessed Zaknafein in action. *You cannot defeat him! Let the drow leave!*

The mind flayers had seen enough of the spirit-wraith's deadly blades; more than a dozen of their comrades had died at Zaknafein's hand already.

This new group standing in Zaknafein's way did not miss the urgency of the telepathic pleas. They parted to either side with all speed—except for one.

The illithid race based its existence on pragmatism founded in vast volumes of communal knowledge. Mind flayers considered base emotions such as pride fatal flaws. It proved to be true again on this occasion.

*Fwoop!* The single illithid blasted the spirit-wraith, determined that none should be allowed to escape.

An instant later, the time of a single, precise swipe of a sword, Zaknafein stepped on the fallen illithid's chest and continued on his way out into the wilds of the Underdark.

No other illithids made any move to stop him.

Zaknafein crouched and carefully picked his path. Drizzt had traveled down this tunnel; the scent was fresh and clear. Even so, in his careful pursuit, where he would often have to pause and check the trail, Zaknafein could not move as swiftly as his intended prey.

But, unlike Zaknafein, Drizzt had to rest.

⚔ ⚔ ⚔ ⚔ ⚔

"Hold!" The tone of Belwar's command left no room for debate. Drizzt and Clacker froze in their tracks, wondering what had put the burrow-warden on sudden alert.

Belwar moved over and put his ear to the rock wall. "Boots," he whispered, pointing to the stone. "Parallel tunnel."

Drizzt joined his friend by the wall and listened intently, but though his senses were keener than almost any other dark elf, he was not nearly as adept at reading the vibrations of the stone as the deep gnome.

"How many?" he asked.

"A few," replied Belwar, but his shrug told Drizzt that he was only making a hopeful approximation.

"Seven," said Clacker from a few paces down the wall, his voice clear and sure. "Duergar—gray dwarves—fleeing from the illithids, as are we."

"How can you . . ." Drizzt started to ask, but he stopped, remembering what Clacker had told him concerning the powers of the pech.

"Do the tunnels cross?" Belwar asked the hook horror. "Can we avoid the duergar?"

Clacker turned back to the stone for the answers. "The tunnels join a short way ahead," he replied, "then continue on as one."

"Then if we stay here, the gray dwarves will probably pass us by," Belwar reasoned.

Drizzt was not so certain of the deep gnome's reasoning.

"We and the duergar share a common enemy," Drizzt remarked, then his eyes widened as a thought came to him suddenly. "Allies?"

"Though often the duergar and drow travel together, gray dwarves do not usually ally with svirfnebli," Belwar reminded him. "Or hook horrors, I would guess!"

"This situation is far from usual," Drizzt was quick to retort. "If the duergar are in flight from the mind flayers, then they are probably ill-equipped and unarmed. They might welcome such an alliance, to the gain of both groups."

"I do not believe they will be as friendly as you assume," Belwar replied with a sarcastic snicker, "but concede I will that this narrow tunnel is not a defensible region, more suited to the size of a duergar than to the long blades of a drow and the longer-still arms of a hook horror. If the duergar double back at the crossroad and head toward us, we may have to do battle in an area that will favor them."

"Then to the place where the tunnels join," said Drizzt, "and let us learn what we may."

The three companions soon came into a small, oval-shaped chamber. Another tunnel, the one in which the duergar were traveling, entered the area right beside the companions' tunnel, and a third passage ran out from the back of the room. The friends moved across into the shadows of this farthest tunnel even as the shuffling of boots echoed in their ears.

A moment later, the seven duergar came into the oval chamber. They were haggard, as Drizzt had suspected, but they were not unarmed. Three carried clubs, another a dagger, two held swords, and the last sported two large rocks.

Drizzt held his friends back and stepped out to meet the strangers. Though neither race held much love for the other, drow and duergar often formed mutually gainful alliances. Drizzt guessed that the chances of forming a peaceful alliance would be greater if he went out alone.

His sudden appearance startled the weary gray dwarves. They rushed all about frantically, trying to form some defensive posture. Swords and clubs came up at the ready, and the dwarf holding the rocks cocked his arm back for a throw.

"Greetings, duergar," Drizzt said hoping that the gray dwarves would understand the drow tongue. His hand rested easily on the hilts of his sheathed scimitars; he knew he could get to them quickly enough if he needed them.

"Who might ye be?" one of the sword-wielding gray dwarves asked in shaky but understandable drow.

"A refugee, as yourselves," replied Drizzt, "fleeing from the slavery of the cruel mind flayers."

"Then ye know our hurry," snarled the duergar, "so be standin' outa our way!"

"I offer to you an alliance," said Drizzt. "Surely greater numbers will only aid us when the illithids come."

"Seven's as good as eight," the duergar stubbornly replied. Behind the speaker, the rock thrower pumped his arm threateningly.

"But not as good as ten," Drizzt reasoned calmly.

"Ye got friends?" asked the duergar, his tone noticeably softening. He glanced about nervously, looking for a possible ambush. "More drow?"

"Hardly," Drizzt answered.

"I seen him!" cried another of the group, also in the drow tongue, before Drizzt could begin to explain. "He runned out with the beaked monster an' the svirfneblin!"

"Deep gnome!" The leader of the duegar spat at Drizzt's feet. "Not a friend o' the duergar or the drow!"

Drizzt would have been willing to let the failed offer go at that, when he and his friends moving on their way and the gray dwarves going their own. But the well-earned reputation of the duergar labeled them as neither peaceful nor overly intelligent. With the illithids not far behind, this band of gray dwarves hardly needed more enemies.

A rock sailed at Drizzt's head. A scimitar flashed out and deflected it harmlessly aside.

*"Bivrip!"* came the burrow-warden's cry from the tunnel, Belwar and

Clacker rushed out, not surprised in the least by the sudden turn of events.

In the drow Academy, Drizzt, like all dark elves, had spent months learning the ways and tricks of the gray dwarves. That training saved him now, for he was the first to strike, lining all seven of his diminutive opponents in the harmless purple flames of faerie fire.

Almost at the same time, three of the duergar faded from view, exercising their innate talents of invisibility. The purple flames remained, though, clearly outlining the disappearing dwarves.

A second rock flew through the air, slamming into Clacker's chest. The armored monster would have smiled at the pitiful attack if a beak could smile, and Clacker continued his charge straight ahead into the duergar's midst.

The rock thrower and the dagger wielder fled out of the hook horror's way, having no weapons that could possibly hurt the armored giant. With other foes readily available, Clacker let them go. They came around the side of the chamber, bearing straight in at Belwar, thinking the svirfneblin the easiest of the targets.

The swipe of a pickaxe abruptly stopped their charge. The unarmed duergar lunged forward, trying to grab the arm before it could launch a backswing. Belwar anticipated the attempt and crossed over with his hammer-hand, slamming the duergar squarely in the face. Sparks flew, bones crumbled, and gray skin burned and splattered. The duergar flew to his back and writhed about frantically, clutching his broken face.

The dagger wielder was not so anxious anymore.

Two invisible duergar came at Drizzt. With the outline of purple flames, Drizzt could see their general movement, and he had prudently marked these two as the sword-wielders. But Drizzt was at a clear disadvantage, for he could not distinguish subtle thrusts and cuts. He backed away, putting distance between himself and his companions.

He sensed an attack and threw out a blocking scimitar, smiling at his luck when he heard the ring of weapons. The gray dwarf came into view for just a moment, to show Drizzt his wicked smile, then faded quickly away.

"How many does ye think ye can block?" the other invisible duergar asked smugly.

"More than you, I suspect," Drizzt replied, and then it was the drow's turn to smile. His enchanted globe of absolute darkness descended over all three of the combatants, stealing the duergar advantage.

In the wild rush of the battle, Clacker's savage hook horror instincts took full control of his actions. The giant did not understand the significance of the empty purple flames that marked the third invisible duergar, and he charged instead at the two remaining gray dwarves, both holding clubs.

Before the hook horror ever got there, a club smashed into his knee, and the invisible duergar chuckled in glee. The other two began to fade from sight, but Clacker now paid them no heed. The invisible club struck again, this time smashing into the hook horror's thigh.

Possessed by the instincts of a race that had never been concerned with finesse, the hook horror howled and fell forward, burying the purple flames under his massive chest. Clacker hopped and dropped several times, until he was satisfied that the unseen enemy was crushed to death.

But then a flurry of clubbing blows rained down upon the back of the hook horror's head.

The dagger-wielding duergar was no novice to battle. His attacks came in measured thrusts, forcing Belwar, wielding heavier weapons, to take the initiative. Deep gnomes hated duergar as profoundly as duergar hated deep gnomes, but Belwar was no fool. His pickaxe waved about only to keep his opponent at bay, while his hammer-hand remained cocked and ready.

Thus, the two sparred without gain for several moments, both content to let the other make the first error. When the hook horror cried out in pain, and with Drizzt out of sight, Belwar was forced to act. He stumbled forward, feigning a trip, and lurched ahead with his hammer-hand as his pickaxe dipped low.

The duergar recognized the ploy, but could not ignore the obvious opening in the svirfneblin's defense. The dagger came in over the pickaxe, diving straight at Belwar's throat.

The burrow-warden threw himself backward with equal speed and lifted a leg as he went, his boot clipping the duergar's chin. The gray dwarf kept coming, though, diving down atop the falling deep gnome, his dagger's point leading the way.

Belwar got his pickaxe up only a split second before the jagged weapon found his throat. The burrow-warden managed to move the duergar's arm out wide, but the gray dwarf's considerable weight pressed them together, their faces barely an inch apart.

"Got ye now!" the duergar cried.

"Get this!" Belwar snarled back, and he freed up his hammer-hand enough to launch a short but heavy punch into the duergar's ribs. The duergar slammed his forehead into Belwar's face, and Belwar bit him on the nose in response. The two rolled about, spitting and snarling, and using whatever weapons they could find.

By the sound of ringing blades, any observers outside Drizzt's darkness globe would have sworn that a dozen warriors battled within. The frenzied tempo of swordplay was solely the doing of Drizzt Do'Urden. In such a situation, fighting blindly, the drow reasoned that the best battle method would be to keep all the blades as far away from his body as possible. His scimitars charged out relentlessly and in perfect harmony, pressing the two gray dwarves back on their heels.

Each arm worked its own opponent, keeping the gray dwarves rooted in place squarely in front of Drizzt. If one of his enemies managed to get around to his side, the drow knew, he would be in serious trouble.

Each scimitar swipe brought a ring of metal, and each passing second gave Drizzt more understanding of his opponents' abilities and attack strategies. Out in the Underdark, Drizzt had fought blindly many times, once even donning a hood against the basilisk he'd met.

Overwhelmed by the sheer speed of the drow's attacks, the duergar could only work their swords back and forth and hope that a scimitar didn't slide through.

The blades sang and rang as the two duergar frantically parried and dodged. Then came a sound that Drizzt had hoped for, the sound of a scimitar digging into flesh. A moment later, one sword clanged to the stone and its wounded wielder made the fatal mistake of crying out in pain.

Drizzt's hunter-self rose to the surface at that moment and focused on that cry, and his scimitar shot straight ahead, smashing into the gray dwarf's teeth and on through the back of its head.

The hunter turned on the remaining duergar in fury. Around and around his blades spun in swirling circular motions. Around and around, then one shot out in a sudden straightforward thrust, too quickly for a blocking response. It caught the duergar in the shoulder, gashing a deep wound.

"Give! Give!" the gray dwarf cried, not desiring the same fate as its companion. Drizzt heard another sword drop to the floor. "Please, drow elf!"

At the duergar's words, the drow buried his instinctive urges. "I accept your surrender," Drizzt replied, and he moved close to his opponent, putting the tip of his scimitar to the gray dwarf's chest. Together, they walked out of the area darkened by Drizzt's spell.

Searing agony ripped through Clacker's head, every blow sending waves of pain. The hook horror gurgled out an animal's growl and exploded into furious motion, heaving up from the crushed duergar and spinning over at the newest foes.

A duergar club smashed in again, but Clacker was beyond any sensation of pain. A heavy claw bashed through the purple outline, through the invisible duergar's skull. The gray dwarf came back into view suddenly, the concentration needed to maintain a state of invisibility stolen by death, the greatest thief of all.

The remaining duergar turned to flee, but the enraged hook horror moved faster. Clacker caught the gray dwarf in a claw and hoisted him into the air. Screeching like a frenzied bird, the hook horror hurled the unseen opponent into the wall. The duergar came back into sight, broken and crumbled at the base of the stone wall.

No opponents stood to face the hook horror, but Clacker's savage hunger was far from satiated. Drizzt and the wounded duergar emerged from the darkness then, and the hook horror barreled in.

With the specter of Belwar's combat taking his attention, Drizzt did not realize Clacker's intent until the duergar prisoner screamed in terror.

By then, it was too late.

Drizzt watched his prisoner's head go flying back into the globe of darkness.

"Clacker!" the drow screamed in protest. Then Drizzt ducked and dived backward for his own life as the other claw came viciously swinging across.

Spotting new prey nearby, the hook horror didn't follow the drow into the globe. Belwar and the dagger-wielding duergar were too engaged in their own struggles to notice the approaching crazed giant. Clacker bent low, collected the prone combatants in his huge arms, and heaved them both straight up into the air. The duergar had the misfortune of coming down first, and Clacker promptly batted it across the chamber. Belwar would have found a similar fate, but crossed scimitars intercepted the hook horror's next blow.

The giant's strength slid Drizzt back several feet, but the parry softened the blow enough for Belwar to fall by. Still, the burrow-warden crashed heavily into the floor and spent a long moment too dazed to react.

"Clacker!" Drizzt cried again, as a giant foot came up with the obvious intent of squashing Belwar flat. Needing all his speed and agility, Drizzt dived around to the back of the hook horror, dropped to the floor, and went for Clacker's knees, as he had in their first encounter. Trying to stomp on the prone svirfneblin, Clacker was already a bit off balance, and Drizzt easily tripped him to the stone. In the blink of an eye, the drow warrior sprang atop the monster's chest and slipped a scimitar tip between the armored folds of Clacker's neck.

Drizzt dodged a clumsy swing as Clacker continued to struggle. The drow hated what he had to do, but then the hook horror calmed suddenly and looked up at him with sincere understanding.

"D-d-do . . . it," came a garbled demand. Drizzt, horrified, glanced over to Belwar for support. Back on his feet, the burrow-warden just looked away.

"Clacker?" Drizzt asked the hook horror. "Are you Clacker once again?"

The monster hesitated, then the beaked head nodded slightly.

Drizzt sprang away and looked at the carnage in the chamber. "Let us leave," he said.

Clacker remained prone a moment longer, considering the grim implications of his reprieve. With the battle's conclusion, the hook horror side backed out of its full control of Clacker's consciousness. Those savage instincts lurked, Clacker knew, not far from the surface, waiting for another opportunity to find a firm hold. How many times would the faltering pech side be able to fight those instincts?

Clacker slammed the stone, a mighty blow that sent cracks running through the chamber's floor. With great effort, the weary giant climbed to his feet. In his embarrassment, Clacker didn't look at his companions, but just stormed away down the tunnel, each banging footstep falling like a hammer on a nail in Drizzt Do'Urden's heart.

"Perhaps you should have finished it, dark elf," Belwar suggested, moving beside his drow friend.

"He saved my life in the illithid cavern," Drizzt retorted sharply. "And has been a loyal friend."

"He tried to kill me, and you," the deep gnome said grimly. "*Magga cammara*."

"I am his friend!" Drizzt growled, grabbing the svirfneblin's shoulder. "You ask me to kill him?"

"I ask you to act as his friend," retorted Belwar, and he pulled free of the grasp and started away down the tunnel after Clacker.

Drizzt grabbed the burrow-warden's shoulder again and roughly spun him around.

"It will only get worse, dark elf," Belwar said calmly into Drizzt's grimace. "A firmer hold does the wizard's spell gain with every passing day. Clacker will try to kill us again, I fear, and if he succeeds, the realization of the act will destroy him more fully than your blades ever could!"

"I cannot kill him," Drizzt said, and he was no longer angry. "Nor can you."

"Then we must leave him," the deep gnome replied. "We must let Clacker go free in the Underdark, to live his life as a hook horror. That surely is what he will become, body and spirit."

"No," said Drizzt. "We must not leave him. We are his only chance. We must help him."

"The wizard is dead," Belwar reminded him, and the deep gnome turned away and started again after Clacker.

"There are other wizards," Drizzt replied under his breath, this time making no move to impede the burrow-warden. The drow's eyes narrowed and he snapped his scimitars back into their sheaths. Drizzt knew what he must do, what price his friendship with Clacker demanded, but he found the thought too disturbing to accept.

There were indeed other wizards in the Underdark, but chance meetings were far from common, and wizards capable of dispelling Clacker's polymorphed state would be fewer still. Drizzt knew where such wizards could be found, though.

The thought of returning to his homeland haunted Drizzt with every step he and his companions took that day. Having viewed the consequences of his decision to leave Menzoberranzan, Drizzt never wanted to see the place again, never wanted to look upon the dark world that had so damned him.

But if he chose now not to return, Drizzt knew that he would soon witness a more wicked sight than Menzoberranzan. He would watch Clacker, a friend who had saved him from certain death, degenerate fully into a hook horror. Belwar had suggested abandoning Clacker, and that course seemed preferable to the battle that Drizzt and the deep gnome surely must fight if they were near Clacker when the degeneration became complete.

Even if Clacker were far removed, though, Drizzt knew that he would witness the degeneration. His thoughts would stay on Clacker, the friend he had abandoned, for the rest of his days, just one more pain for the tormented drow.

In all the world, Drizzt could think of nothing he desired less than viewing the sights of Menzoberranzan or conversing with his former people. Given the choice, he would prefer death over returning to the drow city, but the choice was not so simple. It hinged on more than Drizzt's personal desires. He had founded his life on principles, and those principles now demanded loyalty. They demanded that he put Clacker's needs above his own desires, because Clacker had befriended him and because the concept of true friendship far outweighed personal desires.

Later on, when the friends had set camp for a short rest, Belwar noticed that Drizzt was engaged in some inner conflict. Leaving Clacker, who once again was tap-tapping at the stone wall, the svirfneblin moved cautiously by the drow's side.

Belwar cocked his head curiously. "What are you thinking, dark elf?"

Drizzt, too caught up in his emotional turbulence, did not return Belwar's gaze. "My homeland boasts a school of wizardry," Drizzt replied with steadfast determination.

At first the burrow-warden didn't understand what Drizzt hinted at, but then, when Drizzt glanced over to Clacker, Belwar realized the implications of Drizzt's simple statement.

"Menzoberranzan?" the svirfneblin cried. "You would return there, hoping that some dark elf wizard would show mercy upon our pech friend?"

"I would return there because Clacker has no other chance," Drizzt retorted angrily.

"Then no chance at all has Clacker," Belwar roared. "*Magga cammara*, dark elf. Menzoberranzan will not be so quick to welcome you!"

"Perhaps your pessimism will prove valid," said Drizzt. "Dark elves are not moved by mercy, I agree, but there may be other options."

"You are hunted," Belwar said. His tone showed that he hoped his simple words would shake some sense into his drow companion.

"By Matron Malice," Drizzt retorted. "Menzoberranzan is a large place, my little friend, and loyalties to my mother will play no part in any encounter we find beyond those with my own family. I assure you that I have no plans to meet anyone from my own family!"

"And what, dark elf, might we offer in exchange for dispelling Clacker's curse?" Belwar replied sarcastically. "What have we to offer that any dark elf wizard of Menzoberranzan would value?"

Drizzt's reply started with a blurring cut of a scimitar, was heightened by a familiar simmering fire in the drow's lavender eyes, and ended with a simple statement that even stubborn Belwar could not find the words to refute.

"The wizard's life."

# 23

# RIPPLES

Matron Baenre took a long and careful scan of Malice Do'Urden, measuring how greatly the trials of Zin-carla had weighed on the matron mother. Deep lines of worry creased Malice's once smooth face, and her stark white hair, which had been the envy of her generation, was, for one of the very few times in five centuries, frazzled and unkempt. Most striking, though, were Malice's eyes, once radiant and alert but now dark with weariness and sunken in the sockets of her dark skin.

"Zaknafein almost had him," Malice explained, her voice an uncharacteristic whine. "Drizzt was in his grasp, and yet somehow, my son managed to escape!

"But the spirit-wraith is close on his trail again," Malice quickly added, seeing Matron Baenre's disapproving frown. In addition to being the most powerful figure in all of Menzoberranzan, the withered matron mother of House Baenre was considered Lolth's personal representative in the city. Matron Baenre's approval was Lolth's approval, and by the same logic, Matron Baenre's disapproval most often spelled disaster for a house.

"Zin-carla requires patience, Matron Malice," Matron Baenre said calmly. "It has not been so long."

Malice relaxed a bit, until she looked again at her surroundings. She hated the chapel of House Baenre, so huge and demeaning. The entire

Do'Urden complex could fit within this single chamber, and if Malice's family and soldiers were multiplied ten times over, they still would not fill the rows of benches. Directly above the central altar, directly above Matron Malice, loomed the illusionary image of the gigantic spider, shifting into the form of a beautiful drow female, then back again into an arachnid. Sitting here alone with Matron Baenre under that overpowering image made Malice feel even more insignificant.

Matron Baenre sensed her guest's uneasiness and moved to comfort her. "You have been given a great gift," she said sincerely. "The Spider Queen would not bestow Zin-carla, and would not have accepted the sacrifice of SiNafay Hun'ett, a matron mother, if she did not approve of your methods and your intent."

"It is a trial," Malice replied offhandedly.

"A trial you will not fail!" Matron Baenre retorted. "And then the glories you will know, Malice Do'Urden! When the spirit-wraith of he who was Zaknafein has completed his task and your renegade son is dead, you will sit in honor on the ruling council. Many years, I promise you, will pass before any house will dare to threaten House Do'Urden. The Spider Queen will shine her favor upon you for the proper completion of Zin-carla. She will hold your house in the highest regard and will defend you against rivals."

"What if Zin-carla fails?" Malice dared to ask. "Let us suppose . . ." Her voice trailed away as Matron Baenre's eyes widened in shock.

"Speak not the words!" Baenre scolded. "And think not of such impossibilities! You grow distracted by fear, and that alone will spell your doom. Zin-carla is an exercise of willpower and a test of your devotion to the Spider Queen. The spirit-wraith is an extension of your faith and your strength. If you falter in your trust, then the spirit-wraith of Zaknafein will falter in his quest!"

"I will not falter!" Malice roared, her hands clenched around the armrests of her chair. "I accept the responsibility of my son's sacrilege, and with Lolth's help and blessings, I will enact the appropriate punishment upon Drizzt."

Matron Baenre relaxed back in her seat and nodded her approval. She had to support Malice in this endeavor, by the command of Lolth, and she knew enough of Zin-carla to understand that confidence and determination were two of the primary ingredients for success. A matron mother involved in Zin-carla had to proclaim her trust in Lolth and her desire to please Lolth often and sincerely.

Now, though, Malice had another problem, a distraction she could ill afford. She had come to House Baenre of her own volition, seeking aid.

"Then of this other matter," Matron Baenre prompted, fast growing tired of the meeting.

"I am vulnerable," Malice explained. "Zin-carla steals my energy and attention. I fear that another house may seize the opportunity."

"No house has ever attacked a matron mother in the thralls of Zin-carla," Matron Baenre pointed out, and Malice realized that the withered old drow spoke from experience.

"Zin-carla is a rare gift," Malice replied, "given to powerful matrons with powerful houses, almost assuredly in the highest favor of the Spider Queen. Who would attack under such circumstances? But House Do'Urden is far different. We have just suffered the consequences of war. Even with the addition of some of House Hun'ett's soldiers, we are crippled. It is well known that I have not yet regained Lolth's favor but that my house is eighth in the city, putting me on the ruling council, an enviable position."

"Your fears are misplaced," Matron Baenre assured her, but Malice slumped back in frustration in spite of the words. Matron Baenre shook her head helplessly. "I see that my words alone cannot soothe. Your attention must be on Zin-carla. Understand that, Malice Do'Urden. You have no time for such petty worries."

"They remain," said Malice.

"Then I will end them," offered Matron Baenre. "Return to your house now, in the company of two hundred Baenre soldiers. The numbers will secure your battlements, and my soldiers shall wear the house emblem of Baenre. None in the city will dare to strike with such allies."

A wide smile rolled across Malice's face, a grin that diminished a few of those worry lines. She accepted Matron Baenre's generous gift as a signal that perhaps Lolth still did favor House Do'Urden.

"Go back to your home and concentrate on the task at hand," Matron

Baenre continued. "Zaknafein must find Drizzt again and kill him. That is the deal you offered to the Spider Queen. But fear not for the spirit-wraith's last failure or the time lost. A few days, or tendays, is not very long in Lolth's eyes. The proper conclusion of Zin-carla is all that matters."

"You will arrange for my escort?" Malice asked, rising from her chair.

"It is already waiting," Matron Baenre assured her.

Malice walked down from the raised central dais and out through the many rows of the giant chapel. The huge room was dimly lit, and Malice could barely see, as she exited, another figure moving toward the central dais from the opposite direction. She assumed it to be Matron Baenre's companion illithid, a common figure in the great chapel. If Malice had known that Matron Baenre's mind flayer had left the city on some private business in the west, she might have paid more heed to the distant figure.

Her worry lines would have increased tenfold.

"Pitiful," Jarlaxle remarked as he ascended to sit beside Matron Baenre. "This is not the same Matron Malice Do'Urden that I knew only a few short months ago."

"Zin-carla is not cheaply given," Matron Baenre replied.

"The toll is great," Jarlaxle agreed. He looked straight at Matron Baenre, reading her eyes as well as her forthcoming reply. "Will she fail?"

Matron Baenre chuckled aloud, a laugh that sounded more like a wheeze. "Even the Spider Queen could only guess at the answer. My—our—soldiers should lend Matron Malice enough comfort to complete the task. That is my hope at least. Malice Do'Urden once was in Lolth's highest regard, you know. Her seat on the ruling council was demanded by the Spider Queen."

"Events do seem to lead to the completion of Lolth's will," Jarlaxle snickered, remembering the battle between House Do'Urden and House Hun'ett, in which Bregan D'aerthe had played the pivotal role. The consequences of that victory, the elimination of House Hun'ett, had put House Do'Urden in the city's eighth position and thus, had placed Matron Malice on the ruling council.

"Fortunes smile on the favored," Matron Baenre remarked.

Jarlaxle's grin was replaced by a suddenly serious look. "And is

Malice—Matron Malice," he quickly corrected, seeing Baenre's immediate glower, "now in the Spider Queen's favor? Will fortunes smile on House Do'Urden?"

"The gift of Zin-carla removed both favor and disfavor, I would assume," Matron Baenre explained. "Matron Malice's fortunes are for her and her spirit-wraith to determine."

"Or, for her son—this infamous Drizzt Do'Urden—to destroy," Jarlaxle completed. "Is this young warrior so very powerful? Why has Lolth not simply crushed him?"

"He has forsaken the Spider Queen," Baenre replied, "fully and with all his heart. Lolth has no power over Drizzt and has determined him to be Matron Malice's problem."

"A rather large problem, it would seem," Jarlaxle chuckled with a quick shake of his bald head. The mercenary noticed immediately that Matron Baenre did not share his mirth.

"Indeed," she replied somberly, and her voice trailed off on the word as she sank back for some private thoughts. She knew the dangers, and the possible profits, of Zin-carla better than anyone in the city. Twice before Matron Baenre had asked for the Spider Queen's greatest gift, and twice before she had seen Zin-carla through to successful completion. With the unrivaled grandeur of House Baenre all about her, Matron Baenre could not forget the gains of Zin-carla's success. But every time she saw her withered reflection in a pool or a mirror, she was vividly reminded of the heavy price.

Jarlaxle did not intrude on the matron mother's reflections. The mercenary contemplated on his own at that moment. In a time of trial and confusion such as this, a skilled opportunist would find only gain. By Jarlaxle's reckoning, Bregan D'aerthe could only profit from the granting of Zin-carla to Matron Malice. If Malice proved successful and reinforced her seat on the ruling council, Jarlaxle would have another very powerful ally within the city. If the spirit-wraith failed, to the ruin of House Do'Urden, the price on this young Drizzt's head certainly would escalate to a level that might tempt the mercenary band.

⚔ ⚔ ⚔ ⚔ ⚔

As she had on her journey to the first house of the city, Malice imagined ambitious gazes following her return through the winding streets of Menzoberranzan. Matron Baenre had been quite generous and gracious. Accepting the premise that the withered old matron mother was indeed Lolth's voice in the city, Malice could barely contain her smile.

Undeniably, though, the fears still remained. How readily would Matron Baenre come to Malice's aid if Drizzt continued to elude Zaknafein, if Zin-carla ultimately failed? Malice's position on the ruling council would be tenuous then—as would the continued existence of House Do'Urden.

The caravan passed House Fey-Branche, ninth house of the city and most probably the greatest threat to a weakened House Do'Urden. Matron Halavin Fey-Branche was no doubt watching the procession beyond her adamantite gates, watching the matron mother who now held the coveted eighth seat on the ruling council.

Malice looked at Dinin and the ten soldiers of House Do'Urden, walking by her side as she sat atop the floating magical disc. She let her gaze wander to the two hundred soldiers, warriors openly bearing the proud emblem of House Baenre, marching with disciplined precision behind her modest troupe.

What must Matron Halavin Fey-Branche be thinking at such a sight? Malice wondered. She could not contain her ensuing smile.

"Our greatest glories are soon to come," Malice assured her warrior son. Dinin nodded and returned the wide smile, wisely not daring to steal any of the joy from his volatile mother.

Privately, though, Dinin couldn't ignore his disturbing suspicions that many of the Baenre soldiers, drow warriors he had never had the occasion to meet before, looked vaguely familiar. One of them even shot a sly wink at the elderboy of House Do'Urden.

Jarlaxle's magical whistle being blown on the balcony of House Do'Urden came vividly to Dinin's mind.

# 24

# Faith

Drizzt and Belwar did not have to remind each other of the significance of the green glow that appeared far ahead up the tunnel. Together they quickened their pace to catch up with and warn Clacker, who continued his approach with strides quickened by curiosity. The hook horror always led the party now; Clacker simply had become too dangerous for Drizzt and Belwar to allow him to walk behind.

Clacker turned abruptly at their sudden approach, waved a claw menacingly, and hissed.

"Pech," Belwar whispered, speaking the word he had been using to strike a recollection in his friend's fast-fading consciousness. The troupe had turned back toward the east, toward Menzoberranzan, as soon as Drizzt had convinced the burrow-warden of his determination to aid Clacker. Belwar, having no other options, had finally agreed with the drow's plan as Clacker's only hope, but though they had turned immediately and had quickened their march, both now feared that they would not arrive in time. The transformation in Clacker had been dramatic since the confrontation with the duergar. The hook horror could barely speak and often turned threateningly on his friends.

"Pech," Belwar said again as he and Drizzt neared the anxious monster.

The hook horror paused, confused.

"Pech!" Belwar growled a third time, and he tapped his hammer-hand against the stone wall.

As if a light of recognition had suddenly gone on within the turmoil that was his consciousness, Clacker relaxed and dropped his heavy arms to his sides.

Drizzt and Belwar looked past the hook horror to the green glow and exchanged concerned glances. They had committed themselves fully to this course and had little choice in their actions now.

"Corbies live in the chamber beyond," Drizzt began quietly, speaking each word slowly and distinctly to ensure that Clacker understood. "We have to get directly across and out the other side swiftly, for if we hope to avoid a battle, we have no time for delays. Take care in your steps. The only walkways are narrow and treacherous."

"C-C-Clac—" the hook horror stammered futilely.

"Clacker," Belwar offered.

"L-l-l—" Clacker stopped suddenly and threw a claw out in the direction of the green-glowing chamber.

"Clacker lead?" Drizzt said, unable to bear the hook horror's struggling. "Clacker lead," Drizzt said again, seeing the great head bobbing in accord.

Belwar didn't seem so sure of the wisdom of that suggestion. "We have fought the bird-men before and have seen their tricks," the svirfneblin reasoned. "But Clacker has not."

"The sheer bulk of the hook horror should deter them," Drizzt argued. "Clacker's mere presence may allow us to avoid a fight."

"Not against the corbies, dark elf," said the burrow-warden. "They will attack anything without fear. You witnessed their frenzy, their disregard for their own lives. Even your panther did not deter them."

"Perhaps you are right," Drizzt agreed, "but even if the corbies do attack, what weapons do they possess that could defeat a hook horror's armor? What defense could the birdmen offer against Clacker's great claws. Our giant friend will sweep them aside."

"You forget the stone-riders up above," the burrow-warden pointedly reminded him. "They will be quick to take a ledge down, and take Clacker with it!"

Clacker turned away from the conversation and stared into the stone of the walls in a futile effort to recapture a portion of his former self. He felt a slight urge to begin tap-tapping on the stone, but it was no greater than his continuing urge to smash a claw into the face of either the svirfneblin or the drow.

"I will deal with any corbies waiting above the ledges," Drizzt replied. "You just follow Clacker across—a dozen paces behind."

Belwar glanced over and noticed the mounting tension in the hook horror. The burrow-warden realized that they could not afford any delays, so he shrugged and pushed Clacker off, motioning down the passage toward the green glow. Clacker started away, and Drizzt and Belwar fell into step behind.

"The panther?" Belwar whispered to Drizzt as they rounded the last bend in the tunnel.

Drizzt shook his head briskly, and Belwar, remembering Guenhwyvar's last painful episode in the corby chamber, did not question him further.

Drizzt patted the deep gnome on the shoulder for luck, then moved up past Clacker and was the first to enter the quiet chamber. With a few simple motions, the drow stepped into a levitation spell and floated silently up. Clacker, amazed by this strange place with the glowing lake of acid below him, hardly noticed Drizzt's movements. The hook horror stood perfectly still, glancing all about the chamber and using his keen sense of hearing to locate any possible enemies.

"Move," Belwar whispered behind him. "Delay will bring disaster!"

Clacker started out tentatively, then picked up speed as he gained confidence in the strength of the narrow, unsupported walkway. He took the straightest course he could discern, though even this meandered about before it reached the exiting archway opposite the one they had entered.

"Do you see anything, dark elf?" Belwar called as loudly as he dared a few uneventful moments later. Clacker had passed the midpoint of the chamber without incident and the burrow-warden could not contain his mounting anxiety. No corbies had shown themselves; not a sound had been made beyond the heavy thumping of Clacker's feet and the shuffling of Belwar's worn boots.

Drizzt floated back down to the ledge, far behind his companions. "Nothing," he replied. The drow shared Belwar's suspicions that no dire corbies were about. The hush of the acid-filled cavern was absolute and unnerving. Drizzt ran out toward the center of the chamber, then lifted off again in his levitation, trying to get a better angle on all of the walls.

"What do you see?" Belwar asked him a moment later. Drizzt looked down to the burrow-warden and shrugged.

"Nothing at all."

"*Magga cammara*," grumbled Belwar, almost wishing that a corby would step out and attack.

Clacker had nearly reached the targeted exit by this time, though Belwar, in his conversation with Drizzt, had lagged behind and remained near the center of the huge room. When the burrow-warden finally turned back to the path ahead, the hook horror had disappeared under the arch of the exit.

"Anything?" Belwar called out to both of his companions. Drizzt shook his head and continued to rise. He rotated slowly about, scanning the walls, unable to believe that no corbies lurked in ambush.

Belwar looked back to the exit. "We must have chased them out," he muttered to himself, but in spite of his words, the burrow-warden knew better. When he and Drizzt had taken flight from this room a couple of tendays before, they had left several dozen of the bird-men behind them. Certainly the toll of a few dead corbies would not have chased away the rest of the fearless clan.

For some unknown reason, no corbies had come out to stand against them.

Belwar started off at a quick pace, thinking it best not to question their good fortune. He was about to call out to Clacker, to confirm that the hook horror had indeed moved to safety, when a sharp, terror-filled squeal rolled out from the exit, followed by a heavy crash. A moment later, Belwar and Drizzt had their answers.

The spirit-wraith of Zaknafein Do'Urden stepped under the arch and out onto the ledge.

"Dark elf!" the burrow-warden called sharply.

Drizzt had already seen the spirit-wraith and was descending as rapidly as he could toward the walkway near the middle of the chamber.

"Clacker," Belwar called, but he expected no answer, and received none, from the shadows beyond the archway. The spirit-wraith steadily advanced.

"You murderous beast!" the burrow-warden cursed, setting his feet wide apart and slamming his mithral hands together. "Come out and get your due!" Belwar fell into his chant to empower his hands, but Drizzt interrupted him.

"No!" the drow cried out high above. "Zaknafein is here for me, not you. Move out of his way!"

"Was he here for Clacker?" Belwar yelled back. "A murderous beast, he is, and I have a score to settle!"

"You do not know that," Drizzt replied, increasing his descent as fast as he dared to catch up to the fearless burrow-warden. Drizzt knew that Zaknafein would get to Belwar first, and he could guess easily enough the grim consequences.

"Trust me now, I beg," Drizzt pleaded. "This drow warrior is far beyond your abilities."

Belwar banged his hands together again, but he could not honestly refute Drizzt's words. Belwar had seen Zaknafein in battle only that one time in the illithid cavern, but the monster's blurring movements had stolen his breath. The deep gnome backed away a few steps and turned down a side walkway, seeking another route to the arched exit so that he might learn Clacker's fate.

With Drizzt so plainly in sight, the spirit-wraith paid the little svirfneblin no heed. Zaknafein charged right past the side walkway and continued on to fulfill the purpose of his existence.

Belwar thought to pursue the strange drow, to close from behind and help Drizzt in the battle, but another cry issued from under the archway, a cry so pain-filled and pitiful that the burrow-warden could not ignore it. He stopped as soon as he got back on the main walkway, then looked both ways, torn in his loyalties.

"Go!" Drizzt shouted at him. "See to Clacker. This is Zaknafein, my father." Drizzt noticed a slight hesitation in the spirit-wraith's charge at the mention of those words, a hesitation that brought Drizzt a flicker of understanding.

"Your father? *Magga cammara*, dark elf!" Belwar protested. "Back in the illithid cavern—"

"I am safe enough," Drizzt interjected.

Belwar did not believe that Drizzt was safe at all, but against the protests of his own stubborn pride, the burrow-warden realized that the battle that was about to begin was far beyond his abilities. He would be of little help against this mighty drow warrior, and his presence in the battle might actually prove detrimental to his friend. Drizzt would have a difficult enough time without worrying about Belwar's safety.

Belwar banged his mithral hands together in frustration and rushed toward the archway and the continuing moans of his fallen hook horror companion.

⚔ ⚔ ⚔ ⚔ ⚔

Matron Malice's eyes widened and she uttered a sound so primal that her daughters, gathered by her side in the anteroom, knew immediately that the spirit-wraith had found Drizzt. Briza glanced over at the younger Do'Urden priestesses and dismissed them. Maya obeyed immediately, but Vierna hesitated.

"Go," Briza snarled, one hand dropping to the snakeheaded whip on her belt. "Now."

Vierna looked to her matron mother for support, but Malice was quite lost in the spectacle of the distant events. This was the moment of triumph for Zin-carla and for Matron Malice Do'Urden; she would not be distracted by the petty squabbling of her inferiors.

Briza then was alone with her mother, standing behind the throne and studying Malice as intently as Malice watched Zaknafein.

⚔ ⚔ ⚔ ⚔ ⚔

As soon as he entered the small chamber beyond the archway, Belwar knew that Clacker was dead, or soon would be. The giant hook horror body lay on the floor, bleeding from a single but wickedly precise wound across the neck. Belwar began to turn away, then realized that he owed comfort, at least, to his fallen friend. He dropped to one knee and forced himself to watch as Clacker went into a series of violent convulsions.

Death terminated the polymorph spell, and Clacker gradually reverted to his former self. The huge, clawed arms trembled and jerked, twisted and popped into the long and spindly, yellow-skinned arms of a pech. Hair sprouted through the cracking armor of Clacker's head and the great beak split apart and dissipated. The massive chest, too, fell away, and the whole body compacted with a grinding sound that sent shivers up and down the hardy burrow-warden's spine.

The hook horror was no more, and in death, Clacker was as he had been. He was a bit taller than Belwar, though not nearly as wide, and his features were broad and strange, with pupil-less eyes and a flattened nose.

"What was your name, my friend?" the burrow-warden whispered, though he knew that Clacker would never answer. He bent down and lifted the pech's head in his arms, taking some comfort in the peace that finally had come to the tormented creature's face.

⚔ ⚔ ⚔ ⚔ ⚔

"Who are you that takes the guise of my father?" Drizzt asked as the spirit-wraith stalked across the last few paces.

Zaknafein's snarl was indecipherable, and his response came more clearly in the hacking slice of a sword.

Drizzt parried the attack and jumped back. "Who are you?" he demanded again. "You are not my father!"

A wide smile spread over the spirit-wraith's face. "No," Zaknafein replied in a shaky voice, an answer that was inspired from an anteroom many miles away.

"I am your . . . mother!" The swords came on again in a blinding flurry.

Drizzt, confused by the response, met the charge with equal ferocity and the many sudden hits of sword on scimitar sounded like a single ring.

⚔ ⚔ ⚔ ⚔ ⚔

Briza watched her mother's every movement. Sweat poured down Malice's brow and her clenched fists pounded on the arms of her stone throne even after they had begun to bleed. Malice had hoped that it would be like this, that the final moment of her triumph would shine clearly in her thoughts from across the miles. She heard Drizzt's every frantic word and felt his distress so very keenly. Never had Malice known such pleasure!

Then she felt a slight twinge as Zaknafein's consciousness struggled against her control. Malice pushed Zaknafein aside with a guttural snarl; his animated corpse was her tool!

Briza noted her mother's sudden snarl with more than a passing interest.

⚔ ⚔ ⚔ ⚔ ⚔

Drizzt knew beyond any doubts that this was not Zaknafein Do'Urden who stood before him, yet he could not deny the unique fighting style of his former mentor. Zaknafein was in there—somewhere—and Drizzt would have to reach him if he hoped to get any answers.

The battle quickly settled into a comfortable, measured rhythm, both opponents launching cautious attack routines and paying careful attention to their tenuous footing on the narrow walkway.

Belwar entered the room then, bearing Clacker's broken body. "Kill him, Drizzt!" the burrow-warden cried. "*Magga* . . ." Belwar stopped and was afraid when he witnessed the battle. Drizzt and Zaknafein seemed to intertwine, their weapons spinning and darting, only to be parried away. They seemed as one, these two dark elves that Belwar had considered distinctly different, and that notion unnerved the deep gnome.

When the next break came in the struggle, Drizzt glanced over to the burrow-warden and his gaze locked on the dead pech. "Damn you!" he spat, and he rushed back in, scimitars diving and chopping at the monster who had murdered Clacker.

The spirit-wraith parried the foolishly bold assault easily and worked Drizzt's blades up high, rocking Drizzt back on his heels. This, too, seemed so very familiar to the young drow, a fighting approach that Zaknafein had used against him many times in their sparring matches back in Menzoberranzan. Zaknafein would force Drizzt high, then come in suddenly low with both of his swords. In their early contests, Zaknafein had often defeated Drizzt with this maneuver, the double-thrust low, but in their last encounter in the drow city, Drizzt had found the answering parry and had turned the attack against his mentor.

Now Drizzt wondered if this opponent would follow through with the expected attack routine, and he wondered, too, how Zaknafein would react to his counter. Were any of Zak's memories within the monster he now faced?

Still the spirit-wraith kept Drizzt's blades working defensively high. Zaknafein then took a quick step back and came in low with both blades.

Drizzt dropped his scimitars into a downward X, the appropriate cross-down parry that pinned the attacking swords low. Drizzt kicked his foot up between the hilts of his blades and straight at his opponent's face.

The spirit-wraith somehow anticipated the countering attack and was out of reach before the boot could connect. Drizzt believed that he had an answer, for only Zaknafein Do'Urden could have known.

"You *are* Zaknafein!" Drizzt cried. "What has Malice done to you?"

The spirit-wraith's hands trembled visibly in their hold on the swords and his mouth twisted as though he was trying to say something.

⚔ ⚔ ⚔ ⚔ ⚔

"No!" Malice screamed, and she violently tore back the control of her monster, walking the delicate and dangerous line between Zaknafein's physical abilities and the consciousness of the being he once had been.

"You are mine, wraith," Malice bellowed, "and by the will of Lolth, you shall complete the task!"

⚔⚔⚔⚔⚔

Drizzt saw the sudden regression of the murderous spirit-wraith. Zaknafein's hands no longer trembled and his mouth locked into a thin and determined grimace once again.

"What is it, dark elf?" Belwar demanded, confused by the strange encounter. Drizzt noticed that the deep gnome had placed Clacker's body on a ledge and was steadily approaching. Sparks flew from Belwar's mithral hands whenever they bumped together.

"Stay back!" Drizzt called to him. The presence of an unknown enemy could ruin the plans that were beginning to formulate in Drizzt's mind. "It is Zaknafein," he tried to explain to Belwar. "Or at least a part of it is!"

In a voice too low for the burrow-warden to hear, Drizzt added, "And I believe I know how to get to that part." Drizzt came on in a flurry of measured attacks that he knew Zaknafein could easily deflect. He did not want to destroy his opponent, but rather he sought to inspire other memories of fighting routines that would be familiar to Zaknafein.

He put Zaknafein through the paces of a typical training session, talking all the while in the same way that he and the weapon master used to talk back in Menzoberranzan. Malice's spirit-wraith countered Drizzt's familiarity with savagery, and matched Drizzt's friendly words with animal-like snarls. If Drizzt thought he could lull his opponent with complacency, he was badly mistaken.

Swords rushed at Drizzt inside and out, seeking a hole in his expert defenses. Scimitars matched their speed and precision, catching and stopping each arcing cut and deflecting every straightforward thrust harmlessly wide.

A sword slipped through and nicked Drizzt in the ribs. His fine armor held back the weapon's razor edge, but the weight of the blow would leave a deep bruise. Rocked back on his heels, Drizzt saw that his plan would not be so easily executed.

"You are my father!" he shouted at the monster. "Matron Malice is your enemy, not I!"

The spirit-wraith mocked the words with an evil laugh and came on wildly. From the very beginning of the battle, Drizzt had feared this moment, but now he stubbornly reminded himself that this was not really his father that stood before him.

Zaknafein's careless offensive charge inevitably left gaps in his defenses, and Drizzt found them, once and then again, with his scimitars. One blade gashed a hole in the spirit-wraith's belly, another slashed deeply into the side of his neck.

Zaknafein only laughed again, louder, and came on.

Drizzt fought in sheer panic, his confidence faltering. Zaknafein was nearly his equal, and Drizzt's blades barely hurt the thing! Another problem quickly became evident as well, for time was against Drizzt. He did not know exactly what it was that he faced, but he suspected that it would not tire.

Drizzt pressed with all his skill and speed. Desperation drove him to new heights of swordsmanship. Belwar started out again to join in, but he stopped a moment later, stunned by the display.

Drizzt hit Zaknafein several more times, but the spirit-wraith seemed not to notice, and as Drizzt stepped up the tempo, the spirit-wraith's intensity grew to match his own. Drizzt could hardly believe that this was not Zaknafein Do'Urden fighting against him; he could recognize the moves of his father and former mentor so very clearly. No other soul could move that perfectly muscled drow body with such precision and skill.

Drizzt was backing away again, giving ground and waiting patiently for his opportunities. He reminded himself over and over that it was not Zaknafein that he faced, but some monster created by Matron Malice for the sole purpose of destroying him. Drizzt had to be ready; his only chance of surviving this encounter was to trip his opponent from the ledge. With the spirit-wraith fighting so brilliantly, though, that chance seemed remote indeed.

The walkway turned slightly around a short bend, and Drizzt felt it carefully with one foot, sliding it along. Then a rock right under Drizzt's foot broke free from the side of the walkway.

Drizzt stumbled, and his leg, to the knee, slipped down beside the bridge. Zaknafein came upon him in a rush. The whirling swords soon had Drizzt down on his back across the narrow walkway, his head hanging precariously over the lake of acid.

"Drizzt!" Belwar screamed helplessly. The deep gnome rushed out, though he could not hope to arrive in time or defeat Drizzt's killer. "Drizzt!"

Perhaps it was that call of Drizzt's name, or maybe it was just the moment of the kill, but the former consciousness of Zaknafein flickered to life in that instant and the sword arm, readied for a killing plunge that Drizzt could not have deflected, hesitated.

Drizzt didn't wait for any explanations. He punched out with a scimitar hilt, then the other, both connecting squarely on Zaknafein's jaw and moving the spirit-wraith back. Drizzt was up again, panting and favoring a twisted ankle.

"Zaknafein!" Confused and frustrated by the hesitation, Drizzt screamed at his opponent.

"Driz—" the spirit-wraith's mouth struggled to reply. Then Malice's monster rushed back in, swords leading.

Drizzt defeated the attack and slipped away again. He could sense his father's presence; he knew that the true Zaknafein lurked just below the surface of this creature, but how could he free that spirit? Clearly, he could not hope to continue this struggle much longer.

"It is you," Drizzt whispered. "No one else could fight so. Zaknafein is there, and Zaknafein will not kill me." Another thought came to Drizzt then, a notion he had to believe.

Once again, the truth of Drizzt's convictions became the test.

Drizzt slipped his scimitars back into their sheaths.

The spirit-wraith snarled; his swords danced about in the air and cut viciously, but Zaknafein did not come on.

⚔ ⚔ ⚔ ⚔ ⚔

"Kill him!" Malice squealed in glee, thinking her moment of victory at hand. The images of the combat, though, flitted away from her suddenly, and she was left with only darkness. She had given too much back to

Zaknafein when Drizzt had stepped up the tempo of the combat. She had been forced to allow more of Zak's consciousness back into her animation, needing all of Zaknafein's fighting skills to defeat her warrior son.

Now Malice was left with blackness, and with the weight of impending doom hanging precariously over her head. She glanced back at her too-curious daughter, then sank back within her trance, fighting to regain control.

⚔ ⚔ ⚔ ⚔ ⚔

"Drizzt," Zaknafein said, and the word felt so very good indeed to the animation. Zak's swords went into their sheaths, though his hands had to struggle against the demands of Matron Malice every inch of the way.

Drizzt started toward him, wanting nothing more than to hug his father and dearest friend, but Zaknafein put out a hand to keep him back.

"No," the spirit-wraith explained. "I do not know how long I can resist. The body is hers, I fear," Zaknafein replied.

Drizzt did not understand at first. "Then you are—?"

"I am dead," Zaknafein stated bluntly. "At peace, be assured. Malice has repaired my body for her own vile purposes."

"But you defeated her," Drizzt said, daring to hope. "We are together again"

"A temporary stay, and no more." As if to accentuate the point, Zaknafein's hand involuntarily shot to his sword hilt. He grimaced and snarled, and stubbornly fought back, gradually loosening his grip on the weapon. "She is coming back, my son. That one is always coming back!"

"I cannot bear to lose you again," Drizzt said. "When I saw you in the illithid cavern—"

"It was not me that you saw," Zaknafein tried to explain. "It was the zombie of Malice's evil will. I am gone, my son. I have been gone for many years."

"You are here," Drizzt reasoned.

"By Malice's will, not . . . my own." Zaknafein growled, and his face contorted as he struggled to push Malice away for just a moment longer.

Back in control, Zaknafein studied the warrior that his son had become. "You fight well," he remarked. "Better than I had ever imagined. That is good, and it is good that you had the courage to run—" Zaknafein's face contorted again suddenly, stealing the words. This time, both of his hands went to his swords, and this time, both weapons came flashing out.

"No!" Drizzt pleaded as a mist welled in his lavender eyes. "Fight her."

"I . . . cannot," the spirit-wraith replied. "Flee from this place, Drizzt. Flee to the very . . . ends of the world! Malice will never forgive. She . . . will never stop—"

The spirit-wraith leaped forward, and Drizzt had no choice but to draw his weapons. But Zaknafein jerked suddenly before he got within reach of Drizzt.

"For us!" Zak cried in startling clarity, a call that pealed like a trumpet of victory in the green-glowing chamber and echoed across the miles to Matron Malice's heart like the final toll of a drum signaling the onset of doom. Zaknafein had wrested control again, for just a fleeting instant—one that allowed the charging spirit-wraith to veer off the walkway.

# 25
# Consequences

Matron Malice could not even scream her denial. A thousand explosions pounded her brain when Zaknafein went into the acid lake, a thousand realizations of impending and unavoidable disaster. She leaped from her stone throne, her slender hands twisting and clenching in the air as though she were trying to find something tangible to grasp, something that wasn't there.

Her breath rasped in labored gasps and wordless snarls issued from her gulping mouth. After a moment in which she could not calm herself, Malice heard one sound more clearly than the din of her own contortions. Behind her came the slight hiss of the small, wicked snake heads of a high priestess's whip.

Malice spun about, and there stood Briza, her face grimly and determinedly set and her whip's six living snake heads waving in the air.

"I had hoped that my time of ascension would be many years away," the eldest daughter said calmly. "But you are weak, Malice, too weak to hold House Do'Urden together in the trials that will follow our—your—failure."

Malice wanted to laugh in the face of her daughter's foolishness; snake-headed whips were personal gifts from the Spider Queen and could not be used against matron mothers. For some reason, though, Malice could not find the courage or conviction to refute her daughter at that moment. She watched, mesmerized, as Briza's arm slowly reared back and then shot forward.

The six snake heads uncoiled toward Malice. It was impossible! It went against all tenets of Lolth's doctrine! The fanged heads came on eagerly and dived into Malice's flesh with all the Spider Queen's fury behind them. Searing agony coursed through Malice's body, jolting and racking her and leaving an icy numbness in its wake.

Malice teetered on the brink of consciousness, trying to hold firmly against her daughter, trying to show Briza the futility and stupidity of continuing the attack.

The snake-whip snapped again and the floor rushed up to swallow Malice. Briza muttered something, Malice heard, some curse or chant to the Spider Queen.

Then came a third crack, and Malice knew nothing more. She was dead before the fifth strike, but Briza pounded on for many minutes, venting her fury to let the Spider Queen be assured that House Do'Urden truly had forsaken its failing matron mother.

By the time Dinin, unexpectedly and unannounced, burst into the room, Briza had settled comfortably into the stone throne. The elderboy glanced over at his mother's battered body, then back to Briza, his head shaking in disbelief, and a wide, knowing grin splayed across his face.

"What have you done, sis—Matron Briza?" Dinin asked, catching his slip of the tongue before Briza could react to it.

"Zin-carla has failed," Briza growled as she glared at him. "Lolth would no longer accept Malice."

Dinin's laughter, which seemed founded in sarcasm, cut to the marrow of Briza's bones. Her eyes narrowed further and she let Dinin see her hand clearly as it moved down to the hilt of her whip.

"You have chosen the perfect moment for ascension," the elderboy explained calmly, apparently not at all worried that Briza would punish him. "We are under attack."

"Fey-Branche?" Briza cried, springing excitedly from her seat. Five minutes in the throne as matron mother, and already Briza faced her first test. She would prove herself to the Spider Queen and redeem House Do'Urden from much of the damage that Malice's failures had caused.

"No, sister," Dinin said quickly, without pretense. "Not House Fey-Branche."

Her brother's cool response put Briza back in the throne and twisted her grin of excitement into a grimace of pure dread.

"Baenre." Dinin, too, no longer smiled.

⚔ ⚔ ⚔ ⚔ ⚔

Vierna and Maya looked out from House Do'Urden's balcony to the approaching forces beyond the adamantite gate. The sisters did not know their enemy, as Dinin had, but they understood from the sheer size of the force that some great house was involved. Still, House Do'Urden boasted two hundred fifty soldiers, many trained by Zaknafein himself. With two hundred more well-trained and well-armed troops on loan from Matron Baenre, both Vierna and Maya figured that their chances were not so bad. They quickly outlined defense strategies, and Maya swung one leg over the balcony railing, meaning to descend to the courtyard and relay the plans to her captains.

Of course, when she and Vierna suddenly realized that they had two hundred enemies already within their gates—enemies they had accepted on loan from Matron Baenre—their plans meant little.

Maya still straddled the railing when the first Baenre soldiers came up on the balcony. Vierna drew her whip and cried for Maya to do the same. But Maya was not moving, and Vierna, on closer inspection, noticed several tiny darts protruding from her sister's body.

Vierna's own snake-headed whip turned on her then, its fangs slicing across her delicate face. Vierna understood at once that House Do'Urden's downfall had been decreed by Lolth herself. "Zin-carla," Vierna mumbled, realizing the source of the disaster. Blood blurred her vision and a wave of dizziness overtook her as darkness closed in all about her.

⚔ ⚔ ⚔ ⚔ ⚔

"This cannot be!" Briza cried. "House Baenre attacks? Lolth has not given me—"

"We had our chance!" Dinin yelled at her. "Zaknafein was our chance—" Dinin looked to his mother's torn body—"and the wraith has failed, I would assume."

Briza growled and lashed out with her whip. Dinin expected the strike, though—he knew Briza so very well—and he darted beyond the weapon's range. Briza took a step toward him.

"Does your anger require more enemies?" Dinin asked, swords in hand. "Go out to the balcony, dear sister, where you will find a thousand awaiting you!"

Briza cried out in frustration but turned away from Dinin and rushed from the room, hoping to salvage something out of this terrible predicament.

Dinin did not follow. He stooped over Matron Malice and looked one final time into the eyes of the tyrant who had ruled his entire life. Malice had been a powerful figure, confident and wicked, but how fragile her rule had proved, broken by the antics of a renegade child.

Dinin heard a commotion out in the corridor, then the anteroom door swung open again. The elderboy did not have to look to know that enemies were in the room. He continued to stare at his dead mother, knowing that he soon would share the same fate.

The expected blow did not fall, however, and several agonizing moments later, Dinin dared to glance back over his shoulder.

Jarlaxle sat comfortably on the stone throne.

"You are not surprised?" the mercenary asked, noting that Dinin's expression did not change.

"Bregan D'aerthe was among the Baenre troops, perhaps all of the Baenre troops," Dinin said casually. He covertly glanced around the room at the dozen or so soldiers who had followed Jarlaxle in. If only he could get to the mercenary leader before they killed him! Dinin thought. Watching the death of the treacherous Jarlaxle might bring some measure of satisfaction to this whole disaster.

"Observant," Jarlaxle said to him. "I hold to my suspicions that you knew all along that your house was doomed."

"If Zin-carla failed," Dinin replied.

"And you knew it would?" the mercenary asked, almost rhetorically.

Dinin nodded. "Ten years ago," he began, wondering why he was telling all this to Jarlaxle, "I watched as Zaknafein was sacrificed to the Spider Queen. Rarely has any house in all of Menzoberranzan seen a greater waste."

"The weapon master of House Do'Urden had a mighty reputation," the mercenary put in.

"Well earned, do not doubt," replied Dinin. "Then Drizzt, my brother—"

"Another mighty warrior."

Again Dinin nodded. "Drizzt deserted us, with war at our gates. Matron Malice's miscalculation could not be ignored. I knew then that House Do'Urden was doomed."

"Your house defeated House Hun'ett, no small feat," reasoned Jarlaxle.

"Only with the help of Bregan D'aerthe," Dinin corrected. "For most of my life, I have watched House Do'Urden, under Matron Malice's steady guidance, ascend through the city hierarchy. Every year, our power and influence grew. For the last decade, though, I have seen us spiral down. I have watched the foundations of House Do'Urden crumble. The structure had to follow the descent."

"As wise as you are skilled with the blade," the mercenary remarked. "I have said that before of Dinin Do'Urden, and it seems that I am proved correct once again."

"If I have pleased you, I ask one favor," Dinin said, rising to his feet. "Grant it if you will."

"Kill you quickly and without pain?" Jarlaxle asked through a widening smile.

Dinin nodded for the third time.

"No," Jarlaxle said simply.

Not understanding, Dinin brought his sword flashing up and ready.

"I'll not kill you at all," Jarlaxle explained.

Dinin kept his sword up high and studied the mercenary's face, looking for some hint as to his intent. "I am a noble of the house," Dinin said. "A witness to the attack. No house elimination is complete if nobles remain alive."

"A witness?" Jarlaxle laughed. "Against House Baenre? To what gain?"

Dinin's sword dropped low.

"Then what is my fate?" he asked. "Will Matron Baenre take me in?" Dinin's tone showed that he was not excited about that possibility.

"Matron Baenre has little use for males," Jarlaxle replied. "If any of your sisters survive—and I believe the one named Vierna has—they may find themselves in Matron Baenre's chapel. But the withered old mother of House Baenre would never see the value of a male such as Dinin, I fear."

"Then what?" Dinin demanded.

"I know your value," Jarlaxle stated casually. He led Dinin's gaze around to the concurring grins of his troops.

"Bregan D'aerthe?" Dinin balked. "Me, a noble, to become a rogue?"

Quicker than Dinin's eye could follow, Jarlaxle whipped a dagger into the body at his feet. The blade buried itself up to the hilt in Malice's back.

"A rogue or a corpse," Jarlaxle casually explained.

It was not so difficult a choice.

⚔ ⚔ ⚔ ⚔ ⚔

A few days later, Jarlaxle and Dinin looked back on the ruined adamantite gate of House Do'Urden. Once it had stood so proud and strong, with its intricate carvings of spiders and the two formidable stalagmite pillars that served as guard towers.

"How fast it changed," Dinin remarked. "I see all my former life before me, yet it is all gone."

"Forget what has gone before," Jarlaxle suggested. The mercenary's sly wink told Dinin that he had something specific in mind as he completed the thought. "Except that which may aid in your future."

Dinin did a quick visual inspection of himself and the ruins. "My battle gear?" he asked, fishing for Jarlaxle's intent. "My training."

"Your brother."

"Drizzt?" Again the cursed name reared up to bring anguish to Dinin!

"It would seem that there is still the matter of Drizzt Do'Urden to be reconciled," Jarlaxle explained. "He's a high prize in the eyes of the Spider Queen."

"Drizzt?" Dinin asked again, hardy believing Jarlaxle's words.

"Why are you so surprised?" Jarlaxle asked. "Your brother is still alive, else why was Matron Malice brought down?"

"What house could be interested in him?" Dinin asked bluntly. "Another mission for Matron Baenre?"

Jarlaxle's laugh belittled him. "Bregan D'aerthe may act without the guidance—or the purse—of a recognized house," he replied.

"You plan to go after my brother?"

"It may be the perfect opportunity for Dinin to show his value to my little family," said Jarlaxle to no one in particular. "Who better to catch the renegade that brought down House Do'Urden? Your brother's value increased many times over with the failure of Zin-carla."

"I have seen what Drizzt has become," said Dinin. "The cost will be great."

"My resources are limitless," Jarlaxle answered smugly, "and no cost is too high if the gain is higher." The eccentric mercenary went silent for a short while, allowing Dinin's gaze to linger over the ruins of his once proud house.

"No," Dinin said suddenly.

Jarlaxle turned a wary eye on him.

"I'll not go after Drizzt," Dinin explained.

"You serve Jarlaxle, the master of Bregan D'aerthe," the mercenary calmly reminded him.

"As I once served Malice, the matron of House Do'Urden," Dinin replied with equal calm. "I would not venture out again after Drizzt for my mother—" He looked at Jarlaxle squarely, unafraid of the consequences—"and I shall not do it again for you."

Jarlaxle spent a long moment studying his companion. Normally the mercenary leader would not tolerate such brazen insubordination, but Dinin was sincere and adamant, beyond doubt. Jarlaxle had accepted Dinin into Bregan D'aerthe because he valued the elderboy's experience and skill; he could not now readily dismiss Dinin's judgment.

"I could have you put to a slow death," Jarlaxle replied, more to see Dinin's reaction than to make any promises. He had no intention of destroying one as valuable as Dinin.

"No worse than the death and disgrace I would find at Drizzt's hands," Dinin answered calmly.

Another long moment passed as Jarlaxle considered the implications of Dinin's words. Perhaps Bregan D'aerthe should rethink its plans for hunting the renegade; perhaps the price would prove too high.

"Come, my soldier," Jarlaxle said at length. "Let us return to our home, to the streets, where we might learn what adventures our futures hold."

# 26
# Lights in the Ceiling

Belwar ran along the walkways to get to his friend. Drizzt did not watch the svirfneblin's approach. He kneeled on the narrow bridge, looking down to the bubbling spot in the green lake where Zaknafein had fallen. The acid sputtered and rolled, the scorched hilt of a sword came up into view, then disappeared under the opaque veil of green.

"He was there all along," Drizzt whispered to Belwar. "My father!"

"A mighty chance you took, dark elf," the burrow-warden replied. "*Magga cammara*! When you put your blades away, I thought he would surely strike you down."

"He was there all along," Drizzt said again. He looked up at his svirfneblin friend. "You showed me that."

Belwar screwed up his face in confusion.

"The spirit cannot be separated from the body," Drizzt tried to explain. "Not in life." He looked back to the ripples in the acid lake. "And not in undeath. In my years alone in the wilds, I had lost myself, so I believed. But you showed me the truth. The heart of Drizzt was never gone from this body, and so I knew it to be true with Zaknafein."

"Other forces were involved this time," remarked Belwar. "I would not have been so certain."

"You did not know Zaknafein," Drizzt retorted. He rose to his feet, the moisture rimming his lavender eyes diminished by the sincere smile that widened across his face. "I did. Spirit, not muscles, guides a warrior's blades, and only he who was truly Zaknafein could move with such grace. The moment of crisis gave Zaknafein the strength to resist my mother's will."

"And you gave him the moment of crisis," reasoned Belwar. "Defeat Matron Malice or kill his own son." Belwar shook his bald head and crinkled up his nose. "*Magga cammara*, but you are brave, dark elf." He shot Drizzt a wink. "Or stupid."

"Neither," replied Drizzt. "I only trusted in Zaknafein." He looked back to the acid lake and said no more.

Belwar fell silent and waited patiently while Drizzt finished his private eulogy. When Drizzt finally looked away from the lake, Belwar motioned for the drow to follow and started off along the walkway. "Come," the burrow-warden said over his shoulder. "Witness the truth of our slain friend."

Drizzt thought the pech a beautiful thing, a beauty inspired by the peaceful smile that at last had found its way onto his tormented friend's face. He and Belwar said a few words, mumbled a few hopes to whatever gods might be listening, and gave Clacker to the acid lake, thinking it a preferable fate to the bellies of the carrion eaters that roamed the Underdark corridors.

Drizzt and Belwar set off again alone, as they had been when they first departed the svirfneblin city, and arrived in Blingdenstone a few days later.

The guards at the city's mammoth gates, though obviously thrilled, seemed confused at their return. They allowed the two companions entrance on the burrow-warden's promise that he would go straight off and inform King Schnicktick.

"This time, he will let you stay, dark elf," Belwar said to Drizzt. "You beat the monster." He left Drizzt at his house, vowing that he would return soon with welcome news.

Drizzt wasn't so sure of any of it. Zaknafein's final warning that Matron Malice would never give up her hunt remained clearly in his thoughts, and he could not deny the truth. Much had happened in the tendays that he and Belwar had been out of Blingdenstone, but none of it, as far as Drizzt knew, diminished the very real threat to the svirfneblin city. Drizzt had only agreed to follow the Belwar back to Blingdenstone because it seemed a proper first step to the plan he had decided upon.

"How long shall we battle, Matron Malice?" Drizzt asked the blank stone when the burrow-warden had gone. He needed to hear his reasoning spoken aloud, to convince himself beyond doubt that his decision had been a wise one. "Neither gains in the conflict, but that is the way of the drow, is it not?" Drizzt fell back onto one of the stools beside the little table and considered the truth of his words.

"You will hunt me, to your ruin or to mine, blinded by the hatred that rules your life. There can be no forgiveness in Menzoberranzan. That would go against the edict of your foul Spider Queen.

"And this is the Underdark, your world of shadows and gloom, but it is not all the world, Matron Malice, and I shall see how long your evil arms can reach!"

Drizzt sat silent for many minutes, remembering his first lessons at the drow Academy. He tried to find some clue that would lead him to believe that the stories of the surface world were no more than lies. The masters' deceptions at the drow Academy had been perfected over centuries and were infallibly complete. Drizzt soon came to realize that he simply would have to trust his feelings.

When Belwar returned, grim-faced, a few hours later, Drizzt's resolve was firm.

"Stubborn, orc-brained . . ." the burrow-warden gnashed through his teeth as he crossed through the stone door.

Drizzt stopped him with a heartfelt laugh.

"They will not hear of your staying!" Belwar yelled at him, trying to steal his mirth.

"Did you truly expect otherwise?" Drizzt asked him. "My fight is not over, dear Belwar. Do you believe that my family could be so easily defeated?"

"We will go back out," Belwar growled, moving over to take the stool near Drizzt. "My generous—" the word dripped of sarcasm—"king agreed that you could remain in the city for a tenday. A single tenday!"

"When I leave, I leave alone," Drizzt interrupted. He pulled the onyx figurine out of his pouch and reconsidered his words. "Almost alone."

"We had this argument before, dark elf," Belwar reminded him.

"That was different."

"Was it?" retorted the burrow-warden. "Will you survive any better alone in the wilds of the Underdark now than you did before? Have you forgotten the burdens of loneliness?"

"I'll not be in the Underdark," Drizzt replied.

"Back to your homeland you mean to go?" Belwar cried, leaping to his feet and sending his stool skidding across the stone.

"No, never!" Drizzt laughed. "Never will I return to Menzoberranzan, unless it is at the end of Matron Malice's chains."

The burrow-warden retrieved his seat and eased back into it, curious.

"Neither will I remain in the Underdark," Drizzt explained. "This is Malice's world, more fitting to the dark heart of a true drow."

Belwar began to understand, but he couldn't believe what he was hearing. "What are you saying?" he demanded. "Where do you mean to go?"

"The surface," Drizzt replied evenly. Belwar leaped up again, sending his stone stool bouncing even farther across the floor.

"I was up there once," Drizzt continued, undaunted by the reaction. He calmed the svirfneblin with a determined gaze. "I partook of a drow massacre. Only the actions of my companions bring pain to my memories of that journey. The scents of the wide world and the cool feel of the wind bring no dread to my heart."

"The surface," Belwar muttered, his head lowered and his voice almost a groan. "*Magga cammara*. Never did I plan to travel there—it is not the place of a svirfneblin." Belwar pounded the table suddenly and looked up, a determined smile on his face. "But if Drizzt will go, then Belwar will go by his side!"

"Drizzt will go alone," the drow replied. "As you just said, the surface is not the place of a svirfneblin."

"Nor a drow," the deep gnome added pointedly.

"I do not fit the usual expectations of drow," Drizzt retorted. "My heart is not their heart, and their home is not mine. How far must I walk through the endless tunnels to be free of my family's hatred? And if, in fleeing Menzoberranzan, I chance upon another of the great dark elf cities, Ched Nasad or some similar place, will those drow, too, take up the hunt to fulfill the Spider Queen's desires that I be slain? No, Belwar, I will find no peace in the close ceilings of this world. You, I fear, would never be content removed from the stone of the Underdark. Your place is here, a place of deserved honor among your people."

Belwar sat quietly for a long time, digesting all that Drizzt had said. He would follow Drizzt willingly if Drizzt desired it so, but he truly did not wish to leave the Underdark. Belwar could raise no argument against Drizzt's desires to go. A dark elf would find many trials up on the surface, Belwar knew, but would they outweigh the pains Drizzt would ever experience in the Underdark?

Belwar reached into a deep pocket and took out the light-giving brooch. "Take this, dark elf," he said softly, flipping it to Drizzt, "and do not forget me."

"Never for a single day in all the centuries of my future," Drizzt promised. "Never once."

⚔ ⚔ ⚔ ⚔ ⚔

The tenday passed all too quickly for Belwar, who was reluctant to see his friend go. The burrow-warden knew that he would never look upon Drizzt again, but he knew also that Drizzt's decision was a sound one. As a friend, Belwar took it upon himself to see that Drizzt had the best chance of success. He took the drow to the finest provisioners in all of Blingdenstone and paid for the supplies out of his own pocket.

Belwar then procured an even greater gift for Drizzt. Deep gnomes had traveled to the surface on occasion, and King Schnicktick possessed several copies of rough maps leading out of the Underdark tunnels.

"The journey will take you many tendays," Belwar said to Drizzt when he handed him the rolled parchment, "but I fear that never would you find your way at all without this."

Drizzt's hands trembled as he unrolled the map. It was true, he now dared to believe. He was indeed going to the surface. He wanted to tell Belwar at that moment to come along; how could he say good-bye to so dear a friend?

But principles had carried Drizzt this far in his travels, and principles demanded that he not be selfish now.

He walked out of Blingdenstone the next day, promising Belwar that if he ever came this way again, he would return to visit. Both of them knew he would never return.

⚔ ⚔ ⚔ ⚔ ⚔

Miles and days passed uneventfully. Sometimes Drizzt held the magical brooch Belwar had given to him high; sometimes he walked in the quiet darkness. Whether coincidence or kind fate, he met no monsters along the course laid out on the rough map. Few things had changed in the Underdark, and though the parchment was old, even ancient, the trail was easily followed.

Shortly after breaking camp on his thirty-third day out of Blingdenstone, Drizzt felt a lightening of the air, a sensation of that cold and vast wind he so vividly remembered.

He pulled the onyx figurine from his pouch and summoned Guenhwyvar to his side. Together they walked on anxiously, expecting the ceiling to disappear around every bend.

They came into a small cave, and the darkness beyond the distant archway was not nearly as gloomy as the darkness behind them. Drizzt held his breath and led Guenhwyvar out.

Stars twinkled through the broken clouds of the night sky, the moon's silvery light splayed out in a duller glow behind one large cloud, and the wind howled a mountain song. Drizzt was high up in the Realms, perched on the side of a tall mountain in the midst of a mighty range.

He minded not at all the bite of the breeze, but stood very still for a long time and watched the meandering clouds pass him on their slow aerial trek to the moon.

Guenhwyvar stood beside him, unjudging, and Drizzt knew the panther always would.

SOJOURN
THE LEGEND OF DRIZZT BOOK III

# PRELUDE

The dark elf sat on the barren mountainside, watching anxiously as the line of red grew above the eastern horizon. This would be perhaps his hundredth dawn, and he knew well the sting the searing light would bring to his lavender eyes—eyes that had known only the darkness of the Underdark for more than four decades.

The drow did not turn away, though, when the upper rim of the flaming sun crested the horizon. He accepted the light as his purgatory, a pain necessary if he was to follow his chosen path, to become a creature of the surface world.

Gray smoke wafted up before the drow's dark-skinned face. He knew what it meant without even looking down. His *piwafwi*, the magical drow-made cloak that had so many times in the Underdark shielded him from probing enemy eyes, had finally succumbed to the daylight. The magic in the cloak had begun fading tendays before, and the fabric itself was simply melting away. Wide holes appeared as patches of the garment dissolved, and the drow pulled his arms in tightly to salvage as much as he could.

It wouldn't make any difference, he knew; the cloak was doomed to waste away in this world so different from where it had been created. The drow clung to it desperately, somehow viewing it as an analogy to his own fate.

The sun climbed higher and tears rolled out of the drow's squinting lavender eyes. He could not see the smoke anymore, could see nothing beyond the blinding glare of that terrible ball of fire. Still he sat and watched, right through the dawn.

To survive, he had to adapt.

He pushed his toe painfully down against a jag in the stone and focused his attention away from his eyes, from the dizziness that threatened to overcome him. He thought of how thin his finely woven boots had become and knew that they, too, would soon dissipate into nothingness.

Then his scimitars, perhaps? Would those magnificent drow weapons, which had sustained him through so many trials, be no more? What fate awaited Guenhwyvar, his magical panther companion? Unconsciously the drow dropped a hand into his pouch to feel the marvelous figurine, so perfect in every detail, which he used to summon the cat. Its solidity reassured him in that moment of doubt, but if it, too, had been crafted by the dark elves, imbued with the magic so particular to their domain, would Guenhwyvar soon be lost?

"What a pitiful creature I will become," the drow lamented in his native tongue. He wondered, not for the first time and certainly not for the last, about the wisdom of his decision to leave the Underdark, to forsake the world of his evil people.

His head pounded; sweat rolled into his eyes, heightening the sting. The sun continued its ascent and the drow could not endure. He rose and turned toward the small cave he had taken as his home, and he again put a hand absently on the panther figurine.

His *piwafwi* hung in tatters about him, serving as

meager protection from the mountain winds' chill bite. There was no wind in the Underdark except for slight currents rising off pools of magma, and no chill except for the icy touch of an undead monster. This surface world, which the drow had known for several months, showed him many differences, many variables—too many, he often believed.

Drizzt Do'Urden would not surrender. The Underdark was the world of his kin, of his family, and in that darkness he would find no rest. Following the demands of his principles, he had struck out against Lolth, the Spider Queen, the evil deity his people revered above life itself. The dark elves, Drizzt's family, would not forgive his blasphemy, and the Underdark had no holes deep enough to escape their long reach.

Even if Drizzt believed that the sun would burn him away, as it burned away his boots and his precious *piwafwi*, even if he became no more than insubstantial, gray smoke blowing away in the chill mountain breeze, he would retain his principles and dignity, those elements that made his life worthwhile.

Drizzt pulled off his cloak's remains and tossed them down a deep chasm. The chilly wind nipped against his sweat-beaded brow, but the drow walked straight and proud, his jaw firm and his lavender eyes wide open.

This was the fate he preferred.

⚔ ⚔ ⚔ ⚔ ⚔

Along the side of a different mountain, not so far away, another creature watched the rising sun. Ulgulu, too, had left his birthplace, the filthy, smoking rifts that marked the plane of Gehenna, but this monster had not come of his own accord. It was Ulgulu's fate, his penance, to grow in this world until he attained sufficient strength to return to his home.

Ulgulu's lot was murder, feeding on the life force of the weak mortals around him. He was close now to attaining his maturity: huge and strong and terrible.

Every kill made him stronger.

# Part One

## Sunrise

It burned at my eyes and pained every part of my body. It destroyed my piwafwi and boots, stole the magic from my armor, and weakened my trusted scimitars. Still, every day, without fail, I was there, sitting upon my perch, my judgment seat, to await the arrival of the sunrise.

It came to me each day in a paradoxical way. The sting could not be denied, but neither could I deny the beauty of the spectacle. The colors just before the sun's appearance grabbed my soul in a way that no patterns of heat emanations in the Underdark ever could. At first, I thought my entrancement a result of the strangeness of the scene, but even now, many years later, I feel my heart leap at the subtle brightening that heralds the dawn.

I know now that my time in the sun—my daily penance—was more than mere desire to adapt to the ways of the surface world. The sun became the symbol of the difference between the Underdark and my new home. The society that I had run away from, a world of secret dealings and treacherous conspiracies, could not exist in the open spaces under the light of day.

This sun, for all the anguish it brought me physically, came to represent my denial of that other, darker world. Those rays of revealing light reinforced my principles as surely as they weakened the drow-made magical items.

In the sunlight the piwafwi, the shielding cloak that defeated probing eyes, the garment of thieves and assassins, became no more than a worthless rag of tattered cloth.

–Drizzt Do'Urden

# I
# Poignant Lessons

Drizzt crept past the shielding shrubs and over the flat and bare stone that led to the cave now serving as his home. He knew that something had crossed this way recently—very recently. There were no tracks to be seen, but the scent was strong.

Guenhwyvar circled on the rocks up above the hillside cave. Sight of the panther gave the drow a measure of comfort. Drizzt had come to trust Guenhwyvar implicitly and knew that the cat would flush out any enemies hiding in ambush. Drizzt disappeared into the dark opening and smiled as he heard the panther come down behind, watching over him.

Drizzt paused behind a stone just inside the entrance, letting his eyes adjust to the gloom. The sun was still bright, though it was fast dipping into the western sky, but the cave was much darker—dark enough for Drizzt to let his vision slip into the infrared spectrum. As soon as the adjustment was completed, Drizzt located the intruder. The clear glow of a heat source, a living creature, emanated from behind another rock deeper in the one-chambered cave. Drizzt relaxed considerably. Guenhwyvar was only a few steps away now, and considering the size of the rock, the intruder could not be a large beast.

Still, Drizzt had been raised in the Underdark, where every living creature, regardless of its size, was respected and considered dangerous.

He signaled for Guenhwyvar to remain in position near the exit and crept around to get a better angle on the intruder.

Drizzt had never seen such an animal before. It appeared almost cat-like, but its head was much smaller and more sharply pointed. The whole of it could not have weighed more than a few pounds. This fact, and the creature's bushy tail and thick fur, indicated that it was more a forager than a predator. It rummaged now through a pack of food, apparently oblivious to the drow's presence.

"Take ease, Guenhwyvar," Drizzt called softly, slipping his scimitars into their sheaths. He took a step toward the intruder for a better look, though he kept a cautious distance so as not to startle it, thinking that he might have found another companion. If he could only gain the animal's trust . . .

The small animal turned abruptly at Drizzt's call, its short front legs quickly backing it against the wall.

"Take ease," Drizzt said quietly, this time to the intruder. "I'll not harm you." Drizzt took another step in and the creature hissed and spun about, its small hind feet stamping down on the stone floor.

Drizzt nearly laughed aloud, thinking that the creature meant to push itself straight through the cave's back wall. Guenhwyvar bounded over then, and the panther's immediate distress stole the mirth from the drow's face.

The animal's tail came up high; Drizzt noticed in the faint light that the beast had distinctive stripes running down its back. Guenhwyvar whimpered and turned to flee, but it was too late. . . .

About an hour later Drizzt and Guenhwyvar walked along the lower trails of the mountain in search of a new home. They had salvaged what they could, though that wasn't very much. Guenhwyvar kept a good distance to the side of Drizzt. Proximity made the stink only worse.

Drizzt took it all in stride, though the stench of his own body made the lesson a bit more poignant than he would have liked. He didn't know the little animal's name, of course, but he had marked its appearance keenly. He would know better the next time he encountered a skunk.

"What of my other companions in this strange world?" Drizzt whispered to himself. It was not the first time the drow had voiced such concerns. He knew very little of the surface and even less of the creatures that lived here. His months had been spent in and about the cave, with only occasional forays down to the lower, more populated regions. There, in his foraging, he had seen some animals, usually at a distance, and had even observed some humans. He had not yet found the courage to come out of hiding, though, to greet his neighbors, fearing potential rejection and knowing that he had nowhere left to run.

The sound of rushing water led the reeking drow and panther to a fast-running brook. Drizzt immediately found some protective shade and began stripping away his armor and clothing, while Guenhwyvar moved downstream to do some fishing. The sound of the panther fumbling around in the water brought a smile to the drow's severe features. They would eat well this night.

Drizzt gingerly flipped the clasp of his belt and laid his crafted weapons beside his mesh chain mail. Truly, he felt vulnerable without the armor and weapons—he never would have put them so far from his reach in the Underdark—but many months had passed since Drizzt had found any need for them. He looked to his scimitars and was flooded by the bittersweet memories of the last time he had put them to use.

He had battled Zaknafein then, his father and mentor and dearest friend. Only Drizzt had survived the encounter. The legendary weapon master was gone now, but the triumph in that fight belonged as much to Zak as it did to Drizzt, for it was not really Zaknafein who had come after Drizzt on the bridges of an acid-filled cavern. Rather, it was Zaknafein's wraith, under the control of Drizzt's evil mother, Matron Malice. She had sought revenge upon her son for his denouncement of Lolth and of the chaotic drow society in general. Drizzt had spent more than thirty years in Menzoberranzan but had never accepted the malicious and cruel ways that were the norm in the drow city. He had been a constant embarrassment to House Do'Urden despite his considerable skill with weapons. When he ran from the city to live a life of exile in the wilds of the Underdark, he had placed his high priestess mother out of Lolth's favor.

Thus, Matron Malice Do'Urden had raised the spirit of Zaknafein, the weapon master she had sacrificed to Lolth, and sent the undead thing after her son. Malice had miscalculated, though, for there remained enough of Zak's soul within the body to deny the attack on Drizzt. In the instant that Zak managed to wrest control from Malice, he had cried out in triumph and leaped into the lake of acid.

"My father," Drizzt whispered, drawing strength from the simple words. He had succeeded where Zaknafein had failed; he had forsaken the evil ways of the drow where Zak had been trapped for centuries, acting as a pawn in Matron Malice's power games. From Zaknafein's failure and ultimate demise, young Drizzt had found strength; from Zak's victory in the acid cavern, Drizzt had found determination. Drizzt had ignored the web of lies his former teachers at the Academy in Menzoberranzan had tried to spin, and he had come to the surface to begin a new life.

Drizzt shuddered as he stepped into the icy stream. In the Underdark he had known fairly constant temperatures and unvarying darkness. Here, though, the world surprised him at every turn. Already he had noticed that the periods of daylight and darkness were not constant; the sun set earlier every day and the temperature—changing from hour to hour, it seemed—had steadily dipped during the last few tendays. Even within those periods of light and dark loomed inconsistencies. Some nights were visited by a silver-glowing orb and some days held a pall of gray instead of a dome of shining blue.

In spite of it all, Drizzt most often felt comfortable with his decision to come to this unknown world. Looking at his weapons and armor now, lying in the shadows a dozen feet from where he bathed, Drizzt had to admit that the surface, for all of its strangeness, offered more peace than anywhere in the Underdark ever could.

Drizzt was in the wilds now, despite his calm. He had spent four months on the surface and was still alone, except when he was able to summon his magical feline companion. Now, stripped bare except for his ragged pants, with his eyes stinging from the skunk spray, his sense of smell lost within the cloud of his own pungent aroma, and his keen sense of hearing dulled by the din of rushing water, the drow was indeed vulnerable.

"What a mess I must appear," Drizzt mused, roughly running his slender fingers through the mat of his thick, white hair. When he glanced back to his equipment, though, the thought was washed quickly from Drizzt's mind. Five hulking forms straddled his belongings and undoubtedly cared little for the dark elf's ragged appearance.

Drizzt considered the grayish skin and dark muzzles of the dog-faced, seven-foot-tall humanoids, but more particularly, he watched the spears and swords that they now leveled his way. He knew this type of monster, for he had seen similar creatures serving as slaves back in Menzoberranzan. In this situation, however, the gnolls appeared much different, more ominous, than Drizzt remembered them.

He briefly considered a rush to his scimitars but dismissed the notion, knowing that a spear would skewer him before he ever got close. The largest of the gnoll band an eight-foot giant with striking red hair, looked at Drizzt for a long moment, eyed the drow's equipment, then looked back to him.

"What are you thinking?" Drizzt muttered under his breath. Drizzt really knew very little about gnolls. At Menzoberranzan's Academy he had been taught that gnolls were of a goblinoid race, evil, unpredictable, and quite dangerous. He had been told that of the surface elves and humans as well, though—and he now realized, of nearly every race that was not drow. Drizzt almost laughed aloud despite his predicament. Ironically, the race that most deserved that mantle of evil unpredictability was the drow themselves!

The gnolls made no other moves and uttered no commands. Drizzt understood their hesitancy at the sight of a dark elf, and he knew that he must seize that natural fear if he was to have any chance at all. Calling upon the innate abilities of his magical heritage, Drizzt waved his dark hand and outlined all five gnolls in harmless purple-glowing flames.

One of the beasts dropped immediately to the ground, as Drizzt had hoped, but the others halted at a signal from their more experienced leader's outstretched hand. They looked around nervously, apparently wondering about the wisdom of continuing this meeting. The gnoll chieftain, though, had seen harmless faerie fire before, in a fight with an unfortunate—now deceased—ranger, and knew it for what it was.

Drizzt tensed in anticipation and tried to determine his next move.

The gnoll chieftain glanced around at its companions, as if studying how fully they were limned by the dancing flames. Judging by the completeness of the spell, this was no ordinary drow peasant standing in the stream—or so Drizzt hoped the chieftain was thinking.

Drizzt relaxed a bit as the leader dipped its spear and signaled for the others to do likewise. The gnoll then barked a jumble of words that sounded like gibberish to the drow. Seeing Drizzt's obvious confusion, the gnoll called something in the guttural tongue of goblins.

Drizzt understood the goblin language, but the gnoll's dialect was so very strange that he managed to decipher only a few words, "friend" and "leader" being among them.

Cautiously, Drizzt took a step toward the bank. The gnolls gave ground, opening a path to his belongings. Drizzt took another tentative step, then grew more at ease when he noticed a black feline form crouched in the bushes a short distance away. At his command Guenhwyvar, in one great spring, would come crashing into the gnoll band.

"You and I to walk together?" Drizzt asked the gnoll leader, using the goblin tongue and trying to simulate the creature's dialect.

The gnoll replied in a hurried shout, and the only thing that Drizzt thought he understood was the last word of the question: ". . . ally?"

Drizzt nodded slowly, hoping he understood the creature's full meaning.

"Ally!" the gnoll croaked, and all of its companions smiled and laughed in relief and patted each other on the back. Drizzt reached his equipment then, and immediately strapped on his scimitars. Seeing the gnolls distracted, the drow glanced at Guenhwyvar and nodded to the thick growth along the trail ahead. Swiftly and silently, Guenhwyvar took up a new position. No need to give all of his secrets away, Drizzt figured, not until he truly understood his new companions' intentions.

Drizzt walked along with the gnolls down the mountain's lower, winding passes. The gnolls kept far to the drow's sides, whether out of respect for Drizzt and the reputation of his race or for some other reason, he could not know. More likely, Drizzt suspected, they kept their distance simply because of his odor, which the bath had done little to diminish.

The gnoll leader addressed Drizzt every so often, accentuating its excited words with a sly wink or a sudden rub of its thick, padded hands. Drizzt had no idea of what the gnoll was talking about, but he assumed from the creature's eager lip-smacking that it was leading him to some sort of feast.

Drizzt soon guessed the band's destination, for he had often watched from jutting peaks high in the mountains, the lights of a small human farming community in the valley. Drizzt could only guess at the relationship between the gnolls and the human farmers, but he sensed that it was not a friendly one. When they neared the village, the gnolls dropped into defensive positions, followed lines of shrubs, and kept to the shadows as much as possible. Twilight was fast approaching as the troupe made its way around the village's central area to look down upon a secluded farmhouse off to the west.

The gnoll chieftain whispered to Drizzt, slowly rolling out each word so that the drow might understand. "One family," it croaked. "Three men, two women . . ."

"One young woman," another added eagerly.

The gnoll chieftain gave a snarl. "And three young males," it concluded.

Drizzt thought he now understood the journey's purpose, and the surprised and questioning look on his face prompted the gnoll to confirm it beyond doubt.

"Enemies," the leader declared.

Drizzt, knowing next to nothing of the two races, was in a dilemma. The gnolls were raiders—that much was clear—and they meant to swoop down upon the farmhouse as soon as the last daylight faded away. Drizzt had no intention of joining them in their fight until he had a lot more information concerning the nature of the conflict.

"Enemies?" he asked.

The gnoll leader crinkled its brow in apparent consternation. It spouted a line of gibberish in which Drizzt thought he heard "human . . . weakling . . . slave." All the gnolls sensed the drow's sudden uneasiness, and they began fingering their weapons and glancing to each other nervously.

"Three men," Drizzt said.

The gnoll jabbed its spear savagely toward the ground. "Kill oldest! Catch two!"

"Women?"

The evil smile that spread over the gnoll's face answered the question beyond doubt, and Drizzt was beginning to understand where he stood in the conflict.

"What of the children?" He eyed the gnoll leader squarely and spoke each word distinctly. There could be no misunderstanding. His final question confirmed it all, for while Drizzt could accept the typical savagery concerning mortal enemies, he could never forget the one time he had participated in such a raid. He had saved an elven child on that day, had hidden the girl under her mother's body to keep her from the wrath of his drow companions. Of all the many evils Drizzt had ever witnessed, the murder of children had been the worst.

The gnoll thrust its spear toward the ground, its dog-face contorted in wicked glee.

"I think not," Drizzt said simply, fires springing up in his lavender eyes. Somehow, the gnolls noticed, his scimitars had appeared in his hands.

Again the gnoll's snout crinkled, this time in confusion. It tried to get its spear up in defense, not knowing what this strange drow would do next, but was too late.

Drizzt's rush was too quick. Before the gnoll's spear tip even moved, the drow waded in, scimitars leading. The other four gnolls watched in amazement as Drizzt's blades snapped twice, tearing the throat from their powerful leader. The giant gnoll fell backward silently, grasping futilely at its throat.

A gnoll to the side reacted first, leveling its spear and charging at Drizzt. The agile drow easily deflected the straightforward attack but was careful not to slow the gnoll's momentum. As the huge creature lumbered past, Drizzt rolled around beside it and kicked at its ankles. Off balance, the gnoll stumbled on, plunging its spear deep into the chest of a startled companion.

The gnoll tugged at the weapon, but it was firmly embedded, its barbed head hooked around the other gnoll's backbone. The gnoll had no concern for its dying companion; all it wanted was its weapon. It tugged and twisted and cursed and spat into the agonized expressions crossing its companion's face—until a scimitar bashed in the beast's skull.

Another gnoll, seeing the drow distracted and thinking it wiser to engage the foe from a distance, raised its spear to throw. Its arm went up high, but before the weapon ever started forward, Guenhwyvar crashed in, and the gnoll and panther tumbled away. The gnoll smashed heavy punches into the panther's muscled side, but Guenhwyvar's raking claws were more effective by far. In the split second it took Drizzt to turn from the three dead gnolls at his feet, the fourth of the band lay dead beneath the great panther. The fifth had taken flight.

Guenhwyvar tore free of the dead gnoll's stubborn grasp. The cat's sleek muscles rippled anxiously as it awaited the expected command. Drizzt considered the carnage around him, the blood on his scimitars, and the horrible expressions on the faces of the dead. He wanted to let it end, for he realized that he had stepped into a situation beyond his experience, had crossed the paths of two races that he knew very little about. After a moment of consideration, though, the single notion that stood out in the drow's mind was the gnoll leader's gleeful promise of death to the human children. Too much was at stake.

Drizzt turned to Guenhwyvar, his voice more determined than resigned. "Go get him."

⚔ ⚔ ⚔ ⚔ ⚔

The gnoll scrambled along the trails, its eyes darting back and forth as it imagined dark forms behind every tree or stone.

"Drow!" it rasped over and over, using the word itself as encouragement during its flight. "Drow! Drow!"

Huffing and panting, the gnoll came into a copse of trees stretching between two steep walls of bare stone. It tumbled over a fallen log, slipped, and bruised its ribs on the angled slope of a moss-covered stone. Minor pains would not slow the frightened creature, though, not in the least. The gnoll knew it was being pursued, sensed a presence slipping in and out of the shadows just beyond the edges of its vision.

As it neared the end of the copse, the evening gloom thick about it, the gnoll spotted a set of yellow-glowing eyes peering back at it. The gnoll had seen its companion taken down by the panther and could make a guess as to what now blocked its path.

Gnolls were cowardly monsters, but they could fight with amazing tenacity when cornered. So it was now. Realizing that it had no escape—it certainly couldn't turn back in the direction of the dark elf—the gnoll snarled and heaved its heavy spear.

The gnoll heard a shuffle, a thump, and a squeal of pain as the spear connected. The yellow eyes went away for a moment, then a form scurried off toward a tree. It moved low to the ground, almost catlike, but the gnoll realized at once that his mark had been no panther. When the wounded animal got to the tree, it looked back and the gnoll recognized it clearly.

"Raccoon," the gnoll blurted, and it laughed. "I run from raccoon!" The gnoll shook its head and blew away all of its mirth in a deep breath. The sight of the raccoon had brought a measure of relief, but the gnoll could not forget what had happened back down the path. It had to get back to its lair now, back to report to Ulgulu, its gigantic goblin master, its god-thing, about the drow.

It took a step to retrieve the spear, then stopped suddenly, sensing a movement from behind. Slowly the gnoll turned its head. It could see its own shoulder and the moss-covered rock behind.

The gnoll froze. Nothing moved behind it, not a sound issued from anywhere in the copse, but the beast knew that something was back there. The goblinoid's breath came in short rasps; its fat hands clenched and opened at its sides.

The gnoll spun quickly and roared, but the shout of rage became a cry of terror as six hundred pounds of panther leaped down upon it from a low branch.

The impact laid the gnoll out flat, but it was not a weak creature. Ignoring the burning pains of the panther's cruel claws, the gnoll grasped Guenhwyvar's plunging head, held on desperately to keep the deadly maw from finding a hold on its neck.

For nearly a minute the gnoll struggled, its arms quivering under the pressure of the powerful muscles in the panther's neck. The head came down then and Guenhwyvar found a hold. Great teeth locked onto the gnoll's neck and squeezed away the doomed creature's breath.

The gnoll flailed and thrashed wildly; somehow it managed to roll back over the panther. Guenhwyvar remained viselike, unconcerned. The maw held firm.

In a few minutes, the thrashing stopped.

# 2

# Questions of Conscience

Drizzt let his vision slip into the infrared spectrum, the night vision that could see gradations of heat as clearly as he viewed objects in the light. To his eyes, his scimitars now shone brightly with the heat of fresh blood and the torn gnoll bodies spilled their warmth into the open air.

Drizzt tried to look away, tried to observe the trail where Guenhwyvar had gone in pursuit of the fifth gnoll, but every time, his gaze fell back to the dead gnolls and the blood on his weapons.

"What have I done?" Drizzt wondered aloud. Truly, he did not know. The gnolls had spoken of slaughtering children, a thought that had evoked rage within Drizzt, but what did Drizzt know of the conflict between the gnolls and the humans of the village? Might the humans, even the human children, be monsters? Perhaps they had raided the gnolls' village and killed without mercy. Perhaps the gnolls meant to strike back because they had no choice, because they had to defend themselves.

Drizzt ran from the grizzly scene in search of Guenhwyvar, hoping he could get to the panther before the fifth gnoll was dead. If he could find the gnoll and capture it, he might be able to learn some of the answers that he desperately needed to know.

He moved with swift and graceful strides, making barely a rustle as he slipped through the brush along the trail. He found signs of the gnoll's

passing easily enough, and he saw, to his fear, that Guenhwyvar had also discovered the trail. When he came at last to the narrow copse of trees, he fully expected that his search was at its end. Still, Drizzt's heart sank when he saw the cat, reclined beside the final kill.

Guenhwyvar looked at Drizzt curiously as he approached, the drow's stride obviously agitated.

"What have we done, Guenhwyvar?" Drizzt whispered. The panther tilted its head as though it did not understand.

"Who am I to pass such judgment?" Drizzt went on, talking to himself more than to the cat. He turned from Guenhwyvar and the dead gnoll and moved to a leafy bush, where he could wipe the blood from his blades. "The gnolls did not attack me, but they had me at their mercy when they first found me in the stream. And I repay them by spilling their blood!"

Drizzt spun back on Guenhwyvar with the proclamation, as if he expected, even hoped, that the panther would somehow berate him, somehow condemn him and justify his guilt. Guenhwyvar hadn't moved an inch and did not now, and the panther's saucer eyes, shining greenish yellow in the night, did not bore into Drizzt, did not incriminate him for his actions in any way.

Drizzt started to protest, wanting to wallow in his guilt, but Guenhwyvar's calm acceptance would not be shaken. When they had lived out alone in the wilds of the Underdark, when Drizzt had lost himself to savage urges that relished killing, Guenhwyvar had sometimes disobeyed him, had even returned to the Astral Plane once without being dismissed. Now, though, the panther showed no signs of leaving or of disappointment. Guenhwyvar rose to its feet, shook the dirt and twigs from its sleek, black coat, and walked over to nuzzle against Drizzt.

Gradually Drizzt relaxed. He wiped his scimitars once more, this time on the thick grass, and slipped them back into their sheaths, then he dropped a thankful hand onto Guenhwyvar's huge head.

"Their words marked them as evil," the drow whispered to reassure himself. "Their intentions forced my action." His own words lacked conviction, but at that moment, Drizzt had to believe them. He took a deep breath to steady himself and looked inward to find the strength he knew he would need. Realizing then that Guenhwyvar had been at his side for a long time and needed to return to the Astral Plane to rest, he reached into the small pouch at his side.

Before Drizzt ever got the onyx figurine out of his pouch, though, the panther's paw came up and batted it from his grasp. Drizzt looked at Guenhwyvar curiously, and the cat leaned heavily into him, nearly taking him from his feet.

"My loyal friend," Drizzt said, realizing that the weary panther meant to stay beside him. He pulled his hand from the pouch and dropped to one knee, locking Guenhwyvar in a great hug. The two of them, side by side, then walked from the copse.

Drizzt slept not at all that night, but watched the stars and wondered. Guenhwyvar sensed his anxiety and stayed close throughout the rise and set of the moon, and when Drizzt moved out to greet the next dawn, Guenhwyvar plodded along, drawn and tired, at his side. They found a rocky crest in the foothills and sat back to watch the coming spectacle.

Below them the last lights faded from the windows of the farming village. The eastern sky turned to pink, then crimson, but Drizzt found himself distracted. His gaze lingered on the farmhouses far below; his mind tried to piece together the routines of this unknown community and tried to find in that some justification for the previous day's events.

The humans were farmers, that much Drizzt knew, and diligent workers, too, for many of them were already out tending their fields. While those facts brought promise, however, Drizzt could not begin to make sweeping assumptions as to the human race's overall demeanor.

Drizzt came to a decision then, as the daylight stretched wide, illuminating the wooden structures of the town and the wide fields of grain. "I must learn more, Guenhwyvar," he said softly. "If I—if we—are to remain in this world, we must come to understand the ways of our neighbors."

Drizzt nodded as he considered his own words. It had already been proven, painfully proven, that he could not remain a neutral observer to the goings-on of the surface world. Drizzt was often called to action by his conscience, a force he had no power to deny. Yet with so little knowledge of the races sharing this region, his conscience could easily lead him astray.

It could wreak damage against the innocent, thereby defeating the very principles Drizzt meant to champion.

Drizzt squinted through the morning light, eyeing the distant village for some hint of an answer. "I will go there," he told the panther. "I will go and watch and learn."

Guenhwyvar sat silently through it all. If the panther approved or disapproved, or even understood Drizzt's intent, Drizzt could not tell. This time, though, Guenhwyvar made no move of protest when Drizzt reached for the onyx figurine. A few moments later, the great panther was running off through the planar tunnel to its astral home, and Drizzt moved along the trails leading to the human village and his answers. He stopped only once, at the body of the lone gnoll, to take the creature's cloak. Drizzt winced at his own thievery, but the chill night had reminded him that the loss of his *piwafwi* could prove serious.

To this point, Drizzt's knowledge of humans and their society was severely limited. Deep in the bowels of the Underdark, the dark elves had little communication with, or interest in, those of the surface world. The one time in Menzoberranzan that Drizzt had heard anything of humans at all was during his tenure in the Academy, the six months he had spent in Sorcere, the school of wizards. The drow masters had warned the students against using magic "like a human would," implying a dangerous recklessness generally associated with the shorter-lived race.

"Human wizards," the masters had said, "have no fewer ambitions than drow wizards, but while a drow may take five centuries accomplishing those goals, a human has only a few short decades."

Drizzt had carried the implications of that statement with him for a score of years, particularly over the last few months, when he had looked down upon the human village almost daily. If all humans, not just wizards, were as ambitious as so many of the drow—fanatics who might spend the better part of a millennium accomplishing their goals—would they be consumed by a single-mindedness that bordered on hysteria? Or perhaps, Drizzt hoped, the stories he had heard of humans at the Academy were just more of the typical lies that bound his society in a web of intrigue and paranoia. Perhaps humans set their goals at more reasonable levels and found enjoyment and satisfaction in the small pleasures of the short days of their existence.

Drizzt had met a human only once during his travels through the Underdark. That man, a wizard, had behaved irrationally, unpredictably, and ultimately dangerously. The wizard had transformed Drizzt's friend from a pech, a harmless little humanoid creature, into a horrible monster. When Drizzt and his companions went to set things aright at the wizard's tower, they were greeted by a roaring blast of lightning. In the end, the human was killed and Drizzt's friend, Clacker, had been left to his torment.

Drizzt had been left with a bitter emptiness, an example of a man who seemed to confirm the truth of the drow masters' warnings. So it was with cautious steps that Drizzt now traveled toward the human settlement, his steps weighted by the growing fear that he had erred in killing the gnolls.

Drizzt chose to observe the same secluded farmhouse on the western edge of town that the gnolls had selected for their raid. It was a long and low log structure with a single door and several shuttered windows. An open-sided, roofed porch ran the length of the front. Beside it stood a barn, two stories high, with wide and high doors that would admit a huge wagon. Fences of various makes and sizes dotted the immediate yard, many holding chickens or pigs, one corralling a goat, and others encircling straight rows of leafy plants that Drizzt did not recognize.

The yard was bordered by fields on three sides, but the back of the house was near the mountain slopes' thick brush and boulders. Drizzt dug in under the low branches of a pine tree to the side of the house's rear corner, affording him a view of most of the yard.

The three adult men of the house—three generations, Drizzt guessed by their appearances—worked the fields, too far from the trees for Drizzt to discern many details. Closer to the house, though, four children, a daughter just coming into womanhood and three younger boys, quietly went about their chores, tending to the hens and pigs and pulling weeds from a vegetable garden. They worked separately and with minimum interaction for most of the morning, and Drizzt learned little of their family relationships. When a sturdy woman with the same wheat-colored hair as all five children came out on the porch and rang a giant bell, it seemed as if all the spirit that had been cooped up within the workers burst beyond control.

With hoots and shouts, the three boys sprinted for the house, pausing just long enough to toss rotted vegetables at their older sister. At first, Drizzt thought the bombing a prelude to a more serious conflict, but when the young woman retaliated in kind, all four howled with laughter and he recognized the game for what it was.

A moment later, the youngest of the men in the field, probably an older brother, charged into the yard, shouting and waving an iron hoe. The young woman cried encouragement to this new ally and the three boys broke for the porch. The man was quicker, though, and he scooped up the trailing imp in one strong arm and promptly dropped him into the pig trough.

And all the while, the woman with the bell shook her head helplessly and issued an unending stream of exasperated grumbling. An older woman, gray-haired and stick-thin, came out to stand next to her, waving a wooden spoon ominously. Apparently satisfied, the young man draped one arm over the young woman's shoulders and they followed the first two boys into the house. The remaining youngster pulled himself from the murky water and moved to follow, but the wooden spoon kept him at bay.

Drizzt couldn't understand a word of what they were saying, of course, but he figured that the women would not let the little one into the house until he had dried off. The rambunctious youngster mumbled something at the spoon-wielder's back as she turned to enter the house, but his timing was not so great.

The other two men, one sporting a thick, gray beard and the other clean-shaven, came in from the field and sneaked up behind the boy as he grumbled. Up into the air the boy went again and landed with a *splash!* back in the trough. Congratulating themselves heartily, the men went into the house to the cheers of all the others. The soaking boy merely groaned again and splashed some water into the face of a sow that had come over to investigate.

Drizzt watched it all with growing wonderment. He had seen nothing conclusive, but the family's playful manner and the resigned acceptance of even the loser of the game gave him encouragement. Drizzt sensed a common spirit in this group, with all members working toward a common goal. If this single farm proved a reflection of the whole village, then the place surely resembled Blingdenstone, a communal city of the deep gnomes, far more than it resembled Menzoberranzan.

The afternoon went much the same way as the morning, with a mixture of work and play evident throughout the farm. The family retired early, turning down their lamps soon after sunset, and Drizzt slipped deeper into the thicket of the mountainside to consider his observations.

He still couldn't be certain of anything, but he slept more peacefully that night, untroubled by nagging doubts concerning the dead gnolls.

⚔ ⚔ ⚔ ⚔ ⚔

For three days the drow crouched in the shadows behind the farm, watching the family at work and at play. The closeness of the group became more and more evident, and whenever a true fight did erupt among the children, the nearest adult quickly stepped in and mediated it to a level of reasonableness. Invariably, the combatants were back at play together within a short span.

All doubts had flown from Drizzt. "Ware my blades, rogues," he whispered to the quiet mountains one night. The young drow renegade had decided that if any gnolls or goblins—or creatures of any other race at all—tried to swoop down upon this particular farming family, they first would have to contend with the whirling scimitars of Drizzt Do'Urden.

Drizzt understood the risk he was taking by observing the farm family. If the farmer-folk noticed him—a distinct possibility—they surely would panic. At this point in his life, though, Drizzt was willing to take that chance. A part of him may even have hoped to be discovered.

Early on the morning of the fourth day, before the sun had found its way into the eastern sky, Drizzt set out on his daily patrol, circumventing the hills and woodlands surrounding the lone farmhouse. By the time the drow returned to his perch, the work day on the farm was in full swing. Drizzt sat comfortably on a bed of moss and peered from the shadows into the brightness of the cloudless day.

Less than an hour later, a solitary figure crept from the farmhouse and in Drizzt's direction. It was the youngest of the children, the sandy-haired lad who seemed to spend nearly as much time in the trough as out of it, usually not of his own volition.

Drizzt rolled around the trunk of a nearby tree, uncertain of the lad's intent. He soon realized that the youngster hadn't seen him, for the boy slipped into the thicket, gave a snort over his shoulder, back toward the farmhouse, and headed off into the hilly woodland whistling all the while. Drizzt understood then that the lad was avoiding his chores, and Drizzt almost applauded the boy's carefree attitude. In spite of that, though, Drizzt wasn't convinced of the small child's wisdom in wandering away from home in such dangerous terrain. The boy couldn't have been more than ten years old; he looked thin and delicate, with innocent, blue eyes peering out from under his amber locks.

Drizzt waited a few moments, to let the boy get a lead and to see if anyone would be following, then he took up the trail, letting the whistling guide him.

The boy moved unerringly away from the farmhouse, up into the mountains, and Drizzt moved behind him by a hundred paces or so, determined to keep the boy out of danger.

In the dark tunnels of the Underdark Drizzt could have crept right up behind the boy—or behind a goblin or practically anything else—and patted him on the rump before being discovered. But after only a half-hour or so of this pursuit, the movements and erratic speed changes along the trail, coupled with the fact that the whistling had ceased, told Drizzt that the boy knew he was being followed.

Wondering if the boy had sensed a third party, Drizzt summoned Guenhwyvar from the onyx figurine and sent the panther off on a flanking maneuver. Drizzt started ahead again at a cautious pace.

A moment later, when the child's voice cried out in distress, the drow drew his scimitars and threw out all caution. Drizzt couldn't understand any of the boy's words, but the desperate tone rang clearly enough.

"Guenhwyvar!" the drow called, trying to bring the distant panther back to his side. Drizzt couldn't stop and wait for the cat, though, and he charged on.

The trail wound up a steep climb, came out of the trees suddenly, and ended on the lip of a wide gorge, fully twenty feet across. A single log spanned the crevasse, and hanging from it near the other side was the boy. His eyes widened considerably at the sight of the ebony-skinned elf, scimitars in hand. He stammered a few words that Drizzt could not begin to decipher.

A wave of guilt flooded through Drizzt at the sight of the imperiled child; the boy had only landed in this predicament because of Drizzt's pursuit. The gorge was only about as deep as it was wide, but the fall ended on jagged rocks and brambles. At first, Drizzt hesitated, caught off guard by the sudden meeting and its inevitable implications, then the drow quickly put his own problems out of mind. He snapped his scimitars back into their sheaths and folding his arms across his chest in a drow signal for peace, he put one foot out on the log.

The boy had other ideas. As soon as he recovered from the shock of seeing the strange elf, he swung himself to a ledge on the stone bank opposite Drizzt and pushed the log from its perch. Drizzt quickly backed off the log as it tumbled down into the crevasse. The drow understood then that the boy had never been in real danger but had pretended distress to flush out his pursuer. And Drizzt presumed, if the pursuer had been one of the boy's family, as the boy no doubt had suspected, the peril might have deflected any thoughts of punishment.

Now Drizzt was the one in the predicament. He had been discovered. He tried to think of a way to communicate with the boy, to explain his presence and stave off panic. The boy didn't wait for any explanations, though. Wide-eyed and terror-stricken, he scaled the bank—via a path he obviously knew well—and darted off into the shrubbery.

Drizzt looked around helplessly. "Wait!" he cried in the drow tongue, though he knew the boy would not understand and would not have stopped even if he could.

A black feline form rushed out beside the drow and sprang into the air, easily clearing the crevasse. Guenhwyvar padded down softly on the other side and disappeared into the thicket.

"Guenhwyvar!" Drizzt cried, trying to halt the panther. Drizzt had no idea how Guenhwyvar would react to the child. To Drizzt's knowledge, the panther had only encountered one human before, the wizard that Drizzt's companions had subsequently killed. Drizzt looked around for some way to follow. He could scale down the side of the gorge, cross at the bottom, and climb back up, but that would take too long.

Drizzt ran back a few steps, then charged the gorge and leaped into the air, calling on his innate powers of levitation as he went. Drizzt was truly relieved when he felt his body pull free of the ground's gravity. He hadn't used his levitation spell since he had come to the surface. The spell served no purpose for a drow hiding under the open sky. Gradually, Drizzt's initial momentum carried him near the far bank. He began to concentrate on drifting down to the stone, but the spell ended abruptly and Drizzt plopped down hard. He ignored the bruises on his knee, and the questions of why his spell had faltered, and came up running, calling desperately for Guenhwyvar to stop.

Drizzt was relieved when he found the cat. Guenhwyvar sat calmly in a clearing, one paw casually pinning the boy facedown to the ground. The child was calling out again—for help, Drizzt assumed—but appeared unharmed.

"Come, Guenhwyvar," Drizzt said quietly, calmly. "Leave the child alone." Guenhwyvar yawned lazily and complied, padding across the clearing to stand at its master's side.

The boy remained down for a long moment. Then, summoning his courage, he moved suddenly, leaping to his feet and spinning to face the dark elf and the panther. His eyes seemed wider still, almost a caricature of terror, peeking out from his now dirty face.

"What are you?" the boy asked in the common human language.

Drizzt held his arms out to the sides to indicate that he did not understand. On impulse, he poked a finger into his chest and replied, "Drizzt Do'Urden." He noticed that the boy was moving slightly, secretly dropping one foot behind the other and sliding the other back into place. Drizzt was not surprised—and he made certain that he kept Guenhwyvar in check this time—when the boy turned on his heel and sprinted away, screaming "Help! It's a drizzit!" with every stride.

Drizzt looked at Guenhwyvar and shrugged, and the cat seemed to shrug back.

# 3
# The Whelps

Nathak, a spindle-armed goblin, made his way slowly up the steep, rocky incline, every step weighted with dread. The goblin had to report his findings—five dead gnolls could not be ignored—but the unfortunate creature seriously doubted that either Ulgulu or Kempfana would willingly accept the news. Still, what options did Nathak have? He could run away, flee down the other side of the mountain, and off into the wilderness. That seemed an even more desperate course, though, for the goblin knew well Ulgulu's taste for vengeance. The great purple-skinned master could tear a tree from the ground with his bare hands, could tear handfuls of stone from the cave wall, and could readily tear the throat from a deserting goblin.

Every step brought a shudder as Nathak moved beyond the concealing scrub into the small entry room of his master's cave complex.

"Bouts time yez isses back," one of the other two goblins in the room snorted. "Yez been gone fer two days!"

Nathak just nodded and took a deep breath.

"What're ye fer?" the third goblin asked. "Did ye finded the gnolls?"

Nathak's face blanched, and no amount of deep breathing could relieve the fit that came over the goblin. "Ulgulu in there?" he asked squeamishly.

The two goblin guards looked curiously at each other, then back to

Nathak. "He finded the gnolls," one of them remarked, guessing the problem. "Dead gnolls."

"Ulgulu won'ts be glad," the other piped in, and they moved apart, one of them lifting the heavy curtain that separated the entry room from the audience chamber.

Nathak hesitated and started to look back, as though reconsidering this whole course. Perhaps flight would be preferable, he thought. The goblin guards grabbed their spindly companion and roughly shoved him into the audience chamber, crossing their spears behind Nathak to prevent any retreat.

Nathak managed to find a measure of composure when he saw that it was Kempfana, not Ulgulu, sitting in the huge chair across the room. Kempfana had earned a reputation among the goblin ranks as the calmer of the ruling brothers, though Kempfana, too, had impulsively devoured enough of his minions to earn their healthy respect. Kempfana hardly took note of the goblin's entrance, instead busily conversing with Lagerbottoms, the fat hill giant that formerly claimed the cave complex as his own.

Nathak shuffled across the room, drawing the gazes of both the hill giant and the huge—nearly as large as the hill giant—scarlet-skinned goblinoid.

"Yes, Nathak," Kempfana prompted, silencing the hill giant's forthcoming protest with a simple wave of the hand. "What have you to report?"

"Me . . . me," Nathak stuttered.

Kempfana's large eyes suddenly glowed orange, a clear sign of dangerous excitement.

"Me finded the gnolls!" Nathak blurted. "Dead. Killded."

Lagerbottoms issued a low and threatening growl, but Kempfana clutched the hill giant's arm tightly, reminding him of who was in charge.

"Dead?" the scarlet-skinned goblin asked quietly.

Nathak nodded.

Kempfana lamented the loss of such reliable slaves, but the barghest whelp's thoughts at that moment were more centered on his brother's inevitably volatile reaction to the news. Kempfana didn't have long to wait.

*"Dead!"* came a roar that nearly split the stone. All three monsters in the room instinctively ducked and turned to the side, just in time to see a huge boulder, the crude door to another room, burst out and go skipping off to the side.

"Ulgulu!" Nathak squealed, and the little goblin fell face-down to the floor, not daring to look.

The huge, purple-skinned goblinlike creature stormed into the audience chamber, his eyes seething in orange-glowing rage. Three great strides took Ulgulu right up beside the hill giant, and Lagerbottoms suddenly seemed very small and vulnerable.

"Dead!" Ulgulu roared again in rage. As his goblin tribe had diminished, killed either by the humans of the village or by other monsters—or eaten by Ulgulu during his customary fits of anger—the small gnoll band had become the primary capturing force for the lair.

Kempfana cast an ugly glare at his larger sibling. They had come to the Material Plane together, two barghest whelps, to eat and grow. Ulgulu had promptly claimed dominance, devouring the strongest of their victims and thus, growing larger and stronger. By the color of Ulgulu's skin, and by his sheer size and strength, it was apparent that the whelp would soon be able to return to the reeking valley rifts of Gehenna.

Kempfana hoped that day was near. When Ulgulu was gone, he would rule; he would eat and grow stronger. Then Kempfana, too, could escape his interminable weaning period on this cursed plane, could return to compete among the barghests on their rightful plane of existence.

"Dead," Ulgulu growled again. "Get up, wretched goblin, and tell me how! What did this to my gnolls?"

Nathak groveled a minute longer, then managed to rise to his knees. "Me no know," the goblin whimpered. "Gnolls dead, slashed and ripped."

Ulgulu rocked back on the heels of his floppy, oversized feet. The gnolls had gone off to raid a farmhouse, with orders to return with the farmer and his oldest son. Those two hardy human meals would have strengthened the great barghest considerably, perhaps even bringing Ulgulu to the level of maturation he needed to return to Gehenna.

Now, in light of Nathak's report, Ulgulu would have to send Lagerbottoms, or perhaps even go himself, and the sight of either the giant or the purple-skinned monstrosity could prompt the human settlement to dangerous, organized action. "Tephanis!" Ulgulu roared suddenly.

Over on the far wall, across from where Ulgulu had made his crashing entrance, a small pebble dislodged and fell. The drop was only a few feet, but by the time the pebble hit the floor, a slender sprite had zipped out of the small cubby he used as a bedroom, crossed the twenty feet of the audience hall, and run right up Ulgulu's side to sit comfortably atop the barghest's immense shoulder.

"You-called-for-me, yes-you-did, my-master," Tephanis buzzed, too quickly. The others hadn't even realized that the two-foot-tall sprite had entered the room. Kempfana turned away, shaking his head in amazement.

Ulgulu roared with laughter; he so loved to witness the spectacle of Tephanis, his most prized servant. Tephanis was a quickling, a diminutive sprite that moved in a dimension that transcended the normal concept of time. Possessing boundless energy and an agility that would shame the most proficient halfling thief, quicklings could perform many tasks that no other race could even attempt. Ulgulu had befriended Tephanis early in his tenure on the Material Plane—Tephanis was the only member of the lair's diverse tenants that the barghest did not claim rulership over—and that bond had given the young whelp a distinct advantage over his sibling. With Tephanis scouting out potential victims, Ulgulu knew exactly which ones to devour and which ones to leave to Kempfana, and knew exactly how to win against those adventurers more powerful than he.

"Dear Tephanis," Ulgulu purred in an odd sort of grating sound. "Nathak, poor Nathak,"—The goblin didn't miss the implications of that reference—"has informed me that my gnolls have met with disaster."

"And-you-want-me-to-go-and-see-what-happened-to-them, my-master," Tephanis replied. Ulgulu took a moment to decipher the nearly unintelligible string of words, then nodded eagerly.

"Right-away, my-master. Be-back-soon."

Ulgulu felt a slight shiver on his shoulder, but by the time he, or any of the others, realized what Tephanis had said, the heavy drape separating the chamber from the entry room was floating back to its hanging position. One of the goblins poked its head in for just a moment, to see if Kempfana or Ulgulu had summoned it, then returned to its station, thinking the drape's movement a trick of the wind.

Ulgulu roared in laughter again; Kempfana cast him a disgusted glare. Kempfana hated the sprite and would have killed it long ago, except that he couldn't ignore the potential benefits, assuming that Tephanis would work for him once Ulgulu had returned to Gehenna.

Nathak slipped one foot behind the other, meaning to silently retreat from the room. Ulgulu stopped the goblin with a look.

"Your report served me well," the barghest started.

Nathak relaxed, but only for the moment it took Ulgulu's great hand to shoot out, catch the goblin by the throat, and lift Nathak from the floor.

"But it would have served me better if you had taken the time to find out what happened to my gnolls!"

Nathak swooned and nearly fainted, and by the time half of his body had been stuffed into Ulgulu's eager mouth, the spindle-armed goblin wished he had.

⚔ ⚔ ⚔ ⚔ ⚔

"Rub the behind, ease the pain. Switch it brings it back again. Rub the behind, ease the pain. Switch it brings it back again," Liam Thistledown repeated over and over, a litany to take his concentration from the burning sensation beneath his britches, a litany that mischievous Liam knew all too well. This time was different, though, with Liam actually admitting to himself, after a while, that he had indeed run out on his chores.

"But the drizzit was true," Liam growled defiantly.

As if in answer to his statement, the shed's door opened just a crack and Shawno, the second youngest to Liam, and Eleni, the only sister, slipped in.

"Got yourself into it this time," Eleni scolded in her best big-sister voice. "Bad enough you run off when there's work to be done, but coming home with such tales!"

"The drizzit was true," Liam protested, not appreciating Eleni's pseudomothering. Liam could get into enough trouble with just his parents scolding him; he didn't need Eleni's ever-sharp hindsight. "Black as Connor's anvil and with a lion just as black!"

"Quiet, you both," Shawno warned. "If dad's to learn that we're out here talking such, he'll whip the lot of us."

"Drizzit," Eleni huffed doubtfully.

"True!" Liam protested too loudly, bringing a stinging slap from Shawno. The three turned, faces ashen, when the door swung open.

"Get in here!" Eleni whispered harshly, grabbing Flanny, who was a bit older than Shawno but three years Eleni's junior, by the collar and hoisting him into the woodshed. Shawno, always the worrier of the group, quickly poked his head outside to see that no one was watching, then softly closed the door.

"You should not be spying on us!" Eleni protested.

"How'd I know you was in here?" Flanny shot back. "I just came to tease the little one." He looked at Liam, twisted his mouth, and waved his fingers menacingly in the air. "Ware, ware," Flanny crooned. "I am the drizzit, come to eat little boys!"

Liam turned away, but Shawno was not so impressed. "Aw, shut up!" he growled at Flanny, emphasizing his point with a slap on the back of his brother's head. Flanny turned to retaliate, but Eleni stepped between them.

"Stop it!" Eleni cried, so loudly that all four Thistledown children slapped a finger over their lips and said, "Ssssh!"

"The drizzit was true," Liam protested again. "I can prove it—if you're not too scared!"

Liam's three siblings eyed him curiously. He was a notorious fibber, they all knew, but what now would be the gain? Their father hadn't believed Liam, and that was all that mattered as far as the punishment was concerned. Yet Liam was adamant, and his tone told them all that there was substance behind the proclamation.

"How can you prove the drizzit?" Flanny asked.

"We've no chores tomorrow," Liam replied. "We'll go blueberry picking in the mountains."

"Ma and Daddy'd never let us," Eleni put in.

"They would if we can get Connor to go along," said Liam, referring to their oldest brother.

"Connor'd not believe you," Eleni argued.

"But he'd believe you!" Liam replied sharply, drawing another communal "Ssssh!"

"I don't believe you," Eleni retorted quietly. "You're always making things up, always causing trouble and lying to get out of it!"

Liam crossed his little arms over his chest and stamped one foot impatiently at his sister's continuing stream of logic. "But you will believe me," Liam growled, "if you get Connor to go!"

"Aw, do it," Flanny pleaded to Eleni, though Shawno, thinking of the potential consequences, shook his head.

"So we go up into the mountains," Eleni said to Liam, prompting him to continue and thus revealing her agreement.

Liam smiled widely and dropped to one knee, collecting a pile of sawdust in which to draw a rough map of the area where he had encountered the drizzit. His plan was a simple one, using Eleni, casually picking blueberries, as bait. The four brothers would follow secretly and watch as she feigned a twisted ankle or some other injury. Distress had brought the drizzit before; surely with a pretty young girl as bait, it would bring the drizzit again.

Eleni balked at the idea, not thrilled at being planted as a worm on a hook.

"But you don't believe me anyway," Liam quickly pointed out. His inevitable smile, complete with a gaping hole where a tooth had been knocked out, showed that her own stubbornness had cornered her.

"So I'll do it, then!" Eleni huffed. "And I don't believe in your drizzit, Liam Thistledown! But if the lion is real, and I get chewed, I'll tan you good!" With that, Eleni turned and stormed out of the woodshed.

Liam and Flanny spit in their hands, then turned daring glares on Shawno until he overcame his fears. Then the three brothers brought their palms together in a triumphant, wet slap. Any disagreements between them always seemed to vanish whenever one of them found a way to bother Eleni.

None of them told Connor about their planned hunt for the drizzit. Rather, Eleni reminded him of the many favors he owed her and promised that she would consider the debt paid in full—but only after Liam had agreed to take on Connor's debt if they didn't find the drizzit—if Connor would only take her and the boys blueberry picking.

Connor grumbled and balked, complaining about some shoeing that needed to be done to one of the mares, but he could never resist his little sister's batting blue eyes and wide, bright smile, and Eleni's promise of erasing his considerable debt had sealed his fate. With his parents' blessing, Connor led the Thistledown children up into the mountains, buckets in the children's hands and a crude sword belted on his hip.

⚔ ⚔ ⚔ ⚔ ⚔

Drizzt saw the ruse coming long before the farmer's young daughter moved out alone in the blueberry patch. He saw, too, the four Thistledown boys, crouched in the shadows of a nearby grove of maple trees, Connor, somewhat less than expertly, brandishing the crude sword.

The youngest had led them here, Drizzt knew. The day before, the drow had witnessed the boy being pulled out into the woodshed. Cries of "drizzit!" had issued forth after every switch, at least at the beginning. Now the stubborn lad wanted to prove his outrageous story.

The blueberry picker jerked suddenly, then fell to the ground and cried out. Drizzt recognized "Help!" as the same distress call the sandy-haired boy had used, and a smile widened across his dark face. By the ridiculous way the girl had fallen, Drizzt saw the game for what it was. The girl was not injured now; she was simply calling out for the drizzit.

With an incredulous shake of his thick white mane, Drizzt started away, but an impulse grabbed at him. He looked back to the blueberry patch, where the girl sat rubbing her ankle, all the while glancing nervously around or back toward her concealed brothers. Something pulled at Drizzt's heartstrings at that moment, an urge he could not resist. How long had he been alone, wandering without companionship? He longed for Belwar at that moment, the svirfneblin who had accompanied him through many trials in the wilds of the Underdark. He longed for Zaknafein, his father and friend. Seeing the interplay between the caring siblings was more than Drizzt Do'Urden could bear.

The time had come for Drizzt to meet his neighbors.

Drizzt hiked the hood of his oversized gnoll cloak up over his head, though the ragged garment did little to hide the truth of his heritage, and bounded across the field. He hoped that if he could at least deflect the girl's initial reaction to seeing him, he might find some way to communicate with her. The hopes were farfetched at best.

"The drizzit!" Eleni gasped under her breath when she saw him coming. She wanted to cry out loud but found no breath; she wanted to run, but her terror held her firmly.

From the copse of trees, Liam spoke for her. "The drizzit!" the boy cried. "I told you so! I told you so!" He looked to his brothers, and Flanny and Shawno were having the expected excited reactions. Connor's face, though, was locked into a look of dread so profound that one glance at it stole the joy from Liam.

"By the gods," the eldest Thistledown son muttered. Connor had adventured with his father and had been trained to spot enemies. He looked now to his three confused brothers and muttered a single word that explained nothing to the inexperienced boys. "Drow."

Drizzt stopped a dozen paces from the frightened girl, the first human woman he had seen up close, and studied her. Eleni was pretty by any race's standards, with huge, soft eyes, dimpled cheeks, and smooth, golden skin. Drizzt knew there would be no fight here. He smiled at Eleni and crossed his arms gently over his chest. "Drizzt," he corrected, pointing to his chest. A movement to the side turned him away from the girl.

"Run, Eleni!" Connor Thistledown cried, waving his sword and bearing down on the drow. "It is a dark elf! A drow! Run for your life!"

Of all that Connor had cried, Drizzt only understood the word "drow." The young man's attitude and intent could not be mistaken, though, for Connor charged straight between Drizzt and Eleni, his sword tip pointed Drizzt's way. Eleni managed to get to her feet behind her brother, but she did not flee as he had instructed. She, too, had heard of the evil dark elves, and she would not leave Connor to face one alone.

"Turn away, dark elf," Connor growled. "I am an expert swordsman and much stronger than you."

Drizzt held his hands out helplessly, not understanding a word.

"Turn away!" Connor yelled.

On an impulse, Drizzt tried to reply in the drow silent code, an intricate language of hand and facial gestures.

"He's casting a spell!" Eleni cried, and she dived down into the blueberries. Connor shrieked and charged.

Before Connor even knew of the counter, Drizzt grabbed him by the forearm, used his other hand to twist the boy's wrist and take away the sword, spun the crude weapon three times over Connor's head, flipped it in his slender hand then handed it, hilt first, back to the boy.

Drizzt held his arms out wide and smiled. In drow custom, such a show of superiority without injuring the opponent invariably signaled a desire for friendship. To the oldest son of farmer Bartholemew Thistledown, the drow's blinding display brought only awe-inspired terror.

Connor stood, mouth agape, for a long moment. His sword fell from his hand but he didn't notice; his pants, soiled, clung to his thighs, but he didn't notice.

A scream erupted from somewhere within Connor. He grabbed Eleni, who joined in his scream, and they fled back to the grove to collect the others, then farther, running until they crossed the threshold of their own home.

Drizzt was left, his smile fast fading and his arms out wide, standing all alone in the blueberry patch.

⚔ ⚔ ⚔ ⚔ ⚔

A set of dizzily darting eyes had watched the exchange in the blueberry patch with more than a casual interest. The unexpected appearance of a dark elf, particularly one wearing a gnoll cloak, had answered many questions for Tephanis. The quickling sleuth had already examined the gnoll corpses but simply could not reconcile the gnolls' fatal wounds with the crude weapons usually wielded by the simple village farmers. Seeing the magnificent twin scimitars so casually belted on the dark elf's hips and the ease with which the dark elf had dispatched the farm boy, Tephanis knew the truth.

The dust trail left by the quickling would have confused the best rangers in the Realms. Tephanis, never a straightforward sprite, zipped up the mountain trails, spinning circuits around some trees, running up and down the sides of others, and generally doubling, even tripling, his route. Distance never bothered Tephanis; he stood before the purple-skinned barghest whelp even before Drizzt, considering the implications of the disastrous meeting, had left the blueberry patch.

# 4

# Worries

Farmer Bartholemew Thistledown's perspective changed considerably when Connor, his oldest son, renamed Liam's "drizzit" a dark elf. Farmer Thistledown had spent his entire forty-five years in Maldobar, a village fifty miles up the Dead Orc River north of Sundabar. Bartholemew's father had lived here, and his father's father before him. In all that time, the only news any Farmer Thistledown had ever heard of dark elves was the tale of a suspected drow raid on a small settlement of wild elves a hundred miles to the north, in Coldwood. That raid, if it was even perpetrated by the drow, had occurred more than a decade before.

Lack of personal experience with the drow race did not diminish Farmer Thistledown's fears at hearing his children's tale of the encounter in the blueberry patch. Connor and Eleni, two trusted sources old enough to keep their wits about them in a time of crisis, had viewed the elf up close, and they held no doubts about the color of his skin.

"The only thing I can't rightly figure," Bartholemew told Benson Delmo, the fat and cheerful mayor of Maldobar and several other farmers gathered at his house that night, "is why this drow let the children go free. I'm no expert on the ways of dark elves, but I've heard tell enough about them to expect a different sort of action."

"Perhaps Connor fared better in his attack than he believed," Delmo piped in tactfully. They had all heard the tale of Connor's disarming; Liam and the other Thistledown children, except for poor Connor, of course, particularly enjoyed retelling that part.

As much as he appreciated the mayor's vote of confidence, though, Connor shook his head emphatically at the suggestion. "He took me," Connor admitted. "Maybe I was too surprised at the sight of him, but he took me—clean."

"And no easy feat," Bartholemew put in, deflecting any forthcoming snickers from the gruff crowd. "We've all seen Connor at fighting. Just last winter, he took down three goblins and the wolves they were riding!"

"Calm, good Farmer Thistledown," the mayor offered. "We've no doubts of your son's prowess."

"I've my doubts about the truth o' the foe!" put in Roddy McGristle, a bear-sized and bear-hairy man, the most battle-seasoned of the group. Roddy spent more time up in the mountains than tending his farm, a recent endeavor he didn't particularly enjoy, and whenever someone offered a bounty on orc ears, Roddy invariably collected the largest portion of the coffers, often larger than the rest of the town combined.

"Put yer neck hairs down," Roddy said to Connor as the boy began to rise, a sharp protest obviously forthcoming. "I know what ye says ye seen, and I believe that ye seen what ye says. But ye called it a drow, an' that title carries more than ye can begin to know. If it was a drow ye found, my guess's that yerself an' yer kin'd be lying dead right now in that there blueberry patch. No, not a drow, by my guess, but there's other things in them mountains could do what ye says this thing did."

"Name them," Bartholemew said crossly, not appreciating the doubts Roddy had cast over his son's story. Bartholemew didn't much like Roddy anyway. Farmer Thistledown kept a respectable family, and every time crude and loud Roddy McGristle came to pay a visit, it took Bartholemew and his wife many days to remind the children, particularly Liam, about proper behavior.

Roddy just shrugged, taking no offense at Bartholemew's tone. "Goblin, troll—might be a wood elf that's seen too much o' the sun." His laughter, erupting after the last statement, rolled over the group, belittling their seriousness.

"Then how do we know for sure," said Delmo.

"We find out by finding it," Roddy offered. "Tomorrow mornin',"—he pointed around at each man sitting at Bartholemew's table—"we go out an' see what we can see." Considering the impromptu meeting at an end, Roddy slammed his hands down on the table and pushed himself to his feet. He looked back before he got to the farmhouse door, though, and cast an exaggerated wink and a nearly toothless smile back at the group. "And boys," he said, "don't be forgettin' yer weapons!"

Roddy's cackle rolled back in on the group long after the rough-edged mountain man had departed.

"We could call in a ranger," one of the other farmers offered hopefully as the dispirited group began to depart. "I heard there's one in Sundabar, one of Lady Alustriel's sisters."

"A bit too early for that," Mayor Delmo answered, defeating any optimistic smiles.

"Is it ever too early when drow are involved?" Bartholemew quickly put in.

The mayor shrugged. "Let us go with McGristle," he replied. "If anyone can find some truth up in the mountains, it's him." He tactfully turned to Connor. "I believe your tale, Connor. Truly I do. But we've got to know for sure before we put out a call for such distinguished assistance as a sister of the Lady of Silverymoon."

The mayor and the rest of the visiting farmers departed, leaving Bartholemew, his father, Markhe, and Connor alone in the Thistledown kitchen.

"Wasn't no goblin or wood elf," Connor said in a low tone that hinted at both anger and embarrassment.

Bartholemew patted his son on the back, never doubting him.

---

Up in a cave in the mountains, Ulgulu and Kempfana, too, spent a night of worry over the appearance of a dark elf.

"If he's a drow, then he's an experienced adventurer," Kempfana offered to his larger brother. "Experienced enough, perhaps, to send Ulgulu into maturity."

"And back to Gehenna!" Ulgulu finished for his conniving brother. "You do so dearly desire to see me depart."

"You, too, hope for the day when you may return to the smoking rifts," Kempfana reminded him.

Ulgulu snarled and did not reply. The appearance of a dark elf prompted many considerations and fears beyond Kempfana's simple statement of logic. The barghests, like all intelligent creatures on nearly every plane of existence, knew of the drow and maintained a healthy respect for the race. While one drow might not be too much of a problem, Ulgulu knew that a dark elf war party, perhaps even an army, could prove disastrous. The whelps were not invulnerable. The human village had provided easy pickings for the barghest whelps and might continue to do so for some time if Ulgulu and Kempfana were careful about their attacks. But if a band of dark elves showed up, those easy kills could disappear quite suddenly.

"This drow must be dealt with," Kempfana remarked. "If he is a scout, then he must not return to report."

Ulgulu snapped a cold glare on his brother, then called to his quickling. "Tephanis," he cried, and the quickling was upon his shoulder before he had even finished the word.

"You-need-me-to-go-and-kill-the-drow, my-master," the quickling replied. "I-understand-what-you-need-me-to-do!"

"No!" Ulgulu shouted immediately, sensing that the quickling intended to go right out. Tephanis was halfway to the door by the time Ulgulu finished the syllable, but the quickling returned to Ulgulu's shoulder before the last note of the shout had died away.

"No," Ulgulu said again, more easily. "There may be a gain in the drow's appearance."

Kempfana read Ulgulu's evil grin and understood his brother's intent. "A new enemy for the townspeople," the smaller whelp reasoned. "A new enemy to cover Ulgulu's murders?"

"All things can be turned to advantage," the big, purple-skinned barghest replied wickedly, "even the appearance of a dark elf." Ulgulu turned back to Tephanis.

"You-wish-to-learn-more-of-the-drow, my-master," Tephanis spouted excitedly.

"Is he alone?" Ulgulu asked. "Is he a forward scout to a larger group, as we fear, or a lone warrior? What are his intentions toward the townspeople?"

"He-could-have-killed-the-children," Tephanis reiterated. "I-guess-him-to-desire-friendship."

"I know," Ulgulu snarled. "You have made those points before. Go now and learn more! I need more than your guess, Tephanis, and by all accounts, a drow's actions rarely hint at his true intent!"

Tephanis skipped down from Ulgulu's shoulder and paused, expecting further instructions.

"Indeed, dear Tephanis," Ulgulu purred. "Do see if you can appropriate one of the drow's weapons for me. It would prove usef—" Ulgulu stopped when he noticed the flutter in the heavy curtain blocking the entry room.

"An excitable little sprite," Kempfana noted.

"But with his uses," Ulgulu replied, and Kempfana had to nod in agreement.

⚔ ⚔ ⚔ ⚔ ⚔

Drizzt saw them coming from a mile away. Ten armed farmers followed the young man he had met in the blueberry patch on the previous day. Though they talked and joked, the set of their stride was determined and their weapons were prominently displayed, obviously ready to be put to use. Even more insidious, walking to the side of the main band came a barrel-chested, grim-faced man wrapped in thick skins, brandishing a finely crafted axe and leading two large and snarling yellow dogs on thick chains.

Drizzt wanted to make further contact with the villagers, wanted dearly to continue the events he had set in motion the previous day and learn if he might have, at long last, found a place he could call home, but this coming encounter, he realized, was not the place to make such gains. If the farmers found him, there would surely be trouble, and while Drizzt wasn't too worried for his own safety against the ragged band even considering the grim-faced fighter, he did fear that one of the farmers might get hurt.

Drizzt decided that his mission this day was to avoid the group and to deflect their curiosity. The drow knew the perfect diversion to accomplish those goals. He set the onyx figurine on the ground before him and called to Guenhwyvar.

A buzzing noise off to the side, followed by the sudden rustle of brush, distracted the drow for just a moment as the customary mist swirled around the figurine. Drizzt saw nothing ominous approaching, though, and quickly dismissed it. He had more pressing problems, he thought.

When Guenhwyvar arrived, Drizzt and the cat moved down the trail beyond the blueberry patch, where Drizzt guessed that the farmers would begin their hunt. His plan was simple: He would let the farmers mill about the area for a while, let the farmer's son retell his story of the encounter. Guenhwyvar then would make an appearance along the edge of the patch and lead the group on a futile chase. The black-furred panther might cast some doubts on the farm boy's tale; possibly the older men would assume that the children had encountered the cat and not a dark elf and that their imaginations had supplied the rest of the details. It was a gamble, Drizzt knew, but at the very least, Guenhwyvar would cast some doubts about the existence of the dark elf and would get this hunting party away from Drizzt for a while.

The farmers arrived at the blueberry patch on schedule, a few grim-faced and battle-ready but the majority of the group talking casually in conversations filled with laughter. They found the discarded sword, and Drizzt watched, nodding his head, as the farmer's son played through the events of the previous day. Drizzt noticed, too, that the large axe-wielder, listening to the story halfheartedly, circled the group with his dogs, pointing at various spots in the patch and coaxing the dogs to sniff about. Drizzt had no practical experience with dogs, but he knew that many creatures had superior senses and could be used to aid in a hunt.

"Go, Guenhwyvar," the drow whispered, not waiting for the dogs to get a clear scent.

The great panther loped silently down the trail and took up a position in one of the trees in the same grove where the boys had hidden the previous day. Guenhwyvar's sudden roar silenced the group's growing conversation in an instant, all heads spinning to the trees.

The panther leaped out into the patch, shot right past the stunned humans, and darted across the rising rocks of the mountain slopes. The farmers hooted and took up pursuit, calling for the man with the dogs to take the lead. Soon the whole group, dogs baying wildly, moved off and Drizzt went down into the grove near the blueberry patch to consider the day's events and his best course of action.

He thought that a buzzing noise followed him, but he passed it off as the hum of an insect.

By his dogs' confused actions, it didn't take Roddy McGristle long to figure out that the panther was not the same creature that had left the scent in the blueberry patch. Furthermore, Roddy realized that his ragged companions, particularly the obese mayor, even with his aid, had little chance of catching the great cat; the panther could spring across ravines that would take the farmers many minutes to circumvent.

"Go on!" Roddy told the rest of the group. "Chase the thing along this course. I'll take my dogs'n go far to the side and cut the thing off, turn it back to ye!" The farmers hooted their accord and bounded away, and Roddy pulled back the chains and turned his dogs aside.

The dogs, trained for the hunt, wanted to go on, but their master had another route in mind. Several thoughts bothered Roddy at that moment. He had been in these mountains for thirty years but had never seen, or even heard of, such a cat. Also, though the panther easily could have left its pursuers far behind, it always seemed to appear out in the open not too far away, as though it was leading the farmers on. Roddy knew a diversion when he saw it, and he had a good guess of where the perpetrator might be hiding. He muzzled the dogs to keep them silent and headed back the way he had come, back to the blueberry patch.

⚔ ⚔ ⚔ ⚔ ⚔

Drizzt rested against a tree in the shadows of the thick copse and wondered how he might further his exposure to the farmers without causing any more panic among them. In his days of watching the single farm family, Drizzt had become convinced that he could find a place among the humans, of this or of some other settlement, if only he could convince them that his intentions were not dangerous.

A buzz to Drizzt's left brought him abruptly from his contemplations. Quickly he drew his scimitars, then something flashed by him, too fast for him to react. He cried out at a sudden pain in his wrist, and his scimitar was pulled from his grasp. Confused, Drizzt looked down to his wound, expecting to see an arrow or crossbow bolt stuck deep into his arm.

The wound was clean and empty. A high-pitched laughter spun Drizzt to the right. There stood the sprite, Drizzt's scimitar casually slung over one shoulder, nearly touching the ground behind the diminutive creature, and a dagger, dripping blood, in his other hand.

Drizzt stayed very still, trying to guess the thing's next move. He had never seen a quickling, or even heard of the uncommon creatures, but he already had a good idea of his speedy opponent's advantage. Before the drow could form any plan to defeat the quickling, though, another nemesis showed itself.

Drizzt knew as soon as he heard the howl that his cry of pain had revealed him. The first of Roddy McGristle's snarling hounds crashed through the brush, charging in low at the drow. The second, a few running strides behind the first, came in high, leaping toward Drizzt's throat.

This time, though, Drizzt was the quicker. He slashed down with his remaining scimitar, cutting the first dog's head and bashing its skull. Without hesitation, Drizzt threw himself backward, reversing his grip on the blade and bringing it up above his face, in line with the leaping dog. The scimitar's hilt locked fast against the tree trunk, and the dog, unable to turn in its flight, drove hard into the set weapon's other end, impaling itself through the throat and chest. The wrenching impact tore the scimitar from Drizzt's hand and dog and blade bounced away into some scrub to the side of the tree.

Drizzt had barely recovered when Roddy McGristle burst in.

"Ye killed my dogs!" the huge mountain man roared, chopping Bleeder, his large, battle-worn axe, down at the drow's head. The cut came deceptively swiftly, but Drizzt managed to dodge to the side. The drow couldn't understand a word of McGristle's continuing stream of expletives, and he knew that the burly man would not understand a word of any explanations Drizzt might try to offer.

Wounded and unarmed, Drizzt's only defense was to continue to dodge away. Another swipe nearly caught him, cutting through his gnoll cloak, but he sucked in his stomach, and the axe skipped off his fine chain mail. Drizzt danced to the side, toward a tight cluster of smaller trees, where he believed his greater agility might give him some advantage. He had to try to tire the enraged human, or at least make the man reconsider his brutal attack. McGristle's ire did not lessen, though. He charged right after Drizzt, snarling and swinging with every step.

Drizzt now saw the shortcomings of his plan. While he might keep away from the large human's bulky body in the tightly packed trees, McGristle's axe could dive between them quite deftly.

The mighty weapon came in from the side at shoulder level. Drizzt dropped flat down on the ground desperately, narrowly avoiding death. McGristle couldn't slow his swing in time, and the heavy—and heavily ensorceled—weapon smashed into the four-inch trunk of a young maple, felling the tree.

The tightening angle of the buckling trunk held Roddy's axe fast. Roddy grunted and tried to tear the weapon free, and did not realize his peril until the last minute. He managed to jump away from the main weight of the trunk but was buried under the maple's canopy. Branches ripped across his face and the side of his head forming a web around him and pinning him tightly to the ground. "Damn ye, drow!" McGristle roared, shaking futilely at his natural prison.

Drizzt crawled away, still clutching his wounded wrist. He found his remaining scimitar, buried to the hilt in the unfortunate dog. The sight pained Drizzt; he knew the value of animal companions. It took him several heartsick moments to pull the blade free, moments made even more dramatic by the other dog, which, merely stunned, was beginning to stir once again.

"Damn ye, drow!" McGristle roared again.

Drizzt understood the reference to his heritage, and he could guess the rest. He wanted to help the fallen man, thinking that he might make some inroads on opening some more civilized communication, but he didn't think that the awakening dog would be so ready to lend a paw. With a final glance around for the sprite that had started this whole thing, Drizzt dragged himself out of the grove and fled into the mountains.

⚔ ⚔ ⚔ ⚔ ⚔

"We should've got the thing!" Bartholemew Thistledown grumbled as the troupe returned to the blueberry patch. "If McGristle had come in where he said he would, we'd've gotten the cat for sure! Where is that dog pack leader, anyhow?"

An ensuing roar of "Drow! Drow!" from the maple grove answered Bartholemew's question. The farmers rushed over to find Roddy still helplessly pinned by the felled maple tree.

"Damned drow!" Roddy bellowed. "Killed my dog! Damned drow!" He reached for his left ear when his arm was free but found that the ear was no longer attached. "Damned drow!" he roared again.

Connor Thistledown let everyone see the return of his pride at the confirmation of his oft-doubted tale, but the eldest Thistledown child was the only one pleased at Roddy's unexpected proclamation. The other farmers were older than Connor; they realized the grim implications of having a dark elf haunting the region.

Benson Delmo, wiping sweat from his forehead, made little secret of how he stood on the news. He turned immediately to the farmer by his side, a younger man known for his prowess in raising and riding horses. "Get to Sundabar," the mayor ordered. "Find us a ranger straightaway!"

In a few minutes, Roddy was pulled free. By this time, his wounded dog had rejoined him, but the knowledge that one of his prized pets had survived did little to calm the rough man.

"Damned drow!" Roddy roared for perhaps the thousandth time, wiping the blood from his cheek. "I'm gonna get me a damned drow!" He emphasized his point by slamming Bleeder, one-handed, into the trunk of another nearby maple, nearly felling that one as well.

# 5 The Stalk of Doom

The goblin guards dived to the side as mighty Ulgulu tore through the curtain and exited the cave complex. The open, crisp air of the chill mountain night felt good to the barghest, better still when Ulgulu thought of the task before him. He looked to the scimitar that Tephanis had delivered, the crafted weapon appearing tiny in Ulgulu's huge, dark-skinned hand.

Ulgulu unconsciously dropped the weapon to the ground. He didn't want to use it this night; the barghest wanted to put his own deadly weapons—claws and teeth—to use, to taste his victims and devour their life essence so that he could become stronger. Ulgulu was an intelligent creature, though, and his rationale quickly overruled the base instincts that so desired the taste of blood. There was purpose in this night's work, a method that promised greater gains and the elimination of the very real threat that the dark elf's unexpected appearance posed.

With a guttural snarl, a small protest from Ulgulu's base urges, the barghest grabbed the scimitar again and pounded down the mountainside, covering long distances with each stride. The beast stopped on the edge of a ravine, where a single narrow trail wound down along the sheer facing of the cliff. It would take him many minutes to scale down the dangerous trail.

But Ulgulu was hungry.

Ulgulu's consciousness fell back into itself, focusing on that spot of his being that fluctuated with magical energy. He was not a creature of the Material Plane, and extra-planar creatures inevitably brought with them powers that would seem magical to creatures of the host plane. Ulgulu's eyes glowed orange with excitement when he emerged from his trance just a few moments later. He peered down the cliff, visualizing a spot on the flat ground below, perhaps a quarter of a mile away.

A shimmering, multicolored door appeared before Ulgulu, hanging in the air beyond the lip of the ravine. His laughter sounding more like a roar, Ulgulu pushed open the door and found, just beyond its threshold, the spot he had visualized. He moved through, circumventing the material distance to the ravine's floor with a single extradimensional step.

Ulgulu ran on, down the mountain and toward the human village, ran on eagerly to set the gears of his cruel plan turning.

As the barghest approached the lowest mountain slopes, he again found that magical corner of his mind. Ulgulu's strides slowed, then the creature stopped altogether, jerking spasmodically and gurgling indecipherably. Bones ground together with popping noises, skin ripped and reformed, darkening nearly to black.

When Ulgulu started away again, his strides—the strides of a dark elf—were not so long.

⚔ ⚔ ⚔ ⚔ ⚔

Bartholemew Thistledown sat with his father, Markhe, and his oldest son that evening in the kitchen of the lone farmhouse on the western outskirts of Maldobar. Bartholemew's wife and mother had gone out to the barn to settle the animals for the night, and the four youngest children were safely tucked into their beds in the small room off the kitchen.

On a normal night the rest of the Thistledown family, all three generations, would also be snugly snoring in their beds, but Bartholemew feared that many nights would pass before any semblance of normalcy returned to the quiet farm. A dark elf had been spotted in the area, and while Bartholemew wasn't convinced that this stranger meant harm—

the drow easily could have killed Connor and the other children—he knew that the drow's appearance would cause a stir in Maldobar for quite some time.

"We could get back to the town proper," Connor offered. "They'd find us a place, and all of Maldobar'd stand behind us then."

"Stand behind us?" Bartholemew responded with sarcasm. "And would they be leaving their farms each day to come out here and help us keep up with our work? Which of them, do ye think, might ride out here each night to tend to the animals?"

Connor's head drooped at his father's berating. He slipped one hand to the hilt of his sword, reminding himself that he was no child. Still, Connor was silently grateful for the supporting hand his grandfather casually dropped on his shoulder.

"Ye've got to think, boy, before ye make such calls," Bartholemew continued, his tone mellowing as he began to realize the profound effect his harsh words had on his son. "The farm's yer lifeblood, the only thing that matters."

"We could send the little ones," Markhe put in. "The boy's got a right to be fearing, with a dark elf about and all."

Bartholemew turned away and resignedly dropped his chin into his palm. He hated the thought of breaking apart the family. Family was their source of strength, as it had been through five generations of Thistledowns and beyond. Yet, here Bartholemew was berating Connor, even though the boy had spoken only for the good of the family.

"I should have thought better, Dad," he heard Connor whisper, and he knew that his own pride could not hold out against the realization of Connor's pain. "I am sorry."

"Ye needn't be," Bartholemew replied, turning back to the others. "I'm the one should apologize. All of us got our neck hairs up with this dark elf about. Ye're right in yer thinking, Connor. We're too far out here to be safe."

As if in answer came a sharp crack of breaking wood and a muffled cry from outside the house, from the direction of the barn. In that single horrible moment, Bartholemew Thistledown realized that he should have come to his decision earlier, when the revealing light of day still offered his family some measure of protection.

Connor reacted first, running to the door and throwing it open. The farmyard was deathly quiet; not the chirp of a cricket disturbed the surrealistic scene. A silent moon loomed low in the sky, throwing long and devious shadows from every fence post and tree. Connor watched, not daring to breathe, through the passing of a second that seemed like an hour.

The barn door creaked and toppled from its hinges. A dark elf walked out into the farmyard.

Connor shut the door and fell back against it, needing its tangible support. "Ma," he breathed to the startled faces of his father and grandfather. "Drow."

The older Thistledown men hesitated, their minds whirling through the tumult of a thousand horrible notions. They simultaneously leaped from their seats, Bartholemew going for a weapon and Markhe moving toward Connor and the door.

Their sudden action freed Connor from his paralysis. He pulled the sword from his belt and swung the door open, meaning to rush out and face the intruder.

A single spring of his powerful legs had brought Ulgulu right up to the farmhouse door. Connor charged over the threshold blindly, slammed into the creature—which only appeared like a slender drow—and bounced back, stunned, into the kitchen. Before any of the men could react, the scimitar slammed down onto the top of Connor's head with all the strength of the barghest behind it, nearly splitting the young man in half.

Ulgulu stepped unhindered into the kitchen. He saw the old man—the lesser remaining enemy—reaching out for him, and called upon his magical nature to defeat the attack. A wave of imparted emotion swept over Markhe Thistledown, a wave of despair and terror so great that he could not combat it. His wrinkled mouth shot open in a silent scream and he staggered backward, crashing into a wall and clutching helplessly at his chest.

Bartholemew Thistledown's charge carried the weight of unbridled rage behind it. The farmer growled and gasped unintelligible sounds as he lowered his pitchfork and bore down on the intruder that had murdered his son.

The slender, assumed frame that held the barghest did not diminish Ulgulu's gigantic strength. As the pitchfork's tips closed the last inches to the creature's chest, Ulgulu slapped a single hand on the weapon's shaft. Bartholemew stopped in his tracks, the butt end of the pitchfork driving hard into his belly, blowing away his breath.

Ulgulu raised his arm quickly, lifting Bartholemew clear off the floor and slamming the farmer's head into a ceiling beam with enough force to break his neck. The barghest casually tossed Bartholemew and his pitiful weapon across the kitchen and stalked over to the old man.

Perhaps Markhe saw him coming; perhaps the old man was too torn by pain and anguish to register any events in the room. Ulgulu moved to him and opened his mouth wide. He wanted to devour the old man, to feast on this one's life force as he had with the younger woman out in the barn. Ulgulu had lamented his actions in the barn as soon as the ecstacy of the kill had faded. Again the barghest's rationale displaced his base urges. With a frustrated snarl, Ulgulu drove the scimitar into Markhe's chest, ending the old man's pain.

Ulgulu looked around at his gruesome work, lamenting that he had not feasted on the strong young farmers but reminding himself of the greater gains his actions this night would yield. A confused cry led him to the side room, where the children slept.

⚔ ⚔ ⚔ ⚔ ⚔

Drizzt came down from the mountains tentatively the next day. His wrist, where the sprite had stabbed him, throbbed, but the wound was clean and Drizzt was confident that it would heal. He crouched in the brush on the hillside behind the Thistledown farm, ready to try another meeting with the children. Drizzt had seen too much of the human community, and had spent too much time alone, to give up. This was where he intended to make his home if he could get beyond the obvious prejudicial barriers, personified most keenly by the large man with the snarling dogs.

From this angle, Drizzt couldn't see the blasted barn door, and all appeared as it should on the farm in the predawn glow.

The farmers did not come out with the sun, however, and always before they had been out no later than its arrival. A rooster crowed and several animals shuffled around the barnyard, but the house remained silent. Drizzt knew this was unusual, but he figured that the encounter in the mountains on the previous day had sent the farmers into hiding. Possibly the family had left the farm altogether, seeking the shelter of the larger cluster of houses in the village proper. The thoughts weighed heavily on Drizzt; again he had disrupted the lives of those around him simply by showing his face. He remembered Blingdenstone, the city of svirfneblin gnomes, and the tumult and potential danger his appearance had brought to them.

The sunny day brightened, but a chill breeze blew down off the mountains. Still not a person stirred in the farmyard or within the house, as far as Drizzt could tell. The drow watched it all, growing more concerned with each passing second.

A familiar buzzing noise shook Drizzt from his contemplations. He drew his lone scimitar and glanced around. He wished he could call Guenhwyvar, but not enough time had passed since the cat's last visit. The panther needed to rest in its astral home for another day before it would be strong enough to walk beside Drizzt. Seeing nothing in his immediate area, Drizzt moved between the trunks of two large trees, a more defensible position against the sprite's blinding speed.

The buzzing was gone an instant later, and the sprite was nowhere to be seen. Drizzt spent the rest of that day moving about the brush, setting trip wires and digging shallow pits. If he and the sprite were to battle again, the drow was determined to change the outcome.

The lengthening shadows and crimson western sky brought Drizzt's attention back to the Thistledown farm. No candles were lighted within the farmhouse to defeat the deepening gloom.

Drizzt grew ever more concerned. The return of the nasty sprite had poignantly reminded him of the dangers in the region, and with the continuing inactivity in the farmyard, a fear budded within him, took root, and quickly grew into a sense of dread.

Twilight darkened into night. The moon rose and climbed steadily into the eastern sky.

Still not a candle burned in the house, and not a sound came through the darkened windows.

Drizzt slipped out of the brush and darted across the short back field. He had no intentions of getting close to the house; he just wanted to see what he might learn. Perhaps the horses and the farmer's small wagon would be gone, lending evidence to Drizzt's earlier suspicion that the farmers had taken refuge in the village.

When he came around the side of the barn and saw the broken door, Drizzt knew instinctively that this was not the case. His fears grew with every step. He peered through the barn door and was not surprised to see the wagon sitting in the middle of the barn and the stalls full of horses.

To the side of the wagon, though, lay the older woman, crumbled and covered in her own dried blood. Drizzt went to her and knew at once that she was dead, killed by some sharp-edged weapon. Immediately his thoughts went to the evil sprite and his own missing scimitar. When he found the other corpse, behind the wagon, he knew that some other monster, something more vicious and powerful, had been involved. Drizzt couldn't even identify this second, half-eaten body.

Drizzt ran from the barn to the farmhouse, throwing out all caution. He found the bodies of the Thistledown men in the kitchen and to his ultimate horror, the children lying too still in their beds. Waves of revulsion and guilt rolled over the drow when he looked upon the young bodies. The word "drizzit" chimed painfully in his mind at the sight of the sandy-haired lad.

The tumult of Drizzt's emotions were too much for him. He covered his ears against that damning word, "drizzit!" but it echoed endlessly, haunting him, reminding him.

Unable to find his breath, Drizzt ran from the house. If he had searched the room more carefully, he would have found, under the bed, his missing scimitar, snapped in half and left for the villagers.

# Part Two

# The Ranger

Does anything in all the world force a heavier weight upon one's shoulders than guilt? I have felt the burden often, have carried it over many steps, on long roads.

Guilt resembles a sword with two edges. On the one hand it cuts for justice, imposing practical morality upon those who fear it. Guilt, the consequence of conscience, is what separates the goodly persons from the evil. Given a situation that promises gain, most drow can kill another, kin or otherwise, and walk away carrying no emotional burden at all. The drow assassin might fear retribution but will shed no tears for his victim.

To humans—and to surface elves, and to all of the other goodly races—the suffering imposed by conscience will usually far outweigh any external threats. Some would conclude that guilt–conscience–is the primary difference between the varied races of the Realms. In this regard, guilt must be considered a positive force.

But there is another side to that weighted emotion. Conscience does not always adhere to rational judgment. Guilt is always a self-imposed burden, but is not always rightly imposed. So it was for me along the road from Menzoberranzan to Icewind Dale. I carried out of Menzoberranzan guilt for Zaknafein, my father, sacrificed on my behalf. I carried into Blingdenstone guilt for Belwar Dissengulp, the svirfneblin my brother had maimed. Along the many roads there came many other burdens: Clacker, killed by the monster that hunted for me; the gnolls, slain by my own hand; and the farmers–most painfully–that simple farm family murdered by the barghest whelp.

Rationally I knew that I was not to blame, that the actions were beyond my influence, or in some cases, as with the gnolls, that I had acted properly. But rationale is little defense against the weight of guilt.

In time, bolstered by the confidence of trusted friends, I came to throw off many of those burdens. Others remain and always shall. I accept this as inevitable, and use the weight to guide my future steps.

This, I believe, is the true purpose of conscience.

–Drizzt Do'Urden

# 6

# SUNDABAR

"Oh, enough, Fret," the tall woman said to the white-robed, white-bearded dwarf, batting his hands away. She ran her fingers through her thick, brown hair, messing it considerably.

"Tsk, tsk," the dwarf replied, immediately moving his hands back to the dirty spot on the woman's cloak. He brushed frantically, but the ranger's continual shifting kept him from accomplishing much. "Why, Mistress Falconhand I do believe that you would do well to consult a few books on proper behavior."

"I just rode in from Silverymoon," Dove Falconhand replied indignantly, tossing a wink to Gabriel, the other fighter in the room, a tall and stern-faced man. "One tends to collect some dirt on the road."

"Nearly a tenday ago!" the dwarf protested. "You attended the banquet last night in this very cloak!" The dwarf then noticed that in his fuss over Dove's cloak he had smudged his silken robes, and that catastrophe turned his attention from the ranger.

"Dear Fret," Dove went on, licking a finger and casually rubbing it over the spot on her cloak, "you are the most unusual of attendants."

The dwarf's face went beet red, and he stamped a shiny slipper on the tiled floor. "Attendant?" he huffed. "I should say . . ."

"Then do!" Dove laughed.

"I am the most—one of the most—accomplished sages in the north! My thesis concerning the proper etiquette of racial banquets—"

"Or lack of proper etiquette—" Gabriel couldn't help but interrupt. The dwarf turned on him sourly—"at least where dwarves are concerned," the tall fighter finished with an innocent shrug.

The dwarf trembled visibly and his slippers played a respectable beat on the hard floor.

"Oh, dear Fret," Dove offered, dropping a comforting hand on the dwarf's shoulder and running it along the length of his perfectly trimmed, yellow beard.

"Fred!" the dwarf retorted sharply, pushing the ranger's hand away. "Fredegar!"

Dove and Gabriel looked at each other for one brief, knowing moment, then cried out the dwarf's surname in an explosion of laughter. "Rockcrusher!"

"Fredegar Quilldipper would be more to the point!" Gabriel added. One look at the fuming dwarf told the man that the time had passed for leaving, so he scooped up his pack and darted from the room, pausing only to slip one final wink Dove's way.

"I only desired to help." The dwarf dropped his hands into impossibly deep pockets and his head drooped low.

"So you have!" Dove cried to comfort him.

"I mean, you do have an audience with Helm Dwarf-friend," Fret went on, regaining some pride. "One should be proper when seeing the Master of Sundabar."

"Indeed one should," Dove readily agreed. "Yet all I have to wear you see before you, dear Fret, stained and dirtied from the road. I am afraid that I shall not cut a very fine figure in the eyes of Sundabar's master. He and my sister have become such friends." It was Dove's turn to feign a vulnerable pout, and though her sword had turned many a giant into vulture food, the strong ranger could play this game better than most.

"Whatever shall I do?" She cocked her head curiously as she glanced at the dwarf. "Perhaps," she teased. "If only . . ."

Fret's face began to brighten at the hint.

"No," Dove said with a heavy sigh. "I could never impose so upon you."

Fret verily bounced with glee, clapping his thick hands together. "Indeed you could, Mistress Falconhand! Indeed you could!"

Dove bit her lip to forestall any further demeaning laughter as the excited dwarf skipped out of the room. While she often teased Fret, Dove would readily admit that she loved the little dwarf. Fret had spent many years in Silverymoon, where Dove's sister ruled, and had made many contributions to the famed library there. Fret really was a noted sage, known for his extensive research into the customs of various races, both good and evil, and he was an expert on issues demihuman. He also was a fine composer. How many times, Dove wondered with sincere humility, had she ridden along a mountain trail, whistling a cheery melody composed by this very same dwarf?

"Dear Fret," the ranger whispered under her breath when the dwarf returned, a silken gown draped over one arm—but carefully folded so that it would not drag across the floor!—assorted jewelry and a pair of stylish shoes in his other hand a dozen pins sticking out from between his pursed lips, and a measuring string looped over one ear. Dove hid her smile and decided to give the dwarf this one battle. She would tiptoe into Helm Dwarf-friend's audience hall in a silken gown, the picture of Ladydom, with the diminutive sage huffing proudly by her side.

All the while, Dove knew, the shoes would pinch and bite at her feet and the gown would find some place to itch where she could not reach. Alas for the duties of station, Dove thought as she stared at the gown and accessories. She looked into Fret's beaming face then and realized that it was worth all the trouble.

Alas for the duties of friendship, she mused.

⚔ ⚔ ⚔ ⚔ ⚔

The farmer had ridden straight through for more than a day; the sighting of a dark elf often had such effects on simple villagers. He had taken two horses out of Maldobar; one he had left a score of miles behind, halfway between the two towns. If he was lucky, he'd find the animal unharmed on the return trip. The second horse, the farmer's prized stallion, was beginning to tire. Still the farmer bent low in the saddle, spurring the steed on. The torches of Sundabar's night watch, high up on the city's thick stone walls, were in sight.

"Stop and speak your name!" came the formal cry from the captain of the gate guards when the rider approached, half an hour later.

⚔ ⚔ ⚔ ⚔ ⚔

Dove leaned on Fret for support as they followed Helm's attendant down the long and decorated corridor to the audience room. The ranger could cross a rope bridge without handrails, could fire her bow with deadly accuracy atop a charging steed, could scramble up a tree in full chain armor, sword and shield in hand. But she could not, for all of her experience and agility, manage the fancy shoes that Fret had squeezed her feet into.

"And this gown," Dove whispered in exasperation, knowing that the impractical garment would split in six or seven places if she had occasion to swing her sword while wearing it, let alone inhaled too abruptly.

Fret looked up at her, wounded.

"This gown is surely the most beautiful . . ." Dove stuttered, careful not to send the tidy dwarf into a tantrum. "Truly I can find no words suitable to my gratitude, dear Fret."

The dwarf's gray eyes shone brightly, though he wasn't sure that he believed a word of it. Either way, Fret figured that Dove cared enough about him to go along with his suggestions, and that fact was all that really mattered to him.

"I beg a thousand pardons, my lady," came a voice from behind. The whole entourage turned to see the captain of the night watch, a farmer by his side, trotting down the somber hallway.

"Good captain!" Fret protested at the violation of protocol. "If you desire an audience with the lady, you must make an introduction in the hall. Then, and only then, and only if the master allows, you may . . ."

Dove dropped a hand on the dwarf's shoulder to silence him. She recognized the urgency etched onto the men's faces, a look the adventuring heroine had seen many times. "Do go on, Captain," she prompted. To placate Fret, she added, "We have a few moments before our audience is set to begin. Master Helm will not be kept waiting."

The farmer stepped forward boldly. "A thousand pardons for myself, my lady," he began, fingering his cap nervously in his hands. "I am but a farmer from Maldobar, a small village north . . ."

"I know of Maldobar," Dove assured him. "Many times I have viewed the place from the mountains. A fine and sturdy community." The farmer brightened at her description. "No harm has befallen Maldobar, I pray."

"Not as yet, my lady," the farmer replied, "but we've sighted trouble, we're not to doubting." He paused and looked to the captain for support. "Drow."

Dove's eyes widened at the news. Even Fret, tapping his foot impatiently throughout the conversation, stopped and took note.

"How many?" Dove asked.

"Only one, as we have seen. We're fearing he's a scout or spy, and up to no good."

Dove nodded her agreement. "Who has seen the drow?"

"Children first," the farmer replied, drawing a sigh from Fret and setting the dwarf's foot impatiently tapping once again.

"Children?" the dwarf huffed.

The farmer's determination did not waver. "Then McGristle saw him," he said, eyeing Dove directly, "and McGristle's seen a lot!"

"What is a McGristle?" Fret huffed.

"Roddy McGristle," Dove answered, somewhat sourly, before the farmer could explain. "A noted bounty hunter and fur trapper."

"The drow killed one of Roddy's dogs," the farmer put in excitedly, "and nearly cut down Roddy! Dropped a tree right on him! He's lost an ear for the experience."

Dove didn't quite understand what the farmer was talking about, but she really didn't need to. A dark elf had been seen and confirmed in the region, and that fact alone set the ranger into motion. She flipped off her fancy shoes and handed them to Fret, then told one of the attendants to go straight off and find her traveling companions and told the other to deliver her regrets to the Master of Sundabar.

"But Lady Falconhand!" Fret cried.

"No time for pleasantries," Dove replied, and Fret could tell by her obvious excitement that she was not too disappointed at canceling her audience with Helm. Already she was wiggling about, trying to open the catch on the back of her magnificent gown.

"Your sister will not be pleased," Fret growled loudly over the tapping of his boot.

"My sister hung up her backpack long ago," Dove retorted, "but mine still wears the fresh dirt of the road!"

"Indeed," the dwarf mumbled, not in a complimentary way.

"Ye mean to come, then?" the farmer asked hopefully.

"Of course," Dove replied. "No reputable ranger could ignore the sighting of a dark elf! My three companions and I will set out for Maldobar this very night, though I beg that you remain here, good farmer. You have ridden hard—it is obvious—and need sleep." Dove glanced around curiously for a moment, then put a finger to her pursed lips.

"What?" the annoyed dwarf asked her.

Dove's face brightened as her gaze dropped down to Fret. "I have little experience with dark elves," she began, "and my companions, to my knowledge, have never dealt with one." Her widening smile set Fret back on his heels.

"Come, dear Fret," Dove purred at the dwarf. Her bare feet slapping conspicuously on the tiled floor, she led Fret, the captain, and the farmer from Maldobar down the hallway to Helm's audience room.

Fret was confused—and hopeful—for a moment by Dove's sudden change of direction. As soon as Dove began talking to Helm, Fret's master, apologizing for the unexpected inconvenience and asking Helm to send along one who might aid in the mission to Maldobar, the dwarf began to understand.

⚔ ⚔ ⚔ ⚔ ⚔

By the time the sun found its way above the eastern horizon the next morning, Dove's party, which included an elf archer and two powerful human fighters, had ridden more than ten miles from Sundabar's heavy gate.

"Ugh!" Fret groaned when the light increased. He rode a sturdy Adbar pony at Dove's side. "See how the mud has soiled my fine clothes! Surely it will be the end of us all! To die filthy on a gods-forsaken road!"

"Pen a song about it," Dove suggested, returning the widening smiles of her other three companions. "The Ballad of the Five Choked Adventurers, it shall be named."

Fret's angry glare lasted only the moment it took Dove to remind him that Helm Dwarf-friend, the Master of Sundabar himself, had commissioned Fret to travel along.

# 7 Simmering Rage

On the same morning that Dove's party left on the road to Maldobar, Drizzt set out on a journey of his own. The initial horror of his gruesome discovery the previous night had not diminished, and the drow feared that it never would, but another emotion had also entered Drizzt's thinking. He could do nothing for the innocent farmers and their children, nothing except avenge their deaths. That thought was not so pleasing to Drizzt; he had left the Underdark behind, and the savagery as well, he had hoped. With the images of the carnage still so horribly clear in his mind, and all alone as he was, Drizzt could look only to his scimitar for justice.

Drizzt took two precautions before he set out on the murderer's trail. First, he crept back down to the farmyard, to the back of the house, where the farmers had placed a broken plowshare. The metal blade was heavy, but the determined drow hoisted it and carried it away without a thought to the discomfort.

Drizzt then called Guenhwyvar. As soon as the panther arrived and took note of Drizzt's scowl, it dropped into an alert crouch. Guenhwyvar had been around Drizzt long enough to recognize that expression and to believe that they would see battle before it returned to its astral home.

They moved off before dawn, Guenhwyvar easily following the barghest's clear trail, as Ulgulu had hoped. Their pace was slow, with Drizzt hindered by the plowshare, but steady, and as soon as Drizzt caught the sound of a distant buzzing noise, he knew he had done right in collecting the cumbersome item.

Still, the remainder of the morning passed without incident. The trail led the companions into a rocky ravine and to the base of a high, uneven cliff. Drizzt feared that he might have to scale the cliff face—and leave the plowshare behind—but soon he spotted a single narrow trail winding up along the wall. The ascending path remained smooth as it wound around sheer bends in the cliff face, blind and dangerous turns. Wanting to use the terrain to his advantage, Drizzt sent Guenhwyvar far ahead and moved along by himself, dragging the plowshare and feeling vulnerable on the open cliff.

That feeling did nothing to quench the simmering fires in Drizzt's lavender eyes, though, which burned clearly from under the low-pulled cowl of his oversized gnoll cloak. If the sight of the ravine looming just to the side unnerved the drow, he needed only to remember the farmers. A short while later, when Drizzt heard the expected buzzing noise from somewhere lower on the narrow trail, he only smiled.

The buzz quickly closed from behind. Drizzt fell back against the cliff wall and snapped out his scimitar, carefully monitoring the time it took the sprite to close.

Tephanis flashed beside the drow, the quickling's little dagger darting and prodding for an opening in the defensive twists of the waving scimitar. The sprite was gone in an instant, moving up ahead of Drizzt, but Tephanis had scored a hit, nicking Drizzt on one shoulder.

Drizzt inspected the wound and nodded gravely, accepting it as a minor inconvenience. He knew he could not defeat the blinding attack, and he knew, too, that allowing this first strike had been necessary for his ultimate victory. A growl on the path up ahead put Drizzt quickly back on alert. Guenhwyvar had met the sprite, and the panther, with flashing paws that could match the quickling's speed, no doubt had turned the thing back around.

Again Drizzt put his back to the wall, monitoring the buzzing approach. Just as the sprite came around the corner, Drizzt jumped out onto the narrow path, his scimitar at the ready. The drow's other hand was less conspicuous and held steady a metal object, ready to tilt it out to block the opening.

The speeding sprite cut back in toward the wall, easily able, as Drizzt realized, to avoid the scimitar. But in his narrow focus on his target, the sprite failed to notice Drizzt's other hand.

Drizzt hardly registered the sprite's movements, but the sudden "Bong!" and the sharp vibrations in his hand as the creature smacked into the plowshare brought a satisfied grin to his lips. He let the plowshare drop and scooped up the unconscious sprite by the throat, holding it clear of the ground. Guenhwyvar bounded around the bend about the same time the sprite shook the dizziness from his sharp-featured head, his long and pointed ears nearly flopping right over the other side of his head with each movement.

"What creature are you?" Drizzt asked in the goblin tongue, the language that had worked for him with the gnoll band. To his surprise, he found that the sprite understood, though his high-pitched, blurred response came too quickly for Drizzt to even begin to understand.

He gave the sprite a quick jerk to silence him, then growled, "One word at a time! What is your name?"

"Tephanis," the sprite said indignantly. Tephanis could move his legs a hundred times a second, but they didn't do him much good while he was suspended in the air. The sprite glanced down to the narrow ledge and saw his small dagger lying next to the dented plowshare.

Drizzt's scimitar moved in dangerously. "Did you kill the farmers?" he asked bluntly. He almost struck in response to the sprite's ensuing chuckle.

"No," Tephanis said quickly.

"Who did?"

"Ulgulu!" the sprite proclaimed. Tephanis pointed up the path and blurted out a stream of excited words. Drizzt managed to make out a few, "Ulgulu . . . waiting . . . dinner," being the most disturbing of them.

Drizzt really didn't know what he would do with the captured sprite. Tephanis was simply too fast for Drizzt to safely handle. He looked to

Guenhwyvar, sitting casually a few feet up the path, but the panther only yawned and stretched.

Drizzt was about to come back with another question, to try to figure out where Tephanis fit into the whole scenario, but the cocky sprite decided that he had suffered enough of the encounter. His hands moving too fast for Drizzt to react, Tephanis reached down into his boot, produced another knife, and slashed at Drizzt's already injured wrist.

This time, the cocky sprite had underestimated his opponent. Drizzt could not match the sprite's speed, could not even follow the tiny, darting dagger. As painful as the wounds were, though, Drizzt was too filled with rage to take note. He only tightened his grip on the sprite's collar and thrust his scimitar ahead. Even with such limited mobility, Tephanis was quick enough and nimble enough to dodge, laughing wildly all the while.

The sprite struck back, digging a deeper cut into Drizzt's forearm. Finally Drizzt chose a tactic that Tephanis could not counter, one that took the sprite's advantage away. He slammed Tephanis into the wall, then tossed the stunned creature off the cliff.

⚔ ⚔ ⚔ ⚔ ⚔

Some time later, Drizzt and Guenhwyvar crouched in the brush at the base of a steep, rocky slope. At the top, behind carefully placed bushes and branches, lay a cave, and every so often, goblin voices rolled out.

Beside the cave, to the side of the sloping ground was a steep drop. Beyond the cave, the mountain climbed on at an even greater angle. The tracks, though they were sometimes scarce on the bare stone, had led Drizzt and Guenhwyvar to this spot; there could be no doubt that the monster who slaughtered the farmers was in the cave.

Drizzt again fought with his decision to avenge the farmers' deaths. He would have preferred a more civilized justice, a lawful court, but what was he to do? He certainly could not go to the human villagers with his suspicions, nor to anyone else. Crouching in the bush, Drizzt thought again of the farmers, of the sandy-haired boy, of the pretty girl, barely a woman, and of the young man he had disarmed in the blueberry patch. Drizzt fought hard to keep his breathing steady. In the wild Underdark he had sometimes given in to his instinctive urges, a darker side of himself that fought with brutal and deadly efficiency, and Drizzt could feel that alter-ego welling within him once again. At first, he tried to sublimate the rage, but then he remembered the lessons he had learned. This darker side was a part of him, a tool for survival, and was not altogether evil.

It was necessary.

Drizzt understood his disadvantage in the situation, however. He had no idea how many enemies he would encounter, or even what type of monsters they might be. He heard goblins, but the carnage at the farmhouse indicated that something much more powerful was involved. Drizzt's good judgment told him to sit and watch, to learn more of his enemies.

Another fleeting instant of remembrance, the scene at the farmhouse, threw that good judgment aside. Scimitar in one hand the sprite's dagger in another, Drizzt stalked up the stony hill. He didn't slow when he neared the cave, but merely ripped the brush aside and walked straight in.

Guenhwyvar hesitated and watched from behind, confused by the drow's straightforward tactics.

* * * * *

Tephanis felt cool air brushing by his face and thought for a moment that he was enjoying some pleasant dream. The sprite came out of his delusion quickly, though, and realized that he was fast approaching the ground. Fortunately, Tephanis was not far from the cliff. He sent his hands and feet spinning rapidly enough to produce a constant humming sound and clawed and kicked at the cliff in an effort to slow his descent. In the meantime, he began the incantations to a levitation spell, possibly the only thing that could save him.

A few agonizingly slow seconds passed before the sprite felt his body buoyed by the spell. He still hit the ground hard, but he realized that his wounds were minor.

Tephanis stood relatively slowly and dusted himself off. His first thought was to go and warn Ulgulu of the approaching drow, but he reconsidered at once. He could not levitate up to the cave complex in time to warn the barghest, and there was only one path up the cliff face—which the drow was on.

Tephanis had no desire to face that one again.

⚔ ⚔ ⚔ ⚔ ⚔

Ulgulu had not tried to cover his tracks at all. The dark elf had served the barghest's needs; now he planned to make a meal of Drizzt, one that might bring him into maturity and allow him to return to Gehenna.

Ulgulu's two goblin guards were not too surprised at Drizzt's entrance. Ulgulu had told them to expect the drow and to simply delay him out in the entry room until the barghest could come and attend to him. The goblins halted their conversation abruptly, dropped their spears in a blocking cross over the curtain, and puffed out their scrawny chests, foolishly following their boss's instructions as Drizzt approached.

"None can go in—" one of them began, but then, in a single swipe of Drizzt's scimitar, both the goblin and its companion staggered down, clutching at their opened throats. The spear barrier fell away and Drizzt never even slowed as he stalked through the curtain.

In the middle of the inner room, the drow saw his enemy. Scarlet-skinned and giant-sized, the barghest waited with crossed arms and a wicked, confident grin.

Drizzt threw the dagger and charged right in behind it. That throw saved the drow's life, for when the dagger passed harmlessly through his enemy's body, Drizzt recognized the trap. He came in anyway, unable to break his momentum, and his scimitar entered the image without finding anything tangible to cut into.

The real barghest was behind the stone throne at the back of the room. Using another power of his considerable magical repertoire, Kempfana had sent an image of himself into the middle of the room to hold the drow in place.

Immediately Drizzt's instincts told him that he had been set up. This was no real monster he faced but an apparition meant to keep him in the open and vulnerable. The room was sparsely furnished; nothing nearby offered any cover.

Ulgulu, levitating above the drow, came down quickly, lighting softly behind him. The plan was perfect and the target was right in place.

Drizzt, his reflexes and muscles trained and honed to fighting perfection, sensed the presence and dived forward into the image as Ulgulu launched a heavy blow. The barghest's huge hand only clipped Drizzt's flowing hair, but that alone nearly ripped the drow's head to the side.

Drizzt half-turned his body as he dived, rolling back to his feet facing Ulgulu. He met a monster even larger than the giant image, but that fact did nothing to intimidate the enraged drow. Like a stretched cord, Drizzt snapped straight back at the barghest. By the time Ulgulu even recovered from his unexpected miss, Drizzt's lone scimitar had poked him three times in the belly and had dug a neat little hole under his chin.

The barghest roared in rage but was not too badly hurt, for Drizzt's drow-made weapon had lost most of its magic in the drow's time on the surface and only magical weapons—such as Guenhwyvar's claws and teeth—could truly harm a creature from Gehenna's rifts.

The huge panther slammed onto the back of Ulgulu's head with enough force to drop the barghest facedown on the floor. Never had Ulgulu felt such pain as Guenhwyvar's claws raked across his head.

Drizzt moved to join in, when he heard a shuffle from the back of the room. Kempfana came charging out from behind the throne, bellowing in protest.

It was Drizzt's turn to utilize some magic. He threw a globe of darkness in the scarlet-skinned barghest's path, then dived into it himself, crouching on his hands and knees. Unable to slow, Kempfana roared in, stumbled over the braced drow—kicking Drizzt with enough force to blast the air from his lungs—and fell heavily out the other side of the darkness.

Kempfana shook his head to clear it and planted his huge hands to rise. Drizzt was on the barghest's back in no time, hacking away wildly with his vicious scimitar. Blood matted Kempfana's hair by the time he was able to brace himself enough to throw the drow off. He staggered to his feet dizzily and turned to face the drow.

---

Across the room, Ulgulu crawled and tumbled, rolled and twisted. The panther was too quick and too sleek for the giant's lumbering counters. A dozen gashes scarred Ulgulu's face and now Guenhwyvar had its teeth clamped on the back of the giant's neck and all four paws raking at the giant's back.

Ulgulu had another option, though. Bones crackled and reformed. Ulgulu's scarred face became an elongated snout filled with wicked canine teeth. Thick hair sprouted from all over the giant, fending off Guenhwyvar's claw attacks. Flailing arms became kicking paws.

Guenhwyvar battled a gigantic wolf, and the panther's advantage was short-lived.

---

Kempfana stalked in slowly, showing Drizzt new respect.

"You killed them all," Drizzt said in the goblin tongue, his voice so utterly cold that it stopped the scarlet-skinned barghest in his tracks.

Kempfana was not a stupid creature. The barghest recognized the explosive rage in this drow and had felt the sharp bite of the scimitar. Kempfana knew better than to walk straight in, so again he called upon his otherworldly skills. In the blink of an orange-burning eye, the scarlet-skinned barghest was gone, stepping through an extradimensional door and reappearing right behind Drizzt.

As soon as Kempfana disappeared, Drizzt instinctively broke to the side. The blow from behind came quicker, though, landing squarely on Drizzt's back and launching him across the room. Drizzt crashed into the base of one wall and came up into a kneel, gasping for his breath.

Kempfana did stalk straight in this time; the drow had dropped his scimitar halfway to the wall, too far away for Drizzt to grasp.

The great barghest-wolf, nearly twice Guenhwyvar's size, rolled over and straddled the panther. Great jaws snapped near Guenhwyvar's throat and face, the panther batting wildly to hold them at bay. Guenhwyvar could not hope to win an even fight against the wolf. The only advantage the panther retained was mobility. Like a black-shafted arrow, Guenhwyvar darted out from under the wolf and toward the curtain.

Ulgulu howled and gave chase, ripping the curtain down and charging on, toward the waning daylight.

Guenhwyvar came out of the cave as Ulgulu tore through the curtain, pivoted instantly, and leaped straight up to the slopes above the entrance. When the great wolf came out, the panther again crashed down on Ulgulu's back and resumed its raking and slashing.

⚔ ⚔ ⚔ ⚔ ⚔

"Ulgulu killed the farmers, not I," Kempfana growled as he approached. He kicked Drizzt's scimitar across to the other side of the room. "Ulgulu wants you—you who killed his gnolls. But I shall kill you, drow warrior. I shall feast on your life force so that I may gain in strength!"

Drizzt, still trying to find his breath, hardly heard the words. The only thoughts that occurred to him were the images of the dead farmers, images that gave Drizzt courage. The barghest drew near and Drizzt snapped a vile gaze upon him, a determined gaze not lessened in the least by the drow's obviously desperate situation.

Kempfana hesitated at the sight of those narrowed, burning eyes, and the barghest's delay brought Drizzt all the time he needed. He had fought giant monsters before, most notably hook horrors. Always Drizzt's scimitars had ended those battles, but for his initial strikes, he had, every time, used only his own body. The pain in his back was no match for his mounting rage. He rushed out from the wall, remaining in a crouch, and dived through Kempfana's legs, spinning and catching a hold behind the barghest's knee.

Kempfana, unconcerned, lurched down to grab the squirming drow. Drizzt eluded the giant's grasp long enough to find some leverage. Still,

Kempfana accepted the attacks as a mere inconvenience. When Drizzt put the barghest off balance, Kempfana willingly toppled, meaning to crush the wiry little elf. Again Drizzt was too quick for the barghest. He twisted out from under the falling giant, put his feet back under him, and sprinted for the opposite end of the chamber.

"No, you shall not!" Kempfana bellowed, crawling then running in pursuit. Just as Drizzt scooped up his scimitar, giant arms wrapped around him and easily lifted him off the ground.

"Crush you and bite you!" Kempfana roared, and indeed, Drizzt heard one of his ribs crack. He tried to wiggle around to face his foe, then gave up on the notion, concentrating instead on freeing his sword arm.

Another rib snapped; Kempfana's huge arms tightened. The barghest did not want to simply kill the drow, though, realizing the great gains toward maturity he could make by devouring so powerful an enemy, by feeding on Drizzt's life force.

"Bite you, drow." The giant laughed. "Feast!"

Drizzt grasped his scimitar in both hands with strength inspired by the images of the farmhouse. He tore the weapon loose and snapped it straight back over his head. The blade entered Kempfana's open, eager mouth and dived down the monster's throat.

Drizzt twisted it and turned it.

Kempfana whipped about wildly and Drizzt's muscles and joints nearly ripped apart under the strain. The drow had found his focus, though, the scimitar hilt, and he continued to twist and turn.

Kempfana went down heavily, gurgling, and rolled onto Drizzt, trying to squash the life out of him. Pain began to seep into Drizzt's consciousness.

"No!" he cried, grabbing at the image of the sandy-haired boy, slain in his bed. Still Drizzt twisted and turned the blade. The gurgling continued, a wheezing sound of air rising through choking blood. Drizzt knew that this battle was won when the creature above him no longer moved.

Drizzt wanted only to curl up and find his breath but told himself that he was not yet finished. He crawled out from under Kempfana, wiped the blood, his own blood, from his lips, unceremoniously ripped his scimitar free of Kempfana's mouth, and retrieved his dagger.

He knew that his wounds were serious, could prove fatal if he didn't attend to them immediately. His breath continued to come in forced, bloodied gasps. It didn't concern him, though, for Ulgulu, the monster who had killed the farmers, still lived.

⚔ ⚔ ⚔ ⚔ ⚔

Guenhwyvar sprang from the giant wolf's back, again finding a tenuous footing on the steep slope above the cave entrance. Ulgulu spun, snarling, and leaped up at the panther, clawing and raking at the stones in an effort to get higher.

Guenhwyvar leaped out over the barghest-wolf, pivoted immediately, and slashed at Ulgulu's backside. The wolf spun but Guenhwyvar leaped by, again to the slope.

The game of hit-and-run went on for several moments, Guenhwyvar striking, then darting away. Finally, though, the wolf anticipated the panther's dodge. Ulgulu brought the leaping panther down in his massive jaws. Guenhwyvar squirmed and tore free, but came up near the steep gorge. Ulgulu hovered over the cat, blocking any escape.

Drizzt exited the cave as the great wolf bore down, pushing Guenhwyvar back. Pebbles rolled out into the gorge; the panther's back legs slipped and clawed back, trying to find a hold. Even mighty Guenhwyvar could not hold out against the weight and strength of the barghest-wolf, Drizzt knew.

Drizzt saw immediately that he could not get the great wolf off Guenhwyvar in time. He pulled out the onyx figurine and tossed it near the combatants. "Be gone, Guenhwyvar!" he commanded.

Guenhwyvar normally would not desert its master in a time of such danger, but the panther understood what Drizzt had in mind. Ulgulu bore in powerfully, determinedly driving Guenhwyvar from the ledge.

Then the beast was pushing only intangible vapors. Ulgulu lurched forward and scrambled wildly, kicking more stones and the onyx figurine into the gorge. Overbalanced, the wolf could not find a hold, and Ulgulu was falling.

Bones popped again, and the canine fur thinned; Ulgulu could not enact a levitation spell in his canine form. Desperate, the barghest concentrated, reaching for his goblinoid form. The wolf maw shortened into a flat-featured face; paws thickened and reformed into arms.

The half-transformed creature didn't make it, but instead cracked into the stone.

Drizzt stepped off the ledge and into a levitation spell, moving down slowly and close to the rocky wall. As it had before, the spell soon died away. Drizzt bounced and clawed through the last twenty feet of the fall, coming to a hard stop at the rocky bottom. He saw the barghest twitching only a few feet away and tried to rise in defense, but darkness overwhelmed him.

⚔ ⚔ ⚔ ⚔ ⚔

Drizzt could not know how many hours had passed when a thunderous roar awakened him some time later. It was dark now and a cloudy night. Slowly the memories of the encounter came back to the dazed and injured drow. To his relief, he saw that Ulgulu lay still on the stone beside him, half a goblin and half a wolf, obviously quite dead.

A second roar, back up by the cave, turned the drow toward the ledge high above him. There stood Lagerbottoms, the hill giant, returned from a hunting trip and outraged by the carnage he had found.

Drizzt knew as soon as he managed to crawl to his feet that he could not fight another battle this day. He searched around for a moment, found the onyx figurine, and dropped it into his pouch. He wasn't too concerned for Guenhwyvar. He had seen the panther through worse calamities—caught in the explosion of a magical wand pulled into the Plane of Earth by an enraged elemental, even dropped into a lake of hissing acid. The figurine appeared undamaged, and Drizzt was certain that Guenhwyvar was now comfortably at rest in its astral home.

Drizzt, however, could afford no such rest. Already the giant had begun picking its way down the rocky slope. With a final look to Ulgulu, Drizzt felt a sense of vengeance that did little to defeat the agonizing, bitter memories of the slaughtered farmers. He set off, moving farther into the wild mountains, running from the giant and from the guilt.

# 8
# Clues and Riddles

More than a day had passed since the massacre when the first of the Thistledowns' neighbors rode out to their secluded farm. The stench of death alerted the visiting farmer to the carnage even before he looked in the house or barn.

He returned an hour later with Mayor Delmo and several other armed farmers at his side. They crawled through the Thistledown house and across the grounds cautiously, putting cloth over their faces to combat the terrible smell.

"Who could have done this?" the mayor demanded. "What monster?" As if in answer, one of the farmers walked out of the bedroom and into the kitchen, holding a broken scimitar in his hands.

"A drow weapon?" the farmer asked. "We should be getting McGristle."

Delmo hesitated. He expected the party from Sundabar to arrive any day and felt that the famed ranger Dove Falconhand would be better able to handle the situation than the volatile and uncontrollable mountain man.

The debate never really began, though, for the snarl of a dog alerted all in the house that McGristle had arrived. The burly, dirty man stalked into the kitchen, the side of his face horribly scarred and caked with brown, dried blood.

"Drow weapon!" he spat, recognizing the scimitar all too clearly. "Same as he used agin me!"

"The ranger will be in soon," Delmo began, but McGristle hardly listened. He stalked about the room and into the adjoining bedroom, gruffly tapping bodies with his foot and bending low to inspect some minor details.

"Saw the tracks outside," McGristle stated suddenly. "Two sets, I make 'em."

"The drow has an ally," the mayor reasoned. "More cause for us to wait for the party from Sundabar."

"Bah, ye hardly know if they're even comin'!" McGristle snorted. "Got to get after the drow now, while the trail's fine for my dog's nose!"

Several of the gathered farmers nodded their accord—until Delmo prudently reminded them of exactly what they might be facing.

"A single drow took you down, McGristle," the mayor said. "Now you think there's two of them, maybe more, and you want us to go and hunt them?"

"Bad fortune, it was, that took me down!" Roddy snapped back. He looked around, appealing to the now less-than-eager farmers. "I had that drow, had him cleaned an' dressed!"

The farmers milled nervously and whispered to each other as the mayor took Roddy by the arm and led him to the side of the room.

"Wait a day," Delmo begged. "Our chances will be much greater if the ranger comes."

Roddy didn't seem convinced. "My battle's my own to fight," he snarled. "He killed my dog an' left me ugly."

"You want him, and you'll have him," the mayor promised, "but there might be more on the table here than your dog or your pride."

Roddy's face contorted ominously, but the mayor was adamant. If a drow war party was indeed operating in the area, all of Maldobar was in imminent danger. The small group's greatest defense until help could arrive from Sundabar was unity, and that defense would fail if Roddy led a group of men—fighters who were scarce enough already—on a chase through the mountains. Benson Delmo was astute enough to know that he could not appeal to Roddy on those terms, though. While the mountain man had remained in Maldobar for a couple of years, he was, in essence, a drifter and owed no allegiance to the town.

Roddy turned away, deciding that the meeting was at its end, but the mayor boldly grabbed his arm and turned him back around. Roddy's dog bared its teeth and growled, but that threat was a small consideration to the fat man in light of the awful scowl that Roddy shot him.

"You'll have the drow," the mayor said quickly, "but wait for the help from Sundabar, I beg." He switched to terms that Roddy could truly appreciate. "I am a man of no small means, McGristle, and you were a bounty hunter before you got here, and still are, I'd expect."

Roddy's expression quickly changed from outrage to curiosity.

"Wait for the help, then go get the drow." The mayor paused, considering his forthcoming offer. He really had no experience in this sort of thing and while he didn't want to come in too low and spoil the interest he had sparked, he didn't want to tax his own purse strings any more than was necessary. "A thousand gold for the drow's head."

Roddy had played this pricing game many times. He hid his delight well; the mayor's offer was five times his normal fee and he would have gone after the drow in any case, with or without payment.

"Two thousand!" the mountain man grumbled without missing a beat, suspecting that more could be exacted for his troubles. The mayor rocked back on his heels but reminded himself several times that the town's very existence might be at stake.

"And not a copper less!" Roddy added, crossing his burly arms over his chest.

"Wait for Mistress Falconhand" Delmo said meekly, "and you shall have your two thousand."

⚔ ⚔ ⚔ ⚔ ⚔

All through the night, Lagerbottoms followed the wounded drow's trail. The bulky hill giant was not yet certain how it felt about the death of Ulgulu and Kempfana, the unasked for masters who had taken over his lair and his life. While Lagerbottoms feared any enemy who could defeat those two, the giant knew that the drow was sorely wounded.

Drizzt realized he was being followed but could do little to hide his tracks. One leg, injured in his bouncing descent into the ravine, dragged painfully and Drizzt had all he could do to keep ahead of the giant. When dawn came, bright and clear, Drizzt knew that his disadvantage had increased. He could not hope to escape the hill giant through the long and revealing light of day.

The trail dipped into a small grouping of variously sized trees, sprouting up wherever they could find cracks between the numerous boulders. Drizzt meant to go straight through—he saw no option other than continuing his flight—but while he leaned on one of the larger trees for support to catch his breath, a thought came to him. The tree's branches hung limply, supple and cordlike.

Drizzt glanced back along the trail. Higher up and crossing a bare expanse of rock, the relentless hill giant plodded along. Drizzt drew his scimitar with the one arm that still seemed to work and hacked down the longest branch he could find. Then he looked for a suitable boulder.

The giant crashed into the copse about a half-hour later, its huge club swinging at the end of one massive arm. Lagerbottoms stopped abruptly when the drow appeared from behind a tree, blocking the path.

Drizzt nearly sighed aloud when the giant stopped, exactly at the appointed area. He had feared that the huge monster would just continue on and swat him down, for Drizzt, injured as he was, could have offered little resistance. Seizing the moment of the monster's hesitation, Drizzt shouted "Halt!" in the goblin language and enacted a simple spell, limning the giant in blue-glowing, harmless flames.

Lagerbottoms shifted uncomfortably but made no advance toward this strange and dangerous enemy. Drizzt eyed the giant's shuffling feet with more than a casual interest.

"Why do you follow me?" Drizzt demanded. "Do you desire to join the others in the sleep of death?"

Lagerbottoms ran his plump tongue over dry lips. So far, this encounter hadn't gone as expected. Now the giant thought past those first instinctual urges that had led him out here and tried to consider the options. Ulgulu and Kempfana were dead; Lagerbottoms had his cave back. But the gnolls and goblins, too, were gone, and that pesky little quickling sprite hadn't been around for a while. A sudden thought came to the giant.

"Friends?" Lagerbottoms asked hopefully.

Though he was relieved to find that combat might be avoided, Drizzt was more than a little skeptical at the offer. The gnoll band had given him a similar offer, to disastrous ends, and this giant was obviously connected to those other monsters that Drizzt had just killed, those who had slaughtered the farm family.

"Friends to what end?" Drizzt asked tentatively, hoping against all reason that he might find this creature to be motivated by some principles, and not just by blood lust.

"To kill," Lagerbottoms replied, as though the answer had been obvious.

Drizzt snarled and jerked his head about in angry denial, his white mane flying wildly. He snapped the scimitar out of its sheath, hardly caring if the giant's foot had found the loop of his snare.

"Kill you!" Lagerbottoms cried, seeing the sudden turn, and the giant lifted his club and took a huge stride forward, a stride shortened by the vinelike branch pulling tightly around his ankle.

Drizzt checked his desire to rush in, reminding himself that the trap had been set into motion, and reminding himself, too, that in his present condition he would be hard put to survive against the formidable giant.

Lagerbottoms looked down at the noose and roared in outrage. The branch wasn't really a proper cord and the noose wasn't so tight. If Lagerbottoms had simply reached down, the giant easily could have slipped the noose off his foot. Hill giants, however, were never known for their intelligence.

"Kill you!" the giant cried again, and it kicked hard against the strain of the branch. Propelled by the considerable force of the kick, the large rock tied to the branch's other end, behind the giant, pelted forward through the underbrush and sailed into Lagerbottoms's back.

Lagerbottoms had started to cry out a third time, but the menacing threat came out as a *whoosh!* of forced air. The heavy club dropped to the ground and the giant, clutching its kidney area, dropped to one knee.

Drizzt hesitated a moment, not knowing whether to run or finish the kill. He didn't fear for himself; the giant would not be coming after him anytime soon, but he could not forget the lurid expression on the giant's face when the monster had said that they might kill together.

"How many other families will you slaughter?" Drizzt asked in the drow tongue.

Lagerbottoms could not begin to understand the language. He just grunted and snarled through the burning pain.

"How many?" Drizzt asked again, his hand wrenching over the scimitar's pommel and his eyes narrowing menacingly.

He came in fast and hard.

⚔ ⚔ ⚔ ⚔ ⚔

To Benson Delmo's absolute relief, the party from Sundabar—Dove Falconhand her three fighting companions, and Fret, the dwarven sage—came in later that day. The mayor offered the troupe food and rest, but as soon as Dove heard of the massacre at the Thistledown farm, she and her companions set straight out, with the mayor, Roddy McGristle, and several curious farmers close behind.

Dove was openly disappointed when they arrived at the secluded farm. A hundred sets of tracks obscured critical clues, and many of the items in the house, even the bodies, had been handled and moved. Still, Dove and her seasoned company moved about methodically, trying to decipher what they could of the gruesome scene.

"Foolish people!" Fret scolded the farmers when Dove and the others had completed their investigation. "You have aided our enemies!"

Several of the farmer-folk, even the mayor, looked around uncomfortably at the berating, but Roddy snarled and towered over the tidy dwarf. Dove quickly interceded.

"Your earlier presence here has marred some of the clues," Dove explained calmly, disarmingly, to the mayor as she prudently stepped between Fret and the burly mountain man. Dove had heard many tales of McGristle before, and his reputation was not one of predictability or calm.

"We didn't know," the mayor tried to explain.

"Of course not," Dove replied. "You reacted as anyone would have."

"Any novice," Fret remarked.

"Shut yer mouth!" McGristle growled, and so did his dog.

"Be at ease, good sir," Dove bade him. "We have too many enemies beyond the town to need some within."

"Novice?" McGristle barked at her. "I've hunted down a hundred men, an' I know enough o' this damned drow to find him."

"Do we know it was the drow?" Dove asked, genuinely doubting.

On a nod from Roddy, a farmer standing on the side of the room produced the broken scimitar.

"Drow weapon," Roddy said harshly, pointing to his scarred face. "I seen it up close!"

One look at the mountain man's jagged wound told Dove that the fine-edged scimitar had not caused it, but the ranger conceded the point, seeing no gain in further argument.

"And drow tracks," Roddy insisted. "The boot prints match close to the ones by the blueberry patch, where we seen the drow!"

Dove's gaze led all eyes to the barn. "Something powerful broke that door," she reasoned. "And the younger woman inside was not killed by any dark elf."

Roddy remained undaunted. "Drow's got a pet," he insisted. "Big, black panther. Damned big cat!"

Dove remained suspicious. She had seen no prints to match a panther's paws, and the way that a portion of the woman had been devoured, bones and all, did not fit any knowledge that she had of great cats. She kept her thoughts to herself, though, realizing that the gruff mountain man wanted no mysteries clouding his already-drawn conclusions.

"Now, if ye've had enough o' this place, let's get onto the trail," Roddy boomed. "My dog's got a scent, and the drow's got a lead big enough already!"

Dove flashed a concerned glance at the mayor, who turned away, embarrassed, under her penetrating gaze.

"Roddy McGristle's to go with you," Delmo explained, barely able to spit out the words, wishing that he had not made his emotionally inspired deal with Roddy. Seeing the cool-headedness of the woman ranger and her party, so drastically different from Roddy's violent temper, the mayor now thought it better that Dove and her companions handle the situation in their own way. But a deal was a deal.

"He'll be the only one from Maldobar joining your troupe," Delmo continued. "He is a seasoned hunter and knows this area better than any."

Again Dove, to Fret's disbelief, conceded the point.

"The day is fast on the wane," Dove said. She added pointedly to McGristle, "We go at first light."

"Drow's got too much of a lead already!" Roddy protested. "We should get after him now!"

"You assume that the drow is running," Dove replied, again calmly, but this time with a stern edge to her voice. "How many dead men once assumed the same of enemies?" This time, Roddy, perplexed, did not shout back. "The drow, or drow band could be holed up nearby. Would you like to come upon them unexpectedly, McGristle? Would it please you to battle dark elves in the dark of night?"

Roddy just threw up his hands, growled, and stalked away, his dog close on his heels.

The mayor offered Dove and her troupe lodging at his own house, but the ranger and her companions preferred to remain behind at the Thistledown farm. Dove smiled as the farmers departed, and Roddy set up camp just a short distance away, obviously to keep an eye on her. She wondered just how much a stake McGristle had in all of this and suspected that there was more to it than revenge for a scarred face and a lost ear.

"Are you really to let that beastly man come with us?" Fret asked later on, as the dwarf, Dove, and Gabriel sat around the blazing fire in the farmyard. The elven archer and the other member of the troupe were out on perimeter guard.

"It is their town, dear Fret," Dove explained. "And I cannot refute McGristle's knowledge of the region."

"But he is so dirty," the dwarf grumbled. Dove and Gabriel exchanged smiles, and Fret, realizing that he would get nowhere with his argument, turned down his bedroll and slipped in, purposefully spinning away from the others.

"Good old Quilldipper," mumbled Gabriel, but he noted that Dove's ensuing smile did little to diminish the sincere concern on her face.

"You've a problem, Lady Falconhand?" he asked.

Dove shrugged. "Some things do not fit properly in the order of things here," she began.

" 'Twas no panther that killed the woman in the barn," Gabriel remarked, for he, too, had noted some discrepancies.

"Nor did any drow kill the farmer, the one they named Bartholemew, in the kitchen," said Dove. "The beam that broke his neck was nearly snapped itself. Only a giant possesses such strength."

"Magic?" Gabriel asked.

Again Dove shrugged. "Drow magic is usually more subtle, according to our sage," she said, looking to Fret, who was already snoring quite loudly. "And more complete. Fret does not believe that drow magic killed Bartholemew or the woman, or destroyed the barn door. And there is another mystery on the matter of the tracks."

"Two sets," Gabriel said, "and made nearly a day apart."

"And of differing depths," added Dove. "One set, the second, might indeed have been those of a dark elf, but the other, the set of the killer, went too deep for an elf's light steps."

"An agent of the drow?" Gabriel offered. "Conjured denizen of the lower planes, perhaps? Might it be that the dark elf came down the next day to inspect its monster's work?" This time, Gabriel joined Dove in her confused shrug.

"So we shall learn," Dove said. Gabriel lit a pipe then, and Dove drifted off into slumber.

⚔ ⚔ ⚔ ⚔ ⚔

"Oh-master, my-master," Tephanis crooned, seeing the grotesque form of the broken, half-transformed barghest. The quickling didn't really care all that much for Ulgulu or the barghest's brother, but their deaths left some severe implications for the sprite's future path. Tephanis had joined Ulgulu's group for mutual gain. Before the barghests came along, the little sprite had spent his days in solitude, stealing whenever he could from nearby villages. He had done all right for himself, but his life had been a lonely and unexciting existence.

Ulgulu had changed all of that. The barghest army offered protection and companionship, and Ulgulu, always scheming for new and more devious kills, had provided Tephanis with unending important missions.

Now the quickling had to walk away from it all, for Ulgulu was dead and Kempfana was dead, and nothing Tephanis could do would change those simple facts.

"Lagerbottoms?" the quickling asked himself suddenly. He thought that the hill giant, the only member missing from the lair, might prove a fine companion. Tephanis saw the giant's tracks clearly enough, heading away from the cave area and out into the deeper mountains. He clapped his hands excitedly, perhaps a hundred times in the next second, then was off, speeding away to find a new friend.

⚔ ⚔ ⚔ ⚔ ⚔

Far up in the mountains, Drizzt Do'Urden looked upon the lights of Maldobar for the last time. Since he had come down from the high peaks after his unpleasant encounter with the skunk, the drow had found a world of savagery nearly equal to the dark realm he had left behind. Whatever hopes Drizzt had realized in his days watching the farming family were lost to him now, buried under the weight of guilt and the awful images of carnage that he knew would haunt him forever.

The drow's physical pain had lessened a bit; he could draw his breath fully now, though the effort sorely stung, and the cuts on his arms and legs had closed. He would survive.

Looking down at Maldobar, another place that he could never call home, Drizzt wondered if that might be a good thing.

# 9 The Chase

"What is it?" Fret asked, cautiously moving behind the folds of Dove's forest-green cape.

Dove, and even Roddy, also moved tentatively, for while the creature seemed dead, they had never seen anything quite like it. It appeared to be some strange, giant-sized mutation between a goblin and a wolf.

They gained in courage as they neared the body, convinced that it was truly dead. Dove bent low and tapped it with her sword.

"It has been dead for more than a day, by my guess," she announced.

"But what is it?" Fret asked again.

"Half-breed," Roddy muttered.

Dove closely inspected the creature's strange joints. She noted, too, the many wounds inflicted upon the thing—tearing wounds, like those caused by the scratching of a great cat.

"Shape-changer," guessed Gabriel, keeping watch at the side of the rocky area.

Dove nodded. "Killed halfway through."

"I never heared of any goblin wizards," Roddy protested.

"Oh, yes," Fret began, smoothing the sleeves of his soft-clothed tunic. "There was, of course, Grubby the Wiseless, pretended archmage, who . . ."

A whistle from high above stopped the dwarf. Up on the ledge stood

Kellindil, the elven archer, waving his arms about. "More up here," the elf called when he had their attention. "Two goblins and a red-skinned giant, the likes of which I have never seen!"

Dove scanned the cliff. She figured that she could scale it, but one look at poor Fret told her that they would have to go back to the trail, a journey of more than a mile. "You remain here," she said to Gabriel. The stern-faced man nodded and moved off to a defensive position among some boulders, while Dove, Roddy, and Fret headed back along the ravine.

Halfway up the single winding path that moved along the cliff, they met Darda, the remaining fighter of the troupe. A short and heavily muscled man, he scratched his stubbly beard and examined what looked to be a plowshare.

"That's Thistledown's!" Roddy cried. "I seen it out back of his farm, set for fixing!"

"Why is it up here?" Dove asked.

"And why might it be bloodied?" added Darda, showing them the stains on the concave side. The fighter looked over the ledge into the ravine, then back to the plowshare. "Some unfortunate creature hit this hard," Darda mused, "then probably went into the ravine."

All eyes focused on Dove as the ranger pulled her thick hair back from her face, put her chin in her delicate but calloused hand and tried to sort through this newest puzzle. The clues were too few, though, and a moment later, Dove threw her hands up in exasperation and headed off along the trail. The path wound in and left the cliff as it leveled near the top, but Dove walked back over to the edge, right above where they had left Gabriel. The fighter spotted her immediately and his wave told the ranger that all was calm below.

"Come," Kellindil bade them, and he led the group into the cave. Some answers came clear to Dove as soon as she glanced upon the carnage in the inner room.

"Barghest whelp!" exclaimed Fret, looking upon the scarlet-skinned, giant corpse.

"Barghest?" Roddy asked, perplexed.

"Of course," piped in Fret. "That does explain the wolf-giant in the gorge."

"Caught in the change," Darda reasoned. "Its many wounds and the stone floor took it before it could complete the transition."

"Barghest?" Roddy asked again, this time angrily, not appreciating being left out of a discussion he could not understand.

"A creature from another plane of existence," Fret explained. "Gehenna, it is rumored. Barghests send their whelps to other planes, sometimes to our own, to feed and to grow." He paused a moment in thought. "To feed," he said again, his tone leading the others.

"The woman in the barn!" Dove said evenly.

The members of Dove's troupe nodded their heads at the sudden revelation, but grim-faced McGristle held stubbornly to his original theory. "Drow killed 'em!" he growled.

"Have you the broken scimitar?" Dove asked. Roddy produced the weapon from beneath one of the many folds in his layered skin garments.

Dove took the weapon and bent low to examine the dead barghest. The blade unmistakably matched the beast's wounds, especially the fatal wound in the barghest's throat.

"You said that the drow wielded two of these," Dove remarked to Roddy as she held up the scimitar.

"The mayor said that," Roddy corrected, "on account of the story Thistledown's son told. When I seen the drow—" he took back the weapon—"he had just the one—the one he used to kill the Thistledown clan!" Roddy purposely didn't mention that the drow, while wielding just the one weapon, had scabbards for two scimitars on his belt.

Dove shook her head, doubting the theory. "The drow killed this barghest," she said. "The wounds match the blade, the sister blade to the one you hold, I would guess. And if you check the goblins in the front room, you will find that their throats were slashed by a similar curving scimitar."

"Like the wounds on the Thistledowns!" Roddy snarled.

Dove thought it best to keep her budding hypothesis quiet, but Fret, disliking the big man, echoed the thoughts of all but McGristle. "Killed by the barghest," the dwarf proclaimed, remembering the two sets of footprints at the farmyard. "In the form of the drow!"

Roddy glowered at him and Dove cast Fret a leading look, wanting the dwarf to remain silent. Fret misinterpreted the ranger's stare, though, thinking it astonishment of his reasoning power, and he proudly continued. "That explains the two sets of tracks, the heavier, earlier set for the bar—"

"But what of the creature in the gorge?" Darda asked Dove, understanding his leader's desire to shut Fret up. "Might its wounds, too, match the curving blade?"

Dove thought for a moment and managed to subtly nod her thanks to Darda. "Some, perhaps," she answered. "More likely, that barghest was killed by the panther—" she looked directly at Roddy—"the cat you claimed the drow kept as a pet."

Roddy kicked the dead barghest. "Drow killed the Thistledown clan!" he growled. Roddy had lost a dog and an ear to the dark elf and would not accept any conclusions that lessened his chances of claiming the two thousand gold piece bounty that the mayor had levied.

A call from outside the cave ended the debate—both Dove and Roddy were glad of that. After leading the troupe into the lair, Kellindil had returned outside, following up on some further clues he had discovered.

"A boot print," the elf explained, pointing to a small, mossy patch, when the others came out. "And here," he showed them scratches in the stone, a clear sign of a scuffle.

"My belief is that the drow went to the ledge," Kellindil explained. "And over, perhaps in pursuit of the barghest and the panther, though on that point I am merely assuming."

After a moment of following the trail Kellindil had reconstructed, Dove and Darda, and even Roddy, agreed with the assumption.

"We should go back into the ravine," Dove suggested. "Perhaps we will find a trail beyond the stony gorge that will lead us toward some clearer answers."

Roddy scratched at the scabs on his head and flashed Dove a disdainful look that showed her his emotions. Roddy cared not a bit for any of the ranger's promised "clearer answers," having drawn all of the conclusions that he needed long ago. Roddy was determined—beyond anything else, Dove knew—to bring back the dark elf's head.

Dove Falconhand was not so certain about the murderer's identity.

Many questions remained for both the ranger and for the other members of her troupe. Why hadn't the drow killed the Thistledown children when they had met earlier in the mountains? If Connor's tale to the mayor had been true, then why had the drow given the boy back his weapon? Dove was firmly convinced that the barghest, and not the drow, had slaughtered the Thistledown family, but why had the drow apparently gone after the barghest lair?

Was the drow in league with the barghests, a communion that fast soured? Even more intriguing to the ranger—whose very creed was to protect civilians in the unending war between the good races and monsters—had the drow sought out the barghest to avenge the slaughter at the farm? Dove suspected the latter was the truth, but she couldn't understand the drow's motives. Had the barghest, in killing the family, put the farmers of Maldobar on alert, thereby ruining a planned drow raid?

Again the pieces didn't fit properly. If the dark elves planned a raid on Maldobar, then certainly none of them would have revealed themselves beforehand. Something inside Dove told her that this single drow had acted alone, had come out and avenged the slain farmers. She shrugged it off as a trick of her own optimism and reminded herself that dark elves were rarely known for such rangerlike acts.

By the time the five got down the narrow path and returned to the sight of the largest corpse, Gabriel had already found the trail, heading deeper into the mountains. Two sets of tracks were evident, the drow's and fresher ones belonging to a giant, bipedal creature, possibly a third barghest.

"What happened to the panther?" Fret asked, growing a bit overwhelmed by his first field expedition in many years.

Dove laughed aloud and shook her head helplessly. Every answer seemed to bring so many more questions.

* * * * *

Drizzt kept on the move at night, running, as he had for so many years, from yet another grim reality. He had not killed the farmers—he had actually saved them from the gnoll band—but now they were dead. Drizzt could not escape that fact. He had entered their lives, quite of his own will, and now they were dead.

On the second night after his encounter with the hill giant, Drizzt saw a distant campfire far down the winding mountain trails, back in the direction of the barghest's lair. Knowing this sight to be more than coincidence, the drow summoned Guenhwyvar to his side, then sent the panther down for a closer look.

Tirelessly the great cat ran, its sleek, black form invisible in the evening shadows as it rapidly closed the distance to the camp.

⚔ ⚔ ⚔ ⚔ ⚔

Dove and Gabriel rested easily by their campfire, amused by the continuing antics of Fret, who busily cleaned his soft jerkin with a stiff brush and grumbled all the while.

Roddy kept to himself across the way, securely tucked into a niche between a fallen tree and a large rock, his dog curled up at his feet.

"Oh, bother for this dirt!" Fret groaned. "Never, never will I get this outfit clean! I shall have to buy a new one." He looked at Dove, who was futilely trying to hold a straight face. "Laugh if you will, Mistress Falconhand" the dwarf admonished. "The price will come out of your purse, do not doubt!"

"A sorry day it is when one must buy fineries for a dwarf," Gabriel put in, and at his words, Dove burst into laughter.

"Laugh if you will!" Fret said again, and he rubbed harder with the brush, wearing a hole right through the garment. "Drat and bebother!" he cursed, then he threw the brush to the ground.

"Shut yer mouth!" Roddy groused at them, stealing the mirth. "Do ye mean to bring the drow down upon us?"

Gabriel's ensuing glare was uncompromising, but Dove realized that the mountain man's advice, though rudely given, was appropriate. "Let us rest, Gabriel," the ranger said to her fighting companion. "Darda and Kellindil will be in soon and our turn shall come for watch. I expect that tomorrow's road will be no less wearisome—" She looked at Fret and winked—"and no less dirty, than today's."

Gabriel shrugged, hung his pipe in his mouth, and clasped his hands behind his head. This was the life that he and all of the adventuring companions enjoyed, camping under the stars with the song of the mountain wind in their ears.

Fret, though, tossed and turned on the hard ground, grumbling and growling as he moved through each uncomfortable position.

Gabriel didn't need to look at Dove to know that she shared his smile. Nor did he have to glance over at Roddy to know that the mountain man fumed at the continuing noise. It no doubt seemed negligible to the ears of a city-living dwarf but rang out conspicuously to those more accustomed to the road.

A whistle from the darkness sounded at the same time Roddy's dog put its fur up and growled.

Dove and Gabriel were up and over to the side of the camp in a second, moving to the perimeter of the firelight in the direction of Darda's call. Likewise, Roddy, pulling his dog along, slipped around the large rock, out of the direct light so that their eyes could adjust to the gloom.

Fret, too involved with his own discomfort, finally noticed the movements. "What?" the dwarf asked curiously. "What?"

After a brief and whispered conversation with Darda, Dove and Gabriel split up, circling the camp in opposite directions to ensure the integrity of the perimeter.

"The tree," came a soft whisper, and Dove dropped into a crouch. In a moment, she sorted out Roddy, cleverly concealed between the rock and some brush. The big man, too, had his weapon readied, and his other hand held his dog's muzzle tightly, keeping the animal silent.

Dove followed Roddy's nod to the widespread branches of a solitary elm. At first, the ranger could discern nothing unusual among the leafy branches, but then came the yellow flash of feline eyes.

"Drow's panther," Dove whispered. Roddy nodded his agreement. They sat very still and watched, knowing that the slightest movement could alert the cat. A few seconds later, Gabriel joined them, falling into a silent position and following their eyes to the same darker spot on the elm. All three understood that time was their ally; even now, Darda and Kellindil were no doubt moving into position.

Their trap would surely have had Guenhwyvar, but a moment later, the dwarf crashed out of the campsite, stumbling right into Roddy. The mountain man nearly fell over, and when he reflexively threw his weaponless hand out to catch himself, his dog rushed out, baying wildly.

Like a black-shafted arrow, the panther bolted from the tree and flew off into the night. Fortune was not with Guenhwyvar, though, for it crossed straight by Kellindil's position, and the keen-visioned elven archer saw it clearly.

Kellindil heard the barking and shouting in the distance, back by the camp, but had no way of knowing what had transpired. Any hesitation the elf had, however, was quickly dispelled when one voice called out clearly.

"Kill the murdering thing!" Roddy cried.

Thinking then that the panther or its drow companion must have attacked the campsite, Kellindil let his arrow fly. The enchanted dart buried itself deeply into Guenhwyvar's flank as the panther rushed by.

Then came Dove's call, berating Roddy. "Do not!" the ranger shouted. "The panther has done nothing to deserve our ire!"

Kellindil rushed out to the panther's trail. With his sensitive elven eyes viewing in the infrared spectrum, he clearly saw the heat of blood dotting the area of the hit and trailing off away from the camp.

Dove and the others came upon him a moment later. Kellindil's elven features, always angular and beautiful, seemed sharp as his angry glare fell over Roddy.

"You have misguided my shot, McGristle," he said angrily. "On your words, I shot a creature undeserving of an arrow! I warn you once, and once alone, to never do so again." After a final glare to show the mountain man how much he meant his words, Kellindil stalked off along the blood trail.

Angry fires welled in Roddy, but he sublimated them, understanding that he stood alone against the formidable foursome and the tidy dwarf. Roddy did let his glare drop upon Fret, though, knowing that none of the others could disagree with his judgment.

"Keep yer tongue in yer mouth when danger nears!" Roddy growled. "And keep yer stinkin' boots off my back!"

Fret looked around incredulously as the group began to move off after Kellindil. "Stinking," the dwarf asked aloud. He looked down, wounded, to his finely polished boots. "Stinking," he said to Dove, who paused to offer a comforting smile. "Dirtied by that one's back, more likely!"

⚔ ⚔ ⚔ ⚔ ⚔

Guenhwyvar limped back to Drizzt soon after the first rays of dawn peeked through the eastern mountains. Drizzt shook his head helplessly, almost unsurprised by the arrow protruding from Guenhwyvar's flank. Reluctantly, but knowing it a wise course, Drizzt drew out the dagger he had taken from the quickling and cut the bolt free.

Guenhwyvar growled softly through the procedure but lay still and offered no resistance. Then Drizzt, though he wanted to keep Guenhwyvar by his side, allowed the panther to return to its astral home, where the wound would heal faster. The arrow had told the drow all he needed to know about his pursuers, and Drizzt believed that he would need the panther again all too soon. He stood out on a rocky outcropping and peered through the growing brightness to the lower trails to the expected approach of yet another enemy.

He saw nothing, of course; even wounded, Guenhwyvar had easily outdistanced the pursuit and for a man or similar being, the campfire was many hours' travel.

But they would come, Drizzt knew, forcing him into yet another battle he did not want. Drizzt looked all around, wondering what devious traps he could set for them, what advantages he could gain when the encounter came to blows, as every encounter seemed to.

Memories of his last meeting with humans, of the man with the dogs and the other farmers, abruptly altered Drizzt's thinking. On that occasion, the battle had been inspired by misunderstanding, a barrier that Drizzt doubted he could ever overcome. Drizzt had fostered no desire then to fight against the humans and fostered none now, despite Guenhwyvar's wound.

The light was growing and the still-injured drow, though he had rested through the night, wanted to find a dark and comfortable hole. But Drizzt could afford no delays, not if he wanted to keep ahead of the coming battle.

"How far will you follow me?" Drizzt whispered into the morning breeze. He vowed in a somber but determined tone, "We shall see."

# 10
# A Question of Honor

"The panther found the drow," Dove concluded after she and her companions had spent some time inspecting the region near the rocky outcropping. Kellindil's arrow lay broken on the ground, at about the same spot where the panther tracks ended. "And the panther disappeared."

"So it would seem," Gabriel agreed, scratching his head and looking down at the confusing trail.

"Hell cat," Roddy McGristle growled. "Gone back to its filthy home!"

Fret wanted to ask, "Your house?" but he wisely held the sarcastic thought to himself.

The others, too, let the mountain man's proclamation slip by. They had no answers to this riddle, and Roddy's guess was as good as any of them could manage. The wounded panther and the fresh blood trail were gone, but Roddy's dog soon had Drizzt's scent. Baying excitedly, the dog led them on, and Dove and Kellindil, both skilled trackers, often discovered other evidence that confirmed the direction.

The trail lay along the side of the mountain, dipped through some thickly packed trees, and continued on across an expanse of bare stone, ending abruptly at yet another ravine. Roddy's dog moved right to the lip and even down to the first step on a rocky and treacherous descent.

"Damned drow magic," Roddy grumbled. He looked around and

bounced a fist off his thigh, guessing that it would take him many hours to circumvent the steep wall.

"The daylight wanes," Dove offered. "Let us set camp here and find our way down in the morn."

Gabriel and Fret nodded their accord, but Roddy disagreed. "The trail's fresh now!" the mountain man argued. "We should get the dog down there and back on it, at least, before we're taking to our beds."

"That could take hours . . ." Fret began to protest, but Dove hushed the tidy dwarf.

"Come," the ranger bade the others, and she walked off to the west, to where the ground sloped at a steep, but climbable decline.

Dove did not agree with Roddy's reasoning, but she wanted no further arguments with Maldobar's appointed representative.

At the bottom of the ravine they found only more riddles. Roddy spurred his dog off in every direction but could find no trace of the elusive drow. After many minutes of contemplation, the truth sparked in Dove's mind and her smile revealed everything to her other seasoned companions.

"He doubled us!" Gabriel laughed, guessing the source of Dove's mirth. "He led us right to the cliff, knowing we would assume he used some magic to get down!"

"What're ye talkin' about?" Roddy demanded angrily, though the experienced bounty hunter understood exactly what had happened.

"You mean that we have to climb all the way back up there?" Fret asked, his voice a whine.

Dove laughed again but sobered quickly as she looked to Roddy and said, "In the morning."

This time the mountain man offered no objections.

By the time the next dawn had broken, the group had hiked to the top of the ravine and Roddy had his dog back on Drizzt's scent, backtracking the trail in the direction of the rocky outcropping where they had first picked it up. The trick had been simple enough, but the same question nagged at all of the experienced trackers: how had the drow broken away from his track cleanly enough to so completely fool the dog. When they came again into the thickly packed trees, Dove knew that they had their answer.

She nodded to Kellindil, who was already dropping off his heavy pack. The nimble elf picked a low-hanging branch and swung up into the trees, searching for possible routes that the climbing drow might have followed. The branches of many trees twined together, so the options seemed many, but after a while, Kellindil correctly guided Roddy and his dog to the new trail, breaking off to the side of the copse and circling back down the side of the mountain, back in the direction of Maldobar.

"The town!" cried a distressed Fret, but the others didn't seem concerned.

"Not the town," offered Roddy, too intrigued to hold his angry edge. As a bounty hunter, Roddy always enjoyed a worthy opponent, at least during the chase. "The stream," Roddy explained, thinking that now he had figured out the drow's mind-set. "Drow's headed for the stream, to follow it along an' break off clean, back out to the wilder land."

"The drow is a crafty adversary," Darda remarked, wholeheartedly agreeing with Roddy's conclusions.

"And now he has at least a day's lead over us," Gabriel remarked.

After Fret's disgusted sigh finally died away, Dove offered the dwarf some hope. "Fear not," she said. "We are well stocked, but the drow is not. He must pause to hunt or forage, but we can continue on."

"We sleep only when need be!" Roddy put in, determined to not be slowed by the group's other members. "And only for short times!"

Fret sighed heavily again.

"And we begin rationing our supplies immediately," Dove added, both to placate Roddy and because she thought it prudent. "We shall be put to it hard enough just to close on the drow. I do not want any delays."

"Rationing," Fret mumbled under his breath. He sighed for the third time and placed a comforting hand on his belly. How badly the tidy dwarf wished that he could be back in his neat little room in Helm's castle in Sundabar!

⚔ ⚔ ⚔ ⚔ ⚔

Drizzt's every intention was to continue deeper into the mountains until the pursuing party had lost its heart for the chase. He kept up his misdirecting tactics, often doubling back and taking to the trees to begin a second trail in an entirely different direction. Many mountain streams provided further barriers to the scent, but Drizzt's pursuers were not novices, and Roddy's dog was as fine a hunting hound as had ever been bred. Not only did the party keep true to Drizzt's trail, but they actually closed the gap over the next few days.

Drizzt still believed that he could elude them, but their continuing proximity brought other, more subtle, concerns to the drow. He had done nothing to deserve such dogged pursuit; he had even avenged the deaths of the farming family. And despite Drizzt's angry vow that he would go off alone, that he would bring no more danger to anyone, he had known loneliness as too close a companion for too many years. He could not help but look over his shoulder, out of curiosity and not fear, and the longing did not diminish.

At last, Drizzt could not deny his curiosity for the pursuing party. That curiosity, Drizzt realized as he studied the figures moving about the campfire one dark night, might prove to be his downfall. Still, the realization, and the second-guessing, came too late for the drow to do anything about it. His needs had dragged him back, and now the campsite of his pursuers loomed barely twenty yards away.

The banter between Dove, Fret, and Gabriel tugged at Drizzt's heartstrings, though he could not understand their words. Any desire the drow felt to walk into the camp was tempered, though, whenever Roddy and his mean-tempered dog strolled by the light. Those two would never pause to hear any explanations, Drizzt knew.

The party had set two guards, one an elf and one a tall human. Drizzt had sneaked past the human, guessing correctly that the man would not be as adept as the elf in the darkness. Now, though, the drow, again against all caution, picked his way around to the other side of the camp, toward the elven sentry.

Only once before had Drizzt encountered his surface cousins. It had been a disastrous occasion. The raiding party for which Drizzt was a scout had slaughtered every member of a surface elf gathering, except for a single elven girl, whom Drizzt had managed to conceal. Driven by those haunting memories, Drizzt needed to see an elf again, a living and vital elf.

The first indication Kellindil had that someone else was in the area came when a tiny dagger whistled past his chest, neatly severing his bowstring. The elf spun about immediately and looked into the drow's lavender eyes. Drizzt stood only a few paces away.

The red glow of Kellindil's eyes showed that he was viewing Drizzt in the infrared spectrum. The drow crossed his hands over his chest in an Underdark signal of peace.

"At last we have met, my dark cousin," Kellindil whispered harshly in the drow tongue, his voice edged in obvious anger and his glowing eyes narrowing dangerously. Quick as a cat, Kellindil snapped a finely crafted sword, its blade glowing in a fiery red flame, from his belt.

Drizzt was amazed and hopeful when he learned that the elf could speak his language, and in the simple fact that the elf had not spoken loudly enough to alert the camp. The surface elf was Drizzt's size and similarly sharp-featured, but his eyes were narrower and his golden hair wasn't as long or thick as Drizzt's white mane.

"I am Drizzt Do'Urden," Drizzt began tentatively.

"I care nothing for what you are called!" Kellindil shot back. "You are drow. That is all I need to know! Come then, drow. Come and let us learn who is the stronger!"

Drizzt had not yet drawn his blade and had no intention of doing so. "I have no desire to battle with you . . ." Drizzt's voice trailed away, as he realized his words were futile against the intense hatred the surface elf held for him.

Drizzt wanted to explain everything to the elf, to tell his tale completely and be vindicated by some voice other than his own. If only another—particularly a surface elf—would learn of his trials and agree with his decisions, agree that he had acted properly through the course of his life in the face of such horrors, then the guilt would fly from Drizzt's shoulders. If only he could find acceptance among those who so hated—as he himself hated—the ways of his dark people, then Drizzt Do'Urden would be at peace.

But the elf's sword tip did not slip an inch toward the ground, nor did the grimace diminish on his fair elven face, a face more accustomed to smiles.

Drizzt would find no acceptance here, not now and probably not ever. Was he forever to be misjudged? he wondered. Or was he, perhaps, misjudging those around him, giving the humans and this elf more credit for fairness than they deserved?

Those were two disturbing notions that Drizzt would have to deal with another day, for Kellindil's patience had reached its end. The elf came at the drow with his sword tip leading the way.

Drizzt was not surprised—how could he have been? He hopped back, out of immediate reach, and called upon his innate magic, dropping a globe of impenetrable blackness over the advancing elf.

No novice to magic, Kellindil understood the drow's trick. The elf reversed direction, diving out the back side of the globe and coming up, sword at the ready.

The lavender eyes were gone.

"Drow!" Kellindil called out loudly, and those in the camp immediately exploded into motion. Roddy's dog started howling, and that excited and threatening yelp followed Drizzt back into the mountains, damning him to his continuing exile.

Kellindil leaned back against a tree, alert but not too concerned that the drow was still in the area. Drizzt could not know it at that time, but his words and ensuing actions—fleeing instead of fighting—had indeed put a bit of doubt in the kindly elf's not-so-closed mind.

⚔ ⚔ ⚔ ⚔ ⚔

"He will lose his advantage in the dawn's light," Dove said hopefully after several fruitless hours of trying to keep up with the drow. They were in a bowl-shaped, rocky vale now, and the drow's trail led up the far side in a high and fairly steep climb.

Fret, nearly stumbling with exhaustion at her side, was quick to reply. "Advantage?" The dwarf groaned. He looked at the next mountain wall and shook his head. "We shall all fall dead of weariness before we find this infernal drow!"

"If ye can't keep up, then fall an' die!" Roddy snarled. "We're not to be lettin' the stinking drow get away this time!"

It was not Fret, however, but another member of the troupe who unexpectedly went down. A large rock soared into the group suddenly, clipping Darda's shoulder with enough force to lift the man from the ground and spin him right over in the air. He never even got the chance to cry out before he fell facedown in the dust.

Dove grabbed Fret and rolled for a nearby boulder, Roddy and Gabriel doing likewise. Another stone, and several more, thundered into the region.

"Avalanche?" the stunned dwarf asked when he recovered from the shock.

Dove, too concerned with Darda, didn't bother to answer, though she knew the truth of their situation and knew that it was no avalanche.

"He is alive," Gabriel called from behind his protective rock, a dozen feet across from Dove's. Another stone skipped through the area, narrowly missing Darda's head.

"Damn," Dove mumbled. She peeked up over the lip of her boulder, scanning both the mountainside and the lower crags at its base. "Now, Kellindil," she whispered to herself. "Get us some time."

As if in answer came the distant twang of the elf's re-strung bow, followed by an angry roar. Dove and Gabriel glanced over to each other and smiled grimly.

"Stone giants!" Roddy cried, recognizing the deep, grating timbre of the roaring voice.

Dove crouched and waited, her back to the boulder and her open pack in her hand. No more stones bounced into the area; rather, thunderous crashes began up ahead of them, near Kellindil's position. Dove rushed out to Darda and gently turned the man over.

"That hurt," Darda whispered, straining to smile at his obvious understatement.

"Do not speak," Dove replied, fumbling for a potion bottle in her pack. But the ranger ran out of time. The giants, seeing her out in the open, resumed their attack on the lower area.

"Get back to the stone!" Gabriel cried. Dove slipped her arm under the fallen man's shoulder to support Darda as, stumbling with every movement, he crawled for the rock.

"Hurry! Hurry!" Fret cried, watching them anxiously with his back flat against the large stone.

Dove leaned over Darda suddenly, flattening him down to the ground as another rock zipped by just above their ducking heads.

Fret started to bite his fingernails, then realized what he was doing and stopped, a disgusted look on his face. "Do hurry!" he cried again to his friends. Another rock bounced by, too close.

Just before Dove and Darda got to Fret, a stone landed squarely on the backside of the boulder. Fret, his back tight against the rock barrier, flew out wildly, easily clearing his crawling companions. Dove placed Darda down behind the boulder, then turned, thinking she would have to go out again and retrieve the fallen dwarf.

But Fret was already back up, cursing and grumbling, and more concerned with a new hole in his fine garment than in any bodily injury.

"Get back here!" Dove screamed at him.

"Drat and bebother these stupid giants!" was all that Fret replied, stomping purposefully back to the boulder, his fists clenched angrily against his hips.

The barrage continued, both up ahead of the pinned companions and in their area. Then Kellindil came diving in, slipping to the rock beside Roddy and his dog.

"Stone giants," the elf explained. "A dozen at the least." He pointed up to a ridge halfway up the mountainside.

"Drow set us up," Roddy growled, banging his fist on the stone.

Kellindil wasn't convinced, but he held his tongue.

⚔ ⚔ ⚔ ⚔ ⚔

Up on the peak of the rocky rise, Drizzt watched the battle unfolding. He had passed through the lower paths an hour earlier, before the dawn. In the dark, the waiting giants had been no obstacle for the stealthy drow; Drizzt had slipped through their line with little trouble.

Now, squinting through the morning light, Drizzt wondered about his course of action. When he had passed the giants, he fully expected that his pursuers would fall into trouble. Should he have somehow tried to warn them? he wondered. Or should he have veered away from the region, leading the humans and the elf out of the giants' path?

Again Drizzt did not understand where he fit in with the ways of this strange and brutal world. "Let them fight among themselves," he said harshly, as though trying to convince himself. Drizzt purposefully recalled his encounter of the previous night. The elf had attacked despite his proclamation that he did not want to fight. He recalled, too, the arrow he had dug out of Guenhwyvar's flank.

"Let them all kill each other," Drizzt said and he turned to leave. He glanced back over his shoulder one final time and noticed that some of the giants were on the move. One group remained at the ridge, showering the valley floor with a seemingly endless supply of rocks while two other groups, one to the left and one to the right, had fanned out, moving to encircle the trapped party.

Drizzt knew then that his pursuers would not escape. Once the giants had them flanked, they would find no protection against the cross fire.

Something stirred within the drow at that moment, the same emotions that had set him into action against the gnoll band. He couldn't know for certain, but as with the gnolls and their plans to attack the farmhouse, Drizzt suspected that the giants were the evil ones in this fight.

Other thoughts softened Drizzt's determined grimace, memories of the human children at play on the farm, of the sandy-haired boy going into the water trough.

Drizzt dropped the onyx figurine to the ground. "Come, Guenhwyvar," he commanded. "We are needed."

⚔ ⚔ ⚔ ⚔ ⚔

"We're being flanked!" Roddy McGristle snarled, seeing the giant bands moving along the higher trails.

Dove, Gabriel, and Kellindil all glanced around and to each other, searching for some way out. They had battled giants many times in their travels, together and with other parties. Always before, they had gone into the fight eagerly, happy to relieve the world of a few troublesome monsters. This time, though, they all suspected that the result might be different. Stone giants were reputably the best rock-throwers in all the realms and a single hit could kill the hardiest of men. Also, Darda, though alive, could not possibly run away, and none of the others had any intentions of leaving him behind.

"Flee, mountain man," Kellindil said to Roddy. "You owe us nothing."

Roddy looked at the archer incredulously. "I don't run away, elf," he growled. "Not from nothin'!"

Kellindil nodded and fitted an arrow to his bow.

"If they get to the side, we're doomed," Dove explained to Fret. "I beg your forgiveness, dear Fret. I should not have taken you from your home."

Fret shrugged the thought away. He reached under his robes and produced a small but sturdy silver hammer. Dove smiled at the sight, thinking how odd the hammer seemed in the dwarf's soft hands, more accustomed to holding a quill.

⚔ ⚔ ⚔ ⚔ ⚔

On the top ridge, Drizzt and Guenhwyvar shadowed the movements of the stone giant band circling to the trapped party's left flank. Drizzt was determined to help the humans, but he wasn't certain of how effective he could be against the likes of four armed giants. Still, he figured that with Guenhwyvar by his side, he could find some way to disrupt the giant group long enough for the trapped party to make a break.

The valley rolled out wider across the way and Drizzt realized that the giant band circling in the other direction, to the trapped party's right flank, was probably out of rock-throwing range.

"Come, my friend," Drizzt whispered to the panther, and he drew his scimitar and started down a descent of broken and jagged stone. A moment later, though, as soon as he noticed the terrain a short distance ahead of the giant band Drizzt grabbed Guenhwyvar by the scruff and led the panther back up to the top ridge.

Here the ground was jagged and cracked but undeniably stable. Just ahead, however, great boulders and hundreds of loose smaller rocks lay strewn about the steeply sloping ground. Drizzt was not so experienced in the dynamics of a mountainside, but even he could see that the steep and loose landscape verged on collapse.

The drow and the cat rushed ahead, again getting above the giant band. The giants were nearly in position; some of them had even begun to launch rocks at the pinned party. Drizzt crept down to a large boulder and heaved against it, setting it into motion. Guenhwyvar's tactics were far less subtle. The panther charged down the mountainside, dislodging stones with every great stride, leaping onto the back side of rocks and springing away as they began tumbling.

Boulders bounced and bounded. Smaller rocks skipped between them, building the momentum. Drizzt, committed to the action, ran down into the midst of the budding avalanche, throwing stones, pushing against others—whatever he could do to add to the rush. Soon the very ground beneath the drow's feet was sliding and the whole section of the mountainside seemed to be coming down.

Guenhwyvar sped along ahead of the avalanche, a beacon of doom for the surprised giants. The panther sprang out over them, but they took note of the great cat only momentarily, as tons of bouncing rocks slammed into them.

Drizzt knew that he was in trouble; he was not nearly as quick and agile as Guenhwyvar and could not hope to outrun the slide, or to get out of its way. He leaped high into the air from the crest of a small ridge and called upon a levitation spell as he went.

Drizzt fought hard to hold his concentration on the effort. The spell had failed him twice before, and if he couldn't hold it now, if he dropped back into the rush of stones, he knew he would surely die.

Despite his determination, Drizzt felt increasingly heavy on the air. He waved his arms futilely, sought that magical energy within his drow body—but he was coming down.

⚔ ⚔ ⚔ ⚔ ⚔

"Th'only ones that can hit us are up in front!" Roddy cried as a thrown boulder bounced harmlessly short of the right flank. "The ones on the right're too far for throwing, and the ones on the left . . . !"

Dove followed Roddy's logic and his gaze to the rising dust cloud on their left flank. She stared hard and long at the cascading rocks, and at what might have been a dark-cloaked elven form. When she looked back at Gabriel, she knew that he, too, had seen the drow.

"We have to go now," Dove called to the elf.

Kellindil nodded and spun to the side of his barrier boulder, his bowstring taut.

"Quickly," Gabriel added, "before the group to the right gets back in range."

Kellindil's bow twanged once and again. Ahead, a giant howled in pain.

"Stay here with Darda," Dove bade Fret, then she, Gabriel, and Roddy—holding his dog on a tight leash—darted out from their cover and charged the giants straight ahead. They rolled from rock to rock, cutting their course in confusing zigzags to prevent the giants from anticipating their movements. All the while, Kellindil's arrows soared above them, keeping the giants more concerned with ducking than with throwing.

Deep crags marked the mountainside's lower slopes, crags that offered cover but that also split the three fighters apart. Neither could they see the giants, but they knew the general direction and picked their separate ways as best they could.

Rounding a sharp bend between two walls of stone, Roddy came upon one of the giants. Immediately the mountain man freed his dog, and the vicious canine charged fearlessly and leaped high, barely reaching the twenty-foot-tall behemoth's waist.

Surprised by the sudden attack, the giant dropped its huge club and caught the dog in midflight. It would have crushed the troublesome mutt in an instant, except that Bleeder, Roddy's wicked axe, sliced into its thigh with all the force the burly mountain man could muster. The giant lurched and Roddy's dog squirmed loose, climbing and clawing, then snapping at the giant's face and neck. Below, Roddy hacked away, chopping the monster down as he would a tree.

⚔ ⚔ ⚔ ⚔ ⚔

Half-floating and half-dancing atop the bouncing stones, Drizzt rode the rock slide. He saw one giant emerge, stumbling, from the tumult, only to be met by Guenhwyvar. Wounded and stunned, the giant went down in a heap.

Drizzt had no time to savor his desperate plan's success. His levitation spell continued somewhat, keeping him light enough so that he could ride along. Even above the main slide, though, rocks bounced heavily into the drow and dust choked him and stung his sensitive eyes. Nearly blinded, he managed to spot a ridge that could provide some shelter, but the only way he could get to it would be to release his levitation spell and scramble.

Another rock nicked into Drizzt, nearly spinning him over in midair. He could sense the spell failing and knew that he had only that one chance. He regained his equilibrium, released his spell, and hit the ground running.

He rolled and scrambled, coming up in a dead run. A rock skipped into the knee of his already wounded leg, forcing him parallel to the ground. Drizzt was rolling again, trying however he could to get to the safety of the ridge.

His momentum ended far short. He came back up to his feet, meaning to thrust ahead over the final distance, but Drizzt's leg had no strength and it buckled immediately, leaving him stranded and exposed.

He felt the impact on his back and thought his life was at its end. A moment later, dazed, Drizzt realized only that he somehow had landed behind the ridge and that he was buried by something, but not by stones or dirt.

Guenhwyvar stayed on top of its master, shielding Drizzt until the last of the bouncing rocks had rolled to a stop.

⚔ ⚔ ⚔ ⚔ ⚔

As the crags gave way to more open ground, Dove and Gabriel came back in sight of each other. They noticed movement directly ahead, behind a loose-fitted wall of piled boulders a dozen feet high and about fifty feet long.

A giant appeared atop the wall, roaring in rage and holding a rock above its head, readied to throw. The monster had several arrows protruding from its neck and chest, but it seemed not to care.

Kellindil's next shot surely caught the giant's attention, though, for the elf put an arrow squarely into the monster's elbow. The giant howled and clutched at its arm, apparently forgetting about its rock, which promptly dropped with a thud upon its head. The giant stood very still, dazed, and two more arrows knocked into its face. It teetered for a moment, then crashed into the dust.

Dove and Gabriel exchanged quick smiles, sharing their appreciation for the skilled elven archer, then continued their charge, going for opposite ends of the wall.

Dove caught one giant by surprise just around her corner. The monster reached for its club, but Dove's sword beat it to the spot and cleanly severed its hand. Stone giants were formidable foes, with fists that could drive a person straight into the ground and a hide nearly as hard as the rock that gave them their name. But wounded, surprised, and without its cudgel, the giant was no match for the skilled ranger. She sprang atop the wall, which put her even with the giant's face, and set her sword to methodical work.

In two thrusts, the giant was blinded. The third, a deft, sidelong swipe, cut a smile into the monster's throat. Then Dove went on the defensive, neatly dodging and parrying the dying monster's last desperate swings.

Gabriel was not as lucky as his companion. The remaining giant was not close to the corner of the piled rock wall. Though Gabriel surprised the monster when he came charging around, the giant had enough time—and a stone in hand—to react.

Gabriel got his sword up to deflect the missile, and the act saved his life. The stone blew the fighter's sword from his hands and still came on with enough force to throw Gabriel to the ground. Gabriel was a seasoned veteran, and the primary reason he was still alive after so very many battles was the fact that he knew when to retreat. He forced himself through that moment of blurring pain and found his footing, then bolted back around the wall.

The giant, with its heavy club in hand came right behind. An arrow greeted the monster as it turned into the open, but it brushed the pesky dart away as no more than an inconvenience and bore down on the fighter.

Gabriel soon ran out of room. He tried to make it back to the broken paths, but the giant cut him off, trapping him in a small box canyon of huge boulders. Gabriel drew his dagger and cursed his ill luck.

Dove had dispatched her giant by this time and rushed out around the stone wall, immediately catching sight of Gabriel and the giant.

Gabriel saw the ranger, too, but he only shrugged, almost apologetically, knowing that Dove couldn't possibly get to him in time to save him.

The snarling giant took a step in, meaning to finish the puny man, but then came a sharp *crack!* and the monster halted abruptly. Its eyes darted about weirdly for a moment or two, then it toppled at Gabriel's feet, quite dead.

Gabriel looked up to the side, to the top of the boulder wall, and nearly laughed out loud.

Fret's hammer was not a large weapon—its head being only two inches across—but it was a solid thing, and in a single swing, the dwarf had driven it clean through the stone giant's thick skull.

Dove approached, sheathing her sword, equally at a loss.

Looking upon their amazed expressions, Fret was not amused.

"I am a dwarf, after all!" he blurted at them, crossing his arms indignantly. The action brought the brain-stained hammer in contact with Fret's tunic, and the dwarf lost his bluster in a fit of panic. He licked his stubby fingers and wiped at the gruesome stain, then regarded the gore on his hand with even greater horror.

Dove and Gabriel did laugh aloud.

"Know that you are paying for the tunic!" Fret railed at Dove. "Oh, you most certainly are!"

A shout to the side brought them from their momentary relief. The four remaining giants, having seen one group of their companions buried in an avalanche and another group cut down so very efficiently, had lost interest in the ambush and had taken flight.

Right behind them went Roddy McGristle and his howling dog.

⚔ ⚔ ⚔ ⚔ ⚔

A single giant had escaped both the avalanche's thunder and the panther's terrible claws. It ran wildly now across the mountainside, seeking the top ridge.

Drizzt set Guenhwyvar in quick pursuit, then found a stick to use as a cane and managed to get to his feet. Bruised, dusty, and still nursing wounds from the barghest battle—and now a dozen more from his mountain ride—Drizzt started away. A movement at the bottom of the slope caught his attention and held him, though. He turned to face the elf and more pointedly, the arrow nocked in the elf's drawn bow.

Drizzt looked around but had nowhere to duck. He could place a globe of darkness somewhere between himself and the elf, possibly, but he realized that the skilled archer, having drawn a bead on him, would not miss him even with that obstacle. Drizzt steadied his shoulders and turned about slowly, facing the elf squarely and proudly.

Kellindil eased his bowstring back and pulled the arrow from its nock. Kellindil, too, had seen the dark-cloaked form floating above the rock slide.

"The others are back with Darda," Dove said, coming upon the elf at that moment, "and McGristle is chasing . . ."

Kellindil neither answered nor looked to the ranger. He nodded curtly, leading Dove's gaze up the slope to the dark form, which moved again up the mountainside.

"Let him go," Dove offered. "That one was never our enemy."

"I fear to let a drow walk free," Kellindil replied.

"As do I," Dove answered, "but I fear the consequences more if McGristle finds the drow."

"We will return to Maldobar and rid ourselves of that man," Kellindil offered, "then you and the others may return to Sundabar for your appointment. I have kin in these mountains; together they and I will watch out for our dark-skinned friend and see that he causes no harm."

"Agreed," said Dove. She turned and started away, and Kellindil, needing no further convincing, turned to follow.

The elf paused and looked back one final time. He reached into his backpack and produced a flask, then laid it out in the open on the ground. Almost as an afterthought, Kellindil produced a second item, this one from his belt, and dropped it to the ground next to the flask. Satisfied, he turned and followed the ranger.

⚔ ⚔ ⚔ ⚔ ⚔

By the time Roddy McGristle returned from his wild, fruitless chase, Dove and the others had packed everything together and were prepared to leave.

"Back after the drow," Roddy proclaimed. "He's gained a bit o' time, but we'll close on him fast."

"The drow is gone," Dove said sharply. "We shall pursue him no more."

Roddy's face crinkled in disbelief and he seemed on the verge of exploding.

"Darda is badly in need of rest!" Dove growled at him, not backing down a bit. "Kellindil's arrows are nearly exhausted, as are our supplies."

"I'll not so easily forget the Thistledowns!" Roddy declared.

"Neither did the drow," Kellindil put in.

"The Thistledowns have already been avenged," Dove added, "and you know it is true, McGristle. The drow did not kill them, but he most definitely slew their killers!"

Roddy snarled and turned away. He was an experienced bounty hunter and thus, an experienced investigator. He had, of course, figured out the truth long ago, but Roddy couldn't ignore the scar on his face or the loss of his ear—or the heavy bounty on the drow's head.

Dove anticipated and understood his silent reasoning. "The people of

Maldobar will not be so anxious to see the drow brought in when they learn the truth of the massacre," she said, "and not so willing to pay, I would guess."

Roddy snapped a glare at her, but again he could not dispute her logic. When Dove's party set out on the trail back to Maldobar, Roddy McGristle went with them.

⚔ ⚔ ⚔ ⚔ ⚔

Drizzt came back down the mountainside later that day, searching for something that would tell him his pursuers' whereabouts. He found Kellindil's flask and approached it tentatively, then relaxed when he noticed the other item lying next to it, the tiny dagger he had taken from the sprite, the same one he had used to sever the elf's bowstring on their first meeting.

The liquid within the flask smelled sweet, and the drow, his throat still parched from the rock dust, gladly took a quaff. Tingling chills ran through Drizzt's body, refreshing him and revitalizing him. He had barely eaten for several days, but the strength that had seeped from his now-frail form came rushing back in a sudden burst. His torn leg went numb for a moment, and Drizzt felt that, too, grow stronger.

A wave of dizziness washed over Drizzt then, and he shuffled over to the shade of a nearby boulder and sat down to rest.

When he awoke, the sky was dark and filled with stars, and he felt much better. Even his leg, so torn in the ride down the avalanche, would once again support his weight. Drizzt knew who had left the flask and dagger for him, and now that he understood the nature of the healing potion, his confusion and indecision only grew.

# Part Three

## Montolio

To all the varied peoples of the world nothing is so out of reach, yet so deeply personal and controlling, as the concept of god. My experience in my homeland showed me little of these supernatural beings beyond the influences of the vile drow deity, the Spider Queen, Lolth.

After witnessing the carnage of Lolth's workings, I was not so quick to embrace the concept of any god, of any being that could so dictate, codes of behavior and precepts of an entire society. Is morality not an internal force, and if it is, are principles then to be dictated or felt?

So follows the question of the gods themselves: Are these named entities, in truth, actual beings, or are they manifestations of shared beliefs? Are the dark elves evil because they follow the precepts of the Spider Queen, or is Lolth a culmination of the drow's natural evil conduct?

Likewise, when the barbarians of Icewind Dale charge across the tundra to war, shouting the name of Tempus, Lord of Battles, are they following the precepts of Tempus, or is Tempus merely the idealized name they give to their actions?

This I cannot answer, nor, I have come to realize, can any one else, no matter how loudly they—particularly priests of certain gods—might argue otherwise. In the end, to a preacher's ultimate sorrow, the choice of a god is a personal one, and the alignment to a being is in accord with one's internal code of principles. A missionary might coerce and trick would-be disciples, but no rational being can truly follow the determined orders of any god-figure if those orders run contrary to his own tenets. Neither I, Drizzt Do'Urden, nor my father, Zaknafein, could ever have become disciples of the Spider Queen. And Wulfgar of Icewind Dale, my friend of later years, though he still might yell out to the battle god, does not please this entity called Tempus except on those occasions when he puts his mighty war hammer to use.

The gods of the realms are many and varied—or they are the many and varied names and identities tagged onto the same being.

I know not—and care not—which.

—Drizzt Do'Urden

# II
# Winter

Drizzt picked his way through the rocky, towering mountains for many days, putting as much ground between himself and the farm village—and the awful memories—as he could. The decision to flee had not been a conscious one; if Drizzt had been less out of sorts, he might have seen the charity in the elf's gifts, the healing potion and the returned dagger, as a possible lead to a future relationship.

But the memories of Maldobar and the guilt that bowed the drow's shoulders would not be so easily dismissed. The farming village had become simply one more stopover on the search to find a home, a search that he increasingly believed was futile. Drizzt wondered how he could even go down to the next village that he came upon. The potential for tragedy had been played out all too clearly for him. He didn't stop to consider that the presence of the barghests might have been an unusual circumstance, and that, perhaps, in the absence of such fiends, his encounter might have turned out differently.

At this low point in his life, Drizzt's entire thoughts focused around a single word that echoed interminably in his head and pierced him to his heart: "drizzit."

Drizzt's trail eventually led him to a wide pass in the mountains and to a steep and rocky-gorge filled by the mist of some roaring river far below.

The air had been getting colder, something that Drizzt did not understand and the moist vapor felt good to the drow. He picked his way down the rocky cliff, a journey that took him the better part of the day, and found the bank of the cascading river.

Drizzt had seen rivers in the Underdark, but none to rival this. The Rauvin leaped across stones, throwing spray high into the air. It swarmed around great boulders, did a white-faced skip over fields of smaller stones, and dived suddenly into falls five times the drow's height. Drizzt was enchanted by the sight and the sound, but more than that, he also saw the possibilities of this place as a sanctuary. Many culverts edged the river, still pools where water had deflected from the pull of the main stream. Here, too, gathered the fish, resting from their struggles against the strong current.

The sight brought a grumble from Drizzt's belly. He knelt down over one pool, his hand poised to strike. It took him many tries to understand the refraction of sunlight through the water, but the drow was quick enough and smart enough to learn this game. Drizzt's hand plunged down suddenly and came back up firmly grasping a foot-long trout.

Drizzt tossed the fish away from the water, letting it bounce about on the stones, and soon had caught another. He would eat well this night, for the first time since he had fled the region of the farm village, and he had enough clear and cold water to satisfy any thirst.

This place was called Dead Orc Pass by those who knew the region. The title was somewhat of a misnomer, however, for while hundreds of orcs had indeed died in this rocky valley in numerous battles against human legions, thousands more lived here still, lurking in the many mountain caves, poised to strike against intruders. Few people came here, and none of them wisely.

To naive Drizzt, with the easy supply of food and water and the comfortable mist to battle the surprisingly chilling air, this gorge seemed the perfect retreat.

The drow spent his days huddled in the sheltering shadows of the many rocks and small caves, preferring to fish and forage in the dark hours of night. He didn't view this nocturnal style as a reversion to anything he had once been. When he had first stepped out of the Underdark, he had determined that he would live among the surface dwellers as a surface dweller, and thus, he had taken great pains to acclimate himself to the daytime sun. Drizzt held no such illusions now. He chose the nights for his activities because they were less painful to his sensitive eyes and because he knew that the less exposure his scimitar had to the sun, the longer it would retain its edge of magic.

It didn't take Drizzt very long, however, to understand why the surface dwellers seemed to prefer the daylight. Under the sun's warming rays, the air was still tolerable, if a bit chill. During the night, Drizzt found that he often had to take shelter from the biting breeze that whipped down over the steep edges of the mist-filled gorge. Winter was fast approaching the northland but the drow, raised in the seasonless world of the Underdark, couldn't know that.

On one of these nights, with the wind driving a brutal northern blast that numbed the drow's hands, Drizzt came to an important understanding. Even with Guenhwyvar beside him, huddled beneath a low overhang, Drizzt felt the severe pain growing in his extremities. Dawn was many hours away, and Drizzt seriously wondered if he would survive to see the sunrise.

"Too cold, Guenhwyvar," he stuttered through his chattering teeth. "Too cold."

He flexed his muscles and moved vigorously, trying to restore lost circulation. Then he mentally prepared himself, thinking of times past when he was warm, trying to defeat the despair and trick his own body into forgetting the cold. A single thought stood out clearly, a memory of the kitchens in Menzoberranzan's Academy. In the ever-warm Underdark, Drizzt had never even considered fire as a source of warmth. Always before, Drizzt had seen fire as merely a method of cooking, a means of producing light, and an offensive weapon. Now it took on even greater importance for the drow. As the winds continued to blow colder and colder, Drizzt realized, to his horror, that a fire's heat alone could keep him alive.

He looked about for kindling. In the Underdark, he had burned mushroom stalks, but no mushrooms grew large enough on the surface. There were plants, though, trees that grew even larger than the Underdark's fungus.

"Get me . . . limb," Drizzt stuttered to Guenhwyvar, not knowing any words for wood or tree. The panther regarded him curiously.

"Fire," Drizzt begged. He tried to rise but found his legs and feet numb.

Then the panther did understand. Guenhwyvar growled once and sprinted out into the night. The great cat nearly tripped over a pile of branches and twigs that had been set—by whom, Guenhwyvar did not know—just outside the doorway. Drizzt, too concerned with his survival at the time, did not even question the cat's sudden return.

Drizzt tried unsuccessfully to strike a fire for many minutes, smacking his dagger against a stone. Finally he understood that the wind prevented the sparks from catching, so he moved the setup to a more sheltered area. His legs ached now, and his own saliva froze along his lips and chin.

Then a spark took hold in the dry pile. Drizzt carefully fanned the tiny flame, cupping his hands to prevent the wind from coming in too strongly.

⚔ ⚔ ⚔ ⚔ ⚔

"The flames are up," an elf said to his companion.

Kellindil nodded gravely, still not certain if he and his fellow elves had done right in aiding the drow. Kellindil had come right back out from Maldobar, while Dove and the others had set off for Sundabar, and had met with a small elven family, kinfolk of his, who lived in the mountains near Dead Orc Pass. With their expert aid, the elf had little trouble locating the drow, and together he and his kin had watched, curiously, over the last few tendays.

Drizzt's innocuous lifestyle had not dispelled all of the wary elf's doubts, though. Drizzt was a drow, after all, dark-skinned to view and dark-hearted by reputation.

Still, Kellindil's sigh was one of relief when he, too, noted the slight, distant glow. The drow would not freeze; Kellindil believed that this drow did not deserve such a fate.

⚔ ⚔ ⚔ ⚔ ⚔

After his meal later that night, Drizzt leaned on Guenhwyvar—and the panther gladly accepting the shared body heat—and looked up at the stars, twinkling brightly in the cold air. "Do you remember Menzoberranzan?" he asked the panther. "Do you remember when we first met?"

If Guenhwyvar understood him, the cat gave no indication. With a yawn, Guenhwyvar rolled against Drizzt and dropped its head between two outstretched paws.

Drizzt smiled and roughly rubbed the panther's ear. He had met Guenhwyvar in Sorcere, the wizard school of the Academy, when the panther was in the possession of Masoj Hun'ett, the only drow that Drizzt had ever killed. Drizzt purposely tried not to think of that incident now; with the fire burning brightly, warming his toes, this was no night for unpleasant memories. Despite the many horrors he had faced in the city of his birth, Drizzt had found some pleasures there and had learned many useful lessons. Even Masoj had taught him things that now aided him more than he ever would have believed. Looking back to the crackling flames, Drizzt mused that if it had not been for his apprenticeship duties of lighting candles, he would not even have known how to build a fire. Undeniably, that knowledge had saved him from a chilling death.

Drizzt's smile was short-lived as his thoughts continued along those lines. Not so many months after that particularly useful lesson, Drizzt had been forced to kill Masoj.

Drizzt lay back again and sighed. With neither danger nor confusing companionship apparently imminent, this was perhaps the most simple time of his life, but never had the complexities of his existence so fully overwhelmed him.

He was brought from his tranquillity a moment later, when a large bird, an owl with tufted, hornlike feathers on its rounded head, rushed suddenly overhead. Drizzt laughed at his own inability to relax; in the second it had taken him to recognize the bird as no threat, he had leaped to his feet and drawn his scimitar and dagger. Guenhwyvar, too, had reacted to the startling bird, but in a far different manner. With Drizzt suddenly up and out of the way, the panther rolled closer to the heat of the fire, stretched languidly, and yawned again.

* * * * *

The owl drifted silently on unseen breezes, rising with the mist out of the river valley opposite the wall that Drizzt had originally descended. The bird rushed on through the night to a thick grove of evergreens on the side of a mountain, coming to rest on a wood-and-rope bridge constructed across the higher boughs of three of the trees. After a few moments preening itself, the bird rang a little silver bell, attached to the bridge for just such occasions.

A moment later, the bird rang the bell again.

"I am coming," came a voice from below. "Patience, Hooter. Let a blind man move at a pace that best suits him!" As if it understood, and enjoyed, the game, the owl rang the bell a third time.

An old man with a huge and bristling gray mustache and white eyes appeared on the bridge. He hopped and skipped his way toward the bird. Montolio was formerly a ranger of great renown, who now lived out his final years—by his own choice—secluded in the mountains and surrounded by the creatures he loved best (and he did not consider humans, elves, dwarves, or any of the other intelligent races among them). Despite his considerable age, Montolio remained tall and straight, though the years had taken their toll on the hermit, crinkling one hand up so that it resembled the claw of the bird he now approached.

"Patience, Hooter," he mumbled over and over. Anyone watching him nimbly pick his way across the somewhat treacherous bridge never would have guessed that he was blind, and those who knew Montolio certainly would not describe him that way. Rather, they might have said that his eyes did not function, but they quickly would have added that he did not need them to function. With his skills and knowledge, and with his many animal friends, the old ranger "saw" more of the world around him than most of those with normal sight.

Montolio held out his arm, and the great owl promptly hopped onto it, carefully finding its footing on the man's heavy leather sleeve.

"You have seen the drow?" Montolio asked.

The owl responded with a whoo, then went off into a complicated series of chattering hoots and whoos Montolio took it all in, weighing every detail. With the help of his friends, particularly this rather talkative owl, the ranger had monitored the drow for several days, curious as to why a dark elf had wandered into the valley. At first, Montolio had assumed that the drow was somehow connected to Graul, the chief orc of the region, but as time went on, the ranger began to suspect differently.

"A good sign," Montolio remarked when the owl had assured him that the drow had not yet made contact with the orc tribes Graul was bad enough without having any allies as powerful as dark elves!

Still, the ranger could not figure out why the orcs had not sought out the drow. Possibly they had not caught sight of him; the drow had gone out of his way to remain inconspicuous, setting no fires (before this very night) and only coming out after sunset. More likely, Montolio mused as he gave the matter more thought, the orcs had seen the drow but had not yet found the courage to make contact.

Either way, the whole episode was proving a welcome diversion for the ranger as he went about the daily routines of setting up his house for the coming winter. He did not fear the drow's appearance. Montolio did not fear much of anything—and if the drow and the orcs were not allies, the resulting conflict might well be worth the watching.

"By my leave," the ranger said to placate the complaining owl. "Go and hunt some mice!" The owl swooped off immediately, circled once under then back over the bridge, and headed out into the night.

"Just take care not to eat any of the mice I have set to watching the drow!" Montolio called after the bird, and he chuckled, shook his wild-grown gray locks, and turned back toward the ladder at the end of the bridge. He vowed, as he descended, that he would soon strap on his sword and find out what business this particular dark elf might have in the region.

The old ranger made many such vows.

⚔ ⚔ ⚔ ⚔ ⚔

Autumn's warning blasts gave way quickly to the onslaught of winter. It hadn't taken Drizzt long to figure out the significance of gray clouds, but when the storm broke this time, in the form of snow instead of rain, the drow was truly amazed. He had seen the whiteness along the tops of the mountains but had never gone high enough to inspect it and had merely assumed that it was a coloration of the rocks. Now Drizzt watched the white flakes descend on the valley; they disappeared in the rush of the river but gathered on the rocks.

As the snow began to mount and the clouds hung ever lower in the sky, Drizzt came to a dreadful realization. Quickly he summoned Guenhwyvar to his side.

"We must find better shelter," he explained to the weary panther. Guenhwyvar had only been released to its astral home the previous day. "And we must stock it with wood for our fires."

Several caves dotted the valley wall on this side of the river. Drizzt found one, not only deep and dark but sheltered from the blowing wind by a high stone ridge. He entered, pausing just inside to let his eyes adapt from the snow's glaring brightness.

The cave floor was uneven and its ceiling was not high. Large boulders were scattered randomly about, and off to the side, near one of these, Drizzt noticed a darker gloom, indicating a second chamber. He placed his armful of kindling down and started toward it, then halted suddenly, both he and Guenhwyvar sensing another presence.

Drizzt drew his scimitar, slipped to the boulder, and peered around it. With his infravision, the cave's other inhabitant, a warm-glowing ball considerably larger than the drow, was not hard to spot. Drizzt knew at once what it was, though he had no name for it. He had seen this creature from afar several times, watching it as it deftly—and with amazing speed, considering its bulk—snatched fish from the river.

Whatever it might be called, Drizzt had no desire to fight with it over the cave; there were other holes in the area, more easily attainable.

The great brown bear, though, seemed to have different ideas. The creature stirred suddenly and came up to its rear legs, its avalanche growl echoing throughout the cave and its claws and teeth all too noticeable.

Guenhwyvar, the astral entity of the panther, knew the bear as an ancient rival, and one that wise cats took great care to avoid. Still the brave panther sprang right in front of Drizzt, willing to take on the larger creature so that its master might escape.

"No, Guenhwyvar!" Drizzt commanded, and he grabbed the cat and pulled himself back in front.

The bear, another of Montolio's many friends, made no move to attack, but it held its position fiercely, not appreciating the interruption of its long-awaited slumber.

Drizzt sensed something here that he could not explain—not a friendship with the bear, but an eerie understanding of the creature's viewpoint. He thought himself foolish as he sheathed his blade, yet he could not deny the empathy he felt, almost as though he was viewing the situation through the bear's eyes.

Cautiously, Drizzt stepped closer, drawing the bear fully into his gaze. The bear seemed almost surprised, but gradually it lowered its claws and its snarling grimace became an expression that Drizzt understood as curiosity.

Drizzt slowly reached into his pouch and took out a fish that he had been saving for his own supper. He tossed it over to the bear, which sniffed it once, then swallowed it down with hardly a chew.

Another long moment of staring ensued, but the tension was gone. The bear belched once, rolled back down, and was soon snoring contentedly.

Drizzt looked at Guenhwyvar and shrugged helplessly, having no idea of how he had just communicated so profoundly with the animal. The panther had apparently understood the connotations of the exchange, too, for Guenhwyvar's fur was no longer ruffled.

For the rest of the time that Drizzt spent in that cave, he took care, whenever he had spare food, to drop a morsel by the slumbering bear. Sometimes, particularly if Drizzt had dropped fish, the bear sniffed and awakened just long enough to gobble the meal, More often, though, the animal ignored the food altogether, rhythmically snoring and dreaming about honey and berries and female bears, and whatever else sleeping bears dreamed about.

⚔ ⚔ ⚔ ⚔ ⚔

"He took up his home with Bluster?" Montolio gasped when he learned from Hooter that the drow and the ornery bear were sharing the two-chambered cave. Montolio nearly fell over—and would have if he hadn't been so close to the supporting tree trunk. The old ranger leaned there, stunned, scratching at the stubble on his face and pulling at his moustache. He had known the bear for several years, and even he wasn't certain that he would be willing to share quarters with it. Bluster was an easily riled creature, as many of Graul's stupid orcs had learned over the years.

"I guess Bluster is too tired to argue," Montolio rationalized, but he knew that something more was brewing here. If an orc or a goblin had gone into that cave, Bluster would have swatted it dead without a second thought. Yet the drow and his panther were in there, day after day, setting their fires in the outer chamber while Bluster snored contentedly in the inner.

As a ranger, and knowing many other rangers, Montolio had seen and heard of stranger things. Up to now, though, he had always considered that innate ability to mentally connect with wild animals the exclusive domain of those surface elves, sprites, halflings, gnomes, and humans who had trained in the woodland way.

"How would a dark elf know of a bear?" Montolio asked aloud, still scratching at his beard. The ranger considered two possibilities: Either there was more to the drow race than he knew, or this particular dark elf was not akin to his kin. Given the elf's already strange behavior, Montolio assumed the latter, though he greatly wanted to find out for sure. His investigation would have to wait, though. The first snow had already fallen, and the ranger knew the second, and the third, and many more, would not be far behind. In the mountains around Dead Orc Pass, little moved once the snows had begun.

⚔ ⚔ ⚔ ⚔ ⚔

Guenhwyvar proved to be Drizzt's salvation through the coming tendays. On those occasions when the panther walked the Material Plane, Guenhwyvar went out into the frigid, deep snows continually, hunting and more importantly, bringing back wood for the life-giving fire.

Still, things were not easy for the displaced drow. Every day Drizzt had to go down to the river and break up the ice that formed in the slower pools, Drizzt's fishing pools, along its bank. It was not a far walk, but the snow was soon deep and treacherous, often sliding down the slope behind Drizzt to bury him in a chilling embrace. Several times, Drizzt stumbled back to his cave, all feeling gone from his hands and legs. He learned quickly to get the fires blazing before he went out, for on his return, he had no strength to hold the dagger and stone to strike a spark.

Even when Drizzt's belly was full and he was surrounded by the glow of the fire and Guenhwyvar's fur, he was cold and utterly miserable. For the first time in many tendays, the drow questioned his decision to leave the Underdark, and as his desperation grew, he questioned his decision to leave Menzoberranzan.

"Surely I am a homeless wretch," he often complained in those no-longer-so-rare moments of self-pity. "And surely I will die here, cold and alone."

Drizzt had no idea of what was going on in the strange world around him. Would the warmth that he found when he first came to the surface world ever return to the land? Or was this some vile curse, perhaps aimed at him by his mighty enemies back in Menzoberranzan? This confusion led Drizzt to a troublesome dilemma: Should he remain in the cave and try to wait out the storm (for what else could he call the wintry season)? Or should he set out from the river valley and seek a warmer climate?

He would have left, and the trek through the mountains most assuredly would have killed him, but he noticed another event coinciding with the harsh weather. The hours of daylight had lessened and the hours of night had increased. Would the sun disappear completely, engulfing the surface in an eternal darkness and eternal cold? Drizzt doubted that possibility, so, using some sand and an empty flask that he had in his pack, he began measuring the time of light and of darkness.

His hopes sank every time his calculations showed an earlier sunset, and as the season deepened, so did Drizzt's despair. His health diminished as well. He was a wretched thing indeed, thin and shivering, when he first noticed the seasonal turn-around, the winter solstice. He hardly believed his findings—his measurements were not so precise—but after the next few days, Drizzt could not deny what the falling sand told him.

The days were growing longer.

Drizzt's hope returned. He had suspected a seasonal variance since the first cool winds had begun to blow months before. He had watched the bear fishing more diligently as the weather worsened, and now he believed that the creature had anticipated the cold and had stored up its fat to sleep it out.

That belief, and his findings about the daylight, convinced Drizzt that this frozen desolation would not endure.

The solstice did not bring any immediate relief, though. The winds blew harder and the snow continued to pile. But Drizzt grew determined again, and more than a winter would be needed to defeat the indomitable drow.

Then it happened—almost overnight, it seemed. The snows lessened, the river ran freer of ice, and the wind shifted to bring in warmer air. Drizzt felt a surge of vitality and hope, a release from grief and from guilt that he could not explain. Drizzt could not realize what urges gripped him, had no name or concept for it, but he was as fully caught up in the timeless spring as all of the natural creatures of the surface world.

One morning, as Drizzt finished his meal and prepared for bed, his long-dormant roommate plodded out of the side chamber, noticeably more slender but still quite formidable. Drizzt watched the ambling bear carefully, wondering if he should summon Guenhwyvar or draw his scimitar. The bear paid him no heed, though. It shuffled right by him, stopped to sniff at and lick the flat stone Drizzt had used as a plate, and ambled out into the warm sunlight, stopping at the cave exit to give a yawn and a stretch so profound that Drizzt understood that its winter nap was at an end. Drizzt understood, too, that the cave would grow crowded very quickly with the dangerous animal up and about, and he decided that perhaps, with the more hospitable weather, the cave might not be worth fighting for.

Drizzt was gone before the bear returned, but to the bear's delight, he had left one final fish meal. Soon Drizzt was setting up in a more shallow and less protected cave a few hundred yards down the valley wall.

# 12 To Know Your Enemies

Winter gave way as quickly as it had come. The snows lessened daily and the southern wind brought air that had no chill. Drizzt soon settled into a comfortable routine; the biggest problem he faced was the daytime glare of the sun off the still snow-covered ground. The drow had adapted quite well to the sun in his first few months on the surface, moving about—even fighting—in the daylight. Now, though, with the white snow throwing the glaring reflection back in his face, Drizzt could hardly venture out.

He came out only at night and left the daytime to the bear and other such creatures. Drizzt was not too concerned; the snow would be gone soon, he believed, and he could return to the easy life that had marked the last days before winter.

Well fed, well rested, and under the soft light of a shining, alluring moon one night, Drizzt glanced across the river, to the far wall of the valley.

"What is up there?" the drow whispered to himself. Though the river ran strong with the spring melt, earlier that night Drizzt had found a possible way across it, a series of large and closely spaced rocks poking up above the rushing water.

The night was still young; the moon was not halfway up in the sky. Filled with the wanderlust and spirit so typical of the season, Drizzt decided to have a look. He skipped down to the riverbank and jumped lightly and nimbly out onto the stones. To a man or an orc—or most of the other races of the world—crossing on the wet, unevenly spaced, and often rounded stones might have seemed too difficult and treacherous to even make the attempt, but the agile drow managed it quite easily.

He came down on the other bank running, springing over or around the many rocks and crags without a thought or care. How different his demeanor might have been if he had known that he was now on the side of the valley belonging to Graul, the great orc chieftain!

⚔ ⚔ ⚔ ⚔ ⚔

An orc patrol spotted the prancing drow before he was halfway up the valley wall. The orcs had seen the drow before, on occasions when Drizzt was fishing out at the river. Fearful of dark elves, Graul had ordered its minions to keep their distance, thinking the snows would drive the intruder away. But the winter had passed and this lone drow remained, and now he had crossed the river.

Graul wrung his fat-fingered hands nervously when he was told the news. The big orc was comforted a bit by the belief that this drow was alone and not a member of a larger band. He might be a scout or a renegade; Graul could not know for sure, and the implications of either did not please the orc chieftain. If the drow was a scout, more dark elves might follow, and if the drow was a renegade, he might look upon the orcs as possible allies.

Graul had been chieftain for many years, an unusually long tenure for the chaotic orcs. The big orc had survived by taking no chances, and Graul meant to take none now. A dark elf could usurp the leadership of the tribe, a position Graul coveted dearly. This, Graul would not permit. Two orc patrols slipped out of dark holes shortly thereafter, with explicit orders to kill the drow.

⚔ ⚔ ⚔ ⚔ ⚔

A chill wind blew above the valley wall, and the snow was deeper up here, but Drizzt didn't care. Great patches of evergreens rolled out before him, darkening the mountainous valleys and inviting him, after a winter cooped up in the cave, to come and explore.

He had put nearly a mile behind him when he first realized that he was being pursued. He never actually saw anything, except perhaps a fleeting shadow out of the corner of his eye, but those intangible warrior senses told Drizzt the truth beyond doubt. He moved up the side of a steep incline, climbed above a copse of thick trees, and sprinted for the high ridge. When he got there, he slipped behind a boulder and turned to watch.

Seven dark forms, six humanoid and one large canine, came out of the trees behind him, following his trail carefully and methodically. From this distance, Drizzt couldn't tell their race, though he suspected that they were humans. He looked all about, searching for his best course of retreat, or the best defensible area.

Drizzt hardly noticed that his scimitar was in one hand his dagger in the other. When he realized fully that he had drawn the weapons, and that the pursuing party was getting uncomfortably close, he paused and pondered.

He could face the pursuers right here and hit them as they scaled the last few treacherous feet of the slippery climb.

"No," Drizzt growled, dismissing that possibility as soon as it came to him. He could attack, and probably win, but then what burden would he carry away from the encounter? Drizzt wanted no fight, nor did he desire any contact at all. He already carried all the guilt he could handle.

He heard his pursuers' voices, guttural strains similar to the goblin tongue. "Orcs," the drow mouthed silently, matching the language with the creatures' human size.

The recognition did nothing to change the drow's attitudes, though. Drizzt had no love for orcs—he had seen enough of the smelly things back in Menzoberranzan—but neither did he have any reason, any justification, for battling this band. He turned and picked a path and sped off into the night.

The pursuit was dogged; the orcs were too close behind for Drizzt to shake them. He saw a problem developing, for if the orcs were hostile, and by their shouts and snarls, Drizzt believed that to be the case, then Drizzt had missed his opportunity to fight them on favorable ground. The moon had set long ago and the sky had taken on the blue tint of predawn. Orcs did not favor sunlight, but with the glare of the snow all about him, Drizzt would be nearly helpless in it.

Stubbornly the drow ignored the battle option and tried to outrun the pursuit, circling back toward the valley. Here Drizzt made his second error, for another orc band this one accompanied by both a wolf and a much larger form, a stone giant, lay in wait.

The path ran fairly level, one side of it dropping steeply down a rocky slope to the drow's left and the other climbing just as steeply and over ground just as rocky to his right. Drizzt knew his pursuers would have little trouble following him over such a predetermined course, but he relied solely on speed now, trying to get back to his defensible cave before the blinding sun came up.

A snarl warned him a moment before a huge bristle-haired wolf, called a worg, bounded around the boulders just above him and cut him off. The worg sprang at him, its jaws snapping for his head. Drizzt dipped low, under the assault, and his scimitar came out in a flash, slashing across to further widen the beast's huge maw. The worg tumbled down heavily behind the turning drow, its tongue lapping widely at its own gushing blood.

Drizzt whacked it again, dropping it, but the six orcs came rushing in, brandishing spears and clubs. Drizzt turned to flee, then ducked again, just in time, as a hurled boulder flew past, skipping down the rocky decline.

Without a second thought, Drizzt brought a globe of darkness down over his own head.

The four leading orcs plunged into the globe without realizing it. Their remaining two comrades held back, clutching spears and glancing nervously about. They could see nothing inside the magical darkness, but from the rushing thumps of blades and clubs and the wild shouting, it sounded as if an entire army battled in there. Then another sound issued from the darkness, a growling, feline sound.

The two orcs backed away, looking over their shoulders and wishing the stone giant would hurry up and get down to them. One of their orc comrades, and another, came tearing out of the blackness, screaming in terror. The first sped past its startled kin, but the second never made it.

Guenhwyvar latched on to the unfortunate orc and drove it to the ground, tearing the life from it. The panther hardly slowed, leaping out and taking down one of the waiting two as it frantically stumbled to get away. Those remaining outside the globe scrambled and tripped over the rocks, and Guenhwyvar, having finished the second kill, leaped off in pursuit.

Drizzt came out the other side of the globe unscathed, with both his scimitar and dagger dripping orc blood. The giant, huge and square-shouldered, with legs as large as tree trunks, stepped out to face him, and Drizzt never hesitated. He sprang to a large stone, then leaped off, his scimitar leading the way.

His agility and speed surprised the stone giant; the monster never even got its club or its free hand up to block. But luck was not with the drow this time. His scimitar, enchanted in the magic of the Underdark, had seen too much of the surface light. It drove against the stonelike skin of the fifteen-foot giant, bent nearly in half, and snapped at the hilt.

Drizzt bounced back, betrayed for the first time by his trusted weapon.

The giant howled and lifted its club, grinning evilly until a black form soared over its intended victim and crashed into its chest, raking with four cruel claws.

Guenhwyvar had saved Drizzt again, but the giant was hardly finished. It clubbed and thrashed until the panther flew free. Guenhwyvar tried to pivot and come right back in, but the panther landed on the down slope and its momentum broke away the sheet of snow. The cat slid and tumbled, and finally broke free of the slide, unharmed, but far down the mountainside from Drizzt and the battle.

The giant offered no smile this time. Blood seeped from a dozen deep scratches across its chest and face. Behind it, down the trail, the other orc group, led by a second howling worg, was quickly closing.

Like any wise warrior so obviously outnumbered, Drizzt turned and ran.

If the two orcs who had fled from Guenhwyvar had come right back down the slope, they could have cut the drow off. Orcs had never been known for bravery, though, and those two had already crested the ridge of the slope and were still running, not even looking back.

Drizzt sped along the trail, searching for some way he might descend and rejoin the panther. Nowhere on the slope seemed promising, though, for he would have to pick his way slowly and carefully, and no doubt with a giant raining boulders down at him. Going up seemed just as futile with the monster so close behind, so the drow just ran on, along the trail, hoping it wouldn't end anytime soon.

The sun peeked over the eastern horizon then, just another problem—suddenly one of many—for the desperate drow.

Understanding that fortune had turned against him, Drizzt somehow knew, even before he turned the trail's latest sharp corner, that he had come to the end of the road. A rock slide had long ago blocked the trail. Drizzt skidded to a halt and pulled off his pack, knowing that time was against him.

The worg-led orc band caught up to the giant, both gaining confidence in the presence of the other. Together they charged on, with the vicious worg sprinting out to take the lead.

Around a sharp bend the creature sped, stumbling and trying to stop when it tangled suddenly in a looped rope. Worgs were not stupid creatures, but this one didn't fully comprehend the terrible implications as the drow pushed a rounded stone over the ledge. The worg didn't understand that is, until the rope snapped taut and the stone pulled the beast, flying, down behind.

The simple trap had worked to perfection, but it was the only advantage Drizzt could hope to gain. Behind him, the trail was fully blocked, and to the sides, the slopes climbed and dropped too abruptly for him to flee. When the orcs and the giant came around the corner, tentatively after watching their worg go for a rather bumpy ride, Drizzt stood to face them with only a dagger in his hand.

The drow tried to parlay, using the goblin tongue, but the orcs would hear nothing of it. Before the first word left Drizzt's mouth, one of them had launched its spear.

The weapon came in a blur at the sun-blinded drow, but it was a curving shaft thrown by a clumsy creature. Drizzt easily sidestepped and returned the throw with his dagger. The orc could see better than the drow, but it was not as quick. It caught the dagger cleanly, right in the throat. Gurgling, the orc went down, and its closest comrade grabbed at the knife and tore it free, not to save the other orc, but merely to get its hands on so fine a weapon.

Drizzt scooped up the crude spear and planted his feet firmly as the stone giant stalked in.

An owl swooped down above the giant suddenly and gave a hoot, hardly distracting the determined monster. A moment later, though, the giant jerked forward, moved by the weight of an arrow that had suddenly thudded into its back.

Drizzt saw the quivering, black-feathered shaft as the angry giant spun about. The drow didn't question the unexpected aid. He drove his spear with all his strength right into the monster's backside.

The giant would have turned to respond, but the owl swooped in again and hooted and on cue, another arrow whistled in, this one digging into the giant's chest. Another hoot, and another arrow found the mark.

The stunned orcs looked all about for the unseen assailant, but the glaring brightness of the morning sun on the snow offered little assistance to the nocturnal beasts. The giant, struck through the heart, only stood and stared blankly, not even realizing that its life was at an end. The drow drove his spear in again from behind, but that action only served to tumble the monster away from Drizzt.

The orcs looked to each other and all around, wondering which way they could flee.

The strange owl dived in again, this time above an orc, and gave a fourth hoot. The orc, understanding the implications, waved its arms and shrieked, then fell silent with an arrow protruding from its face.

The four remaining orcs broke ranks and fled, one up the slope, another running back the way it had come, and two rushing toward Drizzt.

A deft spin of the spear sent its butt end slamming into the face of one orc, then Drizzt fully completed the spinning motion to deflect the other orc's spear tip toward the ground. The orc dropped the weapon, realizing that it could not get it back in line in time to stop the drow.

⚔ ⚔ ⚔ ⚔ ⚔

The orc climbing the slope understood its doom as the signaling owl closed on it. The terrified creature dived behind a rock upon hearing one hoot, but if it had been a smarter thing, it would have realized its error. By the angle of the shots that had felled the giant, the archer had to be somewhere up on this slope.

An arrow knocked into its thigh as it crouched, dropping it, writhing, to its back. With the orc's growling and thrashing, the unseen and unseeing archer hardly needed the owl's next hoot to place his second shot, this one catching the orc squarely in the chest and silencing it forever.

⚔ ⚔ ⚔ ⚔ ⚔

Drizzt reversed his direction immediately, clipping the second orc with the spear's butt end. In the blink of an eye, the drow reversed his grip a third time and drove the spear tip into the creature's throat, digging upward into its brain. The first orc that Drizzt had hit reeled and shook its head violently, trying to reorient itself to the battle. It felt the drow's hands grab at the front of its dirty bearskin tunic, then it felt a rush of air as it flew out over the ledge, taking the same route as the previously trapped worg.

⚔ ⚔ ⚔ ⚔ ⚔

Hearing the screams of its dying companions, the orc on the trail put its head down and sped on, thinking itself quite clever in taking this route. It changed its mind abruptly, though, when it turned a bend and ran straight into the waiting paws of a huge black panther.

⚔ ⚔ ⚔ ⚔ ⚔

Drizzt leaned back, exhausted, against the stone, holding his spear ready for a throw as the strange owl floated back down the mountainside. The owl kept its distance, though, alighting on the outcropping that forced the trail's sharp bend a dozen steps away.

Movement up above caught the drow's attention. He could hardly see in the blinding light, but he did make out a humanlike form picking a careful path down toward him.

The owl set off again, circling above the drow and calling, and Drizzt crouched, alert and unnerved, as the man slipped down to a position behind the rocky spur. No arrow whistled out to the owl's hooting, though. Instead came the archer.

He was tall, straight, and very old, with a huge gray moustache and wild gray hair. Most curious of all were his milky white and pupilless eyes. If Drizzt had not witnessed the man's archery display, he would have believed the man blind. The old man's limbs seemed quite frail, too, but Drizzt did not let appearances deceive him. The expert archer kept his heavy longbow bowed and ready, an arrow firmly nocked, with hardly any effort. The drow did not have to look far to see the deadly efficiency with which the human could put the powerful weapon to use.

The old man said something in a language that Drizzt could not understand then in a second tongue, then in goblin, which Drizzt understood. "Who are you?"

"Drizzt Do'Urden," the drow replied evenly, taking some hope in the fact that he could at least communicate with this adversary.

"Is that a name?" the old man asked. He chuckled and shrugged. "Whatever it is, and whoever you might be, and whyever you might be here, is of minor consequence."

The owl, noticing movement, started hooting and swooping widely, but it was too late for the old man. Behind him, Guenhwyvar slunk around the bend and closed to within an easy spring, ears flattened and teeth bared.

Seemingly oblivious to the peril, the old man finished his thought. "You are my prisoner now."

Guenhwyvar issued a low, throaty growl and the drow grinned broadly.

"I think not," Drizzt replied.

# 13 Montolio

"Friend of yours?" the old man asked calmly.

"Guenhwyvar," Drizzt explained.

"Big cat?"

"Oh, yes," Drizzt answered.

The old man eased his bowstring straight and let the arrow slowly slip, point down. He closed his eyes, tilted his head back, and seemed to fall within himself. A moment later, Drizzt noticed that Guenhwyvar's ears came up suddenly, and the drow understood that this strange human was somehow making a telepathic link to the panther.

"Good cat, too," the old man said a moment later. Guenhwyvar walked out from around the outcropping—sending the owl flapping away in a frenzy—and casually stalked past the old man, moving to stand beside Drizzt. Apparently, the panther had relinquished all concerns that the old man was an enemy.

Drizzt considered Guenhwyvar's actions curious, viewing them in the same manner as he had his own empathic agreement with the bear in the cave a season ago.

"Good cat," the old man said again.

Drizzt leaned back against the stone and relaxed his grip on the spear.

"I am Montolio," the old man explained proudly, as though the name should carry some weight with the drow. "Montolio DeBrouchee."

"Well met and fare well," Drizzt said flatly. "If we are done with our meeting, then we may go our own ways."

"We may," Montolio agreed, "if we both choose to."

"Am I to be your . . . prisoner . . . once more?" Drizzt asked with a bit of sarcasm in his voice.

The sincerity of Montolio's ensuing laughter brought a smile to the drow's face despite his cynicism. "Mine?" the old man asked incredulously. "No, no, I believe we have settled that issue. But you have killed some minions of Graul this day, a deed that the orc king will want punished. Let me offer you a room at my castle. The orcs will not approach the place." He showed a wry smile and bent over toward Drizzt to whisper, as if to keep his next words a secret between them. "They will not come near me, you know." Montolio pointed to his strange eyes. "They believe me to be bad magic because of my . . ." Montolio struggled for the word that would convey the thought, but the guttural language was limited and he soon grew frustrated.

Drizzt silently recounted the course of the battle, then his jaw drooped open in undeniable amazement as he realized the truth of what had transpired. The old man was indeed blind! The owl, circling over enemies and hooting, had led his shots. Drizzt looked around at the slain giant and orc and his jaw did not close; the old man hadn't missed.

"Will you come?" Montolio asked. "I would like to gain the—" again he had to search for an appropriate term—"purposes . . . a dark elf would have to live a winter in a cave with Bluster the bear."

Montolio cringed at his own inability to converse with the drow, but from the context, Drizzt could pretty much understand what the old man meant, even figuring out unfamiliar terms such as "winter" and "bear."

"Orc king Graul has ten hundred more fighters to send against you," Montolio remarked, sensing that the drow was having a difficult time considering the offer.

"I will not come with you," Drizzt declared at length. The drow truly wanted to go, wanted to learn a few things about this remarkable man, but too many tragedies had befallen those who had crossed Drizzt's path.

Guenhwyvar's low growl told Drizzt that the panther did not approve of his decision.

"I bring trouble," Drizzt tried to explain to the old man, to the panther, and to himself. "You would be better served, Montolio DeBrouchee, to keep away from me."

"Is this a threat?"

"A warning," Drizzt replied. "If you take me in, if you even allow me to remain near to you, then you will be doomed, as were the farmers in the village."

Montolio perked his ears up at the mention of the distant farming village. He had heard that one family in Maldobar had been brutally killed and that a ranger, Dove Falconhand had been called in to help.

"I do not fear doom," Montolio said, forcing a smile. "I have lived through many . . . fights, Drizzt Do'Urden. I have fought in a dozen bloody wars and spent an entire winter trapped on the side of a mountain with a broken leg. I have killed a giant with only a dagger and . . . befriended every animal for five thousand steps in any direction. Do not fear for me." Again came that wry, knowing smile. "But then," Montolio said slowly, "It is not for me that you fear."

Drizzt felt confused and a bit insulted.

"You fear for yourself," Montolio continued, undaunted. "Self-pity? It does not fit one of your prowess. Dismiss and come along with me."

If Montolio had seen Drizzt's scowl, he would have guessed the forthcoming answer. Guenhwyvar did notice it, and the panther bumped hard into Drizzt's leg.

From Guenhwyvar's reaction, Montolio understood the drow's intent. "The cat wants you to come along," he remarked. "It'll be better than a cave," he promised, "and better food than half-cooked fish."

Drizzt looked down at Guenhwyvar and again the panther bumped him, this time voicing a louder and more insistent growl with the action.

Drizzt remained adamant, reminding himself pointedly by conjuring an image of carnage in a farmhouse far away. "I will not come," he said firmly.

"Then I must name you as an enemy, and a prisoner!" Montolio roared, snapping his bow back to a ready position. "Your cat will not aid you this time, Drizzt Do'Urden!" Montolio leaned in and flashed his smile and whispered, "The cat agrees with me."

It was too much for Drizzt. He knew that the old man wouldn't shoot him, but Montolio's flaky charm soon wore away the drow's mental defenses, considerable though they were.

What Montolio had described as a castle turned out to be a series of wooden caves dug around the roots of huge and tightly packed evergreens. Lean-tos of woven sticks furthered the protection and somewhat linked the caves together, and a low wall of stacked rocks ringed the whole complex. As Drizzt neared the place, he noticed several rope-and-wood bridges crossing from tree to tree at various heights, with rope ladders leading up to them from the ground level and with crossbows securely mounted at fairly regular intervals.

The drow didn't complain that the castle was of wood and dirt, though. Drizzt had spent three decades in Menzoberranzan living in a wondrous castle of stone and surrounded by many more breathtakingly beautiful structures, but none of them seemed as welcoming as Montolio's home.

Birds chittered their welcome at the old ranger's approach. Squirrels, even a raccoon, hopped excitedly among the tree branches to get near him—though they kept their distance when they noticed that a huge panther accompanied Montolio.

"I have many rooms," Montolio explained to Drizzt. "Many blankets and much food." Montolio hated the limited goblin tongue. He had so many things he wanted to say to the drow, and so many things he wanted to learn from the drow. This seemed impossible, if not overly tedious, in a language so base and negative in nature, not designed for complex thoughts or notions. The goblin tongue sported more than a hundred words for killing and for hatred, but not a one for higher emotions such as compassion. The goblin word for friendship could be translated to mean either a temporary military alliance or servitude to a stronger goblin, and neither definition fit Montolio's intentions toward the lone dark elf.

The first task then, the ranger decided, was to teach this drow the common tongue.

"We cannot speak"—There was no word for "properly" in Goblin, so Montolio had to improvise ". . . well . . . in this language," he explained to Drizzt, "but it will serve us as I teach you the tongue of humans—if you wish to learn."

Drizzt remained tentative in his acceptance. When he had walked away from the farming village, he had decided that his lot in life would be as a hermit, and thus far he had done pretty well—better than he had expected. The offer was tempting, though, and on a practical level, Drizzt knew that knowing the common language of the region might keep him out of trouble. Montolio's smile nearly took in the ranger's ears when the drow accepted.

Hooter, the owl, however, seemed not so pleased. With the drow—or, more particularly, with the drow's panther—about, the owl would be spending less time in the comforts of the evergreens' lower boughs.

⚔ ⚔ ⚔ ⚔ ⚔

"Cousin, Montolio DeBrouchee has taken the drow in!" an elf cried excitedly to Kellindil. All the group had been out searching for Drizzt's trail since the winter had broken. With the drow gone from Dead Orc Pass, the elves, particularly Kellindil, had feared trouble, had feared that the drow had perhaps taken in with Graul and his orc minions.

Kellindil jumped to his feet, hardly able to grasp the startling news. He knew of Montolio, the legendary if somewhat eccentric ranger, and he knew, too, that Montolio, with all of his animal contacts, could judge intruders quite accurately.

"When? How?" Kellindil asked, barely knowing where to begin. If the drow had confused him through the previous months, the surface elf was thoroughly flustered now.

"A tenday ago," the other elf answered. "I know not how it came about, but the drow now walks in Montolio's grove, openly and with his panther beside him."

"Is Montolio . . ."

The other elf interrupted Kellindil, seeing where his line of concern was heading. "Montolio is unharmed and in control," he assured Kellindil. "He has taken in the drow of his own accord, it would seem, and now it appears that the old ranger is teaching the dark elf the common tongue."

"Amazing," was all that Kellindil could reply.

"We could set a watch over Montolio's grove," the other elf offered. "If you fear for the old ranger's safety—"

"No," Kellindil replied. "No, the drow once again has proven himself no enemy. I have suspected his friendly intentions since I encountered him near Maldobar. Now I am satisfied. Let us get on with our business and leave the drow and the ranger to theirs."

The other elf nodded his agreement, but a diminutive creature listening outside Kellindil's tent was not so certain.

Tephanis came into the elven camp nightly, to steal food and other items that would make him more comfortable. The sprite had heard of the dark elf a few days earlier, when the elves had resumed their search for Drizzt, and he had taken great pains to listen to their conversation ever since, as curious as any about the whereabouts of the one who had destroyed Ulgulu and Kempfana.

Tephanis shook his floppy-eared head violently. "Drat-the-day-that-that-one-returned!" he whispered, sounding somewhat like an excited bumblebee. Then he ran off, his little feet barely touching the ground. Tephanis had made another connection in the months since Ulgulu's demise, another powerful ally that he did not want to lose.

Within minutes he found Caroak, the great, silver-haired winter wolf, on the high peak that they called their home.

"The-drow-is-with-the-ranger," Tephanis spouted, and the canine beast seemed to understand. "Beware-of-that-one-I-say! It-was-he-who-killed-my-former-masters. Dead!"

Caroak looked down the wide expanse to the mountain that held Montolio's grove. The winter wolf knew that place well, and he knew well enough to stay away from it. Montolio DeBrouchee was friends with all sorts of animals, but winter wolves were more monster than animal, and no friend of rangers.

Tephanis, too, looked Montolio's way, worried that he might again have to face the sneaky drow. The mere thought of encountering that one again made the little sprite's head ache (and the bruise from the plowshare had never completely gone away).

⚔ ⚔ ⚔ ⚔ ⚔

As winter eased into spring over the next few tendays, so did Drizzt and Montolio ease into their friendship. The common tongue of the region was not so very different from the goblin tongue, more a shift of inflection than an alteration of complete words, and Drizzt caught on to it quickly, even learning how to read and write. Montolio proved a fine teacher, and by the third tenday, he spoke to Drizzt exclusively in the common tongue and scowled impatiently every time Drizzt reverted to using goblin to get a point across.

For Drizzt, this was a fun time, a time of easy living and shared pleasures. Montolio's collection of books was extensive, and the drow found himself absorbed in adventures of the imagination, in dragon lore, and accounts of epic battles. Any doubts Drizzt might have had were long gone, as were his doubts about Montolio. The shelter in the evergreens was indeed a castle, and the old man as fine a host as Drizzt had ever known.

Drizzt learned many other things from Montolio during those first tendays, practical lessons that would aid him for the rest of his life. Montolio confirmed Drizzt's suspicions about a seasonal weather change, and he even taught Drizzt how to anticipate the weather from day to day by watching the animals, the sky, and the wind.

In this, too, Drizzt caught on quickly, as Montolio had suspected he would. Montolio never would have believed it until he had witnessed it personally, but this unusual drow possessed the demeanor of a surface elf, perhaps even the heart of a ranger.

"How did you calm the bear?" Montolio asked one day, a question that had nagged at him since the very first day he had learned that Drizzt and Bluster were sharing a cave.

Drizzt honestly did not know how to answer, for he still did not understand what had transpired in that meeting. "The same way you calmed Guenhwyvar when first we met," the drow offered at length.

Montolio's grin told Drizzt that the old man understood better than he. "Heart of a ranger," Montolio whispered as he turned away. With his exceptional ears, Drizzt heard the comment, but he didn't fully comprehend.

Drizzt's lessons came faster as the days rolled along. Now Montolio concentrated on the life around them, the animals and the plants. He showed Drizzt how to forage and how to understand the emotions of an animal simply by watching its movements. The first real test came soon after, when Drizzt, shifting the outward branches of a berry bush, found the entrance to a small den and was promptly confronted by an angry badger.

Hooter, in the sky above, issued a series of cries to alert Montolio, and the ranger's first instinct was to go and help his drow friend. Badgers were possibly the meanest creatures in the region, even above the orcs, quicker to anger than Bluster the bear and quite willing to take the offensive against any opponent, no matter how large. Montolio stayed back, though, listening to Hooter's continuing descriptions of the scene.

Drizzt's first instinct sent his hand flashing to his dagger. The badger reared and showed its wicked teeth and claws, hissing and sputtering a thousand complaints.

Drizzt eased back, even put his dagger back in its sheath. Suddenly, he viewed the encounter from the badger's point of view, knew that the animal felt overly threatened. Somehow, Drizzt then further realized that the badger had chosen this den as a place to raise its soon-coming litter of pups.

The badger seemed confused by the drow's deliberate motions. Late in term, the expectant mother did not want a fight, and as Drizzt carefully slipped the berry bush back in place to conceal the den, the badger eased down to all fours, sniffed the air so that it could remember the dark elf's scent, and went back into its hole.

When Drizzt turned around, he found Montolio smiling and clapping. "Even a ranger would be hard put to calm a riled badger," the old man explained.

"The badger was with pups," Drizzt replied. "She wanted to fight less than I."

"How do you know that?" Montolio asked, though he did not doubt the drow's perceptions.

Drizzt started to answer, then realized that he could not. He looked back to the berry bush, then to Montolio helplessly.

Montolio laughed loudly and returned to his work. He, who had followed the ways of the goddess Mielikki for so many years, knew what was happening, even if Drizzt did not.

"The badger could have ripped you, you do know," the ranger said wryly when Drizzt moved beside him.

"She was with pups," Drizzt reminded him, "and not so large a foe."

Montolio's laughter mocked him. "Not so large?" the ranger echoed. "Trust me, Drizzt, you would rather tangle with Bluster than with a mother badger!"

Drizzt only shrugged in response, having no arguments for the more experienced man.

"Do you really believe that puny knife would have been any defense against her?" Montolio asked, now wanting to take the discussion in a different direction.

Drizzt regarded the dagger, the one he had taken from the sprite. Again he could not argue; the knife was indeed puny. He laughed both to and at himself. "It is all that I have, I fear," he replied.

"We shall see about that," the ranger promised, then said no more about it. Montolio, for all his calm and confidence, knew well the dangers of the wild, mountainous region.

The ranger had come to trust in Drizzt without reservations.

⚔ ⚔ ⚔ ⚔ ⚔

Montolio roused Drizzt shortly before sunset and led the drow to a wide tree in the northern end of the grove. A large hole, almost a cave, lay at the base of the tree, cunningly concealed by shrubs and a blanket colored to resemble the tree trunk. As soon as Montolio pushed this aside, Drizzt understood the secrecy.

"An armory?" the drow asked in amazement.

"You fancy the scimitar," Montolio replied, remembering the weapon Drizzt had broken on the stone giant. "I have a good one, too." He crawled inside and fished about for a while, then returned with a fine, curving blade. Drizzt moved in to the hole to survey the marvelous display of weapons as the ranger exited. Montolio possessed a huge variety of weapons, from ornamental daggers to great bardiche axes to crossbows, light and heavy, all polished and cared for meticulously. Set against the back of the inner tree trunk, running right up into the tree, were a variety of spears, including one metal-shafted ranseur, a ten-foot-long pike with a long and pointed head and two smaller barbs sticking out to the sides near the tip.

"Do you prefer a shield, or perhaps a dirk, for your other hand?" Montolio asked when the drow, muttering to himself in sincere admiration, reappeared. "You may have any but those bearing the taloned owl. That shield, sword, and helmet are my own."

Drizzt hesitated a moment, trying to imagine the blind ranger so outfitted for close melee. "A sword," he said at length, "or another scimitar if you have one."

Montolio looked at him curiously. "Two long blades for fighting," he remarked. "You would likely tangle yourself up in them, I would guess."

"It is not so uncommon a fighting style among the drow," Drizzt said.

Montolio shrugged, not doubting, and went back in. "This one is more for show, I fear," he said as he returned, bearing an overly ornamented blade. "You may use it if you choose, or take a sword. I've a number of those."

Drizzt took the scimitar to measure its balance. It was a bit too light and perhaps a bit too fragile. The drow decided to keep it, though, thinking its curving blade a better compliment to his other scimitar than a straight and cumbersome sword.

"I will care for these as well as you have," Drizzt promised, realizing how great a gift the human had given him. "And I will use them," he added, knowing what Montolio truly wanted to hear, "only when I must."

"Then pray that you may never need them, Drizzt Do'Urden," Montolio replied. "I have seen peace and I have seen war, and I can tell you that I prefer the former! Come now, friend. There are so many more things I wish to show you."

Drizzt regarded the scimitars one final time, then slipped them into the sheaths on his belt and followed Montolio.

With summer fast approaching and with such fine and exciting companionship, both the teacher and his unusual student were in high spirits, anticipating a season of valuable lessons and wondrous events.

⚔ ⚔ ⚔ ⚔ ⚔

How diminished their smiles would have been if they had known that a certain orc king, angered at the loss of ten soldiers, two worgs, and a valued giant ally, had its yellow, bloodshot eyes scanning the region, searching for the drow. The big orc was beginning to wonder if Drizzt had gone back to the Underdark or had taken in with some other group, perhaps with the small elven bands known to be in the region, or with the damnable blind ranger, Montolio. If the drow was still in the area, Graul meant to find him. The orc chieftain took no chances, and the mere presence of the drow constituted a risk.

# 14
# Montolio's Test

"Well, I have waited long enough!" Montolio said sternly late one afternoon. He gave the drow another shake.

"Waited?" Drizzt asked, wiping the sleep from his eyes.

"Are you a fighter or a wizard?" Montolio went on. "Or both? One of those multitalented types? The elves of the surface are known for that."

Drizzt's expression twisted in confusion. "I am no wizard," he said with a laugh.

"Keeping secrets, are you?" Montolio scolded, though his continuing smirk lessened his gruff facade. He pointedly straightened himself outside of Drizzt's bedroom hole and folded his arms over his chest. "That will not do. I have taken you in, and if you are a wizard, I must be told!"

"Why do you say that?" asked the perplexed drow. "Wherever did you—"

"Hooter told me!" Montolio blurted. Drizzt was truly confused. "In the fight when first we met," Montolio explained, "you darkened the area around yourself and some orcs. Do not deny it, wizard. Hooter told me!"

"That was no wizard's spell," Drizzt protested helplessly, "and I am no wizard."

"No spell?" echoed Montolio. "A device then? Well, let me see it!"

"Not a device," Drizzt replied, "an ability. All drow, even the lowest ranking, can create globes of darkness. It is not such a difficult task."

Montolio considered the revelation for a moment. He had no experience with dark elves before Drizzt had come into his life. "What other 'abilities' do you possess?"

"Faerie fire," Drizzt replied. "It is a line of—"

"I know of the spell," Montolio said to him. "It is commonly used by woodland priests. Can all drow create this as well?"

"I do not know," Drizzt answered honestly. "Also, I am—or was—able to levitate. Only drow nobles can accomplish that feat. I fear that the power is lost to me, or soon shall be. That ability has begun to fail me since I came to the surface, as my *piwafwi*, my boots, and my drow-crafted scimitars have failed me."

"Try it," Montolio offered.

Drizzt concentrated for a long moment. He felt himself growing lighter, then he lifted off the ground. As soon as he got up, though, his weight returned and he settled back to his feet. He rose no more than three inches.

"Impressive," Montolio muttered.

Drizzt only laughed and shook his white mane. "May I go back to sleep now?" he asked, turning back to his bedroll.

Montolio had other ideas. He had come to further feel out his companion, to find the limits of Drizzt's abilities, wizardly and otherwise. A new plan came to the ranger, but he had to set it into motion before the sun went down.

"Wait," he bade Drizzt. "You can rest later, after sunset. I need you now, and your 'abilities.' Could you summon a globe of darkness, or must you take time to contemplate the spell?"

"A few seconds," Drizzt replied.

"Then get your armor and weapons," Montolio said, "and come with me. Be quick about it. I do not want to lose the advantage of daylight."

Drizzt shrugged and got dressed, then followed the ranger to the grove's northern end, a little used section of the woodland complex.

Montolio dropped to his knees and pulled Drizzt down beside him, pointing out a small hole on the side of a grassy mound.

"A wild boar has taken to living in there," the old ranger explained. "I do not wish to harm it, but I fear to get close enough to make contact with the thing. Boars are unpredictable at best."

A long moment of silence passed. Drizzt wondered if Montolio simply meant to wait for the boar to emerge.

"Go ahead then," the ranger prompted.

Drizzt turned on him incredulously, thinking that Montolio expected him to walk right up and greet their uninvited and unpredictable guest.

"Do it," the ranger continued. "Enact your darkness globe—right in front of the hole—if you please."

Drizzt understood, and his relieved sigh made Montolio bite his lip to hide his revealing chuckle. A moment later, the area before the grassy mound disappeared in blackness. Montolio motioned for Drizzt to wait behind and headed in.

Drizzt tensed, watching and listening. Several high-pitched squeals issued forth suddenly, then Montolio cried out in distress. Drizzt leaped up and charged in headlong, nearly tripping over his friend's prostrate form.

The old ranger groaned and squirmed and did not answer any of the drow's quiet calls. With no boar to be heard anywhere about, Drizzt dropped down to find out what had happened and recoiled when he found Montolio curled up, clutching at his chest.

"Montolio," Drizzt breathed, thinking the old man seriously wounded. He leaned over to speak directly into the ranger's face, then straightened quicker than he had intended as Montolio's shield slammed into the side of his head.

"It is Drizzt!" the drow cried, rubbing his developing bruise. He heard Montolio jump up before him, then heard the ranger's sword come out of its scabbard.

"Of course it is!" Montolio cackled.

"But what of the boar?"

"Boar?" Montolio echoed. "There is no boar, you silly drow. There never was one. We are the opponents here. The time has come for some fun!"

Now Drizzt fully understood. Montolio had manipulated him to use his darkness merely to take away his advantage of sight. Montolio was challenging him, on even terms. "Flat of the blade!" Drizzt replied, quite willing to play along. How Drizzt had loved such tests of skill back in Menzoberranzan with Zaknafein!

"For the sake of your life!" Montolio retorted with a laugh that came straight from his belly. The ranger sent his sword arcing in, and Drizzt's scimitar drove it harmlessly wide.

Drizzt countered with two rapid and short strokes straight up the middle, an attack that would have defeated most foes but did no more than play a two-note tune on Montolio's well-positioned shield. Certain of Drizzt's location, the ranger shield-rushed straight ahead.

Drizzt was pushed back on his heels before he managed to get out of the way. Montolio's sword came in again from the side, and Drizzt blocked it. The old man's shield slammed straight ahead again, and Drizzt deflected its momentum, digging his heels in stubbornly.

The crafty old ranger thrust the shield up high then, taking one of Drizzt's blades, and a good measure of the drow's balance, along with it, then sent his sword screaming across at Drizzt's midsection.

Drizzt somehow sensed the attack. He leaped back on his toes, sucked in his gut, and threw his rump out behind him. For all his desperation, he still felt the rush as the sword whisked past.

Drizzt went to the offensive, launching several cunning and intricate routines that he believed would end this contest. Montolio anticipated each one, though, for all of Drizzt's efforts were rewarded with the same sound of scimitar on shield. The ranger came on then and Drizzt was sorely pressed. The drow was no novice to blind-fighting, but Montolio lived every hour of every day as a blind man and functioned as well and as easily as most men with perfect vision.

Soon Drizzt realized that he could not win in the globe. He thought of moving the ranger out of the spell's area, but then the situation changed suddenly as the darkness expired. Thinking the game over, Drizzt backed up several steps, feeling his way with his feet up a rising tree root.

Montolio regarded his opponent curiously for a moment, noting the change in fighting attitude, then came on, hard and low.

Drizzt thought himself very clever as he dived headlong over the ranger, meaning to roll to his feet behind Montolio and come back in from one side or the other as the confused human spun about, disoriented.

Drizzt didn't get what he expected, though. Montolio's shield met the drow's face as he was halfway over, and Drizzt groaned and fell heavily to the ground. By the time he shook the dizziness away, he became aware that Montolio was sitting comfortably on his back, sword resting across Drizzt's shoulders.

"How . . ." Drizzt started to ask.

Montolio's voice was as sharp-edged as Drizzt had ever heard it. "You underestimated me, drow. You considered me blind and helpless. Never do that again!"

Drizzt honestly wondered, for just a split second, if Montolio meant to kill him, so angry was the ranger. He knew that his condescension had wounded the man, and he realized then that Montolio DeBrouchee, so confident and able, carried his own weight upon his old shoulders. For the first time since he had met the ranger, Drizzt considered how painful it must have been for the man to lose his sight. What else, Drizzt wondered, had Montolio lost?

"So obvious," Montolio said after a short pause. His voice had softened again. "With me charging in low, as I did."

"Obvious only if you sensed that the darkness spell had ended," Drizzt replied, wondering how disabled Montolio truly was. "I would never have attempted the diving maneuver in the darkness, without my eyes to guide me, yet how could a blind man know that the spell was no more?"

"You told me yourself!" Montolio protested, still making no move to get off Drizzt's back. "In attitude! The sudden shuffle of your feet—too lightly to be made in absolute blackness—and your sigh, drow! That sigh belied your relief, though you knew by then that you could not best me without your sight."

Montolio got up from Drizzt, but the drow remained prone, digesting the revelations. He realized how little he knew about his companion, how much he had taken for granted where Montolio was concerned.

"Come along, then," Montolio said. "This night's first lesson is ended. It was a valuable one, but there are other things we must accomplish."

"You said that I could sleep," Drizzt reminded him.

"I had thought you more competent," Montolio replied immediately, casting a smirk the prone drow's way.

⚔ ⚔ ⚔ ⚔ ⚔

While Drizzt eagerly absorbed the many lessons Montolio set out for him, that night and in the days that followed, the old ranger gathered his own information about the drow. Their work was most concerned with the present, Montolio teaching Drizzt about the world around him and how to survive in it. Invariably one or the other, usually Drizzt, would slip in some comment about his past. It became almost a game between the two, remarking on some distant event, more to measure the shocked expression of the other than to make any relevant point. Montolio had some fine anecdotes about his many years on the road, tales of valorous battles against goblins and humorous pranks that the usually serious-minded rangers often played on one another. Drizzt remained a bit guarded about his own past, but still his tales of Menzoberranzan, of the sinister and insidious Academy and the savage wars pitting family against family, went far beyond anything Montolio had ever imagined.

As great as the drow's tales were, though, Montolio knew that Drizzt was holding back, was carrying some great burden on his shoulders. The ranger didn't press Drizzt at first. He kept his patience, satisfied that he and Drizzt shared principles and—as he came to know with the drastic improvement of Drizzt's ranger skills—a similar way of viewing the world.

One night, beneath the moon's silvery light, Drizzt and Montolio rested back in wooden chairs that the ranger had constructed high in the boughs of a large evergreen. The brightness of the waning moon, as it dipped and dodged behind fast-moving, scattered clouds, enchanted the drow.

Montolio couldn't see the moon, of course, but the old ranger, with Guenhwyvar comfortably draped across his lap, enjoyed the brisk night no less. He rubbed a hand absently through the thick fur on Guenhwyvar's muscled neck and listened to the many sounds carried on the breeze, the chatter of a thousand creatures that the drow never even noticed, even though Drizzt's hearing was superior to Montolio's. Montolio chuckled every now and again, once when he heard a field mouse squealing angrily at an owl—Hooter probably—for interrupting its meal and forcing it to flee into its hole.

Looking at the ranger and Guenhwyvar, so at ease and accepting of one another, Drizzt felt the pangs of friendship and guilt. "Perhaps I should never have come," he whispered, turning his gaze back to the moon.

"Why?" Montolio asked quietly. "You do not like my food?" His smile disarmed Drizzt as the drow turned back to him somberly.

"To the surface, I mean," Drizzt explained, managing a laugh in spite of his melancholy. "Sometimes I think my choice a selfish act."

"Survival usually is," Montolio replied. "I have felt that way myself on some occasions. I was once forced to drive my sword into a man's heart. The harshness of the world brings great remorse, but mercifully it is a passing lament and certainly not one to carry into battle."

"How I wish it would pass," Drizzt remarked, more to himself or to the moon than to Montolio.

But the remark hit Montolio squarely. The closer he and Drizzt had become, the more the ranger shared Drizzt's unknown burden. The drow was young by elf standards but was already world-wise and skilled in battle beyond most professional soldiers. Undeniably one of Drizzt's dark heritage would find barriers in an unaccepting surface world. By Montolio's estimation, though, Drizzt should be able to get through these prejudices and live a long and prosperous life, given his considerable talents. What was it, Montolio wondered, that so burdens this elf? Drizzt suffered more than he smiled and punished himself more than he should.

"Is yours an honest lament?" Montolio asked him. "Most are not, you know. Most self-imposed burdens are founded on misperceptions. We—at least we of sincere character—always judge ourselves by stricter standards than we expect others to abide by. It is a curse, I suppose, or a blessing, depending on how one views it." He cast his sightless gaze Drizzt's way. "Take it as a blessing, my friend, an inner calling that forces you to strive to unattainable heights."

"A frustrating blessing," Drizzt replied casually.

"Only when you do not pause to consider the advances that the striving has brought to you," Montolio was quick to reply, as though he had expected the drow's words. "Those who aspire to less accomplish less. There can be no doubt. It is better, I think, to grab at the stars than to sit flustered because you know you cannot reach them." He shot Drizzt his typical wry smile. "At least he who reaches will get a good stretch, a good view, and perhaps even a low-hanging apple for his effort!"

"And perhaps also a low-flying arrow fired by some unseen assailant," Drizzt remarked sourly.

Montolio tilted his head helplessly against Drizzt's unending stream of pessimism. It pained him deeply to see the good-hearted drow so scarred. "He might indeed," Montolio said, a bit more harshly than he had intended, "but the loss of life is only great to those who chance to live it! Let your arrow come in low and catch the huddler on the ground, I say. His death would not be so tragic!"

Drizzt could not deny the logic, nor the comfort the old ranger gave to him. Over the last few tendays, Montolio's offhanded philosophies and way of looking at the world—pragmatically yet heavily edged with youthful exuberance, put Drizzt more at ease than he had been since his earliest training days in Zaknafein's gymnasium. But Drizzt also could not deny the inevitably short life span of that comfort. Words could soothe, but they could not erase the haunting memories of Drizzt's past, the distant voices of dead Zaknafein, dead Clacker, and the dead farmers. A single mental echo of "drizzit" vanquished hours of Montolio's well-intended advice.

"Enough of this cockeyed banter," Montolio went on, seeming perturbed. "I call you friend, Drizzt Do'Urden, and I hope you call me the same. What sort of friend might I be against this weight that stoops your shoulders unless I know more of it? I am your friend, or I am not. The decision is yours, but if I am not, then I see no purpose in sharing nights as wondrous as this beside you. Tell me, Drizzt, or be gone from my home!"

Drizzt could hardly believe that Montolio, normally so patient and relaxed, had put him on such a spot. The drow's first reaction was to recoil, to build a wall of anger in the face of the old man's presumptions and cling to that which he considered personal. As the moments passed, though, and Drizzt got beyond his initial surprise and took the time to sift through

Montolio's statement, he came to understand one basic truth that excused those presumptions: He and Montolio had indeed become friends, mostly through the ranger's efforts.

Montolio wanted to share in Drizzt's past, so that he might better understand and comfort his new friend.

"Do you know of Menzoberranzan, the city of my birth and of my kin?" Drizzt asked softly. Even speaking the name pained him. "And do you know the ways of my people, or the Spider Queen's edicts?"

Montolio's voice was somber as he replied. "Tell me all of it, I beg."

Drizzt nodded—Montolio sensed the motion even if he could not see it—and relaxed against the tree. He stared at the moon but actually looked right past it. His mind wandered back through his adventures, back down that road to Menzoberranzan, to the Academy, and to House Do'Urden. He held his thoughts there for a while, lingering on the complexities of drow family life and on the welcomed simplicity of his times in the training room with Zaknafein.

Montolio watched patiently, guessing that Drizzt was looking for a place to begin. From what he had learned from Drizzt's passing remarks, Drizzt's life had been filled with adventure and turbulent times, and Montolio knew that it would be no easy feat for Drizzt, with his still limited command of the common tongue, to accurately recount all of it. Also, given the burdens, the guilt and the sorrow, the drow obviously carried, Montolio suspected that Drizzt might be hesitant.

"I was born on an important day in the history of my family," Drizzt began. "On that day, House Do'Urden eliminated House DeVir."

"Eliminated?"

"Massacred," Drizzt explained. Montolio's blind eyes revealed nothing, but the ranger's expression was clearly one of revulsion, as Drizzt had expected. Drizzt wanted his companion to understand the horrible depths of drow society, so he pointedly added, "And on that day, too, my brother Dinin drove his sword through the heart of our other brother, Nalfein."

A shudder coursed up Montolio's spine and he shook his head. He realized that he was only just beginning to understand the burdens Drizzt carried.

"It is the drow way," Drizzt said calmly, matter-of-factly, trying to impart the dark elves' casual attitude toward murder. "There is a strict structure of rank in Menzoberranzan. To climb it, to attain a higher rank, whether as an individual or a family, you simply eliminate those above you."

A slight quiver in his voice betrayed Drizzt to the ranger. Montolio clearly understood that Drizzt did not accept the evil practices, and never had.

Drizzt went on with his story, telling it completely and accurately, at least for the more than forty years he had spent in the Underdark. He told of his days under the strict tutelage of his sister Vierna, cleaning the house chapel endlessly and learning of his innate powers and his place in drow society. Drizzt spent a long time explaining that peculiar social structure to Montolio, the hierarchies based on strict rank, and the hypocrisy of drow "law," a cruel facade screening a city of utter chaos. The ranger cringed as he heard of the family wars. They were brutal conflicts that allowed for no noble survivors, not even children. Montolio cringed even more when Drizzt told him of drow "justice," of the destruction wreaked upon a house that had failed in its attempt to eradicate another family.

The tale was less grim when Drizzt told of Zaknafein, his father and dearest friend. Of course, Drizzt's happy memories of his father became only a short reprieve, a prelude to the horrors of Zaknafein's demise. "My mother killed my father," Drizzt explained soberly, his deep pain evident, "sacrificed him to Lolth for my crimes, then animated his corpse and sent it out to kill me, to punish me for betraying the family and the Spider Queen."

It took a while for Drizzt to resume, but when he did, he again spoke truthfully, even revealing his own failures in his days alone in the wilds of the Underdark. "I feared that I had lost myself and my principles to some instinctive, savage monster," Drizzt said, verging on despair. But then the emotional wave that had been his existence rose again, and a smile found his face as he recounted his time beside Belwar, the most honored svirfneblin burrow-warden, and Clacker, the pech who had been polymorphed into a hook horror. Expectedly, the smile proved short lived, for Drizzt's tale eventually led him to where Clacker fell to Matron Malice's undead monster. Another friend had died on Drizzt's behalf.

Appropriately, by the time Drizzt came to his exit from the Underdark, the dawn peeked through the eastern mountains. Now Drizzt picked his words more carefully, not ready to divulge the tragedy of the farming family for fear that Montolio would judge him and blame him, destroying their newfound bond. Rationally, Drizzt could remind himself that he had not killed the farmers, had even avenged their deaths, but guilt was rarely a rational emotion, and Drizzt simply could not find the words—not yet.

Montolio, aged and wise and with animal scouts throughout the region, knew that Drizzt was concealing something. When they had first met, the drow had mentioned a doomed farming family, and Montolio had heard of a family slaughtered in the village of Maldobar. Montolio didn't believe for a minute that Drizzt could have done it, but he suspected that the drow was somehow involved. He didn't press Drizzt, though. Drizzt had been more honest, and more complete, than Montolio had expected, and the ranger was confident that the drow would fill in the obvious holes in his own time.

"It is a good tale," Montolio said at length. "You have been through more in your few decades than most elves will know in three hundred years. But the scars are few, and they will heal."

Drizzt, not so certain, put a lamenting look upon him, and Montolio could only offer a comforting pat on the shoulder as he rose and headed off for bed.

⚔ ⚔ ⚔ ⚔ ⚔

Drizzt was still asleep when Montolio roused Hooter and tied a thick note to the owl's leg. Hooter wasn't so pleased at the ranger's instructions; the journey could take a tenday, valuable and enjoyable time at this height of the mousing and mating season. For all its whining hoots, however, the owl would not disobey.

Hooter ruffled its feathers, caught the first gust of wind, and soared effortlessly across the snow-covered range to the passes that would take it to Maldobar—and beyond that to Sundabar, if need be. A certain ranger of no small fame, a sister of the Lady of Silverymoon, was still in the region, Montolio knew through his animal connections, and he charged Hooter with seeking her out.

✕ ✕ ✕ ✕ ✕

"Will-there-be-no-end-to-it?" the sprite whined, watching the burly human pass along the trail. "First-the-nasty-drow-and-now-this-brute! Am-I-never-to-be-rid-of-these-troublemakers?" Tephanis slapped his head and stamped his feet so rapidly that he dug himself a little hole.

Down on the trail, the big, scarred yellow dog growled and bared its teeth, and Tephanis, realizing that his pouting had been too loud, zipped in a wide semicircle, crossing the trail far behind the traveler and coming up on the other flank. The yellow dog, still looking in the opposite direction, cocked its head and whimpered in confusion.

# 15

# A Shadow Over Sanctuary

Drizzt and Montolio said nothing of the drow's tale over the next couple of days. Drizzt brooded over painfully rekindled memories, and Montolio tactfully gave him the room he needed. They went about their daily business methodically, farther apart, and with less enthusiasm, but the distance was a passing thing, which they both realized.

Gradually they came closer together, leaving Drizzt with hopes that he had found a friend as true as Belwar or even Zaknafein. One morning, though, the drow was awakened by a voice that he recognized all too well, and Drizzt thought at once that his time with Montolio had come to a crashing end.

He crawled to the wooden wall that protected his dugout chamber and peered through.

"Drow elf, Mooshie," Roddy McGristle was saying, holding a broken scimitar out for the old ranger to see. The burly mountain man, looming even larger in the many layers of furs he wore, sat atop a small but muscled horse just outside of the rock wall surrounding the grove. "Ye seen him?"

"Seen?" Montolio echoed sarcastically, giving an exaggerated wink of his milky-white eyes. Roddy was not amused.

"Ye know what I mean!" he growled. "Ye see more'n the rest of us, so don't ye be playin' dumb!" Roddy's dog, showing a wicked scar from where

Drizzt had struck it, caught a familiar scent then and started sniffing excitedly and darting back and forth along the paths of the grove.

Drizzt crouched at the ready, a scimitar in one hand and a look of dread and confusion on his face. He had no desire to fight—he did not even want to strike the dog again.

"Get your dog back to your side!" Montolio huffed.

McGristle's curiosity was obvious. "Seen the dark elf, Mooshie?" he asked again, this time suspiciously.

"Might that I have," Montolio replied. He turned and let out a shrill, barely audible whistle. Immediately, Roddy's dog, hearing the ranger's clear ire in no uncertain terms, dropped its tail between its legs and slunk back to stand beside its master's horse.

"I've a brood of fox pups in there," the ranger lied angrily. "If your dog sets on them . . ." Montolio let the threat hang at that, and apparently Roddy was impressed. He dropped a noose down over the dog's head and pulled it tight to his side.

"A drow, must be the same one, came through here before the first snows," Montolio went on. "You will have a hard hunt for that one, bounty hunter." He laughed. "He had some trouble with Graul, by my knowledge, then set out again, back for his dark home, I would guess. Do you mean to follow the drow down into the Underdark? Certainly your reputation would grow considerably, bounty hunter, though your very life might prove the cost!"

Drizzt relaxed at the words; Montolio had lied for him! He could see that the ranger did not hold McGristle in high regard, and that fact, too, brought comfort to Drizzt. Then Roddy came back forcefully, laying out the story of the tragedy in Maldobar in a blunt and warped way that put Drizzt and Montolio's friendship to a tough test.

"The drow killed the Thistledowns!" Roddy roared at the ranger's smug smile, which vanished in the blink of an eye. "Slaughtered them, and his panther ate one o' them. Ye knew Bartholemew Thistledown, ranger. Shame on ye for talkin' lightly on his murderer!"

"Drow killed them?" Montolio asked grimly.

Roddy held out the broken scimitar once more. "Cut 'em down," he growled. "There's two thousand gold pieces on that one's head—I'll give ye back five hunnerd if ye can find out more for me."

"I have no need of your gold," Montolio quickly replied.

"But do ye have need to see the killer brought in?" Roddy shot back. "Do ye mourn for the deaths o' the Thistledown clan, as fine a family as any?"

Montolio's ensuing pause led Drizzt to believe that the ranger might turn him in. Drizzt decided then that he would not run, whatever Montolio's decision. He could deny the bounty hunter's anger, but not Montolio's. If the ranger accused him, Drizzt would have to face him and be judged.

"Sad day," Montolio muttered. "Fine family, indeed. Catch the drow, McGristle. It would be the best bounty you ever earned."

"Where to start?" Roddy asked calmly, apparently thinking he had won Montolio over. Drizzt thought so, too, especially when Montolio turned and looked back toward the grove.

"You have heard of Morueme's Cave?" Montolio asked.

Roddy's expression visibly dropped at the question. Morueme's Cave, on the edge of the great desert Anauroch, was so named for the family of blue dragons that lived there. "Hunnerd an' fifty miles," McGristle groaned. "Through the Nethers—a tough range."

"The drow went there, or about there, early in the winter," Montolio lied.

"Drow went to the dragons?" Roddy asked, surprised.

"More likely, the drow went to some other hole in that region," Montolio replied. "The dragons of Morueme could possibly know of him. You should inquire there."

"I'm not so quick to bargain with dragons," Roddy said somberly. "Too risky, and even goin', well, it costs too much!"

"Then it seems that Roddy McGristle has missed his first catch," Montolio said. "A good try, though, against the likes of a dark elf."

Roddy reined in his horse and spun the beast about. "Don't ye put yer bets against me, Mooshie!" he roared back over his shoulder. "I'll not let this one get away, if I have to search every hole in the Nethers myself."

"Seems a bit of trouble for two thousand gold," Montolio remarked, not impressed.

"Drow took my dog, my ear, and give me this scar!" Roddy countered, pointing to his torn face. The bounty hunter realized the absurdity of his actions—of course, the blind ranger could not see him—and spun back, setting his horse charging out of the grove.

Montolio waved a hand disgustedly at McGristle's back, then turned to find the drow. Drizzt met him on the edge of the grove, hardly knowing how to thank Montolio.

"Never liked that one," Montolio explained.

"The Thistledown family was murdered," Drizzt admitted bluntly.

Montolio nodded.

"You knew?"

"I knew before you came here," the ranger answered. "Honestly, I wondered if you did it, at first."

"I did not," Drizzt said.

Again Montolio nodded.

The time had come for Drizzt to fill in the details of his first few months on the surface. All the guilt came back to him when he recounted his battle with the gnoll group, and all the pain came rushing back, focused on the word "drizzit," when he told of the Thistledowns and his gruesome discovery. Montolio identified the speedy sprite as a quickling but was quite at a loss to explain the giant goblin and wolf creatures that Drizzt had battled in the cave.

"You did right in killing the gnolls," Montolio said when Drizzt had finished. "Release your guilt for that act and let it fall to nothingness."

"How could I know?" Drizzt asked honestly. "All of my learning ties to Menzoberranzan and still I have not sorted the truth from the lies."

"It has been a confusing journey," Montolio said, and his sincere smile relieved the tension considerably. "Come along, and let me tell you of the races, and of why your scimitars struck for justice when they felled the gnolls."

As a ranger, Montolio had dedicated his life to the unending struggle between the good races—humans, elves, dwarves, gnomes, and halflings being the most prominent members—and the evil goblinoids and giantkind, who lived only to destroy as a bane to the innocent.

"Orcs are my particular unfavorites," Montolio explained. "So now I content myself with keeping an eye—an owl's eye, that is—on Graul and his smelly kin."

So much fell into perspective for Drizzt then. Comfort flooded through the drow, for Drizzt's instincts had proven correct and he could now, for a while and to some measure at least, be free from the guilt.

"What of the bounty hunter and those like him?" Drizzt asked. "They do not seem to fit so well into your descriptions of the races."

"There is good and bad in every race," Montolio explained. "I spoke only of the general conduct, and do not doubt that the general conduct of goblinoids and giantkind is an evil one!"

"How can we know?" Drizzt pressed.

"Just watch the children," Montolio answered. He went on to explain the not-so-subtle differences between children of the goodly races and children of the evil races. Drizzt heard him, but distantly, needing no clarification. Always it seemed to come down to the children. Drizzt had felt better concerning his actions against the gnolls when he had looked upon the Thistledown children at play. And back in Menzoberranzan, what seemed like only a day ago and a thousand years ago at the same time, Drizzt's father had expressed similar beliefs. "Are all drow children evil?" Zaknafein had wondered, and through all of his beleaguered life, Zaknafein had been haunted by the screams of dying children, drow nobles caught in the fire between warring families.

A long, silent moment ensued when Montolio finished, both friends taking the time to digest the day's many revelations. Montolio knew that Drizzt was comforted when the drow, quite unexpectedly, turned to him, smiled widely, and abruptly changed the grim subject.

"Mooshie?" Drizzt asked, recalling the name McGristle had tagged on Montolio at the rock wall.

"Montolio DeBrouchee." The old ranger cackled, tossing a grotesque wink Drizzt's way. "Mooshie, to my friends, and to those like McGristle, who struggle so with any words bigger than 'spit,' 'bear,' or 'kill!' "

"Mooshie," Drizzt mumbled under his breath, taking some mirth at Montolio's expense.

"Have you no chores to do, Drizzit?" the old ranger huffed.

Drizzt nodded and started boisterously away. This time, the ring of "drizzit" did not sting so very badly.

⚔ ⚔ ⚔ ⚔ ⚔

"Morueme's Cave," Roddy griped. "Damned Morueme's Cave!" A split second later, a small sprite sat atop Roddy's horse, staring the stunned bounty hunter in the face. Tephanis had watched the exchange at Montolio's grove and had cursed his luck when the ranger had turned the bounty hunter away. If Roddy could catch Drizzt, the quickling figured, they'd both be out of his way, a fact that did not alarm Tephanis.

"Surely-you-are-not-so-stupid-as-to-believe-that-old-Car?" Tephanis blurted.

"Here!" Roddy cried, grabbing clumsily at the sprite, who merely hopped down, darted back, past the startled dog, and climbed up to sit behind Roddy.

"What in the Nine Hells are you?" the bounty hunter roared. "And sit still!"

"I am a friend," Tephanis said as slowly as he could.

Roddy eyed him cautiously over one shoulder.

"If-you-want-the-drow, you-are-going-the-wrong-way," the sprite said smugly.

A short while later, Roddy crouched in the high bluffs south of Montolio's grove and watched the ranger and his dark-skinned guest going about their chores.

"Good-hunting!" Tephanis offered, then he was gone, back to Caroak, the great wolf that smelled better than this particular human.

Roddy, his eyes fixed upon the distant scene, hardly noticed the quickling's departure. "Ye'll pay for yer lies, ranger," he muttered under his breath. An evil smile spread over his face as he thought of a way to get at the companions. It would be a delicate feat. But then, dealing with Graul always was.

⚔ ⚔ ⚔ ⚔ ⚔

Montolio's messenger returned two days later with a note from Dove Falconhand. Hooter tried to recount the ranger's response, but the excitable owl was completely inept at conveying such long and intricate tales. Flustered and having no other option, Montolio handed the letter to Drizzt and told the drow to read it aloud, and quickly. Not yet a skilled reader, Drizzt was several lines through the creased paper before he realized what it was. The note detailed Dove's accounts of what had happened in Maldobar and along the subsequent chase. Dove's version struck near to the truth, vindicating Drizzt and naming the barghest whelps as the murderers.

Drizzt's relief was so great that he could hardly utter the words as the letter went on to express Dove's pleasure and gratitude that the "deserving drow" had taken in with the old ranger.

"You get your due in the end, my friend," was all that Montolio needed to say.

# Part Four

## Resolutions

I now view my long road as a search for truth—truth in my own heart, in the world around me, and in the larger questions of purpose and of existence. How does one define good and evil?

I carried an internal code of morals with me on my trek, though whether I was born with it or it was imparted to me by Zaknafein—or whether it simply developed from my perceptions—I cannot ever know. This code forced me to leave Menzoberranzan, for though I was not certain of what those truths might have been, I knew beyond doubt that they would not be found in the domain of Lolth.

After many years in the Underdark outside of Menzoberranzan and after my first awful experiences on the surface, I came to doubt the existence of any universal truth, came to wonder if there was, after all, any purpose to life. In the world of drow, ambition was the only purpose, the seeking of material gains that came with increased rank. Even then, that seemed a little thing to me, hardly a reason to exist.

I thank you, Montolio DeBrouchee, for confirming my suspicions. I have learned that the ambition of those who follow selfish precepts is no more than a chaotic waste, a finite gain that must be followed by infinite loss. For there is indeed a harmony in the universe, a concordant singing of common weal. To join that song, one must find inner harmony, must find the notes that ring true.

There is one other point to be made about that truth: Evil creatures cannot sing.

–Drizzt Do'Urden

# 16
# Of Gods and Purpose

The lessons continued to go quite well. The old ranger had lessened the drow's considerable emotional burden, and Drizzt picked up on the ways of the natural world better than anyone Montolio had ever seen. But Montolio sensed that something still bothered the drow, though he had no idea of what it might be.

"Do all humans possess such fine hearing?" Drizzt asked him suddenly as they dragged a huge fallen branch out of the grove. "Or is yours a blessing, perhaps, to make up for your blindness?"

The bluntness of the question surprised Montolio for just the moment it took him to recognize the drow's frustration, an uneasiness caused by Drizzt's failure to understand the man's abilities.

"Or is your blindness, perhaps, a ruse, a deception you use to gain the advantage?" Drizzt pressed relentlessly.

"If it is?" Montolio replied offhandedly.

"Then it is a good one, Montolio DeBrouchee," Drizzt replied. "Surely it aids you against enemies . . . and friends alike." The words tasted bitter to Drizzt, and he suspected that he was letting his pride get the best of him.

"You have not often been bested in battle," Montolio replied, recognizing the source of Drizzt's frustrations as their sparring match. If he could have seen the drow then, Drizzt's expression would have revealed much.

"You take it too hard," Montolio continued after an uneasy silence. "I did not truly defeat you."

"You had me down and helpless."

"You beat yourself," Montolio explained. "I am indeed blind, but not as helpless as you seem to think. You underestimated me. I knew that you would, too, though I hardly believed that you could be so blind."

Drizzt stopped abruptly, and Montolio stopped on cue as the drag on the branch suddenly increased. The old ranger shook his head and cackled. He then pulled out a dagger, spun it high into the air, caught it, and yelling, "Birch!" heaved it squarely into one of the few birch trees by the evergreen grove.

"Could a blind man do that?" Montolio asked rhetorically.

"Then you can see," Drizzt stated.

"Of course not," Montolio retorted sharply. "My eyes have not functioned for five years. But neither am I blind, Drizzt, especially in this place I call my home!

"Yet you thought me blind," the ranger went on, his voice calm again. "In our sparring, when your spell of darkness expired, you believed that you had gained the edge. Did you think that all of my actions—effective actions, I must say—both in the battle against the orcs and in our fight were simply prepared and rehearsed? If I were as crippled as Drizzt Do'Urden believes me, how should I survive another day in these mountains?"

"I did not . . ." Drizzt began, but his embarrassment silenced him. Montolio spoke the truth, and Drizzt knew it. He had, at least on an unconscious level, thought the ranger less than whole since their very first meeting. Drizzt felt he showed his friend no disrespect—indeed, he thought highly of the man—but he had taken Montolio for granted and thought the ranger's limitations greater than his own.

"You did," Montolio corrected, "and I forgive you that. To your credit, you treated me more fairly than any who knew me before, even those who had traveled beside me through uncounted campaigns. Sit now," he bade Drizzt. "It is my turn to tell my tale, as you have told yours.

"Where to begin?" Montolio mused, scratching at his chin. It all seemed so distant to him now, another life that he had left behind. He retained one link to his past, though: his training as a ranger of the goddess Mielikki. Drizzt, similarly instructed by Montolio, would understand.

"I gave my life to the forest, to the natural order, at a very young age," Montolio began. "I learned, as I have begun to teach you, the ways of the wild world and decided soon enough that I would defend that perfection, that harmony of cycles too vast and wonderful to be understood. That is why I so enjoy battling orcs and the like. As I have told you before, they are the enemies of natural order, the enemies of trees and animals as much as of men and the goodly races. Wretched things, all in all, and I feel no guilt in cutting them down!"

Montolio then spent many hours recounting some of his campaigns, expeditions in which he acted singly or as a scout for huge armies. He told Drizzt of his own teacher, Dilamon, a ranger so skilled with a bow that he had never seen her miss, not once in ten thousand shots. "She died in battle," Montolio explained, "defending a farmhouse from a raiding band of giants. Weep not for Mistress Dilamon, though, for not a single farmer was injured and not one of the few giants who crawled away ever showed its ugly face in that region again!"

Montolio's voice dropped noticeably when he came to his more recent past. He told of the Rangewatchers, his last adventuring company, and of how they came to battle a red dragon that had been marauding the villages. The dragon was slain, as were three of the Rangewatchers, and Montolio had his face burned away.

"The clerics fixed me up well," Montolio said somberly. "Hardly a scar to show for my pain." He paused, and Drizzt saw, for the first time since he had met the old ranger, a cloud of pain cross Montolio's face. "They could do nothing for my eyes, though. The wounds were beyond their abilities."

"You came out here to die," Drizzt said, more accusingly than he intended.

Montolio did not refute the claim. "I have suffered the breath of dragons, the spears of orcs, the anger of evil men, and the greed of those who would rape the land for their own gain," the ranger said. "None of those things wounded as deeply as pity. Even my Rangewatcher companions, who had fought beside me so many times pitied me. Even you."

"I did not . . ." Drizzt tried to interject.

"You did indeed," Montolio retorted. "In our battle, you thought yourself superior. That is why you lost! The strength of any ranger is wisdom, Drizzt. A ranger understands himself, his enemies, and his friends. You thought me impaired, else you never would have attempted so brash a maneuver as to jump over me. But I understood you and anticipated the move." That sly smile flashed wickedly. "Does your head still hurt?"

"It does," Drizzt admitted, rubbing the bruise, "though my thoughts seem to be clearing."

"As to your original question," Montolio said, satisfied that his point had been made, "there is nothing exceptional about my hearing, or any of my other senses. I just pay more attention to what they tell than do other folks, and they guide me quite well, as you now understand. Truly, I did not know of their abilities myself when I first came out here, and you are correct in your guess as to why I did. Without my eyes, I thought myself a dead man, and I wanted to die here, in this grove that I had come to know and love in my earlier travels.

"Perhaps it was due to Mielikki, the Mistress of the Forest—though more likely it was Graul, an enemy so close at hand—but it did not take me long to change my intentions concerning my own life. I found a purpose out here, alone and crippled—and I was crippled in those first days. With that purpose came a renewal of meaning in my life, and that in turn led me to realize again my limits. I am old now, and weary, and blind. If I had died five years ago, as I had intended, I would have died with my life incomplete. I never would have known how far I could go. Only in adversity, beyond anything Montolio DeBrouchee had ever imagined, could I have come to know myself and my goddess so well."

Montolio stopped to consider Drizzt. He heard a shuffle at the mention of his goddess, and he took it to be an uncomfortable movement. Wanting to explore this revelation, Montolio reached inside his chain mail and tunic and produced a pendant shaped like a unicorn's head.

"Is it not beautiful?" he pointedly asked.

Drizzt hesitated. The unicorn was perfectly crafted and marvelous in design, but the connotations of such a pendant did not sit easily with the drow. Back in Menzoberranzan Drizzt had witnessed the folly of following the commands of deities, and he liked not at all what he had seen.

"Who is your god, drow?" Montolio asked. In all the tendays he and Drizzt had been together, they had not really discussed religion.

"I have no god," Drizzt answered boldly, "and neither do I want one."

It was Montolio's turn to pause.

Drizzt rose and walked off a few paces.

"My people follow Lolth," he began. "She, if not the cause, is surely the continuation of their wickedness, as this Gruumsh is to the orcs, and as other gods are to other peoples. To follow a god is folly. I shall follow my heart instead."

Montolio's quiet chuckle stole the power from Drizzt's proclamation. "You have a god, Drizzt Do'Urden," he said.

"My god is my heart," Drizzt declared, turning back to him.

"As is mine."

"You named your god as Mielikki," Drizzt protested.

"And you have not found a name for your god yet," Montolio shot back. "That does not mean that you have no god. Your god is your heart, and what does your heart tell you?"

"I do not know," Drizzt admitted after considering the troubling question.

"Think then!" Montolio cried. "What did your instincts tell you of the gnoll band or of the farmers in Maldobar? Lolth is not your deity—that much is certain. What god or goddess then fits that which is in Drizzt Do'Urden's heart?"

Montolio could almost hear Drizzt's continuing shrugs. "You do not know?" the old ranger asked. "But I do."

"You presume much," Drizzt replied, still not convinced.

"I observe much," Montolio said with a laugh. "Are you of like heart with Guenhwyvar?"

"I have never doubted that fact," Drizzt answered honestly.

"Guenhwyvar follows Mielikki."

"How can you know?" Drizzt argued, growing a bit perturbed. He didn't mind Montolio's presumptions about him, but Drizzt considered such labeling an attack on the panther. Somehow to Drizzt, Guenhwyvar seemed to be above gods and all the implications of following one.

"How can I know?" Montolio echoed incredulously. "The cat told me, of course! Guenhwyvar is the entity of the panther, a creature of Mielikki's domain."

"Guenhwyvar does not need your labels," Drizzt retorted angrily, moving briskly to sit again beside the ranger.

"Of course not," Montolio agreed. "But that does not change the fact of it. You do not understand Drizzt Do'Urden. You grew up among the perversion of a deity."

"And yours is the true one?" Drizzt asked sarcastically.

"They are all true, and they are all one, I fear," Montolio replied. Drizzt had to agree with Montolio's earlier observation: He did not understand.

"You view the gods as entities without," Montolio tried to explain. "You see them as physical beings trying to control our actions for their own ends, and thus you, in your stubborn independence, reject them. The gods are within, I say, whether one has named his own or not. You have followed Mielikki all of your life, Drizzt. You merely never had a name to put on your heart."

Suddenly Drizzt was more intrigued than skeptical.

"What did you feel when you first walked out of the Underdark?" Montolio asked. "What did your heart tell you when first you looked upon the sun or the stars, or the forest green?"

Drizzt thought back to that distant day, when he and his drow patrol had come out of the Underdark to raid an elven gathering. Those were painful memories, but within them loomed one sense of comfort, one memory of wondrous elation at the feel of the wind and the scents of newly bloomed flowers.

"And how did you talk to Bluster?" Montolio continued. "No easy feat, sharing a cave with that bear! Admit it or not, you've the heart of a ranger. And the heart of a ranger is a heart of Mielikki."

So formal a conclusion brought back a measure of Drizzt's doubts. "And what does your goddess require?" he asked, the angry edge returned to his voice. He began to stand again, but Montolio slapped a hand over his legs and held him down.

"Require?" The ranger laughed. "I am no missionary spreading a fine word and imposing rules of behavior! Did I not just tell you that gods are within? You know Mielikki's rules as well as I. You have been following them all of your life. I offer you a name for it, that is all, and an ideal of behavior personified, an example that you might follow in times that you stray from what you know is true." With that, Montolio took up the branch and Drizzt followed.

Drizzt considered the words for a long time. He did not sleep that day, though he remained in his den, thinking.

"I wish to know more of your . . . our . . . goddess," Drizzt admitted that next night, when he found Montolio cooking their supper.

"And I wish to teach you," Montolio replied.

⚔ ⚔ ⚔ ⚔ ⚔

A hundred sets of yellow, bloodshot eyes settled to stare at the burly human as he made his way through the encampment, reining his yellow dog tightly to his side. Roddy didn't enjoy coming here, to the fort of the orc king, Graul, but he had no intentions of letting the drow get away this time. Roddy had dealt with Graul several times over the last few years; the orc king, with so many eyes in the wild mountains had proven an invaluable, though expensive, ally in hunting bounties.

Several large orcs purposely crossed Roddy's path, jostling him and angering his dog. Roddy wisely kept his pet still, though he, too, wanted to set upon the smelly orcs. They played this game every time he came in, bumping him, spitting at him, anything to provoke a fight. Orcs were always brave when they outnumbered opponents a hundred to one.

The whole group swept up behind McGristle and followed him closely as he covered the last fifty yards, up a rocky slope, to the entrance of Graul's cave. Two large orcs jumped out of the entrance, brandishing spears, to intercept the intruder.

"Why has yous come?" one of them asked in their native tongue. The other held out its hand as if expecting payment.

"No pay this time," Roddy replied, imitating their dialect perfectly. "This time Graul pay!"

The orcs looked to each other in disbelief, then turned on Roddy and issued snarls that were suddenly cut short when an even larger orc emerged from the cave.

Graul stormed out and threw his guards aside, striding right up to put his oozing snout only an inch from Roddy's nose. "Graul pay?" he snorted, his breath nearly overwhelming Roddy.

Roddy's chuckle was purely for the sake of those excited orc commoners closest to him. He couldn't show any weakness here; like vicious dogs, orcs were quick to attack anyone who did not stand firm against them.

"I have information, King Graul," the bounty hunter said firmly. "Information that Graul would wish to know."

"Speak," Graul commanded.

"Pay?" Roddy asked, though he suspected that he was pushing his luck.

"Speak!" Graul growled again. "If yous wordses has value, Graul will let yous live."

Roddy silently lamented that it always seemed to work this way with Graul. It was difficult to strike any favorable bargain with the smelly chieftain when he was surrounded by a hundred armed warriors. Roddy remained undaunted, though. He hadn't come here for coin—though he had hoped he might extract some—but for revenge. Roddy wouldn't openly strike against Drizzt while the drow was with Mooshie. In these mountains, surrounded by his animal friends, Mooshie was a formidable force, and even if Roddy managed to get past him to the drow, Mooshie's many allies, veterans such as Dove Falconhand would surely avenge the action.

"There be a dark elf in yer domain, mighty orc king!" Roddy proclaimed. He didn't get the shock he had hoped for.

"Rogue," Graul clarified.

"Ye know?" Roddy's wide eyes betrayed his disbelief.

"Drow killed Graul's fighters," the orc chieftain said grimly. All the gathered orcs began stamping and spitting, cursing the dark elf.

"Then why does the drow live?" Roddy asked bluntly. The bounty hunter's eyes narrowed as he came to suspect that Graul did not now know the drow's location. Perhaps he still had something to bargain with.

"Me scouts cannot finds him!" Graul roared, and it was true enough. But any frustration the orc king showed was a finely crafted piece of acting. Graul knew where Drizzt was, even if his scouts did not.

"I have found him!" Roddy roared, and all the orcs jumped and cried in hungry glee. Graul raised his arms to quiet them. This was the critical part, the orc king knew. He scanned the gathering to locate the tribe's shaman, the spiritual leader of the tribe, and found the red-robed orc watching and listening intently, as Graul had hoped.

On advice from that shaman, Graul had avoided any action against Montolio for all these years. The shaman thought the cripple who was not so crippled to be an omen of bad magic, and with their religious leader's warnings, all the orc tribe cowered whenever Montolio was near. But in allying with the drow, and if Graul's suspicions were correct, in helping the drow to win the battle on the high ridge, Montolio had struck where he had no business, had violated Graul's domain as surely as had the renegade drow. Now convinced that the drow was indeed a rogue—for no other dark elves were in the region—the orc king only awaited some excuse that might spur his minions to action against the grove. Roddy, Graul had been informed, might now provide that excuse.

"Speak!" Graul shouted in Roddy's face, to intercept any forthcoming attempts for payment.

"The drow isses with the ranger," Roddy replied. "He sits in the blind ranger's grove!" If Roddy had hoped that his proclamation would inspire another eruption of cursing, jumping, and spitting, he was surely disappointed. The mention of the blind ranger cast a heavy pall over the gathering, and now all the common orcs looked from the shaman to Graul and back again for some guidance.

It was time for Roddy to weave a tale of conspiracy, as Graul had been told he would.

"Ye must goes and gets them!" Roddy cried. "They're not fer . . ."

Graul raised his arms to silence both the muttering and Roddy. "Was it the blind ranger who killded the giant?" the orc king asked Roddy slyly. "And helped the drow to kill me fighters?"

Roddy, of course, had no idea what Graul was talking about, but he was quick enough to catch on to the orc king's intent.

"It was!" he declared loudly. "And now the drow and the ranger plot against ye all! Ye must bash them and smash them before they come and bash yerselves! The ranger'll be bringing his animals, and elveses—lots an' lots of elveses—and dwarveses, too, against Graul!"

The mention of Montolio's friends, particularly the elves and dwarves, which Graul's people hated above everything else in all the world, brought sour expressions on every face and caused more than one orc to look nervously over its shoulder, as if expecting the ranger's army to be encircling the camp even then.

Graul stared squarely at the shaman.

"He-Who-Watches must bless the attack," the shaman replied to the silent question. "On the new moon!" Graul nodded, and the red-robed orc turned about, summoned a score of commoners to his side, and set out to begin the preparations.

Graul reached into a pouch and produced a handful of silver coins for Roddy. Roddy hadn't provided any real information that the king did not already know, but the bounty hunter's declaration of a conspiracy against the orc tribe gave Graul considerable assistance in his attempt to rouse his superstitious shaman against the blind ranger.

Roddy took the pitiful payment without complaint, thinking it well enough that he had achieved his purpose, and turned to leave.

"Yous is to stay," Graul said suddenly at his back. On a motion from the orc king, several orc guards stepped up beside the bounty hunter. Roddy looked suspiciously at Graul.

"Guest," the orc king explained calmly. "Join in the fight."

Roddy wasn't left with many options.

Graul waved his guards aside and went alone back into his cave. The orc guards only shrugged and smiled at each other, having no desire to go back in and face the king's guests, particularly the huge silver-furred wolf.

When Graul had returned to his place within, he turned to speak to his other guest. "Yous was right," Graul said to the diminutive sprite.

"I-am-quite-good-at-getting-information." Tephanis beamed, and silently he added, and-creating-favorable-situations!

Tephanis thought himself clever at that moment, for not only had he informed Roddy that the drow was in Montolio's grove, but he had then arranged with King Graul for Roddy to aid them both. Graul had no love for the blind ranger, Tephanis knew, and with the drow's presence serving as an excuse, Graul could finally persuade his shaman to bless the attack.

"Caroak will help in the fight?" Graul asked, looking suspiciously at the huge and unpredictable silver wolf.

"Of-course," Tephanis said immediately. "It-is-in-our-interest-too-to-see-those-enemies-destroyed!"

Caroak, understanding every word the two exchanged, rose up and sauntered out of the cave. The guards at the entrance did not try to block his way.

"Caroak-will-rouse-the-worgs," Tephanis explained. "A-mighty-force-will-assemble-against-the-blind-ranger. Too-long-has-he-been-an-enemy-of-Caroak."

Graul nodded and mused privately about the coming tendays. If he could get rid of both the ranger and the drow, his valley would be more secure than it had been in many years—since before Montolio's arrival. The ranger rarely engaged the orcs personally, but Graul knew that it was the ranger's animal spies that always alerted the passing caravans. Graul could not remember the last time his warriors had caught a caravan unawares, the preferred orc method. If the ranger was gone, however . . .

With summer, the height of the trading season, fast approaching, the orcs would prey well this year.

All that Graul needed now was confirmation from the shaman, that He-Who-Watches, the orc god Gruumsh One-eye, would bless the attack.

The new moon, a holy time for the orcs and a time when the shaman believed he could learn of the god's pleasures, was more than two tendays away. Eager and impatient, Graul grumbled at the delay, but he knew that he would simply have to wait. Graul, far less religious than others believed, meant to attack no matter the shaman's decision, but the crafty orc king would not openly defy the tribe's spiritual leader unless it was absolutely necessary.

The new moon was not so far away, Graul told himself. Then he would be rid of both the blind ranger and the mysterious drow.

# 17

# Outnumbered

"You seem troubled," Drizzt said to Montolio when he saw the ranger standing on a rope bridge the next morning. Hooter sat in a branch above him.

Montolio, lost in thought, did not immediately answer. Drizzt thought nothing of it. He shrugged and turned away, respecting the ranger's privacy, and took the onyx figurine out of his pocket.

"Guenhwyvar and I will go out for a short hunt," Drizzt explained over his shoulder, "before the sun gets too high. Then I will take my rest and the panther will share the day with you."

Still Montolio hardly heard the drow, but when the ranger noticed Drizzt placing the onyx figurine on the rope bridge, the drow's words registered more clearly and he came out of his contemplations.

"Hold," Montolio said, reaching a hand out. "Let the panther remain at rest."

Drizzt did not understand. "Guenhwyvar has been gone a day and more," he said.

"We may need Guenhwyvar for more than hunting before too long," Montolio began to explain. "Let the panther remain at rest."

"What is the trouble?" Drizzt asked, suddenly serious. "What has Hooter seen?"

"Last night marked the new moon," Montolio said. Drizzt, with his new understanding of the lunar cycles, nodded.

"A holy day for the orcs," Montolio continued. "Their camp is miles away, but I heard their cries last night."

Again Drizzt nodded in recognition. "I heard the strains of their song, but I wondered if it might be no more than the quiet voice of the wind."

"It was the wail of orcs," Montolio assured him. "Every month they gather and grunt and dance wildly in their typical stupor—orcs need no potions to induce it, you know. I thought nothing of it, though they seemed overly loud. Usually they cannot be heard from here. A favorable . . . unfavorable . . . wind carried the tune in, I supposed."

"You have since learned that there was more to the song?" Drizzt assumed.

"Hooter heard them, too," Montolio explained. "Always watching out for me, that one." He glanced at the owl. "He flew off to get a look."

Drizzt also looked up at the marvelous bird, sitting puffed and proud as though it understood Montolio's compliments. Despite the ranger's grave concerns, though, Drizzt had to wonder just how completely Montolio could understand Hooter, and just how completely the owl could comprehend the events around it.

"The orcs have formed a war party," Montolio said, scratching at his bristled beard. "Graul has awakened from the long winter with a vengeance, it seems."

"How can you know?" Drizzt asked. "Can Hooter understand their words?"

"No, no, of course not!" Montolio replied, amused at the notion.

"Then how can you know?"

"A pack of worgs came in, that much Hooter did tell me," Montolio explained. "Orcs and worgs are not the best of friends, but they do get together when trouble is brewing. The orc celebration was a wild one last night, and with the presence of worgs, there can be little doubt."

"Is there a village nearby?" Drizzt asked.

"None closer than Maldobar," Montolio replied. "I doubt the orcs would go that far, but the melt is about done and caravans will be rolling through the pass, from Sundabar to Citadel Adbar and the other way around, mostly. There must be one coming from Sundabar, though I do not believe Graul would be bold enough, or stupid enough, to attack a caravan of heavily armed dwarves coming from Adbar."

"How many warriors has the orc king?"

"Graul could collect thousands if he took the time and had the mind to do it," Montolio said, "but that would take tendays, and Graul has never been known for his patience. Also, he wouldn't have brought the worgs in so soon if he meant to hold off while collecting his legions. Orcs have a way of disappearing while worgs are around, and the worgs have a way of getting lazy and fat with so many orcs around, if you understand my meaning."

Drizzt's shudder showed that he did indeed.

"I would guess that Graul has about a hundred fighters," Montolio went on, "maybe a dozen to a score worgs, by Hooter's count, and probably a giant or two."

"A considerable force to strike at a caravan," Drizzt said, but both the drow and the ranger had other suspicions in mind. When they had first met, two months before, it had been at Graul's expense.

"It will take them a day or two to get ready," Montolio said after an uncomfortable pause. "Hooter will watch them more closely tonight, and I shall call on other spies as well."

"I will go to scout on the orcs," Drizzt added. He saw concern cross Montolio's face but quickly dismissed it. "Many were the times that such duties fell on me as a patrol scout in Menzoberranzan," he said. "It is a task that I feel quite secure in performing. Fear not."

"That was in the Underdark," Montolio reminded him.

"Is the night so different?" Drizzt replied slyly, throwing a wink and a comforting smile Montolio's way. "We shall have our answers."

Drizzt said his "good days" then and headed off to take his rest. Montolio listened to his friend's retreating steps, barely a swish through the thickly packed trees, with sincere admiration and thought it a good plan.

The day passed slowly and uneventfully for the ranger. He busied himself as best he could in considering his defense plans for the grove. Montolio had never defended the place before, except once when a band of foolish thieves had stumbled in, but he had spent many hours formulating and testing different strategies, thinking it inevitable that one day Graul would grow weary of the ranger's meddling and find the nerve to attack.

If that day had come, Montolio was confident that he would be ready.

Little could be done now, though—the defenses could not be put in place before Montolio was certain of Graul's intent—and the ranger found the waiting interminable. Finally, Hooter informed Montolio that the drow was stirring.

"I will set off, then," Drizzt remarked as soon as he found the ranger, noting the sun riding low in the west. "Let us learn what our unfriendly neighbors are planning."

"Have a care, Drizzt," Montolio said, and the genuine concern in his voice touched the drow. "Graul may be an orc, but he is a crafty one. He may well be expecting one of us to come and look in on him."

Drizzt drew his still-unfamiliar scimitars and spun them about to gain confidence in their movement. Then he snapped them back to his belt and dropped a hand into his pocket, taking further comfort in the presence of the onyx figurine. With a final pat on the ranger's back, the scout started off.

"Hooter will be about!" Montolio cried after him. "And other friends you might not expect. Give a shout if you find more trouble than you can handle!"

⚔ ⚔ ⚔ ⚔ ⚔

The orc camp was not difficult to locate, marked as it was by a huge bonfire blazing into the night sky. Drizzt saw the forms, including one of a giant, dancing around the flames, and he heard the snarls and yips of large wolves, worgs, Montolio had called them. The camp was in a small dale, in a clearing surrounded by huge maples and rock walls. Drizzt could hear the orc voices fairly well in the quiet night, so he decided not to get in too close. He selected one massive tree and focused on a lower branch, summoning his innate levitation ability to get him up.

The spell failed utterly, so Drizzt, hardly surprised, slipped his scimitars into his belt and climbed. The trunk branched several times, down low and as high as twenty feet. Drizzt made for the highest break and was just about to start out on a long and winding branch when he heard an intake of breath. Cautiously, Drizzt slipped his head around the large trunk.

On the side opposite him, nestled comfortably in the nook of the trunk and another branch, reclined an orc sentry with its hands clasped behind its head and a blank, bored expression on its face. Apparently the creature was oblivious to the silent-moving dark elf perched less than two feet away.

Drizzt grasped the hilt of a scimitar, then gaining confidence that the stupid creature was too comfortable to even look around, changed his mind and ignored the orc. He focused instead on the events down in the clearing.

The orc language was similar to the goblin tongue in structure and inflection, but Drizzt, no master even at goblin, could only make out a few scattered words. Orcs were ever a rather demonstrative race, though. Two models, effigies of a dark elf and a thin, moustached human, soon showed Drizzt the clan's intent. The largest orc of the gathering, King Graul, probably, sputtered and cursed at the models. Then the orc soldiers and the worgs took turns tearing into them, to the glee of the frenzied onlookers, a glee that turned to sheer ecstacy when the stone giant walked over and flattened the fake dark elf to the ground.

It went on for hours, and Drizzt suspected it would continue until the dawn. Graul and several other large orcs moved away from the main host and began drawing in the dirt, apparently laying battle plans. Drizzt could not hope to get close enough to make out their huddled conversations and he had no intention of staying in the tree with the dawn's revealing light fast approaching.

He considered the orc sentry on the other side of the trunk, now breathing deeply in slumber, before he started down. The orcs meant to attack Montolio's home, Drizzt knew; shouldn't he now strike the first blow?

Drizzt's conscience betrayed him. He came down from the huge maple and fled from the camp, leaving the orc to its snooze in the comfortable nook.

⚔ ⚔ ⚔ ⚔ ⚔

Montolio, Hooter on his shoulder, sat on one of the rope bridges, waiting for Drizzt's return. "They are coming for us," the old ranger declared when the drow finally came in. "Graul has his neck up about something, probably a little incident at Rogee's Bluff." Montolio pointed to the west, toward the high ridge where he and Drizzt had met.

"Do you have a sanctuary secured for times such as this?" Drizzt asked. "The orcs will come this very night, I believe, nearly a hundred strong and with powerful allies."

"Run?" Montolio cried. He grabbed a nearby rope and swung down to stand by the drow, Hooter clutching his tunic and rolling along for the ride. "Run from orcs? Did I not tell you that orcs are my special bane? Nothing in all the world sounds sweeter than a blade opening an orc's belly!"

"Should I even bother to remind you of the odds?" Drizzt said, smiling in spite of his concern.

"You should remind Graul!" Montolio laughed. "The old orc has lost his wits, or grown an oversized set of fortitude, to come on when he is so obviously outnumbered!"

Drizzt's only reply, the only possible reply to such an outrageous statement, came as a burst of laughter.

"But then," Montolio continued, not slowing a beat, "I will wager a bucket of freshly caught trout and three fine stallions that old Graul won't come along for the fight. He will stay back by the trees, watching and wringing his fat hands, and when we blast his forces apart, he will be the first to flee! He never did have the nerve for the real fighting, not since he became king anyway. He's too comfortable, I would guess, with too much to lose. Well, we'll take away a bit of his bluster!"

Again Drizzt could not find the words to reply, and he couldn't have stopped laughing at the absurdity anyway. Still, Drizzt had to admit the rousing and comforting effect Montolio's rambling imparted to him.

"You go and get some rest," Montolio said, scratching his stubbly chin and turning all about, again considering his surroundings. "I will begin the preparations—you will be amazed, I promise—and rouse you in a few hours."

The last mumblings the drow heard as he crawled into his blanket in a dark den put it all in perspective. "Yes, Hooter, I've been waiting for this for a long time," Montolio said excitedly, and Drizzt did not doubt a word of it.

⚔ ⚔ ⚔ ⚔ ⚔

It had been a peaceful spring for Kellindil and his elven kin. They were a nomadic group, ranging throughout the region and taking up shelter where they found it, in trees or in caves. Their love was the open world, dancing under the stars, singing in tune with rushing mountain rivers, hunting harts and wild boar in the thick trees of the mountainsides.

Kellindil recognized the dread, a rarely seen emotion among the carefree group, on his cousin's face as soon as the other elf walked into camp late one night.

All the others gathered about.

"The orcs are stirring," the elf explained.

"Graul has found a caravan?" Kellindil asked.

His cousin shook his head and seemed confused. "It is too early for the traders," he replied. "Graul has other prey in mind."

"The grove," several of the elves said together. The whole group turned to Kellindil then, apparently considering the drow his responsibility.

"I do not believe that the drow was in league with Graul," Kellindil answered their unspoken question. "With all of his scouts, Montolio would have known. If the drow is a friend to the ranger, then he is no enemy to us."

"The grove is many miles from here," one of the others offered. "If we wish to look more closely at the orc king's stirrings, and to arrive in time to aid the old ranger, then we must start out at once."

Without a word of dissent, the wandering elves gathered the necessary supplies, mostly their great long bows and extra arrows. Just a few minutes later, they set off, running through the woods and across the mountain trails, making no more noise than a gentle breeze.

⚔ ⚔ ⚔ ⚔ ⚔

Drizzt awakened early in the afternoon to a startling sight. The day had darkened with gray clouds but still seemed bright to the drow as he crawled out of his den and stretched. High above him he saw the ranger, crawling about the top boughs of a tall pine. Drizzt's curiosity turned to horror, when Montolio, howling like a wild wolf, leaped spread-eagled out of the tree.

Montolio wore a rope harness attached to the pine's thin trunk. As he soared out, his momentum bent the tree, and the ranger came down lightly, bending the pine nearly in two. As soon as he hit the ground, he scrambled to his feet and set the rope harness around some thick roots.

As the scene fully unfolded to Drizzt, he realized that several pines had been bent this way, all pointing to the west and all tied by interconnected ropes. As he carefully picked his way over to Montolio, Drizzt passed a net, several trip wires, and one particularly nasty rope set with a dozen or more double-bladed knives. When the trap was sprung and the trees snapped back up, so would this rope, to the peril of any creatures standing beside it.

"Drizzt?" Montolio asked, hearing the light footsteps. "Ware your steps, now. I would not want to have to rebend all these trees, though I will admit it is a bit of fun."

"You seem to have the preparations well under way," Drizzt said as he came to stand near the ranger.

"I have been expecting this day for a long time," Montolio replied. "I have played through this battle a hundred times in my mind and know the course it will take." He crouched and drew an elongated oval on the ground, roughly the shape of the pine grove. "Let me show you," he explained, and he proceeded to draw the landscape around the grove with such detail and accuracy that Drizzt shook his head and looked again to make sure the ranger was blind.

The grove consisted of several dozen trees, running north-south for about fifty yards and less than half that in width. The ground sloped at a gentle but noticeable incline, with the northern end of the grove being half a tree's height lower than the southern end. Farther to the north the ground was broken and boulder-strewn, with scraggly patches of grass and sudden drops, and crossed by sharply twisting trails.

"Their main force will come from the west," Montolio explained, pointing beyond the rock wall and across the small meadow to a pair of dense copses packed between the many rock ledges and cliff facings. "That is the only way they could come in together."

Drizzt took a quick survey of the surrounding area and did not disagree. Across the grove to the east, the ground was rough and uneven. An army charging from that direction would come into the field of tall grass nearly single-file, straight between two high mounds of stone, and would make an easy target for Montolio's deadly bow. South, beyond the grove, the incline grew steeper, a perfect place for orc spear-throwers and archers, except for the fact that just over the nearest ridge loomed a deep ravine with a nearly unclimbable wall.

"We'll not see any trouble from the south," Montolio piped in, almost as though he had read Drizzt's thoughts. "And if they come from the north, they'll be running uphill to get at us. I know Graul better than that. With such favorable odds, he will charge his host straight in from the west, trying to overrun us."

"Thus the trees," Drizzt remarked in admiration. "And the net and knife-set rope."

"Cunning," Montolio congratulated himself. "But remember, I have had five years to prepare for this. Come along now. The trees are just the beginning. I have duties for you while I finish with the tree trap."

Montolio led Drizzt to another secret, blanket-shielded den. Inside hung lines of strange iron items, resembling animal jaws with a strong chain connected to their bases.

"Traps," Montolio explained. "Pelt hunters set them in the mountains. Wicked things. I find them—Hooter is particularly skilled at spotting them—and take them away. I wish I had eyes to see the hunter scratching his head when he comes for them a tenday later!

"This one belonged to Roddy McGristle," Montolio continued, pulling down the closest of the contraptions. The ranger set it on the ground and carefully maneuvered his feet to pull the jaws apart until they set. "This should slow an orc," Montolio said, grabbing a nearby stick and patting around until he hit the plunger.

The trap's iron jaws snapped shut, the force of the blow breaking the stick cleanly and wrenching the remaining half right out of Montolio's hand. "I have collected more than a score of them," Montolio said grimly, wincing at the evil sound of the iron jaws. "I never thought to put them to use—evil things—but against Graul and his clan the traps might just amend some of the damage they have wrought."

Drizzt needed no further instructions. He brought the traps out into the western meadow, set and concealed them, and staked down the chains several feet away. He put a few just inside the rock wall, too, thinking that the pain they might cause to the first orcs coming over would surely slow those behind.

Montolio was done with the trees by this time; he had bent and tied off more than a dozen of them. Now the ranger was up on a rope bridge that ran north-south, fastening a line of crossbows along the western supports. Once set and loaded, either Montolio or Drizzt could merely trot down the line, firing as he went.

Drizzt planned to go and help, but first he had another trick in mind. He went back to the weapons cache and got the tall and heavy ranseur he had seen earlier. He found a sturdy root in the area where he planned to make his stand and dug a small hole out behind it. He laid the metal-shafted weapon down across this root, with only a foot or so of the butt sticking out over the hole, then covered the whole of it with grass and leaves.

He had just finished when the ranger called to him again.

"Here is the best yet," Montolio said, flashing his sly smile. He brought Drizzt to a split log, hollowed and burned smooth, and pitched to seal any cracks. "Good boat for when the river is high and slow," Montolio explained. "And good for holding Adbar brandy," he added with another smile.

Drizzt, not understanding, eyed him curiously. Montolio had shown Drizzt his kegs of the strong drink more than a tenday before, a gift the ranger had received for warning a Sundabar caravan of Graul's ambush intent, but the dark elf saw no purpose in pouring the drink into a hollowed log.

"Adbar brandy is powerful stuff," Montolio explained. "It burns brighter than all but the finest oil."

Now Drizzt understood. Together, he and Montolio carried the log out and placed it at the end of the only pass from the east. They poured in some brandy, then covered it with leaves and grass.

When they got back to the rope bridge, Drizzt saw that Montolio had already made the preparations on this end. A single crossbow was set facing east, its loaded quarrel headed by a wrapped, oil-soaked rag and a flint and steel resting nearby.

"You will have to sight it in," Montolio explained. "Without Hooter, I cannot be sure, and even with the bird, sometimes the height of my aim is off."

The daylight was almost fully gone now, and Drizzt's keen night vision soon located the split log. Montolio had built the supports along the rope bridge quite well and with just this purpose in mind, and with a few minor adjustments, Drizzt had the weapon locked on its target.

All of the major defenses were in place, and Drizzt and Montolio busied themselves finalizing their strategies. Every so often, Hooter or some other owl would rush in, chattering with news. One came in with the expected confirmation: King Graul and his band were on the march.

"You can call Guenhwyvar now," Montolio said. "They will come in this night."

"Foolish," said Drizzt. "The night favors us. You are blind anyway and in no need of daylight and I surely prefer the darkness."

The owl hooted again.

"The main host will come in from the west," Montolio told Drizzt smugly. "As I said they would. Scores of orcs and a giant besides! Hooter's watching another smaller group that split from the first."

The mention of the giant sent a shudder along Drizzt's spine, but he had every intention and a plan already set, for fighting this one. "I want to draw the giant to me," he said.

Montolio turned to him curiously. "Let us see how the battle goes," the ranger offered. "There is only one giant—you or I will get it."

"I want to draw the giant to me," Drizzt said again, more firmly. Montolio couldn't see the set of the drow's jaw or the seething fires in Drizzt's lavender eyes, but the ranger couldn't deny the determination in Drizzt's voice.

*"Mangura bok woklok,"* he said, and he smiled again, knowing that the strange utterance had caught the drow unaware.

*"Mangura bok woklok,"* Montolio declared again. "'Stupid blockhead: translated word by word. Stone giants hate that phrase—brings them charging in every timed."

*"Mangura bok woklok,"* Drizzt mouthed quietly. He'd have to remember that.

# 18 The Battle of Mooshie's Grove

Drizzt noticed that Montolio looked more than a little troubled after Hooter, back with more news, departed.

"The split of Graul's forces?" he inquired.

Montolio nodded, his expression grim. "Worg-riding orcs—just a handful—circling around to the west."

Drizzt looked out beyond the rock wall, to the pass secured by their brandy trough. "We can stop them," he said.

Still the ranger's expression told of doom. "Another group of worgs—a score or more—is coming from the south." Drizzt did not miss the ranger's fear, as Montolio added, "Caroak is leading them. I never thought that one would fall in with Graul."

"A giant?" Drizzt asked.

"No, winter wolf," Montolio replied. At the words, Guenhwyvar flattened its ears and growled angrily.

"The panther knows," Montolio said as Drizzt looked on in amazement. "A winter wolf is a perversion of nature, a blight against creatures following the natural order, and thus, Guenhwyvar's enemy."

The black panther growled again.

"It's a large creature," Montolio went on, "and too smart for a wolf. I have fought Caroak before. Alone he could give us a time of it! With the worgs around him, and us busy fighting orcs, he might have his way."

Guenhwyvar growled a third time and tore the ground with great claws.

"Guenhwyvar will deal with Caroak," Drizzt remarked.

Montolio moved over and grabbed the panther by the ears, holding Guenhwyvar's gaze with his own sightless expression. "Ware the wolf's breath," the ranger said. "A cone of frost, it is, that will freeze your muscles to your bones. I have seen a giant felled by it!" Montolio turned to Drizzt and knew that the drow wore a concerned expression.

"Guenhwyvar has to keep them away from us until we can chase off Graul and his group," the ranger said, "then we can make arrangements for Caroak." He released his hold on the panther's ears and swatted Guenhwyvar hard on the scruff of the neck.

Guenhwyvar roared a fourth time and darted off through the grove, a black arrow aimed at the heart of doom.

⚔ ⚔ ⚔ ⚔ ⚔

Graul's main attack force came, as expected, from the west, whooping and hollering and trampling the brush in its path. The troops approached in two groups, one through each of the dense copses.

"Aim for the group on the south!" Montolio called up to Drizzt, in position on the crossbow-laden rope bridge. "We've friends in the other!"

As if in confirmation of the ranger's decree, the northern copse erupted suddenly in orc cries that sounded more like terrified shrieks than battle calls. A chorus of throaty growls accompanied the screams. Bluster the bear had come to Montolio's call, Drizzt knew, and by the sounds in the copse, he had brought a number of friends.

Drizzt wasn't about to question their good fortune. He positioned himself behind the closest crossbow and let the quarrel fly as the first orcs emerged from the southern copse. Right down the line the drow ran, clicking off his shots in rapid succession. From down below, Montolio arced a few arrows over the wall.

In the sudden swarm of orcs, Drizzt couldn't tell how many of their shots actually hit, but the buzzing bolts did slow the orc charge and scattered their ranks. Several orcs dropped to their bellies; a few turned and headed straight back into the trees. The bulk of the group, though, and some running to join from the other copse, came on.

Montolio fired one last time, then felt his way back into a sheltered run behind the center of his bent tree traps, where he would be protected on three sides by walls of wood and trees. His bow in one hand he checked his sword and reached around to touch a rope at his other side.

Drizzt noticed the ranger moving into position twenty feet below him and to the side, and he figured that this might be his last free opportunity. He sorted out an object hanging above Montolio's head and dropped a spell over it.

The quarrels had brought minimum chaos to the field of charging orcs, but the traps proved more effective. First one, then another, orc stepped in, their cries rising over the din of the charge. As other orcs saw their companions' pain and peril, they slowed considerably or stopped altogether.

With the commotion growing in the field, Drizzt paused and carefully considered his final shot. He noticed a large, finely outfitted orc watching from the closest boughs of the northern copse. Drizzt knew this was Graul, but his attention shifted immediately to the figure standing next to the orc king. "Damn," the drow muttered, recognizing McGristle. Now he was torn, and he moved the crossbow back and forth between the adversaries. Drizzt wanted to shoot at Roddy, wanted to end his personal torment then and there. But Roddy was not an orc, and Drizzt found himself repulsed by the thought of killing a human.

"Graul is the more important target," the drow told himself, more to distract his inner torment than for any other reason. Quickly, before he could find any more arguments, he took aim and fired. The quarrel whistled long and far, knocking into the trunk of a tree just inches above Graul's head. Roddy promptly grabbed the orc king and pulled him back into the deeper shadows. In their stead came a roaring stone giant, rock in hand.

The boulder clipped the trees beside Drizzt, shaking the branches and bridge alike. A second shot followed at once, this one taking a supporting post squarely and dropping the front half of the bridge.

Drizzt had seen it coming, though he was amazed and horrified by the uncanny accuracy at so far a range. As the front half of the bridge fell away beneath him, Drizzt leaped out, catching a hold in a tangle of branches. When he finally sorted himself out, he was faced by a new problem. From the east came the worg-riders, brandishing torches.

Drizzt looked to the log trap, then to the crossbow. It and the post securing it had survived the boulder hit, but the drow could not hope to cross to it on the faltering bridge.

⚔ ⚔ ⚔ ⚔ ⚔

The leaders of the main host, now behind Drizzt, reached the rock wall then. Fortunately, the first orc leaping over landed squarely into another of the wicked jaw traps, and its companions were not so quick to follow.

Guenhwyvar leaped around and between the many broken crags of stone marking the descent to the north. The panther caught the distant first cries of battle back at the grove, but more intently, Guenhwyvar heard the ensuing howls of the approaching wolf pack. The panther sprang up to a low ledge and waited.

Caroak, the huge silver canine beast, led the charge. Focused on the distant grove, the winter wolf's surprise was complete when Guenhwyvar dropped upon it, scratching and raking wildly.

Clumps of silver fur flew about under the assault. Yelping, Caroak dived into a sidelong roll. Guenhwyvar rode the wolf as a lumberjack might foot-roll a log in a pool, slashing and kicking with each step. But Caroak was a wizened old wolf, a veteran of a hundred battles. As the monster rolled about to its back, a blast of icy frost came at the panther.

Guenhwyvar dodged aside, both from the frost and the onslaught of several worgs. The frost got the panther on the side of the face, though, numbing Guenhwyvar's jaw. Then the chase was on, with Guenhwyvar leaping and tumbling right around the wolf pack, and the worgs, and angry Caroak, nipping at the panther's heels.

⚔ ⚔ ⚔ ⚔ ⚔

Time was running out for Drizzt and Montolio. Above all else, the drow knew that he must protect their rear flank. In synchronous movements, Drizzt kicked off his boots, took the flint in one hand and put a piece of steel in his mouth, and leaped up to a branch that would take him out over the lone crossbow.

He got above it a moment later. Holding with one hand he struck the flint hard. Sparks rolled down, close to the mark. Drizzt struck again and again, and finally, a spark hit the oil-soaked rags tipping the loaded quarrel squarely enough to ignite them.

Now the drow was not so lucky. He rocked and twisted but could not get his foot close enough to the trigger.

Montolio could see nothing, of course, but he knew well enough the general situation. He heard the approaching worgs at the back of the grove and knew that those in front had breached the wall. He sent another bow shot through the thick canopy of bent trees, just for good measure, and hooted loudly three times.

In answer, a group of owls swooped down from the pines, bearing down on the orcs along the rock wall. Like the traps, the birds could only cause minimal real damage, but the confusion bought the defenders a little more time.

⚔ ⚔ ⚔ ⚔ ⚔

To this point, the only clear advantage for the grove's defenders came in the northernmost copse, where Bluster and three of his closest and largest bear buddies had a dozen orcs down and a score more running about blindly.

One orc, in flight from a bear, came around a tree and nearly crashed into Bluster. The orc kept its wits enough to thrust its spear ahead, but the creature hadn't the strength to drive the crude weapon through Bluster's thick hide.

Bluster responded with a heavy swipe that sent the orc's head flying through the trees.

Another great bear ambled by, its huge arms wrapped in front of it. The only clue that the bear held an orc in the crushing hug was the orc's feet, which hung out and kicked wildly below the engulfing fur.

Bluster caught sight of another enemy, smaller and quicker than an orc. The bear roared and charged, but the diminutive creature was long gone before he ever got close.

Tephanis had no intentions of joining the battle. He had come with the northernmost group mostly to keep out of Graul's sight, and had planned all along to remain in the trees and wait out the fighting. The trees didn't seem so safe anymore, so the sprite lighted out, meaning to get into the southern copse.

About halfway to the other woods, the sprite's plans were foiled again. Sheer speed nearly got him past the trap before the iron jaws snapped closed, but the wicked teeth just caught the end his foot. The ensuing jolt blasted the breath from him and left him dazed, facedown in the grass.

⚔ ⚔ ⚔ ⚔ ⚔

Drizzt knew how revealing that little fire on the quarrel would prove, so he was hardly surprised when another giant-hurled rock thundered in. It struck Drizzt's bending branch, and with a series of cracks, the limb swung down.

Drizzt hooked the crossbow with his foot as he dropped, and he hit the trigger immediately, before the weapon was deflected too far aside. Then he stubbornly held his position and watched.

The fiery quarrel reached out into the darkness beyond the eastern rock wall. It skidded in low, sending sparks up through the tall grass, then thudded into the side—the outside—of the brandy-filled trough.

The first half of the worg-riders got across the trap, but the remaining three were not so lucky, bearing in just as flames licked over the side of the dugout. The brandy and kindling roared to life as the riders plunged through. Worgs and orcs thrashed about in the tall grass, setting other pockets of fire.

Those who had already come through spun about abruptly at the sudden conflagration. One orc rider was thrown heavily, landing on its own torch, and the other two barely kept their seats. Above all else, worgs hated fire, and the sight of three of their kin rolling about, furry balls of flame, did little to strengthen their resolve for this battle.

⚔ ⚔ ⚔ ⚔ ⚔

Guenhwyvar came to a small, level area dominated by a single maple. Onlookers to the panther's rush would have blinked incredulously, wondering if the vertical tree trunk was really a log lying on its side, so fast did Guenhwyvar run up it.

The worg pack came in soon after, sniffing and milling about, certain that the cat was up the tree but unable to pick out Guenhwyvar's black form among the dark boughs.

The panther showed itself soon enough, though, again dropping heavily to the back of the winter wolf, and this time taking care to lock its jaws onto Caroak's ear.

The winter wolf thrashed and yelped as Guenhwyvar's claws did their work. Caroak managed to turn about and Guenhwyvar heard the sharp intake of breath, the same as the one preceding the previous chilling blast.

Guenhwyvar's huge neck muscles flexed, forcing Caroak's open jaws to the side. The foul breath came anyway, blasting three charging worgs right in the face.

Guenhwyvar's muscles reversed and flexed again suddenly, and the panther heard Caroak's neck snap. The winter wolf plopped straight down, Guenhwyvar still atop it.

Those three worgs closest to Guenhwyvar, the three who had caught Caroak's icy breath, posed no threat. One lay on its side, gasping for air that would not move through its frozen lungs, another turned tight circles, fully blinded, and the last stood perfectly still, staring down at its forelegs, which, for some reason, would not answer its call to move.

The rest of the pack, though, nearly a score strong, came in methodically, surrounding the panther in a deadly ring. Guenhwyvar looked all about for some escape, but the worgs did not rush frantically, leaving openings.

They worked in harmony, shoulder to shoulder, tightening the ring.

The leading orcs milled about the tangle of bent trees, looking for some way through. Some had begun to make progress, but the whole of the trap was interconnected, and any one of a dozen trip wires would send all the pines springing up.

One of the orcs found Montolio's net, then, the hard way. It stumbled over a rope, fell facedown on the net, then went high into the air, one of its companions caught beside it. Neither of them could have imagined how much better off they were than those they had left behind, particularly the orc unsuspectingly straddling the knife-set rope. When the trees sprang up, so did this devilish trap, gutting the creature and lifting it head over heels into the air.

Even those orcs not caught by the secondary traps did not fare well. Tangled branches, bristling with prickly pine needles, shot up all about them, sending a few on a pretty fair ride and scratching and disorienting the others.

Even worse for the orcs, Montolio used the sound of the rushing trees as his signal to open fire. Arrow after arrow whistled down the sheltered run, more hitting the mark than not. One orc lifted its spear to throw, then caught one arrow in the face and another in the chest. Another beast turned and fled, crying "Bad magic!" frantically.

To those crossing the rock wall, the screamer seemed to fly, its feet kicking above the ground. Its startled companions understood when the orc came back down in a heap, a quivering arrow shaft protruding from its back.

Drizzt, still on his tenuous perch, didn't have time to marvel at the efficient execution of Montolio's well-laid plans. From the west, the giant was now on the move and back the other way, the two remaining worg-riders had settled enough to resume their charges, torches held high.

The ring of snarling worgs tightened. Guenhwyvar could smell their stinking breath. The panther could not hope to charge through the thick ranks, nor could the cat get over them quickly enough to flee.

Guenhwyvar found another route. Hind paws tamped down on Caroak's still-twitching body and the panther arrowed straight up into the air, twenty feet and more. Guenhwyvar caught the maple's lowest branch with long front claws, hooked on, and pulled itself up. Then the panther disappeared into the boughs, leaving the frustrated pack howling and growling.

Guenhwyvar reappeared quickly though, out from the side and back to the ground, and the pack took up the pursuit. The panther had come to know this terrain quite well over the last few tendays and now Guenhwyvar had figured out exactly where to lead the wolves.

They ran along a ridge, with a dark and brooding emptiness on their left flank. Guenhwyvar marked well the boulders and the few scattered trees. The panther couldn't see the chasm's opposite bank and had to trust fully in its memory. Incredibly fast, Guenhwyvar pivoted suddenly and sprang out into the night, touching down lightly across the wide way and speeding off toward the grove. The worgs would have a long jump—too long for most of them—or a long way back around if they meant to follow.

They inched up snarling and scratching at the ground. One poised on the lip and meant to try the leap, but an arrow exploded into its side and destroyed its determination.

Worgs were not stupid creatures, and the sight of the arrow put them on the defensive. The ensuing shower by Kellindil and his kin was more than they expected. Dozens of arrows whistled in, dropping the worgs where they stood. Only a few escaped that barrage, and they promptly scattered to the corners of the night.

Drizzt called upon another magical trick to stop the torch-bearers. Faerie fire, harmless dancing flames, appeared suddenly below the torch fires, rolling down the wooden instrument to lick at the orcs' hands. Faerie fire did not burn—was not even warm—but when the orcs saw the flames engulfing their hands, they were far from rational.

One of them threw its torch out wide, and the jerking motion cost it its seat. It tumbled down in the grass, and the worg turned yet another time and snarled in frustration.

The other orc simply dropped its torch, which fell on top of its mount's head. Sparks and flames erupted from the worg's thick coat, stinging its eyes and ears, and the beast went crazy. It dropped into a headlong roll, bouncing right over the startled orc.

The orc staggered back to its feet, dazed and bruised and holding its arms out wide as if in apology. The singed worg wasn't interested in hearing any, however. It sprang straight in and clamped its powerful jaws on the orc's face.

Drizzt didn't see any of it. The drow could only hope that his trick had worked, for as soon as he had cast the spell, he released his foothold on the crossbow and let the torn branch carry him down to the ground.

Two orcs, finally seeing a target, rushed at the drow as he landed, but as soon as Drizzt's hands were free of the branch, they held his scimitars. The orcs came in, oblivious, and Drizzt slapped their weapons aside and cut them down. The drow waded through more scattered resistance as he made his way to his prepared spot. A grim smile found his face when at last he felt the ranseur's metal shaft under his bare feet. He remembered the giants back in Maldobar that had slain the innocent family, and he took comfort that now he would kill another of their evil kin.

*"Mangura bok woklok!"* Drizzt cried, placing one foot on the root fulcrum and the other on the butt of the hidden weapon.

⚔ ⚔ ⚔ ⚔ ⚔

Montolio smiled when he heard the drow's call, gaining confidence in the proximity of his powerful ally. His bow sang out a few more times, but the ranger sensed that the orcs were coming in at him in a roundabout way, using the thick trees as cover. The ranger waited, baiting them in. Then, just before they closed, Montolio dropped his bow, whipped out his sword and slashed the rope at his side, right below a huge knot. The severed rope rolled up into the air, the knot catching on a fork in the lowest branch, and Montolio's shield, empowered with one of Drizzt's darkness spells, dropped down to hang at precisely the right height for the ranger's waiting arm.

Darkness held little influence over the blind ranger, but the few orcs that had come in at Montolio found themselves in a precarious position. They jostled and swung wildly—one cut down its own brother—while Montolio calmly sorted out the melee and went to methodical work. In the matter of a minute, four of the five who had come in were dead or dying and the fifth had taken flight.

Far from sated, the ranger and his portable ball of darkness followed, searching for voices or sounds that would lead him to more orcs. Again came the cry that made Montolio smile.

⚔ ⚔ ⚔ ⚔ ⚔

*"Mangura bok woklok."* Drizzt yelled again. An orc tossed a spear at the drow, which Drizzt promptly swatted aside. The distant orc was now unarmed, but Drizzt would not pursue, determinedly holding his position.

*"Mangura bok woklok!"* Drizzt cried again. "Come in, stupid blockhead!" This time the giant, approaching the wall in Montolio's direction, heard the words. The great monster hesitated a moment, regarding the drow curiously.

Drizzt didn't miss the opportunity. *"Mangura bok woklok!"*

With a howl and a stamp that shook the earth, the giant kicked a hole in the rock wall and strode toward Drizzt.

*"Mangura bok woklok!"* Drizzt said for good measure, angling his feet properly.

The giant broke into a dead run, scattering terrified orcs before it and slamming its stone and its club together angrily. It sputtered a thousand curses at Drizzt in those few seconds, words that the drow would never decipher. Three times the drow's height and many times his weight, the giant loomed over Drizzt, and its rush seemed as though it would surely bury Drizzt where he calmly stood.

When the giant got only two long strides from Drizzt, committed fully to its collision course, Drizzt dropped all of his weight onto his back foot. The ranseur's butt dropped into the hole. Its tip angled up.

Drizzt leaped back at the moment the giant plowed into the ranseur. The weapon's tip and hooked barbs disappeared into the giant's belly, drove upward through its diaphragm and into its heart and lungs. The metal shaft bowed and seemed as if it would break as its butt end was driven a foot and more into the ground.

The ranseur held, and the giant was stopped cold. It dropped its club and rock, reached helplessly for the metal shaft with hands that had not the strength to even close around it. Huge eyes bulged in denial, in terror, and in absolute surprise. The great mouth opened wide and contorted weirdly, but could not even find the wind to scream.

Drizzt, too, almost cried out, but caught the words before he uttered them. "Amazing," he said, looking back to where Montolio was fighting, for the cry he nearly shouted was a praise to the goddess Mielikki. Drizzt shook his head helplessly and smiled, stunned by the acute perceptions of his not-so-blind companion.

With those thoughts in mind and a sense of righteousness in his heart, Drizzt ran up the shaft and slashed at the giant's throat with both weapons. He continued on, stepping right on the giant's shoulder and head and leaping off toward a group of watching orcs, whooping as he went.

The sight of the giant, their bully, quivering and gasping, had already unnerved the orcs, but when this ebony-skinned and wild-eyed drow monster leaped at them, they broke rank altogether. Drizzt's charge got him to the closest two, and he promptly cut them down and charged on.

Twenty feet to the drow's left, a ball of blackness rolled out of the trees, leading a dozen frightened orcs before it. The orcs knew that to fall within that impenetrable globe was to fall within the blind hermit's reach and to die.

⚔ ⚔ ⚔ ⚔ ⚔

Two orcs and three worgs, all that remained of the torch bearers, regrouped and slipped quietly toward the grove's eastern edge. If they could get in behind the enemy, they believed the battle still could be won.

The orc farthest to the north never even saw the rushing black form. Guenhwyvar plowed it down and charged on, confident that that one would never rise again.

A worg was next in line. Quicker to react than the orc, the worg spun and faced the panther, its teeth bared and jaws snapping.

Guenhwyvar snarled, pulling up short right before it. Great claws came in alternately in a series of slaps. The worg could not match the cat's speed. It swung its jaws from side to side, always a moment too late to catch up to the darting paws. After only five slaps, the worg was defeated. One eye had closed forever, its tongue, half torn, lolled helplessly out one side of its mouth, and its lower jaw was no longer in line with its upper. Only the presence of other targets saved the worg, for when it turned and fled the way it had come, Guenhwyvar, seeing closer prey, did not follow.

Drizzt and Montolio had flushed most of the invading force back out over the rock wall. "Bad magic!" came the general orc cry, voices edged on desperation. Hooter and his owl companions aided the growing frenzy, flapping down all of a sudden in orc faces, nipping with a talon or beak, then rushing off again into the sky. Still another orc discovered one of the traps as it tried to flee. It went down howling and shrieking, its cries only heightening its companions' terror.

"No!" Roddy McGristle cried in disbelief. "Ye've let two beat up yer whole force!"

Graul's glare settled on the burly man.

"We can turn 'em back," Roddy said. "If they see ye, they'll go back to the fight." The mountain man's appraisal was not off the mark. If Graul and Roddy had made their entrance then, the orcs, still numbering more than fifty, might have regrouped. With most of their traps exhausted, Drizzt and Montolio would have been in a sore position indeed! But the orc king had seen another brewing problem to the north and had decided, despite Roddy's protests, that the old man and the dark elf simply weren't worth the effort.

Most of the orcs in the field heard the newest danger before they saw it, for Bluster and his friends were a noisy lot. The largest obstacle the bears found as they rolled through the orc ranks was picking out a single target in the mad rush. They swatted orcs as they passed, then chased them into the copse and beyond, all the way back to their holes by the river. It was high spring; the air was charged with energy and excitement, and how these playful bears loved to swat orcs!

⚔ ⚔ ⚔ ⚔ ⚔

The whole horde of rushing bodies swarmed right past the fallen quickling. When Tephanis awoke, he found that he was the only one alive on the blood-soaked field. Growls and shouts wafted in from the west, the fleeing band and sounds of battle still sounded in the ranger's grove. Tephanis knew that his part in the battle, minor though it had been, was over. Tremendous pain rolled up the sprite's leg, more pain than he had ever known. He looked down to his torn foot and to his horror realized that the only way out of the wicked trap was to complete the gruesome cut, losing the end of his foot and all five of his toes in the process. It was not a difficult job—the foot was hanging by a thin piece of skin—and Tephanis did not hesitate, fearing that the drow would come out at any moment and find him.

The quickling stifled his scream and covered the wound with his torn shirt, then ambled—slowly—off into the trees.

⚔ ⚔ ⚔ ⚔ ⚔

The orc crept along silently, glad for the covering noises of the fight between the panther and a worg. All thoughts of killing the old man or the drow had flown from this orc now; it had seen its comrades chased away by a pack of bears. Now the orc only wanted to find a way out, not an easy feat in the thick, low tangle of pine branches.

It stepped on some dry leaves as it came into one clear area and froze at the resounding crackle. The orc glanced to the left, then slowly brought its head back around to the right. All of a sudden, it jumped and spun, expecting an attack from the rear. But all was clear as far as it could tell and all, except for the distant panther growls and worg yelps, was quiet. The orc let out a profound sigh of relief and sought the trail once again.

It stopped suddenly on instinct and threw its head way back to look up. A dark form crouched on a branch just above the orc's head, and the silvery flash shot down before the orc could begin to react. The curve of the scimitar's blade proved perfect for slipping around the orc's chin and diving into its throat.

The orc stood very still, arms wide and twitching, and tried to scream, but the whole length of its larynx was torn apart. The scimitar came out in a rush and the orc fell backward into death.

Not so far away, another orc finally extracted itself from the hanging net and quickly cut free its buddy. The two of them, enraged and not as anxious to run away without a fight, crept in quietly.

"In the dark," the first explained as they came through one thicket and found the landscape blotted out by an impenetrable globe. "Deep."

Together, the orcs raised their spears and threw, grunting savagely with the effort. The spears disappeared into the dark globe, dead center, one banging into a metallic object but the other striking something softer.

The orcs' cries of victory were cut short by two twangs of a bowstring. One of the creatures lurched forward, dead before it hit the ground, but the other, stubbornly holding its footing, managed to look down to its chest, to the protruding point of an arrowhead. It lived long enough to see Montolio casually stride past and disappear into the darkness to retrieve his shield.

Drizzt watched the old man from a distance, shaking his head and wondering.

⚔ ⚔ ⚔ ⚔ ⚔

"It is ended," the elven scout told the others when they caught up to him among the boulders just south of Mooshie's Grove.

"I am not so certain," Kellindil replied, looking curiously back to the west and hearing the echoes of bear growls and orc screams. Kellindil suspected that something beyond Graul was behind this attack and feeling somewhat responsible for the drow, he wanted to know what it might be.

"The ranger and drow have won the grove," the scout explained.

"Agreed," said Kellindil, "and so your part is ended. Go back, all of you, to the campsite."

"And will you join us?" one of the elves asked, though he had already guessed the answer.

"If the fates decree it," Kellindil replied. "For now, I have other business to attend."

The others did not question Kellindil further. Rarely did he come to their realm and never did he remain with them for long. Kellindil was an adventurer; the road was his home. He set off at once, running to catch up to the fleeing orcs, then paralleling their movements just south of them.

⚔ ⚔ ⚔ ⚔ ⚔

"Ye let just two of them beat ye!" Roddy griped when he and Graul had a moment to stop and catch their breath. "Two of them!"

Graul's answer came in the swing of a heavy club. Roddy partially blocked the blow, but its weight knocked him backward.

"Ye're to pay for that!" the mountain man growled, tearing Bleeder from his belt. A dozen of Graul's minions appeared beside the orc king then and immediately understood the situation.

"Yous has brought ruin to us!" Graul snapped at Roddy. Then to his orcs, he shouted, "Kill him!"

Roddy's dog tripped the closest of the group and Roddy didn't wait for the others to catch up. He turned and sprinted off into the night, using every trick he knew to get ahead of the pursuing band.

His efforts were quickly successful—the orcs really didn't want any more battles this night—and Roddy would have been wise to stop looking over his shoulder.

He heard a rustle up ahead and turned just in time to catch the pommel of a swinging sword squarely in the face. The weight of the blow, multiplied by Roddy's own momentum, dropped the mountain man straight to the ground and into unconsciousness.

"I am not surprised," Kellindil said over the writhing body.

# 19 SEPARATE WAYS

Eight days had done nothing to ease the pain in Tephanis's foot. The sprite ambled about as best he could, but whenever he broke into a sprint, he inevitably veered to one side and more often than not crashed into a bush or, worse, the unbending trunk of a tree.

"Will-you-please-quit-growling-at-me, stupid-dog!" Tephanis snapped at the yellow canine he had been with since the day after the battle. Neither had become comfortable around the other. Tephanis often lamented that this ugly mutt was in no way akin to Caroak.

But Caroak was dead; the quickling had found the winter wolf's torn body. Another companion gone, and now the sprite was alone again. "Alone-except-for-you, stupid-dog," he lamented.

The dog bared its teeth and growled.

Tephanis wanted to slice its throat, wanted to run up and down the length of the mangy animal, cutting and slashing at every inch. He saw the sun riding low in the sky, though, and knew that the beast might soon prove valuable.

"Time-for-me-to-go!" the quickling spouted. Faster than the dog could react, Tephanis darted by it, grabbed at the rope he had hung about the dog's neck, and zipped three complete circuits of a nearby tree. The dog went after him, but Tephanis easily kept out of its reach until the leash snapped taut, flipping the dog right over. "Be-back-soon, you-stupid-thing!"

Tephanis sped along the mountain paths, knowing that this night might be his last chance. The lights of Maldobar burned in the far distance, but it was a different light, a campfire, that guided the quickling. He came upon the small camp just a few minutes later, glad to see that the elf was not around.

He found Roddy McGristle sitting at the base of a huge tree, his arms pulled behind him and tied at the wrists around the trunk. The mountain man seemed a wretched thing—as wretched as the dog—but Tephanis was out of options. Ulgulu and Kempfana were dead, Caroak was dead, and Graul, after the disaster at the grove, had actually placed a bounty on the quickling's head.

That left only Roddy—not much of a choice, but Tephanis had no desire to survive on his own ever again. He sped, unnoticed, to the back of the tree and whispered in the mountain man's ear. "You-will-be-in-Maldobar-tomorrow."

Roddy froze at the unexpected, squeaky voice.

"You will be in Maldobar tomorrow," Tephanis said again, as slowly as he could.

"Go away," Roddy growled at him, thinking that the sprite was teasing him.

"You-should-be-kinder-to-me, oh-you-should!" Tephanis snapped right back. "The-elf-means-to-imprison-you, you-know. For-crimes-against-the-blind-ranger."

"Shut yer mouth," McGristle growled, louder than he had intended.

"What are you about?" came Kellindil's call from not so far away.

"There, you-have-done-it-now, silly-man!" Tephanis whispered.

"I told ye to go away!" Roddy replied.

"I-might, and-then-where-would-you-be? In-prison?" Tephanis said angrily. "I-can-help-you-now, if-you-want-my-help."

Roddy was beginning to understand. "Untie my hands," he ordered.

"They-already-are-untied," Tephanis replied, and Roddy found the sprite's words to be true. He started to rise but changed his mind abruptly as Kellindil entered the camp.

"Keep-still," Tephanis advised. "I-will-distract-your-captor." Tephanis had moved as he spoke the words and Roddy heard only an unintelligible murmur. He kept his hands behind him, though, seeing no other course available with the heavily armed elf approaching.

"Our last night on the road," Kellindil remarked, dropping by the fire the coney he had shot for a meal. He moved in front of Roddy and bent low. "I will send for Lady Falconhand once we have arrived in Maldobar," he said. "She names Montolio DeBrouchee as a friend and will be interested to learn of the events in the grove."

"What do ye know?" Roddy spat at him. "The ranger was a friend o' mine, too!"

"If you are a friend of orc king Graul, then you are no friend of the ranger in the grove," Kellindil retorted.

Roddy had no immediate rebuttal, but Tephanis supplied one. A buzzing noise came from behind the elf and Kellindil, dropping a hand to his sword, spun about.

"What manner of being are you?" he asked the quickling, his eyes wide in amazement.

Kellindil never learned the answer, for Roddy came up suddenly behind him and slammed him to the ground. Kellindil was a seasoned fighter, but in close he was no match for the sheer brawn of Roddy McGristle. Roddy's huge and dirty hands closed on the slender elf's throat.

"I-have-your-dog," Tephanis said to Roddy when the foul business was done. "Tied-it-to-a-tree."

"Who are ye?" Roddy asked, trying to hide his elation, both for his freedom and for the knowledge that his dog still lived. "And what do ye want with me?"

"I-am-a-little-thing, you-can-see-that-to-be-true," Tephanis explained. "I-like-keeping-big-friends."

Roddy considered the offer for a moment. "Well, ye've earned it, he said with a laugh. He found Bleeder, his trusted axe, among the dead elf's belongings and rose up huge and grim-faced. "Come on then, let's get back to the mountains. I've a drow to deal with."

A sour expression crossed the quickling's delicate features, but Tephanis hid it before Roddy could notice. Tephanis had no desire to go anywhere near the blind ranger's grove. Aside from the fact that the orc king had placed a bounty on his head, he knew that the other elves might get suspicious if Roddy showed up without Kellindil. More than that, Tephanis found the pain in his head and foot even more acute at the mere thought of facing the dark elf again.

"No!" the sprite blurted. Roddy, not used to being disobeyed, eyed him dangerously.

"No-need," Tephanis lied. "The-drow-is-dead, killed-by-a-worg."

Roddy didn't seem convinced.

"I-led-you-to-the-drow-once," Tephanis reminded him.

Truly Roddy was disappointed, but he no longer doubted the quickling. If it hadn't been for Tephanis, Roddy knew, he never would have located Drizzt. He would be more than a hundred miles away, sniffing around Morueme's Cave and spending all of his gold on dragon lies. "What about the blind ranger?" Roddy asked.

"He-lives, but-let-him-live," Tephanis replied. "Many-powerful-friends-have-joined-him." He led Roddy's gaze to Kellindil's body. "Elves, many-elves."

Roddy nodded his assent. He had no real grudge against Mooshie and had no desire to face Kellindil's kin.

They buried Kellindil and all of the supplies they couldn't take with them, found Roddy's dog, and set out later that same night for the wide lands to the west.

⚔ ⚔ ⚔ ⚔ ⚔

Back at Mooshie's grove, the summer passed peacefully and productively, with Drizzt coming into the ways and methods of a ranger even more easily than optimistic Montolio had believed. Drizzt learned the name for every tree or bush in the region, and every animal, and more importantly, he learned how to learn, how to observe the clues that Mielikki gave him. When he came upon an animal that he had not encountered before, he found that simply by watching its movements and actions he could quickly discern its intent, demeanor, and mood.

"Go and feel its coat," Montolio whispered to him one day in the gray and blustery twilight. The old ranger pointed across a field, to the tree line and the white flicking of a deer's tail. Even in the dim light, Drizzt had trouble seeing the deer, but he sensed its presence, as Montolio obviously had.

"Will it let me?" Drizzt whispered back. Montolio smiled and shrugged.

Drizzt crept out silently and carefully, following the shadows along the edge of the meadow. He chose a northern, downwind approach, but to get north of the deer, he had to come around from the east. He knew his error when he was still two dozen yards from the deer. It lifted its head suddenly, sniffed, and flicked its white tail.

Drizzt froze and waited for a long moment while the deer resumed its grazing. The skittish creature was on the alert now, and as soon as Drizzt took another measured step, the deer bolted away.

But not before Montolio, taking the southern approach, had gotten close enough to pat its rump as it ran past.

Drizzt blinked in amazement. "The wind favored me!" he protested to the smug ranger.

Montolio shook his head. "Only over the last twenty yards, when you came north of the deer," he explained. "West was better than east until then."

"But you could not get north of the deer from the west," Drizzt said.

"I did not have to," Montolio replied. "There is a high bluff back there," he pointed to the south. "It cuts the wind at this angle—swirls it back around."

"I did not know."

"You have to know," Montolio said lightly. "That is the trick of it. You have to see as a bird might and look down upon all the region before you choose your course "

"I have not learned to fly," Drizzt replied sarcastically.

"Nor have I!" roared the old ranger. "Look above you."

Drizzt squinted as he turned his eyes to the gray sky. He made out a solitary form, gliding easily with great wings held wide to catch the breeze.

"A hawk," the drow said.

"Rode the breeze from the south," Montolio explained, "then banked west on the breaking currents around the bluff. If you had observed its flight, you might have suspected the change in terrain."

"That is impossible," Drizzt said helplessly.

"Is it?" Montolio asked, and he started away—to hide his smile. Of course the drow was correct; one could not tell the topography of the terrain by the flight patterns of a hawk. Montolio had learned of the shifting wind from a certain sneaky owl who had slipped in at the ranger's bidding right after Drizzt had started out across the meadow, but Drizzt didn't have to know that. Let the drow consider the fib for a while, the old ranger decided. The contemplation, recounting all he had learned, would be a valuable lesson.

"Hooter told you," Drizzt said a half-hour later, on the trail back to the grove. "Hooter told you of the wind and told you of the hawk."

"You seem sure of yourself."

"I am," Drizzt said firmly. "The hawk did not cry—I have become aware enough to know that. You could not see the bird, and I know that you did not hear the rush of wind over its wings, whatever you may say!"

Montolio's laughter brought a smile of confirmation to the drow's face.

"You have done well this day," the old ranger said.

"I did not get near the deer," Drizzt reminded him.

"That was not the test," Montolio replied. "You trusted in your knowledge to dispute my claims. You are sure of the lessons you have learned. Now hear some more. Let me tell you a few tricks when approaching a skittish deer."

They talked all the way back to the grove and far into the night after that. Drizzt listened eagerly, absorbing every word as he was let in on still more of the world's wondrous secrets.

A tenday later, in a different field, Drizzt placed one hand on the rump of a doe, the other on the rump of its speckle-coated fawn. Both animals lit out at the unexpected touch, but Montolio "saw" Drizzt's smile from a hundred yards away.

Drizzt's lessons were far from complete when the summer waned, but

Montolio no longer spent much time instructing the drow. Drizzt had learned enough to go out and learn on his own, listening and watching the quiet voices and subtle signs of the trees and the animals. So caught up was Drizzt in his unending revelations that he hardly noticed the profound changes in Montolio. The ranger felt much older now. His back would hardly straighten on chill mornings and his hands often went numb. Montolio remained stoic about it all, hardly one for self-pity and hardly lamenting what he knew was to come.

He had lived long and fully, had accomplished much, and had experienced life more vividly than most men ever would.

"What are your plans?" he said unexpectedly to Drizzt one night as they ate their dinner, a vegetable stew that Drizzt had concocted.

The question hit Drizzt hard. He had no plans beyond the present, and why should he, with life so easy and enjoyable—more so than it had ever been for the beleaguered drow renegade? Drizzt really didn't want to think about the question, so he threw a biscuit at Guenhwyvar to change the subject. The panther was getting a bit too comfortable on Drizzt's bedroll, wrapping up in the blankets to the point where Drizzt worried that the only way to get Guenhwyvar out of the tangle would be to send it back to the astral plane.

Montolio was persistent. "What are your plans, Drizzt Do'Urden?" the old ranger said again firmly. "Where and how will you live?"

"Are you throwing me out?" Drizzt asked.

"Of course not."

"Then I will live with you," Drizzt replied calmly.

"I mean after," Montolio said, growing flustered.

"After what?" Drizzt asked, thinking that Mooshie knew something he did not.

Montolio's laughter mocked his suspicions. "I am an old man," the ranger explained, "and you are a young elf. I am older than you, but even if I were a babe, your years would far outdistance my own. Where will Drizzt Do'Urden go when Montolio DeBrouchee is no more?"

Drizzt turned away. "I do not . . ." he began tentatively. "I will stay here."

"No," Montolio replied soberly. "You have much more before you than this, I hope. This life would not do."

"It has suited you," Drizzt snapped back, more forcefully than he had intended.

"For five years," Montolio said calmly, taking no offense. "Five years after a life of adventure and excitement."

"My life has not been so quiet," Drizzt reminded him.

"But you are still a child," Montolio said. "Five years is not five hundred, and five hundred is what you have remaining. Promise me now that you will reconsider your course when I am no more. There is a wide world out there, my friend, full of pain, but filled with joy as well. The former keeps you on the path of growth, and the latter makes the journey tolerable.

"Promise me now," Montolio said, "that when Mooshie is no more, Drizzt will go and find his place."

Drizzt wanted to argue, to ask the ranger how he was so certain that this grove was not Drizzt's 'place.' A mental scale dipped and leveled, then dipped again within Drizzt at that moment. He weighed the memories of Maldobar, the farmers' deaths, and all the memories before that of the trials he had faced and the evils that had so persistently followed him. Against this, Drizzt considered his heartfelt desire to go back out in the world. How many other Mooshies might he find? How many friends? And how empty would be this grove when he and Guenhwyvar had it to themselves?

Montolio accepted the silence, knowing the drow's confusion. "Promise me that when the time is upon you, you will at least consider what I have said."

Trusting in Drizzt, Montolio did not have to see his friend's affirming nod.

⚔ ⚔ ⚔ ⚔ ⚔

The first snow came early that year, just a light dusting from broken clouds that played hide-and-seek with a full moon. Drizzt, out with Guenhwyvar, reveled in the seasonal change, enjoyed the reaffirmation of the endless cycle. He was in high spirits when he bounded back to the grove, shaking the snow from the thick pine branches as he picked his way in.

The campfire burned low; Hooter sat still on a low branch and even the wind seemed not to make a sound. Drizzt looked to Guenhwyvar for some explanation, but the panther only sat by the fire, somber and still.

Dread is a strange emotion, a culmination of too-subtle clues that brings as much confusion as fear.

"Mooshie?" Drizzt called softly, approaching the old ranger's den. He pushed aside the blanket and used it to screen the light from the embers of the dying campfire, letting his eyes slip into the infrared spectrum.

He remained there for a very long time, watching the last wisps of heat depart from the ranger's body. But if Mooshie was cold, his contented smile emanated warmth.

Drizzt fought back many tears over the next few days, but whenever he remembered that last smile, the final peace that had come over the aged man, he reminded himself that the tears were for his own loss and not for Mooshie.

Drizzt buried the ranger in a cairn beside the grove, then spent the winter quietly, tending to his daily chores and wondering. Hooter came by less and less frequently, and on one occasion the departing look Hooter cast at Drizzt told the drow beyond doubt that the owl would never return to the grove.

In the spring, Drizzt came to understand Hooter's sentiments. For more than a decade, he had been searching for a home, and he had found one with Montolio. But with the ranger gone, the grove no longer seemed so hospitable. This was Mooshie's place, not Drizzt's.

"As I promised," Drizzt mumbled one morning. Montolio had asked him to consider his course carefully when the ranger was no more, and Drizzt now held to his word. He had become comfortable in the grove and was still accepted here, but the grove was no longer his home. His home was out there, he knew, out in that wide world that Montolio had assured him was "full of pain, but filled with joy as well."

Drizzt packed a few items—practical supplies and some of the ranger's more interesting books—belted on his scimitars, and slung the longbow over his shoulder. Then he took a final walk around the grove, viewing one last time the rope bridges, the armory, the brandy barrel and trough, the tree root where he had stopped the charging giant, the sheltered run where Mooshie had made his stand. He called Guenhwyvar, and the panther understood as soon as it arrived.

They never looked back as they moved down the mountain trail, toward the wide world of pains and joys.

# Part Five

# Sojourn

How different the trail seemed as I departed Mooshie's Grove from the road that had led me there. Again I was alone, except when Guenhwyvar came to my call. On this road, though, I was alone only in body.

In my mind I carried a name, the embodiment of my valued principles. Mooshie had called Mielikki a goddess; to me she was a way of life.

She walked beside me always along the many surface roads I traversed. She led me out to safety and fought off my despair when I was chased away and hunted by the dwarves of Citadel Adbar, a fortress northeast of Mooshie's Grove. Mielikki, and my belief in my own value, gave me the courage to approach town after town throughout the northland. The receptions were always the same: shock and fear that quickly turned to anger. The more generous of those I encountered told me simply to go away; others chased me with weapons bared. On two occasions I was forced to fight, though I managed to escape without anyone being badly injured.

The minor nicks and scratches were a small price to pay. Mooshie had bidden me not to live as he had, and the old ranger's perceptions, as always, proved true. On my journeys throughout the northland I retained something—hope—that I never would have held if I had remained a hermit in the evergreen grove. As each new village showed on the horizon, a tingle of anticipation quickened my steps. One day, I was determined, I would find acceptance and find my home.

It would happen suddenly, I imagined. I would approach a gate, speak a formal greeting, then reveal myself as a dark elf. Even my fantasy was tempered by reality, for the gate would not swing wide at my approach. Rather, I would be allowed guarded entry, a trial period much like the one I endured in Blingdenstone, the svirfneblin city. Suspicions would linger about me for many months, but in the end, principles would be seen and accepted for what they were; the character of the person would outweigh the color of his skin and the reputation of his heritage.

I replayed that fantasy countless times over the years. Every word of every meeting in my imagined town became a litany against the continued rejections. It would not have been enough, but always there was Guenhwyvar, and now there was Mielikki.

—Drizzt Do'Urden

# 20

# Years and Miles

The Harvest Inn in Westbridge was a favorite gathering place for travelers along the Long Road that stretched between the two great northern cities of Waterdeep and Mirabar. Aside from comfortable bedding at reasonable rates, the Harvest offered Derry's Tavern and Eatery, a renowned story-swapping bar where on any night of any tenday a guest might find adventurers from regions as varied as Luskan and Sundabar. The hearth was bright and warm, the drinks were plentiful, and the yarns woven in Derry's were ones that would be told and retold all across the realms.

Roddy kept the cowl of his worn traveling cloak pulled low about him, hiding his scarred face, as he tore into his mutton and biscuits. The old yellow dog sat on the floor beside him, growling, and every now and Roddy absently dropped it a piece of meat.

The ravenous bounty hunter rarely lifted his head from the plate, but Roddy's bloodshot eyes peered suspiciously from the shadows of his cowl. He knew some of the ruffians gathered in Derry's this night, personally or by reputation, and he wouldn't trust them any more than they, if they were wise, would trust him.

One tall man recognized Roddy's dog as he passed the table and stopped, thinking to greet the bounty hunter. The tall man walked away silently, though, realizing that miserable McGristle wasn't really worth the effort. No one knew exactly what had happened those years before in the mountains near Maldobar, but Roddy had come out of that region deeply scarred, physically and emotionally. Always a surly one, McGristle now spent more time growling than talking.

Roddy gnawed a bit longer then dropped the thick bone down to his dog and wiped his greasy hands on his cloak, inadvertently brushing back the side of his cowl that hid his gruesome scars. Roddy quickly pulled the cowl back down, his gaze darting about for anyone who might have noticed. A single disgusted glance had cost several men their lives where Roddy's scars were concerned.

No one seemed to notice, though, not this time. Most of those who weren't busily eating were over at the bar, arguing loudly.

"Never was it!" one man growled.

"I told you what I saw!" another shot back. "And I told you right!"

"To yer eyes!" the first shouted back, and still another put in, "Ye'd not know one if ye seen one!" Several of the men closed in, bumping chest to chest.

"Stand quiet!" came a voice. A man pushed out of the throng and pointed straight at Roddy, who, not recognizing the man, instinctively dropped his hand to Bleeder, his well-worn axe.

"Ask McGristle!" the man cried. "Roddy McGristle. He knows about dark elves better than any."

A dozen conversations sprouted up at once as the whole group, looking like some amorphous rolling blob, slid over toward Roddy. Roddy's hand was off Bleeder again, crossing fingers with the other one on the table in front of him.

"Ye're McGristle, are ye?" the man asked Roddy, showing the bounty hunter a good measure of respect.

"Might that I am," Roddy replied calmly, enjoying the attention. He hadn't been surrounded by a group so interested in what he had to say since the Thistledown clan had been found murdered.

"Aw," a disgruntled voice piped in from somewhere in the back, "what's he know about dark elves."

Roddy's glare sent those in front back a step, and he noticed the movement. He liked the feeling, liked being important again, respected.

"Drow elf killed my dog," he said gruffly. He reached down and yanked up the old yellow hound's head, displaying the scar. "And dented this one's head. Damned dark elf—" he said deliberately, easing the cowl back from his face—"gave me this." Normally Roddy hid the hideous scars, but the crowd's gasps and mumbles sounded immensely satisfying to the wretched bounty hunter. He turned to the side, gave them a full view, and savored the reaction for as long as he could.

"Black-skinned and white-haired?" asked a short, fat-bellied man, the one who had begun the debate back at the bar with his own tale of a dark elf.

"Would have to be if he was a dark elf," Roddy huffed back. The man looked about triumphantly.

"That is what I tried to tell them," he said to Roddy. "They claim that I saw a dirty elf, or an orc maybe, but I knew it was a drow!"

"If ye see a drow," Roddy said grimly and deliberately, weighing every word with importance, "then ye know ye seen a drow. And ye'll not forget that ye seen a drow! And let any man that doubts yer words go and find a drow for himself. He'll come back to ye with a word of bein' sorry!"

"Well, I seen a dark elf," the man proclaimed. "I was camping in Lurkwood, north of Grunwald. Peaceful enough night, I thought, so I let the fire up a bit to beat the cold wind. Well, in walked this stranger without a warning, without a word!"

Every man in the group hung on the words now, hearing them in a different light now that the drow-scarred stranger had somewhat confirmed the tale.

"Without a word, or a bird call, or nothing!" the fat-bellied man went on. "He had his cloak pulled low, suspicious, so I said to him, 'What are you about?'"

"'Searching for a place that my companions and I may camp the night,' " he answered, calm as you may. Seemed reasonable enough to me, but I still did not like that low cowl."

"'Pull back your hood then,," I told him. 'I share nothing without seeing a man's face.' He considered my words a minute, then he moved his hands up, real slow,"—the man imitated the movement dramatically, glancing around to ensure that he had everyone's attention.

"I needed to see nothing more!" the man cried suddenly, and everyone, though they had heard the same tale told the same way only a moment before, jumped back in surprise. "His hands were as black as coal and as slender as an elf's. I knew then, but I know not how I knew so surely, that it was a drow before me. A drow, I say, and let any man who doubts my words go and find a dark elf for himself!"

Roddy nodded his approval as the fat-bellied man stared down his former doubters. "Seems I've heard too much about dark elves lately," the bounty hunter grumbled.

"I've heared of just the one," another man piped in. "Until we spoke to you, I mean, and heard of your battle. That makes two drow in six years."

"As I said," Roddy remarked grimly, "seems I've heard too much about dark—" Roddy never finished as the group exploded into exaggerated laughter around him. It seemed like the grand old times to the bounty hunter, the days when everyone about him hung tense on his every word.

The only man who wasn't laughing was the fat-bellied storyteller, too shook up from his own recounting of his meeting with the drow. "Still," he said above the commotion, "when I think of those purple eyes staring out at me from under that cowl!"

Roddy's smile disappeared in the blink of an eye. "Purple eyes?" he barely managed to gasp. Roddy had encountered many creatures that used infravision, the heat-sensing sight most common among denizens of the Underdark, and he knew that normally, such eyes showed as dots of red. Roddy still remembered vividly the purple eyes looking down at him when he was trapped under the maple tree. He knew then, and he knew now, that those strange-hued orbs were a rarity even among the dark elves.

Those in the group closest to Roddy stopped their laughing, thinking that Roddy's question shed doubt on the truth of the man's tale.

"They were purple," the fat-bellied man insisted, though there was little conviction in his shaky voice. The men around him waited for Roddy's agreement or rebuttal, not knowing whether or not to laugh at the storyteller.

"What weapons did the drow wield?" Roddy asked grimly, rising ominously to his feet.

The man thought for a moment. "Curved swords," he blurted.

"Scimitars?"

"Scimitars," the other agreed.

"Did the drow say his name?" Roddy asked, and when the man hesitated, Roddy grabbed him by the collar and pulled him over the table. "Did the drow say his name?" the bounty hunter said again, his breath hot on the fat-bellied man's face.

"No . . . er, uh, Driz . . ."

"Drizzit?"

The man shrugged helplessly, and Roddy threw him back to his feet. "Where?" the bounty hunter roared. "And when?"

"Lurkwood," the quivering, full-bellied man said again. "Three tendays ago. Drow's going to Mirabar with the Weeping Friars, I would guess." Most of the crowd groaned at the mention of the fanatic religious group. The Weeping Friars were a ragged band of begging sufferers who believed—or claimed to believe—that there was a finite amount of pain in the world. The more suffering they took on themselves, the friars said, the less remained for the rest of world to endure. Nearly everyone scorned the order. Some were sincere, but some begged for trinkets, promising to suffer horribly for the good of the giver.

"Those were the drow's companions," the fat-bellied man continued. "They always go to Mirabar, go to find the cold, as winter comes on."

"Long way," someone remarked.

"Longer," said another. "The Weeping Friars always take the tunnel route."

"Three hundred miles," the first man who had recognized Roddy put in, trying to calm the agitated bounty hunter. But Roddy never even heard him. His dog in tow, he spun away and stormed out of Derry's, slamming the door behind him and leaving the whole group mumbling to each other in absolute surprise.

"It was Drizzit that took Roddy's dog and ear," the man went on, now turning his attention to the group. He had no previous knowledge of the strange drow's name; he merely had made an assumption based on Roddy's reaction. Now the group flowed around him, holding their collective breath for him to tell them of the tale of Roddy McGristle and the purple-eyed drow. Like any proper patron of Derry's, the man didn't let lack of real knowledge deter him from telling the tale. He hooked his thumbs into his belt and began, filling in the considerable blanks with whatever sounded appropriate.

A hundred more gasps and claps of appreciation and startled delight echoed on the street outside of Derry's that night, but Roddy McGristle and his yellow dog, their wagon wheels already thick in the mud of the Long Road, heard none of them.

"Hey, what-are-you-doing?" came a weary complaint from a sack behind Roddy's bench. Tephanis crawled out. "Why-are-we-leaving?"

Roddy twisted about and took a swipe, but Tephanis, even sleepy-eyed, had no trouble darting out of harm's way.

"Ye lied to me, ye cousin to a kobold!" Roddy growled. "Ye telled me that the drow was dead. But he's not! He's on the road to Mirabar, and I mean to catch him!"

"Mirabar?" Tephanis cried. "Too-far, too-far!" The quickling and Roddy had passed through Mirabar the previous spring. Tephanis thought it a perfectly miserable place, full of grim-faced dwarves, sharp-eyed men, and a wind much too cold for his liking. "We-must-go-south-for-the-winter. South-where-it-is-warm!"

Roddy's ensuing glare silenced the sprite. "I'll forget what ye did to me," he snarled, then he added an ominous warning, "if we get the drow." He turned from Tephanis then, and the sprite crawled back into his sack, feeling miserable and wondering if Roddy McGristle was worth the trouble.

Roddy drove through the night, bending low to urge his horse onward and muttering "Six years!" over and over.

⚔ ⚔ ⚔ ⚔ ⚔

Drizzt huddled close to the fire that roared out of an old ore barrel the group had found. This would be the drow's seventh winter on the surface, but still he remained uncomfortable in the chill. He had spent decades, and his people had lived for many millennia, in the seasonless and warm Underdark. Though winter was still months away, its approach was evident in the chill winds blowing down from the Spine of the World Mountains. Drizzt wore only an old blanket, thin and torn, over his clothes, chain mail, and weapon belt.

The drow smiled when he noticed his companions fidgeting and huffing over who got the next draw on a bottle of wine they had begged and how much the last drinker had taken. Drizzt was alone at the barrel now; the Weeping Friars, while not actually shunning the drow, didn't often go near him. Drizzt accepted this and knew that the fanatics appreciated his companionship for practical, if not aesthetic, reasons. Some of the band actually enjoyed attacks by the various monsters of the land viewing them as opportunities for some true suffering, but the more pragmatic of the group appreciated having the armed and skilled drow around for protection.

The relationship was acceptable to Drizzt, if not fulfilling. He had left Mooshie's Grove years ago filled with hope, but hope tempered by the realities of his existence. Time after time, Drizzt had approached a village only to be put out behind a wall of harsh words, curses, and drawn weapons. Every time, Drizzt shrugged away the snubbing. True to his ranger spirit—for Drizzt was indeed a ranger now, in training as well as in heart—he accepted his lot stoically.

The last rejection had shown Drizzt that his resolve was wearing thin, though. He had been turned away from Luskan, on the Sword Coast, but not by any guards, for he had never even approached the place. Drizzt's own fears had kept him away, and that fact had frightened him more than any swords he had ever faced. On the road outside the city, Drizzt had met up with this handful of Weeping Friars, and the outcasts had tentatively accepted him, as much because they had no means to keep him out as because they were too full of their own wretchedness to care about any racial differences. Two of the group had even thrown themselves at Drizzt's feet, begging him to unleash his "dark elf terrors" and make them suffer.

Through the spring and summer, the relationship had evolved with Drizzt serving as silent guardian while the friars went about their begging and suffering ways. All in all, it was quite distasteful, even sometimes deceitful, to the principled drow, but Drizzt had found no other options.

Drizzt stared into the leaping flames and considered his fate. He still had Guenhwyvar at his call and had put his scimitars and bow to gainful use many times. Every day he told himself that beside the somewhat helpless fanatics, he was serving Mielikki, and his own heart, well. Still, he did not hold the friars in high regard and did not call them friends. Watching the five men now, drunk and slobbering all over each other, Drizzt suspected that he never would.

"Beat me! Slash me!" one of the friars cried suddenly, and he ran over toward the barrel, stumbling into Drizzt. Drizzt caught him and steadied him, but only for a moment.

"Loosh your dwow whickedniss on me head!" the dirty, unshaven friar sputtered, and his lanky frame tumbled down in an angular heap.

Drizzt turned away, shook his head, and unconsciously dropped a hand into his pouch to feel the onyx figurine, needing the touch to remind him that he was not truly alone. He was surviving, fighting an endless and lonely battle, but was far from contented. He had found a place, perhaps, but not a home.

"Like the grove without Montolio," the drow mused. "Never a home."

"Did you say something?" asked a portly friar, Brother Mateus, coming over to collect his drunken companion. "Please excuse Brother Jankin, friend. He has imbibed too much, I fear."

Drizzt's helpless smile told that he had taken no offense, but his next words caught Brother Mateus, the leader and most rational member—if not the most honest—of the group, off guard.

"I will complete the trip to Mirabar with you," Drizzt explained, "then I will leave."

"Leave?" asked Mateus, concerned.

"This is not my place," Drizzt explained.

"Ten-Towns ish the place!" Jankin blurted.

"If anyone has offended you . . ." Mateus said to Drizzt, taking no heed of the drunken man.

"No one," Drizzt said and smiled again. "There is more for me in this life, Brother Mateus. Do not be angry, I beg, but I am leaving. It was not a decision I came to lightly."

Mateus took a moment to consider the words. "As you choose," he said, "but might you at least escort us through the tunnel into Mirabar?"

"Ten-Towns!" Jankin insisted. "Thast the place fer sufferin'! You'd like it, too, drow. Land o' rogues, where a rogue might find hish place!"

"Often there are rakes in the shadows who would prey on unarmed friars," Mateus interrupted, giving Jankin a rough shake.

Drizzt paused a moment, transfixed on Jankin's words. Jankin had collapsed, though, and the drow looked up to Mateus. "Is that not why you take the tunnel route into the city?" Drizzt asked the portly friar. The tunnel was normally reserved for mine carts, rolling down from the Spine of the World, but the friars always went through it, even in situations such as this, when they had to make a complete circuit of the city just to get to the long route's entrance. "To fall victim and suffer?" Drizzt continued. "Surely the road is clear and more convenient with winter still months away." Drizzt did not like the tunnel to Mirabar. Any wanderers they met on that road would be too close for the drow to hide his identity. Drizzt had been accosted there on both his previous trips through.

"The others insist that we go through the tunnel, though it is many miles out of our way," replied Mateus, a sharp edge to his tone. "But I prefer more personal forms of suffering and would appreciate your company through to Mirabar."

Drizzt wanted to scream at the phony friar. Mateus considered missing a single meal a harsh suffering and only used his facade because many gullible people handed coins to the cloaked fanatics, more often than not just to be rid of the smelly men.

Drizzt nodded and watched as Mateus hauled Jankin away. "Then I leave," he whispered under his breath. He could tell himself over and over that he was serving his goddess and his heart by protecting the seemingly helpless band but their behavior often flew in the face of those words.

"Dwow! Dwow!" Brother Jankin slobbered as Mateus dragged him back to the others.

# 21
# Hephaestus

Tephanis watched the party of six—the five friars and Drizzt—make their slow way toward the tunnel on the western approach to Mirabar. Roddy had sent the quickling ahead to scout out the region, telling Tephanis to turn the drow, if he found the drow, back toward Roddy. "Bleeder'll be taking care of that one," Roddy had snarled, slapping his formidable axe across his palm.

Tephanis wasn't so sure. The sprite had watched Ulgulu, a master arguably more powerful than Roddy McGristle, dispatched by the drow, and another mighty master, Caroak, had been torn apart by the drow's black panther. If Roddy got his wish and met the drow in battle, Tephanis might soon be searching for yet another master.

"Not-this-time, drow," the sprite whispered suddenly, an idea coming to mind. "This-time-I-get-you!" Tephanis knew the tunnel to Mirabar—he and Roddy had used it the winter before last, when snow had buried the western road—and had learned many of its secrets, including one that the sprite now planned to use to his advantage.

He made a wide circuit around the group, not wanting to alert the sharp-eared drow, and still made the tunnel entrance long before the others. A few minutes later, the sprite was more than a mile in, picking at an intricate lock, one that seemed clumsy to the skilled quickling, on a portcullis crank.

⚔ ⚔ ⚔ ⚔ ⚔

Brother Mateus led the way into the tunnel, with another friar at his side and the remaining three completing a shielding circle around Drizzt. Drizzt had requested this so that he could remain inconspicuous if anyone happened by. He kept his cloak pulled up tightly and his shoulders hunched. He stayed low in the middle of the group.

They met no other travelers and moved along the torch-lit passage at a steady pace. They came to an intersection and Mateus stopped abruptly, seeing the raised portcullis to a passage on the right side. A dozen steps in, an iron door swung wide, and the passage beyond that was pitch black, not torch-lit like the main tunnel.

"How curious," Mateus remarked.

"Careless," another corrected. "Let us pray that no other travelers, who might not know the way as well as we, happen by here and take the wrong path!"

"Perhaps we should close the door," still another offered.

"No," Mateus quickly interjected. "There may be some down there, merchants perhaps, who would not be so pleased if we followed that plan."

"No!" Brother Jankin cried suddenly and ran to the front of the group. "It is a sign! A sign from God! We are beckoned, my brethren, to Phaestus, the ultimate suffering!"

Jankin turned to charge down the tunnel, but Mateus and one other, hardly surprised by Jankin's customarily wild outburst, immediately sprang upon him and bore him to the ground.

"Phaestus!" Jankin cried wildly, his long and shaggy black hair flying all about his face. "I am coming!"

"What is it?" Drizzt had to ask, having no idea of what the friars were talking about, though he thought he recognized the reference. "Who, or what, is Phaestus?"

"Hephaestus," Brother Mateus corrected.

Drizzt did know the name. One of the books he had taken from Mooshie's Grove was of dragon lore, and Hephaestus, a venerable red dragon living in the mountains northwest of Mirabar, had an entry.

"That is not the dragon's real name, of course," Mateus went on between grunts as he struggled with Jankin. "I do not know that, nor does anyone else anymore." Jankin twisted suddenly, throwing the other monk aside, and promptly stomped down on Mateus's sandal.

"Hephaestus is an old red dragon who has lived in the caves west of Mirabar for as long as anyone, even the dwarves, can remember," explained another friar, Brother Herschel, one less engaged than Mateus. "The city tolerates him because he is a lazy one and a stupid one, though I would not tell him so. Most cities, I presume, would choose to tolerate a red if it meant not fighting the thing! But Hephaestus is not much for pillaging—none can recall the last time he even came out of his hole—and he even does some ore-melting for hire, though the fee is steep."

"Some pay it, though," added Mateus, having Jankin back under control, "especially late in the season, looking to make the last caravan south. Nothing can separate metal like a red dragon's breath!" His laughter disappeared quickly as Jankin slugged him, dropping him to the ground.

Jankin bolted free, for just a moment. Quicker than anyone could react, Drizzt threw off his cloak and rushed after the fleeing monk, catching him just inside the heavy iron door. A single step and twisting maneuver put Jankin down hard on his back and took the wild-eyed friar's breath away.

"Let us get by this region at once," the drow offered, staring down at the stunned friar. "I grow tired of Jankin's antics—I might just allow him to run down to the dragon!"

Two of the others came over and gathered Jankin up, then the whole troupe turned to depart.

"Help!" came a cry from farther down the dark tunnel.

Drizzt's scimitars came out in his hands. The friars all gathered around him, peering down into the gloom.

"Do you see anything?" Mateus asked the drow, knowing that Drizzt's night vision was much keener than his own.

"No, but the tunnel turns a short way from here," Drizzt replied.

"Help!" came the cry again. Behind the group, around the corner in the main tunnel, Tephanis had to suppress his laughter. Quicklings were adept ventriloquists, and the biggest problem Tephanis had in deceiving the group was keeping his cries slow enough to be understood.

Drizzt took a cautious step in, and the friars, even Jankin, sobered by the distress call, followed right behind. Drizzt motioned for them to go back, even as he suddenly realized the potential for a trap.

But Tephanis was too quick. The door slammed with a resounding thud and before the drow, two steps away, could push through the startled friars, the sprite already had the door locked. A moment later, Drizzt and the friars heard a second crash as the portcullis came down.

Tephanis was back out in the daylight a few minutes later, thinking himself quite clever and reminding himself to keep a puzzled expression when he explained to Roddy that the drow's party was nowhere to be found.

⚔ ⚔ ⚔ ⚔ ⚔

The friars grew tired of yelling as soon as Drizzt reminded them that their screams might arouse the occupant at the other end of the tunnel. "Even if someone happens by the portcullis, he will not hear you through this door," the drow said, inspecting the heavy portal with the single candle Mateus had lit. A combination of iron, stone, and leather, and perfectly fitted, the door had been crafted by dwarves. Drizzt tried pounding on it with the pommel of a scimitar, but that produced only a dull thud that went no farther than the screams.

"We are lost," groaned Mateus. "We have no way out, and our stores are not too plentiful."

"Another sign!" Jankin blurted suddenly, but two of the friars knocked him down and sat on him before he could run off toward the dragon's den.

"Perhaps there is something to Brother Jankin's thinking," Drizzt said after a long pause.

Mateus looked at him suspiciously. "Are you thinking that our stores would last longer if Brother Jankin went to meet Hephaestus?" he asked.

Drizzt could not hold his laughter. "I have no intention of sacrificing anyone," he said and looked at Jankin struggling under the friars. "No matter how willing! But we have only one way out, it would seem."

Mateus followed Drizzt's gaze down the dark tunnel. "If you plan no sacrifices, then you are looking the wrong way," the portly friar huffed. "Surely you are not thinking to get past the dragon!"

"We shall see," was all that the drow answered. He lit another candle from the first one and moved a short distance down the tunnel. Drizzt's good sense argued against the undeniable excitement he felt at the prospect of facing Hephaestus, but it was an argument that he expected simple necessity to overrule. Montolio had fought a dragon, Drizzt remembered, had lost his eyes to a red. The ranger's memories of the battle, aside from his wounds, were not so terrible. Drizzt was beginning to understand what the blind ranger had told him about the differences between survival and fulfillment. How valuable would be the five hundred years Drizzt might have left to live?

For the friar's sake, Drizzt did hope that someone would come along and open the portcullis and door. The drow's fingers tingled with promised thrills, though, when he reached into his sack and pulled out a book on dragon lore he had taken from the grove.

The drow's sensitive eyes needed little light, and he could make out the script with only minor difficulty. As he suspected, there was an entry for the venerable red who lived west of Mirabar. The book confirmed that Hephaestus was not the dragon's real name, rather the name given to it in reference to some obscure god of blacksmiths.

The entry was not extensive, mostly tales from the merchants who went in to hire the dragon for its breath, and other tales of merchants who apparently said the wrong thing or haggled too much about the cost—or perhaps the dragon was merely hungry or in a foul mood—for they never came back out. Most importantly to Drizzt, the entry confirmed the friar's description of the beast as lazy and somewhat stupid. According to the notes, Hephaestus was overly proud, as dragons usually were, and able to speak the common tongue, but "lacking in the area of suspicious insight normally associated with the breed, particularly with venerable reds."

"Brother Herschel is attempting to pick the lock," Mateus said, coming over to Drizzt. "Your fingers are nimble. Would you give it a try?"

"Neither Herschel nor I could get through that lock," Drizzt said absently, not looking up from the book.

"At least Herschel is trying," Mateus growled, "and not huddled off by himself wasting candles and reading some worthless tome!"

"Not so worthless to any of us who mean to get out of here alive," Drizzt said, still not looking up. He had the portly friar's attention.

"What is it?" Mateus asked, leaning closely over Drizzt's shoulder, even though he could not read.

"It tells of vanity," Drizzt replied.

"Vanity? What does vanity have to do . . ."

"Dragon vanity," Drizzt explained. "A very important point, perhaps. All dragons possess it in excess, evil ones more than good ones."

"Wielding claws as long as swords and breath that can melt a stone, well they should," grumbled Mateus.

"Perhaps," Drizzt conceded, "but vanity is a weakness—do not doubt—even to a dragon. Several heroes have exploited this trait to a dragon's demise."

"Now you're thinking of killing the thing," Mateus gawked.

"If I must," Drizzt said, again absently. Mateus threw up his hands and walked away, shaking his head to answer the questioning stares of the others.

Drizzt smiled privately and returned to his reading. His plans were taking definite form now. He read the entire entry several times, committing every word of it to memory.

Three candles later, Drizzt was still reading and the friars were growing impatient and hungry. They prodded Mateus, who stood, hiked his belt up over his belly, and strode toward Drizzt.

"More vanity?" he asked sarcastically.

"Done with that part," Drizzt answered. He held up the book, showing Mateus a sketch of a huge black dragon curled up around several fallen trees in a thick swamp. "I am learning now of the dragon that may aid our cause."

"Hephaestus is a red," Mateus remarked scornfully, "not a black."

"This is a different dragon," Drizzt explained. "Mergandevinasander of Chult, possibly a visitor to converse with Hephaestus."

Brother Mateus was at a complete loss. "Reds and blacks do not get on well," he snipped, his skepticism obvious. "Every fool knows that."

"Rarely do I listen to fools," Drizzt replied, and again the friar turned and walked away, shaking his head.

"There is something more that you do not know, but Hephaestus most probably will," Drizzt said quietly, too low for anyone to hear. "Mergandevinasander has purple eyes!" Drizzt closed the book, confident that it had given him enough understanding to make his attempt. If he had ever witnessed the terrible splendor of a venerable red before, he would not have been smiling at that moment. But both ignorance and memories of Montolio bred courage in the young drow warrior who had so little to lose, and Drizzt had no intention of giving in to starvation for fear of some unknown danger. He wouldn't go forward either, not yet.

Not until he had time to practice his best dragon voice.

⚔ ⚔ ⚔ ⚔ ⚔

Of all the splendors Drizzt had seen in his adventurous life, none—not the great houses of Menzoberranzan, the cavern of the illithids, even the lake of acid—began to approach the awe-inspiring spectacle of the dragon's lair. Mounds of gold and gems filled the huge chamber in rolling waves, like the wake of some giant ship on the sea. Weapons and armor, gleaming magnificently, were piled all about, and the abundance of crafted items—chalices, goblets and the like—could have fully stocked the treasure rooms of a hundred rich kings.

Drizzt had to remind himself to breathe when he looked upon the splendor. It wasn't the riches that held him so—he cared little for material things—but the adventures that such wondrous items and wealth hinted at tugged Drizzt in a hundred different directions. Looking at the dragon's lair belittled his simple survival on the road with the Weeping Friars and his simple desire to find a peaceful and quiet place to call his home. He thought again of Montolio's dragon tale, and of all the other adventurous tales the blind ranger had told him. Suddenly he needed those adventures for himself.

Drizzt wanted a home, and he wanted to find acceptance, but he realized then, looking at the spoils, that he also desired a place in the books of the bards. He hoped to travel roads dangerous and exciting and even write his own tales.

The chamber itself was immense and uneven, rolling back around blind corners. The whole of it was dimly lit in a smoky, reddish golden glow. It was warm, uncomfortably so when Drizzt and the others took the time to consider the source of that heat.

Drizzt turned back to the waiting friars and winked, then pointed down to his left, to the single exit. "You know the signal," he mouthed silently.

Mateus nodded tentatively, still wondering if it had been wise to trust the drow. Drizzt had been a valuable ally to the pragmatic friar on the road these last few months, but a dragon was a dragon.

Drizzt surveyed the room again, this time looking past the treasures. Between two piles of gold he spotted his target, and that was no less splendid than the jewels and gems. Lying in the valley of those mounds was a huge, scaled tail, red-gold like the hue of the light, swishing slightly and rhythmically back and forth, each swipe piling the gold deeper around it.

Drizzt had seen pictures of dragons before; one of the wizard masters in the Academy had even created illusions of the various dragon types for the students to inspect. Nothing, though, could have prepared the drow for this moment, his first view of a living dragon. In all the known realms there was nothing more impressive, and of all the dragon types, huge reds were perhaps the most imposing.

When Drizzt finally managed to tear his gaze from the tail, he sorted out his path into the chamber. The tunnel exited high on the side of a wall, but a clear trail led down to the floor. Drizzt studied this for a long moment, memorizing every step. Then he scooped two handfuls of dirt into his pockets, removed an arrow from his quiver, and placed a darkness spell over it. Carefully and quietly, Drizzt picked his blind steps down the trail, guided by the continuing swish of the scaly tail. He nearly stumbled when he reached the first pile of gems and heard the tail come to an abrupt stop.

"Adventure," Drizzt reminded himself quietly, and he went on, concentrating on his mental image of his surroundings. He imagined the dragon rearing up before him, seeing through his darkness-globe disguise. He winced instinctively, expecting a burst of flame to engulf him and shrivel him where he stood. But he pressed on, and when he at last came over the gold pile, he was glad to hear the easy, thunderlike, breathing of the slumbering dragon.

Drizzt started up the second mound slowly, letting a spell of levitation form in his thoughts. He didn't really expect the spell to work very well—it had been failing more completely each time he attempted it. Any help he could get would add to the effect of his deception. Halfway up the mound, Drizzt broke into a run, spraying coins and gems with every step. He heard the dragon rouse, but didn't slow, drawing his bow as he went.

When he reached the ridge, he leaped out and enacted the levitation, hanging motionless in the air for a split second before the spell failed. Then Drizzt dropped, firing the bow and sending the darkness globe soaring across the chamber.

He never would have believed that a monster of such size could be so nimble, but when he crashed heavily onto a pile of goblets and jeweled trinkets, he found himself staring into the face of a very angry beast.

Those eyes! Like twin beams of damnation, their gaze latched onto Drizzt, bored right through him, impelled him to fall on his belly and grovel for mercy, and to reveal every deception, to confess every sin to Hephaestus, this god-thing. The dragon's great, serpentine neck angled slightly to the side, but the gaze never let go of the drow, holding him as firmly as one of Bluster the bear's hugs.

A voice sounded faintly but firmly in Drizzt's thoughts, the voice of a blind ranger spinning tales of battle and heroism. At first, Drizzt hardly heard it, but it was an insistent voice, reminding Drizzt in its own special way that five other men depended on him now. If he failed, the friars would die.

This part of the plan was not too difficult for Drizzt, for he truly believed in his words. "Hephaestus!" he cried in the common tongue. "Can it be, at long last? Oh, most magnificent! More magnificent than the tales, by far."

The dragon's head rolled back a dozen feet from Drizzt, and a confused expression came into those all-knowing eyes, revealing the facade. "You know of me?" Hephaestus boomed, the dragon's hot breath blowing Drizzt's white mane behind him.

"All know of you, mighty Hephaestus!" Drizzt cried, scrambling to his knees but not daring to stand. "It was you whom I sought, and now I have found you and am not disappointed!"

The dragon's terrible eyes narrowed suspiciously. "Why would a dark elf seek Hephaestus, Destroyer of Cockleby, Devourer of Ten Thousand Cattle, He Who Crushed Angalander the Stupid Silver, He Who . . ." It went on for many minutes, with Drizzt bearing the foul breath stoically, all the while feigning enchantment with the dragon's listing of his many wicked accomplishments.. When Hephaestus was done, Drizzt had to pause a moment to remember the initial question.

His real confusion only added to the deception at the time. "Dark elf?" he asked as if he didn't understand. He looked up at the dragon and repeated the words, even more confused. "Dark elf?"

The dragon looked all around, his gaze falling like twin beacons across the treasure mounds, then lingering for some time on Drizzt's blackness globe, halfway across the room. "I mean you!" Hephaestus roared suddenly, and the force of the yell knocked Drizzt over backward. "Dark elf!"

"Drow?" Drizzt said, recovering quickly and daring now to stand. "No, not I." He surveyed himself and nodded in sudden recognition. "Yes, of course," he said. "So often do I forget this mantle I wear!"

Hephaestus issued a long, low, increasingly impatient growl and Drizzt knew he had better move quickly.

"Not a drow," he said. "Though soon I might be if Hephaestus cannot help me!" Drizzt could only hope that he had piqued the dragon's curiosity. "You have heard of me, I am sure, mighty Hephaestus. I am, or was and hope to be again, Mergandevinasander of Chult, an old black of no small fame."

"Mergandevin . . . ?" Hephaestus began, but the dragon let the word trail away. Hephaestus had heard of the black, of course; dragons knew the names of most of the other dragons in all the world. Hephaestus knew, too, as Drizzt had hoped he would, that Mergandevinasander had purple eyes.

To aid him through the explanation, Drizzt recalled his experiences with Clacker, the unfortunate pech who had been transformed by a wizard into the form of a hook horror. "A wizard defeated me," he began somberly. "A party of adventurers entered my lair. Thieves! I got one of them, though, a paladin!"

Hephaestus seemed to like this little detail, and Drizzt, who had just thought of it, congratulated himself silently.

"How his silvery armor sizzled under the acid of my breath!"

"Pity to so waste him," Hephaestus interjected. "Paladins do make such fine meals!"

Drizzt smiled to hide his uneasiness at the thought. How would a dark elf taste? he could not help but wonder with the dragon's mouth so very near. "I would have killed them all—and a fine treasure take it would have been—but for that wretched wizard! It was he that did this terrible thing to me!" Drizzt looked at his drow form reprovingly.

"Polymorph?" Hephaestus asked, and Drizzt noted a bit of sympathy—he prayed—in the voice.

Drizzt nodded solemnly. "An evil spell. Took my form, my wings, and my breath. Yet I remained Mergandevinasander in thought, though . . ." Hephaestus widened his eyes at the pause, and the pitiful, confused look that Drizzt gave actually backed the dragon up.

"I have found this sudden affinity to spiders," Drizzt muttered. "To pet them and kiss them . . ." So that is what a disgusted red dragon looks like, Drizzt thought when he glanced back up at the beast. Coins and trinkets tinkled all throughout the room as an involuntary shudder coursed through the dragon's spine.

⚔ ⚔ ⚔ ⚔ ⚔

The friars in the low tunnel couldn't see the exchange, but they could make out the conversation well enough and understood what the drow had in mind. For the first time that any of them could recall, Brother Jankin was stricken speechless, but Mateus managed to whisper a few words, echoing their shared sentiments.

"He has got a measure of fortitude, that one!" The portly friar chuckled, and he slapped a hand across his own mouth, fearing that he had spoken too loudly.

⚔ ⚔ ⚔ ⚔ ⚔

"Why have you come to me?" Hephaestus roared angrily. Drizzt skidded backward under the force but managed to hold his balance this time.

"I beg, mighty Hephaestus!" Drizzt pleaded. "I have no choice. I traveled to Menzoberranzan, the city of drow, but this wizard's spell was powerful, they told me, and they could do nothing to dispel it. So I come to you, great and powerful Hephaestus, renowned for your abilities with spells of transmutation. Perhaps one of my own kind . . ."

"A black?" came the thunderous roar, and this time, Drizzt did fall. "Your own kind?"

"No, no, a dragon," Drizzt said quickly, retracting the apparent insult and hopping back to his feet—thinking that he might be running soon. Hephaestus's continuing growl told Drizzt that he needed a diversion, and he found it behind the dragon, in the deep scorch marks along the walls and back of a rectangular alcove. Drizzt figured this was where Hephaestus earned his considerable pay melting ores. The drow couldn't help but shudder as he wondered how many unfortunate merchants or adventurers might have found their end between those blasted walls.

"What caused such a cataclysm?" Drizzt cried in awe. Hephaestus dared not turn away, suspecting treachery. A moment later, though, the dragon realized what the dark elf had noticed and the growl disappeared.

"What god has come down to you, mighty Hephaestus, and blessed you with such a spectacle of power? Nowhere in all the realms is there stone so torn! Not since the fires that formed the world . . ."

"Enough!" Hephaestus boomed. "You who are so learned does not know the breath of a red?"

"Surely fire is the means of a red," Drizzt replied, never taking his gaze from the alcove, "but how intense might the flames be? Surely not so as to wreak such devastation!"

"Would you like to see?" came the dragon's answer in a sinister, smoking hiss.

"Yes!" Drizzt cried, then, "No!" he said, dropping into a fetal curl. He knew he was walking a tentative line here, but he knew it was a necessary gamble. "Truly I would desire to witness such a blast, but truly I fear to feel its heat."

"Then watch, Mergandevinasander of Chult!" Hephaestus roared. "See your better!" The sharp intake of the dragon's breath pulled Drizzt two steps forward, brought his white hair stinging around into his eyes, and nearly tore the blanket-cloak from his back. On the mound behind him, coins toppled forward in a noisy rush.

Then the dragon's serpentine neck swung about in a long and wide arc, putting the great red's head in line with the alcove.

The ensuing blast stole the air from the chamber; Drizzt's lungs burned and his eyes stung, both from the heat and the brightness. He continued to watch, though, as the dragon fire consumed the alcove in a roaring, thunderous blaze. Drizzt noted, too, that Hephaestus closed his eyes tightly when he breathed his fire.

When the conflagration was finished, Hephaestus swung back triumphantly. Drizzt, still looking at the alcove, at the molten rock running down the walls and dripping from the ceiling, did not have to feign his awe.

"By the gods!" he whispered harshly. He managed to look back at the dragon's smug expression. "By the gods," he said again. "Mergandevinasander of Chult, who thought himself supreme, is humbled."

"And well he should be!" Hephaestus boomed. "No black is the equal of a red! Know that now, Mergandevinasander. It is a fact that could save your life if ever a red comes to your door!"

"Indeed," Drizzt promptly agreed. "But I fear that I shall have no door." Again he looked down at his form and scowled with disdain. "No door beyond one in the city of dark elves!"

"That is your fate, not mine," Hephaestus said. "But I shall take pity on you. I shall let you depart alive, though that is more than you deserve for disturbing my slumber!"

This was the critical moment, Drizzt knew. He could have taken

Hephaestus up on the offer; at that moment, he wanted nothing more than to be out of there. But his principles and Mooshie's memory wouldn't let him go. What of his companions in the tunnel? he reminded himself. And what of the adventures for the bards' books?

"Devour me then," he said to the dragon, though he could hardly believe the words as he spoke them. "I who have known the glory of dragonkind cannot be content with life as a dark elf."

Hephaestus's huge maw inched forward.

"Alas for all the dragonkind!" Drizzt wailed. "Our numbers ever decreasing, while the humans multiply like vermin. Alas for the treasures of dragons, to be stolen by wizards and paladins!" The way he spat that last word gave Hephaestus pause.

"And alas for Mergandevinasander," Drizzt continued dramatically, "to be struck down thus by a human wizard whose power outshines even that of Hephaestus, mightiest of dragonkind!"

"Outshines!" Hephaestus cried, and the whole chamber trembled under the power of that roar.

"What am I to believe?" Drizzt yelled back, somewhat pitifully compared to the dragon's volume. "Would Hephaestus not aid one of his own diminishing kind? Nay, that I cannot believe, that the world shall not believe!" Drizzt aimed a pointed finger at the ceiling above him, preaching for all he was worth. He did not have to be reminded of the price of failure. "They will say, one and all from all the wide realms, that Hephaestus dared not try to dispel the wizard's magic, that the great red dared not reveal his weakness against so powerful a spell for fear that his weakness would invite that same wizard-led party to come north for another haul of dragon plunder!

"Ah!" Drizzt shouted, wide-eyed. "But will not Hephaestus's perceived surrender also give the wizard and his nasty thieving friends hope of such plunder? And what dragon possesses more to steal than Hephaestus, the red of rich Mirabar?"

The dragon was at a loss. Hephaestus liked his way of life, sleeping on treasures ever-growing from high-paying merchants. He didn't need the likes of heroic adventurers poking around in his lair! Those were the exact sentiments Drizzt had been counting on.

"Tomorrow!" the dragon roared. "This day I contemplate the spell and tomorrow Mergandevinasander shall be a black once more! Then he shall depart, his tail aflame, if he dares utter one more blasphemous word! Now I must take my rest to recall the spell. You shall not move, dragon in drow form. I smell you where you are and hear as well as anything in all the world. I am not as sound a sleeper as many thieves have wished!"

Drizzt did not doubt a word of it, of course, so while things had gone as well as he had hoped, he found himself in a bit of a mess. He couldn't wait a day to resume his conversation with the red, nor could his friends. How would proud Hephaestus react, Drizzt wondered, when the dragon tried to counter a spell that didn't even exist? And what, Drizzt told himself as he neared panic, would he do if Hephaestus actually did change him into a black dragon?

"Of course, the breath of a black has advantages over a red's," Drizzt blurted as Hephaestus swung away.

The red came back at him in a frightening flash and with frightening fury.

"Would you like to feel my breath?" Hephaestus snarled. "How great would come your boasts then, I must wonder?"

"No, not that," Drizzt replied. "Take no insult, mighty Hephaestus. Truly the spectacle of your fires stole my pride! But the breath of a black cannot be underestimated. It has qualities beyond even the power of a red's fire!"

"How say you?"

"Acid, O Hephaestus the Incredible, Devourer of Ten Thousand Cattle," Drizzt replied. "Acid clings to a knight's armor, digs through in lasting torment."

"As dripping metal might?" Hephaestus asked sarcastically. "Metal melted by a red's fire?"

"Longer, I fear," Drizzt admitted, dropping his gaze. "A red's breath comes in a burst of destruction, but a black's lingers, to the enemy's dismay."

"A burst?" Hephaestus growled. "How long can your breath last, pitiful black? Longer can I breathe, I know!"

"But . . ." Drizzt began, indicating the alcove. This time, the dragon's sudden intake pulled Drizzt several steps forward and nearly whipped him from his feet. The drow kept his wits enough to cry out the appointed signal, "Fires of the Nine Hells!" as Hephaestus swung his head back in line with the alcove.

⚔ ⚔ ⚔ ⚔ ⚔

"The signal!" Mateus said above the tumult. "Run for your lives! Run!"

"Never!" cried the terrified Brother Herschel, and the others, except for Jankin, didn't disagree.

"Oh, to suffer so!" the shaggy-haired fanatic wailed, stepping from the tunnel.

"We have to! On our lives!" Mateus reminded them, catching Jankin by the hair to keep him from going the wrong way.

They struggled at the tunnel exit for several seconds and the other friars, realizing that perhaps their only hope soon would pass them by, burst out of the tunnel and the whole group tumbled out and down the sloping path from the wall. When they recovered, they were surely in a fix, and they danced about aimlessly, not sure of whether to climb back up to the tunnel or light out for the exit. Their desperate scrambling hardly made any headway up the slope, especially with Mateus still trying to rein in Jankin, so the exit was the only way. Tripping all over themselves, the friars fled across the room.

Even their terror did not prevent each of them, even Jankin, from scooping up a pocketful of baubles as he passed.

⚔ ⚔ ⚔ ⚔ ⚔

Never had there been such a blast of dragon fire! Hephaestus, eyes closed, roared on and on, disintegrating the stone in the alcove. Great gouts of flame burst out into the room—Drizzt was nearly overcome by the heat—but the angry dragon did not relent, determined to humble the annoying visitor once and for all.

The dragon peeked once, to witness the effects of his display. Dragons knew their treasure rooms better than anything in the world, and Hephaestus did not miss the image of five fleeting figures darting across the main chamber toward the exit.

The breath stopped abruptly and the dragon swung about. "Thieves!" he roared, splitting stone with his thunderous voice.

Drizzt knew that the game was up.

The great, spear-filled maw snapped at the drow. Drizzt stepped to the side and leaped, having nowhere else to go. He caught one of the dragon's horns and rode up with the beast's head. Drizzt managed to scramble on top of it and held on for all his life as the outraged dragon tried to shake him free. Drizzt reached for a scimitar but found a pocket instead, and he pulled out a handful of dirt. Without the slightest hesitation, the drow flung the dirt down into the dragon's evil eye.

Hephaestus went berserk, snapping his head violently, up and down and all about. Drizzt held on stubbornly, and the devious dragon discerned a better method.

Drizzt understood Hephaestus's intent as the head shot up into the air at full speed. The ceiling was not so high—not compared with Hephaestus's serpentine neck. It was a long fall, but a preferable fate by far, and Drizzt dropped off just before the dragon's head slammed into the rock.

Drizzt dizzily regained his feet as Hephaestus, hardly slowed by the crushing impact, sucked in his breath. Luck saved the drow, and not for the first or the last time, as a considerable chunk of stone fell from the battered ceiling and crashed into the dragon's head. Hephaestus's breath blurted out in a harmless puff and Drizzt darted with all speed over the treasure mound, diving down behind.

Hephaestus roared in rage and loosed the rest of his breath, without thinking, straight for the mound. Gold coins melted together; enormous gemstones cracked under the pressure. The mound was fully twenty feet thick and tightly packed, but Drizzt, against the opposite side, felt his back aflame. He jumped out from the pile, leaving his cloak smoking and meshed with molten gold.

Out came Drizzt, scimitars drawn, as the dragon reared. The drow rushed straight in bravely, stupidly, whacking away with all his strength. He stopped, stunned, after only two blows, both scimitars ringing painfully in his hands; he might as well have banged them against a stone wall!

Hephaestus, head high, had paid the attack no heed. "My gold!" the dragon wailed. Then the beast looked down, his lamplight gaze boring through the drow once more. "My gold!" Hephaestus said again, wickedly.

Drizzt shrugged sheepishly, then he ran.

Hephaestus snapped his tail about, slamming it into yet another mound of treasure and showering the room in flying gold and silver coins and gemstones. "My gold!" the dragon roared over and over as he slammed his way through the tight piles.

Drizzt fell behind another mound. "Help me, Guenhwyvar," he begged, dropping the figurine.

"I smell you, thief!" The dragon purred—as if a thunder storm could purr—not far from Drizzt's mound.

In response, the panther came to the top of the mound, roared in defiance, then sprang away. Drizzt, down at the bottom, listened carefully, measuring the steps, as Hephaestus rushed forward.

"I shall chew you apart, shape-changer!" the dragon bellowed, and his gaping mouth snapped down at Guenhwyvar.

But teeth, even dragon teeth, had little effect on the insubstantial mist that Guenhwyvar suddenly became.

Drizzt managed to pocket a few baubles as he rushed out, his retreat covered by the din of the frustrated dragon's tantrum. The chamber was large and Drizzt was not quite gone when Hephaestus recovered and spotted him. Confused but no less enraged, the dragon roared and started after Drizzt.

In the goblin tongue, knowing from the book that Hephaestus spoke it but hoping that the dragon wouldn't know he knew, Drizzt yelled, "When the stupid beast follows me out, come out and get the rest!"

Hephaestus skidded to a stop and spun about, eyeing the low tunnel that led to the mines. The stupid dragon was in a frightful fit, wanting to munch on the imposing drow but fearing a robbery from behind. Hephaestus stalked over to the tunnel and slammed his scaly head into the wall above it, for good measure, then moved back to think things over.

The thieves had made the exit by now, the dragon knew; he would have to go out under the wide sky if he wanted to catch them—not a wise proposition at this time of year, considering the dragon's lucrative business. In the end, Hephaestus settled the dilemma as he settled every problem: He vowed to thoroughly eat the next merchant party that came his way. His pride restored in that resolution, one that he undoubtedly would forget as soon as he returned to his sleep, the dragon moved back about his chamber, repiling the gold and salvaging what he could from the mounds he inadvertently had melted.

# 22 HOMEWARD BOUND

"You got us through!" Brother Herschel cried. All of the friars except Jankin threw a great hug on Drizzt as soon as the drow caught up to them in a rocky vale west of the dragon lair's entrance.

"If ever there is a way that we can repay you . . . !"

Drizzt emptied his pockets in response, and five sets of eager eyes widened as gold trinkets and baubles rolled forth, glittering in the afternoon sun. One gem in particular, a two-inch ruby, promised wealth beyond anything the friars had ever known.

"For you," Drizzt explained. "All of it. I have no need of treasures."

The friars looked about guiltily, none of them willing to reveal the booty stored in his own pockets. "Perhaps you should keep a bit," Mateus offered, "if you still plan to strike out on your own."

"I do," Drizzt said firmly.

"You cannot stay here," reasoned Mateus. "Where will you go?"

Drizzt really hadn't given it much thought. All he really knew was that his place was not among the Weeping Friars. He pondered a while, recalling the many dead-end roads he had traveled. A thought popped into his head.

"You said it," Drizzt remarked to Jankin. "You named the place a tenday before we entered the tunnel."

Jankin looked at him curiously, hardly remembering.

"Ten-Towns," Drizzt said. "Land of rogues, where a rogue might find his place."

"Ten-Towns?" Mateus balked. "Surely you should reconsider your course, friend. Icewind Dale is not a welcoming place, nor are the hardy killers of Ten-Towns."

"The wind is ever blowing," Jankin added with a wistful look in his dark and hollow eyes, "filled with stinging sand and an icy bite. I will go with you!"

"And the monsters!" added one of the others, slapping Jankin on the back of the head. "Tundra yeti and white bears, and fierce barbarians! No, I would not go to Ten-Towns if Hephaestus himself tried to chase me there!"

"Well the dragon might," said Herschel, glancing nervously back toward the not-so-distant lair. "There are some farmhouses nearby. Perhaps we could stay there the night and get back to the tunnel tomorrow."

"I'll not go with you," Drizzt said again. "You name Ten-Towns an unwelcoming place, but would I find any warmer reception in Mirabar?"

"We will go to the farmers this night," Mateus replied, reconsidering his words. "We will buy you a horse there, and the supplies you will need. I do not wish you to go away at all," he said, "but Ten-Towns seems a good choice—" He looked pointedly at Jankin—"for a drow. Many have found their place there. Truly it is a home for he who has none."

Drizzt understood the sincerity in the friar's voice and appreciated Mateus's graciousness. "How do I find it?" he asked.

"Follow the mountains," Mateus replied. "Keep them always at your right hand's reach. When you get around the range, you have entered Icewind Dale. Only a single peak marks the flat land north of the Spine of the World. The towns are built around it. May they be all that you hope!"

With that, the friars prepared to leave. Drizzt clasped his hands behind his head and leaned back against the valley wall. It was indeed time for his parting with the friars, he knew, but he could not deny both the guilt and loneliness that the prospect offered. The small riches they had taken from the dragon's lair would greatly change his companions' lives, would give them shelter and all the necessities, but wealth could do nothing to alter the barriers that Drizzt faced.

Ten-Towns, the land that Jankin had named a house for the homeless, a gathering ground for those who had nowhere else to go, brought the drow a measure of hope. How many times had fate kicked him? How many gates had he approached hopefully only to be turned away at the tip of a spear? This time will be different, Drizzt told himself, for if he could not find a place in the land of rogues, where then might he turn?

For the beleaguered drow, who had spent so very long running from tragedy, guilt, and prejudices he could not escape, hope was not a comfortable emotion.

⚔ ⚔ ⚔ ⚔ ⚔

Drizzt camped in a small copse that night while the friars went into the small farming village. They returned the next morning leading a fine horse, but with one of their group conspicuously absent.

"Where is Jankin?" Drizzt asked, concerned.

"Tied up in a barn," Mateus replied. "He tried to get away last night, to go back . . ."

"To Hephaestus," Drizzt finished for him.

"If he is still in a mind for it this day, we might just let him go," added a disgusted Herschel.

"Here is your horse," Mateus said, "if the night has not changed your mind."

"And here is a new wrap," offered Herschel. He handed Drizzt a fine, fur-lined cloak. Drizzt knew how uncharacteristically generous the friars were being, and he almost changed his mind. He could not dismiss his other needs, though, and he would not satisfy them among this group.

To display his resolve, the drow moved straight to the animal, meaning to climb right on. Drizzt had seen a horse before, but never so close. He was amazed by the beast's sheer strength, the muscles rippling along the animal's neck, and he was amazed, too, by the height of the animal's back.

He spent a moment staring into the horse's eyes, communicating his intent as best he could. Then, to everyone's shock, even Drizzt's, the horse bent low, allowing the drow to climb easily into the saddle.

"You have a way with horses," remarked Mateus. "Never did you mention that you were a skilled rider."

Drizzt only nodded and did his very best to remain in the saddle when the horse started into a trot. It took the drow many moments to figure out how to control the beast and he had circled far to the east—the wrong way—before he managed to turn about. Throughout the circuit, Drizzt tried hard to keep up his facade, and the friars, never ones for horses themselves, merely nodded and smiled.

Hours later, Drizzt was riding hard to the west, following the southern edge of the Spine of the World.

⚔ ⚔ ⚔ ⚔ ⚔

"The Weeping Friars," Roddy McGristle whispered, looking down from a stony bluff at the band as they made their way back toward Mirabar's tunnel later that same tenday.

"What?" Tephanis gawked, rushing from his sack to join Roddy. For the very first time, the sprite's speed proved a liability. Before he even realized what he was saying, Tephanis blurted, "It-cannot-be! The-dragon . . ."

Roddy's glare fell over Tephanis like the shadow of a thundercloud.

"I-mean-I-assumed . . ." Tephanis sputtered, but he realized that Roddy, who knew the tunnel better than he and knew, too, the sprite's ways with locks, had pretty much guessed the indiscretion.

"Ye took it on yerself to kill the drow," Roddy said calmly.

"Please, my-master," Tephanis replied. "I-did-not-mean . . . I-feared-for-you. The-drow-is-a-devil, I-say! I-sent-them-down-the-dragon's-tunnel. I-thought-that-you . . ."

"Forget it," Roddy growled. "Ye did what ye did, and no more about it. Now get in yer sack. Mighten that we can fix what ye done, if the drow's not dead."

Tephanis nodded, relieved, and zipped back into the sack. Roddy scooped it up and called his dog to his side.

"I'll get the friars talking," the bounty hunter vowed, "but first . . ." Roddy whipped the sack about, slamming it into the stone wall.

"Master!" came the sprite's muffled cry.

"Ye drow-stealin . . ." Roddy huffed, and he beat the sack mercilessly against the unyielding stone. Tephanis squirmed for the first few whacks, even managed to begin a tear with his little dagger. But then the sack darkened with wetness and the sprite struggled no more.

"Drow-stealing mutant," Roddy mumbled, tossing the gory package away. "Come on, dog. If the drow's alive, the friars'll know where to find him."

⚔ ⚔ ⚔ ⚔ ⚔

The Weeping Friars were an order dedicated to suffering, and a couple of them, particularly Jankin, had indeed suffered much in their lives. None of them, though, had ever imagined the level of cruelty they found at the hands of wild-eyed Roddy McGristle, and before an hour had passed, Roddy, too, was driving hard to the west along the southern edge of the mountain range.

⚔ ⚔ ⚔ ⚔ ⚔

The cold eastern wind filled his ears with its endless song. Drizzt had heard it every second since he had rounded the western edge of the Spine of the World and turned north and east, into the barren stretch of land named for this wind, Icewind Dale. He accepted the mournful groan and the wind's freezing bite willingly, for to Drizzt the rush of air came as a gust of freedom.

Another symbol of that freedom, the sight of the wide sea, came as the drow rounded the mountain range. Drizzt had visited the shoreline once, on his passage to Luskan, and now he wanted to pause and go the few miles to its shores again. But the cold wind reminded him of the impending winter, and he understood the difficulty he would find in traveling the dale once the first snows had fallen.

Drizzt spotted Kelvin's Cairn, the solitary mountain on the tundra north of the great range, the first day after he had turned into the dale. He made for it anxiously, visualizing its singular peak as the marking post to the land he would call home. Tentative hope filled him whenever he focused on that mountain.

He passed several small groups, solitary wagons or a handful of men on horseback, as he neared the region of Ten-Towns along the caravan route, a southwestern approach. The sun was low in the west and dim, and Drizzt kept the cowl of his fine cloak pulled low, hiding his ebony skin. He nodded curtly as each traveler passed.

Three lakes dominated the region, along with the peak of rocky Kelvin's Cairn, which rose a thousand feet above the broken plain and was capped with snow even through the short summer. Of the ten towns that gave the area its name, only the principle city, Bryn Shander, stood apart from the lakes. It sat above the plain, on a short hill, its flag whipping defiantly against the stiff wind. The caravan route, Drizzt's trail, led to this city, the region's principle marketplace.

Drizzt could tell from the rising smoke of distant fires that several other communities were within a few miles of the city on the hill. He considered his course for a moment, wondering if he should go to one of these smaller, more secluded towns instead of continuing straight on to the principle city.

"No," the drow said firmly, dropping a hand into his pouch to feel the onyx figurine. Drizzt kicked his horse ahead, up the hill to the walled city's forbidding gates.

"Merchant?" asked one of the two guards standing bored before the iron-bound portal. "Ye're a bit late in the year for trading."

"No merchant," Drizzt replied softly, losing a good measure of his nerve now that the hour was upon him. He reached up slowly to his hood, trying to keep his trembling hand moving.

"From what town, then?" the other guard asked. Drizzt dropped his hand back, his courage deflected by the blunt question.

"From Mirabar," he answered honestly, and before he could stop himself and before the guards posed another distracting question, he reached up and pulled back his hood.

Four eyes popped wide and hands immediately dropped to belted swords.

"No!" Drizzt retorted suddenly. "No, please." A weariness came into both his voice and his posture that the guards could not understand. Drizzt had no strength left for senseless battles of misunderstanding. Against a goblin horde or a marauding giant, the drow's scimitars came easily into his hands, but against one who only battled him because of misperceptions, his blades weighed heavily indeed.

"I have come from Mirabar," Drizzt continued, his voice growing steadier with each syllable, "to Ten-Towns to reside in peace." He held his hands out wide, offering no threat.

The guards hardly knew how to react. Neither of them had ever seen a dark elf—though they knew beyond doubt that Drizzt was one—or knew more about the race than fireside tales of the ancient war that had split the elven peoples apart.

"Wait here," one of the guards breathed to the other, who didn't seem to appreciate the order. "I will go inform Spokesman Cassius." He banged on the iron-bound gate and slipped inside as soon as it was opened wide enough to let him through. The remaining guard eyed Drizzt unblinking, his hand never leaving his sword hilt.

"If you kill me, a hundred crossbows will cut you down," he declared, trying but utterly failing to sound confident.

"Why would I?" Drizzt asked innocently, keeping his hands wide apart and his posture unthreatening. This encounter had gone well so far, he believed. In every other village he had dared approach, those first seeing him had fled in terror or chased him with bared weapons.

The other guard returned a short time later with a small and slender man, clean-shaven and with bright blue eyes that scanned continuously, taking in every detail. He wore fine clothes, and from the respect the two guards showed the man, Drizzt knew at once that he was of high rank.

He studied Drizzt for a long while, considering every move and every feature. "I am Cassius," he said at length, "Spokesman of Bryn Shander and Principle Spokesman of Ten-Towns' Ruling Council."

Drizzt dipped a short bow. "I am Drizzt Do'Urden," he said, "of Mirabar and points beyond, now come to Ten-Towns."

"Why?" Cassius asked sharply, trying to catch him off guard.

Drizzt shrugged. "Is a reason required?"

"For a dark elf, perhaps," Cassius replied honestly.

Drizzt's accepting smile disarmed the spokesman and quieted the two guards, who now stood protectively close to his sides. "I can offer no reason for coming, beyond my desire to come," Drizzt continued. "Long has been my road, Spokesman Cassius. I am weary and in need of rest. Ten-Towns is the place of rogues, I have been told, and do not doubt that a dark elf is a rogue among the dwellers of the surface."

It seemed logical enough, and Drizzt's sincerity came through clearly to the observant spokesman. Cassius dropped his chin in his palm and thought for a long while. He didn't fear the drow, or doubt the elf's words, but he had no intention of allowing the stir that a drow would cause in his city.

"Bryn Shander is not your place," Cassius said bluntly, and Drizzt's lavender eyes narrowed at the unfair proclamation. Undaunted, Cassius pointed to the north. "Go to Lonelywood, in the forest on the northern banks of Maer Dualdon," he offered. He swung his gaze to the southeast. "Or to Good Mead or Dougan's Hole on the southern lake, Redwaters. These are smaller towns, where you will cause less stir and find less trouble."

"And when they refuse my entry?" Drizzt asked. "Where then, fair spokesman? Out in the wind to die on the empty plain?"

"You do not know—"

"I know," Drizzt interrupted. "I have played this game many times. Who will welcome a drow, even one who has forsaken his people and their ways and who desires nothing more than peace?" Drizzt's voice was stern and showed no self-pity, and Cassius again understood the words to be true.

Truly Cassius sympathized. He himself had been a rogue once and had been forced to the ends of the world, to forlorn Icewind Dale, to find a home. There were no ends farther than this; Icewind Dale was a rogue's last stop. Another thought came to Cassius then, a possible solution to the dilemma that would not nag at his conscience.

"How long have you lived on the surface?" Cassius asked, sincerely interested.

Drizzt considered the question for a moment, wondering what point the spokesman meant to make. "Seven years," he replied.

"In the northland?"

"Yes."

"Yet you have found no home, no village to take you in," Cassius said. "You have survived hostile winters and doubtless, more direct enemies. Are you skilled with those blades you hang on your belt?"

"I am a ranger," Drizzt said evenly.

"An unusual profession for a drow," Cassius remarked.

"I am a ranger," Drizzt said again, more forcefully, "well trained in the ways of nature and in the use of my weapons."

"I do not doubt," Cassius mused. He paused, then said, "There is a place offering shelter and seclusion." The spokesman led Drizzt's gaze to the north, to the rocky slopes of Kelvin's Cairn. "Beyond the dwarven vale lies the mountain," Cassius explained, "and beyond that the open tundra. It would do Ten-Towns well to have a scout on the mountain's northern slopes. Danger always seems to come from that direction."

"I came to find my home," Drizzt interrupted. "You offer me a hole in a pile of rock and a duty to those whom I owe nothing." In truth, the suggestion appealed to Drizzt's ranger spirit.

"Would you have me tell you that things are different?" Cassius replied. "I'll not let a wandering drow into Bryn Shander."

"Would a man have to prove himself worthy?"

"A man does not carry so grim a reputation," Cassius replied evenly, without hesitation. "If I were so magnanimous, if I welcomed you on your words alone and threw my gates wide, would you enter and find your home? We both know better than that, drow. Not everyone in Bryn Shander would be so open-hearted, I promise. You would cause an uproar wherever you went and whatever your demeanor and intent, you would be forced into battles.

"It would be the same in any of the towns," Cassius went on, guessing that his words had struck a chord of truth in the homeless drow. "I offer you a hole in a pile of rock, within the borders of Ten-Towns, where your actions, good or bad, will become your reputation beyond the color of your skin. Does my offer seem so shallow now?"

"I shall need supplies," Drizzt said, accepting the truth of Cassius's words. "And what of my horse? I do not think the slopes of a mountain are a proper place for such a beast."

"Trade your horse then," Cassius offered. "My guard will get a fair price and return here with the supplies you will need."

Drizzt thought about the suggestion for a moment, then handed the reins to Cassius.

The spokesman left then, thinking himself quite clever. Not only had he averted any immediate trouble, he had convinced Drizzt to guard his borders, all in a place where Bruenor Battlehammer and his clan of grim-faced dwarves could certainly keep the drow from causing any trouble.

⚔ ⚔ ⚔ ⚔ ⚔

Roddy McGristle pulled his wagon into a small village nestled in the shadows of the mountain range's western end. Snow would come soon, the bounty hunter knew, and he had no desire to be caught halfway up the dale when it began. He'd stay here with the farmers and wait out the winter. Nothing could leave the dale without passing this area, and if Drizzt had gone there, as the friars had revealed, he had nowhere left to run.

⚔ ⚔ ⚔ ⚔ ⚔

Drizzt set out from the gates that night, preferring the darkness for his journey, despite the cold. His direct approach to the mountain took him along the eastern rim of the rocky gorge that the dwarves had claimed as their home. Drizzt took extra care to avoid any guards the bearded folk might have set. He had encountered dwarves only once before, when he had passed Citadel Adbar on his earliest wanderings out of Mooshie's Grove, and it had not been a pleasant experience. Dwarven patrols had chased him off without waiting for any explanations, and they had dogged him through the mountains for many days.

For all his prudence in getting past the valley, though, Drizzt could not ignore a high mound of rocks he came upon, a climb with steps cut into the piled stones. He was less than halfway to the mountain, with several miles and hours of night still to go, but Drizzt moved up the detour, step over step, enchanted by the widening panorama of town lights about him.

The climb was not high, only fifty feet or so, but with the flat tundra and clear night Drizzt was afforded a view of five cities: two on the banks of the lake to the east, two to the west on the largest lake, and Bryn Shander, on its hillock a few miles to the south.

How many minutes passed Drizzt did not know, for the sights sparked too many hopes and fantasies for him to notice. He had been in Ten-Towns for barely a day, but already he was feeling comfortable with the sights, with knowing that thousands of people about the mountain would hear of him and possibly come to accept him.

A grumbling, gravelly voice shook Drizzt from his contemplations. He dropped into a defensive crouch and circled behind a rock. The stream of complaints marked the coming figure clearly. He was wide-shouldered and about a foot shorter than Drizzt, though obviously heavier than the drow. Drizzt knew it was a dwarf even before the figure paused to adjust its helmet—by slamming its head into a stone.

"Dagnaggit blasted," the dwarf muttered, "adjusting" the helmet a second time.

Drizzt was certainly intrigued, but he was also smart enough to realize that a grumbling dwarf wouldn't likely welcome an uninvited drow in the middle of a dark night. As the dwarf moved for yet another adjustment, Drizzt skipped off, running lightly and silently along the side of the trail. He passed close by the dwarf but then was gone with no more rustle than the shadow of a cloud.

"Eh?" the dwarf mumbled when he came back up, this time satisfied with his headgear's fit. "Who's that? What're ye about?" He went into a series of short, spinning hops, eyes darting alertly all about.

There was only the darkness, the stones, and the wind.

# 23

# A Memory Come To Life

The season's first snow fell lazily over Icewind Dale, large flakes drifting down in mesmerizing zigzag dances, so different from the wind-whipped blizzards most common to the region. The young girl, Catti-brie, watched it with obvious enchantment from the doorway of her cavern home, the hue of her deep-blue eyes seeming even purer in the reflection of the ground's white blanket.

"Late in comin', but hard when it gets here," grumbled Bruenor Battlehammer, a red-bearded dwarf, as he came up behind Catti-brie, his adopted daughter. "Suren to be a hard season, as are all in this place for white dragons!"

"Oh, me Daddy!" replied Catti-brie sternly. "Stop yer whining! Suren 'tis a beautiful fall, and harmless enough without the wind to drive it."

"Humans," huffed the dwarf derisively, still behind the girl. Catti-brie could not see his expression, tender toward her even as he grumbled, but she didn't need to. Bruenor was nine parts bluster and one part grouch, by Catti-brie's estimation.

Catti-brie spun on the dwarf suddenly, her shoulder-length, auburn locks twirling about her face. "Can I go out to play?" she asked, a hopeful smile on her face. "Oh, please, me Daddy!"

Bruenor forced on his best grimace. "Go out!" he roared. "None but a fool'd look for an Icewind Dale winter as a place for playin'! Show some sense, girl! The season'd freeze yer bones! "

Catti-brie's smile disappeared, but she refused to surrender so easily. "Well said for a dwarf," she retorted, to Bruenor's horror. "Ye're well enough fit for the holes and the less ye see o' the sky, the more ye're smiling. But I've a long winter ahead, and this might be me last chance to see the sky. Please, Daddy?"

Bruenor could not hold his snarling visage against his daughter's charm, but he did not want her to go out. "I'm fearing there's something prowlin' out there," he explained, trying to sound authoritative. "Sensed it on the climb a few nights back, though I never seen it. Mighten be a white lion, or a white bear. Best to . . ." Bruenor never finished, for Catti-brie's disheartened look more than destroyed the dwarf's imagined fears.

Catti-brie was no novice to the dangers of the region. She had lived with Bruenor and his dwarven clan for more than seven years. A raiding goblin band had killed Catti-brie's parents when she was only a toddler, and though she was human, Bruenor had taken her in as his own.

"Ye're a hard one, me girl," Bruenor said in answer to Catti-brie's relentless, sorrow-filled expression. "Go out and find yer play, then, but don't ye be goin' too far! On yer word, ye spirited filly, keep the caves in sight and a sword and horn on yer belt."

Catti-brie rushed over and planted a wet kiss on Bruenor's cheek, which the taciturn dwarf promptly wiped away, grumbling at the girl's back as she disappeared into the tunnel. Bruenor was the leader of the clan, as tough as the stone they mined. But every time Catti-brie planted an appreciative kiss on his cheek, the dwarf realized he had given in to her.

"Humans!" the dwarf growled again, and he stomped down the tunnel to the mine, thinking to batter a few pieces of iron, just to remind himself of his toughness.

⚔ ⚔ ⚔ ⚔ ⚔

It was easy for the spirited young girl to rationalize her disobedience when she looked back across the valley from the lower slopes of Kelvin's Cairn, more than three miles from Bruenor's front door. Bruenor had told

Catti-brie to keep the caves in sight, and they were, or at least the wider terrain around them was, from this high vantage point.

But Catti-brie, happily sliding down one bumpy expanse, soon found a flaw in not heeding to her experienced father's warnings. She had come to the bottom, a delightful ride, and was briskly rubbing the stinging chill out of her hands, when she heard a low and ominous growl.

"White lion," Catti-brie mouthed silently, remembering Bruenor's suspicion. When she looked up, she saw that her father's guess had not quite hit the mark. It was indeed a great feline the girl saw looking down at her from a bare, stony mound, but the cat was black, not white, and a huge panther, not a lion.

Defiantly, Catti-brie pulled her knife from its sheath. "Keep yerself back, cat!" she said, only the slightest tremor in her voice, for she knew that fear invited attack from wild animals.

Guenhwyvar flattened its ears and plopped to its belly, then issued a long and resounding roar that echoed throughout the stony region.

Catti-brie could not respond to the power in that roar, or to the very long and abundant teeth the panther showed. She searched around for some escape but knew that no matter which way she ran she could not get beyond the panther's first mighty spring.

"Guenhwyvar!" came a call from above. Catti-brie looked back up the snowy expanse to see a slender, cloaked form picking a careful route toward her. "Guenhwyvar!" the newcomer called again. "Be gone from here!"

The panther growled a throaty reply, then bounded away, leaping the snow-covered boulders and springing up small cliffs as easily as if it were running across a smooth and flat field.

Despite her continuing fears, Catti-brie watched the departing panther with sincere admiration. She had always loved animals and had often studied them, but the interplay of Guenhwyvar's sleek muscles was more majestic than anything she had ever imagined. When she at last came out of her trance, she realized that the slender figure was right behind her. She whirled about, knife still in hand.

The blade dropped from her grasp and her breathing halted abruptly as soon as she looked upon the drow.

Drizzt, too, found himself stunned by the encounter. He wanted to make certain that the girl was all right, but when he looked upon Catti-brie, all thoughts of his purpose faded away in a flood of memories.

She was about the same age as the sandy-haired boy on the farm, Drizzt noted initially, and that thought inevitably brought back the agonizing memories of Maldobar. When Drizzt looked more closely, though, into Catti-brie's eyes, his thoughts were sent flying back further into his past, to his days marching alongside his dark kin. Catti-brie's eyes possessed that same joyful and innocent sparkle that Drizzt had seen in the eyes of an elven child, a girl he had rescued from the savage blades of his raiding kin. The memory overwhelmed Drizzt, sent him whirling back to that bloody glade in the elven wood, where his brother and fellow drow had brutally slaughtered an elven gathering. In the frenzy, Drizzt had almost killed the elven child, had almost put himself forever on that same dark road that his kin so willingly followed.

Drizzt shook himself free of the recollection and reminded himself that this was a different child of a different race. He meant to speak a greeting, but the girl was gone.

That damning word, "drizzit," echoed in the drow's thoughts several times as he made his way back to the cave he had set up as his home on the mountain's northern face.

⚔ ⚔ ⚔ ⚔ ⚔

That same night, the onslaught of the season began in full. The cold eastern wind blowing off the Reghed Glacier drove the snow into high, impassable drifts.

Catti-brie watched the snow forlornly, fearing that many tendays might pass before she could again go to Kelvin's Cairn. She hadn't told Bruenor or any of the other dwarves about the drow, for fear of punishment and that Bruenor would drive the drow away. Looking at the piling snow, Catti-brie wished that she had been braver, had remained and talked to the strange elf. Every howl of the wind heightened that wish and made the girl wonder if she had lost her only chance.

⚔ ⚔ ⚔ ⚔ ⚔

"I'm off to Bryn Shander," Bruenor announced one morning more than two months later. An unexpected break had come in Icewind Dale's normal seven-month winter, a rare January thaw. Bruenor eyed his daughter suspiciously for a long moment. "Ye're meanin' to go out yerself this day?" he asked.

"If I may," Catti-brie answered. "The caves're tight around me and the wind's not so cold."

"I'll get a dwarf or two to go with ye," Bruenor offered.

Catti-brie, thinking that now might be her chance to go back to investigate the drow, balked at the notion. "They're all for mendin' their doors!" she retorted, more sharply than she intended. "Don't ye be botherin' them for the likes of meself!"

Bruenor's eyes narrowed. "Ye've too much stubbornness in ye."

"I get it from me dad," Catti-brie said with a wink that shot down any more forthcoming arguments.

"Take care, then," Bruenor began, "and keep—"

". . . the caves in sight!" Catti-brie finished for him. Bruenor spun about and stomped out of the cave, grumbling helplessly and cursing the day he had ever taken a human in for a daughter. Catti-brie only laughed at the unending facade.

Once again it was Guenhwyvar who first encountered the auburn-haired girl. Catti-brie had set straight out for the mountain and was making her way around its western most trails when she spotted the black panther above her, watching her from a rock spur.

"Guenhwyvar," the girl called, remembering the name the drow had used. The panther growled lowly and dropped from the spur, moving closer.

"Guenhwyvar?" Catti-brie said again, less certain, for the panther was only a few dozen strides away. Guenhwyvar's ears came up at the second mention of the name and the cat's taut muscles visibly relaxed.

Catti-brie approached slowly, one deliberate step at a time. "Where's the dark elf, Guenhwyvar?" she asked quietly. "Can ye take me to him?"

"And why would you want to go to him?" came a question from behind.

Catti-brie froze in her tracks, remembering the smooth-toned, melodic voice, then turned slowly to face the drow. He was only three steps behind her, his lavender-eyed gaze locking onto hers as soon as they met. Catti-brie had no idea of what to say, and Drizzt, absorbed again by memories, stood quiet, watching and waiting.

"Be ye a drow?" Catti-brie asked after the silence became unbearable. As soon as she heard her own words, she privately berated herself for asking such a stupid question.

"I am," Drizzt replied. "What does that mean to you?"

Catti-brie shrugged at the strange response. "I've heard that drow be evil, but ye don't seem so to me."

"Then you have taken a great risk in coming out here all by yourself," Drizzt remarked. "But fear not," he quickly added, seeing the girl's sudden uneasiness, "for I am not evil and will bring no harm to you." After the months alone in his comfortable but empty cave, Drizzt did not want this meeting to end quickly.

Catti-brie nodded, believing his words. "Me name's Catti-brie," she said. "Me dad is Bruenor, King o' Clan Battlehammer."

Drizzt cocked his head curiously.

"The dwarves," Catti-brie explained, pointing back to the valley. She understood Drizzt's confusion as soon as she spoke the words. "He's not me real dad," she said. "Bruenor took me in when I was just a babe, when me real parents were . . ."

She couldn't finish, and Drizzt didn't need her to, understanding her pained expression.

"I am Drizzt Do'Urden," the drow interjected. "Well met, Catti-brie, daughter of Bruenor. It is good to have another to talk with. For all these tendays of winter, I have had only Guenhwyvar, there, when the cat is around, and my friend does not say much, of course!"

Catti-brie's smile nearly took in her ears. She glanced over her shoulder to the panther, now reclining lazily in the path. "She's a beautiful cat," Catti-brie remarked.

Drizzt did not doubt the sincerity in the girl's tone, or in the admiring gaze she dropped on Guenhwyvar. "Come here, Guenhwyvar," Drizzt said, and the panther stretched and slowly rose. Guenhwyvar walked right beside Catti-brie, and Drizzt nodded to answer her unspoken but obvious desire. Tentatively at first, but then firmly, Catti-brie stroked the panther's sleek coat, feeling the beast's power and perfection. Guenhwyvar accepted the petting without complaint, even bumped into Catti-brie's side when she stopped for a moment, prodding her to continue.

"Are you alone?" Drizzt asked.

Catti-brie nodded. "Me dad said to keep the caves in sight." She laughed. "I can see them well enough, by me thinkin'!"

Drizzt looked back into the valley, to the far rock wall several miles away. "Your father would not be pleased. This land is not so tame. I have been on the mountain for only two months, and I have fought twice already shaggy white beasts I do not know."

"Tundra yeti," Catti-brie replied. "Ye must be on the northern side. Tundra yeti don't come around the mountain."

"Are you so certain?" Drizzt asked sarcastically.

"I've not ever seen one," Catti-brie replied, "but I'm not fearing them. I came to find yerself, and now I have."

"You have," said Drizzt, "and now what?"

Catti-brie shrugged and went back to petting Guenhwyvar's sleek coat.

"Come," Drizzt offered. "Let us find a more comfortable place to talk. The glare off the snow stings my eyes."

"Ye're used to the dark tunnels?" Catti-brie asked hopefully, eager to hear tales of lands beyond the borders of Ten-Towns, the only place Catti-brie had ever known.

Drizzt and the girl spent a marvelous day together. Drizzt told Catti-brie of Menzoberranzan and Catti-brie answered his tales with stories of Icewind Dale, of her life with the dwarves. Drizzt was especially interested in hearing about Bruenor and his kin, since the dwarves were his closest, and most-feared, neighbors.

"Bruenor talks rough as stone, but I'm knowin' him better than all that!" Catti-brie assured the drow. "He's a right fine one, and so's the rest o' the clan."

Drizzt was glad to hear it, and glad, too, that he had made this connection, both for the implications of having such a friend and even more so because he truly enjoyed the charming and spirited lass's company. Catti-brie's energy and zest for life verily bubbled over. In her presence, the drow could not recall his haunting memories, could only feel good about his decision to save the elven child those many years before. Catti-brie's singsong voice and the careless way she flipped her flowing hair about her shoulders lifted the burden of guilt from Drizzt's back as surely as a giant could have hoisted a rock.

Their tales could have gone on all that day and night, and for many tendays afterward, but when Drizzt noticed the sun riding low along the western horizon, he realized that the time had come for the girl to head back to her home.

"I will take you," Drizzt offered.

"No," Catti-brie replied. "Ye best not. Bruenor'd not understand and ye'd get me in a mountain o' trouble. I can get back, don't ye be worrying! I know these trails better'n yerself, Drizzt Do'Urden, and ye couldn't keep up to me if ye tried!"

Drizzt laughed at the boast but almost believed it. He and the girl set out at once, moving to the mountain's southern most spur and saying their good-byes with promises that they would meet again during the next thaw, or in the spring if none came sooner.

Truly the girl was skipping lightly when she entered the dwarven complex, but one look at her surly father stole a measure of her delight. Bruenor had gone to Bryn Shander that morning on business with Cassius. The dwarf wasn't thrilled to learn that a dark elf had made a home so close to his door, but he guessed that his curious—too curious—daughter would think it a grand thing.

"Keep yerself away from the mountain," Bruenor said as soon as he noticed Catti-brie, and she was in despair.

"But me Dad—" she tried to protest.

"On yer word, girl!" the dwarf demanded. "Ye'll not set foot on that mountain again without me permission! There's a dark elf there, by Cassius's telling. On yer word!"

Catti-brie nodded helplessly, then followed Bruenor back to the dwarven complex, knowing she would have a hard time changing her father's mind, but knowing, too, Bruenor held views far from justified where Drizzt Do'Urden was concerned.

⚔ ⚔ ⚔ ⚔ ⚔

Another thaw came a month later and Catti-brie heeded her promise. She never put one foot on Kelvin's Cairn, but from the valley trails around it, she called out to Drizzt and to Guenhwyvar. Drizzt and the panther, looking for the girl with the break in the weather, were soon beside her, in the valley this time, sharing more tales and a picnic lunch that Catti-brie had packed.

When Catti-brie got back to the dwarven mines that evening, Bruenor suspected much and asked her only once if she had kept her word. The dwarf had always trusted his daughter, but when Catti-brie answered that she had not been on Kelvin's Cairn, his suspicions did not diminish.

# 24
# REVELATIONS

Bruenor ambled along the lower slopes of Kelvin's Cairn for the better part of the morning. Most of the snow was melted now with spring thick in the air, but stubborn pockets still made the trails difficult. Axe in one hand and shield, emblazoned with the foaming mug standard of Clan Battlehammer, in the other, Bruenor trudged on, spitting curses at every slick spot, at every boulder obstacle, and at dark elves in general.

He rounded the northwesternmost spur of the mountain, his long, pointed nose cherry-red from the biting wind and his breath coming hard. "Time for a rest," the dwarf muttered, spotting a stone alcove sheltered by high walls from the relentless wind.

Bruenor wasn't the only one who had noticed the comfortable spot. Just before he reached the ten-foot-wide break in the rock wall, a sudden flap of leathery wings brought a huge, insectlike head rising up before him. The dwarf fell back, startled and wary. He recognized the beast as a remorhaz, a polar worm, and was not so eager to jump in against it.

The remorhaz came out of the cubby in pursuit, its snakelike, forty-foot-long body rolling out like an ice-blue ribbon behind it. Multifaceted bug eyes, shining bright white, honed in on the dwarf. Short, leathery wings kept the creature's front half reared and ready to strike while dozens of scrambling legs propelled the remainder of the long torso.

Bruenor felt the increasing heat as the agitated creature's back began to glow, first to a dull brown, then brightening to red.

"That'll stop the wind for a bit!" the dwarf chuckled, realizing that he could not outrun the beast. He stopped his retreat and waved his axe threateningly.

The remorhaz came straight in, its formidable maw, large enough to swallow the diminutive target whole, snapping down hungrily.

Bruenor jumped aside and angled his shield and body to keep the maw from snapping off his legs, while slamming his axe right between the monster's horns.

The wings beat ferociously, lifting the head back up. The remorhaz, hardly injured, poised to strike again quickly, but Bruenor beat it to the spot. He snatched his bulky axe with his shield hand drew a long dagger, and dived forward, right between the monster's first set of legs.

The great head came down in a rush, but Bruenor had already slipped under the low belly, the beast's most vulnerable spot. "Ye get me point?" Bruenor chided, driving the dagger up between the scale ridge.

Bruenor was too tough and too well armored to be seriously injured by the worm's thrashing, but then the creature began to roll, meaning to put its glowing-hot back on the dwarf.

"No, ye don't, ye confused dragon-worm-bird-bug!" Bruenor howled, scrambling to keep away from the heat. He came to the creature's side and heaved with all his strength, tumbling the off-balance remorhaz right over.

Snow sputtered and sizzled when the fiery back touched down. Bruenor kicked and swatted his way past the thrashing legs to get to the vulnerable underside. The dwarf's many-notched axe smashed in, opening a wide and deep gash.

The remorhaz coiled and snapped its long body to and fro, throwing Bruenor to the side. The dwarf was up in an instant, but not quickly enough, as the polar worm rolled at him. The searing back caught Bruenor on the thigh as he tried to leap away, and the dwarf came out limping, grabbing at his smoking leather leggings.

Then they faced off again, both showing considerably more respect for the other.

The maw gaped; with a quick snap, Bruenor's axe took a tooth from it and deflected it aside. The dwarf's wounded leg buckled with the blow, though, and a stumbling Bruenor could not get out of the way. A long horn hooked Bruenor under the arm and hurled him far to the side.

He crashed amid a small field of rocks, recovered, and purposely banged his head against a large stone to adjust his helmet and knock the dizziness away.

The remorhaz left a trail of blood, but it did not relent. The huge maw opened and the creature hissed, and Bruenor promptly chucked a stone down its gullet.

⚔ ⚔ ⚔ ⚔ ⚔

Guenhwyvar alerted Drizzt to the trouble down at the northwestern spur. The drow had never seen a polar worm before, but as soon as he spotted the combatants, from a ridge high above, he knew that the dwarf was in trouble. Lamenting that he had left his bow back in the cave, Drizzt drew his scimitars and followed the panther down the mountainside as quickly as the slippery trails would allow.

⚔ ⚔ ⚔ ⚔ ⚔

"Come on, then!" the stubborn dwarf roared at the remorhaz, and indeed the monster did charge. Bruenor braced himself, meaning to get in at least one good shot before becoming worm food.

The great head came down at him, but then the remorhaz, hearing a roar from behind, hesitated and looked away.

"Fool move!" the dwarf cried in glee, and Bruenor slashed with his axe at the monster's lower jaw, splitting it cleanly between two great incisors. The remorhaz screeched in pain; its leathery wings flapped wildly, trying to get the head out of the wicked dwarf's reach.

Bruenor hit it again, and a third time, each blow cutting huge creases in the maw and driving the head down.

"Think ye're to bite at me, eh?" the dwarf cried. He lashed out with his shield hand and grabbed at a horn as the remorhaz head began to rise again. A quick jerk turned the monster's head at a vulnerable angle and the knotted muscles in Bruenor's arm snapped viciously, cleaving his mighty axe into the polar worm's skull.

The creature shuddered and thrashed for a second longer, then lay still, its back still glowing hotly.

A second roar from Guenhwyvar took the proud dwarf's eyes from his kill. Bruenor, injured and tentative, looked up to see Drizzt and the panther fast approaching, the drow with both scimitars drawn.

"Come on!" Bruenor roared at them both, misunderstanding their charge. He banged his axe against his heavy shield. "Come on and feel me blade!"

Drizzt stopped abruptly and called for Guenhwyvar to do the same. The panther continued to stalk, though, ears flattened.

"Be gone, Guenhwyvar!" Drizzt commanded.

The panther growled indignantly one final time and sprang away.

Satisfied that the cat was gone, Bruenor snapped his glare on Drizzt, standing at the other end of the fallen polar worm.

"Yerself and me, then?" the dwarf spat. "Ye got the belly to face me axe, drow, or do little girls be more to yer liken'?"

The obvious reference to Catti-brie brought an angry light to Drizzt's eyes, and his grasp on his weapons tightened.

Bruenor swung his axe easily. "Come on," he chided derisively. "Ye got the belly to come and play with a dwarf?"

Drizzt wanted to scream out for all the world to hear. He wanted to spring over the dead monster and smash the dwarf, deny the dwarf's words with sheer and brutal force, but he couldn't. Drizzt couldn't deny Mielikki and couldn't betray Mooshie. He had to sublimate his rage once again, had to take the insults stoically and with the realization that he, and his goddess, knew the truth of what lay in his heart.

The scimitars spun into their sheaths and Drizzt walked away, Guenhwyvar coming up beside him.

Bruenor watched the pair go curiously. At first he thought the drow a coward, but then, as the excitement of the battle gradually diminished,

Bruenor came to wonder about the drow's intent. Had he come down to finish off both combatants, as Bruenor had first assumed? Or had he, possibly, come down to Bruenor's aid?

"Nah," the dwarf muttered, dismissing the possibility. "Not a dark elf!"

The walk back was long for the limping dwarf, giving Bruenor many opportunities to replay the events around the northwestern spur. When he finally arrived back at the mines, the sun had long set and Catti-brie and several dwarves were gathered, ready to go out to look for him.

"Ye're hurt," one of the dwarves remarked. Catti-brie immediately imagined a fight between Drizzt and her father.

"Polar worm," the dwarf explained casually. "Got him good, but got a bit of a burn for me effort."

The other dwarves nodded admiringly at their leader's battle prowess—a polar worm was no easy kill—and Catti-brie sighed audibly.

"I saw the drow!" Bruenor growled at her, suspecting the source of that sigh. The dwarf remained confused about his meeting with the dark elf, and confused, too, about where Catti-brie fit into all of this. Had Catti-brie actually met the dark elf? he wondered.

"I seen him, I did!" Bruenor continued, now speaking more to the other dwarves. "Drow and the biggest an' blackest cat me eyes ever set on. He came down for me, just as I dropped the worm."

"Drizzt would not!" Catti-brie interrupted before her father could get into his customary story-telling roll.

"Drizzt?" Bruenor asked, and the girl turned away, realizing that her lie was up. Bruenor let it go—for the moment.

"He did, I say!" the dwarf continued. "Came in at me with both his blades drawn! I chased that one an' the cat off!"

"We could hunt him down," offered one of the dwarves. "Run him off the mountain!" The others nodded and mumbled their agreement, but Bruenor, still struggling with the drow's intent, cut them short.

"He's got the mountain," Bruenor told them. "Cassius gave it to him, and we need no trouble with Bryn Shander. As long as the drow stays put and stays outa our way, we'll leave him be.

"But" Bruenor continued, eyeing Catti-brie directly, "ye're not to speak to, ye're not to go near, that one again!"

"But—" Catti-brie started futilely.

"Never!" Bruenor roared. "I'll have yer word now, girl, or by Moradin, I'll have that dark elf's head!"

Catti-brie hesitated, horribly trapped.

"Tell me!" Bruenor demanded.

"Ye have me word," the girl mumbled, and she fled back to the dark shelter of the cave.

⚔ ⚔ ⚔ ⚔ ⚔

"Cassius, Spokesman o' Bryn Shander, sent me yer way," the gruff man explained. "Says ye'd know the drow if any would."

Bruenor glanced around his formal audience hall to the many other dwarves in attendance, none of them overly impressed by the rude stranger. Bruenor dropped his bearded chin into his palm and yawned widely, determined to remain outside this apparent conflict. He might have bluffed the crude man and his smelly dog out of the halls without further bother, but Catti-brie, sitting at her father's side, shuffled uneasily.

Roddy McGristle did not miss her revealing movement. "Cassius says ye must've seen the drow, him bein' so close."

"If any of me people have," Bruenor replied absently, "they've spoke not a bit of it. If yer drow's about, he's been no bother."

Catti-brie looked curiously at her father and breathed easier.

"No bother?" Roddy muttered, a sly look coming into his eye. "Never is, that one." Slowly and dramatically, the mountain man peeled back his hood, revealing his scars. "Never a bother, until ye don't expect what ye get!"

"Drow give ye that?" Bruenor asked, not overly alarmed or impressed. "Fancy scars—better'n most I seen."

"He killed my dog!" Roddy growled.

"Don't look dead to me," Bruenor quipped, drawing chuckles from every corner.

"My other dog," Roddy snarled, understanding where he stood with this stubborn dwarf. "Ye care not a thing for me, and well ye shouldn't. But it's not for myself that I'm hunting this one, and not for any bounty on his head. Ye ever heared o' Maldobar?"

Bruenor shrugged.

"North o' Sundabar," Roddy explained. "Small, peaceable place. Farmers all. One family, the Thistledowns, lived on the side o' town, three generations in a single house, as good families will. Bartholemew Thistledown was a good man, I tell ye, as his pa afore him, an' his children, four lads and a filly—much like yer own—standing tall and straight with a heart of spirit and a love o' the world."

Bruenor suspected where the burly man was leading, and by Catti-brie's uncomfortable shifting beside him, he figured that his perceptive daughter knew as well.

"Good family," Roddy mused, feigning a wispy, distant expression. "Nine in the house." The mountain man's visage hardened suddenly and he glared straight at Bruenor. "Nine died in the house," he declared. "Hacked by yer drow, and one ate up by his devil cat!"

Catti-brie tried to respond, but her words came out in a garbled shriek. Bruenor was glad of her confusion, for if she had spoken clearly, her argument would have given the mountain man more than Bruenor wanted him to know. The dwarf laid a hand across his daughter's shoulders, then answered Roddy calmly. "Ye've come to us with a dark tale. Ye shook me daughter, and I'm not for liking me daughter shook!"

"I beg yer forgivings kingly dwarf," Roddy said with a bow, "but ye must be told of the danger on yer door. Drow's a bad one, and so's his devil cat! I want no repeating o' the Maldobar tragedy."

"And ye'll get none in me halls," Bruenor assured him. "We're not simple farmers, take to yer heart. Drow won't be botherin' us any more'n ye've bothered us already."

Roddy wasn't surprised that Bruenor wouldn't help him, but he knew well that the dwarf, or at least the girl, knew more about Drizzt's whereabouts than they had let on. "If not for me, then for Bartholemew Thistledown, I beg ye, good dwarf. Tell me if ye know where I might find the black demon. Or if ye don't know, then give me some soldiers to help me sniff him out."

"Me dwarves've much to do with the melt," Bruenor explained. "Can't be spared chasin' another's fiends." Bruenor really didn't care one way or another for Roddy's gripe with the drow, but the mountain man's story did confirm the dwarf's belief that the dark elf should be avoided, particularly by his daughter. Bruenor actually might have helped Roddy and been done with it, more to get them both out of his valley than for any moral reasons, but he couldn't ignore Catti-brie's obvious distress.

Roddy unsuccessfully tried to hide his anger, looking for some other option. "Where would ye go if ye was runnin', King Bruenor?" he asked. "Ye know the mountain better'n any living, so Cassius telled me. Where should I look?"

Bruenor found that he liked seeing the unpleasant human so distressed. "Big valley," he said cryptically. "Wide mountain. Lot o' holes." He sat quiet for a long moment, shaking his head.

Roddy's facade blew away altogether. "Ye'd help the murderin' drow?" he roared. "Ye call yerself a king, but ye'd . . ."

Bruenor leaped up from his stone throne, and Roddy backed away a cautious step and dropped a hand to Bleeder's handle.

"I've the word o' one rogue against another rogue!" Bruenor growled at him. "One's as good—as bad!—as the other, by me guess!"

"Not by a Thistledown's guess!" Roddy cried, and his dog, sensing his outrage, bared its teeth and growled menacingly.

Bruenor looked at the strange, yellow beast curiously. It was getting near dinnertime and arguments did so make Bruenor hungry! How might a yellow dog fill his belly? he wondered.

"Have ye nothing more to give to me?" Roddy demanded.

"I could give ye me boot," Bruenor growled back. Several well-armed dwarf soldiers moved in close to make certain that the volatile human didn't do anything foolish. "I'd offer ye supper," Bruenor continued, "but ye smell too bad for me table, and ye don't seem the type what'd be takin' a bath."

Roddy yanked his dog's rope and stormed away, banging his heavy boots and slamming through each door he came upon. At Bruenor's nod, four soldiers followed the mountain man to make certain that he left without any unfortunate incidents. In the formal audience hall, the others laughed and howled about the way their king had handled the human.

Catti-brie didn't join in on the mirth, Bruenor noted, and the dwarf thought he knew why. Roddy's tale, true or not, had instilled some doubts in the girl.

"So now ye have it," Bruenor said to her roughly, trying to push her over the edge in their running argument. "The drow's a hunted killer. Now ye'll take me warnings to heart, girl!"

Catti-brie's lips disappeared in a bitter bite. Drizzt had not told her much about his life on the surface, but she could not believe that this drow whom she had come to know would be capable of murder. Neither could Catti-brie deny the obvious: Drizzt was a dark elf, and to her more experienced father, at least, that fact alone gave credence to McGristle's tale.

"Ye hear me, girl?" Bruenor growled.

"Ye've got to get them all together," Catti-brie said suddenly. "The drow and Cassius, and ugly Roddy McGristle. Ye've got to—"

"Not me problem!" Bruenor roared, cutting her short. Tears came quickly to Catti-brie's soft eyes in the face of her father's sudden rage. All the world seemed to turn over before her. Drizzt was in danger, and more so was the truth about his past. Just as stinging to Catti-brie, her father, whom she had loved and admired for all her remembered life, seemed now to turn a deaf ear to the calls for justice.

In that horrible moment, Catti-brie did the only thing an eleven-year-old could do against such odds—she turned from Bruenor and fled.

⚔ ⚔ ⚔ ⚔ ⚔

Catti-brie didn't really know what she meant to accomplish when she found herself running along the lower trails of Kelvin's Cairn, breaking her promise to Bruenor. Catti-brie could not refuse her desire to come, though she had little to offer Drizzt beyond a warning that McGristle was looking for him.

She couldn't sort through all the worries, but then she stood before the drow and understood the real reason she had ventured out. It was not for Drizzt that she had come, though she wanted him safe. It was for her own peace.

"Ye never speaked o' the Thistledowns of Maldobar," she said icily in greeting, stealing the drow's smile. The dark expression that crossed Drizzt's face clearly showed his pain.

Thinking that Drizzt, by his melancholy, had accepted blame for the tragedy, the wounded girl spun and tried to flee. Drizzt caught her by the shoulder, though, turned her about, and held her close. He would be a damned thing indeed if this girl, who had accepted him with all her heart, came to believe the lies.

"I killed no one," Drizzt whispered above Catti-brie's sobs, "except the monsters that slew the Thistledowns. On my word!" He recounted the tale then, in full, even telling of his flight from Dove Falconhand's party.

"And now I am here," he concluded, "wishing to put the experience behind me, though never, on my word, shall I ever forget it!"

"Ye weave two tales apart," Catti-brie replied. "Yerself an' McGristle, I mean."

"McGristle?" Drizzt gasped as though his breath had been blasted from his body. Drizzt hadn't seen the burly man in years and had thought Roddy to be a thing of his distant past.

"Came in today," Catti-brie explained. "Big man with a yellow dog. He's hunting ye."

The confirmation overwhelmed Drizzt. Would he ever escape his past? he wondered. If not, how could he ever hope to find acceptance?

"McGristle said ye killed them," Catti-brie continued.

"Then you have our words alone," Drizzt reasoned, "and there is no evidence to prove either tale." The ensuing silence seemed to go for hours.

"Never did like that ugly brute." Catti-brie sniffed, and she managed her first smile since she had met McGristle.

The affirmation of their friendship struck Drizzt profoundly, but he could not forget the trouble that was now hovering all about him. He would have to fight Roddy, and maybe others if the bounty hunter could stir up resentment—not a difficult task considering Drizzt's heritage. Or Drizzt would have to run away, again accept the road as his home.

"What'll ye do?" Catti-brie asked, sensing his distress.

"Do not fear for me," Drizzt assured her, and he gave her a hug as he spoke, one that he knew might be his way of saying good-bye. "The day grows long. You must get back to your home."

"He'll find ye," Catti-brie replied grimly.

"No," Drizzt said calmly. "Not soon anyway. With Guenhwyvar by my side, we will keep Roddy McGristle away until I can figure my best course. Now, be off! The night comes swiftly and I do not believe that your father would appreciate your coming here."

The reminder that she would have to face Bruenor again set Catti-brie in motion. She bid Drizzt farewell and turned away, then rushed back up to the drow and threw a hug around him. Her step was lighter as she moved back down the mountain. She hadn't resolved anything for Drizzt, at least as far as she knew, but the drow's troubles seemed a distant second compared to her own relief that her friend was not the monster some claimed him to be.

The night would be dark indeed for Drizzt Do'Urden. He had thought McGristle a long-distant problem, but the menace was here now, and none save Catti-brie had jumped to his defense.

He would have to stand alone—again—if he meant to stand at all. He had no allies beyond Guenhwyvar and his own scimitars, and the prospects of battling McGristle—win or lose—did not appeal to him.

"This is no home," Drizzt muttered to the frosty wind. He pulled out the onyx figurine and called to his panther companion. "Come, my friend," he said to the cat. "Let us be away before our adversary is upon us."

Guenhwyvar kept an alert guard while Drizzt packed up his possessions, while the road-weary drow emptied his home.

# 25 Dwarven Banter

Catti-brie heard the growling dog, but she had no time to react when the huge man leaped out from behind a boulder and grabbed her roughly by the arm. "I knowed ye knowed!" McGristle cried, putting his foul breath right in the girl's face.

Catti-brie kicked him in the shin. "Ye let me go!" she retorted. Roddy was surprised that she had no trace of fear in her voice. He gave her a good shake when she tried to kick him again.

"Ye came to the mountain for a reason," Roddy said evenly, not relaxing his grip. "Ye came to see the drow—I knowed that ye was friends with that one. Seen it in yer eyes! "

"Ye know not a thing!" Catti-brie spat in his face. "Ye talk in lies."

"So the drow told ye his story o' the Thistledowns, eh?" Roddy replied, easily guessing the girl's meaning. Catti-brie knew then that she had erred in her anger, had given the wretch confirmation of her destination.

"The drow?" Catti-brie said absently. "I'm not for guessing what ye're speaking about."

Roddy's laughter mocked her. "Ye been with the drow, girl. Ye've said it plain enough. And now ye're goin' to take me to see him."

Catti-brie sneered at him, drawing another rough shake.

Roddy's grimace softened then, suddenly, and Catti-brie liked even less the look that came into his eye. "Ye're a spirited girl, ain't ye?" Roddy purred, grabbing Catti-brie's other shoulder and turning her to face him squarely. "Full o' life, eh? Ye'll take me to the drow, girl, don't ye doubt. But mighten be there's other things we can do first, things to show ye not to cross the likes o' Roddy McGristle." His caress on Catti-brie's cheek seemed ridiculously grotesque, but horribly and undeniably threatening, and Catti-brie thought she would gag.

It took every bit of Catti-brie's fortitude to face up to Roddy at that moment. She was only a young girl but had been raised among the grim-faced dwarves of Clan Battlehammer, a proud and rugged group. Bruenor was a fighter, and so was his daughter. Catti-brie's knee found Roddy's groin, and as his grip suddenly relaxed, the girl brought one hand up to claw at his face. She kneed him a second time, with less effect, but Roddy's defensive twist allowed her to pull away, almost free.

Roddy's iron grip tightened suddenly around her wrist, and they struggled for just a moment. Then Catti-brie felt an equally rough grab at her free hand and before she could understand what had happened, she was pulled from Roddy's grasp and a dark form stepped by her.

"So ye come to face yer fate," Roddy snarled delightedly at Drizzt.

"Run off," Drizzt told Catti-brie. "This is not your affair." Catti-brie, shaken and terribly afraid, did not argue.

Roddy's gnarled hands clenched Bleeder's handle. The bounty hunter had faced the drow in battle before and had no intention of trying to keep up with that one's agile steps and twists. With a nod, he loosed his dog.

The dog got halfway to Drizzt, was just about to leap at him, when Guenhwyvar buried it, rolling it far to the side. The dog came back to its feet, not seriously wounded but backing off several steps every time the panther roared in its face.

"Enough of this," Drizzt said, suddenly serious. "You have pursued me through years and leagues. I salute your resilience, but your anger is misplaced, I tell you. I did not kill the Thistledowns. Never would I have raised a blade against them!"

"To Nine Hells with the Thistledowns!" Roddy roared back. "Ye think that's what this is about?"

"My head would not bring you your bounty," Drizzt retorted.

"To Nine Hells with the gold!" Roddy yelled. "Ye took my dog, drow, an' my ear!" He banged a dirty finger against the side of his scarred face.

Drizzt wanted to argue, wanted to remind Roddy that it was he who had initiated the fight, and that his own axe swing had felled the tree that had torn his face. But Drizzt understood Roddy's motivation and knew that mere words would not soothe. Drizzt had wounded Roddy's pride, and to a man like Roddy that injury far outweighed any physical pain.

"I want no fight," Drizzt offered firmly. "Take your dog and be gone, on your word alone that you'll pursue me no longer."

Roddy's mocking laughter sent a shudder up Drizzt's spine. "I'll chase ye to the ends o' the world, drow!" Roddy roared. "And I'll find ye every time. No hole's deep enough to keep me from ye. No sea's wide enough! I'll have ye, drow. I'll have ye now or, if ye run, I'll have ye later!"

Roddy flashed a yellow-toothed smile and cautiously stalked toward Drizzt. "I'll have ye drow," the bounty hunter growled again quietly. A sudden rush brought him close and Bleeder swiped across wildly. Drizzt hopped back.

A second strike promised similar results, but Roddy, instead of following through, came with a deceptively quick backhand that glanced Drizzt's chin.

He was on Drizzt in an instant, his axe whipping furiously every which way. "Stand still!" Roddy cried as Drizzt deftly sidestepped, hopped over, or ducked under each blow. Drizzt knew that he was taking a dangerous chance in not countering the wicked blows, but he hoped that if he could tire the burly man, he might still find a more peaceful solution.

Roddy was agile and quick for a big man, but Drizzt was far quicker, and the drow believed that he could play the game a good while longer.

Bleeder came in a side swipe, diving across at Drizzt's chest. The attack was a feint, with Roddy wanting Drizzt to duck under so that he might kick the drow in the face.

Drizzt saw through the deception. He leaped instead of ducked, turned a somersault above the cutting axe, and came down lightly, even closer to Roddy. Now Drizzt did wade in, punching with both scimitar hilts straight into Roddy's face. The bounty hunter staggered backward, feeling warm blood rolling out of his nose.

"Go away," Drizzt said sincerely. "Take your dog back to Maldobar, or wherever it is that you call home."

If Drizzt believed that Roddy would surrender in the face of further humiliation, he was badly mistaken. Roddy bellowed in rage and charged straight in, dipping his shoulder in an attempt to bury the drow.

Drizzt pounded his weapon hilts down onto Roddy's dipped head and launched himself into a forward roll right over Roddy's back. The bounty hunter went down hard but came quickly to his knees, drawing and firing a dagger at Drizzt even as the drow turned back.

Drizzt saw the silvery flicker at the last instant and snapped a blade down to deflect the weapon. Another dagger followed, and another after that, and each time, Roddy advanced a step on the distracted drow.

"I'm knowing yer tricks, drow," Roddy said with an evil grin. Two quick steps brought him right up to Drizzt and Bleeder again sliced in.

Drizzt dived into a sidelong roll and came up a few feet away. Roddy's continuing confidence began to unnerve Drizzt; he had hit the bounty hunter with blows that would have dropped most men, and he wondered how much damage the burly human could withstand. That thought led Drizzt to the inevitable conclusion that he might have to start hitting Roddy with more than his scimitar hilts.

Again Bleeder came from the side. This time, Drizzt did not dodge. He stepped within the arc of the axe blade and blocked with one weapon, leaving Roddy open for a strike with the other scimitar. Three quick right jabs closed one of Roddy's eyes, but the bounty hunter only grinned and charged, catching hold of Drizzt and bearing the lighter combatant to the ground.

Drizzt squirmed and slapped, understanding that his conscience had betrayed him. In such close quarters, he could not match Roddy's strength, and his limited movements destroyed his advantage of speed. Roddy held his position on top and maneuvered one arm to chop down with Bleeder.

A yelp from his yellow dog was the only warning he got, and that didn't register enough for him to avoid the panther's rush. Guenhwyvar bowled Roddy off Drizzt, slamming him to the ground. The burly man kept his wits enough to swipe at the panther as it continued past, nicking Guenhwyvar on the rear flank.

The stubborn dog came rushing in, but Guenhwyvar recovered, pivoted right around Roddy, and drove it away.

When Roddy turned back to Drizzt, he was met by a savage flurry of scimitar blows that he could not follow and could not counter. Drizzt had seen the strike on the panther and the fires in his lavender eyes no longer indicated compromise. A hilt smashed Roddy's face, followed by the flat of the other blade. A foot kicked his stomach, his chest, and his groin in what seemed a single motion. Impervious, Roddy accepted it all with a snarl, but the enraged drow pressed on. One scimitar caught again under the axe head, and Roddy moved to charge, thinking to bear Drizzt to the ground once more.

Drizzt's second weapon struck first, though, slicing across Roddy's forearm. The bounty hunter recoiled, grasping at his wounded limb as Bleeder fell to the ground.

Drizzt never slowed. His rush caught Roddy off guard and several kicks and punches left the man reeling. Drizzt then leaped high into the air and kicked straight out with both feet, connecting squarely on Roddy's jaw and dropping him heavily to the ground. Still Roddy shrugged it off and tried to rise, but this time, the bounty hunter felt the edges of two scimitars come to rest on opposite sides of his throat.

"I told you to be on your way," Drizzt said grimly, not moving his blades an inch but letting Roddy feel the cold metal acutely.

"Kill me," Roddy said calmly, sensing a weakness in his opponent, "if ye got the belly for it!"

Drizzt hesitated, but his scowl did not soften. "Be on your way," he said with as much calm as he could muster, calm that denied the coming trial he knew he would face.

Roddy laughed at him. "Kill me, ye black-skinned devil!" he roared, bulling his way, though he remained on his knees, toward Drizzt. "Kill me or I'll catch ye! Not for doubtin', drow. I'll hunt ye to the corners o' the world and under it if need!"

Drizzt blanched and glanced at Guenhwyvar for support.

"Kill me!" Roddy cried, bordering on hysteria. He grabbed Drizzt's wrists and pulled them forward. Lines of bright blood appeared on both sides of the man's neck. "Kill me as ye killed my dog!"

Horrified, Drizzt tried to pull away, but Roddy's grip was like iron.

"Ye got not the belly for it?" the bounty hunter bellowed. "Then I'll help ye!" He jerked the wrists sharply against Drizzt's pull, cutting deeper lines, and if the crazed man felt pain, it did not show through his unyielding grin.

Waves of jumbled emotions assaulted Drizzt. He wanted to kill Roddy at that moment, more out of stupefied frustration than vengeance, and yet he knew that he could not. As far as Drizzt knew, Roddy's only crime was an unwarranted hunt against him and that was not reason enough. For all that he held dear, Drizzt had to respect a human life, even one as wretched as Roddy McGristle's.

"Kill me!" Roddy shouted over and over, taking lewd pleasure in the drow's growing disgust.

"No!" Drizzt screamed in Roddy's face with enough force to silence the bounty hunter. Enraged to a point where he could not contain his trembling, Drizzt did not wait to see if Roddy would resume his insane cry. He drove a knee into Roddy's chin, pulled his wrists free of Roddy's grasp, then slammed his weapon hilts simultaneously into the bounty hunter's temples.

Roddy's eyes crossed, but he did not swoon, stubbornly shaking the blow away. Drizzt slammed him again and again, finally beating him down, horrified at his own actions and at the bounty hunter's continuing defiance.

When the rage had played itself out, Drizzt stood over the burly man, trembling and with tears rimming his lavender eyes. "Drive that dog far away!" he yelled to Guenhwyvar. Then he dropped his bloodied blades in horror and bent down to make sure that Roddy was not dead.

⚔ ⚔ ⚔ ⚔ ⚔

Roddy awoke to find his yellow dog standing over him. Night was fast falling and the wind had picked up again. His head and arm ached, but he dismissed the pain, wanting only to resume his hunt, confident now that

Drizzt would never find the strength to kill him. His dog caught the scent at once, leading back to the south, and they set off. Roddy's nerve dissipated only a little when they came around a rocky outcropping and found a red-bearded dwarf and a girl waiting for him.

"Ye don't be touchin' me girl, McGristle," Bruenor said evenly. "Ye just shouldn't be touchin' me girl."

"She's in league with the drow!" Roddy protested. "She told the murdering devil of my comin'!"

"Drizzt's not a murderer!" Catti-brie yelled back. "He never did kill the farmers! He says ye're saying that just so others'll help ye to catch him!" Catti-brie realized suddenly that she had just admitted to her father that she had met with the drow. When Catti-brie had found Bruenor, she had told him only of McGristle's rough handling.

"Ye went to him," Bruenor said, obviously wounded. "Ye lied to me, an' ye went to the drow! I telled ye not to. Ye said ye wouldn't . . ."

Bruenor's lament stung Catti-brie profoundly, but she held fast to her beliefs. Bruenor had raised her to be honest, but that included being honest to what she knew was right. "Once ye said to me that everyone gets his due," Catti-brie retorted. "Ye telled me that each is different and each should be seen for what he is. I've seen Drizzt, and seen him true, I tell ye. He's no killer! And he's—" She pointed accusingly at McGristle—"a liar! I take no pride in me own lie, but never could I let Drizzt get caught by this one!"

Bruenor considered her words for a moment, then wrapped one arm about her waist and hugged her tightly. His daughter's deception still stung, but the dwarf was proud that his girl had stood up for what she believed. In truth, Bruenor had come out here, not looking for Catti-brie, whom he believed was sulking in the mines, but to find the drow. The more he recounted his fight with the remorhaz, the more Bruenor became convinced that Drizzt had come down to help him, not to fight him. Now, in light of recent events, few doubts remained.

"Drizzt came and pulled me free of that one," Catti-brie went on. "He saved me."

"Drow's got her mixed," Roddy said, sensing Bruenor's growing attitude and wanting no fight with the dangerous dwarf. "He's a murderin' dog, I say, and so would Bartholemew Thistledown if a dead man could!"

"Bah!" Bruenor snorted. "Ye don't know me girl or ye'd be thinking the better than to call her a liar. And I telled ye before, McGristle, that I don't like me daughter shook! Me thinkin's that ye should be gettin' outa me valley. Me thinkin's that ye should be goin' now."

Roddy growled and so did his dog, which sprung between the mountain man and the dwarf and bared its teeth at Bruenor. Bruenor shrugged, unconcerned, and growled back at the beast, provoking it further.

The dog lurched at the dwarf's ankle, and Bruenor promptly put a heavy boot in its mouth and pinned its bottom jaw to the ground. "And take yer stinkin' dog with ye!"

Bruenor roared, though in admiring the dog's meaty flank, he was thinking again that he might have better use for the surly beast.

"I go where I choose, dwarf!" Roddy retorted. "I'm gonna get me a drow, and if the drow's in yer valley, then so am I!"

Bruenor recognized the clear frustration in the man's voice, and he took closer note then of the bruises on Roddy's face and the gash on his arm. "The drow got away from ye," the dwarf said, and his chuckle stung Roddy acutely.

"Not for long," Roddy promised. "And no dwarf'll stand in my way!"

"Get along back to the mines," Bruenor said to Catti-brie. "Tell the others I mighten be a bit late for dinner." The axe came down from Bruenor's shoulder.

"Get him good," Catti-brie mumbled under her breath, not doubting her father's prowess in the least. She kissed Bruenor atop his helmet, then rushed off happily. Her father had trusted her; nothing in all the world could be wrong.

⚔ ⚔ ⚔ ⚔ ⚔

Roddy McGristle and his three-legged dog left the valley a short while later. Roddy had seen a weakness in Drizzt and thought he could win against the drow, but he saw no such signs in Bruenor Battlehammer. When Bruenor had Roddy down, a feat that hadn't taken very long, Roddy did not doubt for a second that if he had asked the dwarf to kill him, Bruenor gladly would have complied.

From the top of the southern climb, where he had gone for his last look at Ten-Towns, Drizzt watched the wagon roll out of the vale, suspecting that it was the bounty hunter's. Not knowing what it all meant, but hardly believing that Roddy had undergone a change of heart, Drizzt looked down at his packed belongings and wondered where he should turn next.

The lights of the towns were coming on now, and Drizzt watched them with mixed emotions. He had been on this climb several times, enchanted by his surroundings and thinking he had found his home. How different now was this view! McGristle's appearance had given Drizzt pause and reminded him that he was still an outcast, and ever to be one.

"Drizzit," he mumbled to himself, a damning word indeed. At that moment, Drizzt did not believe he would ever find a home, did not believe that a drow who was not in heart a drow had a place in all the realms, surface or Underdark. The hope, ever fleeting in Drizzt's weary heart, had flown altogether.

"Bruenor's Climb, this place is called," said a gruff voice behind Drizzt. He spun about, thinking to flee, but the red-bearded dwarf was too close for him to slip by. Guenhwyvar rushed to the drow's side, teeth bared.

"Put yer pet away, elf," Bruenor said. "If cat tastes as bad as dog, I'll want none of it!

"My place, this is," the dwarf went on, "me bein' Bruenor and this bein' Bruenor's Climb!"

"I saw no sign of ownership," Drizzt replied indignantly, his patience exhausted from the long road that now seemed to grow longer. "I know your claim now, and so I will leave. Take heart, dwarf. I shall not return."

Bruenor put a hand up, both to silence the drow and to stop him from leaving. "Just a pile o' rocks," he said, as close to an apology as Bruenor had ever given. "I named it as me own, but does that make it so? Just a damned piled o' rocks!"

Drizzt cocked his head at the dwarf's unexpected rambling.

"Nothin's what it seems, drow!" Bruenor declared. "Nothin'! Ye try to follow what ye know, ye know? But then ye find that ye know not what ye thought ye knowed! Thought a dog'd be tastin' good—looked good enough—but now me belly's cursing me every move!"

The second mention of the dog sparked a sudden revelation concerning Roddy McGristle's departure. "You sent him away," Drizzt said, pointing down to the route out of the vale. "You drove McGristle off my trail."

Bruenor hardly heard him, and certainly wouldn't have admitted the kind-hearted deed, in any case. "Never trusted humans," he said evenly. "Never know what one's about, and when ye find out, too many's the time it's too late for fixin'! But always had me thoughts straight about other folks. An elf's an elf, after all, and so's a gnome. And orcs are straight-out stupid and ugly. Never knew one to be otherways, an' I known a few!" Bruenor patted his axe, and Drizzt did not miss his meaning.

"So was me thoughts about the drow," Bruenor continued. "Never met one—never wanted to. Who would, I ask? Drow're bad, mean-hearted, so I been telled by me dad an' by me dad's dad, an' by any who's ever telled me." He looked out to the lights of Termalaine on Maer Dualdon in the west, shook his head, and kicked a stone. "Now I heared a drow's prowlin' about me valley, and what's a king to do? Then me daughter goes to him!" A sudden fire came into Bruenor's eyes, but it mellowed quickly, almost as if in embarrassment, as soon as he looked at Drizzt. "She lies in me face—never has she done that afore, and never again if she's a smart one!"

"It was not her fault," Drizzt began, but Bruenor waved his hands about wildly to dismiss the whole thing.

"Thought I knowed what I knowed," Bruenor continued after a short pause, his voice almost a lament. "Had the world figured, sure enough. Easy to do when ye stay in yer own hole."

He looked back to Drizzt, straight into the dim shine of the drow's lavender eyes. "Bruenor's Climb?" the dwarf asked with a resigned shrug. "What's it mean, drow, to put a name on a pile o' rocks? Thought I knowed, I did, an' thought a dog'd taste good." Bruenor rubbed a hand over his belly and frowned. "Call it a pile o' rocks then, an' I've no claim on it more'n yerself! Call it Drizzt's Climb then, an' ye'd be kicking me out!"

"I would not," Drizzt replied quietly. "I do not know that I could if I wished to!"

"Call it what ye will!" Bruenor cried, suddenly distressed. "And call a dog a cow—that don't change the way the thing'll taste!" Bruenor threw up his hands, flustered, and turned away, stomping down the rock path, grumbling with every step.

"And ye be keepin' yer eyes on me girl," Drizzt heard Bruenor snarl above his general grumbles, "if she's so orc-headed as to keep goin' to the stinkin' yeti an' worm-filled mountain! Be knowin' that I hold yerself . . ." The rest faded away as Bruenor disappeared around a bend.

Drizzt couldn't begin to dig his way through that rambling dialogue, but he didn't need to put Bruenor's speech in perfect order. He dropped a hand on Guenhwyvar, hoping that the panther shared the suddenly wondrous panoramic view. Drizzt knew then that he would sit up on the climb, Bruenor's Climb, many times and watch the lights flicker to life, for, adding up all that the dwarf had said, Drizzt surmised one phrase clearly, words he had waited so many years to hear:

Welcome home.

# Epilogue

Of all the races in the known realms, none is more confusing, or more confused, than humans. Mooshie convinced me that gods, rather than being outside entities, are personifications of what lies in our hearts. If this is true, then the many, varied gods of the human sects—deities of vastly different demeanors—reveal much about the race.

If you approach a halfling, or an elf, or a dwarf, or any of the other races, good and bad, you have a fair idea of what to expect. There are exceptions, of course; I name myself as one most fervently! But a dwarf is likely to be gruff, though fair, and I have never met an elf, or even heard of one, that preferred a cave to the open sky. A human's preference, though, is his own to know—if even he can sort it out.

In terms of good and evil, then, the human race must be judged most carefully. I have battled vile human assassins, witnessed human wizards so caught up in their power that they mercilessly destroyed all other beings in their paths, and seen cities where groups of humans preyed upon the unfortunate of their own race, living in kingly palaces while other men and women, and even children, starved and died in the gutters of the muddy streets. But

I have met other humans—Catti-brie, Mooshie, Wulfgar, Agorwal of Termalaine—whose honor could not be questioned and whose contributions to the good of the realms in their short life spans will outweigh that of most dwarves and elves who might live a half a millennium and more.

They are indeed a confusing race, and the fate of the world comes more and more into their ever-reaching hands. It may prove a delicate balance, but certainly not a dull one. Humans encompass the spectrum of character more fully than any other beings; they are the only "goodly" race that wages war upon itself—with alarming frequency.

The surface elves hold out hope in the end. They who have lived the longest and seen the birth of many centuries take faith that the human race will mature to goodness, that the evil in it will crush itself to nothingness, leaving the world to those who remain.

In the city of my birth I witnessed the limitations of evil, the self-destruction and inability to achieve higher goals, even goals based upon the acquisition of power. For this reason, I, too, will hold out hope for the humans, and for the realms. As they are the most varied, so too are humans the most malleable, the most able to disagree with that within themselves that they learn to be false.

My very survival has been based upon my belief that there is a higher purpose to this life: that principles are a reward in and of themselves. I cannot, therefore, look forward in despair, but rather with higher hopes for all in mind and with the determination that I might help to reach those heights.

This is my tale, then, told as completely as I can recall and as completely as I choose to divulge. Mine has been a long road filled with ruts and barriers, and only now that I have put so much so far behind me am I able to recount it honestly.

I will never look back on those days and laugh; the toll was too great for humor to seep through. I do often remember Zaknafein, though, and Belwar and Mooshie, and all the other friends I have left behind.

I have often wondered, too, of the many enemies I have faced, of the many lives my blades have ended. Mine has been a violent life in a violent world, full of enemies to myself and to all that I hold dear. I have been praised for the perfect cut of my scimitars, for my abilities in battle, and I must admit that I have many times allowed myself to feel pride in those hard-earned skills.

Whenever I remove myself from the excitement and consider the whole more fully, though, I lament that things could not have been different. It pains me to remember Masoj Hun'ett, the only drow I ever killed; it was he who initiated our battle and he certainly would have killed me if I had not proven the stronger. I can justify my actions on that fated day, but never will I be comfortable with their necessity. There should be a better way than the sword.

In a world so filled with danger, where orcs and trolls loom, seemingly, around every bend in the road, he who can fight is most often hailed as the hero and given generous applause. There is more to the mantle of "hero," I say, than strength of arm or prowess in battle. Mooshie was a hero, truly, because he overcame adversity, because he never blinked at unfavorable odds, and mostly because he acted within a code of clearly defined principles. Can less be said of Belwar Dissengulp, the handless deep gnome who befriended a renegade drow? Or of Clacker, who offered his own life rather than bring danger to his friends?

Similarly, I name Wulfgar of Icewind Dale a hero, who adhered to principle above battle lust. Wulfgar overcame the misperceptions of his savage boyhood, learned to see the world as a place of hope rather than a field of potential conquests. And Bruenor, the dwarf who taught Wulfgar that important difference, is as rightful a king as ever there was in all the realms. He embodies those tenets that his people hold most dear, and they will gladly defend Bruenor with their very lives, singing a song to him even with their dying breaths.

In the end, when he found the strength to deny Matron Malice, my father, too, was a hero. Zaknafein, who had lost his battle for principles and identity throughout most of his life, won in the end.

None of these warriors, though, outshines a young girl I came to know when I first traveled across Ten-Towns. Of all the people I have ever met, none has held themselves to higher standards of honor and decency than Catti-brie. She has seen many battles, yet her eyes sparkle clearly with innocence and her smile shines untainted. Sad will be the day, and let all the world lament, when a discordant tone of cynicism spoils the harmony of her melodic voice.

Often those who call me a hero speak solely of my battle prowess and know nothing of the principles that guide my blades. I accept their mantle for what it is worth, for their satisfaction and not my own. When Catti-brie names me so, then will I allow my heart to swell with the satisfaction of knowing that I have been judged for my heart and not my sword arm; then will I dare to believe that the mantle is justified.

And so my tale ends—do I dare to say? I sit now in comfort beside my friend, the rightful king of Mithral Hall, and all is quiet and peaceful and prosperous. Indeed this drow has found his home and his place. But I am young, I must remind myself. I may have ten times the years remaining as those that have already passed. And for all my present contentment, the world remains a dangerous place, where a ranger must hold to his principles, but also to his weapons.

Do I dare to believe that my story is fully told?

I think not.

—Drizzt Do'Urden